挑戰 NEW TOEIC 新制多益

U0033658

聽力滿分

10回模擬試題1000題 解析版

作者 Kim su hyeon | 譯者 林育珊／關亭薇

MP3

寂天雲 APP

如何下載 MP3 音檔

❶ 寂天雲 APP 聆聽：掃描書上 QR Code 下載「寂天雲－英日語學習隨身聽」APP。加入會員後，用 APP 內建掃描器再次掃描書上 QR Code，即可使用 APP 聆聽音檔。

❷ 官網下載音檔：請上「寂天閱讀網」（www.icosmos.com.tw），註冊會員／登入後，搜尋本書，進入本書頁面，點選「MP3 下載」下載音檔，存於電腦等其他播放器聆聽使用。

Part 1 模擬試題

目錄

新制多益介紹

✅ 改制後如下

類別	Part	舊制多益		新制多益		時間	分數
		題型	題數	題型	題數		
聽力	1	照片描述	10	照片描述	6	45分鐘	495分
	2	應答問題	30	應答問題	25		
	3	簡短對話	30	簡短對話	39		
	4	簡短獨白	30	簡短獨白	30		
閱讀	5	句子填空（文法和單字）	40	句子填空（文法和單字）	30	75分鐘	495分
	6	段落填空	12	段落填空	16		
	7	閱讀　單篇閱讀	28	閱讀　單篇閱讀	29		
		雙篇閱讀	20	多篇閱讀	25		
TOTAL		7 Parts	200題	7 Parts	200題	120分鐘	990分

✅ 題型變更重點

聽力測驗

- Part 1, 2 題數減少（**Part 1**：10 題→ 6 題／ **Part 2**：30 題→ 25 題）
- Part 3 題數增加（**Part 3**：30 題→ 39 題）
- 部分對話長度減短、對話次數增加
- 部分對話中將出現母音省略（如：going to → gonna）
- 新增三人對話 NEW
- 新增對話、說明加上圖表（表格或曲線圖等）的整合題型 NEW
- 新增詢問說話者意圖的題型 NEW

閱讀測驗

- Part 5 題數減少（**Part 5**：40 題→ 30 題）
- Part 6, 7 題數增加（**Part 6**：12 題→ 16 題／ **Part 7**：48 題→ 54 題）
- 文法題比例增加
- 新增判斷上下文意的題型 NEW
  1. 在文章內放入符合上下文意的句子
  2. 將句子放入適當的段落位置
- 新增文字簡訊、線上聊天、通訊軟體多人對話題型 NEW
- 新增整合三篇文章的閱讀題型 NEW

PART 1 高分策略

實戰式高分Point 徹底熟悉動詞類型及時態!

✅ 使用「刪去法」,從中選出最佳解答。

Part 1 為看照片,選出最適當的英文描述。然而在多益測驗中,一看到相關描述便急著選出答案,反而容易答錯。因為隨著多益難度的提升,錯誤選項經常會包含照片中顯而易見的單字,正確答案反而是看完照片當下,難以直接聯想到的用法,因此請善用刪去法作答。即便選項中出現關鍵單字,一旦有錯誤的描述請立即刪除該選項;如未出現關鍵單字,請從選項中挑出一個最佳解答。

（難度較低）
They are painting the wall. (O)
他們正在油漆牆壁。

（難度較高）
The walls are being painted. (O)
牆壁正在被油漆。
They are using tools to paint the wall. (O)
他們正在用工具油漆牆壁。
There are paintings on the wall. (X)
牆上有畫。

- **學會各類動詞!**熟記表示行為或狀態的動詞,聽到當下要能立刻反應是主動或被動語態、進行式或完成式。

  行為動詞:表示動作,如 play(玩)、run(跑)等。
  狀態動詞:表示過程,如 become(變成)、appear(看起來)等。
  主動語態:現在式(動詞現在式)、進行式(be + ing)、完成式(have + p.p.)。
  被動語態:現在式被動語態(be + p.p.)、進行式被動語態(be + being + p.p.)、
  　　　　　完成式被動語態(have been + p.p.)。

  當出現行為動詞,如「paint」(油漆),此時選項中若有某物「being painted」的敘述,由於此行為需要人物在場才能發生,故此說法含有「人物在場」之意,而若照片中未出現人物,則可立刻判定該選項不符照片。

  ➡ 請徹底弄懂錯誤選項的時態,並與照片進行對照。

- **了解句型的結構**,「盡可能」找出錯誤之處。

  把句型結構當成「主詞+動詞+受詞+副詞片語」,一旦發現錯誤的地方,便立即刪除該選項。如果該選項沒有任何錯誤、有聽不太懂的地方,或是無法與照片對照時,請將其暫時保留,最後在未刪除的選項中選出最佳解答。

  ➡ 訓練如何找出錯誤之處。

實戰式高分Point ｜ 試著熟悉高難度單字！

✅ 熟記與風景相關的高難度單字。

✅ 嘗試解答高難度題型，熟悉正確答案的形式。

✅ 仔細觀察照片。

平時要多練習解答難度相似或是難度較高的試題，以免在正式考試時答不出高難度的題目。就算碰到困難的題目，也勿驚慌失措。Part 1 中，除了人物照和常見的日常生活照之外，還有施工現場或是渡船頭之類的戶外風景照，屬於會使用「特定用法」的高難度照片。由於大多為不常使用的單字和句型，請務必訓練自己冷靜找出正確答案。

Mountains overlook the lake. (O)
山巒立於湖上。

Trees are reflected on the water. (O)
樹倒映在水上。

A boat is secured at a dock. (O)
船固定在碼頭邊。

- **風景照**——出題頻率偏低，但屬於超高難度題型。

  施工現場：pushing a wheelbarrow（推手推車）、digging the soil/dirt/earth（挖土／泥／地）
  渡船頭：be tied/docked/anchored（拴／停靠碼頭／拋錨泊船）
  街上／樓梯／橋墩的描寫：The path extends/leads to/curves/runs
  （路徑延伸／通往／彎曲／通過）

  ➡ 掌握與風景相關的單字，熟悉無法直接從照片看出的正解形式。

- **照片細節**——勿忽略照片中的角落、天花板、地板等。

  天空的描寫：clouds in the sky（天上的雲）、smoke rising in the air（在空中飄升的煙霧）
  地板的描寫：casting shadows（蒙上陰影）、tracks left on the ground（地板上遺留的蹤跡）
  角落物品的描寫：power cord has been plugged in（電源線已插上）

  ➡ 練習解出答案為細部描寫的題目，訓練自己多多留意題目陷阱。

PART 2 高分策略

實戰式高分Point | 掌握問題開頭&熟悉常見錯誤選項！

✅ 問句開頭的三、四個單字 ➡ 決定答案主詞、時態與內容。

✅ 排除常見誤導回答。

雖然 Part 2 必須仰賴聽力的實力，但光靠聽力好並無法輕易取得高分。碰上難度較低的題目時，正解通常會是自己所想的那個答案；然而越是高難度的題目，越會出現一時想像不到的回答。此時最安全的方式就是避開常見的錯誤選項，找出正確答案。請將問題與答案視為一個組合，熟記問答形式，累積一定的基礎後，再善用刪去法作答。注意有時重複題目單字、延伸單字字義或使用發音相似單字的選項，反而是誤導作答的陷阱。

Q. **When will we add** another writer to our department?

(A) **As soon as we find someone who's qualified.**

(B) A 2-page article with some photographs.

(C) Several years of writing experience.

問題：我們部門什麼時候才要再增加一位作者？
(A) 一旦我們找到合格的人選。
(B) 圖文並茂的兩頁文章。
(C) 幾年的寫作經驗。

➡ **1 掌握提問重點 & 答案形式！**
確認〈疑問詞＋助動詞＋主詞＋主要動詞〉

以刪去法解題

➡ **2 刪除相關字詞：**
選項未回答時間點，使用與 write 相關的詞彙

➡ **3 刪除發音相似的字詞：**
選項未回答時間點，使用發音相似的字詞 write/writing experience

- **只要聽清楚開頭的三、四個單字，等於掌握八成以上的題目關鍵與答句形式！**

    最有利的答題方式便是聽懂題目再找出正確答案。請訓練自己聽清楚開頭的三、四個單字，一次掌握問句的類型／時態／主詞。建議事先熟記多益測驗中的高頻率答案。
    各類疑問詞的問句：確認疑問詞為 Who/Where/When/How/Why/Which/What（不可用 Yes 或 No 回答）。
    Yes 或 No 的問句：確認問句的形式為選擇問句／建議或勸告／肯定句／否定句／附加問句／間接問句／直述句。

    ➡ 前半部題目（7–25 題）通常可以直接選出答案；後半部題目（26–31 題）則要使用刪去法作答。請將答錯的題目寫在錯誤筆記上，徹底熟悉這兩部分的題型模式。

- **請務必熟悉錯誤選項和正確答案，兩者一樣重要。**

    尚未熟悉多益考題的考生，經常會以刪去法作為答題技巧，優先刪除有發音相似或是相關字詞的選項。但是對追求滿分的考生而言，一味使用刪去法並非恰當的作法，因為選項中很有可能沒有任何發音相似的字詞，又或是三個選項都有發音相似的字詞。因此除了優先排除發音相似或是相關字詞之外，還有更為保險的高分技巧，那就是事先整理出錯誤選項的形式，確切掌握答題的陷阱。

    ➡ 排除常見的發音相似／相關字詞選項，並訓練自己熟悉錯誤選項的單字／句型，才好用刪去法找出正解。

實戰式高分Point 努力消除容易失誤的「弱點」！

✅ 熟悉「直述句」常見回覆。

✅ 熟悉Yes/No問句中，不以Yes或No回答的答句。

聽力測驗中，Part 2 屬於難易度範圍最廣的一個大題。基本上要答對七成以上的題目並非難事，重點在於加強自己的弱點，確保能夠一併答對其他題目。近年來出題頻率最高的題型為「直述句」，因為答案有各式各樣的回答方式（response），如把重點放在句子開頭，則通常無法順利掌握題意，屬於高難度的題型。

Q. I hear that the city plans to build a new park.

(A) At the city council meeting.

(B) When will it be finished?

(C) You can park on the left side.

問題：我聽說本市計劃要蓋一座新公園。
(A) 在市政廳會議。
(B) 什麼時候會完成？
(C) 你可以把車停在左側。

1 直述句：聽到主詞＋動詞＋受詞（作為受詞的片語）
常見的回答：反問對方以表達關心

以刪去法解題

2 刪除發音相似的字詞：
重複使用單字 city

3 刪除發音相似的字詞：
park 公園（名詞）與停車（動詞）並無關聯

• **面對最大的敵人「直述句」，請熟悉反問細節、列出條件等「常見回覆」。**

直述句分成以下幾種類型：①指出問題 ②好消息 ③壞消息 ④表示意見 ⑤傳達事實等。
請如同學習其他題型的方式，熟悉各類型直述句以及常見回覆。
例如：預計九點開會──回覆通常會是詢問地點／與會者有誰／事前準備事項等。

➡ 只要分別將直述句的正確答案／錯誤選項統整出來，就能輕易突破解題障礙。

• **訓練自己看懂省略 Yes 或 No 的直接回答。**

各大考試取得高分的關鍵在於懂得確實細分各類題型。大部分的學生並不會特別將 Yes/No 問句獨立成一種題型，而是單純依靠中文解釋解題，因此只要題目難度稍微變高，就會感到措手不及。口語上 Yes/No 問句的回答，常省略 Yes 或 No，但在句中仍會透露出 Yes 或 No 的意涵，請訓練自己從直接回答中判斷答案。
例如：Was it a long journey?—It certainly was. 回答中雖省略「Yes」但仍有表達出肯定句意。

➡ Yes/No 問句中的高難度答案，僅為稍加變化的常見回覆，請記錄在錯誤筆記上，才能戰勝難題。

PART 3 高分策略

✅ 請在音檔播出前抓住題目重點並記下內容。

✅ 新制多益的準備方式一樣是「先看題目」。

✅ 看到圖表先預測可能的考法。

2018 年新多益改制後，Part 3 為聽力測驗中題數最多（39 題）、難度最高的大題。然而在難度提高的新制多益中，如果仍舊優先看完每一道題目，實在難以集中精神聆聽兩至三人的長篇對話。在 Part 3 和 Part 4 中，只要抓住題目的重點，就可以事先掌握對話的主題，並同時預測答案。以 Part 3 為例，聽起來像是有很多人聚在一起討論，但是其實不需要從頭到尾仔細聆聽並下結論，只要「準確抓出關鍵」，聆聽與題目相關的部分即可解題。

Company	Location
Gourmet W	Newton
Sky View	Summerville
Tao Ling Food	Medford
Jessica's Cafe	Boston

Questions 68 through 70 refer to the following conversation and a list.

M: Heather, I'm excited about the race our company is sponsoring. A lot of people will be running in it. So it'll be great publicity.

W: That reminds me. Have you looked over this list of catering firms we are considering to hire for the event?

M: I can look at it now. Hmm . . . Sky View has the best options, but we need a company that's a little less expensive. Our budget is being reduced since last year's race.

W: Good point. Let's go for the one that is right here in Medford. They have a good reputation and their prices are reasonable.

68. What event is the company sponsoring?

    (A) A race

69. What is the man concerned about?

    (C) A limited budget

70. Look at the graphic. Which company will the speakers choose?

    (A) Gourmet W
    (B) Sky View
    (C) Tao Ling Food
    (D) Jessica's Cafe

男：海瑟，我很期待公司贊助的賽跑活動。有很多人會來跑，所以這會是很好的宣傳。

女：這提醒了我，你看過這個活動要找的外燴公司清單了嗎？

男：我可以現在看看。嗯……空景的菜單選得最好，但我們需要一家不那麼貴的公司。因為自從去年的賽跑活動後，我們的預算就減少了。

女：說得沒錯。我們就選在梅德福的這家吧。他們的聲譽很好，而且價格合理。

- **記下問題重點，試著預測線索出現形式。**

看懂題目後將題目分類，請一邊思考「對話中將會出現哪些答題線索」，一邊聆聽對話。
針對新增的圖表題，請在看完「題目和圖表」後，思考對話中可能會聽到哪些圖表內容。

➡ 請從對話中找尋答題線索，訓練自己一看題目便能準確命中答案。

實戰式高分Point	迅速閱讀選項並能「換句話說」！

✅ 碰到閱讀型題目時，請訓練自己快速看完(A)、(B)、(C)、(D)四個選項，並掌握題目重點。

✅ 請試著將你聽到的單字換成「廣義」的同義字。

本大題要在看完題目當下掌握題目重點，並在聆聽的過程中完成作答。而 Part 3 分成各種不同的難度，增加題目難度的方式有：①增加題目句子的長度和難度，或是②將對話中的單字換成同義字選項，因此即便先看過題目，做好完全準備，仍然聽不出答案。尤其對初學者而言，由於閱讀速度較慢，只要碰上①的情況就束手無策；而高分族群則難以應付②的同義詞變化，碰上②的情況時，就算聽得懂每字每句，可能依然無法找出適當的答案。為戰勝此類高難度題型，請訓練自己面對「高難度」的對話，試著選出正確的選項。

70. Why does the woman direct the man to the company's website?

(A) To make an online payment

(B) To get directions to the store

換句話說

(C) To view available design options

(D) To revise an existing policy

W: If you visit our company website, you'll be able to search through the designs we do offer.

女：如果您上我們的公司網站，就能搜索我們提供的設計款式。

- **訓練自己熟悉閱讀型題目。**

  使用本書時，如碰上較長的選項，請先標記出句子中的主詞和動詞，試著快速瀏覽題目並作答，題目通常有三大類：

  ① 詢問對話中提及的重點（What is mentioned/said about the . . .？）

  ② 詢問說話者的意圖（What does the woman mean when she says, ". . ."？）

  ③ 使用疑問詞 Why/What 詢問對話目的或原因（What made the speaker do . . .？）

  如果無法迅速看完較長的句子，不僅是聽力測驗，就連 Part 6, 7 也難以獲得高分。

  請訓練自己熟悉原文句子，不要將中文解釋一併寫進錯誤筆記中。

  ➡ **內容偏長時，請訓練自己找出題且及各選項的重點。**

- **訓練自己從選項中找出最適當的「換句話說」（Paraphrasing）。**

  看完題目後，大致上可以得知會有哪些人進行對話，並聽出每道題目所對應的對話段落。但是只要選項沒有直接寫出對話中的單字時，就會發生一時選不出答案的窘境。準備聽力測驗時，單純背誦高頻率同義詞是行不通的，因為真正厲害的題目並非只使用同義詞，而是「換句話說」，因此請先聽完對話，再從選項中找出最適當的答案。

  ➡ **熟記常考的「換句話說」，訓練自己可以在選項中找出最適當的答案。**

9

PART 4 高分策略

實戰式高分Point 預先記下題目做好萬全準備！

✔ 請在音檔播出前抓住題目重點並記下內容。

✔ 熟悉各大主題的題型和單字，有助於找出正解。

2018 年新多益改制後，Part 3 和 Part 4 新增了圖表資訊，以及詢問說話者意圖的題型。有別於 Part 3 的多人對話，Part 4 僅由一名說話者（speaker）針對單一主題表達看法。兩大題相比起來，Part 3 的對話具有延伸性；而 Part 4 的獨白則偏向在眾人面前發表演說（speech）的內容，屬於書面語的形式。因此內容較為制式化，不太會出現一時難以招架的題目。只要克服略為艱澀的書面用語，答題的準確率反而能高於 Part 3。

Program	
Presenter	**Time**
Dr. Randolph	9:30 a.m.
Ms. Nelson	11:00 a.m.
Break	12:00–1:30 p.m.
Workshops	2:00 p.m.

98. What is the purpose of this announcement?

   (C) To provide a schedule overview

99. Look at the graphic. Which program has the incorrect information?

   (A) Dr. Randolph's

   (B) Ms. Nelson's

   (C) Lunch break

   (D) Workshops

100. Where can the listeners find information on local restaurants?

   (C) In the conference program

Thank you for coming to the opening day of public speaking seminar. As you can see in your program, we have an exciting day ready for you today. But before we start, I have a brief announcement about the schedule. Dr. Steve Randolph's speech on image training will be at 10 o'clock instead of 9:30 due to some technical difficulties in the meeting room B. But, I'm sure his speech will worth the wait. There will be a break for lunch at 12:00 noon as scheduled. For your convenience, we've provided a list of local restaurants on the back page of the program, or you can visit the downstairs cafeteria. In the afternoon, we will break into groups and you can either take intensive workshops around 2 o'clock, or visit the exhibition halls. I hope you enjoy the best of what we have prepared for you.

歡迎各位來到公開演講研討會的揭幕日。如您在節目手冊上所見，各位將度過精彩刺激的一天。不過在我們開始之前，我想針對時程宣告一些事項。由於會議室 B 發生一些技術問題，史提夫・藍道夫博士圖像訓練的演講將從 9:30 改至 10 點。但我相信他的演講一定值得等待。如同預定，中午 12 點將有午休時間。為了各位方便起見，我們在節目手冊背面提供了當地餐廳的清單，或是您也可以前往樓下的餐廳用餐。下午，大家將進行小組活動，您可以選擇參加 2 點的密集工作坊，或是參訪展覽館。希望各位滿意我們盡心準備的活動。

• **記下問題重點，並利用表格推敲出獨白主題。**

看懂題目後將題目分類，請一邊思考「對話中將會出現哪些答題線索」一邊聆聽對話。尤其在 Part 4 中，同一主題經常會使用相同的題目與句型。針對新增加的圖表題，請在看完「題目和圖表」後，思考對話中可能會聽到哪些圖表內容。

➡ 請從獨白中找尋答題線索，訓練自己一看題目便能準確命中答案。

徹底熟悉難度較高的主題！

☑ 征服90題之後難度較高的主題。

☑ 碰到閱讀型題目時，請訓練自己快速看完(A)、(B)、(C)、(D)四個選項，並掌握題目重點。

本大題要在看完題目當下掌握題目重點，並在聆聽的過程中完成作答。Part 4 增加題目難度的方式通常是：①獨白的語速刻意加快，或是②出現較難的單字或較複雜的詞句。對於初學者而言，若碰上①的情況可能會緊張慌亂，因此平常就要習慣多聆聽正常甚至是語速更快的英文，才能在考試時不致慌了手腳；面對②的挑戰，則需熟悉獨白常出現的高頻率字詞及語句。為戰勝此類高難度題型，請訓練自己面對「高難度」的獨白，試著選出正確的選項。

---

98. Where do the speakers most likely work?

    (A) A food processing plant

    (B) A financial services corporation

    (C) A corporate law firm

    (D) A video production company

I have a few words to say about our meeting with the representatives from Wang's Foods next week. Let's remember that Wang's Foods is our video production's biggest client. It is critical that we get the contract.

針對下週與王記食品代表人員開會的事宜，我有幾句話要說。我們要謹記，王記食品是我們影像製作最大的客戶。拿到他們的合約是相當重要的事情。

- **請熟悉與新聞議題相關的主題。**

  ① **商業新聞（Business News）：**由記者（reporter）或新聞主播（announcer）轉述企業 CEO 提供的消息，內容包含企業收購、合併、新商品、工廠設備等重大決策。

  ② **當地新聞（Local News）：**內容為振興地方發展，由市長（mayor）或市議會（city council）提出、通過各類建設或文化議題。
     雖然單字和用詞上較為艱澀難懂，但是此類高難度題型同樣會出現在 Part 6 和 Part 7 當中，因此請務必熟悉相關內容，以朝高分邁進。

  ➡ 請熟悉地方社區（local community）以及企業商業活動等相關主題。

- **請就業務分配（project assignment）的角度，**
  區分客戶（client）與代理商／供應商（agency/supplier）之間的關係。

  ① **員工會議（Staff Meeting）：**掌握其相關內容，包括指派工作項目（project）給特定企業指定部門的哪位人士，以及各家企業的部門特色，有助於找出正確答案。

  ② **簽署合約（Contract）：**主題為簽約時，確認簽約雙方（both parties）的關係，將有助於回答推論題型。此主題亦會出現在 Part 6 當中。

  ➡ 請培養自己的商業知識，將可輕鬆掌握特定企業的合約業務內容。

ACTUAL TEST

答對題數表

PART 1	
PART 2	
PART 3	
PART 4	
總題數	

01

LISTENING TEST

In the Listening test, you will be asked to demonstrate how well you understand spoken English. The entire Listening test will last approximately 45 minutes. There are four parts, and directions are given for each part. You must mark your answers on the separate answer sheet. Do not write your answers in your test book.

PART 1 01

Directions: For each question in this part, you will hear four statements about a picture in your test book. When you hear the statements, you must select the one statement that best describes what you see in the picture. Then find the number of the question on your answer sheet and mark your answer. The statements will not be printed in your test book and will be spoken only one time.

Sample Answer

Statement (B), "They're shaking hands," is the best description of the picture, so you should select answer (B) and mark it on your answer sheet.

1.

2.

Go on to the next page

3.

4.

5.

6.

Go on to the next page

17

PART 2 ∩ 02

Directions: You will hear a question or statement and three responses spoken in English. They will not be printed in your test book and will be spoken only one time. Select the best response to the question or statement and mark the letter (A), (B), or (C) on your answer sheet.

7. Mark your answer on your answer sheet.

8. Mark your answer on your answer sheet.

9. Mark your answer on your answer sheet.

10. Mark your answer on your answer sheet.

11. Mark your answer on your answer sheet.

12. Mark your answer on your answer sheet.

13. Mark your answer on your answer sheet.

14. Mark your answer on your answer sheet.

15. Mark your answer on your answer sheet.

16. Mark your answer on your answer sheet.

17. Mark your answer on your answer sheet.

18. Mark your answer on your answer sheet.

19. Mark your answer on your answer sheet.

20. Mark your answer on your answer sheet.

21. Mark your answer on your answer sheet.

22. Mark your answer on your answer sheet.

23. Mark your answer on your answer sheet.

24. Mark your answer on your answer sheet.

25. Mark your answer on your answer sheet.

26. Mark your answer on your answer sheet.

27. Mark your answer on your answer sheet.

28. Mark your answer on your answer sheet.

29. Mark your answer on your answer sheet.

30. Mark your answer on your answer sheet.

31. Mark your answer on your answer sheet.

PART 3 ∩03

Directions: You will hear some conversations between two or more people. You will be asked to answer three questions about what the speakers say in each conversation. Select the best response to each question and mark the letter (A), (B), (C), or (D) on your answer sheet. The conversations will not be printed in your test book and will be spoken only one time.

32. What mode of transportation will the speakers use?
(A) Aircraft
(B) Car
(C) Boat
(D) Train

33. What time do the speakers plan to travel?
(A) At 5:00 A.M.
(B) At 9:00 A.M.
(C) At 11:30 A.M.
(D) At 12:00 P.M.

34. What will the woman probably do next?
(A) Attend a meeting
(B) Have lunch
(C) Travel to Detroit
(D) Book tickets

35. What is the main topic of the conversation?
(A) An upcoming corporate merger
(B) A round of layoffs
(C) The promotion of a coworker
(D) Plans for summer vacation

36. When will the discussed event happen?
(A) Immediately
(B) In a week
(C) In three weeks
(D) In the New Year

37. What is the timing of the event dependent upon?
(A) Someone's retirement
(B) The opening of a location
(C) The redecoration of an office
(D) The completion of training

38. Why is the woman calling?
(A) To request a refund
(B) To request a service visit
(C) To ask for directions to the store
(D) To get help with a product

39. What did the woman have trouble with?
(A) Activating the lighting display
(B) Deciding what ingredients to add
(C) Assembling the product
(D) Setting the timer

40. What did the woman say she had already done?
(A) Spoken to a service technician
(B) Looked over the manual
(C) Turned the product off and on
(D) Exchanged the product

41. What is the main topic of the conversation?
(A) Arranging a date
(B) Seeing a doctor
(C) Signing up for a training
(D) Finishing an assignment

42. What is the due date?
(A) Friday
(B) Monday
(C) Tuesday
(D) Thursday

43. What will the woman probably do next?
(A) Send an e-mail
(B) Go to a doctor
(C) Visit a director
(D) Go to a movie

Go on to the next page

44. What job does Jinny most likely do?

(A) Factory worker
(B) Dental assistant
(C) Doctor's receptionist
(D) Personal trainer

45. What day can the man come in?

(A) Friday
(B) Monday
(C) Tuesday
(D) Wednesday

46. What does the woman ask the man to do?

(A) Call another branch of the business
(B) Call to advise them of any changes
(C) Consult a specialist
(D) Pay a deposit in advance

47. What is the man asking about?

(A) Why the CEO wants to see him
(B) Where to buy cleaning supplies
(C) The date and time of a meeting
(D) The status of a utility bill

48. What department is the man the head of?

(A) Marketing
(B) Maintenance
(C) Accounting
(D) Public relations

49. What idea does the woman have?

(A) Having a meeting with the CEO
(B) Reorganizing the department
(C) Reducing air conditioning and heating
(D) Finding cheaper suppliers for cleaning
supplies

50. What event will happen the day after tomorrow?

(A) A training seminar
(B) A management meeting
(C) A cooking lesson
(D) A meal with employees

51. Where will the event most likely happen?

(A) At a Chinese restaurant
(B) At a Mongolian buffet
(C) At the company cafeteria
(D) In the manager's home

52. What does the man mean when he says, "When I was there last, we were packed into one that should have had about six fewer people in it"?

(A) The food was not good.
(B) Some of the staff didn't show up.
(C) The room was too small.
(D) The wait staff was not polite.

53. What is the main topic of the conversation?

(A) A retirement party
(B) A printing order
(C) An employee training seminar
(D) The promotion of a colleague

54. What is the company in the process of doing?

(A) Signing a contract
(B) Hiring new employees
(C) Relocating its offices
(D) Changing its phone number

55. What will the man probably do next?

(A) Order lunch
(B) Contact a company
(C) Go home for the day
(D) Arrange a meeting

56. What is the main topic of the conversation?
    (A) A new staff member
    (B) A rescheduled meeting
    (C) A job description
    (D) A new training program

57. What does the man mean when he says, "He'll probably want to try out a few of the ideas that he has been working on"?
    (A) Company travel will be reduced.
    (B) New office furniture will be ordered.
    (C) New ideas will be implemented.
    (D) Staff numbers will be reduced.

58. What has Mr. Aimes recently done?
    (A) Completed his MBA
    (B) Quit his full-time job
    (C) Canceled a sales seminar
    (D) Trained a new secretary

59. Where does the woman most likely work?
    (A) At a doctor's office
    (B) At a post office
    (C) At a ski resort
    (D) At a health club

60. How much extra does the receipt confirmation cost?
    (A) $0.00
    (B) $5.00
    (C) $10.75
    (D) $15.65

61. What does the woman ask the man to do?
    (A) Attend a seminar
    (B) Submit a report
    (C) Deliver a letter
    (D) Complete a form

Company	Location
Supreme Design	New York
Modern Art	Philadelphia
Hoo Design	Miami
Great View Art	San Francisco

62. What type of event is the company sponsoring?
    (A) A musical event
    (B) An auction
    (C) A theater performance
    (D) An art exhibition

63. What is the man concerned about?
    (A) A lack of volunteers
    (B) A customer complaint
    (C) A limited budget
    (D) A delayed concert

64. Look at the graphic. Which company do the speakers choose?
    (A) Great View Art
    (B) Hoo Design
    (C) Supreme Design
    (D) Modern Art

Go on to the next page

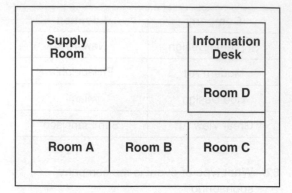

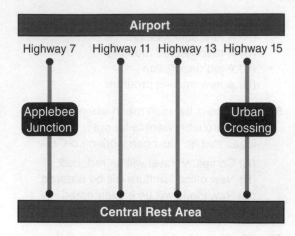

65. According to the man, what will the woman be doing today?

(A) Shopping for some office supplies
(B) Reporting a renovation plan
(C) Taking public transportation
(D) Preparing a press release

66. Look at the graphic. Which office has been assigned to the man?

(A) Room A
(B) Room B
(C) Room C
(D) Room D

67. What does the woman say will take place next week?

(A) A new product launch
(B) A retirement party
(C) A conference call
(D) A staff meeting

68. Where does the conversation take place?

(A) At an airport
(B) At a business office
(C) At a hotel
(D) At a rest area

69. Look at the graphic. Which route does the man suggest the woman take?

(A) Highway 7
(B) Highway 11
(C) Highway 13
(D) Highway 15

70. Why is the woman going to Seoul?

(A) To attend a meeting
(B) To visit a relative
(C) To interview for a job
(D) To hold a wedding

PART 4 ∩04

Directions: You will hear some talks given by a single speaker. You will be asked to answer three questions about what the speaker says in each talk. Select the best response to each question and mark the letter (A), (B), (C), or (D) on your answer sheet. The talks will not be printed in your test book and will be spoken only one time.

71. What is the report mainly about?
    (A) Traffic
    (B) Political protests
    (C) The weather
    (D) Transportation costs

72. According to the announcer, what has caused a problem?
    (A) Closed bridges
    (B) Bad weather
    (C) Construction
    (D) A rally

73. What will the listeners probably hear next?
    (A) A music program
    (B) The weather report
    (C) A game show
    (D) The local news

74. What is the advertisement about?
    (A) An exercise program
    (B) A rafting tour
    (C) A holiday sale
    (D) A job opportunity

75. What qualifications should applicants have?
    (A) Previous experience
    (B) Physical fitness
    (C) A pilot's license
    (D) Their own vehicle

76. What are people interested in the job asked to do?
    (A) Come to a job fair
    (B) Contact the company
    (C) Check the Web site
    (D) Complete a test

77. Where does the speaker most likely work?
    (A) At a pharmacy
    (B) At a dentist
    (C) At a doctor's office
    (D) At a beauty salon

78. Why is the woman calling?
    (A) To request a payment
    (B) To arrange an appointment
    (C) To cancel a test
    (D) To book a surgery

79. What does the woman mean when she says, "Don't forget that the clinic has moved since you were last here"?
    (A) To let the customer know the appointment has been changed
    (B) To remind the customer of the new location of the hospital
    (C) To let the listener know the doctor is not available
    (D) To confirm that the customer must not be late

80. Who most likely is the speaker?
    (A) A flight attendant
    (B) An aviator
    (C) A customs officer
    (D) A businessman

81. Where are the listeners going?
    (A) Tokyo
    (B) Taipei
    (C) Bangkok
    (D) Havana

82. What most likely will happen next?
    (A) Passengers will get off the plane.
    (B) The plane will land.
    (C) Safety procedures will be demonstrated.
    (D) The passengers will receive lunch.

Go on to the next page

83. What is the talk mainly about?

    (A) Events at the conference
    (B) The dinner menu
    (C) Accommodation arrangements
    (D) Rules for the conference

84. What does the man mean when he says, "Welcome to the World Technology Conference"?

    (A) Scientists are attending the conference.
    (B) Musicians are attending the conference.
    (C) Construction workers are attending the conference.
    (D) Fitness coaches are attending the conference.

85. What is the first event of the conference?

    (A) A technology demonstration
    (B) A meal with attendees
    (C) An award presentation
    (D) A roundtable debate

---

86. What type of work will the interns be doing?

    (A) Laboratory research
    (B) Navigation
    (C) Advertising
    (D) Police work

87. What does the man mean when he says, "I learned the ability to do more than one thing at the same time"?

    (A) He has lab techniques.
    (B) He is good at multitasking.
    (C) He has an ability to keep the records accurately.
    (D) He is available 24 hours a day.

88. How long is the internship program?

    (A) Two weeks
    (B) One month
    (C) Two months
    (D) Three months

---

89. Who is the intended audience of this talk?

    (A) Potential clients
    (B) Law enforcement officers
    (C) Company employees
    (D) Company shareholders

90. What does the company probably sell?

    (A) Software
    (B) Cars
    (C) Carpet
    (D) Appliances

91. What will Mr. Anderson probably do next?

    (A) Submit a report
    (B) Conduct an interview
    (C) Receive an award
    (D) Award a prize

---

92. Who most likely is the speaker?

    (A) A bank teller
    (B) A cafeteria employee
    (C) A museum guide
    (D) A marketing manager

93. How long will the tour be?

    (A) 20 minutes
    (B) 45 minutes
    (C) A half hour
    (D) An hour and a half

94. What will the tour members probably do last?

    (A) Go to the airport
    (B) Fill out a form
    (C) Book a tour
    (D) Visit the souvenir shop

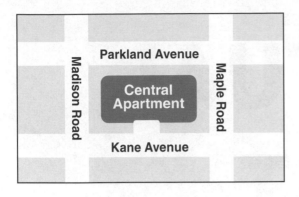

EXPENSE REPORT		
DATE	DESCRIPTION	AMOUNT
May 3	Parking	$30
May 6	Meal	$90
May 8	Car rental	$180
May 10	Accommodations	$250

95. What will take place on April 15?

(A) A flea market
(B) A press conference
(C) Some road construction
(D) A sporting event

96. Look at the graphic. Which street will be closed?

(A) Kane Avenue
(B) Madison Road
(C) Maple Road
(D) Parkland Avenue

97. What does the speaker suggest?

(A) Heading for the office late
(B) Making a detour
(C) Using public transportation
(D) Considering joining a car pool

98. Why is the speaker calling?

(A) Some paperwork did not have a signature.
(B) A reservation has changed.
(C) A certain receipt was not included.
(D) The dates of the business trip were wrong.

99. Look at the graphic. Which expense needs to be confirmed?

(A) Car rental
(B) Meal
(C) Parking
(D) Accommodations

100. What does the speaker say he can do?

(A) Cancel a reservation
(B) Handle a complaint
(C) Hire a new employee
(D) Explain a process

ACTUAL TEST

答對題數表

PART 1	
PART 2	
PART 3	
PART 4	
總題數	

02

LISTENING TEST

In the Listening test, you will be asked to demonstrate how well you understand spoken English. The entire Listening test will last approximately 45 minutes. There are four parts, and directions are given for each part. You must mark your answers on the separate answer sheet.
Do not write your answers in your test book.

PART 1 ∩ 05

Directions: For each question in this part, you will hear four statements about a picture in your test book. When you hear the statements, you must select the one statement that best describes what you see in the picture. Then find the number of the question on your answer sheet and mark your answer. The statements will not be printed in your test book and will be spoken only one time.

Sample Answer

Statement (B), "They're shaking hands, is the best description of the picture, so you should select answer (B) and mark it on your answer sheet.

1.

2.

Go on to the next page

3.

4.

5.

6.

Go on to the next page

PART 2 ∩ 06

Directions: You will hear a question or statement and three responses spoken in English. They will not be printed in your test book and will be spoken only one time. Select the best response to the question or statement and mark the letter (A), (B), or (C) on your answer sheet.

7. Mark your answer on your answer sheet.

8. Mark your answer on your answer sheet.

9. Mark your answer on your answer sheet.

10. Mark your answer on your answer sheet.

11. Mark your answer on your answer sheet.

12. Mark your answer on your answer sheet.

13. Mark your answer on your answer sheet.

14. Mark your answer on your answer sheet.

15. Mark your answer on your answer sheet.

16. Mark your answer on your answer sheet.

17. Mark your answer on your answer sheet.

18. Mark your answer on your answer sheet.

19. Mark your answer on your answer sheet.

20. Mark your answer on your answer sheet.

21. Mark your answer on your answer sheet.

22. Mark your answer on your answer sheet.

23. Mark your answer on your answer sheet.

24. Mark your answer on your answer sheet.

25. Mark your answer on your answer sheet.

26. Mark your answer on your answer sheet.

27. Mark your answer on your answer sheet.

28. Mark your answer on your answer sheet.

29. Mark your answer on your answer sheet.

30. Mark your answer on your answer sheet.

31. Mark your answer on your answer sheet.

PART 3 ∩ 07

Directions: You will hear some conversations between two or more people. You will be asked to answer three questions about what the speakers say in each conversation. Select the best response to each question and mark the letter (A), (B), (C), or (D) on your answer sheet. The conversations will not be printed in your test book and will be spoken only one time.

32. Why is the man calling?

(A) To invite the woman to an event
(B) To book a table
(C) To order takeout food
(D) To cancel a reservation

33. What is the problem?

(A) No tables are available at 8:15.
(B) The business closes at eight o'clock.
(C) The restaurant is out of lobster.
(D) The woman has lost her job.

34. What does the woman suggest?

(A) Coming another day
(B) Coming half an hour later
(C) Trying another location
(D) Reserving seats online

35. What does the man need help with?

(A) A printer
(B) Internet access
(C) A filing system
(D) An answering machine

36. When will the woman most likely return from her meeting?

(A) The next day
(B) In an hour
(C) At 7 P.M.
(D) On Thursday

37. What will the man probably do to solve the problem?

(A) Call the IT department
(B) Consult the manufacturer's Web page
(C) Buy a new router
(D) Use the fax machine

38. What are the women looking for?

(A) An order form
(B) A filing cabinet
(C) A photocopier
(D) A wardrobe

39. Where most likely are the speakers?

(A) In a restaurant
(B) In a grocery store
(C) In an office storeroom
(D) In a boutique

40. What does the man offer to do?

(A) Place an order
(B) Build something
(C) Contact a specialist
(D) Ask his assistant

41. Where did the man expect the woman to be?

(A) In the conference room
(B) In San Francisco
(C) At a training session
(D) At a job interview

42. Why is the woman at the office?

(A) She had a meeting there.
(B) Her conference was canceled.
(C) Her conference was pushed back.
(D) She had to pack her bags.

43. Why won't she take a trip next week?

(A) She has to move to a new office.
(B) Her schedule will be too busy.
(C) She has to talk with a client.
(D) Her office will be renovated.

Go on to the next page

44. What does the woman ask about?
    (A) Directions to the subway
    (B) The duration of a trip
    (C) The cost of a ticket
    (D) The bus schedule

45. Where most likely is the woman?
    (A) On a bus
    (B) In a subway station
    (C) In a cab
    (D) At an airport

46. What will the woman probably do next?
    (A) Pay the bill
    (B) Take a taxi
    (C) Collect her change
    (D) Go into the subway station

47. Why is the woman calling?
    (A) She wants a new job.
    (B) She wants to buy a home.
    (C) She wants to arrange a flight.
    (D) She wants to ask for directions.

48. Where does the man most likely work?
    (A) At a furniture shop
    (B) At a moving company
    (C) At a real estate agency
    (D) At an interior decorating company

49. What will the man most likely do next?
    (A) Apply for a job
    (B) Travel to Los Angeles
    (C) Buy a house
    (D) Arrange a meeting time

50. What does the man say he just did?
    (A) Made a telephone call
    (B) Filed a report
    (C) Finished his work
    (D) Canceled an order

51. Why did Mtech call?
    (A) To check on an order
    (B) To cancel a meeting
    (C) To confirm a price
    (D) To hire a new employee

52. What does the man mean when he says, "No problem"?
    (A) He doesn't understand the problem.
    (B) He can't cancel the order.
    (C) He will advise the woman.
    (D) He will help the woman install the material.

53. What does the woman ask the man to do?
    (A) Give her the weekend off
    (B) Suggest some kitchen appliances
    (C) Allow her to work at a trade show
    (D) Pay for her hotel costs

54. Why does the woman want to go to Las Vegas?
    (A) She wants to apply for a job.
    (B) She wants to stay at a hotel.
    (C) She wants to enjoy some trade shows.
    (D) She wants to see her relative.

55. What does the man remind the woman about?
    (A) That she will have to work
    (B) That she must arrive on time
    (C) That she has a meeting this weekend
    (D) That her brother no longer lives in Las Vegas

56. What are the speakers discussing?

    (A) Their favorite actors
    (B) The movie they are watching
    (C) The performance they've just seen
    (D) A rock concert

57. What does the woman mean when she says, "I'm not particularly surprised"?

    (A) She thought it was very sad.
    (B) She thought it was excellent.
    (C) She thought it was too long.
    (D) She didn't like it.

58. What will the speakers most likely do next?

    (A) Hire a babysitter
    (B) Go to a pub
    (C) See a movie
    (D) Go to a musical

---

59. Why is the woman calling?

    (A) To make a job offer
    (B) To order food
    (C) To cancel a meeting
    (D) To collect an outstanding bill

60. When does the woman want to meet with Ms. Wharton?

    (A) This Monday
    (B) Next Monday
    (C) Next Tuesday
    (D) Over the weekend

61. What does the man say he will do?

    (A) Arrange an interview
    (B) Receive a delivery for Ms. Wharton
    (C) Give Ms. Wharton a message
    (D) Come to the office to meet Ms. Felling

E-1	Lens Malfunction
E-2	No Flash
E-3	Low Battery
E-4	Memory Card Problem

62. Who most likely is the man?

    (A) A mechanic
    (B) A store clerk
    (C) An electrician
    (D) A photo artist

63. Look at the graphic. Which error code is the camera displaying?

    (A) E-1
    (B) E-2
    (C) E-3
    (D) E-4

64. What will the man most likely do next?

    (A) Replace an item
    (B) Purchase a new item
    (C) Read a manual
    (D) Wrap up a camera

Go on to the next page

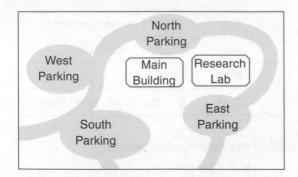

North
Parking

West
Parking

Main
Building

Research
Lab

East
Parking

South
Parking

Miracle Office Complex Directory

Office	Location
Kim's Stationery	1F
P&T Restaurant	2F
Miracle Fitness Center	3F
Jane's Clinic	4F

65. Look at the graphic. Which parking area will be closed?

(A) North
(B) East
(C) South
(D) West

66. What is the woman concerned about?

(A) Encountering road construction
(B) Paying parking fees
(C) Walking a long distance
(D) Facing heavy traffic

67. What does the man say the board will do?

(A) Change the company's policy
(B) Offer complimentary shuttles
(C) Provide a bonus
(D) Reimburse employees

68. What is the purpose of the man's visit?

(A) He is meeting with an accountant.
(B) He has to pay for parking.
(C) He will work out.
(D) He is eating some food.

69. What does the woman say about the parking policy?

(A) It has a time restriction.
(B) It isn't available for residents.
(C) It is for visitors only.
(D) It is complimentary for visitors.

70. Look at the graphic. Which office name has to be updated on the building directory?

(A) Kim's Stationery
(B) P&T Restaurant
(C) Miracle Fitness Center
(D) Jane's Clinic

PART 4 ᎒ 08

Directions: You will hear some talks given by a single speaker. You will be asked to answer three questions about what the speaker says in each talk. Select the best response to each question and mark the letter (A), (B), (C), or (D) on your answer sheet. The talks will not be printed in your test book and will be spoken only one time.

71. Why is the woman calling?

(A) To buy an appliance
(B) To cancel a delivery
(C) To report a problem
(D) To order food

72. What product is the woman discussing?

(A) An exercise bike
(B) A microwave oven
(C) A stereo system
(D) A washing machine

73. What does the speaker want the store to do?

(A) Send spare parts
(B) Send a service person
(C) Order a part
(D) Deliver a replacement

74. What is the purpose of the meeting?

(A) To announce new management
(B) To announce a new building project
(C) To explain a change in policies
(D) To announce the closure of the facility

75. What type of businesses does Angela Tiller work for?

(A) A building supply company
(B) A hospital
(C) A retirement home
(D) A delivery service

76. Why did Ms. Tiller's predecessor leave?

(A) He was transferred.
(B) He went into retirement.
(C) He had a personal matter.
(D) He was dismissed.

77. What is the purpose of the talk?

(A) To order new equipment
(B) To announce layoffs
(C) To discuss the sales results
(D) To discuss tax returns

78. According to the speaker, what positive results were there?

(A) Overseas sales increased.
(B) Domestic sales have hit a target.
(C) Expenses were reduced.
(D) The sales force was increased.

79. What course of action does the speaker announce?

(A) Restrictions on corporate travel
(B) Taking over another company
(C) Hiring additional employees
(D) A series of planning meetings

80. What is the speaker calling about?

(A) Car rental
(B) Emergency arrangements
(C) Airline tickets
(D) A package delivery

81. What information does the speaker require?

(A) A shipping address
(B) A telephone number
(C) A family member's name
(D) A list of contents

82. How does the speaker request that Mr. Wilson contact him?

(A) By online chat
(B) By mail
(C) By telephone
(D) By e-mail

Go on to the next page

83. Where would this talk most likely be heard?

    (A) On the radio
    (B) In a medical seminar
    (C) At a construction site
    (D) In a hospital

84. What field does Sandra Beard work in?

    (A) Geology
    (B) Chemistry
    (C) Environmental science
    (D) Medicine

85. What did Sandra Beard do recently?

    (A) Started a company
    (B) Returned from Africa
    (C) Wrote a book
    (D) Invented a product

86. Who is Mr. Harrison?

    (A) A professional athlete
    (B) A journalist
    (C) A magazine editor
    (D) A photographer

87. What does the caller want to discuss with Mr. Harrison?

    (A) Political issues
    (B) Contract amendments
    (C) Current affairs
    (D) Writing assignments

88. What should Mr. Harrison do if Ms. Phelps does not answer the phone?

    (A) Press 3
    (B) Leave a message
    (C) Call back later
    (D) Send a letter

89. Who is Mr. Pratha?

    (A) The CEO of the company
    (B) A shipping manager
    (C) A clerical worker
    (D) One of the executives of the company

90. What does the speaker say about Mr. Pratha?

    (A) He is being offered a promotion.
    (B) He was with the company for 25 years.
    (C) He recently joined the company.
    (D) He has not been very reliable.

91. What does the man mean when he says, "Here is Mr. Pratha to say a few words"?

    (A) Mr. Pratha will install a new word processor software.
    (B) Mr. Pratha will type on a keyboard.
    (C) Mr. Pratha will make a speech at the ceremony.
    (D) Mr. Pratha will talk to guests one-on-one.

92. Who most likely is the speaker?

    (A) A human resources director
    (B) A computer programmer
    (C) A safety worker
    (D) A salesperson

93. What is the announcement about?

    (A) A problem with the plumbing
    (B) A fire drill
    (C) The elevators being serviced
    (D) A staff meeting

94. What does the man mean when he says, "I will take attendance"?

    (A) The activity is mandatory.
    (B) The activity was postponed.
    (C) The activity was canceled.
    (D) The activity will go smoothly.

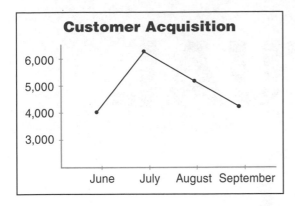

Customer Acquisition

9:00	
10:00	**Staff meeting**
11:00	
12:00	
13:00	**Lunch with a client**
14:00	
15:00	**Conference call**
16:00	

Thursday Schedule

95. Where most likely does the speaker work?

(A) At an insurance company
(B) At a home appliance company
(C) At a supermarket
(D) At a design company

96. Look at the graphic. When was the promotional event held?

(A) In June
(B) In July
(C) In August
(D) In September

97. According to the speaker, what is the company going to do to improve their Web site?

(A) Hold an emergency meeting
(B) Launch a new product
(C) Conduct a promotional event
(D) Employ some experts

98. Where most likely does the speaker work?

(A) At a shipping company
(B) At an accounting firm
(C) At an event planning agency
(D) At a law firm

99. What would the speaker like to discuss with the listener?

(A) A recruiting process
(B) A staff layoff
(C) A project budget
(D) A client claim

100. Look at the graphic. What time does the speaker want to meet?

(A) At 9:00
(B) At 11:00
(C) At 12:00
(D) At 14:00

ACTUAL TEST

答對題數表

PART 1	
PART 2	
PART 3	
PART 4	
總題數	

03

LISTENING TEST

In the Listening test, you will be asked to demonstrate how well you understand spoken English. The entire Listening test will last approximately 45 minutes. There are four parts, and directions are given for each part. You must mark your answers on the separate answer sheet.
Do not write your answers in your test book.

PART 1

Directions: For each question in this part, you will hear four statements about a picture in your test book. When you hear the statements, you must select the one statement that best describes what you see in the picture. Then find the number of the question on your answer sheet and mark your answer. The statements will not be printed in your test book and will be spoken only one time.

Sample Answer
Ⓐ ● Ⓒ Ⓓ

Statement (B), "They're shaking hands," is the best description of the picture, so you should select answer (B) and mark it on your answer sheet.

1.

2.

Go on to the next page

3.

4.

5.

6.

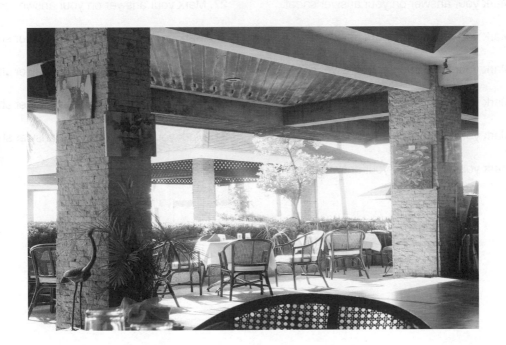

Go on to the next page

PART 2 ∩ 10

Directions: You will hear a question or statement and three responses spoken in English. They will not be printed in your test book and will be spoken only one time. Select the best response to the question or statement and mark the letter (A), (B), or (C) on your answer sheet.

7. Mark your answer on your answer sheet.

8. Mark your answer on your answer sheet.

9. Mark your answer on your answer sheet.

10. Mark your answer on your answer sheet.

11. Mark your answer on your answer sheet.

12. Mark your answer on your answer sheet.

13. Mark your answer on your answer sheet.

14. Mark your answer on your answer sheet.

15. Mark your answer on your answer sheet.

16. Mark your answer on your answer sheet.

17. Mark your answer on your answer sheet.

18. Mark your answer on your answer sheet.

19. Mark your answer on your answer sheet.

20. Mark your answer on your answer sheet.

21. Mark your answer on your answer sheet.

22. Mark your answer on your answer sheet.

23. Mark your answer on your answer sheet.

24. Mark your answer on your answer sheet.

25. Mark your answer on your answer sheet.

26. Mark your answer on your answer sheet.

27. Mark your answer on your answer sheet.

28. Mark your answer on your answer sheet.

29. Mark your answer on your answer sheet.

30. Mark your answer on your answer sheet.

31. Mark your answer on your answer sheet.

PART 3 ∩ 11

Directions: You will hear some conversations between two or more people. You will be asked to answer three questions about what the speakers say in each conversation. Select the best response to each question and mark the letter (A), (B), (C), or (D) on your answer sheet. The conversations will not be printed in your test book and will be spoken only one time.

32. Why is the man talking to the woman?

(A) To deliver a package
(B) To see a doctor
(C) To reserve a spot at a conference
(D) To make an appointment for tomorrow

33. Why does the man decide not to see Dr. Paulson the next morning?

(A) He will be at the conference with Dr. Chung.
(B) He needs prompt assistance.
(C) He has a meeting.
(D) He will be out of town.

34. What will the man most likely do?

(A) Come back tomorrow morning
(B) Visit a nearby pharmacy
(C) Meet with a different physician
(D) Call Dr. Paulson on the phone

35. Why does the woman want to see Ms. Maeda?

(A) To ask about a court date
(B) To sign a contract
(C) To give her some documents
(D) To tell her she is leaving the country

36. Where is Ms. Maeda?

(A) Overseas
(B) At home
(C) At a legal conference
(D) In her office

37. What will the man do next?

(A) Write a note
(B) Call Ms. Maeda
(C) Ask for assistance
(D) Deliver a message

38. What is the woman working on?

(A) Next year's budget
(B) A set of presentation slides
(C) A meeting agenda
(D) A speech

39. What does the woman promise to do?

(A) Reassign some work to Cathy
(B) Make a copy of the agenda
(C) Update the man on her work progress
(D) Meet the man at the board meeting

40. What does the man ask the woman to do?

(A) Include names on the agenda
(B) Rehearse for a speech
(C) Send the agenda out before speaking to Cathy
(D) Let him revise the agenda

41. What does Professor Van Saint teach?

(A) Spanish
(B) Business marketing
(C) French
(D) Accounting

42. Why is the class canceled?

(A) Bad weather
(B) Marriage of the professor's relative
(C) Sickness of the professor
(D) Public holiday

43. How long was the class supposed to be?

(A) 60 minutes
(B) 90 minutes
(C) 30 minutes
(D) 2 hours

Go on to the next page

44. Where does the conversation take place?

    (A) At a museum
    (B) At a department store
    (C) At a library
    (D) At a bookstore

45. What does the man imply when he says, "Oh, I think I know that one"?

    (A) He knows what she is talking about.
    (B) The store has only one copy remaining.
    (C) The man knows the woman well.
    (D) The man will show the woman a review.

46. What will the woman most likely do?

    (A) Go to another store
    (B) Buy two copies
    (C) Ask the man to call her husband
    (D) Purchase a gift

---

47. What are the speakers discussing?

    (A) A trip to Korea
    (B) A language course
    (C) Lecture schedules
    (D) A management meeting

48. When will the classes start?

    (A) The middle of next month
    (B) Tomorrow
    (C) Next week
    (D) On Tuesday

49. What is mentioned about the hotel?

    (A) It is located in Korea.
    (B) Its marketing has focused on Korea recently.
    (C) It has only three employees.
    (D) It has been accommodating many foreign guests.

50. Where most likely do the speakers work?

    (A) At a restaurant
    (B) At a limo service
    (C) At a hotel
    (D) At a wedding hall

51. Why is Micron Technologies calling?

    (A) To book a wedding
    (B) To reserve rooms for next week
    (C) To ask about a car service
    (D) To complain about poor service

52. What will the man probably do next?

    (A) Contact a car company
    (B) Call Micron Technologies back
    (C) Reschedule a wedding
    (D) Clean a hotel room

---

53. What type of business do the speakers probably work in?

    (A) A restaurant
    (B) A hotel
    (C) A newspaper
    (D) A travel agency

54. According to the woman, what did the critic say?

    (A) He is friends with the chef.
    (B) The menu was innovative.
    (C) The service was fantastic.
    (D) The food was ordinary.

55. What does one of the men say he will do?

    (A) Close down the business
    (B) Write something on the wall
    (C) Think of new menu items
    (D) Post the article

---

56. Where does the conversation probably take place?

    (A) At a university
    (B) At a large hospital
    (C) At a clinic
    (D) At an exam center

57. What does the man propose that the woman do?

    (A) Come back tomorrow
    (B) Go to a different institution
    (C) Decide which tests she wants
    (D) Take medicine regularly

58. What will the man probably do next?

    (A) Prepare a document
    (B) See another patient
    (C) Call the general hospital
    (D) Conduct a specialized test

---

59. What does the man mention about the snowstorm?

    (A) It covered the bakery in snow.
    (B) The bakery is not doing very well.
    (C) The price of strawberries nearly doubled.
    (D) The price of strawberry pies has gone up.

60. What does the woman imply?

    (A) They may need to close down the bakery.
    (B) They should apply cost-cutting measures.
    (C) The price of strawberries is going to continue to rise.
    (D) They have already started losing customers.

61. What does the man say he will do tonight?

    (A) Call a few customers
    (B) Cut down on the number of ingredients
    (C) Buy more strawberries
    (D) Review financial records

---

62. What are the speakers trying to do?

    (A) Organize a group lunch
    (B) Choose between soda and juice
    (C) Prepare for a presentation
    (D) Reserve a meeting room

63. What does the woman imply when she says, "I'm way ahead of you"?

    (A) She already took care of it.
    (B) She is in front of the man.
    (C) She is almost done.
    (D) She will win the race.

64. What will the woman do next?

    (A) Distribute copies of the presentation
    (B) Order snacks and drinks
    (C) Give a presentation
    (D) Help the man with the projector

ACTUAL TEST 03

PART 3

Go on to the next page

Program	
Performer	**Time**
Henry	1:00–1:30
Melissa	1:40–2:10
Martha	2:20–2:50
Michael	3:00–3:30

Type	Office Furniture Type	Price
A	Standard office chair	$100
B	Standard office desk with drawers	$575
C	Large, executive desk with drawers	$720
D	Large, president-style office chair	$350

65. Look at the graphic. Who will be performing right before Michael?

(A) Henry
(B) Melissa
(C) Martha
(D) Nobody

66. What kind of performance will Martha do?

(A) Dancing
(B) Singing
(C) Musical instrument
(D) Monologue

67. Why did the program change?

(A) The show has been postponed.
(B) Martha still needs to practice her piece.
(C) Melissa is sick.
(D) Martha will go over the allotted time.

68. What does the department head want?

(A) A stapler
(B) A desk
(C) A new job
(D) A comfortable chair

69. What did the man last order from the catalog?

(A) Staples
(B) Printer paper
(C) An office desk
(D) Staplers

70. Look at the graphic. What item will the woman probably order?

(A) A
(B) B
(C) C
(D) D

PART 4 ⌒ 12

Directions: You will hear some talks given by a single speaker. You will be asked to answer three questions about what the speaker says in each talk. Select the best response to each question and mark the letter (A), (B), (C), or (D) on your answer sheet. The talks will not be printed in your test book and will be spoken only one time.

71. Where is the announcement being made?
    (A) At a stadium
    (B) At a restaurant
    (C) At a university library
    (D) At a museum

72. What does the speaker ask the listeners to do?
    (A) Be careful when touching the sculptures
    (B) Not eat but feel free to drink anywhere
    (C) Be at the appointed place on time
    (D) Go directly home after viewing the exhibits

73. When must the listeners leave the building?
    (A) 12:00 P.M.
    (B) 3:00 P.M.
    (C) 4:00 P.M.
    (D) 8:00 P.M.

74. Where is the announcement being made?
    (A) On a local bus
    (B) At a monorail station
    (C) At a hotel
    (D) On a monorail train

75. Why was the announcement made?
    (A) The train will stop and wait.
    (B) The train will head back.
    (C) The train will continue on to the hotel.
    (D) The train needs to be repaired.

76. According to the speaker, what can listeners do?
    (A) Wait two hours on the train
    (B) Walk back to the monorail station
    (C) Help the workers repair the track
    (D) Take a bus or taxi to the hotel

77. Who is James Cotton?
    (A) A pastor
    (B) A cotton farmer
    (C) A therapist
    (D) A magazine editor

78. What happened to James Cotton last month?
    (A) He won an award.
    (B) He was featured in a magazine.
    (C) He opened the Cottonwood Clinic.
    (D) He was out of town.

79. How can patients get a discount?
    (A) By calling next Monday
    (B) By presenting a coupon
    (C) By bringing a copy of a book
    (D) By making an appointment this week

80. Where can this morning's recital be heard?
    (A) In the auditorium
    (B) On the radio
    (C) In Japan
    (D) At Carnegie Hall

81. What does the speaker say about Dimitry Olanov?
    (A) He lives in Russia.
    (B) He does not perform outside Canada.
    (C) He does not play a musical instrument.
    (D) He won only one competition.

82. What will Dimitry Olanov most likely do this morning?
    (A) Talk about his childhood
    (B) Travel to Canada
    (C) Discuss his love for Vivaldi
    (D) Play a musical instrument

Go on to the next page

51

83. Who most likely are the listeners?

(A) Clients
(B) Consultants
(C) Salespeople
(D) Children

84. Why does the speaker say, "we could not have achieved this level of success without each and every one of you"?

(A) She wants to achieve success.
(B) She has a new project for the team.
(C) She wants to praise the team members.
(D) She is ready for a vacation.

85. What will the listeners do in October?

(A) Go on vacation
(B) Finish up the project
(C) Lower costs
(D) Start on a new project

---

86. What is the speaker mainly talking about?

(A) A subway station
(B) A boutique law firm
(C) An office relocation
(D) A prestigious building

87. What is the merit of the change?

(A) Smaller space
(B) More publicity
(C) Decreased rent
(D) Parking

88. What does the speaker say about the Conway Center?

(A) It is on top of a train station.
(B) It is next to a shopping mall.
(C) It is the tallest building in the city.
(D) It is on the other side of town.

---

89. What is the report mainly about?

(A) A new construction project
(B) A business merger
(C) An innovative software product
(D) Social media platforms

90. What can be inferred about GenuTech's future plans?

(A) It will focus more on online marketing.
(B) It will seek to merge with Veriline.
(C) It will market only in the United States.
(D) It will hire someone new as its first CEO.

91. What does the speaker suggest about the reason behind GenuTech's formation?

(A) To increase sales revenues
(B) To deal with a market competitor
(C) To streamline costs
(D) To come up with global marketing strategies

Time	Music
0:00	BGM 1
2:12	BGM 2
5:25	BGM 3
5:50	BGM 4
6:41	BGM 3
7:01	BGM 1

92. Why does the speaker say, "I need to make one change, though"?

(A) He wants to revise the chart.
(B) He has to change his background.
(C) He needs change for the vending machine.
(D) He wants to make a new song.

93. What does the speaker expect the listener to do?

(A) Pay him $100
(B) Compose background music
(C) Complete the task by Thursday
(D) Help him shoot a video

94. Look at the graphic. What can you tell about the speaker's request?

(A) BGM 4 should be the opening music.
(B) BGM 2 comes after BGM 4.
(C) BGM 2 should be played in two spots.
(D) Background music should be inserted 5 times.

	Monday	Tuesday
8:00 A.M.–10:00 A.M.	Italian Cuisine	Singing in Italian
12:00 P.M.–2:00 P.M.	Italian 101	Italian Opera
2:00 P.M.–4:00 P.M.	Italian Opera	Italian 301
3:30 P.M.–5:30 P.M.	Italian 201	Italian 101
7:00 P.M.–9:00 P.M.	Singing in Italian	Italian Cuisine

	Saturday, April 1	Sunday, April 2	Monday, April 3
Hawaii to Seattle	10:00 P.M.	4:00 P.M.	9:00 A.M.
Hawaii to Los Angeles	10:00 A.M.	11:00 A.M.	5:00 P.M.
Hawaii to Atlanta	3:30 P.M.	3:30 P.M.	3:30 P.M.

95. Who are the listeners?

(A) Italian teachers
(B) Foreigners
(C) Students
(D) Employees

96. What is mentioned about the classes?

(A) New students can take up to two classes.
(B) Students may take Italian 201 and Italian 301 simultaneously.
(C) The first day of classes is on Saturday.
(D) No more than ten students are allowed in one class.

97. Look at the graphic. Which of the following combinations is possible for a new student?

(A) Italian 101 (Mon), Singing in Italian (Mon), and Italian Cuisine (Tues)
(B) Italian 101 (Mon) and Italian 301 (Tues)
(C) Italian 101 (Mon) and Italian 201 (Tues)
(D) Italian Cuisine (Mon) and Italian 101 (Tues)

98. Why did Megan make a phone call?

(A) To say she is going to be leaving early
(B) To say she has lost some luggage
(C) To report that her flight schedule got delayed
(D) To say she will be traveling next to Boston

99. What does Megan say about her schedule?

(A) She was originally scheduled to leave today.
(B) She is transferring in Hawaii.
(C) Her final destination is Seattle.
(D) She can depart from Hawaii tomorrow if she wants to.

100. Look at the graphic. Which day will Megan go home?

(A) Saturday
(B) Sunday
(C) Monday
(D) Tuesday

ACTUAL TEST

答對題數表

PART 1	
PART 2	
PART 3	
PART 4	
總題數	

04

LISTENING TEST

In the Listening test, you will be asked to demonstrate how well you understand spoken English. The entire Listening test will last approximately 45 minutes. There are four parts, and directions are given for each part. You must mark your answers on the separate answer sheet. Do not write your answers in your test book.

PART 1 13

Directions: For each question in this part, you will hear four statements about a picture in your test book. When you hear the statements, you must select the one statement that best describes what you see in the picture. Then find the number of the question on your answer sheet and mark your answer. The statements will not be printed in your test book and will be spoken only one time.

Sample Answer

Statement (B), "They're shaking hands," is the best description of the picture, so you should select answer (B) and mark it on your answer sheet.

1.

2.

Go on to the next page ➜

3.

4.

5.

6.

PART 2 ∩ 14

Directions: You will hear a question or statement and three responses spoken in English. They will not be printed in your test book and will be spoken only one time. Select the best response to the question or statement and mark the letter (A), (B), or (C) on your answer sheet.

7. Mark your answer on your answer sheet.

8. Mark your answer on your answer sheet.

9. Mark your answer on your answer sheet.

10. Mark your answer on your answer sheet.

11. Mark your answer on your answer sheet.

12. Mark your answer on your answer sheet.

13. Mark your answer on your answer sheet.

14. Mark your answer on your answer sheet.

15. Mark your answer on your answer sheet.

16. Mark your answer on your answer sheet.

17. Mark your answer on your answer sheet.

18. Mark your answer on your answer sheet.

19. Mark your answer on your answer sheet.

20. Mark your answer on your answer sheet.

21. Mark your answer on your answer sheet.

22. Mark your answer on your answer sheet.

23. Mark your answer on your answer sheet.

24. Mark your answer on your answer sheet.

25. Mark your answer on your answer sheet.

26. Mark your answer on your answer sheet.

27. Mark your answer on your answer sheet.

28. Mark your answer on your answer sheet.

29. Mark your answer on your answer sheet.

30. Mark your answer on your answer sheet.

31. Mark your answer on your answer sheet.

PART 3 ∩ 15

Directions: You will hear some conversations between two or more people. You will be asked to answer three questions about what the speakers say in each conversation. Select the best response to each question and mark the letter (A), (B), (C), or (D) on your answer sheet. The conversations will not be printed in your test book and will be spoken only one time.

32. Why did the woman call the man?

(A) To get help fixing a problem
(B) To replace a device with a new one
(C) To send him an urgent document
(D) To purchase a monitor

33. According to the woman, what did she do in the morning?

(A) Turned on her computer
(B) Came in earlier than usual
(C) Tried connecting her monitor again
(D) Printed the weekly report from her computer

34. What will the man probably do next?

(A) Submit the report for Stella
(B) Meet Stella in her office
(C) Bring his computer to the 2nd floor
(D) Try plugging the computer into another outlet

35. Why does the woman ask the man for help?

(A) A coworker is not feeling well.
(B) She is very sick.
(C) She is out of town this afternoon.
(D) She will take some time off.

36. What does the man need?

(A) A key to a truck
(B) A telephone number
(C) A director's contact information
(D) Directions to a store

37. What does the woman remind the man to do?

(A) Get a signature
(B) Notify his manager
(C) Become a member
(D) Sign the contract

38. Why will the man visit the woman's house?

(A) To verify her name and address
(B) To reschedule an appointment
(C) To improve the network speed
(D) To sell a telecommunication device

39. Why does the man ask the woman's name?

(A) He is trying to be polite.
(B) Some information is not accurate.
(C) He'll write her a letter afterwards.
(D) He wants to record the woman's voice.

40. What time does the woman want the upgrade to be finished by?

(A) By 2:00 P.M.
(B) By 2:20 P.M.
(C) By 2:30 P.M.
(D) By 3:00 P.M.

41. Where are the speakers working?

(A) At an advertising agency
(B) At a law firm
(C) At an architectural company
(D) At a design school

42. What does the woman mean when she says, "I really can't say"?

(A) She is not allowed to reveal certain information.
(B) She should cancel the appointment.
(C) She cannot make a commitment yet.
(D) She has to revise some mistakes.

43. What does the man propose?

(A) Making an itinerary
(B) Preparing a negotiation
(C) Delaying a meeting
(D) Reviewing the project together

Go on to the next page

ACTUAL TEST 04

PART 3

44. What problem are the speakers mainly discussing?
    (A) They must launch a Web site in a hurry.
    (B) There are not as many participants as they expected.
    (C) They have made a change in a plan.
    (D) The president won't be able to deliver a speech.

45. Why does the man say, "it was worth a try"?
    (A) He is comforting the woman.
    (B) He doesn't want to take the risk.
    (C) He knew that Mr. Dice would turn them down.
    (D) He regrets he had to meet the speaker in person.

46. What does the woman say she will do?
    (A) Send text messages
    (B) Update a Web page
    (C) Contact the president
    (D) Convince Mr. Dice to attend the event

47. Who most likely is the woman?
    (A) A pharmacist
    (B) An optician
    (C) A receptionist
    (D) An appraiser

48. When is the man supposed to come?
    (A) Wednesday morning
    (B) Wednesday evening
    (C) Thursday morning
    (D) Thursday evening

49. What is suggested about the clinic?
    (A) Dr. Jenkins is the only doctor working there.
    (B) This is the first time Mr. Ortega has contacted it.
    (C) It is open from 10 A.M. to 8 P.M. on weekends.
    (D) It keeps some patients' medical records.

50. Who most likely are Chris and Nancy?
    (A) Apartment managers
    (B) Interior designers
    (C) Realtors
    (D) Potential buyers

51. What are Chris and Nancy concerned about?
    (A) The placement of smoke detectors
    (B) The size of a property
    (C) The expense of renovation
    (D) The range of interior design companies

52. What is mentioned about the owner?
    (A) She owns several stores.
    (B) She'll start a new business.
    (C) She can recommend qualified workers.
    (D) She wants to change the interior.

53. What is the woman unable to do?
    (A) Log on to her computer
    (B) Organize a workshop
    (C) Print a document
    (D) Create a password

54. According to the man, what happened yesterday?
    (A) The power went out.
    (B) Some servers were changed.
    (C) Some equipment was broken.
    (D) Computers were installed.

55. What does the man say he will do?
    (A) Restart a computer
    (B) Install new software
    (C) Call a coworker
    (D) Put in a help request

56. What are the speakers mainly talking about?

(A) The cost of living
(B) Overseas branches
(C) An online business
(D) A proposed budget

57. What does the man say about the Rome expenses?

(A) They have been underestimated.
(B) They are the same as last year's.
(C) The quotes look good.
(D) The living costs were not in the budget.

58. What does the woman say she will do?

(A) Spend less money
(B) Estimate a price
(C) Use last year's records
(D) Update some information

---

59. Why is the woman calling the man?

(A) To report an equipment malfunction
(B) To check a device
(C) To request personal information
(D) To set up a meeting

60. What does the woman imply when she says, "I'm interviewing someone here in 10 minutes"?

(A) She needs help urgently.
(B) She does not want to be interrupted.
(C) She is not satisfied with an assignment.
(D) She will not attend another meeting.

61. What does the woman say is unique about the interview?

(A) It will be recorded.
(B) It will be filmed.
(C) It will be conducted face-to-face.
(D) It will last for more than an hour.

Departure	Gate	Time	Status
Melbourne	A8	15:30	Delayed
Sydney	B14	15:45	On time
Perth	A9	16:00	Canceled
Brisbane	C10	17:00	On time

62. Where is the conversation taking place?

(A) At a bus terminal
(B) At an airport
(C) At a business conference
(D) At a train station

63. Why isn't the man staying for the entire conference?

(A) He has a scheduling conflict.
(B) He is about to go on holiday.
(C) He has a presentation.
(D) He could not find a later flight.

64. Look at the graphic. What city are the speakers going to?

(A) Melbourne
(B) Sydney
(C) Perth
(D) Brisbane

Go on to the next page

	stairs	restroom
Room 301 (Sales Department)	Room 302	Room 303
stairs	elevators	
Room 304	copy room	Room 305	staff lounge

From	Subject
Brian Swann	Budget Report
Yianni Ellenikiotis	Conference Agenda
Helen Yang	ATTACHED: Quarterly Sales figures
Brittany Seymour	DELAYED: Management workshop

65. Look at the graphic. Which room are the speakers moving into on Monday?

(A) Room 302
(B) Room 303
(C) Room 304
(D) Room 305

66. According to the woman, what would her colleagues say about their new room?

(A) They're glad to take the biggest room.
(B) They are pleased to be situated near the stairs.
(C) They're not happy to be located near the staff lounge.
(D) They enjoy the advantages of soundproof insulation.

67. Why does the man have to leave early today?

(A) He has to meet a client at two o'clock.
(B) He has an appointment in the afternoon.
(C) He has to pack up his belongings in advance.
(D) He has to pick up something in the staff lounge.

68. Why is the man unable to access his e-mail?

(A) He's using an incorrect password.
(B) His Internet connection isn't available.
(C) He forgot to update some software.
(D) His computer is malfunctioning.

69. Look at the graphic. Who sent the e-mail the speakers are referring to?

(A) Brian Swann
(B) Yianni Ellenikiotis
(C) Helen Yang
(D) Brittany Seymour

70. What does the man ask the woman to do?

(A) Call the technician
(B) Present the quarterly sales figures
(C) Print out a document
(D) Arrange a meeting this afternoon

PART 4 ∩ 16

Directions: You will hear some talks given by a single speaker. You will be asked to answer three questions about what the speaker says in each talk. Select the best response to each question and mark the letter (A), (B), (C), or (D) on your answer sheet. The talks will not be printed in your test book and will be spoken only one time.

71. What is the purpose of the talk?

   (A) To ask for donations
   (B) To publicize the museum
   (C) To discuss modern art
   (D) To introduce an exhibit

72. What will the speaker distribute?

   (A) Entrance tickets
   (B) A brochure
   (C) A map of the museum
   (D) An audio player

73. According to the speaker, what will begin at two o'clock?

   (A) An auction
   (B) A concert
   (C) A talk
   (D) A reception

74. Why did the speaker leave a message?

   (A) To talk about a problem with an order
   (B) To find out when to make a delivery
   (C) To get more information about furniture
   (D) To ask for help choosing a new chair

75. When does the speaker say he can deliver similar chairs?

   (A) In four weeks
   (B) Tomorrow
   (C) This evening
   (D) In two days

76. What does the speaker say he will do today?

   (A) Work at the store all day long
   (B) Record some messages
   (C) Send the package
   (D) Deliver items

77. How long has the business been operating?

   (A) For twelve years
   (B) For two decades
   (C) For a decade
   (D) For fifteen years

78. What type of business is being advertised?

   (A) An airline
   (B) A bus company
   (C) A travel agency
   (D) A bookstore

79. What special offer is the business making now?

   (A) Free calling cards
   (B) Reduced rates on certain flights
   (C) Package tours to Asia and other countries in Europe
   (D) Free accommodation in Venice and Florence

80. What does the speaker say will happen at the end of the month?

   (A) A new City Hall will be built.
   (B) Traffic congestion will take place.
   (C) Construction on new bus lanes will commence.
   (D) A hotel association will select a new president.

81. Who is Tom Kenny?

   (A) A local politician
   (B) A news reporter
   (C) A bus driver
   (D) A city spokesperson

82. What will listeners probably hear next?

   (A) A sports game
   (B) A local news report
   (C) A sponsor's message
   (D) A weather forecast

Go on to the next page

83. What type of business does the speaker work for?

(A) A recruiting agency
(B) A computer retailer
(C) An office equipment manufacturer
(D) An education center

84. Why does the speaker say, "The copier is in room 305"?

(A) He was asked if a copier is available.
(B) The attendees will learn how to make copies today.
(C) The teaching assistants need to copy the roll book.
(D) Some people should go to another room to prepare some document.

85. What does the speaker ask the listeners to do?

(A) Sign the contract
(B) Introduce themselves
(C) Team up with their colleagues
(D) Submit their applications in advance

---

86. What does the speaker mainly talk about?

(A) Building a welfare center
(B) Drawing more volunteers
(C) Organizing a fundraising event
(D) Becoming a teacher

87. What problem does the welfare center have?

(A) There are not many schools in the area.
(B) It cannot afford free meals for the beneficiaries.
(C) The center hasn't launched any education programs yet.
(D) They don't have enough money for a plan.

88. What are the listeners asked to do?

(A) Contact the schools in the area
(B) Look for a suitable contractor
(C) Attract more young teens
(D) Ask for their parents' support

---

89. What is the speaker doing for Ms. Shirley?

(A) Finding a place to live
(B) Reserving a hotel room
(C) Buying an office building
(D) Renovating an interior design

90. What does the speaker imply when she says, "But it's not a problem"?

(A) She wants to recommend a moving company.
(B) She asks for a specific reason.
(C) She feels disappointed.
(D) She thinks that she can resolve the issue.

91. What does the speaker ask Ms. Shirley to do?

(A) Arrange an appointment
(B) Leave a message
(C) Choose the color of the wallpaper
(D) Update contact information

---

92. Why is the speaker calling?

(A) To schedule a meeting
(B) To confirm the listener's presence at a conference
(C) To arrange suitable travel date
(D) To reschedule a conference call

93. What did Mr. Reece's secretary tell Mr. Stanton?

(A) His availability is uncertain.
(B) His interest is negligible.
(C) His attendance is mandatory.
(D) His schedule is canceled.

94. What does the speaker say he will do?

(A) Mail the proposed agenda
(B) Arrange a flight
(C) Send information electronically
(D) Check the time difference

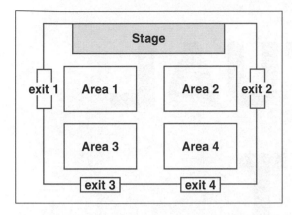

Survey Results	
Design	40%
Color Scheme	25%
Durability	15%
Material	20%

95. Who most likely are the listeners?

(A) Photographers
(B) Performers
(C) Ushers
(D) Audience members

96. Look at the graphic. What section does the speaker want the listeners to sit in?

(A) Area 1
(B) Area 2
(C) Area 3
(D) Area 4

97. What are listeners asked to do when the show ends?

(A) Have some refreshments
(B) Sign autographs
(C) Revise a magazine
(D) Attend a photo shoot

98. According to the speaker, why did the company conduct the survey?

(A) To satisfy consumers
(B) To release the running shoes
(C) To cut operating expenses
(D) To correct a questionnaire

99. Look at the graphic. Which survey result does the speaker want to address now?

(A) Design
(B) Color Scheme
(C) Durability
(D) Material

100. What does the speaker ask the listeners to do?

(A) Conduct safety inspections
(B) Give some feedback
(C) Mention some potential employees
(D) Contact the product development team

ACTUAL
TEST

答對題數表

PART 1	
PART 2	
PART 3	
PART 4	
總題數	

05

LISTENING TEST

In the Listening test, you will be asked to demonstrate how well you understand spoken English. The entire Listening test will last approximately 45 minutes. There are four parts, and directions are given for each part. You must mark your answers on the separate answer sheet.
Do not write your answers in your test book.

PART 1 ∩ 17

Directions: For each question in this part, you will hear four statements about a picture in your test book. When you hear the statements, you must select the one statement that best describes what you see in the picture. Then find the number of the question on your answer sheet and mark your answer. The statements will not be printed in your test book and will be spoken only one time.

Sample Answer

 Ⓐ ● Ⓒ Ⓓ

Statement (B), "They're shaking hands," is the best description of the picture, so you should select answer (B) and mark it on your answer sheet.

1.

2.

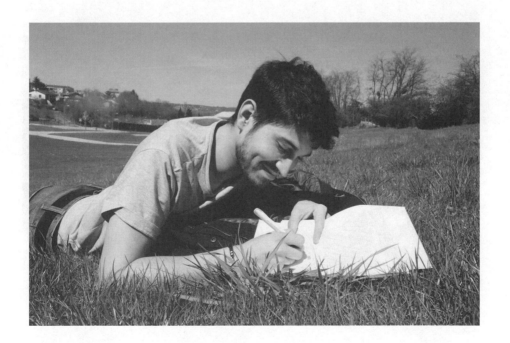

Go on to the next page

3.

4.

5.

6.

Go on to the next page

PART 2 ∩18

Directions: You will hear a question or statement and three responses spoken in English. They will not be printed in your test book and will be spoken only one time. Select the best response to the question or statement and mark the letter (A), (B), or (C) on your answer sheet.

7. Mark your answer on your answer sheet.

8. Mark your answer on your answer sheet.

9. Mark your answer on your answer sheet.

10. Mark your answer on your answer sheet.

11. Mark your answer on your answer sheet.

12. Mark your answer on your answer sheet.

13. Mark your answer on your answer sheet.

14. Mark your answer on your answer sheet.

15. Mark your answer on your answer sheet.

16. Mark your answer on your answer sheet.

17. Mark your answer on your answer sheet.

18. Mark your answer on your answer sheet.

19. Mark your answer on your answer sheet.

20. Mark your answer on your answer sheet.

21. Mark your answer on your answer sheet.

22. Mark your answer on your answer sheet.

23. Mark your answer on your answer sheet.

24. Mark your answer on your answer sheet.

25. Mark your answer on your answer sheet.

26. Mark your answer on your answer sheet.

27. Mark your answer on your answer sheet.

28. Mark your answer on your answer sheet.

29. Mark your answer on your answer sheet.

30. Mark your answer on your answer sheet.

31. Mark your answer on your answer sheet.

PART 3 ∩ 19

Directions: You will hear some conversations between two or more people. You will be asked to answer three questions about what the speakers say in each conversation. Select the best response to each question and mark the letter (A), (B), (C), or (D) on your answer sheet. The conversations will not be printed in your test book and will be spoken only one time.

32. Why does the man choose to shop at the store?
- (A) It is conveniently located.
- (B) The staff is very kind.
- (C) He saw an online advertisement.
- (D) One of his colleagues recommended the store.

33. What does the woman ask about?
- (A) An identification card
- (B) A receipt
- (C) A discount coupon
- (D) An advertisement flyer

34. Why does the man say he will go home?
- (A) He wants to come with his parents.
- (B) He has to answer the phone.
- (C) He left something behind.
- (D) He doesn't want to buy this product.

35. Where is the conversation most likely taking place?
- (A) At a coffee shop
- (B) At an office
- (C) At a clothing factory
- (D) At a dry cleaner's

36. What is the woman doing on Friday?
- (A) Meeting a client
- (B) Interviewing for a job
- (C) Going on a vacation
- (D) Visiting relatives

37. What does the man offer to do?
- (A) Exchange a defective product
- (B) Cancel a reservation
- (C) Offer an express service
- (D) Place a special order

38. Why will the man visit the woman's office?
- (A) To set up appliances
- (B) To make a repair
- (C) To deliver a speech
- (D) To get a refund

39. What does the woman say she will do?
- (A) Buy some refrigerators
- (B) Stay in the company
- (C) Talk to a security officer
- (D) Provide a receipt

40. What does the woman ask the man to leave with the security guard?
- (A) An estimate
- (B) A manual
- (C) An invoice
- (D) An agreement

41. What is the woman shopping for?
- (A) Stationery
- (B) Wrapping paper
- (C) Children's book
- (D) Paint

42. What does Christopher say about the items?
- (A) They're sold out.
- (B) They're offered at a discounted price.
- (C) They've already been delivered.
- (D) They're on a different floor.

43. What additional service does Christopher mention?
- (A) Express delivery
- (B) Free packaging
- (C) A free estimate
- (D) On-site repair

Go on to the next page

44. What are the speakers organizing?

(A) A job interview
(B) A speech contest
(C) A conference
(D) A career fair

45. What problem does the woman mention?

(A) An event has been delayed.
(B) A flight was canceled.
(C) Hotels are all booked up.
(D) A speaker has canceled.

46. What most likely will the man do next?

(A) Send an invitation card
(B) Make a phone call
(C) Make a reservation
(D) Prepare a meeting

47. Where do the speakers most likely work?

(A) At a fitness center
(B) At a sporting goods store
(C) At a department store
(D) At a heavy equipment facility

48. What does the man imply when he says, "I can't do it alone"?

(A) He is asking for a pay increase.
(B) He wants to know the exact number of members.
(C) He thinks that the task is impossible.
(D) He is satisfied with his current position.

49. What does the woman offer to do?

(A) Change the schedule
(B) Move the equipment
(C) Clean up the facility
(D) Recruit more members

50. What are the speakers discussing?

(A) Selecting a new computer system
(B) Checking maintenance information
(C) Starting a business
(D) Finishing a report

51. Why was the man unable to complete a task?

(A) Sales revenue has decreased.
(B) A system was not working properly.
(C) A colleague was out of town.
(D) A meeting was canceled.

52. What does the woman say she will do?

(A) Prepare for a meeting
(B) Change a reservation
(C) Contact the Maintenance Department
(D) E-mail a report

53. What does the man say he will do next month?

(A) Participate in a medical forum
(B) Go away on business
(C) Move to a different city
(D) Finish a medical course

54. According to the conversation, what did Jennifer do in the morning?

(A) She rescheduled an appointment.
(B) She prescribed some medicine.
(C) She printed some documents.
(D) She treated a patient.

55. What does Jennifer ask the man to do?

(A) Make a payment
(B) Wait for a while
(C) Sign a form
(D) Call a doctor's office

56. Why is the man calling?

    (A) He wants to buy another product.
    (B) His order has not yet been delivered.
    (C) He needs to know the store's Web
         site address.
    (D) He was charged twice for a purchase.

57. What does the woman explain about?

    (A) A technical issue
    (B) A renovation project
    (C) An inventory shortage
    (D) A credit card expiration date

58. What does the woman ask the man to do?

    (A) Return a product
    (B) Respond to a survey
    (C) Visit a Web site
    (D) Keep a receipt

---

59. Where most likely is the woman?

    (A) At a building entrance
    (B) In a meeting room
    (C) At an airport
    (D) In an elevator

60. What does the man ask for?

    (A) A department name
    (B) An employee number
    (C) A password
    (D) A telephone number

61. Why does the man say, "It's against the company policy"?

    (A) To postpone a meeting
    (B) To refuse a request
    (C) To ask for a help
    (D) To make up for a mistake

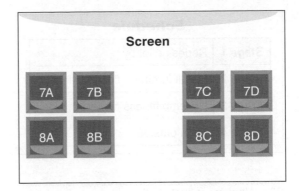

Screen

7A 7B 7C 7D

8A 8B 8C 8D

62. What is the purpose of the conversation?

    (A) To explain refund regulations
    (B) To introduce a new film
    (C) To offer a special discount
    (D) To resolve a problem

63. Look at the graphic. What seat was the woman originally assigned to?

    (A) 7A
    (B) 7B
    (C) 8A
    (D) 8B

64. What does the woman ask the man to do?

    (A) Check the time when the movie starts
    (B) Choose another movie
    (C) Request a discount coupon
    (D) Change the seat

Go on to the next page

Schedule

Stage 1	Redesign lobby
Stage 2	Install furniture, flooring, lighting
Stage 3	Revamp fitness center
Stage 4	Paint outside

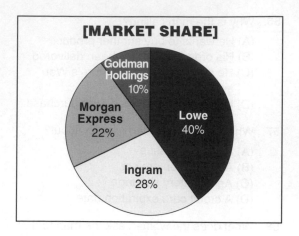

[MARKET SHARE]

Goldman Holdings 10%

Morgan Express 22%

Lowe 40%

Ingram 28%

65. What most likely is the man's profession?

(A) Engineer
(B) Construction manager
(C) Real estate agent
(D) Salesperson

66. Look at the graphic. What stage of the renovation will begin next week?

(A) Stage 1
(B) Stage 2
(C) Stage 3
(D) Stage 4

67. What does the woman ask the man to send?

(A) An estimated price
(B) Some photos
(C) A schedule
(D) A hotel address

68. What are the speakers mainly discussing?

(A) An annual plan
(B) Unemployment rates
(C) A business acquisition
(D) A budget report

69. Look at the graphic. Where do the speakers work?

(A) Lowe
(B) Ingram
(C) Morgan Express
(D) Goldman Holdings

70. Why does the man say he is not convinced?

(A) He didn't read the report.
(B) Some information is inaccurate.
(C) The man is not good at analyzing data.
(D) A company's profits have reduced recently.

PART 4 ∩ 20

Directions: You will hear some talks given by a single speaker. You will be asked to answer three questions about what the speaker says in each talk. Select the best response to each question and mark the letter (A), (B), (C), or (D) on your answer sheet. The talks will not be printed in your test book and will be spoken only one time.

71. What service is being advertised?

(A) Home delivery
(B) A recycling program
(C) Product repair
(D) An education course

72. How can listeners get a discount?

(A) By making a donation
(B) By taking a class
(C) By purchasing a certain item
(D) By recommending a company

73. What does the speaker say is available on a Web site?

(A) A product line
(B) A discount coupon
(C) A promotional video
(D) A list of locations

74. Where is the announcement probably being made?

(A) At an airport
(B) At a bus station
(C) At a taxi stand
(D) At a ticket office

75. What does the speaker ask listeners to do?

(A) Meet with a representative
(B) Cancel a ticket
(C) Visit the company's Web site
(D) Book a hotel

76. According to the speaker, what will be offered?

(A) A free dinner
(B) Free refreshments
(C) An itinerary
(D) Maps

77. What is the purpose of the message?

(A) To set up a meeting
(B) To receive an order
(C) To get an approval
(D) To make a contract

78. What does the speaker imply when she says, "we have only three months left before the opening of the new branch"?

(A) She should find a place to conduct an interview.
(B) She wants the listener to visit a branch.
(C) A branch office should be opened soon.
(D) A decision should be made as soon as possible.

79. What most likely will the speaker do next?

(A) Make a list of candidates
(B) E-mail some documents
(C) Call a branch office
(D) Fill out an application

80. Where does the speaker work?

(A) At a museum
(B) At a hotel
(C) At a store
(D) At a factory

81. What will the listeners be doing today?

(A) Making a flyer
(B) Going on a tour
(C) Distributing leaflets
(D) Taking pictures

82. What has the speaker done for the listeners?

(A) Made a reservation for a restaurant
(B) Ordered gifts
(C) Provided complimentary tickets
(D) Circled places on a map

Go on to the next page

83. What kind of business does the speaker work for?

(A) An advertising agency
(B) A furniture store
(C) A library
(D) A financial institution

84. What is the speaker announcing?

(A) An award winner
(B) A resignation
(C) A promotion
(D) A retirement

85. What does the speaker say about Emmy Kunis's work?

(A) It optimized the production lines.
(B) It led to changes in a company's regulations.
(C) It took advantage of the latest technology.
(D) It helped its client boost profits.

---

86. What is the main topic of the meeting?

(A) A new department
(B) A user manual
(C) Survey results
(D) Product defects

87. What feature of the product does the speaker mention?

(A) An energy-saving function
(B) A digital display
(C) Its durability
(D) A removable rack

88. What does the speaker imply when she says, "So the related department is now editing this"?

(A) The manual can only be viewed online.
(B) The manual is available in multiple languages.
(C) The manual should be shortened.
(D) Customers should read it thoroughly.

---

89. What is the talk mainly about?

(A) Attracting foreign companies
(B) Opening an art gallery
(C) Building a park
(D) Solving traffic congestion

90. What problem does the speaker mention?

(A) A delayed schedule
(B) A transportation system
(C) Lack of funds
(D) A manpower shortage

91. What are the listeners asked to do?

(A) Hold a meeting
(B) Carry out a survey
(C) Come up with a list of local businesses
(D) Purchase items

---

92. What type of business does the speaker work for?

(A) A law firm
(B) A hospital
(C) An employment agency
(D) A manufacturer

93. What does the speaker imply when he says, "this process could take some time"?

(A) He wants the listeners to be patient.
(B) He points out that the office is very busy.
(C) He says that the scheduled date could be canceled.
(D) He suggests that the listeners be ready anytime.

94. What does the speaker ask the listeners to do?

(A) Submit their application
(B) Receive a letter of recommendation
(C) Make a copy of their identification
(D) Fill out some documents

- Order form -

Item	Quantity
Chocolate bar	100
Milk in bottles	200
Cups	300
Cereal flakes	250

95. Look at the graphic. Which quantity of the order form will be changed?

(A) 100
(B) 200
(C) 300
(D) 250

96. What is the speaker doing next week?

(A) She is going on a vacation.
(B) She is moving to a different country.
(C) She is remodeling her house.
(D) She is changing her job.

97. What does the speaker say about John?

(A) He will be dealing with some accounts.
(B) He will cancel an order.
(C) He will print some documents.
(D) He will introduce a new product.

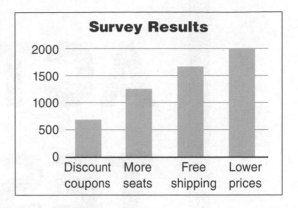

98. Where does the talk take place?

(A) At a bookstore
(B) At a factory
(C) At a hotel
(D) At the airport

99. Look at the graphic. Which suggestions will the company begin to work on?

(A) Discount coupons
(B) More seats
(C) Free shipping
(D) Lower prices

100. What will the people receive for completing the survey?

(A) A complimentary book
(B) A discount coupon
(C) Refreshments
(D) A store gift card

ACTUAL TEST

答對題數表

PART 1	
PART 2	
PART 3	
PART 4	
總題數	

06

LISTENING TEST

In the Listening test, you will be asked to demonstrate how well you understand spoken English. The entire Listening test will last approximately 45 minutes. There are four parts, and directions are given for each part. You must mark your answers on the separate answer sheet. Do not write your answers in your test book.

PART 1 21

Directions: For each question in this part, you will hear four statements about a picture in your test book. When you hear the statements, you must select the one statement that best describes what you see in the picture. Then find the number of the question on your answer sheet and mark your answer. The statements will not be printed in your test book and will be spoken only one time.

Sample Answer

Ⓐ ● Ⓒ Ⓓ

Statement (B), "They're shaking hands," is the best description of the picture, so you should select answer (B) and mark it on your answer sheet.

1.

2.

Go on to the next page

3.

4.

5.

6.

Go on to the next page

PART 2 ∩ 22

Directions: You will hear a question or statement and three responses spoken in English. They will not be printed in your test book and will be spoken only one time. Select the best response to the question or statement and mark the letter (A), (B), or (C) on your answer sheet.

7. Mark your answer on your answer sheet.

8. Mark your answer on your answer sheet.

9. Mark your answer on your answer sheet.

10. Mark your answer on your answer sheet.

11. Mark your answer on your answer sheet.

12. Mark your answer on your answer sheet.

13. Mark your answer on your answer sheet.

14. Mark your answer on your answer sheet.

15. Mark your answer on your answer sheet.

16. Mark your answer on your answer sheet.

17. Mark your answer on your answer sheet.

18. Mark your answer on your answer sheet.

19. Mark your answer on your answer sheet.

20. Mark your answer on your answer sheet.

21. Mark your answer on your answer sheet.

22. Mark your answer on your answer sheet.

23. Mark your answer on your answer sheet.

24. Mark your answer on your answer sheet.

25. Mark your answer on your answer sheet.

26. Mark your answer on your answer sheet.

27. Mark your answer on your answer sheet.

28. Mark your answer on your answer sheet.

29. Mark your answer on your answer sheet.

30. Mark your answer on your answer sheet.

31. Mark your answer on your answer sheet.

PART 3 ∩ 23

Directions: You will hear some conversations between two or more people. You will be asked to answer three questions about what the speakers say in each conversation. Select the best response to each question and mark the letter (A), (B), (C), or (D) on your answer sheet. The conversations will not be printed in your test book and will be spoken only one time.

32. Why is the woman at the shop?

(A) To buy a mobile phone
(B) To ask about a device
(C) To sell a computer
(D) To charge a battery

33. What is the problem with the computer?

(A) It turns off by itself.
(B) It ran out of battery.
(C) It is not connected to the Internet.
(D) It was not fully charged.

34. What will the man probably do next?

(A) Give a full refund
(B) Replace the battery
(C) Update the device
(D) Report the problem to the manufacturer

35. Why is the man calling?

(A) To ask about a membership card
(B) To sign up for an exhibition
(C) To check a ticket reservation
(D) To inquire about a delivery service

36. What will happen next month?

(A) A museum exhibition
(B) A book signing
(C) An international music festival
(D) A pottery-making demonstration

37. What additional information does the woman ask for?

(A) A price estimate
(B) An e-mail address
(C) The sizes of some items
(D) The man's seating number

38. Why is the man calling the woman?

(A) To return her résumé
(B) To reject her application
(C) To ask her to visit him again
(D) To give details about the job opening

39. Why is the woman unavailable tomorrow?

(A) She will be traveling.
(B) She will be working.
(C) She will be giving a presentation.
(D) She will be finishing an assignment.

40. What does the man ask the woman to do?

(A) Submit a résumé
(B) Write an article
(C) Read an employee handbook
(D) Write a novel

41. What are the speakers mainly discussing?

(A) The cover of a booklet
(B) Bad weather
(C) Driving to the airport
(D) Revising a document

42. What is suggested by the speakers?

(A) The woman revised the marketing report.
(B) The rain has finally stopped.
(C) The man has finished the report.
(D) There will be a meeting at three o'clock.

43. What will the woman probably do next?

(A) See an executive at the airport
(B) Correct errors in a paper
(C) Tell the man an e-mail address
(D) Book a flight

Go on to the next page

44. What type of event are the speakers attending?

(A) A professional conference
(B) An employee orientation
(C) A book signing
(D) A staff meeting

45. Why does the man say, "Let's just sit in this row"?

(A) He thinks they have no choice.
(B) He wants to encourage the woman to work harder.
(C) He is disappointed in the presentation.
(D) He thinks his team is more competent than other teams.

46. What does the man say about the seats?

(A) They are all occupied.
(B) They are available near the entrance.
(C) They are not enough for everyone.
(D) They are broken.

47. Why will the woman probably be late?

(A) She is buying a present on the way.
(B) She is held up by a traffic jam.
(C) She had a computer malfunction.
(D) She needs to give a message to Elizabeth.

48. What does the woman recommend?

(A) Taking a taxi instead
(B) Going to her office
(C) Calling her again later
(D) Getting a message from Elizabeth

49. What does the man imply when he says, "They are for the last part of the event"?

(A) Jessica doesn't need to prepare the congratulatory message.
(B) Jessica doesn't need to be at the event from the beginning.
(C) Jessica doesn't need to tell him the password to her computer.
(D) Jessica doesn't need to meet Elizabeth at the ceremony.

50. What is suggested about the book?

(A) It is a used book.
(B) It is expensive.
(C) It has a defect.
(D) It was on sale.

51. What does the man ask the woman to do?

(A) Switch the item
(B) Make a copy
(C) Buy a book
(D) Give a discount

52. What does the woman ask for?

(A) A credit card number
(B) Proof of purchase
(C) A billing address
(D) An exchange

53. What has the man recently done?

(A) Relocated to a new place
(B) Sent a package
(C) Had a medical check-up
(D) Seen a doctor

54. What problem does the woman mention?

(A) An appointment was delayed.
(B) A payment was not received.
(C) An address is incorrect.
(D) A document has not been signed.

55. What does the woman say she will do?

(A) Introduce a new doctor
(B) Update the medical records
(C) Email a document
(D) Send something by express mail

56. Where do the women most likely work?

(A) At an electronics store
(B) At a movie production company
(C) At a TV station
(D) At a movie theater

57. What job requirement do the speakers discuss?

(A) Being professionally certified
(B) Using the proper equipment
(C) Having camera operation skills
(D) Handling some urgent tasks

58. What will the man do next?

(A) Show his work sample
(B) Make a video
(C) Meet a director
(D) Buy a laptop

59. What will happen next month?

(A) A dedication
(B) A holiday party
(C) A company outing
(D) A retirement celebration

60. What is the man considering?

(A) Whether to use a catering company
(B) Where to hold an event
(C) When to order food
(D) Who should be invited

61. What does the woman imply when she says, "That's a good point"?

(A) She agrees with the man's opinion.
(B) She wants to bring some food.
(C) She'll send an e-mail.
(D) She suggests ordering some food.

Admission Price per Person	
Children under 12	$8
Group of 10 or more	$12
Member	$15
Non-member	$20

62. What type of event are the speakers discussing?

(A) A theater performance
(B) A museum exhibition
(C) A new movie
(D) A live music concert

63. Look at the graphic. What ticket price will the speakers probably pay?

(A) $16
(B) $24
(C) $30
(D) $40

64. What does the woman say she will do?

(A) Leave work early
(B) Purchase the tickets
(C) Pay with a credit card
(D) Visit the theater

Go on to the next page

Parramatta Park	
April 5	Ashifield Consulting
April 12	Burwood Church
April 19	SummerMax Advertising
April 26	Amax Accounting

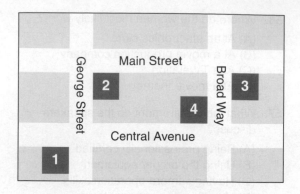

65. Why is the woman calling?

(A) To cancel the event
(B) To change the location
(C) To change the date
(D) To give an invitation

66. According to the woman, what will her company do in May?

(A) Relocate to a different city
(B) Expand a budget
(C) Enlarge a work area
(D) Hire additional workers

67. Look at the graphic. When will the woman use the park?

(A) April 5
(B) April 12
(C) April 19
(D) April 26

68. What do the speakers want to do?

(A) Plan a party for customers
(B) Celebrate a company's anniversary
(C) Express their gratitude
(D) Send out invitations

69. What does the man suggest doing?

(A) Making a presentation
(B) Purchasing a present
(C) Setting up a gift shop
(D) Giving an award

70. Look at the graphic. Where is the gift shop located?

(A) 1
(B) 2
(C) 3
(D) 4

PART 4 ∩ 24

Directions: You will hear some talks given by a single speaker. You will be asked to answer three questions about what the speaker says in each talk. Select the best response to each question and mark the letter (A), (B), (C), or (D) on your answer sheet. The talks will not be printed in your test book and will be spoken only one time.

71. Where does the speaker work?
    (A) At an electronics store
    (B) At a hardware store
    (C) At a car repair shop
    (D) At a car rental company

72. What does the speaker say he has done?
    (A) Scheduled an appointment
    (B) Completed a repair
    (C) Replaced a light
    (D) Ordered a part

73. What does the speaker offer?
    (A) A rental car service
    (B) An extended warranty
    (C) A free inspection
    (D) An express delivery

74. What is the speaker mainly discussing?
    (A) A change to project timelines
    (B) Plans to use teleconferencing
    (C) Some expected job opportunities
    (D) Camera installation

75. According to the speaker, what will happen next week?
    (A) Employees will learn new procedures.
    (B) Salespeople will meet with clients.
    (C) Designers will create video materials.
    (D) Technicians will replace old computers.

76. What does the speaker ask the listeners to do?
    (A) Distribute handouts
    (B) Compile sales data
    (C) Set up the equipment
    (D) Refer to the instructions

77. Where is the tour most likely taking place?
    (A) At a nature center
    (B) In a parking area
    (C) At a flower shop
    (D) At an outdoor market

78. Where will the group have lunch?
    (A) At a mountain cabin
    (B) At a waterfall
    (C) At the summit
    (D) In a parking lot

79. What are the listeners asked to do?
    (A) Throw away trash when they return
    (B) Refrain from picking flowers on the trail
    (C) Not interrupt while the speaker is talking
    (D) Take a group photo after the hike

80. Who is this advertisement for?
    (A) Traffic police
    (B) Driving instructors
    (C) Auto mechanics
    (D) New drivers

81. What is being advertised?
    (A) A discount on driving instruction
    (B) A sale on used cars
    (C) Automobile insurance
    (D) A job opening for driving instructors

82. How can the listeners sign up for a service?
    (A) By visiting an office
    (B) By sending for a brochure
    (C) By visiting a Web site
    (D) By making a phone call

83. What kind of business does the speaker work for?

(A) A repair center
(B) A home appliance company
(C) A market research firm
(D) A cleaning company

84. What is the most popular feature of the current model?

(A) Waterproof motor
(B) Self-cleaning
(C) Detachable parts
(D) High power consumption

85. What does the speaker imply when she says, "strengthen the strengths and make up for the weaknesses"?

(A) She believes the new model has to be more expensive.
(B) She doesn't want to give up the advantages of the previous model.
(C) She regrets the Brown 150 model was designed too poorly.
(D) She doesn't agree with the customers about their complaints.

86. Why is the speaker calling?

(A) To receive a message
(B) To apologize to a customer
(C) To order some items
(D) To inquire about a product

87. What problem does the speaker mention?

(A) Some items are faulty.
(B) A machine is broken.
(C) A shipment is late.
(D) Some items are out of stock.

88. Why does the speaker say, "We can just handle everything"?

(A) To make up for a mistake
(B) To purchase the item
(C) To provide a sample
(D) To give a special gift

89. What type of business is being discussed?

(A) A fabric manufacturer
(B) An ice cream factory
(C) A local business
(D) A cooking school

90. What can be inferred about the company?

(A) It has never operated in this city before.
(B) Its headquarters moved to another city.
(C) It is celebrating its 10th anniversary.
(D) It is expanding a building.

91. What will some customers receive before noon?

(A) A free sample
(B) Some coupons
(C) A promotional brochure
(D) Complimentary recipes

92. What kind of work needs to be done?

(A) Electrical maintenance
(B) Computer system upgrades
(C) Software installation
(D) Floor cleaning

93. When will the work begin?

(A) Tonight
(B) Tomorrow
(C) This weekend
(D) Next week

94. What are some listeners asked to do?

(A) Hire the technicians
(B) Use personal electronics
(C) Attend the meeting in the conference room
(D) Remove important documents from the computer

Order Form

Item	Item code	Quantity
Ink cartridge	FC505	1
Colored pencils, Set (12 colors)	PW74	3
Stapler	HK250	2
Paper cups	DC303	150

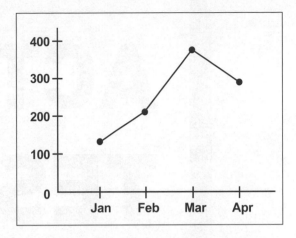

95. Look at the graphic. Which item does the speaker want to be checked?

(A) FC505
(B) PW74
(C) HK250
(D) DC303

96. What is suggested about Tim Falcon?

(A) He has ordered from this store before.
(B) He has a new printer in his office.
(C) He works for a printing company.
(D) He works until 9:30.

97. Why would Tim Falcon call back?

(A) To check the working hours
(B) To order more stationery
(C) To receive a new printer
(D) To confirm an item code

98. Where most likely does the speaker work?

(A) At an advertising agency
(B) At a beauty parlor
(C) At a cosmetics store
(D) At a supermarket

99. Look at the graphic. When was the discount event held?

(A) In January
(B) In February
(C) In March
(D) In April

100. What does the business plan to do next quarter?

(A) Offer a free dyeing event
(B) Open a new branch
(C) Use eco-friendly items
(D) Upgrade a Web site

ACTUAL
TEST

答對題數表

PART 1	
PART 2	
PART 3	
PART 4	
總題數	

07

LISTENING TEST

In the Listening test, you will be asked to demonstrate how well you understand spoken English. The entire Listening test will last approximately 45 minutes. There are four parts, and directions are given for each part. You must mark your answers on the separate answer sheet.
Do not write your answers in your test book.

PART 1 25

Directions: For each question in this part, you will hear four statements about a picture in your test book. When you hear the statements, you must select the one statement that best describes what you see in the picture. Then find the number of the question on your answer sheet and mark your answer. The statements will not be printed in your test book and will be spoken only one time.

Sample Answer
Ⓐ ● Ⓒ Ⓓ

Statement (B), "They're shaking hands," is the best description of the picture, so you should select answer (B) and mark it on your answer sheet.

1.

2.

Go on to the next page

3.

4.

5.

6.

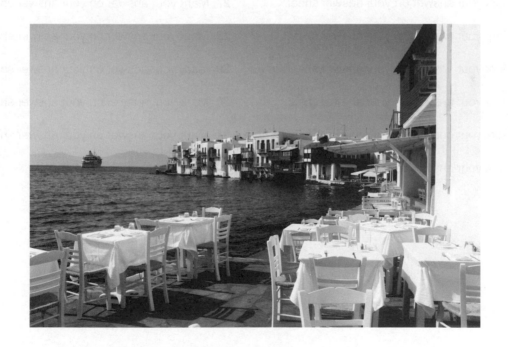

Go on to the next page

PART 2 ∩ 26

Directions: You will hear a question or statement and three responses spoken in English. They will not be printed in your test book and will be spoken only one time. Select the best response to the question or statement and mark the letter (A), (B), or (C) on your answer sheet.

7. Mark your answer on your answer sheet.

8. Mark your answer on your answer sheet.

9. Mark your answer on your answer sheet.

10. Mark your answer on your answer sheet.

11. Mark your answer on your answer sheet.

12. Mark your answer on your answer sheet.

13. Mark your answer on your answer sheet.

14. Mark your answer on your answer sheet.

15. Mark your answer on your answer sheet.

16. Mark your answer on your answer sheet.

17. Mark your answer on your answer sheet.

18. Mark your answer on your answer sheet.

19. Mark your answer on your answer sheet.

20. Mark your answer on your answer sheet.

21. Mark your answer on your answer sheet.

22. Mark your answer on your answer sheet.

23. Mark your answer on your answer sheet.

24. Mark your answer on your answer sheet.

25. Mark your answer on your answer sheet.

26. Mark your answer on your answer sheet.

27. Mark your answer on your answer sheet.

28. Mark your answer on your answer sheet.

29. Mark your answer on your answer sheet.

30. Mark your answer on your answer sheet.

31. Mark your answer on your answer sheet.

PART 3 ∩ 27

Directions: You will hear some conversations between two or more people. You will be asked to answer three questions about what the speakers say in each conversation. Select the best response to each question and mark the letter (A), (B), (C), or (D) on your answer sheet. The conversations will not be printed in your test book and will be spoken only one time.

32. Where most likely does the woman work?

(A) At a library
(B) At a stadium
(C) At a performance hall
(D) At a music shop

33. What is the purpose of the man's call?

(A) To ask for a refund
(B) To cancel a reservation
(C) To sign up for a class
(D) To inquire about tickets

34. What will the man probably do next?

(A) Verify a seating chart
(B) Check his calendar
(C) Talk with his friends
(D) Buy tickets online

35. Who most likely is the woman?

(A) A staff trainer in a local company
(B) A radio producer
(C) A maintenance engineer
(D) A TV reporter

36. What items would probably be serviced by Good Hands?

(A) Toys
(B) Bicycles
(C) Photocopiers
(D) Vehicles

37. According to the man, how does Good Hands differ from its competitors?

(A) It provides extended guarantees.
(B) It has a lot of state-of-the-art equipment.
(C) It provides faster on-site service than its competitors.
(D) It has very skilled employees.

38. What does the woman ask the man to do?

(A) Accept a package
(B) Attend a morning meeting
(C) Take a phone call
(D) Enter some data

39. What information does the man request?

(A) A time
(B) A contact number
(C) An address
(D) A price

40. What does the woman say she will do?

(A) Postpone a meeting
(B) Redirect her phone
(C) Check her schedule
(D) Cancel an appointment

41. What type of business does the woman most likely work for?

(A) A used car dealer
(B) A repair shop
(C) A car rental agency
(D) A paid parking lot

42. What is the man concerned about?

(A) Being charged for a repair
(B) Doing some paperwork
(C) Attending an important meeting
(D) Driving to Oregon from his company

43. For how long is the man renting the car?

(A) One day
(B) Two days
(C) Three days
(D) Four days

Go on to the next page

44. Why is the woman moving out?

(A) Her rental agreement has expired.
(B) She has found a less expensive house.
(C) Her husband decided to relocate.
(D) She wants a bigger house.

45. What does the woman offer to do?

(A) Move out as soon as possible
(B) Help look for a new tenant
(C) Contact a moving company
(D) Pay the rent fee for two months

46. According to the man, why would the woman be willing to help him?

(A) To find a new house in Atlanta
(B) To get a new job
(C) To save the excessive rental fee
(D) To renovate her house within 4 weeks

47. What impressed the women about the man?

(A) His appearance
(B) His managing skills
(C) His previous career
(D) His upcoming performances

48. According to the man, why did he apply to this company?

(A) He wants to earn more money.
(B) He is eager to try overnight shoots.
(C) He wants to lead his own team.
(D) He wants to work for a bigger company.

49. What does the new job require of the man?

(A) Excellent presentation skills
(B) Experience in health matters
(C) The willingness to work overtime
(D) Frequent overseas performances

50. What does the man like about the updated Web site?

(A) The clear images
(B) The faster response time
(C) The easier usability
(D) The detailed floor guide

51. What does the man imply when he says, "It didn't work for me"?

(A) He did not work yesterday.
(B) He already tried pressing the F5 key.
(C) He wants to consult with Jim.
(D) He had the same issue before the update.

52. What does the woman recommend?

(A) Installing some new software
(B) Checking for computer viruses
(C) Restarting his desktop computer
(D) Including an image with his report

53. Where most likely does the man work?

(A) At a laboratory
(B) At a farm
(C) At a fried chicken restaurant
(D) At a government agency

54. What has the man recently done?

(A) Called to confirm the management number
(B) Moved to a new location
(C) Sold a number of eggs
(D) Bred a lot of poultry

55. What does the woman say she is unable to do?

(A) Vaccinate the animals
(B) Offer a discount
(C) Provide financial support
(D) Verify the information of the farm

56. Where does the man most likely work?

(A) At a food store
(B) At a car repair shop
(C) At a cold storage facility
(D) At a delivery service

57. What does the man imply when he says, "I was expecting you"?

(A) He is ready to take the order.
(B) They already know each other.
(C) He knew Ms. Williams would come.
(D) He will deliver the items to Ms. Williams' house himself.

58. What is the woman most likely to do next?

(A) Go home
(B) Provide her telephone number
(C) Pick up the items at the warehouse
(D) Ask for a door-to-door delivery

59. What is the purpose of the contest?

(A) To create a themed campaign
(B) To reduce expenditure
(C) To increase the customer base
(D) To recruit additional employees

60. Why is the woman unsure about participating?

(A) She is going on vacation.
(B) She will be changing jobs.
(C) She does not have any related experience.
(D) She has a deadline for work.

61. What will the winner receive?

(A) A plaque
(B) A hotel voucher
(C) A trip abroad
(D) A cash bonus

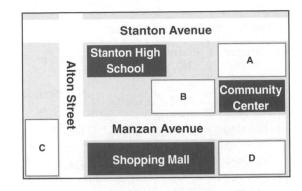

62. What are the speakers mainly talking about?

(A) The woman's new apartment
(B) Joining a sports club
(C) Driving a long distance
(D) A newly arrived student

63. What is the woman concerned about?

(A) The cost of joining a gym
(B) The amount of spare time she has
(C) The location of the new office
(D) The distance she would travel

64. Look at the graphic. Where is the Hillsberry Building?

(A) A
(B) B
(C) C
(D) D

Go on to the next page

Attachment: Pictures Checklist

Branch Name	Phone No.	Manager	Taken at
Alpha Center	7590-4761	Martin Clause	Nighttime
Glanstown	(N/A)	Laura Bright	Daytime
McMillan	7550-8761	(N/A)	Daytime
Unicorn Building	7575-4561	Aaron Smith	Daytime

Floor Guide:

4F	Cafeteria
3F	Auditorium
2F	Counseling Office
1F	Administration Office
B1	Parking lot

65. What most likely is the man's job?

(A) Branch manager
(B) Office interior designer
(C) Photographer
(D) Web site developer

66. What does the woman ask the man to help with?

(A) Assigning a manager
(B) Photocopying some images
(C) Getting some photographs
(D) Installing a telephone

67. Look at the graphic. Which site's photograph is not suitable to be posted on the Web site?

(A) Alpha Center branch
(B) Glanstown branch
(C) McMillan branch
(D) Unicorn Building branch

68. What document will be issued to the man?

(A) An application form
(B) A work permit
(C) A membership card
(D) A recommendation letter

69. Look at the graphic. Where should the man go to meet the woman on Tuesday?

(A) 1st floor
(B) 2nd floor
(C) 3rd floor
(D) 4th floor

70. What does the woman ask the man to do?

(A) Submit an application as soon as possible
(B) Mail extra copies of his certificates
(C) Attend a training session
(D) Give her his autograph

PART 4 ∩ 28

Directions: You will hear some talks given by a single speaker. You will be asked to answer three questions about what the speaker says in each talk. Select the best response to each question and mark the letter (A), (B), (C), or (D) on your answer sheet. The talks will not be printed in your test book and will be spoken only one time.

71. What type of business is being advertised?
    (A) A cold storage facility
    (B) A catering firm
    (C) A web design service
    (D) A cooking institute

72. According to the advertisement, what does Exo-Spices guarantee?
    (A) Unlimited beverages
    (B) Discount vouchers
    (C) A full refund
    (D) Nutritious food

73. What can listeners do online?
    (A) Customize a set menu
    (B) Order samples of some food
    (C) Leave comments
    (D) Track an order

74. What is being rebuilt in Eunice?
    (A) A shopping mall
    (B) A swimming pool
    (C) A playground
    (D) An environmental center

75. Why was the renovation delayed?
    (A) The location was too remote.
    (B) Local residents objected to the renovation.
    (C) Harmful substances were detected.
    (D) Funding was insufficient.

76. According to the speaker, what will take place in July?
    (A) A weekly prize drawing
    (B) An opening ceremony
    (C) A series of lectures
    (D) A charity event

77. What is the purpose of the upcoming event?
    (A) To promote an art class
    (B) To encourage class participation
    (C) To introduce a new lecturer
    (D) To test students' performances

78. What will some students receive?
    (A) Tickets to a musical performance
    (B) Theater discounts
    (C) A complimentary class
    (D) Reduced tuition fees

79. What are the listeners asked to do when entering a class?
    (A) Play the guitar
    (B) Accompany a friend
    (C) Stop by the office
    (D) Apply an ID card

80. Why are the callers unable to speak to a representative immediately?
    (A) More people are calling than usual.
    (B) A hotline system is faulty.
    (C) The shuttles are out of service.
    (D) The Internet connection is unavailable.

81. Why would callers press 4 on their phones?
    (A) To check the shuttle schedules
    (B) To get advice on road travel
    (C) To check the weather forecast
    (D) To locate a nearby shelter

82. What does the speaker mention about the Web site?
    (A) It is updated every day.
    (B) It is currently inaccessible.
    (C) You need to log on to check the contents.
    (D) It provides the current weather status.

Go on to the next page

83. Who most likely are the listeners?

(A) Fashion designers
(B) Corporate executives
(C) Factory workers
(D) Salespeople

84. What will happen this spring?

(A) A womenswear collection will be discontinued.
(B) A new client list will be introduced.
(C) A new range will be launched.
(D) A new outlet will be opened.

85. What will the listeners do next?

(A) Visit their clients
(B) View sample items
(C) Report their sales strategies
(D) Attend a regular meeting

86. What type of business does the speaker work for?

(A) An advertising company
(B) A photography studio
(C) A clothing company
(D) A travel agency

87. What should the listener submit to join the contest?

(A) A series of photographs
(B) A sketch
(C) A video clip
(D) A travel essay

88. What will the winner receive?

(A) Cash
(B) Coupons
(C) Flight tickets
(D) Camping equipment

89. Who most likely is the speaker?

(A) A stadium vendor
(B) A sports announcer
(C) A football player
(D) A match referee

90. What prize is being offered?

(A) Dinner with an athlete
(B) Tickets for the final
(C) A two-week trip
(D) Autographed football shirts

91. What does the man imply when he says, "It couldn't be simpler"?

(A) Everyone can send the message free of charge.
(B) The rules for soccer are not complicated.
(C) It is easy to join the event.
(D) All the names of the players need to be memorized.

92. What is being announced?

(A) A meeting schedule
(B) An increase in salaries
(C) A new working arrangement
(D) An overtime project

93. Why is a change being made?

(A) To attract new employees
(B) To create a survey
(C) To improve working practices
(D) To reward hard-working employees

94. What does the woman imply when she says, "there would be no difficulty in that"?

(A) It is impossible to comply with the change.
(B) The survey was conducted without any trouble.
(C) The change will cause some confusion.
(D) A shorter lunch break is not a big deal.

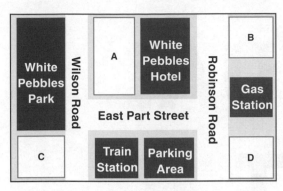

Renovation Schedule	
Noise Inspection	May 24 (Mon.)
Painting the walls	May 25 (Tue.)
Painting the ceilings	May 26 (Wed.)
Replacing the windows	May 27 (Thu.)

95. Why does the speaker recommend the property?

(A) It is in a flood-prone area.
(B) The landlord wants to sell it cheap.
(C) The building is in a good condition.
(D) There is a subway station nearby.

96. What disadvantage does the speaker mention?

(A) The deposit is too high.
(B) The flood risk is high.
(C) The landlord has another buyer.
(D) Parking lot is not included.

97. Look at the graphic. Where most likely is the property?

(A) A
(B) B
(C) C
(D) D

98. What problem is the Management responding to?

(A) Noise from a factory
(B) A shortage of office supplies
(C) Renovation expenses
(D) Broken windows

99. Look at the graphic. When will Mr. Coleman remove the curtains?

(A) Monday
(B) Tuesday
(C) Wednesday
(D) Thursday

100. What does the speaker encourage listeners to do?

(A) Clear the blinds
(B) Wash the curtains
(C) Change the windows
(D) Work from home

ACTUAL TEST

答對題數表

PART 1	
PART 2	
PART 3	
PART 4	
總題數	

08

LISTENING TEST

In the Listening test, you will be asked to demonstrate how well you understand spoken English. The entire Listening test will last approximately 45 minutes. There are four parts, and directions are given for each part. You must mark your answers on the separate answer sheet. Do not write your answers in your test book.

PART 1 ᴒ 29

Directions: For each question in this part, you will hear four statements about a picture in your test book. When you hear the statements, you must select the one statement that best describes what you see in the picture. Then find the number of the question on your answer sheet and mark your answer. The statements will not be printed in your test book and will be spoken only one time.

Sample Answer

Statement (B), "They're shaking hands," is the best description of the picture, so you should select answer (B) and mark it on your answer sheet.

1.

2.

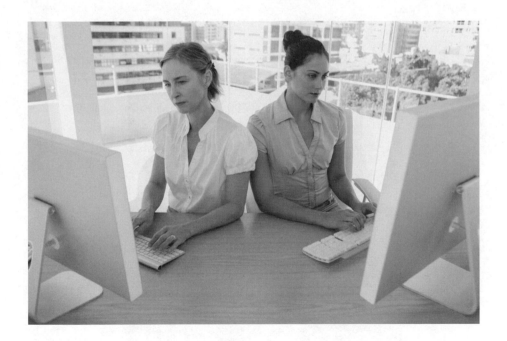

Go on to the next page

3.

4.

5.

6.

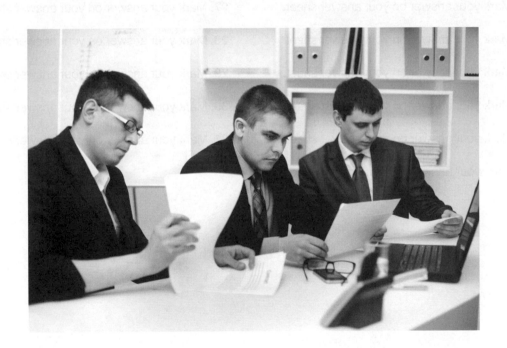

Go on to the next page

PART 2 ∩ 30

Directions: You will hear a question or statement and three responses spoken in English. They will not be printed in your test book and will be spoken only one time. Select the best response to the question or statement and mark the letter (A), (B), or (C) on your answer sheet.

7. Mark your answer on your answer sheet.

8. Mark your answer on your answer sheet.

9. Mark your answer on your answer sheet.

10. Mark your answer on your answer sheet.

11. Mark your answer on your answer sheet.

12. Mark your answer on your answer sheet.

13. Mark your answer on your answer sheet.

14. Mark your answer on your answer sheet.

15. Mark your answer on your answer sheet.

16. Mark your answer on your answer sheet.

17. Mark your answer on your answer sheet.

18. Mark your answer on your answer sheet.

19. Mark your answer on your answer sheet.

20. Mark your answer on your answer sheet.

21. Mark your answer on your answer sheet.

22. Mark your answer on your answer sheet.

23. Mark your answer on your answer sheet.

24. Mark your answer on your answer sheet.

25. Mark your answer on your answer sheet.

26. Mark your answer on your answer sheet.

27. Mark your answer on your answer sheet.

28. Mark your answer on your answer sheet.

29. Mark your answer on your answer sheet.

30. Mark your answer on your answer sheet.

31. Mark your answer on your answer sheet.

PART 3 ∩ 31

Directions: You will hear some conversations between two or more people. You will be asked to answer three questions about what the speakers say in each conversation. Select the best response to each question and mark the letter (A), (B), (C), or (D) on your answer sheet. The conversations will not be printed in your test book and will be spoken only one time.

32. What is the woman concerned about?

(A) A family matter
(B) A newspaper page
(C) A travel itinerary
(D) A group presentation

33. What does the woman ask the man to do?

(A) Take some pictures
(B) Revise an article
(C) Buy some food
(D) Work overtime

34. What does the woman say she will do?

(A) Read a proposal
(B) Mail a package
(C) Arrange for some food
(D) Create an advertisement

35. Who is Patrick Spencer?

(A) A computer engineer
(B) A DVD seller
(C) A health trainer
(D) An ad executive

36. What did Patrick Spencer advise the woman to do?

(A) Sit up straight in her chair
(B) Work on her computer
(C) Lean against a wall
(D) Upgrade her computer

37. What does the woman offer to do?

(A) Share some information with her colleagues
(B) Assist in preparing a demonstration
(C) Buy the man a computer
(D) Make a list of interested employees

38. What are the clients worried about?

(A) The color of the paint
(B) The cost of the work
(C) The deadline for the project
(D) The material of the wallpaper

39. What does the man imply when he says, "I would like to allay their worries"?

(A) He wants to satisfy the clients.
(B) He needs more time to finish the project.
(C) He's going to ask for a budget increase.
(D) He doesn't want to work for Starwood.

40. What does the man suggest?

(A) Finding a different hotel
(B) Consulting with the supplier
(C) Ignoring the customer's expectations
(D) Postponing the meeting

41. What is the conversation mainly about?

(A) Getting a general checkup
(B) Designing a book
(C) Publishing an article
(D) Giving a talk

42. What are the speakers worried about?

(A) The length of a text
(B) The difficulty of an article
(C) The access to an online forum
(D) The deadline for publishing

43. What does the man offer to do?

(A) Participate in the research
(B) Carry a different article
(C) Provide a list of words
(D) Vaccinate the patients

Go on to the next page

44. What are the speakers discussing?

(A) A renovation project
(B) A job interview
(C) A road development
(D) A work schedule

45. What is the woman impressed by?

(A) The improved environment of the office
(B) How quickly the job was performed
(C) The professionalism of the workers
(D) How little the construction cost

46. What does the man say he will suggest?

(A) Rescheduling some appointments
(B) Moving to a new building
(C) Calling the maintenance office
(D) Employing the same company again

47. What was the purpose of the man's trip?

(A) To look at the new factory sites
(B) To source new suppliers
(C) To sell goods abroad
(D) To arrange interviews

48. What does the man say about the company in Copenhagen?

(A) It has many manufacturing plants.
(B) It is favorably located.
(C) It welcomes business from abroad.
(D) It is close to an airport.

49. What does the woman remind the man to do?

(A) Ask for an extended vacation
(B) Report the loss of his luggage
(C) Submit his report
(D) Update his current client details

50. What department does the man work in?

(A) Maintenance
(B) Customer Service
(C) Reception
(D) Human Resources

51. What does the woman ask about?

(A) The start date of a job
(B) The qualifications for a job
(C) The name of the Human Resources Manager
(D) The location of the training session

52. What does the woman say she will probably do?

(A) Hand over her present duties to her colleague
(B) Teach the man how to do his job properly
(C) Move to a new location
(D) Submit a job application

53. Who most likely is the man?

(A) An administrative assistant
(B) A sales representative
(C) An interior designer
(D) A maintenance employee

54. What problem does the woman mention?

(A) A project is not complete.
(B) An office is locked.
(C) Some electric equipment is defective.
(D) Some materials are not available.

55. According to the woman, what is scheduled to take place in the afternoon?

(A) A safety check
(B) A meeting
(C) A job interview
(D) A power outage

56. What problem is the woman talking about?

   (A) She cannot meet her manager today.

   (B) She cannot find any problem with her mobile phone.

   (C) She cannot contact her clients from the office.

   (D) She cannot fix the defective cables.

57. What does the woman imply when she says, "That's no good to me"?

   (A) She has to leave early today.

   (B) She can't wait for the cables to be repaired.

   (C) She will visit the clients in person.

   (D) She doesn't want to use a three-way call.

58. What will the woman probably do next?

   (A) Check the telephone downstairs

   (B) Contact the telephone company again

   (C) Make a speech at the conference

   (D) List some time-sensitive issues

59. What type of company is Amberhues?

   (A) A travel agency

   (B) A moving company

   (C) A decorating firm

   (D) A hotel

60. Why did the woman choose Amberhues?

   (A) It has been in operation for a long time.

   (B) It is convenient to her office.

   (C) It has a branch in Miami.

   (D) It is the most competitively priced.

61. Why will the work start in July?

   (A) The company has to give approval.

   (B) Furniture cannot be delivered earlier.

   (C) The woman will be away until then.

   (D) The company is busy with other work.

Restaurant Suggestions

Wang's Castle	Chinese	Delicious noodles, Not spicy
Beefy Porky	Barbecue	Outdoor restaurant, Fairly cheap
Indiana's	Steakhouse	Lunchtime discount, Rooms available
Chili Chili	Spicy Ribs	Best for spice lovers, Mexican style

62. According to the woman, what is the purpose of the event?

   (A) To organize an awards ceremony

   (B) To taste some exotic food

   (C) To open a new business

   (D) To celebrate a birthday

63. Look at the graphic. Which place would be most suitable for the event?

   (A) Wang's Castle

   (B) Beefy Porky

   (C) Indiana's

   (D) Chili Chili

64. Why does the woman disagree with the man's idea?

   (A) The restaurant is not big enough.

   (B) They won't be able to get a discount.

   (C) The president doesn't like Japanese food.

   (D) They have no time to book a room.

Go on to the next page

Pearson Elementary School	A	Milton Hotel
B	Tinderbox Restaurant	C
Prime Hotel	Gas Station	D

Item	Quantity	Subtotal
Speaker	6	$180
Keyboard	2	$50
Mouse	1	$35
Webcam	1	$75
Delivery		$0
Total		**$340**

65. What most likely is the man's occupation?

    (A) Real estate agent
    (B) Building constructor
    (C) Cooking teacher
    (D) Hotel worker

66. Look at the graphic. Where most likely is the Diana Complex?

    (A) A
    (B) B
    (C) C
    (D) D

67. When does the man say he can visit the Diana Complex?

    (A) This evening
    (B) Later tomorrow
    (C) The day after tomorrow
    (D) The week after

68. Who most likely is the man?

    (A) A storekeeper
    (B) A bank teller
    (C) A delivery man
    (D) A computer repairman

69. What does the woman ask about?

    (A) The delivery time
    (B) The payment options
    (C) The availability of items
    (D) A card approval

70. Look at the graphic. Which information on the list has to be changed now?

    (A) $180
    (B) $50
    (C) $35
    (D) $75

PART 4 ∩ 32

Directions: You will hear some talks given by a single speaker. You will be asked to answer three questions about what the speaker says in each talk. Select the best response to each question and mark the letter (A), (B), (C), or (D) on your answer sheet. The talks will not be printed in your test book and will be spoken only one time.

71. What is the announcement mainly about?
    (A) A machine installation
    (B) A company closure
    (C) A safety inspection
    (D) A vehicle check

72. What does the man imply when he says, "Without any doubt, this is good news"?
    (A) He can fix his car by himself now.
    (B) He will gladly do the overtime work.
    (C) They have purchased the machine at a low price.
    (D) The new machine will help them complete the work in less time.

73. What does the speaker ask the listeners to do?
    (A) Attend an opening ceremony
    (B) Welcome a new supervisor
    (C) Work overtime hours
    (D) Review an operations manual

74. Where does the speaker most likely work?
    (A) At a radio station
    (B) At an employment agency
    (C) At a charity organization
    (D) At a publishing house

75. According to the speaker, what will Mr. Elder discuss?
    (A) A community building
    (B) A fundraising event
    (C) A marketing report
    (D) A new plan

76. Why are volunteers needed?
    (A) To advise young people
    (B) To distribute brochures
    (C) To conduct interviews
    (D) To recruit office workers

77. Who is the speaker?
    (A) A government officer
    (B) A head of a certain society
    (C) A police officer
    (D) A lighting expert

78. What permission has the group received?
    (A) Hosting a fundraising event
    (B) Supporting a sports team
    (C) Submitting a bid for funding
    (D) Sponsoring a lighting company

79. Why should listeners contact Megan Bishop?
    (A) To apply to the committee
    (B) To help in preparing the bid
    (C) To purchase some lighting
    (D) To contribute to the newsletter

80. Who is the intended audience for the talk?
    (A) Prospective writers
    (B) A proofreading team
    (C) A book club
    (D) A Marketing Department

81. According to the speaker, why is the new book unique?
    (A) It is being serialized in the newspaper.
    (B) It is available in e-book format.
    (C) It is the prequel to a series.
    (D) It is written in a different language.

82. What will the speaker most likely do next?
    (A) Review work assignments
    (B) Meet with the editing team
    (C) Distribute copies of a book
    (D) Work out a budget

Go on to the next page

83. What is the announcement mainly about?

(A) A product recall
(B) A brand introduction
(C) A store promotion
(D) A sales training session

84. What were employees recently trained to do?

(A) Design a new promotion
(B) Prepare some cosmetic items
(C) Offer makeovers
(D) Inspect some equipment

85. What is the speaker concerned about?

(A) Finding a new supplier
(B) Having sufficient seating
(C) Lowering operating costs
(D) Providing continuous supplies

86. What item is the speaker calling about?

(A) An outfit
(B) A wardrobe
(C) A television
(D) An e-mail account

87. Where has the item been advertised?

(A) In a magazine
(B) In a local shop
(C) On a bus window
(D) On a notice board

88. What does the speaker request?

(A) Some photographs
(B) A delivery date
(C) Pricing information
(D) The size of the item

89. What does the speaker's company produce?

(A) Medical appliances
(B) Office equipment
(C) Drug supplies
(D) Audio systems

90. What does the speaker want to arrange?

(A) An on-site demonstration
(B) A factory tour
(C) A payment plan
(D) A meeting schedule

91. What does the speaker say about the company's products?

(A) They are highly recommended.
(B) They are covered by a guarantee.
(C) They can be replaced every year.
(D) They are easily transportable.

92. What type of organization did the listener call?

(A) An artistic group
(B) A writers' community
(C) A tutoring program
(D) A sporting club

93. What does the woman imply when she says, "we are always looking for new people"?

(A) To inform the listener that they are newly opened
(B) To find a new place to hold an exhibition
(C) To reschedule the next event
(D) To invite more members to the meeting

94. According to the speaker, what is available on the organization's Web site?

(A) A display of artwork
(B) A calendar of events
(C) An application form
(D) A date for the next meeting

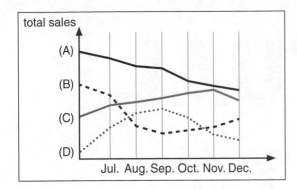

total sales

(A)
(B)
(C)
(D)

Jul. Aug. Sep. Oct. Nov. Dec.

Lunchtime Speaker Series

Room 407
12:15 P.M. ~ 12:45 P.M.

Mon.	Research Dept.	Leah Bennett
Wed.	Marketing Dept.	Justin Hunt
Fri.	Sales Dept.	Brody West

* Refreshments provided

95. What does the speaker want to discuss in this meeting?

(A) Moving up the release date of the new item
(B) Criticizing the Sales Department for the poor performance
(C) Making a successful marketing plan
(D) Deciding which products should be discontinued

96. Look at the graphic. Which line indicates the sales results of the computers?

(A) A
(B) B
(C) C
(D) D

97. What does the speaker say about the new item?

(A) It will be released in February.
(B) It won't meet the customers' expectations.
(C) It is the bestseller as usual.
(D) It only took 6 months to be developed.

98. What will happen later today?

(A) Mr. Hunt will leave for Chicago.
(B) The current marketing plans will be changed.
(C) A speech will be given by Ms. Bennett.
(D) A seminar will be postponed to the following week.

99. Look at the graphic. Which information needs to be changed?

(A) Room 407
(B) Leah Bennett
(C) Wed.
(D) Refreshments provided

100. According to the speaker, why would the listeners contact Julia Watson?

(A) To report an urgent matter
(B) To notify her of their availability
(C) To reschedule a session
(D) To make inquiries to Mr. Hunt

ACTUAL TEST

答對題數表

PART 1	
PART 2	
PART 3	
PART 4	
總題數	

09

LISTENING TEST

In the Listening test, you will be asked to demonstrate how well you understand spoken English. The entire Listening test will last approximately 45 minutes. There are four parts, and directions are given for each part. You must mark your answers on the separate answer sheet.
Do not write your answers in your test book.

PART 1 ∩ 33

Directions: For each question in this part, you will hear four statements about a picture in your test book. When you hear the statements, you must select the one statement that best describes what you see in the picture. Then find the number of the question on your answer sheet and mark your answer. The statements will not be printed in your test book and will be spoken only one time.

Sample Answer

Ⓐ ● Ⓒ Ⓓ

Statement (B), "They're shaking hands," is the best description of the picture, so you should select answer (B) and mark it on your answer sheet.

1.

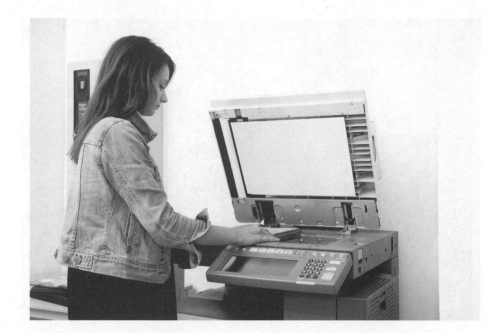

2.

Go on to the next page

3.

4.

5.

6.

Go on to the next page

PART 2 ∩ 34

Directions: You will hear a question or statement and three responses spoken in English. They will not be printed in your test book and will be spoken only one time. Select the best response to the question or statement and mark the letter (A), (B), or (C) on your answer sheet.

7. Mark your answer on your answer sheet.

8. Mark your answer on your answer sheet.

9. Mark your answer on your answer sheet.

10. Mark your answer on your answer sheet.

11. Mark your answer on your answer sheet.

12. Mark your answer on your answer sheet.

13. Mark your answer on your answer sheet.

14. Mark your answer on your answer sheet.

15. Mark your answer on your answer sheet.

16. Mark your answer on your answer sheet.

17. Mark your answer on your answer sheet.

18. Mark your answer on your answer sheet.

19. Mark your answer on your answer sheet.

20. Mark your answer on your answer sheet.

21. Mark your answer on your answer sheet.

22. Mark your answer on your answer sheet.

23. Mark your answer on your answer sheet.

24. Mark your answer on your answer sheet.

25. Mark your answer on your answer sheet.

26. Mark your answer on your answer sheet.

27. Mark your answer on your answer sheet.

28. Mark your answer on your answer sheet.

29. Mark your answer on your answer sheet.

30. Mark your answer on your answer sheet.

31. Mark your answer on your answer sheet.

PART 3 ∩ 35

Directions: You will hear some conversations between two or more people. You will be asked to answer three questions about what the speakers say in each conversation. Select the best response to each question and mark the letter (A), (B), (C), or (D) on your answer sheet. The conversations will not be printed in your test book and will be spoken only one time.

32. What type of event are the speakers planning to attend?

(A) A trade exhibition
(B) An opening ceremony
(C) A budget committee
(D) An office opening

33. What problem does the man mention?

(A) A venue is fully booked.
(B) The cost has increased.
(C) A company has gone bankrupt.
(D) An exhibition has been canceled.

34. What does the woman recommend?

(A) Reducing the size of the display
(B) Contacting other venues
(C) Promoting the event on television
(D) Asking for a discount

35. What kind of product is the woman inquiring about?

(A) Computer software
(B) Flooring materials
(C) Lab equipment
(D) Hotel pieces

36. What does the man offer to do?

(A) Stop by the hotel
(B) Send the woman an order form
(C) Provide some samples
(D) Consult a flooring expert

37. What does the woman request?

(A) An instruction manual
(B) A use of a product
(C) An online tutorial
(D) A tile specialist

38. What problem is mentioned about the airport?

(A) The check-in line is too long.
(B) The baggage area is blocked.
(C) An airplane has been delayed.
(D) An employee has not arrived.

39. What does the man ask the woman about?

(A) Payment options
(B) Business hours
(C) Round-trip airfares
(D) Beverage choices

40. What does the woman say she will do?

(A) Find another airline
(B) Lend the man some money
(C) Contact her office
(D) Use a credit card

41. What does the woman want to do?

(A) Purchase a product
(B) Read a product review
(C) Complain about a device
(D) Return an item

42. What did the woman read about the Hurricane Power?

(A) It is inexpensive.
(B) It is complicated to use.
(C) It is unreliable.
(D) It is the most popular model.

43. What does the man suggest the woman do?

(A) Post messages on a forum
(B) Browse online
(C) Contact a sales assistant
(D) Visit a specific store

Go on to the next page

44. What type of business does the man work for?

(A) A food supply company
(B) A post office
(C) A bookstore
(D) A courier service

45. What policy does the man mention?

(A) Delivered goods must be put in the mailbox.
(B) The invoice must be issued on delivery.
(C) Damaged items must be returned to the supplier.
(D) A signature must be provided.

46. What does the woman want to check?

(A) Her shipping receipt
(B) Her son's availability
(C) Her order form
(D) Her tracking number

47. What was the woman asked to do?

(A) Drive a coworker to the airport
(B) Prepare a presentation
(C) Hire additional workers
(D) Visit a production facility

48. What does the man imply when he says, "That makes sense"?

(A) He will pick the woman up at the airport.
(B) He thinks renting a car is a good idea.
(C) He knows taking a taxi costs less.
(D) He can send a taxi for the woman.

49. What does the woman decide to do?

(A) Leave a meeting early
(B) Get back to a branch manager
(C) Use another form of transportation
(D) Make extra copies of a report

50. What does the woman want to discuss with the man?

(A) A refund policy
(B) A travel itinerary
(C) A checklist sheet
(D) An insurance claim

51. When does the woman say she submitted the paperwork?

(A) In June
(B) Yesterday
(C) Last week
(D) Last month

52. According to the man, what may have caused the delay?

(A) Regular procedure
(B) Computer errors
(C) Lost paperwork
(D) Staff negligence

53. Who does the woman want to take to the Cebuana Lounge?

(A) Clients
(B) The management team
(C) Family members
(D) Colleagues

54. What does the man want to know about the restaurant?

(A) Its menu
(B) Its opening hours
(C) Its prices
(D) Its location

55. What does the woman suggest?

(A) Using her mobile phone
(B) Booking a table
(C) Making a phone call
(D) Checking room availability

56. What is the woman mainly notifying the men of?

(A) Financial confidentiality
(B) Recycling guidelines
(C) Client information
(D) Presentation schedules

57. What are the men advised to do with confidential documents?

(A) Keep them in their desk
(B) Give them to the director
(C) File them in a locked cabinet
(D) Keep them in a special container

58. What does Mike imply when he says, "Thanks for the information"?

(A) He's glad to be informed about the change.
(B) He's not asked to comply with the regulations.
(C) He's going to update all the financial documents.
(D) He's allowed to store all the documents in a cabinet.

59. What is the man interested in purchasing?

(A) A coat
(B) A hat
(C) A sweater
(D) A scarf

60. What is the problem?

(A) A product is faulty.
(B) An item is unavailable in a certain color on site.
(C) Some merchandise has been misplaced.
(D) Some clothes are too expensive.

61. What does the woman suggest the man do?

(A) Check on the store's Web site
(B) Go to a different store
(C) Return within a week
(D) Choose another color

Expense Report, 6–9 May

Round-trip ticket	$340
Hotel (2 nights)	$300
Car rental (with insurance)	$120
Meals (2.5 days *3)	$85

62. What does the woman have to do in the morning?

(A) Meet with a client
(B) Fill out an expense form
(C) Use her computer
(D) Organize a training session

63. Look at the graphic. Which item didn't the woman attach a receipt for?

(A) Round-trip ticket
(B) Hotel
(C) Car rental
(D) Meals

64. What does the man say he will do?

(A) Contact a colleague
(B) Create a database
(C) Reschedule his meeting
(D) Meet the woman in the afternoon

Go on to the next page

	Admission	Guided Tour
Event Hall A	$60	Not available
Event Hall B	Free	Free. 11:00 A.M., 7:00 P.M.
Event Hall C	$50	Free. 10:00 A.M., 3:00 P.M., 7:00 P.M.
Event Hall D	$20	$10, booklets provided

65. What problem does the man mention?

(A) A piece of art is missing.
(B) A staff member is unavailable.
(C) Some displays are faulty.
(D) An exhibition is crowded.

66. Look at the graphic. Where is the exhibition the woman wants to see being held?

(A) Event Hall A
(B) Event Hall B
(C) Event Hall C
(D) Event Hall D

67. What will the woman do next?

(A) Stay with the man
(B) Get a free ticket at the box office
(C) Come back tomorrow
(D) Go and see another exhibit

Boxing Equipment	Regular price
Boxing Gloves	$54
Protective Gear	$64
Sandbags	$152
Boxing Shoes	$162

68. What is the man calling about?

(A) Taking sports lessons
(B) Moving into the Graham Complex
(C) Returning a pair of boxing gloves
(D) Leaving his office earlier than usual

69. Look at the graphic. How much is the man going to pay for the equipment he needs?

(A) $44
(B) $64
(C) $152
(D) $162

70. What is suggested about the gym?

(A) It closes at 6 P.M.
(B) It's on the first floor.
(C) It's near the Graham Complex.
(D) It is far from Mr. Phillips's office.

PART 4 🔊 36

Directions: You will hear some talks given by a single speaker. You will be asked to answer three questions about what the speaker says in each talk. Select the best response to each question and mark the letter (A), (B), (C), or (D) on your answer sheet. The talks will not be printed in your test book and will be spoken only one time.

71. What special event is being held?

   (A) A retirement event
   (B) A training session
   (C) A grand opening ceremony
   (D) A promotion party

72. What is Charles Bailey's profession?

   (A) Computer specialist
   (B) Office manager
   (C) Mechanic
   (D) Factory operative

73. What will most likely happen next?

   (A) Some refreshments will be offered.
   (B) An interview will be conducted.
   (C) A seminar will take place.
   (D) A gift will be presented.

74. What kind of business is the speaker calling?

   (A) A holiday resort
   (B) A medical clinic
   (C) An employment agency
   (D) A pharmaceutical company

75. What does the speaker ask about?

   (A) Vaccination requirements
   (B) Better medication
   (C) A medicine price
   (D) A return to work

76. When does the speaker say she will be available?

   (A) This morning
   (B) This afternoon
   (C) Tomorrow morning
   (D) Tomorrow afternoon

77. What will happen on October 11?

   (A) Lunchtime will be extended.
   (B) Paychecks will be distributed.
   (C) A leaflet will be sent out.
   (D) A demonstration will take place.

78. What does the woman imply when she says, "This also applies to the temporary staff"?

   (A) They are not included in a lunchtime session.
   (B) They are required to fill out a form.
   (C) They will receive less pay.
   (D) They must be in attendance.

79. What are listeners asked to read?

   (A) A customer questionnaire
   (B) A health and safety document
   (C) An instruction flyer
   (D) Dismissal procedures

80. What will happen at the event?

   (A) A sustainable program will be reviewed.
   (B) A magazine will be introduced.
   (C) Awards will be presented.
   (D) New legislation will be announced.

81. What can listeners find on their seats?

   (A) Information about past projects
   (B) Results of a questionnaire
   (C) A membership form
   (D) A list of nominations

82. What is mentioned about *Good Energy Magazine*?

   (A) It is a leading magazine in the environment.
   (B) It is supporting the event.
   (C) It is recruiting new practitioners.
   (D) It is found on the seats.

Go on to the next page

83. Who is the speaker most likely addressing?

   (A) Safety inspectors
   (B) Interior designers
   (C) Factory workers
   (D) Laundry staff

84. What is the main topic of the talk?

   (A) Car painting
   (B) Appliance repairs
   (C) Factory inspections
   (D) Safety procedures

85. Where will listeners find the guidelines?

   (A) Near the chemicals
   (B) In the preservatives
   (C) On a bulletin board
   (D) In front of the paint shop

---

86. Where is the fitness center located?

   (A) In the vicinity of Danao City
   (B) Near a subway station
   (C) Right next to the city hall
   (D) In front of the community center

87. What class is newly offered?

   (A) Aerobics
   (B) Yoga
   (C) Squash
   (D) Tae-Bo

88. Why would listeners press one?

   (A) To cancel a class
   (B) To arrange a tutorial
   (C) To enroll in a class
   (D) To get directions

---

89. What has Shiny Clean accomplished over the quarter?

   (A) It launched a new range of products.
   (B) It relocated to Wilmington.
   (C) It increased its share in a specific market.
   (D) It recruited more employees.

90. Who is encouraged to apply for the new position in Wilmington?

   (A) Employees with several years' experience
   (B) Current staff willing to relocate
   (C) Sales managers with an interest in cleaning products
   (D) Those with experience in managing stores

91. What does the man imply when he says, "I have good news for everyone"?

   (A) He's pleased to let everyone know about their success.
   (B) He's willing to move to the headquarters.
   (C) He's glad to have more staff in the new branch.
   (D) He's happy to have a lot of candidates.

---

92. What kind of service is being advertised?

   (A) Online reservations
   (B) Aerial tours
   (C) Vehicle rental
   (D) Boat rides

93. According to the speaker, what is special about the service?

   (A) It is exclusively a daytime trip.
   (B) It is a brand-new service.
   (C) It takes off once a week.
   (D) It takes place at dusk.

94. What are listeners asked to do?

   (A) Provide a health certificate
   (B) Carry identification
   (C) Reserve a place
   (D) Arrive early

Suppliers list		
Miller's Joy	657-0932	Organic bakery
Herbalist's Delight	458-4273	Artificial flowers, other decorations
Mrs. Millers'	352-1853	Flour, Oil, Spices
Harmony	574-3753	Fruits & Vegetables

95. Who is the speaker?

(A) A delivery man
(B) A restaurant manager
(C) A grocer
(D) A millworker

96. What does the speaker intend to do?

(A) Offer an online service
(B) Alter a menu
(C) Deliver to local bakeries
(D) Change his supplier

97. Look at the graphic. Which store is the man most likely calling?

(A) Miller's Joy
(B) Herbalist's Delight
(C) Mrs. Millers'
(D) Harmony

Healthy Habits

11:00–11:45 P.M., Mon.–Fri.

Weekly Schedule	
Mon.	Child Obesity – A New Threat
Tue.	LIVE Lecture: Eating Habits of Adults
Wed.	Smoking, a Silent Killer
Thu.	LIVE Lecture: Vegetarianism. Is It a MUST?
Fri.	Dietholic

98. According to the speaker, what has Professor Holt recently done?

(A) Delivered a lecture
(B) Organized a seminar
(C) Participated in a university debate
(D) Published an article

99. Look at the graphic. When does Mr. James say he wants to meet Professor Holt?

(A) Tuesday
(B) Wednesday
(C) Thursday
(D) Friday

100. What does the speaker ask Professor Holt to do?

(A) Contribute to a TV program
(B) Undertake a newspaper interview
(C) Review some books
(D) Take a university lecture

ACTUAL
TEST

答對題數表

PART 1	
PART 2	
PART 3	
PART 4	
總題數	

10

LISTENING TEST

In the Listening test, you will be asked to demonstrate how well you understand spoken English. The entire Listening test will last approximately 45 minutes. There are four parts, and directions are given for each part. You must mark your answers on the separate answer sheet. Do not write your answers in your test book.

PART 1 ∩ 37

Directions: For each question in this part, you will hear four statements about a picture in your test book. When you hear the statements, you must select the one statement that best describes what you see in the picture. Then find the number of the question on your answer sheet and mark your answer. The statements will not be printed in your test book and will be spoken only one time.

Sample Answer

Statement (B), "They're shaking hands," is the best description of the picture, so you should select answer (B) and mark it on your answer sheet.

1.

2.

Go on to the next page

3.

4.

5.

6.

Go on to the next page

PART 2 ∩ 38

Directions: You will hear a question or statement and three responses spoken in English. They will not be printed in your test book and will be spoken only one time. Select the best response to the question or statement and mark the letter (A), (B), or (C) on your answer sheet.

7. Mark your answer on your answer sheet.

8. Mark your answer on your answer sheet.

9. Mark your answer on your answer sheet.

10. Mark your answer on your answer sheet.

11. Mark your answer on your answer sheet.

12. Mark your answer on your answer sheet.

13. Mark your answer on your answer sheet.

14. Mark your answer on your answer sheet.

15. Mark your answer on your answer sheet.

16. Mark your answer on your answer sheet.

17. Mark your answer on your answer sheet.

18. Mark your answer on your answer sheet.

19. Mark your answer on your answer sheet.

20. Mark your answer on your answer sheet.

21. Mark your answer on your answer sheet.

22. Mark your answer on your answer sheet.

23. Mark your answer on your answer sheet.

24. Mark your answer on your answer sheet.

25. Mark your answer on your answer sheet.

26. Mark your answer on your answer sheet.

27. Mark your answer on your answer sheet.

28. Mark your answer on your answer sheet.

29. Mark your answer on your answer sheet.

30. Mark your answer on your answer sheet.

31. Mark your answer on your answer sheet.

PART 3 ∩ 39

Directions: You will hear some conversations between two or more people. You will be asked to answer three questions about what the speakers say in each conversation. Select the best response to each question and mark the letter (A), (B), (C), or (D) on your answer sheet. The conversations will not be printed in your test book and will be spoken only one time.

32. What did the man write about?
    (A) His favorite pets
    (B) Visiting famous museums
    (C) How to make various dishes
    (D) Writing stories on a blog

33. Why is the man delighted?
    (A) He was given a prize for his writings.
    (B) His work will be published.
    (C) His articles earned favorable reviews.
    (D) He was promoted to editor in a publishing company.

34. Why does the woman want to meet with the man?
    (A) To talk about a future project
    (B) To ask for some cooking advice
    (C) To receive some samples
    (D) To organize an exhibition

35. What are the speakers discussing?
    (A) A shopping list
    (B) A tourist attraction
    (C) A doctor's prescription
    (D) A canceled appointment

36. Why is the man behind schedule?
    (A) A staff member is out sick.
    (B) A doctor didn't write her a prescription.
    (C) He went out for lunch.
    (D) The pharmacy has been busy.

37. What does the woman say she will do?
    (A) Visit the doctor's office
    (B) Go to a nearby store
    (C) Make a phone call
    (D) Make an appointment

38. Why is the man calling?
    (A) To schedule a meeting
    (B) To complain about a product
    (C) To check a delivery schedule
    (D) To advertise a special promotion

39. What types of products does the man's company sell?
    (A) Home appliances
    (B) Computer
    (C) Office supplies
    (D) Furniture

40. What does the man offer to do for the woman?
    (A) Send a message
    (B) Refund her in full
    (C) Offer free delivery
    (D) Call her office

41. What is the man's complaint?
    (A) His room is dirty.
    (B) His reservation was canceled.
    (C) His air conditioner is broken.
    (D) His room is too small.

42. What does the woman offer to the man?
    (A) A free meal
    (B) A free shuttle bus to the airport
    (C) A room upgrade
    (D) A gift certificate

43. What does the man request?
    (A) Help with his luggage
    (B) A room change
    (C) Free Internet service
    (D) A discount coupon

Go on to the next page

44. Where does the woman work?

(A) At a travel agency
(B) At a department store
(C) At a national museum
(D) At a health clinic

45. What does the man say he will be doing next month?

(A) Participating in a conference
(B) Making a presentation
(C) Traveling overseas
(D) Getting vaccinated

46. What does the man imply when he says, "that's not going to work"?

(A) He needs a different appointment.
(B) He does not work on that day.
(C) He prefers to work on schedule.
(D) He will go abroad.

---

47. Why does the woman want to save money?

(A) To replace a computer
(B) To purchase a house
(C) To go on vacation
(D) To buy a car

48. What does the man recommend?

(A) Applying for a loan
(B) Selling a house
(C) Using an online program
(D) Cutting down on expenses

49. What is the woman concerned about?

(A) Web site reliability
(B) Service costs
(C) Scheduling conflicts
(D) A program's expiration date

---

50. Who most likely is the woman?

(A) A graphic designer
(B) An advertising agent
(C) A store owner
(D) A writer

51. What is the woman pleased about?

(A) A final draft of an advertisement
(B) Recent online reviews
(C) A store location
(D) Contact information

52. What does the man offer to do?

(A) Install a computer program
(B) Confirm service request
(C) Print an advertisement
(D) Enlarge an image

---

53. What does the woman imply when she says, "I'm really concerned"?

(A) She is able to do volunteer work.
(B) She is proud of attending the event.
(C) She is indifferent about the matter.
(D) She is worried about the complaints.

54. What is the woman concerned about?

(A) Making a presentation
(B) Responding to client complaints
(C) Translating a different language
(D) Doing multiple tasks at the same time

55. What does the man say he will do tomorrow?

(A) Submit some paperwork
(B) Bring a problem up at a meeting
(C) Prepare the event
(D) Conduct a customer survey

56. Where do the interviewers most likely work?

  (A) At a bookstore
  (B) At a kindergarten
  (C) At a publisher
  (D) At a broadcasting company

57. What job requirement do the speakers discuss?

  (A) Possessing the proper license
  (B) Owning the film equipment
  (C) Having related experience
  (D) Being able to work extra hours

58. What does the man agree to do next?

  (A) Show some previous work
  (B) Conduct a survey
  (C) Watch a presentation
  (D) Meet a president

59. What problem does the woman mention?

  (A) Business is unusually slow.
  (B) A restaurant received several complaints.
  (C) A restaurant is short-staffed.
  (D) The rent has been gone up.

60. What does the man suggest?

  (A) Offering an outdoor event
  (B) Moving into a different location
  (C) Lowering prices
  (D) Acquiring popular restaurants

61. What does the woman ask the man to do?

  (A) Hire a manager
  (B) Train employees
  (C) Get ready for the holiday season
  (D) Prepare some food samples

62. What industry do the speakers most likely work in?

  (A) Pharmaceutical
  (B) Finance
  (C) Construction
  (D) Entertainment

63. What does the woman say will happen within two years?

  (A) Some research will receive a prize.
  (B) A new product will be introduced.
  (C) A company will hire more employees.
  (D) Another conference will be held.

64. What does the woman imply when she says, "Didn't Martial participate in this project"?

  (A) Some results are not promising.
  (B) A project will be finished soon.
  (C) A slide is missing some information.
  (D) The man must attend the conference.

Go on to the next page

Office	Location
Prudential Finance	Suite 101
York Foods	Suite 108
UK Express	Suite 111
Morris International	Suite 114

ITEM	PRICE
Computer hard case	$50
Computer bag	$80
Extended warranty	$200
Computer	$1500
Total	**$1830**

65. What is the purpose of the woman's visit?

(A) To deliver a package
(B) To have a client meeting
(C) To go to the pharmacy
(D) To have a medical appointment

66. What does the man say about parking?

(A) It is available on the street near the building.
(B) It is free for visitors with a validated parking ticket.
(C) It is for tenants in the building.
(D) It has a time limit.

67. Look at the graphic. Which office name has to be updated on the building directory?

(A) Prudential Finance
(B) York Foods
(C) UK Express
(D) Morris International

68. Who most likely is the woman?

(A) A salesperson
(B) An engineer
(C) A bank clerk
(D) A computer programmer

69. What does the man ask about?

(A) A contract renewal
(B) A payment method
(C) Computer accessories
(D) The price of a computer

70. Look at the graphic. Which amount will be removed from the invoice?

(A) $50
(B) $80
(C) $200
(D) $1500

PART 4 ∩ 40

Directions: You will hear some talks given by a single speaker. You will be asked to answer three questions about what the speaker says in each talk. Select the best response to each question and mark the letter (A), (B), (C), or (D) on your answer sheet. The talks will not be printed in your test book and will be spoken only one time.

71. Where does the speaker work?
    (A) At a radio station
    (B) At a bookstore
    (C) At a university
    (D) At a consulting firm

72. What will Dr. Dooling be discussing?
    (A) Career management
    (B) Publishing books
    (C) Communication skills
    (D) Time management

73. What does the speaker encourage listeners to do?
    (A) Call in with questions
    (B) Register in advance
    (D) Save money
    (D) Buy more books

74. What is the man waiting for?
    (A) His passport to be issued
    (B) His airline ticket to be purchased
    (C) His colleagues to arrive
    (D) His luggage to be returned

75. What is scheduled for Monday?
    (A) A meeting
    (B) A product presentation
    (C) A doctor's appointment
    (D) A press conference

76. Why does the man say, "I know it's a difficult job"?
    (A) To advise the listener to finish the job quickly
    (B) To warn that the job is unnecessary
    (C) To apologize for an inconvenience
    (D) To remind the listener of its risks

77. What is the talk mainly about?
    (A) A wage system
    (B) Security enhancements
    (C) Head office relocation
    (D) A training schedule

78. According to the speaker, what will happen on Tuesday?
    (A) Additional staff will be employed.
    (B) An inspection will be carried out.
    (C) Office supplies will be purchased.
    (D) New procedures will take effect.

79. What must employees do this week?
    (A) Use a different entrance
    (B) Update company's accounts
    (C) Register their fingerprints
    (D) Apply for the program

80. What does the speaker say the company is considering?
    (A) Buying a new product
    (B) Changing the lunch time
    (C) Starting a new business
    (D) Extending business hours

81. What can listeners receive for free tomorrow?
    (A) A laptop
    (B) A T-shirt with a company logo
    (C) Stationery
    (D) Beverages

82. Why should listeners visit Belotti's office?
    (A) To pick up an employee ID card
    (B) To sign up for an employee program
    (C) To donate money
    (D) To submit a form

Go on to the next page

83. Where most likely is this announcement being made?

(A) At a customer service center
(B) At a factory
(C) At a department store
(D) At an auto repair shop

84. What problem does the speaker mention?

(A) Some supplies are sold out.
(B) A manager is sick.
(C) Inclement weather is expected.
(D) Some equipment is not working.

85. What will employees be informed about by assembly managers?

(A) Test results
(B) Safety regulations
(C) Work schedule changes
(D) Hygiene inspection

---

86. What is the news report about?

(A) A celebrity's recipe book
(B) A new seafood restaurant
(C) Tips for selecting vegetables
(D) Healthy eating habits

87. What does Dr. Watson recommend that people do?

(A) Prepare meals at home
(B) Buy special equipment
(C) Enroll in a cooking class
(D) Download recipes online

88. According to the speaker, what can listeners do on a Web site?

(A) Make a reservation
(B) Place an order
(C) Read some survey questions
(D) Sign up for a subscription

---

89. Why is the president coming for a visit?

(A) A project has been completed.
(B) A facility has been moved.
(C) A manager will retire.
(D) A sales record has been accomplished.

90. Why does the speaker say, "this is not a formal visit"?

(A) To settle a dispute
(B) To reassure employees
(C) To apologize for problems
(D) To check a procedure

91. What event have the listeners been invited to?

(A) A retirement party
(B) An opening ceremony
(C) A welcome reception
(D) A dinner party

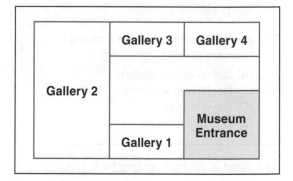

92. What did the listeners see on the tour?

(A) Sculptures
(B) Paintings
(C) Photographs
(D) Pottery

93. What does the guide recommend listeners do to learn more about the exhibition?

(A) Visit a Web site
(B) Attend a program
(C) Buy a book
(D) Watch a related movie

94. Look at the graphic. In which room is the exhibition on the works of Chagall?

(A) Gallery 1
(B) Gallery 2
(C) Gallery 3
(D) Gallery 4

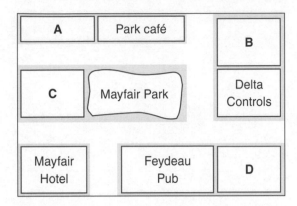

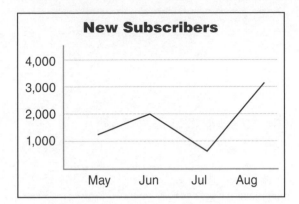

95. Why is the announcement being made?

(A) To inform listeners about a change in working hours
(B) To encourage employees to take part in the parade
(C) To notify listeners of the unavailability of a parking space
(D) To check the off-site duties for today

96. According to the speaker, what is going to happen in the area today?

(A) Delta Controls will be closed.
(B) There will be a big parade all day long.
(C) Vehicles will be regulated for about 3 hours.
(D) The streets will get jammed with cars during rush hour.

97. Look at the graphic. Which parking area was recommended by the speaker?

(A) A
(B) B
(C) C
(D) D

98. Where most likely does the speaker work?

(A) At an advertising company
(B) At a magazine publisher
(C) At a leisure supplies manufacturer
(D) At a market research institute

99. Look at the graphic. When did the company have its 5th anniversary?

(A) In May
(B) In June
(C) In July
(D) In August

100. According to the speaker, what does the business plan to do next month?

(A) Offer a promotional event
(B) Launch a new product
(C) Get new advertisers
(D) Conduct a survey

挑戰 NEW TOEIC
新制多益
聽力滿分
10回模擬試題1000題 解析版

作者 Kim su hyeon ｜ 譯者 林育珊 / 關亭薇

Part 2

Script ＋ 中譯 ＋ 解析 ＋ 核心單字

Part 2

Script + 中譯 + 解析 + 核心單字

目錄

ACTUAL TEST
1

1

(A) She's throwing a ball.
(B) She's appreciating the paintings.
(C) She's leaning against the wall.
(D) She's painting the wall.

(A) 她正在丟球。
(B) 她正在欣賞畫作。
(C) 她正靠著牆。
(D) 她正在油漆牆壁。

• **throw a ball** 丟球　**appreciate** 欣賞　**painting** 畫作　**lean against . . .** 倚靠著……

照片中的女人正對著牆壁粉刷油漆。**(A)** 照片中並未出現球。如果選項中出現照片中沒有的單字，則該選項非正確答案。**(B)** 照片中並未出現畫作。**(C)** 照片中雖然有一面牆，但是女人並未倚靠在牆上。正確答案為 **(D)**。

2

(A) People are singing together.
(B) People are playing different instruments.
(C) People are facing each other.
(D) People are marching in formation.

(A) 人們正在一起唱歌。
(B) 人們正在演奏不同樂器。
(C) 人們正面對著彼此。
(D) 人們正列隊行進。

• **play an instrument** 演奏樂器　**face each other** 面對彼此　**march** 行進　**in formation** 列隊

照片中人們正在演奏樂器。**(A)** 人們並不是在唱歌，而是在演奏樂器。**(C)** 人們全都面向前方，所以不是正確答案。**(D)** 人們全部都坐著。正確答案為 **(B)**。

3

(A) Bicycles are being assembled.
(B) Bicycles are attached to bicycle racks.
(C) The road is being paved.
(D) Bicycles are against the wall.

(A) 腳踏車正在被組裝。
(B) 腳踏車固定在腳踏車架上。
(C) 馬路正在鋪設中。
(D) 腳踏車靠著牆壁。

• **assemble** 組裝　**be attached to . . .** 被固定在……　**bicycle rack** 腳踏車架　**pave** 鋪設

照片中的腳踏車被鎖在保管架上。**(A)** 照片中出現了腳踏車，但並不是正在組裝的照片。照片中沒有出現人，但是選項卻提及需要人才能完成的行為，所以不是正解。**(C)** 照片中雖然可看見道路，但是看不出來正在進行鋪平工程。**(D)** 照片中雖然出現腳踏車，但是並沒有牆壁。正確答案為 **(B)**。

4

(A) There is merchandise on the shelves.
(B) The people are all carrying backpacks.
(C) One of the women is paying for some items.
(D) One of the women is mopping the floor.

(A) 架上有商品。
(B) 人們都背著後背包。
(C) 其中一位女士正在付款買東西。
(D) 其中一位女士正在拖地。

• **merchandise** 商品　**pay for . . .** 付款買……　**mop** 拖（地）

照片中的展示架上放置著商品，遠方有些女人圍站著。**(B)** 照片中雖然出現一些人，但是沒有人背著背包。**(C)** 照片裡沒有正在結帳的女人。**(D)** 照片裡沒有正在拖地的女人。正確答案為 **(A)**。

🎧 01

5

(A) The frame is being cut.
(B) The man is removing his gloves.
(C) The ladder is being made.
(D) The man is welding.

(A) 框架正在被裁剪。
(B) 這位男士正脫下手套。
(C) 梯子正在製作中。
(D) 這位男士正在焊接。

• **frame** 框架　**remove** 移開；去除　**ladder** 梯子　**weld** 焊接

此為一名男子正在進行焊接的照片。**(A)** 照片中未出現框架，也無法確定男子是否在進行裁切。**(B)** 男子戴著手套。**(C)** 照片中雖然出現類似梯子的物品，但是無法確定。正確答案為 **(D)**。

6

(A) An airplane is landing.
(B) An aircraft is parked at the airport.
(C) People are waving their hands from the airplane.
(D) People are exiting the plane.

(A) 一架飛機正在降落。
(B) 一架飛機停在機場。
(C) 人們從飛機上揮手。
(D) 人們正在下飛機。

• **land** 降落　**wave one's hand** 揮手　**exit the plane** 下飛機

此為一台飛機停在機場的照片。**(A)** 雖然照片中出現了飛機，但是並非正在降落中。**(C)** 雖然照片中出現了飛機，但是並未出現正在揮手的人。**(D)** 照片中並未出現人。此選項提及照片中未出現的單字，故為非正確答案。正確答案為 **(B)**。

7 ---

Are you satisfied with your new wallet?
(A) Absolutely! I'm very happy with it.
(B) Yes, for our customer satisfaction.
(C) No, it's hanging on the wall.

你喜歡你的新皮夾嗎？
(A) 當然！我非常滿意。
(B) 是的，為了讓客戶滿意。
(C) 不，它就掛在牆上。

• **be satisfied with . . .** 對……感到滿意　**absolutely** 當然；絕對地　**customer satisfaction** 顧客滿意度

(A) 題目詢問是否喜歡新皮夾，回答「當然喜歡」最為適當，故此選項為正確解答。(B) 為利用和問句中的「satisfied」發音相似的「satisfaction」誘導，非正確答案。(C) 為利用和問句中的「wallet」發音相似的「wall」誘導，非正確答案。正確答案為 (A)。

8 ---

Do you happen to know who's in charge of revising the budget report?
(A) Yes, I was overcharged.
(B) No, you don't need to go over the report.
(C) I guess Mr. Carter is responsible for that.

你知不知道是誰負責修訂預算報告？
(A) 是的，我被多收錢了。
(B) 不，你不用核對那份報告。
(C) 我想卡特先生負責此事。

• **happen to** 偶然；恰巧　**overcharge** 索價過高　**be in charge of . . .** 負責……　**go over** 核對

(A) 為利用和問句中的「charge」發音相似的「overcharged」誘導。(B) 為利用題目中出現過的「report」誘導。(C) 題目詢問負責人為誰，回答「卡特先生負責此事」最為適當，故正確答案為 (C)。

9 ---

Who will be making the first speech?
(A) Mr. Hernandez from the Singapore branch.
(B) Yes, I will make a phone call to you later.
(C) Melanie missed the first class.

誰要發表第一場演說？
(A) 新加坡分公司的赫南德茲先生。
(B) 是的，我晚點會打電話給你。
(C) 梅蘭妮錯過第一堂課了。

• **make a speech** 發表演說　**branch** 分公司　**make a phone call** 打電話

(A) 題目詢問演講者為誰，回答特定人名最為適當，故此選項為正確解答。(B) 疑問詞問句無法使用 Yes/No 回答。(C) 句中雖然提及人名，但是與題目問句毫無關聯，故不正確。正確答案為 (A)。

10

What's the weather like there in Toronto?
(A) She likes living in Toronto.
(B) I don't know whether it will rain tomorrow.
(C) It's cold and snowy.

多倫多那裡的天氣如何？
(A) 她喜歡住在多倫多。
(B) 我不知道明天是否會下雨。
(C) 很冷又下雪。

(A) 為利用和問句中的「like」發音相似的「likes」誘導。(B) 為利用和問句中的「weather」發音相似的「whether」誘導。(C) 題目詢問多倫多天氣如何，回答「很冷又下雪」最為適當，正確答案為 (C)。

11

When is the next flight scheduled to leave?
(A) No, he left 10 minutes ago.
(B) I think we're behind schedule.
(C) At 7:30 P.M. sharp.

下一班飛機預定何時起飛？
(A) 不，他十分鐘前就走了。
(B) 我想我們進度落後了。
(C) 晚上7:30整。

• **be scheduled to V** 計畫做⋯⋯　　**behind schedule** 進度落後；比預定時間晚　　**sharp** 準時地

(A) 疑問詞問句無法使用 Yes/No 回答。(B) 為利用和問句中的「scheduled」發音相似的「schedule」誘導，非正確答案。(C) 題目詢問飛機起飛時間，回答確切時間最為適當，故正確答案為 (C)。

12

Where is the instruction manual for the new copier?
(A) I guess it's in the bottom drawer.
(B) I don't like coffee.
(C) I think he is a good instructor.

新影印機的操作手冊在哪裡？
(A) 我想是在底層的抽屜裡。
(B) 我不喜歡咖啡。
(C) 我想他是個不錯的講師。

• **instruction manual** 操作手冊　　**copier** 影印機　　**bottom drawer** 底層的抽屜　　**instructor** 講師

(A) 題目詢問說明書在何處，回答「在底層的抽屜」最為適當。(B) 為利用和和問句中的「copier」發音相似的「coffee」誘導。(C) 為利用和和問句中的「instruction」發音相似的「instructor」誘導。正確答案為 (A)。

13 --

How long have you worked for this company?　你在這家公司服務多久了？
(A) Approximately 30 years ago.　(A) 大約30年前。
(B) Around 11 P.M.　(B) 大約晚上11點。
(C) About 5 years.　(C) 大約五年了。

• **approximately** 大約

(A) 題目詢問工作資歷，故回答過去某時間點並不適當。(B) 回答某時間點並不適當。(C) 回答「大約五年了」最為適當，故正確答案為 (C)。

14 --

Why did Christine cancel her trip to Hawaii?　克莉絲汀為什麼取消去夏威夷的旅程？
(A) She was born in Hawaii.　(A) 她在夏威夷出生。
(B) She had the flu.　(B) 她得了流行性感冒。
(C) The meeting was canceled.　(C) 會議被取消了。

• **flu** 流行性感冒

(A) 雖題目中出現過的「Hawaii」，但是題目並非詢問出生地。(B) 題目詢問行程取消原因，回答「得了流行性感冒」最為適當，故此選項為正確解答。(C) 此選項「canceled」雖曾出現於題目中，但僅為誘導。正確答案為 (B)。

15 --

Which caterer is supplying food for the wedding reception?　哪一家外燴業者供應婚宴的食物？
(A) A small amount of food.　(A) 少量的食物。
(B) The same one we used last month.　(B) 跟我們上個月找的同一家。
(C) The orders have come in online.　(C) 訂單從網路上進來。

• **caterer** 外燴業者　**supply** 供應　**reception** 宴會

(A) 此選項「food」雖曾出現於題目中，但僅為誘導。(B) 題目詢問合作業者為誰，回答「跟我們上個月找的同一家」最為適當。(C) 與題目毫無關聯的內容。正確答案為 (B)。

16 --

I think we'd better get there by subway.　我想我們最好搭地鐵到那裡。
(A) Okay, I'll pick it up.　(A) 好，我會去拿。
(B) I left my bag in the subway.　(B) 我把包包忘在地鐵上了。
(C) Yes, if you want to avoid traffic.　(C) 沒錯，如果你想避開車潮的話。

• **had better V** 最好……　**avoid** 避開

(A) pick up 的有一種用法為 pick sth up，指的是撿或拿起某物，另一種是 pick sb up，意思為開車去接某人，此選項應是想用後者來誤導，全句內容與題目無關。(B) 雖有題目中出現過的「subway」，但是內容與題目毫無關聯。(C) 題目說「最好搭地鐵」，而此選項附和提議，故正確答案為 (C)。

17 --

You're going to the concert after work, aren't you?
(A) Sorry, I didn't watch the concert last night.
(B) No, I have some overtime work.
(C) No, tickets are still available.

你下班後要去演唱會，不是嗎？
(A) 抱歉，我昨晚沒有看演唱會。
(B) 不，我要加班。
(C) 不，還有票。

• **overtime work** 加班　**available** 可取得的；可用的

(A) 此選項「concert」雖曾出現於題目，但僅為誘導。(B) 題目詢問是否前往演唱會，回答「要加班不能去」最為適當，故此選項為正確解答。(C) 雖有回答「No」，但後續句沒有回答到不去參加的原因。正確答案為 (B)。

18 --

Do you happen to know how I can access the company's files?
(A) At the accessory shop.
(B) You can accompany me.
(C) You should enter the code first.

你知不知道我要如何取得公司的檔案？
(A) 在飾品店。
(B) 你可以陪我。
(C) 你應該先輸入密碼。

• **access** 取得　**accompany** 陪伴　**code** 密碼

(A) 為利用和問句中的「access」發音相似的「accessory」誘導。(B) 為利用和問句中的「company」發音相似的「accompany」誘導。(C) 題目詢問如何取得公司檔案，回答「先輸入密碼」最為適當，故正確答案為 (C)。

19 --

Which do you prefer, a table in the middle or by the window?
(A) A table for three, please.
(B) I don't have a preference.
(C) Yes, that sounds great.

你比較喜歡中間的座位，還是靠窗的？
(A) 三個人的位子，謝謝。
(B) 我沒有特別偏好。
(C) 是的，那聽起來很棒。

• **prefer**〔動詞〕偏好　**preference**〔名詞〕偏好

(A) 此選項「table」雖曾出現於題目中，但僅為誘導。(B) 題目詢問喜歡的座位，回答「沒有特別偏好」最為適當，故此選項為正確解答。(C) 選擇問句不可用 Yes/No 回答。正確答案為 (B)。

9

20

What was J&J Company's final offer for the bid?

(A) Approximately 10 million dollars.

(B) We've accepted the offer.

(C) At the final stage.

J&J公司對投標的最終出價是多少？

(A) 大約一千萬元。

(B) 我們接受了那個報價

(C) 在最後階段。

• **bid** 投標　**approximately** 大約

(A) 題目詢問最終投標價，回答具體金額最為適當，故此選項為正確解答。(B) 此選項「offer」雖曾出現在題目中，但僅為誘導。(C) 此選項「final」雖曾出現在題目中，但僅為誘導。正確答案為 (A)。

21

Was it a long journey?

(A) It certainly was.

(B) Yes, hurry up.

(C) No, he has a long beard.

那是一段很長的旅程嗎？

(A) 的確是。

(B) 是的，快一點。

(C) 不，他留長鬍子。

(A) 題目詢問旅程是否漫長，此選項附和「的確是」，故為正確解答。(B) 與題目毫無關聯的內容。(C) 雖有題目中出現過的「long」，但僅為誘導。正確答案為 (A)。

22

I strongly believe she wears contact lenses.

(A) I swear I'll accept your offer.

(B) I don't wear perfume at all.

(C) How can you tell?

我非常確定她戴隱形眼鏡。

(A) 我發誓我會接受你的提議。

(B) 我完全不擦香水。

(C) 你怎麼知道？

• **swear** 發誓　**wear perfume** 擦香水　**tell** 辨別

(A) 為利用和問句中的「wears」發音相似的「swear」誘導。(B) 雖有題目中出現過的「wear」，但僅為誘導，兩句不具對話關係。(C) 題目表示確定女子戴了隱形眼鏡，此選項反問「你怎麼知道」，故正確答案為 (C)。

23

Why don't we go over the résumés over lunch?

(A) We'll review the applications tonight.

(B) That sounds great.

(C) Lunch was terrific.

我們何不在午餐時看那些履歷呢？

(A) 我們今晚會檢視那些應徵函。

(B) 聽起來不錯。

(C) 午餐很棒。

• **go over** 仔細審查　**résumé** 履歷　**review** 檢視　**application** 應徵函　**terrific** 很棒的

(A) 選項中的「go over」雖和題目的「review」意思相近，但題目透露出邀請的語氣，此處沒有表示答應或拒絕的意願，故非正確答案。(B) 對於題目中提議，回應「聽起來不錯」，表示接受，故為正確解答。(C) 雖有題目中出現過的「lunch」，但僅為誘導。正確答案為 (B)。

24

Wouldn't this platter be good for a wedding gift?
(A) It's really good for your health.
(B) I think it couldn't be better.
(C) Yes, he is planning to go there.

這個淺盤不是很適合當結婚禮物嗎？
(A) 這真的對你的健康有益。
(B) 我想是的。
(C) 是的，他正打算去那裡。

• platter 淺盤

(A) 雖有題目中出現過的「good for」，但僅為誘導。(B) 題目表示淺盤是作為結婚禮物的好選擇，此選項附和，故為正確解答。(C) 與問句毫無關聯的內容。正確答案為 (B)。

25

Should I send this package by regular mail or by courier?
(A) No, your career is excellent.
(B) Yes, you've got mail.
(C) It depends on how urgent it is.

我應該用平信還是快遞寄這個包裹？
(A) 不，你的工作很棒。
(B) 是的，你有郵件。
(C) 要看有多緊急。

• courier 快遞　depend on . . . 視……而定　urgent 緊急的

(A) 選擇問句不可用 Yes/No 回答。(B) 選擇問句不可用 Yes/No 回答。(C) 題目詢問郵件的寄送方式，回答「看有多緊急」最為適當，故正確答案為 (C)。

26

Who will accompany you to the airport?
(A) My colleague at work is taking me.
(B) It's a publishing company.
(C) My friend will pick me up at the airport.

誰會陪你去機場？
(A) 我公司同事要帶我去。
(B) 是一家出版社。
(C) 我朋友會在機場接我。

• accompany 陪伴　colleague 同事　pick up 接送

(A) 題目詢問同前往機場的人，回答同事最為適當，故此選項為正確解答。(B) 為利用和問句中的「accompany」發音相似的「company」誘導，非正確答案。(C) 雖有題目中出現過的「airport」，但僅為誘導。正確答案為 (A)。

27

Did you consider applying for the job in marketing?
(A) A ten percent discount applies to this item.
(B) Why? Do they have an opening?
(C) No, I don't need to purchase office supplies.

你有考慮應徵行銷工作嗎？
(A) 這件商品適用九折優惠。
(B) 怎麼了？他們有空缺嗎？
(C) 不，我不需要購買辦公用品。

• apply for 應徵　apply to 適用於　office supplies 辦公用品

(A) 為利用和問句中的「apply for」發音相似的「apply to」誘導，非正確答案。(B) 題目詢問對工作的應徵意願，反問是否有職缺釋出為合適回應，故為正確解答。(C) 為利用和問句中的「apply」發音相似的「supplies」誘導。正確答案為 (B)。

28

When is your company planning to announce the merger?
(A) It's an emergency meeting.
(B) Three days ago.
(C) We're holding a press conference next month.

貴公司打算何時宣布合併？
(A) 這是個緊急會議。
(B) 三天前。
(C) 我們下個月才會開記者會。

• merger （公司、企業的）合併　emergency 緊急狀況　press conference 記者會

(A) 此選項中的「meeting」雖與題目中的「company」相關，但此處僅為誘導。(B) 題目問句內容的時態為未來式，但是此選項為過去式，故為非正確答案。(C) 題目詢問消息公開時間，回答「下個月才會開記者會」最為適當，故正確答案為 (C)。

29

The train left on time, didn't it?
(A) At the training session.
(B) No, he didn't.
(C) Yes, like always.

火車準時出發了，不是嗎？
(A) 在訓練講習。
(B) 不，他沒有。
(C) 是的，一如往常。

• on time 準時　training session 訓練講習

(A) 為利用和問句中的「train」發音相似的「training」誘導，非正確答案。(B) 雖有題目中出現過的「didn't」，但僅為誘導。(C) 題目詢問火車是否已準時出發，回答「（火車）一如往常」最為適合，故正確答案為 (C)。

30

Where can I find Professor Eugene's office?
(A) Mondays between 1 and 3.
(B) I'm afraid he's on vacation.
(C) Did you check the lost and found?

尤金教授的辦公室在哪裡？
(A) 每週一一點到三點。
(B) 他恐怕正在休假中。
(C) 你找過失物招領處了嗎？

• **on vacation** 休假　**lost and found** 失物招領處

(A) 題目以疑問詞「Where」開頭詢問地點，而此選項以時段回答，並不合適，故此非正確答案。
(B) 題目詢問教授辦公室的位置，此選項回答「他恐怕正在休假」，暗指教授目前不在辦公室，去了恐怕也是白跑一趟，故此為正確答案。(C) 為利用和問句中的「find」發音相似的「found」誘導。正確答案為 (B)。

31

Haven't you found your briefcase yet?
(A) No, I failed to find it.
(B) It will be a brief meeting.
(C) Yes, it was founded two years ago.

你還沒找到公事包嗎？
(A) 還沒，我找不到。
(B) 那會是個簡短的會議。
(C) 是的，它創立於兩年前。

• **briefcase** 公事包　**brief** 簡短的　**found** 創立、創辦 (found-founded-founded)

(A) 題目詢問是否找到公事包，回答「沒有找到」最為合適，故此選項為正確解答。(B) 為利用和問句中的「briefcase」發音相似的「brief」誘導。(C) 為利用和問句中的「found」發音相似的「founded」誘導。正確答案為 (A)。

PART 3 03

32–34 conversation	38–40 對話
M Which flight do you think we should take?	男 妳認為我們應該搭哪一班飛機？
W Well, there are two to Detroit. One is at 9 A.M., and the other leaves at 11:30 A.M.	女 到底特律有兩班。一班是早上9點，另一班是早上11:30起飛。
M Let's take the one at nine o'clock. That way, we'll have time to grab some lunch before that noon meeting starts.	男 我們搭9點那班吧。這樣一來，我們就有時間在午會開始前吃點午餐了。
W That sounds like a nice plan. I'll make the reservations.	女 聽起來是個不錯的計畫。那我來訂機票。
M Okay, thank you.	男 好的，謝謝妳。

• **flight** 班機   **grab** 利用（機會做某事）；（借機）趕緊……   **reservation** 預訂

32
- -

What mode of transportation will the speakers use?

(A) Aircraft
(B) Car
(C) Boat
(D) Train

說話者將採用何種交通運輸方式？

(A) 飛機
(B) 汽車
(C) 船
(D) 火車

男子的第一句台詞「Which flight do you think we should take?」詢問對方應該要搭乘哪一班飛機，故可得知對話者將搭乘飛機，因此正確答案為 (A)。

33
- -

What time do the speakers plan to travel?

(A) At 5:00 A.M.
(B) At 9:00 A.M.
(C) At 11:30 A.M.
(D) At 12:00 P.M.

說話者打算何時出發？

(A) 早上5:00
(B) 早上9:00
(C) 早上11:30
(D) 中午12:00

男子的第二句台詞説：「Let's take the one at nine o'clock.」，故可得知對話者將於九點出發，正確答案為 (B)。

34
- -

What will the woman probably do next?

(A) Attend a meeting
(B) Have lunch
(C) Travel to Detroit
(D) Book tickets

這位女士接下來可能會做什麼？

(A) 參加會議
(B) 吃午餐
(C) 到底特律
(D) 訂機票

女子的最後一句台詞提到「I'll make the reservations.」，故可得知將由女子訂機票，故此題正確答案為 (D)。

14

35-37 conversation with three speakers (NEW)

35–37 三人對話

W	Did you hear the news? Jim got that promotion he applied for. He's going to be the senior manager of Human Resources at the head office. I just heard about it from Jane in Accounting.
M1	Wow, he must be really excited. When will he be starting the new position?
W	They need him there in three weeks. The previous manager will be retiring then.
M2	Good for Jim.
M1	Why don't we throw him a party?
W	That sounds like a great idea.

女	你聽說了那個消息嗎？吉姆申請的升遷獲准了。他將成為總公司人力資源部的資深經理。我剛從會計部的珍那裡聽來的。
男1	哇，他一定很興奮。他的新職何時開始？
女	他們需要他三週後到任。之前的經理屆時會退休。
男2	這對吉姆來說是好消息。
男1	我們何不為他辦個派對呢？
女	聽起來是個好主意。

• promotion 升遷　apply for . . . 申請……　senior manager 資深經理　accounting 會計
coworker 同事

35 ---

What is the main topic of the conversation?
(A) An upcoming corporate merger
(B) A round of layoffs
(C) The promotion of a coworker
(D) Plans for summer vacation

這段對話的主題是什麼？
(A) 即將到來的企業合併
(B) 一輪的裁員
(C) 同事的升遷
(D) 暑假的規畫

從女子的第一句台詞「Jim got that promotion he applied for」中，可知這是升遷相關的對話，再從後續言談可推斷，談話者與吉姆應為同事關係，故正確答案為 (C)。

36 ---

When will the discussed event happen?
(A) Immediately
(B) In a week
(C) In three weeks
(D) In the New Year

這個討論的事件將於何時發生？
(A) 立刻
(B) 一週後
(C) 三週後
(D) 新年期間

從女子的第二句台詞「They need him there in three weeks.」可知吉姆將在三週後升遷，故正確答案為 (C)。

37 ---

What is the timing of the event dependent upon?
(A) Someone's retirement
(B) The opening of a location
(C) The redecoration of an office
(D) The completion of training

這事件發生的時間將依什麼而定？
(A) 某人退休
(B) 店家開幕
(C) 辦公室重新裝潢
(D) 訓練結束

女子的第二句台詞「They need him there in three weeks. The previous manager will be retiring then.」中提及，前經理將在三週後離職，屆時即需要吉姆接任，故可得知前經理卸任後，吉姆將獲得晉升。

15

M	Future World Home Furnishings and Appliances. This is Gary speaking. How can I help you today?	男	未來世界家飾家電用品館。我是格瑞。今日有什麼可為您效勞之處呢？
W	Um, yeah, I bought a bread maker machine at your downtown store. It's the Happy Home brand, model 435. I read the manual, but I can't seem to figure out how to set the auto-start timer.	女	呃，是的。我在你們市中心的門市買了一台麵包機。品牌型號是快樂家435。我看了使用手冊，但是我似乎弄不懂要怎麼設定自動啟動定時器。
M	Okay, let me just access the manual for that item. Let's see. . . . first, you need to press the "Mode" button until "Auto-Start" appears in the lower right of the LCD screen. Then, press the "Set" button until the display shows the number of hours later you want the unit to start.	男	好，讓我看一下那件商品的使用手冊。我們來看一下⋯⋯首先，您要按著「模式」按鈕，直到「自動啟動」出現在LCD螢幕的右下方為止。然後再按著「設定」按鈕，直到螢幕顯示出您希望機器在幾個小時後啟動的數字。
W	Okay, here we go. . . . Oh, that was easy; I can't believe I couldn't figure that out. Thanks so much.	女	好，換我試試看⋯⋯噢，那還真簡單。我真不敢相信我居然搞不懂。真是太感謝你了。

• appliances 家用電器　bread maker 麵包機　downtown 市中心　manual 使用手冊
figure out 理解；想出

38 --

Why is the woman calling?　這位女士為什麼要打這通電話？
(A) To request a refund　(A) 要求退款
(B) To request a service visit　(B) 要求到府服務
(C) To ask for directions to the store　(C) 詢問到店家的交通路線
(D) To get help with a product　(D) 尋求商品的相關協助

女子的第一句台詞「I read the manual, but I can't seem to figure out how to set the auto-start timer.」表示雖然已經她閱讀了使用說明書，但是仍然不知道該如何設定自動定時器，故可推測女子是為了獲得產品使用上的協助才撥打這通電話。對話中使用的「bread maker」即為選項 (D) 中的「product」。此題正確答案為 (D)。

39 --

What did the woman have trouble with?　這位女士在哪個部分碰到問題？
(A) Activating the lighting display　(A) 啟動照明顯示
(B) Deciding what ingredients to add　(B) 決定該加什麼材料
(C) Assembling the product　(C) 組裝產品
(D) Setting the timer　(D) 設定定時器

女子的第一句台詞「I read the manual, but I can't seem to figure out how to set the auto-start timer.」表示雖然她已經閱讀了使用說明書，但是仍然不知道該如何設定自動定時器，故可得知女子在設定定時器方面遇到困難。正確答案為 (D)。

40 --

What did the woman say she had already done?   這位女士說她已經做了什麼事？
(A) Spoken to a service technician   (A) 跟維修技術人員談話
(B) Looked over the manual   (B) 看過使用手冊
(C) Turned the product off and on   (C) 開關產品
(D) Exchanged the product   (D) 更換產品

女子的第一句台詞「I read the manual, but I can't seem to figure out how to set the auto-start timer.」，表示雖然已經閱讀了使用說明書，但是仍然不知道該如何設定自動定時器。對話中使用的「read」意同選項 (B) 中的「looked over」。正確答案為 (B)。

41-43 conversation   **41–43 對話**

🎧 03

M How are you doing with the final project for our new promotional event?	男 公司新宣傳活動的最終企畫進行得如何了？
W Not good at all. I've only just glanced at the proposal. I've just got so much other stuff going on right now. I really don't think I'll finish it in time.	女 一點都不順利。我只草草看過企畫案。我現在手上有好多其他的事在進行。我真的覺得自己無法及時完成了。
M No kidding. I'm busy, too. It's due this Monday morning, isn't it? Why don't you ask to get an extension?	男 說真的，我也很忙。下週一早上截止，不是嗎？妳何不要求延期呢？
W It's hard to say, but I'll stop by now and ask the director. You should come with me.	女 很難開口說，不過我現在要過去問問主管了。你應該和我一起去。
M I'm afraid I can't. I have a doctor's appointment.	男 我恐怕無法。我預約了要看醫生。

• **glance** 草草看過　**in time** 及時　**extension** 延期　**director** 主管　**doctor's appointment** 預約看診

41 --

What is the main topic of the conversation?   這段對話的主題是什麼？
(A) Arranging a date   (A) 安排約會
(B) Seeing a doctor   (B) 看醫生
(C) Signing up for a training   (C) 報名教育訓練
(D) Finishing an assignment   (D) 完成任務

男子的第一句台詞「How are you doing with the final project for our new promotional event?」是在詢問宣傳活動最終企畫的進度，故可得知此段對話應與工作完成有關。對話中使用的「final project」即為選項中 (D) 的「assignment」。正確答案為 (D)。

42

What is the due date?
(A) Friday
(B) Monday
(C) Tuesday
(D) Thursday

截止日期是何時？
(A) 星期五
(B) 星期一
(C) 星期二
(D) 星期四

男子的第二句台詞提及「It's due this Monday morning」，故可得知截止日為星期一，
正確答案為 (B)。

43

What will the woman probably do next?
(A) Send an e-mail
(B) Go to a doctor
(C) Visit a director
(D) Go to a movie

這位女士接下來可能會做什麼？
(A) 寄發電子郵件
(B) 去看醫生
(C) 找主管
(D) 去看電影

女子的最後一句台詞提到「I'll stop by now and ask the director.」，表示她將拜訪主管並進行諮詢。
對話中的「stop by」意同選項 (C) 中的「visit」。正確答案為 (C)。

44-46 conversation

44–46 對話

M Hi Jinny, this is Sam Billings calling. I need to have Dr. Jones take a look at my foot. When do you think I would be able to get in to see him? I'd like to get in as soon as possible. **W** Well, he's available this Friday at 3 P.M., next Monday at 2 P.M., or next Wednesday at 5:30. **M** I can't really get in during the workday, so I guess I'll have to come in on Wednesday. **W** Wednesday it is then. Please let us know as soon as possible if anything comes up that won't let you make the appointment.	**男** 嗨，吉妮，我是山姆·比林斯。我需要讓瓊斯醫生看看我的腳。妳覺得何時可以安排我過去見他呢？我想盡快過去。 **女** 嗯，他這週五下午3點、下週一下午2點或下週三的5:30都有空。 **男** 我真的無法在上班時間過去，所以我想我得下週三過去了。 **女** 好，那就下週三。若您有事無法赴約的話，請盡早告訴我們。

• get in 進入　take a look at . . . 看一看　as soon as possible 盡快　advise . . . of . . . 告知(某人)(某事)

44

What job does Jinny most likely do?
(A) Factory worker
(B) Dental assistant
(C) Doctor's receptionist
(D) Personal trainer

吉妮最可能從事何種工作？
(A) 工廠員工
(B) 牙醫助理
(C) 診所接待員
(D) 私人教練

女子的第一句台詞「Well, he's available this Friday at 3 P.M., next Monday at 2 P.M., or next Wednesday at 5:30.」中提到可以預約醫生看診的時間，再從她最後一句台詞「Please let us know as soon as possible if anything comes up that won't let you make the appointment.」，代表女子應為診所接待，故正確答案為 (C)。

45 ---

What day can the man come in?
(A) Friday
(B) Monday
(C) Tuesday
(D) Wednesday

這位男士何時可以過去？
(A) 星期五
(B) 星期一
(C) 星期二
(D) 星期三

男子的第二句台詞提到「so I guess I'll have to come in on Wednesday.」可得知他將於週三前往看診，正確答案 (D)。

46 ---

What does the woman ask the man to do?
(A) Call another branch of the business
(B) Call to advise them of any changes
(C) Consult a specialist
(D) Pay a deposit in advance

這位女士要求男士做什麼？
(A) 打電話到另一家分院所
(B) 來電告知異動
(C) 諮詢專業人士
(D) 預先支付訂金

女子的最後一句台詞說：「Please let us know as soon as possible if anything comes up that won't let you make the appointment.」如果男子不能赴約，女子要求男子盡快與她連絡。對話中使用的「let us know」指的就是選項 (B) 中的「call to advise them of . . .」。正確答案為 (B)。

47-49 conversation

M	Hey, Betsy, this note on my desk says that the CEO of the company wants to meet with me. Do you have any idea what that's all about?
W	Apparently, he's bringing in all the heads of the departments to discuss ideas to save money. He's going to want to know what you think you can do here in Maintenance.
M	I'm not sure how much we can do here. I think I run a pretty tight ship. I suppose I could try to see if I can find cheaper suppliers for some of the cleaning products we use.
W	That's a good idea. We could also cut back a bit more on heating and air conditioning on the weekends. Maybe restrict it to some special work areas for the few people who do come in.

47–49 對話

男	嘿，貝琪，我桌上的字條寫說公司的執行長想見我。妳知道是什麼事嗎？
女	看樣子，他要召集所有部門主管一起討論省錢的方法。他想知道你認為維修部可以做些什麼。
男	我不確定我們這裡可以做到多少。我想我的管理已經很嚴格了。我可以看看是不是能為目前所使用的清潔產品找到更便宜的供應商。
女	這倒是個好主意。我們還可以在週末時間削減暖氣和冷氣的費用。也許限用於少數人到班的一些特殊工作區域就好。

• **apparently** 顯然地；看樣子　**maintenance** 維護管理　**run a tight ship** 嚴格管理　**restrict** 限制

What is the man asking about?

(A) Why the CEO wants to see him
(B) Where to buy cleaning supplies
(C) The date and time of a meeting
(D) The status of a utility bill

這位男士詢問什麼事？

(A) 執行長為什麼想見他
(B) 去哪裡買清潔用品
(C) 會議的日期及時間
(D) 水電費帳單的狀況

男子的第一句台詞說：「Hey, Betsy, this note on my desk says that the CEO of the company wants to meet with me. Do you have any idea what that's all about?」，可知男子想知道執行長為何要見他，故正確答案為 (A)。

What department is the man the head of?

(A) Marketing
(B) Maintenance
(C) Accounting
(D) Public Relations

這位男士是哪個部門的主管？

(A) 行銷
(B) 維修
(C) 會計
(D) 公關

女子的第一句台詞「Apparently, he's bringing in all the heads of the departments to discuss ideas to save money. He's going to want to know what you think you can do here in Maintenance.」提到，執行長最近約見各部門管理階層，並且想和男子討論維修部門可以負責的事項，故男子應為維修部主管，正確答案為 (B)。

What idea does the woman have?

(A) Having a meeting with the CEO
(B) Reorganizing the department
(C) Reducing air conditioning and heating
(D) Finding cheaper suppliers for cleaning
   supplies

這位女士有什麼想法？

(A) 和執行長開會
(B) 重組部門
(C) 減少冷氣與暖氣的使用
(D) 找到更便宜的清潔用品供應商

女子的最後一句台詞「We could also cut back a bit more on heating and air conditioning on the weekends.」中，提到可以減少週末的冷氣與暖氣費用。對話中使用的「cut back」即為選項 (C) 中的「reduce」。正確答案為 (C)。

50-52 conversation

M Jessica, we're supposed to have that staff dinner the day after tomorrow, aren't we? What time is that supposed to start?

W I booked a room at the Red Dragon Chinese Restaurant for 7:30. I know you requested that we have it at that Mongolian buffet place, but they were all booked up that day. I ate at the Red Dragon not too long ago, and it was really good.

M That sounds fine to me. Just make sure we get a big enough room. (52) **When I was there last, we were packed into one that should have had about six fewer people in it.**

W I've already checked; the room has plenty of space for us all.

50–52 對話

男 潔西卡，我們要在後天舉辦員工晚宴，不是嗎？那是幾點開始？

女 我在紅龍中菜館訂了一間包廂，時間是7:30。我知道你要求我們在蒙古自助餐廳舉辦，但他們那天已經全預約額滿了。我不久前才在紅龍吃過，真的不錯。

男 聽起來還可以。只是要確定我們的包廂夠大。(52)我上次去那裡時，我們被塞進了一間至少要再少六人的包廂。

女 我已經確認過了；這間包廂有足夠的空間容納我們所有人。

 03

• book 預訂　packed 被塞滿的

50 --

What event will happen the day after tomorrow?

(A) A training seminar
(B) A management meeting
(C) A cooking lesson
(D) A meal with employees

後天要舉辦什麼活動？

(A) 教育訓練講座
(B) 管理會議
(C) 烹飪課程
(D) 員工餐會

從男子第一句台詞「Jessica, we're supposed to have that staff dinner the day after tomorrow, aren't we?」可得知後天將舉辦員工聚餐。對話中使用的「dinner」即為選項中的「meal」。正確答案為 (D)。

51 --

Where will the event most likely happen?

(A) At a Chinese restaurant
(B) At a Mongolian buffet
(C) At the company cafeteria
(D) In the manager's home

這個活動最可能在哪裡舉辦？

(A) 中菜館
(B) 蒙古自助餐廳
(C) 公司員工餐廳
(D) 經理的家

女子的第一句台詞提到「I booked a room at the Red Dragon Chinese Restaurant for 7:30.」，故正確解答為 (A)。

52 [NEW] ---

What does the man mean when he says, "When I was there last, we were packed into one that should have had about six fewer people in it"?
(A) The food was not good.
(B) Some of the staff didn't show up.
(C) The room was too small.
(D) The wait staff was not polite.

當這位男士說：「我上次去那裡時，我們被塞進了一間至少要再少六人的包廂」，是什麼意思？
(A) 食物不好吃。
(B) 有些員工沒有出席。
(C) 包廂太小。
(D) 服務生沒有禮貌。

男子的最後一句台詞：「When I was there last, we were packed into one that should have had about six fewer people in it.」中，表示上次去的時候被安排在過小的包廂裡，故正確答案為 (C)。

53-55 conversation / 53–55 對話

W	Darren, I thought you told me that the flyers with the new phone number for the delivery service were supposed to be ready today.	**女**	達倫，我記得你跟我說那些印有新電話號碼準備要寄送的傳單，應該是今天會準備好。
M	They were, but the printing company has a backlog of orders. They've promised to get them to us sometime tomorrow afternoon.	**男**	是準備好了，但印刷公司有一堆積累的訂單。他們答應明天下午會給我們。
W	I guess that will be alright, but they definitely need to be sent out before the old number is deactivated. If not, we'll lose a lot of business.	**女**	我想這沒問題，但他們一定要在舊號碼失效前寄出。如果沒有的話，我們就會失去很多生意。
M	No worries. I'll double-check with the printer now, and I'll arrange for the delivery service to be ready as soon as the flyers are.	**男**	別擔心。我現在就跟印刷公司再確認一次，我也會安排好等傳單一準備好就寄送出去。

• **flyer** 傳單   **backlog** 積累的工作   **deactivate** 失效

53 ---

What is the main topic of the conversation?
(A) A retirement party
(B) A printing order
(C) An employee training seminar
(D) The promotion of a colleague

這段對話的主題是什麼？
(A) 退休派對
(B) 印刷訂單
(C) 員工訓練研習會
(D) 同事的升遷

從女子的第一句台詞中的「the flyers」與男子第一句台詞中的「the printing company」可以知道，對話主題應和交由印刷公司製作的傳單有關，故正確答案為 (B)。

54 ---

What is the company in the process of doing?
(A) Signing a contract
(B) Hiring new employees
(C) Relocating its offices
(D) Changing its phone number

這家公司正在做什麼？
(A) 簽訂合約
(B) 聘用新員工
(C) 辦公室搬遷
(D) 更改電話號碼

女子的第一句台詞「Darren, I thought you told me that the flyers with the new phone number for the delivery service were supposed to be ready today.」提到，印有新電話號碼的傳單應在今天準備完成，故可得知該公司更改了電話號碼，正確答案為 (D)。

55

What will the man probably do next?	這位男士接下來可能會做什麼？
(A) Order lunch	(A) 訂午餐
(B) Contact a company	(B) 聯絡一家公司
(C) Go home for the day	(C) 下班回家
(D) Arrange a meeting	(D) 安排會議

男子的最後一句台詞「I'll double-check with the printer now」，表示他將和印刷公司確認，故可得知他會連絡廠商。對話中使用的「double-check with the printer」意即為選項 (B) 中的「keep in touch with the company」，故正確答案為 (B)。

56-58 conversation / 56–58 對話

| **W** Hey, John, what do you think of the new head of Accounting, Mr. Aimes? He just started yesterday.
M He seems like a really capable guy. I heard he just finished an MBA program at the same time as holding down his full-time job. That's quite impressive.
W Right. There's no way I could do that. It's all I can do to change out of my work clothes at the end of the day. How do you think he'll handle the department?
M I imagine he'll make a few changes. People coming out of MBA programs often have been studying very up-to-date approaches to things. **(57) He'll probably want to try out a few of the ideas that he has been working on.** | 女 嘿，約翰，你覺得會計部新來的主管艾米斯先生如何？他昨天才剛到職。
男 他看起來是個很有能力的人。我聽說他剛讀完MBA的學程，同時還保有全職的工作。這相當令人敬佩。
女 沒錯，我絕對做不到。下班後我能做的就只有換下工作服了。你想他會如何管理這部門？
男 我想他應該會做些改變。從MBA畢業的人通常都學到了一些最新的做事方法。**(57)**他可能會想試試他所學到的一些觀念吧。 |

• full-time 全職的　up-to-date 最新的　implement 實施

56

What is the main topic of the conversation?	這段對話的主題是什麼？
(A) A new staff member	(A) 新同事
(B) A rescheduled meeting	(B) 重新安排的會議
(C) A job description	(C) 職務說明
(D) A new training program	(D) 新訓練課程

從女子的第一句台詞「Hey, John, what do you think of the new head of accounting? He just started yesterday.」可看出，兩人正在討論新來的會計部主管，也就是新的同事，故正確解答為 (A)。

57 (NEW) ---

What does the man mean when he says, "He'll probably want to try out a few of the ideas that he has been working on"?
(A) Company travel will be reduced.
(B) New office furniture will be ordered.
(C) New ideas will be implemented.
(D) Staff numbers will be reduced.

當這位男士說:「他可能會想試試他所學到的一些觀念吧」,是什麼意思?
(A) 將減少員工旅遊
(B) 將訂購新的辦公家具
(C) 將實施新觀念
(D) 將減少員工人數

從男子的第一句台詞「I heard he just finished an MBA program」,最後又說「People coming out of MBA programs often have been studying very up-to-date approaches to things.」指剛從 MBA 畢業的人通常學到了新觀念,連貫看下來可推知,題幹引用的句子指的是新任主管會想實施新的理念。

對話中使用主動語態的「try out a few of the ideas」,指的就是選項 (C) 中改用被動語態的「new ideas will be implemented」。正確答案為 (C)。

58 ---

What has Mr. Aimes recently done?
(A) Completed his MBA
(B) Quit his full-time job
(C) Canceled a sales seminar
(D) Trained a new secretary

艾米斯先生最近做了什麼?
(A) 完成MBA學位
(B) 辭去全職工作
(C) 取消銷售研討會
(D) 訓練新秘書

男子的第一句台詞「I heard he just finished an MBA program at the same time as holding down his full-time job.」提及聽說新會計部長剛結束 MBA 課程。對話中使用的「finished」意同選項 (A) 中的「completed」。正確答案為 (A)。

59-61 conversation

59–61 對話

M	Hi, I'd like to get this letter to my sister in Manila before the end of the week. Is that possible?
W	Yes, that would be our express service. It's guaranteed to be there within three days. It's not cheap, though. The cost for that is $15.65. Will that be okay?
M	Wow, that certainly isn't cheap. How much does it cost to have a confirmation of her receiving the letter?
W	Oh, that's actually included in the cost of our express service. Please fill out this form.

男	妳好,我希望這封信能在週末前送到我在馬尼拉的妹妹手中。這有可能嗎?
女	可以,那就是我們的快遞服務了,保證三天內送達。不過,不便宜喔。快遞的費用要15.65元。這樣可以嗎?
男	哇,那的確不便宜。如果要確認她收到信函的話,費用又是多少?
女	噢,這其實已經包含在快遞服務中了。請填寫這張表格。

• **express service** 快遞服務 **guarantee** 保證 **confirmation** 確認 **fill out** 填寫

59

Where does the woman most likely work?
(A) At a doctor's office
(B) At a post office
(C) At a ski resort
(D) At a health club

這位女士最有可能在哪裡工作？
(A) 在診所
(B) 在郵局
(C) 在滑雪度假中心
(D) 在健康俱樂部

男子的第一句台詞「I'd like to get this letter to my sister in Manila before the end of the week.」提及信件寄送，故可得知此段對話發生在郵局。對話中的「get this letter」與「express service」皆描述郵政服務內容，選項 (B) 中則改用地點「post office」點出。正確答案為 (B)。

60

How much extra does the receipt confirmation cost?
(A) $0.00
(B) $5.00
(C) $10.75
(D) $15.65

確認收件需要額外支付多少錢？
(A) 0元
(B) 5元
(C) 10.75元
(D) 15.65元

女子於最後一句台詞「Oh, that's actually included in the cost of our express service.」中提及，收貨確認費用已經包含在急件費用中，故可得知不須再支付額外費用，故正確答案為 (A)。

61

What does the woman ask the man to do?
(A) Attend a seminar
(B) Submit a report
(C) Deliver a letter
(D) Complete a form

這位女士要求男士做什麼？
(A) 參加研討會
(B) 送交報告
(C) 遞送郵件
(D) 填寫表格

女子的最後一句台詞「Please fill out this form.」中，要求男子填寫表格。對話中使用的「fill out」即為選項 (D) 中的「complete」，故正確答案為 (D)。

M Jessie, I'm very excited about the concert our company is supporting. A lot of fans will be joining it. So, it definitely will be great publicity.	男 潔西,我非常期待公司資助的演唱會。很多粉絲會參加。所以這絕對會是很棒的宣傳。
W Thanks for reminding me. Have you checked the list of graphic design firms we are considering to design the concert souvenirs? We need to hire one soon so the souvenirs will be ready in time.	女 謝謝你提醒我。你看過我們考慮用來設計演唱會紀念品的平面設計公司名單了嗎?我們需要盡快僱請一家,這樣紀念品才能及時準備好。
M Oh, sorry, I was busy with the budget report, but I can look at it now. I think Hoo Design is great to work with, but that we need a company that's a little less expensive. As you know, we have a tight budget.	男 噢,抱歉。我忙著做預算報告,不過我現在可以看一下。我想呼設計是適合合作的對象,但是我們需要一家不那麼貴的公司。妳知道的,我們的預算不多。
W You're right. Why don't we go for the one in New York? I'm pretty sure this firm has a good reputation, and its prices are very reasonable.	女 你說的沒錯。那我們何不就找在紐約的這家呢?我很確定這家公司聲譽良好,價格也很合理。

Company	Location
Supreme Design	New York
Modern Art	Philadelphia
Hoo Design	Miami
Great View Art	San Francisco

公司	地點
卓越設計	紐約
現代藝術	費城
呼設計	邁阿密
大視野藝術	舊金山

• **support** 資助　**publicity** 宣傳;推廣　**remind** 提醒　**souvenir** 紀念品　**tight budget** 預算不多
reputation 聲譽　**reasonable** 合理的

62 --

What type of event is the company sponsoring?   這家公司贊助的是哪一類活動?

(A) A musical event   (A) 音樂盛會
(B) An auction   (B) 拍賣活動
(C) A theater performance   (C) 劇場表演
(D) An art exhibition   (D) 藝術展覽

男子的第一句台詞說:「I'm very excited about the concert our company is supporting.」,故可得知男子的公司是一家協辦演唱會的公司,正確答案為 **(A)**。

63 --

What is the man concerned about?   這位男士擔心的是什麼?

(A) A lack of volunteers   (A) 沒有志工
(B) A customer complaint   (B) 顧客投訴
(C) A limited budget   (C) 預算有限
(D) A delayed concert   (D) 演唱會延期

男子的第二句台詞説：「I think Hoo Design is great to work with, but that we need a company that's a little less expensive. As you know, we have a tight budget.」，由此可知公司的預算相當吃緊。題目中使用的「tight budget」即為選項 (C) 中的「limited budget」，故正確答案為 (C)。

64 NEW --

Look at the graphic. Which company do the speakers choose?
(A) Great View Art
(B) Hoo Design
(C) Supreme Design
(D) Modern Art

看一下圖表，說話者選擇哪一家公司？
(A) 大視野藝術
(B) 呼設計
(C) 卓越設計
(D) 現代藝術

女子的最後一句台詞説：「Why don't we go for the one in New York? I'm pretty sure this firm has a good reputation, and its prices are very reasonable.」提議選擇位於紐約的公司承接紀念品設計。從表格中可以知道，位於紐約的公司為卓越設計，故正確答案為 (C)。

65-67 conversation and floor plan

65–67 對話及樓層平面圖

M Catherine, I know you're heading to the express bus terminal soon to visit a client in Boston, but do you have time to approve the room assignment for our improvement?	男 凱瑟琳，我知道妳現在就要去快捷客運站搭車去拜訪波士頓的客戶，但妳有時間批准公司辦公室分配的改善方案嗎？
W No problem. So, what are we looking at here?	女 沒問題。那麼，我們要看什麼？
M Rooms A and B have been assigned to the Human Resources Department. And you've got the office next to the Information Desk.	男 A、B室都已經分配給人力資源部了，而妳的辦公室就在服務台旁。
W That's good for me. So, that leaves the corner office for you, right?	女 我沒問題。所以，角落的辦公室是留給你的，對吧？
M Yes, I thought it would be good for me to be close to both the HR team and you.	男 是的，我想離妳跟人力資源部近點會比較好。
W That sounds like a great idea. I think our members of staff will be very happy to hear about the assignments at the meeting next Wednesday.	女 聽起來是不錯的主意。我想員工們在下週三的會議中聽到這個分配方案應該會很開心。

Supply Room		Information Desk
		Room D
Room A	Room B	Room C

供應室		服務台
		D室
A室	B室	C室

• **approve** 同意；批准　**assignment** 分配　**improvement** 改善

27

---

65 --

According to the man, what will the woman be doing today?

(A) Shopping for some office supplies
(B) Reporting a renovation plan
(C) Taking public transportation
(D) Preparing a press release

根據這位男士所言，這位女士今天要做什麼？

(A) 買一些辦公用品
(B) 報告整修計畫
(C) 搭乘公共交通運輸工具
(D) 準備新聞稿

男子的第一句台詞説：「Catherine, I know you're heading to the express bus terminal soon to visit a client in Boston」，由此可知，女子為了拜訪客戶，正要去客運站搭車，故正確解答為 (C)。

66 (NEW) ---

Look at the graphic. Which office has been assigned to the man?

(A) Room A
(B) Room B
(C) Room C
(D) Room D

看一下圖表，哪一間辦公室是分配給這位男士的？

(A) A室
(B) B室
(C) C室
(D) D室

從男子的第二句台詞可以知道 A 與 B 室分配給了人力資源部，女子的辦公室則在服務台旁，也就是 D 室。男子隨後也附和自己的辦公室應安排於角落，故此題正確答案為 (C)。

67 --

What does the woman say will take place next week?

(A) A new product launch
(B) A retirement party
(C) A conference call
(D) A staff meeting

這位女士說下週會發生什麼事？

(A) 一項新產品上市
(B) 一場退休派對
(C) 一場電話會議
(D) 一場員工會議

從女子的最後一句台詞中的「the meeting next Wednesday」可知下週將舉行會議，故正確答案為 (D)。

68-70 conversation and map

68–70 對話及地圖

W I'm so glad I ran into you, Mark. This rest area is quite confusing. I'm on my way to the airport, but I'm not sure which highway I should take. I usually take highway 11, but it's closed for repaving the road.	**女** 馬克，我好高興碰到你。這個休息站太混亂了。我正要去機場，但我不確定該走哪條公路。我通常是走11號公路，但這條公路因為道路重鋪的關係關閉了。
M Well, I have a highway map with me. I always take this route. Even though it's not an expressway, it doesn't take that long. And you can stop at Urban Crossing if you want to.	**男** 嗯，我帶了張公路地圖。我一向走這條路。雖然不是快速道路，但也不會花太多時間。如果願意的話，妳還可以在都市交會點停一下。
W Thanks for the tip. I don't want to miss my flight to Seoul.	**女** 謝謝你的提點。我可不想錯過到首爾的班機。
M Why are you going there?	**男** 妳為什麼要去那裡？
W Actually, I'm going to my cousin's wedding. I'll tell you all about it at our next regular staff meeting.	**女** 事實上，我要去參加我表哥的婚禮。下次員工定期會議時，我再告訴你所有的事。
M I'll look forward to it. Have a great trip!	**男** 我很期待。祝妳旅途愉快！

03

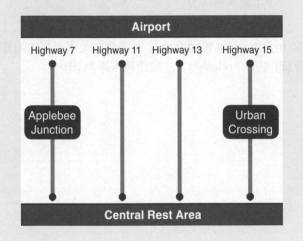

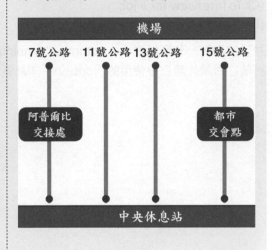

• **run into** 偶然遇見　**rest area** 休息站　**highway** 公路　**repave** 重新鋪路　**expressway** 快速道路　**relative** 親戚

68 --

Where does the conversation take place?
(A) At an airport
(B) At a business office
(C) At a hotel
(D) At a rest area

這段對話在哪裡出現？
(A) 機場
(B) 辦公室
(C) 飯店
(D) 休息站

女子的第一句台詞說：「This rest area is quite confusing. I'm on my way to the airport, but I'm not sure which highway I should take.」提及休息站令人感到混亂，故正確解答為 (D)。

NEW --

Look at the graphic. Which route does the man suggest the woman take?

(A) Highway 7
(B) Highway 11
(C) Highway 13
(D) Highway 15

看一下圖表，這位男士建議女士走哪一條路？

(A) 7號公路
(B) 11號公路
(C) 13號公路
(D) 15號公路

男子的第一句台詞説：「I always take this route. Even though it's not an expressway, it doesn't take that long. And you can stop at Urban Crossing if you want to.」，表示男子建議的路線會經過都市交會點，故可得知此道路應為 15 號公路，正確答案為 (D)。

70 --

Why is the woman going to Seoul?

(A) To attend a meeting
(B) To visit a relative
(C) To interview for a job
(D) To hold a wedding

這位女士為什麼要去首爾？

(A) 去參加會議
(B) 去探訪親戚
(C) 去面試工作
(D) 去舉辦婚禮

女子的最後一句台詞説：「Actually, I'm going to my cousin's wedding.」，表示她是因表哥的婚禮而前往首爾。題目中使用的「cousin」即為選項 (B) 中的「relative」，故正確答案為 (B)。

PART 4

71-73 report

Welcome to CKDU's Homeward Bound traffic report. Traffic is moving surprisingly well for a long weekend Friday. The McKay and McDonald bridges are both busy but steady. The one area where commuters will encounter some delays is the downtown area near Barrington Street. Traffic is still moving but is being hampered by a group of protesters. Apparently, the group is protesting new reductions to unemployment benefits. Try to avoid that area if at all possible. The construction that was slowing down Bay Road has finally been completed, and that road is also moving well. Enjoy the long weekend. This is Debra Bartlett for CKDU, your best source for news and information. Stay tuned for Joe Haskins with the weather.

71-73 報導

歡迎收聽CKDU的《歸途》交通報導。就連續假期的週五來說，交通令人意外地順暢。麥凱伊與麥當勞兩座大橋雖然車流量高卻通行平穩。通勤者可能會碰上延誤的區域，是在靠近巴靈頓街的市中心一帶。車流雖然移動中，但卻受到一群示威抗議者影響而壅塞。這群人顯然正在抗議失業救濟金的新刪減方案。如果可以，請盡量避開該地區。造成海灘路交通減速的施工工程終於結束，而該路段目前也運行順暢。好好享受連續假期。我是CKDU的黛博拉‧巴特莉特，您最佳的新聞與資訊來源。不要轉台，請繼續收聽喬‧海斯金斯的氣象報導。

• **commuter** 通勤者　**encounter** 遭遇　**hamper** 阻礙　**stay tuned** 敬請關注　**rally** 集會；群眾大會

71 --

What is the report mainly about?
(A) Traffic
(B) Political protests
(C) The weather
(D) Transportation costs

這篇報導主要和什麼有關？
(A) 交通
(B) 政治抗議
(C) 天氣
(D) 交通運輸費用

一開始的部分提及「Welcome to CKDU's Homeward Bound traffic report.」故可得知此文章是與交通相關的報導，正確答案為 (A)。

72 --

According to the announcer, what has caused a problem?
(A) Closed bridges
(B) Bad weather
(C) Construction
(D) A rally

根據播報員所說，造成問題的是什麼原因？
(A) 封閉的大橋
(B) 惡劣的天氣
(C) 施工工程
(D) 大集會

中間部分提及「traffic is still moving but is being hampered by a group of protesters.」，表示交通狀況雖然可以通行，但是因為示威團體而有所受阻。題目中使用的「a group of protesters」指的即是選項 (D) 中的「rally」，故正確答案為 (D)。

31

What will the listeners probably hear next?
(A) A music program
(B) The weather report
(C) A game show
(D) The local news

聽者接下來可能會聽到什麼？
(A) 音樂節目
(B) 氣象報告
(C) 遊戲節目
(D) 地方新聞

後半部提及「Stay tuned for Joe Haskins with the weather.」故可得知接下來將可收聽天氣資訊，故正確答案為 (B)。

74-76 advertisement

74-76 廣告

Are you a university student? Are you looking for something different than the average summer job? Backwoods Tours is looking for physically fit and outgoing people to serve as guides on river rafting excursions in the British Columbia interior. Our clientele includes people from all over the world and we offer trips with varying levels of challenge. Experience is preferred; however, we can provide full training. If you think you have what it takes to fill this satisfying and challenging position, call us today at 406-755-1244 to arrange an interview, or send your résumé and cover letter to application@ backwoodstours.com. Make that call today and get ready for the adventure of a lifetime.	你是大學生嗎？你正在找不同於一般暑期打工的工作嗎？後林旅行社正在徵求體能佳且外向的人，來擔任卑詩省內陸的泛舟旅遊團導遊。我們的客人來自世界各地，而本公司提供各種不同等級的挑戰活動。具經驗者尤佳，但本公司亦提供全面的訓練課程。如果你認為自己符合這個令人滿意又具挑戰性的職位，今天就來電406-755-1244以安排面試，或將履歷與求職函寄到application@ backwoodstours.com。今天就來電，準備迎向冒險人生吧。

• **average** 一般的　**fit** 健康的　**outgoing** 外向的　**excursion** 短程旅行；遠足　**lifetime** 終生

74 ---

What is the advertisement about?
(A) An exercise program
(B) A rafting tour
(C) A holiday sale
(D) A job opportunity

這則廣告和什麼有關？
(A) 健身計畫
(B) 泛舟之旅
(C) 節日拍賣
(D) 就業機會

一開始的部分提及「Are you looking for something different than the average summer job?」，故可得知此文章內容與求職相關，正確答案為 (D)。

75

What qualifications should applicants have?
(A) Previous experience
(B) Physical fitness
(C) A pilot's license
(D) Their own vehicle

應徵者應具備什麼資格條件？
(A) 過去的工作經驗
(B) 體能狀態
(C) 飛行員執照
(D) 自用車

中間部分提及「Backwoods Tours is looking for physically fit and outgoing people」，可得知應徵者需要身體健康且個性外向。題目中使用的「physically fit」即是選項 (B) 中改用的「physical fitness」，正確答案為 (B)。

76

What are people interested in the job asked to do?
(A) Come to a job fair
(B) Contact the company
(C) Check the Web site
(D) Complete a test

對這份工作有興趣的人被要求做什麼？
(A) 參加就業博覽會
(B) 聯絡該公司
(C) 查看網站
(D) 完成測驗

後半部提及「If you think you have what it takes to fill this satisfying and challenging position, call us today at 406-755-1244 to arrange an interview, or send your résumé and cover letter to application@backwoodstours.com.」，請求職者以電話或信件聯絡，故正確解答為 (B)。

77-79 telephone message

77-79 電話留言

Hi, this is Dana calling from the Downtown Health Clinic. According to your file, you are due for your annual physical. We have an appointment available next Tuesday at 2:00. Please give me a call at 555-7414 to let me know if this would be suitable for you. **(79) Don't forget that the clinic has moved since you were last here.** We're still in the State Building, but we're on the ninth floor now and not the twelfth floor.	您好，我是市中心健康診所的黛娜。根據您的檔案顯示，您的年度健檢已經到期了。我們下週二下午兩點還有空檔可預約，請來電555-7414告訴我那時間您是否方便。**(79)**別忘了，在您上次來過後，本診所就已搬遷了。我們仍位於國家大廈內，但非12樓，而是在9樓。

• **annual** 一年一度的　**physical** 體檢　**suitable** 適宜的

77

Where does the speaker most likely work?
(A) At a pharmacy
(B) At a dentist
(C) At a doctor's office
(D) At a beauty salon

說話者最有可能在哪裡工作？
(A) 藥局
(B) 牙醫診所
(C) 醫生診所
(D) 美容院

從開頭提及「Hi, this is Dana calling from the Downtown Health Clinic.」可以得知此通電話是由診所撥打。題目中使用的「clinic」即選項 (C) 中的「doctor's office」，故正確答案為 (C)。

Why is the woman calling?
(A) To request a payment
(B) To arrange an appointment
(C) To cancel a test
(D) To book a surgery

這位女士為什麼打這通電話？
(A) 要求付款
(B) 安排預約
(C) 取消考試
(D) 預約手術

中間部分提及「We have an appointment available next Tuesday at 2:00. Please give me a call at 555–7414 to let me know if this would be suitable for you.」，透露可以預約的時段，並請聽話方告知該時間是否可行。由此可知，此通電話是為了敲定預約時間。正確答案為 (B)。

79 [NEW] --

What does the woman mean when she says, "Don't forget that the clinic has moved since you were last here"?
(A) To let the customer know the appointment has been changed
(B) To remind the customer of the new location of the hospital
(C) To let the listener know the doctor is not available
(D) To confirm that the customer must not be late

當這位女士說：「別忘了，在您上次來過後，本診所就已搬遷了」，是什麼意思？
(A) 讓客人知道預約已經變更了
(B) 提醒客人醫院的新位置
(C) 讓聽者知道醫生沒有空
(D) 確認客人不可遲到

可從該句後方的「We're still in the State Building, but we're on the ninth floor now」得知醫院已搬至新位置，故正確答案為 (B)。

80-82 announcement

80–82 宣告

Ladies and gentlemen, this is your captain, Vincent McKenzie, speaking. On behalf of myself and the entire crew, I would like to welcome you aboard Eva Air flight 867 from Taipei to Bangkok. We will be departing shortly, and we'll touch down in Bangkok at approximately 8:15 P.M. with a total flying time of approximately three hours and fifteen minutes. The weather today in Bangkok is hot and humid at 32 degrees Celsius. Your flight attendants will go through the safety procedures with you shortly. And about 30 minutes after takeoff, meals will be served. While you may feel free to move about the cabin while the seatbelt light is off, please return to your seat immediately when you see the seatbelt light activated. Thanks for flying with Eva Air and enjoy your flight.	各位先生女士，我是機長文森·麥肯基，謹代表全體機組員與個人歡迎各位搭乘長榮航空自台北飛往曼谷的867班機。我們即將起飛，大約於晚間8:15抵達曼谷，總飛行時間約3小時又15分鐘。曼谷今日天氣濕熱，溫度來到攝氏32度。空服員即將為各位講解安全程序。在起飛大約30分鐘後，我們將提供餐點。雖然在安全帶燈號熄滅後，各位可自由在艙內走動，但當您見到安全帶燈號亮起時，請立即回到座位上。感謝您搭乘長榮航空，並祝您飛航愉快。

• **on behalf of . . .** 代表…… **approximately** 大約 **go through** 講解 **procedure** 程序 **aviator** 飛行員 **demonstrate** 示範

80 --

Who most likely is the speaker?

(A) A flight attendant

(B) An aviator

(C) A customs officer

(D) A businessman

說話者最有可能是誰？

(A) 空服員

(B) 飛行員

(C) 海關官員

(D) 商人

一開始說話者提及「Ladies and gentlemen, this is your captain, Vincent McKenzie, speaking.」即告知聽話者自己是機長。題目中出現的「captain」即是選項 (B) 的「aviator」，故正確答案為 (B)。

81 --

Where are the listeners going?

(A) Tokyo

(B) Taipei

(C) Bangkok

(D) Havana

聽眾要去哪裡？

(A) 東京

(B) 台北

(C) 曼谷

(D) 哈瓦那

04

從廣播第二句中的「Eva Air flight 867 from Taipei to Bangkok.」可得知這班飛機的目的地為曼谷，故正確答案為 (C)。

82 --

What most likely will happen next?

(A) Passengers will get off the plane.

(B) The plane will land.

(C) Safety procedures will be demonstrated.

(D) The passengers will receive lunch.

接下來最有可能發生什麼事？

(A) 乘客即將下飛機。

(B) 飛機即將降落。

(C) 將示範安全程序。

(D) 乘客將拿到午餐。

廣播的中間部分提及「Your flight attendants will go through the safety procedures with you shortly.」，表示空服員將解說飛機上的安全程序。題目中使用以空服員為主詞的主動語態「go through」，表示空服員解說程序，而選項 (C) 中改用以安全程序為主詞的被動語態「be demonstrated」指程序被示範，但兩者句意最為相似，故正確答案為 (C)。

Greetings, everyone. **(84)Welcome to the World Technology Conference.** Over the course of the weekend, you will have the chance to learn about some of the most amazing breakthroughs in technology that have been made over the last year. Companies and institutes from over 30 countries are represented here. You will have the chance to experience demonstrations, roundtable debates, and presentations. The first order of business, however, will be a welcome banquet followed by a cocktail party, where those of you who already know each other can get reacquainted and those of you who have not met yet can make your introductions. Dinner will be served in about 30 minutes in the Paradise Room.

大家好。**(84)** 歡迎來到世界科技大會。在整個週末期間,各位將有機會了解在過去這一年間,科技界最驚人的一些突破性進展。來自30多個國家的公司與學術機構代表出席此會議,各位將有機會體驗操作示範、圓桌辯論與簡報介紹。而活動的第一件事是歡迎晚宴,接著是雞尾酒派對。在宴會上,已經認識的可敘舊,而還未認識的各位也可彼此介紹。晚宴將於30分鐘後在天堂廳舉行。

• **breakthrough** 突破 **demonstration** 示範 **banquet**（正式的）宴會 **reacquaint** 敘舊 **reception** 招待會

 83 --

What is the talk mainly about?
(A) Events at the conference
(B) The dinner menu
(C) Accommodation arrangements
(D) Rules for the conference

這段談話主要和什麼有關?
(A) 大會活動
(B) 晚餐菜單
(C) 住宿安排
(D) 會議規則

整段內容先是歡迎與會者,接著介紹了出席人員及將進行的活動（體驗、辯論與簡報）,最後說明晚宴與派對的進行,故可知道此段談話主要在簡介大會的活動,正確答案為 (A)。

84 (NEW) --

What does the man mean when he says, "Welcome to the World Technology Conference"?
(A) Scientists are attending the conference.
(B) Musicians are attending the conference.
(C) Construction workers are attending the conference.
(D) Fitness coaches are attending the conference.

當這位男士說:「歡迎來到世界科技大會」,是什麼意思?
(A) 科學家正在參加會議。
(B) 音樂家正在參加會議。
(C) 營建工人正在參加會議。
(D) 健身教練正在參加會議。

由於大會名稱為「世界科技大會」,故與會者最有可能為科學家,而題幹引述的句子旨在歡迎來賓,故正確答案為 (A)。

85 ---

What is the first event of the conference?
(A) A technology demonstration
(B) A meal with attendees
(C) An award presentation
(D) A roundtable debate

大會的第一個活動是什麼？
(A) 技術示範
(B) 與會者聚餐
(C) 頒獎
(D) 圓桌辯論

後半部中，說話者提及「The first order of business, however, will be a welcome banquet.」，由此可知，第一項日程為歡迎宴會。題目中出現的「banquet」指的即為選項 (B) 中的「meal」，故正確答案為 (B)。

86–88 talk

86–88 談話

I'd like to welcome our research interns to the summer program at Healthcom Technologies. I've been a researcher here at Healthcom for more than 15 years now. During that time, I never learned more than when I was an intern here in the summer program myself. Through the course of that summer I became acquainted with technologies far ahead of what I was exposed to at my university. More importantly, I developed a work ethic that has served me well throughout my research career. **(87)I learned the ability to do more than one thing at the same time** and to work in a team environment with other researchers. You will all work very hard over the next 2 months and you will not be paid a great deal of money, but I believe that you will take something away from here that money cannot buy.

歡迎各位研究實習生參與健康科技公司的暑期專案計畫。我個人已經在健康科技擔任研究員超過15年之久。
我在這段期間所學到的，絕不會比自己當年在暑期專案中擔任實習生時還多。在那年的暑假期間，我所學到的技術遠比我在大學裡所接觸到的領先很多。更重要的是，我培養了在整個研究生涯中非常受用的工作倫理。**(87)我學到了同時並行多事的能力，並且學習如何與其他研究者在團隊合作下工作**。在接下來的兩個月裡，各位將會非常辛勤地工作，也無法領到豐厚的薪水，但我相信各位將從這裡帶走金錢買不到的東西。

• **acquaint** 認識；熟悉 **expose** 接觸 **throughout** 自始至終 **multitask** 同時並行多事

86 ---

What type of work will the interns be doing?
(A) Laboratory research
(B) Navigation
(C) Advertising
(D) Police work

實習生將做哪一類的工作？
(A) 實驗室研究
(B) 導航
(C) 廣告
(D) 治安工作

從開頭「I'd like to welcome our research interns to the summer program at Healthcom Technologies.」，表示歡迎研究實習生，故可推測實習生最有可能在實驗室進行研究。題目中出現「research」指的應是選項 (A) 中的「laboratory research」，故正確答案為 (A)。

- -

What does the man mean when he says, "I learned the ability to do more than one thing at the same time"?

(A) He has lab techniques.
(B) He is good at multitasking.
(C) He has an ability to keep the records accurately.
(D) He is available 24 hours a day.

當這位男士說:「我學到了同時並行多事的能力」,是什麼意思?

(A) 他有實驗技術。
(B) 他擅長同時處理多事。
(C) 他具備精確記錄的能力。
(D) 他整天都有空。

談話後半部中,說話者提及「I learned the ability to do more than one thing at the same time」,表示自己學到一心多用的本事。題目中出現的「do more than one thing at the same time」意同選項 (B) 的「multitask」,故正確答案為 (B)。

88 -

How long is the internship program?

(A) Two weeks
(B) One month
(C) Two months
(D) Three months

實習計畫的期間是多長?

(A) 兩週
(B) 一個月
(C) 兩個月
(D) 三個月

從談話後半部的「You will all work very hard over the next 2 months.」可知,實習生的實習期間為兩個月,正確答案為 (C)。

89–91 talk | 89–91 談話

Ladies and gentlemen, thank you for attending this celebration. I am very pleased to announce that this has been the most profitable year in the history of HighTechno Computers. We could not have done it without each and every one of you. Thanks to your efforts, profits are up 27% over last year. Furthermore, we are ready to release our newest computer program package, Super Bits, more than a month ahead of schedule. Now, here to present the highly coveted award for Employee of the Year is Dean Anderson, head of Human Resources. Everyone, let's give Dean a warm welcome.	各位先生女士,感謝各位參加這個慶祝會。我非常高興宣布,這是高科技電腦公司史上營利最豐碩的一年。沒有各位,我們就無法辦到。由於各位的努力,我們的利潤較去年提高27%。此外,我們也比預定時間提早了一個多月準備好要發表最新電腦套裝程式——超級位元。現在,為我們頒發大家期盼已久的年度最佳員工獎的是人力資源部的主管,狄恩·安德森。各位,讓我們熱烈歡迎狄恩。

• **celebration** 慶祝會　**profitable** 獲利的　**furthermore** 此外　**coveted** 夢寐以求的
  award 〔名詞〕獎項;〔動詞〕頒(獎)

89 ---

Who is the intended audience of this talk?
(A) Potential clients
(B) Law enforcement officers
(C) Company employees
(D) Company shareholders

這段對話所針對的聽眾是誰？
(A) 潛在客戶
(B) 執法人員
(C) 公司員工
(D) 公司股東

談話開頭「Ladies and gentlemen, thank you for attending this celebration」以及「this has been the most profitable year in the history of High Techno Computers」，再根據中間部分的「We could not have done it without each and every one of you.」可以得知，此段談話的聽眾是公司員工，故正確答案為 (C)。

90 ---

04

What does the company probably sell?
(A) Software
(B) Cars
(C) Carpet
(D) Appliances

這家公司可能販售什麼產品？
(A) 軟體
(B) 汽車
(C) 地毯
(D) 器具設備

從談話中間部分的「Furthermore, we are ready to release our newest computer program package, Super Bits」可知公司將推出最新的電腦程式，故這應是間軟體銷售公司。題目中使用的「computer program」即為選項 (A) 中的「software」，故正確答案為 (A)。

91 ---

What will Mr. Anderson probably do next?
(A) Submit a report
(B) Conduct an interview
(C) Receive an award
(D) Award a prize

安德森先生接下來可能會做什麼？
(A) 提交報告
(B) 進行面談
(C) 領獎
(D) 頒獎

從倒數第二句的「Now, here to present the highly coveted award for Employee of the Year is Dean Anderson」可知安德森先生將頒發年度最佳員工獎。題目中使用的「present an award」即為選項 (D) 中的「award a prize」，故正確答案為 (D)。

92-94 talk

Welcome to the Museum of Modern Art, or MOMA, as we like to call it around here. Today's tour will last approximately thirty minutes and will focus primarily on our current exhibition of some of the pioneers of modern painting. This includes some of the works of Edvard Munch, Gustav Klimt, Toulouse-Lautrec, and Kandinsky. We will also touch on some of the works of some important sculptors and lithograph makers. After the tour, please don't forget to visit the gift shop. There are some excellent books that deal with some of the individual artists that we have here as well as others that deal with specific areas of our permanent collection. If you follow me, first off, we have a collection of some of the works of Edvard Munch.

92-94 談話

歡迎來到現代美術館，或是我們這裡喜歡稱呼的MOMA。今天的導覽將進行30分鐘左右，主要將集中於本館目前展出的現代繪畫先驅的作品，包括愛德華·孟克、古斯塔夫·克林姆、土魯斯－羅特列克和康丁斯基的部分作品。我們也會概略介紹一些重要雕刻家以及平版畫家的作品。在導覽後，請記得到禮品部。那裡有一些很棒的書籍，是有關我們目前館內的一些個別藝術家，還有一些是有關我們特定區域的永久收藏品。如果各位跟著我，首先，我們將看到愛德華·孟克的部分作品。

• **approximately** 大約　**primarily** 主要的　**pioneer** 先驅　**sculptor** 雕刻家　**lithograph** 石版畫　**specific** 特定的

 92 --

Who most likely is the speaker?
(A) A bank teller
(B) A cafeteria employee
(C) A museum guide
(D) A marketing manager

說話者最有可能是誰？
(A) 銀行行員
(B) 員工餐廳員工
(C) 博物館導覽員
(D) 行銷經理

一開始的「Today's tour will last approximately thirty minutes and will focus primarily on our current exhibition of some of the pioneers of modern painting.」即在告知聽者今天的導覽將進行 30 分鐘，故可推測說話者最可能為博物館導覽員，正確答案為 (C)。

 93 --

How long will the tour be?
(A) 20 minutes
(B) 45 minutes
(C) A half hour
(D) An hour and a half

這趟導覽要多久的時間？
(A) 20分鐘
(B) 45分鐘
(C) 半小時
(D) 一個半小時

從第二句的「Today's tour will last approximately thirty minutes」可知導覽將進行 30 分鐘。題目中使用的「thirty minutes」意同選項 (C) 中的「a half hour」，故正確答案為 (C)。

94 ----------

What will the tour members probably do last?
(A) Go to the airport
(B) Fill out a form
(C) Book a tour
(D) Visit the souvenir shop

導覽的團員們最後可能會做什麼？
(A) 去機場
(B) 填寫表格
(C) 預約行程
(D) 參觀紀念品店

倒數第三句的「After the tour, please don't forget to visit the gift shop.」推薦聽者前往紀念品店，而題目中使用的「gift shop」即為選項 (D) 中的「souvenir shop」，故正確答案為 (D)。

95-97 announcement and map

95–97 宣告及地圖

04

Attention, Central Apartment residents. This is a reminder that the city's annual marathon race will be taking place on April 15. The road that runs in front of the main entrance will be closed for the competition from 9:00 A.M. to 3:00 P.M. The other streets around our apartment complex will still remain open. So drivers who use that road should think about taking an alternate route. Whatever route you decide to take to work, you have to allow more time to commute. Otherwise, you will be stuck in heavy traffic because of this event. We'll keep you updated.

中央公寓大樓的住戶，請注意。在此再次提醒大家，全市年度馬拉松比賽將於4月15日舉行。大門口前的馬路將因比賽的關係，自上午9:00至下午3:00封閉。本大樓周圍其他道路仍維持開放。因此使用該道路的駕駛人應考慮使用替代道路。不論您選擇哪一條路線上班，都必須預留更多通勤時間。否則將因本活動而陷於車陣中。我們將隨時提供最新資訊。

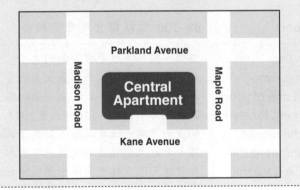

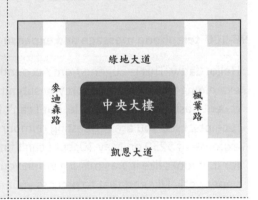

• **resident** 住戶　**annual** 一年一度的　**apartment complex** 公寓大樓　**alternate** 替代的　**commute** 通勤
otherwise 否則　**detour** 繞行的路

95 ----------

What will take place on April 15?
(A) A flea market
(B) A press conference
(C) Some road construction
(D) A sporting event

4月15日將舉辦什麼？
(A) 跳蚤市場
(B) 記者會
(C) 部分道路施工
(D) 運動賽事

開頭第二句的「This is a reminder that the city's annual marathon race will be taking place on April 15.」，表示馬拉松比賽將於 4 月 15 日舉辦，又因題目中使用的「marathon race」正屬於選項 (D) 的「sporting event」，故正確答案為 (D)。

96 (NEW) --

Look at the graphic. Which street will be closed? | 看一下圖表，哪一條道路將封閉？
(A) Kane Avenue | (A) 凱恩大道
(B) Madison Road | (B) 麥迪森路
(C) Maple Road | (C) 楓葉路
(D) Parkland Avenue | (D) 綠地大道

從第三句「The road that runs in front of the main entrance will be closed for the competition from 9:00 A.M. to 3:00 P.M.」可知大門口前的馬路將被封鎖，故正確解答為 (A)。

97 --

What does the speaker suggest? | 說話者建議什麼？
(A) Heading for the office late | (A) 晚點上班
(B) Making a detour | (B) 繞道
(C) Using public transportation | (C) 使用大眾運輸交通工具
(D) Considering joining a car pool | (D) 考慮共乘

後半部提及「So drivers who use that road should think about taking an alternate route.」建議駕駛人考慮走別的道路，此意最接近選項 (B)，故正確解答為 (B)。

98-100 telephone message and expense report | **98–100 電話留言及費用報告**

Hello, Cathy. This is Eugene from Accounting. I'm examining the expense report you submitted for your recent business trip to Seattle, but I can't find one of your receipts. I see you are requesting reimbursement for an expense of $250 on May 10, but I can't find the receipt for it. It looks like it was missing when you submitted the paperwork. I'll need that to process your request for the reimbursement. If you don't have it now, can you call me at extension 3 and then I'll tell you what the procedure is for requesting reimbursement without a receipt. I'm looking forward to hearing from you soon.

哈囉，凱西。我是會計部的尤金。我正在審查妳最近到西雅圖出差的費用報告，但是我找不到其中一張收據。我發現妳申請了5月10日一筆250元的支出津貼，但是我找不到這筆的收據。看起來應該是妳在提出書面報告時遺失了。我需要那份資料才能處理妳的津貼申請。如果妳現在手上沒有的話，可以麻煩撥打3號分機給我嗎？我再告訴妳沒有收據的請款方式。希望很快有妳的消息。

EXPENSE REPORT

DATE	DESCRIPTION	AMOUNT
May 3	Parking	$30
May 6	Meal	$90
May 8	Car rental	$180
May 10	Accommodations	$250

費用報告

日期	明細	金額
5 月 3 日	停車	30 元
5 月 6 日	餐點	90 元
5 月 8 日	租車	180 元
5 月 10 日	住宿	250 元

• **expense report** 支出報告　**receipt** 收據　**submit** 提交　**reimbursement** 報銷；津貼

98 --

Why is the speaker calling?
(A) Some paperwork did not have a signature.
(B) A reservation has changed.
(C) A certain receipt was not included.
(D) The dates of the business trip were wrong.

說話者為什麼打這通電話？
(A) 有些文件沒有簽名。
(B) 預約已更動。
(C) 特定的收據沒附上。
(D) 出差日期有誤。

從留言的第二句「I'm examining the expense report you submitted for your recent business trip to Seattle, but I can't find one of your receipts.」可知，男子因找不到收據而打電話給女子，故正確解答為 (C)。

99 (NEW) --

Look at the graphic. Which expense needs to be confirmed?
(A) Car rental
(B) Meal
(C) Parking
(D) Accommodations

看一下圖表，哪一筆費用需要確認？
(A) 租車
(B) 餐點
(C) 停車
(D) 住宿

04

男子於第四句「I see you are requesting reimbursement for an expense of $250 on May 10, but I can't find the receipt for it.」透露他找不到 5 月 10 日、花費 250 美元的收據。對照表格可得知此為住宿費用，故正確答案為 (D)。

100 ---

What does speaker say he can do?
(A) Cancel a reservation
(B) Handle a complaint
(C) Hire a new employee
(D) Explain a process

說話者說他可以做什麼？
(A) 取消預約
(B) 處理客訴
(C) 僱用新員工
(D) 說明流程

男子在倒數第二句「If you don't have it now, can you call me at extension 3 and then I'll tell you what the procedure is for requesting reimbursement without a receipt.」表示，自己可以教女子沒有收據如何進行報銷，故正確解答為 (D)。

ACTUAL TEST

2

PART 1 🎧 05

1

(A) A man is looking for some ads in the magazine.
(B) A man is standing next to the column.
(C) A street is crowded with many people.
(D) A man is examining a newspaper.

(A) 一位男士正在找雜誌上的某類廣告。
(B) 一位男士正站在柱子旁。
(C) 一條街擠滿了許多人。
(D) 一位男士正在細讀報紙。

• look for . . . 找尋……　ad 廣告　column 柱子　be crowded with . . . 擠滿了……　examine 仔細地看

此為男子正在看報紙的照片。(A) 無法確定正在看報紙的哪一個部分，故無法成為正確答案。(B) 男子坐在椅子上，而且旁邊沒有柱子。(C) 照片中出現的人物只有男子一個人。正確答案為 (D)。

2

(A) Some people are waiting at a traffic light.
(B) There are many vehicles on the road.
(C) There are benches in front of the building.
(D) Some people are resting on the grass.

(A) 一些人正在等紅綠燈。
(B) 路上有很多車輛。
(C) 建築物前有長椅。
(D) 一些人在草地上休息。

• traffic light 紅綠燈　vehicle 車輛　in front of . . . 在……前面　rest 休息

照片裡幾個人正在等著交通號誌轉變，準備過馬路。(B) 照片中雖然出現道路，但是並沒有看到車輛。(C) 雖然是在建築物前拍攝的照片，但是並未出現長凳。(D) 照片中雖然出現人物，但是並不是待在草地上。如果聽到照片沒有出現的單字，則該選項為錯誤答案。正確答案為 (A)。

3

(A) Buildings are being torn down.
(B) Cars are being inspected by a mechanic.
(C) Some people are fishing from a boat.
(D) Cars are parked along the pier.

(A) 建築物正在被拆除。
(B) 汽車正在被技師檢查。
(C) 一些人正在船上釣魚。
(D) 汽車沿著碼頭停放。

• tear down 拆除　inspect 檢查　mechanic 技師　along the pier 沿著碼頭

照片中出現好幾台車沿著碼頭停放。(A) 照片中雖然出現建築物，但是並非正在拆除中。(B) 照片中雖然出現車輛，但是並沒有人在檢查車子。(C) 照片中雖然出現幾艘船，但是並沒有人在釣魚。正確答案為 (D)。

4

(A) All seats are occupied in an office.
(B) People are gathered in an office.
(C) The woman is taking notes.
(D) A group of people has gathered in a laboratory.

(A) 辦公室所有的座位都有人坐。
(B) 人們聚集在辦公室裡。
(C) 這位女士正在做筆記。
(D) 一群人聚集在實驗室裡。

• **occupied** 有人使用的　**be gathered** 聚集　**laboratory** 實驗室

此為人們聚集在辦公室中的照片。(A) 並不是每一張椅子都有人坐。(C) 照片中雖然出現女人，但是並非正在寫筆記。(D) 人們雖然聚集在一起，但是照片中的場所並非實驗室。正確答案為 (B)。

5

(A) People are watching a performance.
(B) A man is paying for a purchase.
(C) A man is signing up for a conference.
(D) One of the women is buying a present.

(A) 人們正在看表演。
(B) 一位男士正在為所買的東西付款。
(C) 一位男士正在報名參加會議。
(D) 其中一位女士正在買禮物。

• **pay for . . .** 為⋯⋯付款　**sign up for** 報名參加

此為一位客人正在結帳的照片。(A) 此處並未出現正在表演的場面。(C) 無法看出男士正在登記參加會議。(D) 照片中雖然出現幾名女子，但是無法看出她們在購買禮物。正確答案為 (B)。

6

(A) Food is being served to the guests.
(B) Glasses are being filled.
(C) There are utensils on the table.
(D) Meat is being roasted on the grill.

(A) 正為賓客上菜中。
(B) 玻璃杯正在被添滿。
(C) 桌上有餐具。
(D) 肉正在烤架上燒烤。

• **utensil** 餐具　**roast** 烘；烤

此為桌上擺放著食物與餐具的照片。(A) 照片中並未出現人物。(B) 照片中雖然出現幾個杯子，但是杯子內已有液體。且此選項提及未發生的「動作」，故非正確答案。(D) 肉品已經被烹調為菜餚，而不是正在燒烤的樣子。正確答案為 (C)。

PART 2 🎧 06

7

Aren't you supposed to be in Prague?
(A) Prague is in the Czech Republic.
(B) They will supposedly arrive in Prague.
(C) The conference was put off until next month.

你應該要在布拉格吧？
(A) 布拉格在捷克共和國。
(B) 他們應該會抵達布拉格。
(C) 會議延到下個月了。

• conference 會議　put off 延期

(A) 此以問句中出現的「Prague」誘導。(B) 此以問句中出現的「suppose」誘導。(C) 此為反問「不是應該要……」的「be supposed to V」句型。題目詢問「你應該在布拉格吧？」，此處回答「會議延後」以解釋不在布拉格的原因，故正確答案為 (C)。

8

Would you like to go to the beach with me?
(A) I'm afraid I don't have enough time.
(B) I'd like to go out.
(C) Yes, I'll go tomorrow.

你要不要跟我去海邊？
(A) 我的時間恐怕不夠。
(B) 我想出去。
(C) 是的，我明天去。

• would like to V . . . 想要……　beach 海邊　enough 足夠的

(A) 題目利用「would like to V」的句型提議一起去海邊，對方回答「沒有時間」為適當答案。(B) 此以問句出現過的「like to」誘導。(C) 雖然回答了「Yes」但是後半句與題目無關，且以文句中出現過的「go」誘導。正確答案為 (A)。

9

Who is going to chair the meeting on the recruitment plans?
(A) Andrew Park from Human Resources.
(B) They are new recruits.
(C) I don't know the person sitting there.

誰要主持招聘計畫會議？
(A) 人力資源部的安德魯·帕克。
(B) 他們是新員工。
(C) 我不認識坐在那裡的人。

• chair 主持（會議）　recruitment 招募　recruit 新成員

(A) 作為疑問詞「Who」的回答，正確解答應為人名。請記得問句「Who」的答句通常為各種人名或職位，以及代名詞「I」、「You」等。(B) 此為利用和問題中出現的「recruitment」相似的「recruit」誘導。(C) 雖然出現「the person」，但句子內容與題目毫無關聯。正確答案為 (A)。

10

What does a one-way ticket from Shanghai to Beijing cost?
(A) All tickets were sold out.
(B) Sorry, the deadline has passed.
(C) I'm afraid I have no idea.

從上海到北京的單程票要多少錢？
(A) 所有的票都賣光了。
(B) 抱歉，截止期限已經過了。
(C) 恐怕我也不知道。

• **one-way ticket** 單程票　**sold out** 賣光　**deadline** 截止期限

(A) 此為利用與問句中出現的「ticket」相似的「tickets」誘導。(B) 與問題完全無關的回答。(C) 題目為利用「What . . . cost?」的句型詢問費用的問句，故「不知道」為適當回答，正確解答為 (C)。

11

When will the sales meeting take place?
(A) In the boardroom.
(B) In two weeks.
(C) For three hours.

業務會議將於何時舉行？
(A) 在會議室。
(B) 兩週後。
(C) 三個小時。

• **boardroom** 會議室　**take place** 舉行

(A) 題目詢問的是時間，回答場所並不合適。(B) 本題為使用時間相關疑問詞「When」的問句，故「兩週後」為適當回答。(C) 問句詢問的是會議舉行的時間點，對方回答的卻是一段期間，故此選項非正確答案。正確答案為 (B)。

12

Where does Susan work?
(A) It's on her desk.
(B) In an office building downtown.
(C) From 8:30 to 6:00.

蘇珊在哪裡上班？
(A) 在她桌上。
(B) 在市中心的辦公大樓裡。
(C) 從8:30到6:00。

• **office building** 辦公大樓　**downtown** 市中心

(A) 句子的內容和題目完全無關。(B) 題目以疑問詞「Where」詢問地點，準確說出「在市中心的辦公大樓」為適當答案。(C) 題目為詢問場所的問句，此選項卻提及時間，故非正確答案。正確答案為 (B)。

13

How often do you visit Singapore on business?
(A) Usually just to show my wares.
(B) Last June, I think.
(C) A couple of times a year.

你多常到新加坡出差？
(A) 通常只是去展示貨品。
(B) 我想是去年六月。
(C) 一年幾次吧。

• on business 出差　usually 通常　wares 貨品

(A) 題目詢問頻繁程度，回答卻只說明原因，故非正確答案。(B) 對於詢問頻率的問句，卻只以特定時間回答，非正確答案。(C) 題目以詢問頻率的「How often . . .」提問，準確說出「一年兩次左右」為適當答案，故正確答案為 (C)。

14

Why is it so humid in this room?
(A) There is no air conditioning in here.
(B) Yes, it's quite cold, isn't it?
(C) Because the argument was heated.

這個房間為什麼這麼潮濕？
(A) 這裡沒有空調。
(B) 是的，相當冷，不是嗎？
(C) 因為爭論激烈。

• humid 潮濕的　air conditioning 空調　argument 爭論

(A) 題目以疑問詞「Why」詢問潮濕理由，準確回答出「沒有空調」為適當答案。(B) 由疑問詞帶出的問句，無法用 Yes/No 回答。(C) 與問句毫不相關的回答。正確答案為 (A)。

15

Which novel are you reading in your book club?
(A) You should read it carefully.
(B) The health club is on the 5th floor.
(C) The one you also read last week.

你們的讀書會正在看哪一本小說？
(A) 你應該仔細閱讀。
(B) 健康俱樂部在五樓。
(C) 你們上週看的那本。

(A) 此為利用與問句中的「reading」發音相似的「read」誘導。(B) 此為利用曾出現於問句的「club」誘導。(C) 題目以疑問詞「Which」詢問「哪個」，回答「the one」（那個）最為合適，故正確答案為 (C)。

16

Jane always arrives at work at eight o'clock sharp.
(A) Her desk is near the entrance.
(B) Is the walk tiresome?
(C) Are all your staff as punctual?

珍總是八點整到公司。
(A) 她的辦公桌在入口附近。
(B) 這趟步行很累人嗎？
(C) 你的員工全都這麼準時嗎？

• sharp 整（時刻）　tiresome 累人的　punctual 準時的

(A) 回答內容與題目毫無關係。(B) 此為利用與題目中出現的「work」讀音相似的「walk」誘導。
(C) 此題以直述句引導對方再提出問題，難易度較高。題目表達「珍總是八點整到公司」，此選項的
回覆最相關且合適，故正確答案為 (C)。

17 --

This firm was established about 7 years ago, wasn't it?
(A) Yes, by Stephen Lee.
(B) Yes, I work at a law firm.
(C) It was built in Switzerland.

這家公司是在七年前成立的，不是嗎？
(A) 是的，由史蒂芬・李成立的。
(B) 是的，我在律師事務所工作。
(C) 它蓋在瑞士。

• **establish** 成立　**law firm** 律師事務所

此為附加問句題型。請記住，附加問句不論是以肯定或否定方式詢問，只要回答內容為肯定，則以
「Yes ＋肯定內容」回答；如為否定，則以「No ＋否定內容」回答。對於「公司是在七年前成立
的，不是嗎？」，(A) 回答「是的」並告知創辦人的名字，此為合適回答，正確答案為 (A)。

(B) 此為利用問題中出現的「firm」誘導。(C) 題目詢問時間，回答地點並不合適。

18 --

Can you please tell me where I can buy tickets for a baseball game?
(A) Proceed to a box office.
(B) Tickets were sold out.
(C) I know where Ms. Kim is.

可以麻煩你告訴我在哪裡買得到棒球賽的票嗎？
(A) 到售票室去。
(B) 票已售完。
(C) 我知道金女士在哪裡。

• **box office** 售票室　**proceed to . . .**（朝特定方向）前進　**sold out** 售完

(A) 題目為間接問句，遇到這種句型務必要聽清楚疑問詞。此題以疑問詞「where」詢問買票地點，
故回答「售票室」最為適當。(B) 此為利用與題目字彙發音相似的「tickets」誘導。(C) 此為利用問
題中出現過的疑問詞誘導。正確答案為 (A)。

19 --

Should I put these boxes on your desk or put them somewhere else?
(A) Let me put them down first.
(B) Either is fine.
(C) No, the package hasn't arrived yet.

我應該把這些箱子放在你的桌上，還是其他地方？
(A) 讓我先把它們放下來。
(B) 兩者皆可。
(C) 不，包裹還沒送達。

• **somewhere** 在某處　**Either is fine** 兩者皆可

(A) 此為利用題目中出現過的「put them」誘導。(B) 題目為選擇疑問句，通常要求從兩者中選擇其
一的情況較多，但是最近「Both sound great.」（兩者皆可）或是「Either is fine.」（任一皆可）等
答案也常常出現，故需多加留意。(C) 選擇疑問句不可以用 Yes/No 回答。正確答案為 (B)。

20

What did you do with the extra folders?
(A) I put them in the warehouse.
(B) No, I didn't.
(C) I did it myself.

你怎麼處理多的文件夾？
(A) 我把它們放進倉庫了。
(B) 不，我沒有。
(C) 我自己做的。

• **extra** 額外的；多餘的　**warehouse** 倉庫

(A) 題目使用疑問詞「What」詢問做了什麼動作，以做過的行動回答屬於常見的解答類型。更重要的是，一定要熟悉疑問詞後面出現的動詞時態。此題題目為過去式，此選項也以過去式回覆，故為合適答案。(B) 疑問詞問句不可以用 Yes/No 回答。(C) 題目詢問做了什麼，只回答是自己做的，卻沒有明確說出做了什麼行動。正確答案為 (A)。

Were you supposed to leave for L.A. yesterday?
(A) Yes, but I changed my mind.
(B) No, it was yesterday.
(C) Where are you heading?

你是昨天要去洛杉磯嗎？
(A) 是的，但我改變主意了。
(B) 不，是昨天。
(C) 你要去哪裡？

• **be supposed to V** 應該、預計（做某事）　**leave for . . .** 前往……　**change one's mind** 改變主意

(A) 題目為可用 Yes/No 回答的疑問句。題目詢問「昨天要去洛杉磯嗎」，故「我改變心意了」為合適回答。(B) 此為利用與題目字彙發音相似的「yesterday」誘導。(C) 與題目毫不相關的回答。正確答案為 (A)。

22

Feel free to call us if you have any queries.
(A) Perhaps I could.
(B) No, that might happen.
(C) Thanks, I'll do that.

若您有任何問題，請隨時打電話給我們。
(A) 也許我會。
(B) 不，那可能會發生。
(C) 謝了，我會的。

• **query** 疑問　**feel free to V . . .** 無須拘束（做某事）

(A) 與題目毫無關係的回答。(B) 雖然題目可以用 Yes/No 回答，但是此選項後續內容與題目毫無關聯。(C) 此題必須聽完整句才能找出正確答案。對於「有任何問題，請隨時打電話」這句話，通常該表示感謝並告知會這麼做，故正確答案為 (C)。

23

Why don't you think the offer over before you make a decision?

(A) Two days wasn't enough.

(B) The disagreement occurred yesterday.

(C) Actually, I've already made up my mind.

在你做決定前，何不仔細考慮一下那個提議呢？

(A) 兩天不夠。

(B) 昨天發生爭論。

(C) 事實上，我已經決定好了。

• **think . . . over** 仔細考慮……　　**disagreement** 爭論　　**make up one's mind** 下定決心

(A) 此選項的時態為過去式，內容也與題目毫無關聯，故非正確答案。(B) 雖然此句使用了與「decision」相關的「disagreement」，但內容與題目無關。(C) 表示勸誘的「Why don't you . . . ?」問句會有特定答案，但可能以各種形式出現，所以最好仔細聽完所有選項再作答。題目詢問「何不仔細考慮」，回答「我已經決定好」代表不會再多考慮，此為合適回覆，故正確答案為 (C)。

24

Have you just been promoted?

(A) Yes, I'll start in my new position on Monday.

(B) Yes, the clothing promotion was a success.

(C) Yes, I am.

你剛獲得升職嗎？

(A) 是的，我將於週一開始新職。

(B) 是的，服飾促銷活動非常成功。

(C) 是的，我是。

• **promote** 晉升　　**promotion** 促銷活動　　**success** 成功

(A) 題目詢問是否晉升，故「週一開始新職」，為合適回覆。(B) 此為利用與題目中的「promoted」相似的「promotion」誘導。(C) 因為題目中以現在完成式進行詢問，應以相同時態回答。正確答案為 (A)。

25

Which carpet do you think matches this floor, blue or black?

(A) I don't think so.

(B) I think either would be nice.

(C) I watched a tennis match on TV.

你覺得哪一塊地毯與這地板比較搭，藍色或黑色？

(A) 我不這麼認為

(B) 我覺得兩者都不錯。

(C) 我看了電視上的網球賽。

• **match . . .** 和……相配　　**tennis match** 網球比賽

(A) 此為利用題目出現過的字彙「think」誘導。(B) 題目以「Which」帶出的選擇疑問句，此選項雖然並未從提示選項擇一，但「兩者都可以」也為合適答覆。(C) 此為利用與題目出現過的「match」誘導。正確答案為 (B)。

Who is the new employee at our office?
(A) His name is Leonardo.
(B) We are all employed here.
(C) In the office.

辦公室裡的新員工是誰？
(A) 他叫李奧納多。
(B) 我們都在這裡上班。
(C) 在辦公室裡。

(A) 以「Who」開頭的疑問句，主要在詢問代名詞、職稱、姓名等。此題詢問新員工是誰，回答確切名字為合適答覆。(B) 題目詢問新員工是誰，回答卻毫不相關。(C) 題目詢問人物，回答卻是場所，故非正確答案。正確答案為 (A)。

27

Could you assist Mr. Johnson with the coffee machine?
(A) Yes, he needs four copies.
(B) Yes, my assistant did it.
(C) I'd be glad to.

你可以幫強生先生處理一下咖啡機嗎？
(A) 是的，他需要四份。
(B) 是的，我的助理做的。
(C) 我很樂意。

• assist 協助　assistant 助理

(A) 此為利用題目中出現過的「coffee」相似的「copies」誘導。(B) 雖然用「Yes」回答，但是回答的內容和題目完全無關。(C) 對於可以用 Yes/No 回答的助動詞疑問句，此選項為常見的回答。
題目詢問是否可以幫助某人，故「很樂意」為合適回答，正確答案為 (C)。

28

When are the sales figures for last month coming out?
(A) 300 million dollars.
(B) Yes, if they are wrong.
(C) In about three days.

上個月的銷售額何時會出來？
(A) 三億元。
(B) 是的，如果它們錯了。
(C) 約三天內。

• sales figures 銷售額　come out 公布；揭曉

(A) 與題目完全無關的答案。(B)「When」疑問句無法用 Yes/No 回答。(C) 題目詢問上個月銷售結果「何時」出來，故「約三天內」為合適回答，正確答案為 (C)。

29

You've printed out the minutes from the last meeting, haven't you?
(A) It took three hours.
(B) No, I'll do it first thing tomorrow.
(C) The printer takes a minute to warm up.

你已經把上次的會議紀錄印出來了，不是嗎？
(A) 花了三個小時。
(B) 不，我明天會先做這件事。
(C) 印表機需要一分鐘暖機。

• print out 印出　minute 會議記錄　warm up（機器等）預熱

(A) 與題目完全無關的回答。(B) 此為附加問句，故通常以 Yes/No 回答。題目詢問上次會議紀錄是否已經印出，回答還沒並表示「明天會先做這件事」，此為合適答覆。(C) 此為利用與題目中的「printed」相似的「printer」誘導。故正確解答為 (B)。

30

Where should I put my signature?
(A) Your sign goes here.
(B) In the drawer, please.
(C) At the bottom of the page.

我要在哪裡簽名？
(A) 你的指標顯示是這裡。
(B) 麻煩，在抽屜裡。
(C) 在這頁的底部。

• **signature** 簽名　**sign** 指標　**drawer** 抽屜

(A) 此為利用與題目中的「signature」相似的「sign」引導，非正確答案。許多人會把「sign」的意思誤解為「簽名」，但作為名詞時，sign 的意思為「招牌」或是「告示牌」，需多加注意。

(B) 雖然回答提及了場所，但是「在抽屜裡簽名」的描寫不合常理，故非正確答案。(C) 以詢問場所的「Where」開頭的問句，通常回答確切地點。此題詢問該在哪裡簽名，故「在這頁的底部」為適當回答，故正確解答為 (C)。

31

Wasn't Ms. Tucker supposed to lead the investigation?
(A) It was decided she lacked the experience.
(B) I've already been considered.
(C) The investment was sound.

塔克女士不是要帶領這個調查活動嗎？
(A) 最後決定她缺乏經驗。
(B) 我已經被列入考慮。
(C) 那項投資非常穩當。

• **be supposed to V** 應該、預計（做某事）　**investigation** 調查　**lack** 缺乏
investment 投資　**sound** 健全的

(A) 否定的疑問句可先理解為肯定句，再尋找答案。題目詢問「塔克女士不是要帶領這個調查嗎」，回答「她缺乏經驗」代表此調查並不由塔克女士主導，所以此選項為正確解答。(B) 與題目完全無關的回答。(C) 此為利用與題目中出現的「investigation」發音相似的「investment」誘導。正確答案為 (A)。

32-34 conversation   **32–34 對話**

W Hello, this is Surf and Turf Restaurant. How can I help you?	女 您好，這裡是海陸總匯餐廳。有什麼可以為您服務的嗎？
M I'd like to make a reservation for this Friday evening for four people at 8:15.	男 我想要訂這週五晚上8:15，四個人的位子。
W Oh, I'm afraid we're full at that time. I could fit you in at 8:45, though. Would that be suitable for your party?	女 噢，很抱歉我們那個時段已經訂滿了，但我可以為您安排到8:45。那時間方便嗎？
M I'll have to get in touch with my friends and get back to you. I'm not entirely sure if that will work for everyone else.	男 我得先聯絡朋友再回覆妳。我無法完全確定那時間每個人都可以。

- **make a reservation** 預約   **fit . . . in** 安排時間（見某人／做某事）   **suitable** 合適的
  get in touch with . . . 聯絡……   **takeout food** 外帶餐點   **be out of . . .** 缺乏……
  entirely 完全地   **book** 預訂

32 -

Why is the man calling?   **這位男士為什麼要打這通電話？**
(A) To invite the woman to an event   (A) 邀請這位女士參加活動
(B) To book a table   (B) 預約位子
(C) To order takeout food   (C) 點外帶餐點
(D) To cancel a reservation   (D) 取消預約

男子的第一句台詞提及「I'd like to make a reservation for this Friday evening for four people at 8:15.」可看出男子想預約時間。對話中使用的「make a reservation」即選項 (B) 的「book a table」，故正確答案為 (B)。

33 -

What is the problem?   **出現什麼問題？**
(A) No tables are available at 8:15.   (A) 8:15已經沒有空位。
(B) The business closes at eight o'clock.   (B) 店家8點結束營業。
(C) The restaurant is out of lobster.   (C) 餐廳沒有龍蝦了。
(D) The woman has lost her job.   (D) 這位女士失業了。

男子的第一句台詞提及「I'd like to make a reservation for this Friday evening for four people at 8:15.」女子則說：「Oh, I'm afraid we're full at that time.」，由此可知，男子想預約的時間已經沒有空位，正確答案為 (A)。

34

What does the woman suggest?
(A) Coming another day
(B) Coming half an hour later
(C) Trying another location
(D) Reserving seats online

這位女士提出什麼建議？
(A) 改天再來
(B) 半個小時後再來
(C) 試試其他地點
(D) 上網訂位

女子的第二句台詞雖然告知無法預約 8 點 15 分的時段，但是又提到「I could fit you in at 8:45, though.」所以 8 點 45 分有空位，故正確答案為 (B)。

35-37 conversation

35–37 對話

M Cindy, could you give me a hand with this Internet connection? I can't seem to figure out what's wrong with it. And I can't even get online to see what the problem might be.	男 辛蒂，妳可以幫我看一下網路連線嗎？我好像找不出哪裡有問題。我甚至無法連上線查查可能是什麼問題。
W I have to go to a meeting right now, but I could help you when I get back in about an hour.	女 我現在得去參加一個會議，不過我大概一個小時後回來，到時可以幫你看看。
M Actually, I have to be able to get online right away. I'll call someone in the IT department and see if they can send someone to help me.	男 事實上，我現在就得連上線。我來打電話給資訊科技部的人，看看他們是否能派人過來幫我。
W Okay. Sorry I couldn't help you.	女 好的。很抱歉無法幫上忙。

• **connection** 聯結 **figure out** 想出；明白 **right away** 立刻 **consult** 查閱

35

What does the man need help with?
(A) A printer
(B) Internet access
(C) A filing system
(D) An answering machine

這位男士需要什麼協助？
(A) 印表機
(B) 連線上網
(C) 檔案系統
(D) 答錄機

男子的第一句台詞「could you give me a hand with this Internet connection?」在要求對方幫忙連結網路。對話中使用的「Internet connection」即選項 (B) 的「Internet access」，正確答案為 (B)。

36

When will the woman most likely return from her meeting?
(A) The next day
(B) In an hour
(C) At 7 P.M.
(D) On Thursday

這位女士最有可能何時結束會議回來？
(A) 隔天
(B) 一個小時後
(C) 晚上7點
(D) 星期四

女子的第一句台詞「I have to go to a meeting right now, but I could help you when I get back in about an hour.」，由此可知，她一個小時後可以回來幫助男子，故正確答案為 (B)。

37 --

What will the man probably do to solve the problem?

(A) Call the IT department
(B) Consult the manufacturer's Web page
(C) Buy a new router
(D) Use the fax machine

這位男士可能會做什麼來解決問題？

(A) 打電話給資訊科技部
(B) 查閱廠商的網頁
(C) 買一台新的路由器
(D) 使用傳真機

從男子的第二句台詞「I'll call someone in the IT department and see if they can send someone to help me.」可知，他將打電話給資訊科技部，故正確答案為 (A)。

38-40 conversation with three speakers `NEW`　　　**38-40 三人對話**

W1	Hi, Bill. We were wondering if there was a filing cabinet in here.	**女1**	嗨，比爾。我們想知道這裡有沒有檔案櫃？
M	Actually, we have a few. What size were you looking for?	**男**	事實上，我們有好幾個。你們要的是哪種尺寸？
W1	We were hoping to get one of those ones that's about four and a half feet tall and has four drawers.	**女1**	我們想要一個4.5英尺高，有四個抽屜的那種。
M	Oh, I don't think we have one that big. All of the ones that we have only have three drawers and are a lot shorter than that.	**男**	噢，我想我們沒有那麼大的。我們現有的都只有三個抽屜，而且比妳要的矮很多。
W2	I'm sorry to hear that. However, we definitely need it for storing some office supplies.	**女2**	真可惜。不過，我們就是需要那種的來存放一些辦公用品。
M	In that case, I could order one for you from our supplier, and it would probably be here by the end of the week.	**男**	這樣的話，我可以幫你們向供應商訂購一個，應該這週末前就可以到貨。

• **filing cabinet** 檔案櫃　**drawer** 抽屜　**definitely** 肯定地　**office supplies** 辦公用品
in that case 這樣的話　**wardrobe** 衣櫃

38 --

What are the women looking for?

(A) An order form
(B) A filing cabinet
(C) A photocopier
(D) A wardrobe

這兩位女士在找什麼？

(A) 訂購單
(B) 檔案櫃
(C) 影印機
(D) 衣櫃

女子的第一句台詞說：「We were wondering if there was a filing cabinet in here.」，由此可知，她正在尋找檔案櫃，正確答案為 (B)。

39

Where most likely are the speakers?

(A) In a restaurant
(B) In a grocery store
(C) In an office storeroom
(D) In a boutique

說話者最有可能在哪裡？

(A) 餐廳
(B) 雜貨店
(C) 公司儲藏室
(D) 精品店

從對話中可知道女子想尋找檔案櫃，而男子回覆「we have a few」，代表此為可以放置檔案櫃等辦公家具的地方，故正確解答為 (C)。

40

What does the man offer to do?

(A) Place an order
(B) Build something
(C) Contact a specialist
(D) Ask his assistant

這位男士提議做什麼事？

(A) 下訂單
(B) 建造東西
(C) 聯絡專家
(D) 詢問他的助理

男子最後說：「In that case, I could order one for you from our supplier, and it would probably be here by the end of the week.」，由此可見，男子將會幫忙向供應商訂購檔案櫃。對話中使用的「order（動詞）」即選項 (A) 中的「place an order（名詞）」，故正確答案為 (A)。

41-43 conversation

M	Wendy, I thought you were supposed to be at that training session in Los Angeles by now.
W	was supposed to be, but they postponed it by a week because they had a problem with one of the speakers.
M	Oh, that must be a real hassle. You had to change your entire schedule around to accommodate this training session.
W	Yeah, I won't even be able to go now. My schedule is just too packed.
M	Cheer up! It happens all the time.

41-43 對話

男	溫蒂，我以為妳現在應該是在洛杉磯的教育訓練講座上。
女	本來是的，但是因為其中一位講者有狀況，所以他們往後延一週了。
男	噢，那一定很麻煩。妳必須更改整個行程來配合這個訓練講座。
女	是啊，我現在甚至無法出席了。我的行程太滿了。
男	振作點！這是常有的事。

• **training session** 訓練講座　**by now** 此時　**postpone** 延後　**hassle** 麻煩　**packed** 塞得滿滿的
all the time 一直；向來

41

Where did the man expect the woman to be?

(A) In the conference room
(B) In San Francisco
(C) At a training session
(D) At a job interview

這位男士以為這位女士會在哪裡？

(A) 會議室
(B) 舊金山
(C) 教育訓練講座
(D) 工作面談

男子的第一句台詞説：「I thought you were supposed to be at that training session in Los Angeles by now.」，由此可知，男子認為女子現在應該去參加講座，故正確答案為 (C)。

42 -

Why is the woman at the office?
(A) She had a meeting there.
(B) Her conference was canceled.
(C) Her conference was pushed back.
(D) She had to pack her bags.

這位女士為什麼會在公司？
(A) 她在那裡開會。
(B) 她的會議取消了。
(C) 她的會議延後了。
(D) 她必須打包行李。

女子的第一句台詞「I was supposed to be, but they postponed it by a week」告知會議已經延期。對話中使用的「postponed」即選項 (C) 中的「pushed back」，故正確答案為 (C)。

43 -

Why won't she take a trip next week?
(A) She has to move to a new office.
(B) Her schedule will be too busy.
(C) She has to talk with a client.
(D) Her office will be renovated.

她下週為什麼無法成行？
(A) 她必須搬到新的辦公室。
(B) 她的行程太滿了。
(C) 她必須和客戶談話。
(D) 她的辦公室將進行整修。

女子的第二句台詞説：「I won't even be able to go now. My schedule is just too packed.」，由此可知，女子因為排滿行程，無法參加研習，故正確答案為 (B)。

44-46 conversation

44–46 對話

W	Driver, how long do you think it will be before we get to the Empire State Building?
M	Well, ma'am, usually it would be about fifteen minutes, but with this traffic it might take us closer to an hour.
W	Oh, that's just too long. I'm sorry; I'm going to have to get you to let me out at a subway station.
M	No problem at all. You're in luck; the station's right over there. That'll be $11.50, please.
W	Here you are. Keep the change.

女	司機，你認為我們還要多久才會到帝國大廈？
男	女士，通常是15分鐘左右，但以這個交通流量我們可能要花上近一個小時的時間。
女	噢，那太久了。很抱歉，我得麻煩你讓我在地鐵站下車了。
男	沒問題。妳運氣很好，車站就在那裡。總共是11.5元。
女	這給你。不用找了。

• **be in luck** 運氣好　**change**〔名詞〕零錢　**duration** 持續期間　**cab** 計程車

44 -

What does the woman ask about?
(A) Directions to the subway
(B) The duration of a trip
(C) The cost of a ticket
(D) The bus schedule

這位女士詢問了什麼事？
(A) 到地鐵的路線
(B) 一段行程的時間
(C) 票價
(D) 公車時刻表

女子的第一句台詞說：「Driver, how long do you think it will be before we get to the Empire State Building?」，由此可知，女子將前往帝國大廈，並且詢問需要花多少時間，故正確答案為 (B)。

45 --

Where most likely is the woman?
(A) On a bus
(B) In a subway station
(C) In a cab
(D) At an airport

這位女士最有可能在哪裡？
(A) 公車上
(B) 地鐵站
(C) 計程車上
(D) 機場

女子開頭已稱對方為「Driver」，又在第二句台詞「Oh, that's just too long. I'm sorry; I'm going to have to get you to let me out at a subway station.」請對方讓她在地鐵站下車，且對方隨後和她收費，故可推知女子應在計程車上，正確答案為 (C)。

46 --

What will the woman probably do next?
(A) Pay the bill
(B) Take a taxi
(C) Collect her change
(D) Go into the subway station

這位女士接下來可能會做什麼？
(A) 付款
(B) 搭計程車
(C) 拿找給她的錢
(D) 進入地鐵站

女子的第二句台詞說：「I'm going to have to get you to let me out at a subway station.」，由此可知，女子將前往地鐵站，正確答案為 (D)。

47-49 conversation

47–49 對話

M Hello, Hillcrest Properties.	男 希爾克雷斯特房屋，您好。
W Hello, my name is Dana Wilkins. My friend George Perry recommended you. My company is relocating me to Houston, and he mentioned that you would be able to help me find a new home there. He said you gave him excellent service and got him a fair price for his house.	女 你好，我叫黛娜・威金斯。我的朋友喬治・派瑞推薦了貴公司。我的公司將我調到休士頓，而他提到貴公司可以幫我在那找到新房子。他說你們提供他很棒的服務，還為他的房子拿到了合理的價格。
M Oh, yes. I remember George. That's very kind of him. We helped him sell his house when he moved from here to Los Angeles. What sort of home are you looking for?	男 喔，是的。我記得喬治。他人真好。當他從這裡搬到洛杉磯時，我們幫忙賣掉了他的房子。您想找哪一類的房子呢？
W I'm looking for a studio apartment somewhere near the downtown area. I'll be in town next week. Would you have time to show me some units?	女 我想找市中心附近的小套房。我下週會進城去。你有時間帶我看一些物件嗎？

• **property** 房地產　**recommend** 推薦　**relocate** 調職　**studio apartment** 小套房
moving company 搬家公司

47

Why is the woman calling? | 這位女士為什麼要打這通電話？
(A) She wants a new job. | (A) 她想要一份新工作。
(B) She wants to buy a home. | (B) 她想要買房子。
(C) She wants to arrange a flight. | (C) 她想安排班機。
(D) She wants to ask for directions. | (D) 她想詢問路線。

女子的第三句台詞「he mentioned that you would be able to help me find a new home there.」中，女子表示曾聽說男子可幫她尋找新房子，故可推測正確答案為 (B)。

Where does the man most likely work? | 這位男士最有可能在哪裡工作？
(A) At a furniture shop | (A) 家具店
(B) At a moving company | (B) 搬家公司
(C) At a real estate agency | (C) 房地產仲介
(D) At an interior decorating company | (D) 室內裝潢公司

從男子第一句台詞「Hello, Hillcrest Properties.」可以看出他接起了電話，並告知對方自己為房屋仲介公司。對話中使用的「properties」即選項 (C) 中的「real estate」，故正確答案為 (C)。

49

What will the man most likely do next? | 這位男士接下來最有可能做什麼？
(A) Apply for a job | (A) 應徵工作
(B) Travel to Los Angeles | (B) 去洛杉磯
(C) Buy a house | (C) 買房子
(D) Arrange a meeting time | (D) 安排會面時間

女子的最後一句台詞問道：「I'm looking for a studio apartment somewhere near the downtown area. I'll be in town next week. Would you have time to show me some units?」，由於女子詢問是否有時間可以看房，故可推測男子應會安排會面，故正確答案為 (D)。

50-52 conversation | 50–52 對話

W James, I just got a call from Mtech. They want to know when the marble flooring they ordered will be in. Do you know?	女 詹姆斯，我剛接到M科技公司的電話。他們想知道他們訂購的大理石地板何時會到貨。你知道嗎？
M I just talked to the supplier on the phone. Hopefully I'll hear back within the hour. Do you want me to give them a call when I hear back?	男 我剛和供應商通過電話。應該在這小時內就可以有消息回覆。妳要我在收到回覆後打電話給他們嗎？
W No, that's okay. Let me know when you hear, and I'll call them. I have to give them a price for some wallpaper as well.	女 不，沒關係。你收到消息時再跟我說一聲，我會打電話給他們。我還要跟他們說壁紙的價格。
M (52)No problem.	男 (52) 沒問題。

• order 訂購 supplier 供應商 on the phone 透過電話 advise 通知 install 安裝

50 --

What does the man say he just did?

(A) Made a telephone call
(B) Filed a report
(C) Finished his work
(D) Canceled an order

這位男士說他剛做了什麼？

(A) 打電話
(B) 提交報告
(C) 完成工作
(D) 取消訂單

從男子的第一句台詞「I just talked to the supplier on the phone.」可以看出男子剛結束與供應商的通話。對話中使用的「talked to . . . on the phone」指的就是選項 (A) 中的「made a phone call」，故正確答案為 (A)。

51 --

Why did Mtech call?

(A) To check on an order
(B) To cancel a meeting
(C) To confirm a price
(D) To hire a new employee

M科技公司為什麼打電話來？

(A) 查詢訂單
(B) 取消會議
(C) 確認價格
(D) 僱用新員工

女子的第一句話「James, I just got a call from Mtech. They want to know when the marble flooring they ordered will be in. Do you know?」中，提及她接到 M 科技的電話，且對方在電話中詢問訂購物品的送達時間。由此可知，M 科技是為了確定訂單詳情而撥打電話，正確答案為 (A)。

52 NEW --

What does the man mean when he says, "No problem"?

(A) He doesn't understand the problem.
(B) He can't cancel the order.
(C) He will advise the woman.
(D) He will help the woman install the material.

當這位男士說：「沒問題」，是什麼意思？

(A) 他聽不懂問題。
(B) 他無法取消訂單。
(C) 他會通知這位女士。
(D) 他將協助這位女士安裝建材。

女子的第二句話說：「Let me know when you hear, and I'll call them. I have to give them a price for some wallpaper as well.」要求男子如果聽到任何消息，要盡快告訴她。而男子回答「No problem.」表示會告知女子。對話中使用的「let . . . know」即選項 (C) 中的「advise」，故正確答案為 (C)。

53-55 conversation

W Dave, I was wondering if it would be okay if I came along to work at the kitchen appliance trade show next week.

M Umm . . . I had already assigned everybody to the trade show that I thought we would need. Why?

W Well, it's in Las Vegas, and my cousin lives there. I haven't seen him in a while. I could stay with him and we wouldn't have to pay for a hotel.

M I guess that should be okay. Just remember that you'll be there to get some work done.

W I'll keep that in mind.

53-55 對話

女 戴夫,我想知道我是否可以跟著參加下週的廚房電器用品貿易展。

男 嗯……我已經指派大家去那個我認為我們應該要去的貿易展了。怎麼了?

女 嗯,因為是在拉斯維加斯舉行,而我表哥就住那裡。我已經好一陣子沒見到他了。我可以住他那,公司不需要支付飯店的錢。

男 我想應該可以,只要記得妳是去那工作的。

女 我會牢記在心的。

• **appliance** 家用電器 **assign** 指派 **in a while** 一陣子 **remind A of B** 提醒 A 關於 B
keep in mind 牢記

53 --

What does the woman ask the man to do?
(A) Give her the weekend off
(B) Suggest some kitchen appliances
(C) Allow her to work at a trade show
(D) Pay for her hotel costs

這位女士要求男士做什麼?
(A) 讓她在週末放假
(B) 推薦一些廚房電器用品
(C) 允許她在貿易展工作
(D) 支付她住宿飯店的錢

女子的第一句台詞說:「Dave, I was wondering if it would be okay if I came along to work at the kitchen appliance trade show next week.」,表示她想知道能否一同去下週舉行的廚房用品展,故正確答案為 (C)。

54 --

Why does the woman want to go to Las Vegas?
(A) She wants to apply for a job.
(B) She wants to stay at a hotel.
(C) She wants to enjoy some trade shows.
(D) She wants to see her relative.

這位女士為什麼想去拉斯維加斯?
(A) 她想應徵工作。
(B) 她想住在飯店。
(C) 她想參觀貿易展。
(D) 她想探望親戚。

女子的第二句台詞說:「Well, it's in Las Vegas, and my cousin lives there. I haven't seen him in a while.」,表示她很久沒有和表哥見面。對話中提到的「cousin」即選項 (D) 中的「relative」,正確答案為 (D)。

---

55 -

What does the man remind the woman about?　　這位男士提醒女士什麼事？

(A) That she will have to work　　(A) 她必須工作

(B) That she must arrive on time　　(B) 她必須準時抵達

(C) That she has a meeting this weekend　　(C) 她本週末要開會

(D) That her brother no longer lives in Las Vegas　　(D) 她哥哥已經不住在拉斯加斯了

男子的第二句台詞說：「Just remember that you'll be there to get some work done.」，要女子記得自己是為了工作才去，而不是為了見表哥，故正確答案為 (A)。

56-58 conversation   56-58 對話

M	Wow, that musical was fantastic! I'm really surprised there were so few people here.	男 哇，那音樂劇好棒！我真的很驚訝居然這麼少人來。
W	**(57)I'm not particularly surprised.** It got terrible reviews in the paper, and I wasn't very impressed with it myself.	女 (57)我倒不特別驚訝。它在報上得到了很糟的評論，我個人對它也沒有深刻的好印象。
M	Well, I don't care what you or the reviews say; I loved it. Anyway, would you like to stop for a drink before we head home? We could swing by Jenny's Bar and Grill on 5th Street. We haven't been there in ages.	男 好吧，我不在乎妳或評論怎麼說；我愛死了。不管怎樣，妳想不想在回家前去喝個東西？我們可以順路去第五街的珍妮燒烤酒吧。我們好久沒去那兒了。
W	That sounds like a good idea. The babysitter isn't expecting us home for at least another hour and a half, and we could even have a game of pool.	女 聽起來不錯。保母應該以為我們至少還要一個半小時才會到家，我們甚至還有時間打場撞球。

• **fantastic** 極好的　**particularly** 特別地　**review** 評論　**babysitter** 保母　**swing by** 順路快速拜訪某地　**pool** 撞球　**performance** 表演

---

56 -

What are the speakers discussing?　　說話者在討論什麼？

(A) Their favorite actors　　(A) 他們最喜歡的男演員

(B) The movie they are watching　　(B) 他們正在看的電影

(C) The performance they've just seen　　(C) 他們剛看完的演出

(D) A rock concert　　(D) 搖滾演唱會

男子的第一句台詞說：「Wow, that musical was fantastic!」，由此可知，兩人對話的主題是剛才一起觀賞的音樂劇。對話中使用的「musical」即選項 (C) 中的「performance」，正確答案為 (C)。

---

57 (NEW) -

What does the woman mean when she says, "I'm not particularly surprised"?　　當這位女士說：「我倒不特別驚訝」，是什麼意思？

(A) She thought it was very sad.　　(A) 她覺得那非常悲傷。

(B) She thought it was excellent.　　(B) 她覺得那非常棒。

(C) She thought it was too long.　　(C) 她覺得那太長了。

(D) She didn't like it.　　(D) 她並不喜歡。

男子覺得音樂劇很精彩，但驚訝觀眾不多，而女子回覆「I'm not particularly surprised.」且後方又補上「I wasn't very impressed with it myself.」可見女子並沒有很喜歡，故正確答案為 (D)。

58

What will the speakers most likely do next?
(A) Hire a babysitter
(B) Go to a pub
(C) See a movie
(D) Go to a musical

說話者接下來最有可能做什麼？
(A) 僱用保母
(B) 去酒吧
(C) 看電影
(D) 去看音樂劇

男子的第二句台詞說：「Anyway, would you like to stop for a drink before we head home? We could swing by Jenny's Bar and Grill on 5th Street.」，由此可知，男子想在回家前先去珍妮燒烤酒吧小酌。對話中使用的「bar」即選項 (B) 中的「pub」，故正確答案為 (B)。

59-61 conversation

59–61 對話

M Hello, Wharton residence. **W** Hello, is Diane Wharton available? **M** I'm afraid not. She's out right now. I'm her husband. I'll definitely let her know. **W** My name is Jenny Felling, and I'm calling from the Human Resources Department of Growtech Pharmaceuticals. She interviewed with us last week. We'd like to offer her the position, and we were wondering if she would be able to come in next Tuesday to sign the contract, if she is still interested in the job. **M** Really? That's great. She'll be very happy about the news. I'll definitely let her know. Thanks.	**男** 華頓家，您好。 **女** 您好，請問黛安‧華頓在嗎？ **男** 不在，她出門了。我是她先生。我一定會轉告她的。 **女** 我叫珍妮‧費林，這裡是成長科技製藥人力資源部。她上週曾來本公司面試。我們想提供她這份工作，我們想知道，如果她對這工作還有興趣的話，下週二是否有空來簽約。 **男** 真的嗎？那太好了。她會非常開心聽到這個消息的。我一定會轉告她。謝謝。

• **residence** 住所 **pharmaceutical** 製藥公司 **be interested in . . .** 對……感興趣 **outstanding** 未支付的

59

Why is the woman calling?
(A) To make a job offer
(B) To order food
(C) To cancel a meeting
(D) To collect an outstanding bill

這位女士為什麼打這通電話？
(A) 提供工作機會
(B) 訂購食物
(C) 取消會議
(D) 收取未付帳單

女子的第二句台詞說：「We'd like to offer her the position」，表示想提供工作機會，故正確答案為 (A)。

60

When does the woman want to meet with Ms. Wharton?
(A) This Monday
(B) Next Monday
(C) Next Tuesday
(D) Over the weekend

這位女士希望何時與華頓女士見面？
(A) 這星期一
(B) 下星期一
(C) 下星期二
(D) 週末期間

女子的第二句台詞說：「we were wondering if she would be able to come in next Tuesday to sign the contract, if she is still interested in the job.」，由此可知，女子想在下週二約定會面，故正確答案為 (C)。

61

What does the man say he will do?
(A) Arrange an interview
(B) Receive a delivery for Ms. Wharton
(C) Give Ms. Wharton a message
(D) Come to the office to meet Ms. Felling

這位男士說他會做什麼？
(A) 安排面試
(B) 幫華頓女士收件
(C) 給華頓女士留言
(D) 到辦公室見費林女士

男子的第二句台詞「She's out right now. I'm her husband. I'll definitely let her know.」告知女子他將代為轉達，故正確答案為 (C)。

07

62-64 conversation and chart

62–64 對話及圖表

M	Welcome to Samson Electronics. What can I do for you?
W	I just bought this digital camera last month from your store. But when I try to save the photos I've taken, an error code displays on the screen.
M	Oh, really? Let me take a look first. I have a chart here of all the codes. Perhaps it'll tell us what's going on. I think I found the problem. According to the chart, it seems that there is something wrong with the memory card.
W	Oh, do I need to purchase a new memory card?
M	Well, let me change it for a new one for free because it is under warranty.

男	歡迎來到參孫電器。我可以為您服務嗎？
女	我上個月在你們店裡買了這台數位相機。但在我試著儲存所拍的照片時，螢幕上出現了一個錯誤代碼。
男	喔，真的嗎？先讓我看一下。我這裡有一張代碼表，也許它可以告訴我們到底怎麼了。我想我找到問題了。根據這張表，應該是記憶卡有問題。
女	喔，那我需要買一張新的記憶卡嗎？
男	因為還在保固期限內，我可以免費幫您換張新的。

E-1	Lens Malfunction
E-2	No Flash
E-3	Low Battery
E-4	Memory Card Problem

E-1	鏡頭故障
E-2	沒有閃光燈
E-3	電力不足
E-4	記憶卡問題

• **error code** 錯誤代碼　**display**（螢幕）顯示　**according to . . .** 根據……　**purchase** 購買
under warranty 在保固期內

Who most likely is the man?
(A) A mechanic
(B) A store clerk
(C) An electrician
(D) A photo artist

這位男士最有可能是誰？
(A) 技師
(B) 商店店員
(C) 電工
(D) 攝影藝術家

男子的第一句台詞「Welcome to Samson Electronics. What can I do for you?」是商店店員的典型台詞。由此可知，故正確答案為 (B)。

 NEW

Look at the graphic. Which error code is the camera displaying?
(A) E-1
(B) E-2
(C) E-3
(D) E-4

看一下圖表，相機顯示的是哪一個錯誤代碼？
(A) E-1
(B) E-2
(C) E-3
(D) E-4

男子的第二句台詞說：「I think I found the problem. According to the chart, it seems that there is something wrong with the memory card.」，表示記憶卡出現問題，對照圖表可知正確答案為 (D)。

64

What will the man most likely do next?
(A) Replace an item
(B) Purchase a new item
(C) Read a manual
(D) Wrap up a camera

這位男士接下來最有可能做什麼？
(A) 更換物件
(B) 購買新物品
(C) 閱讀使用手冊
(D) 包裝相機

男子的第三句台詞說：「Well, let me change it for a new one for free because it is under warranty.」告知將會為對方更換新的記憶卡，故正確答案為 (A)。

65-67 conversation and map | **65–67 對話及地圖**

M Amy, the hospital will be closing the parking lot in front of our research lab for construction next month. Can you send an e-mail to tell the rest of your staff members?

W No problem. Did they find a place to park for everyone until the construction is finished?

M Yes. I think we're supposed to use the West Parking lot instead.

W That's quite far from the lab. It is very inconvenient for everyone to get there on foot. In addition, it is winter now.

M Don't worry. The board of directors decided to provide free shuttle buses from the West Parking lot to our building. Could you let your team members know this decision as well?

男 艾咪，醫院將因下個月的工程關閉我們研究實驗室前的停車場。妳可以寄封電子郵件告訴其他的同事嗎？

女 沒問題。到工程結束前，他們有幫大家找到停車的地方嗎？

男 是的，我想我們應該會改用西區停車場。

女 那離實驗室還蠻遠的。要走路到那裡對大家都不方便。而且，現在還是冬天。

男 別擔心。董事會已經決定提供從西區停車場到這棟大樓的免費接駁公車。妳可以一併告訴組員們這個決定嗎？

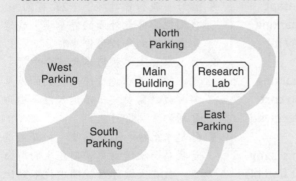
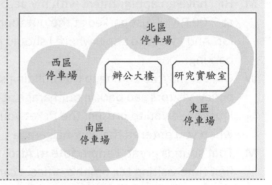

• construction 建造　inconvenient 不方便的　on foot 步行　in addition 此外
the board of directors 董事會

65 [NEW]

Look at the graphic. Which parking area will be closed? 看一下圖表，哪一區的停車場即將關閉？

(A) North
(B) East
(C) South
(D) West

(A) 北
(B) 東
(C) 南
(D) 西

男子的第一句台詞說：「the hospital will be closing the parking lot in front of our research lab for construction next month.」提及實驗室前面的停車區域，故可推測正確答案為 (B)。

66

What is the woman concerned about? 這位女士擔心什麼事？

(A) Encountering road construction
(B) Paying parking fees
(C) Walking a long distance
(D) Facing heavy traffic

(A) 碰到道路工程
(B) 付停車費
(C) 走一段遠路
(D) 面臨交通阻塞

女子的第三句台詞說：「That's quite far from our office. It is very inconvenient for everyone to get to the office on foot.」，表示西區停車場距離實驗室太遠，不便徒步前往，故正確答案為 (C)。

 67 --

What does the man say the board will do?
(A) Change the company's policy
(B) Offer complimentary shuttles
(C) Provide a bonus
(D) Reimburse employees

這位男士說董事會將做什麼事？
(A) 改變公司規定
(B) 提供免費接駁車
(C) 提供額外的津貼
(D) 讓員工報帳

男子的第三句話說：「The board of directors decided to provide free shuttle buses from the West Parking lot to our building.」告知董事會已經決定提供免費的接駁巴士。對話中使用的「free」即選項 (B) 中的「complimentary」，故正確答案為 (B)。

68-70 conversation and building directory 　　68–70 對話及樓層說明

M Hi, I have an appointment with my accountant at 2:00 P.M. I just parked at the outdoor parking lot. And I want to know where I should pay for parking.	男 妳好，我和會計師下午2點有約。我剛把車停在外面的停車場。我想知道應該到哪裡付停車費。
W Oh, actually, according to this building's parking policy, visitors can park in our garage at no cost. I just need you to present the ticket you received when you entered the parking garage.	女 喔，事實上，根據本大樓停車規定，訪客可以免費使用我們的停車場。我只需要您出示進入停車場時拿到的票券即可。
M That sounds great; I appreciate it. Also, this is my first time visiting Mr. Smith's office. I can't find his name on the building directory. Could you tell me where his office is?	男 聽起來很棒，真是感謝。另外，這是我第一次造訪史密斯先生的辦公室。我在大樓樓層說明中找不到他的名字。妳可以告訴我他的辦公室在哪嗎？
W Mr. Smith just moved in three days ago, and we haven't had time to change the directory yet. His office is on the third floor.	女 史密斯先生三天前才搬進來。我們還沒有時間更換樓層說明。他的辦公室在三樓。

Miracle Office Complex Directory

Office	Location
Kim's Stationery	1F
P&T Restaurant	2F
Miracle Fitness Center	3F
Jane's Clinic	4F

奇蹟辦公大樓樓層說明

公司行號	樓層
金文具行	1樓
P&T餐廳	2樓
奇蹟健身中心	3樓
珍診所	4樓

• **appointment**（尤指正式的）約會　**outdoor** 外面的　**policy** 規定　**garage** 停車場　**present** 出示　**building directory** 大樓樓層說明

68 --

What is the purpose of the man's visit?
(A) He is meeting with an accountant.
(B) He has to pay for parking.
(C) He will work out.
(D) He is eating some food.

這位男士造訪的目的是什麼？
(A) 他要與會計師見面。
(B) 他必須付停車費。
(C) 他將要健身。
(D) 他正在吃東西。

從男子的第一句台詞「I have an appointment with my accountant at 2:00 P.M.」可知，男子是來拜訪會計師的，故正確答案為 (A)。

69 --

What does the woman say about the parking policy?
(A) It has a time restriction.
(B) It isn't available for residents.
(C) It is for visitors only.
(D) It is complimentary for visitors.

這位女士提到什麼與停車規定有關的事？
(A) 有時間限制。
(B) 住戶無法使用。
(C) 只提供給訪客使用。
(D) 訪客可免費使用。

女子的第一句台詞說：「Oh, actually, according to this building's parking policy, visitors can park in our garage at no cost.」告知對方訪客可以免費停車，故正確答案為 (D)。

70 NEW --

Look at the graphic. Which office name has to be updated on the building directory?
(A) Kim's Stationery
(B) P&T Restaurant
(C) Miracle Fitness Center
(D) Jane's Clinic

看一下圖表，大樓樓層說明中哪間公司名稱必須被更新？
(A) 金文具行
(B) P&T餐廳
(C) 奇蹟健身中心
(D) 珍診所

女子的最後一句台詞說：「Mr. Smith just moved in three days ago, and we haven't had time to change the directory yet. His office is on the third floor.」，表示因為史密斯先生才剛搬來，他們還來不及修改樓層說明，並告訴對方史密斯先生的辦公室位在三樓。故可推測樓層說明中，三樓的「Miracle Fitness Center」應該進行修改，故正確答案為 (C)。

71-73 message

71–73 留言

Hi, this is Janet Wilson. I bought a washing machine at your store yesterday. My husband's hooked it up, but it's just not working properly. It just keeps beeping and displaying some sort of error code. Could you send someone over right away to look at it? I don't want to have to bring it back to the store, and the warranty says that home service is included for the first year. You can reach me at 555-1254. Thanks very much.	嗨,我是珍娜·威爾森。我昨天在你們店裡買了一台洗衣機。是我先生接的線,但它就是無法順利運轉。它不斷地發出嗶聲,還顯示某種錯誤代碼。你可以馬上派人來查看嗎?我不想送回店裡,而且保證書上說第一年是含到府服務的。你可以撥打555-1254與我聯絡。非常感謝你。

• **hook up . . .** 將……接線   **work properly** 順利運轉   **send . . . over** 派(某人)前往   **warranty** 保證書

71 --

Why is the woman calling?
(A) To buy an appliance
(B) To cancel a delivery
(C) To report a problem
(D) To order food

這位女士為什麼打這通電話?
(A) 要購買家電
(B) 要取消配送
(C) 要回報問題
(D) 要訂購食物

第三句留言説:「My husband's hooked it up, but it's just not working properly. It just keeps beeping . . .」,表示洗衣機無法正常使用。由此可知,女子是為了回報問題而撥打電話,故正確答案為 (C)。

72 --

What product is the woman discussing?
(A) An exercise bike
(B) A microwave oven
(C) A stereo system
(D) A washing machine

這位女士在談論何種產品?
(A) 健身腳踏車
(B) 微波爐
(C) 音響系統
(D) 洗衣機

女子開頭便説:「I bought a washing machine at your store yesterday.」告知洗衣機無法正常啟動,故正確答案為 (D)。

73 --

What does the speaker want the store to do?
(A) Send spare parts
(B) Send a service person
(C) Order a part
(D) Deliver a replacement

說話者要店家做什麼?
(A) 寄送備用零件
(B) 派遣服務人員
(C) 訂購零件
(D) 配送替換商品

從「Could you send someone over right away to look at it?」中可看出,女子要求店家派遣服務人員來進行檢查,故正確答案為 (B)。

74-76 announcement

74–76 宣告

Good morning, everyone. Thanks so much for coming to this residents' meeting. My name is Angela Tiller, and I am the new director of the Shady Acres retirement home. As I am sure you have heard by now, Dan Green, the previous director, has left Shady Acres for personal reasons. I understand that he was very popular with all the residents here, and I'll do my best to fill his shoes. At this point, I have no intention of changing any of the policies or programs that Dan set up; however, I may make some modifications as time goes on. In the meantime, I want you to know that my door is always open for questions or to hear your concerns.

大家早，非常感謝大家來參加住戶大會。我是安琪拉‧提勒，是雪帝艾可斯安養院新來的主任。我相信大家已經聽說了，前主任丹‧格林已經因為個人因素離開雪帝艾可斯。我知道他深受這裡所有住戶的歡迎，我也會竭盡全力頂替他的位置。目前，我無意更動丹所設立的各種規定或計畫；但隨著時間推移，我可能會做些調整。在此同時，我想讓大家知道我的辦公室門永遠是敞開的，歡迎各位提出問題或聆聽您們的疑慮。

- retirement home 安養院　**previous** 先前的　**fill one's shoes** 接替（某人）的工作　**intention** 意圖　**modification** 調整；修改　**in the meantime** 於此同時　**as time goes on** 隨著時間推移

08

74

What is the purpose of the meeting?
(A) To announce new management
(B) To announce a new building project
(C) To explain a change in policies
(D) To announce the closure of the facility

這個會議的目的是什麼？
(A) 宣布新管理人員
(B) 宣布新建設計畫
(C) 說明政策上的變動
(D) 宣布場地的關閉

女子開頭提到「My name is Angela Tiller, and I am the new director of the Shady Acres retirement home.」，表明自己是安養院的新主任，並由下文可知，這場會議的目的是宣布新管理人員上任。題目中使用的「new director」即選項 (A) 中的「new management」，故正確答案為 (A)。

75

What type of businesses does Angela Tiller work for?
(A) A building supply company
(B) A hospital
(C) A retirement home
(D) A delivery service

安琪拉‧提勒在哪個行業工作？
(A) 建築材料公司
(B) 醫院
(C) 安養院
(D) 貨運服務

女子開頭提到「I am the new director of the Shady Acres retirement home.」，可知她在安養院工作，故正確答案為 (C)。

76 --

Why did Ms. Tiller's predecessor leave?
(A) He was transferred.
(B) He went into retirement.
(C) He had a personal matter.
(D) He was dismissed.

提勒女士的前任者為什麼離開？
(A) 他被轉調。
(B) 他退休了。
(C) 他有個人因素。
(D) 他被解僱。

中間部分提到「Dan Green, the previous director, has left Shady Acres for personal reasons.」，表示前任者因為個人因素而離職。題目使用的「personal reasons」即選項 (C) 中的「personal matter」，故正確答案為 (C)。

77-79 talk   ## 77-79 談話

Hi, everyone, and welcome to our yearly sales review meeting. As I'm sure you're all aware, this year's results have been somewhat mixed. We have significantly expanded our overseas sales; however, domestic sales have stagnated and in some areas actually declined. Overall sales levels have remained almost the same as last year's, so we definitely did not hit our growth targets for the year. Over the next month, we are going to have a series of meetings to hammer out a plan to improve our position over the next year.	大家好，歡迎參加本公司年度業務審查會議。我相信大家都知道，今年的成果有點繁雜。我們大幅地拓展了海外業務，但國內的銷售量卻沉滯不前，實際上，在某些地區還是衰退的。總體業績幾乎與去年持平，我們顯然並未達到年度的成長目標。在下個月內，我們將舉行一連串會議以商研出一個計畫來改善明年的狀況。

• **somewhat** 有點 **significantly** 大幅地 **overseas** 海外的 **domestic** 國內的 **decline** 衰退
  stagnate 停滯 **overall** 總體的 **a series of** 一連串的 **hammer out**（討論後）達成（協定或解決方法）

77 --

What is the purpose of the talk?
(A) To order new equipment
(B) To announce layoffs
(C) To discuss the sales results
(D) To discuss tax returns

這段談話的目的是什麼？
(A) 訂購新設備
(B) 宣布解僱
(C) 討論業績成效
(D) 討論退稅

一開始提到「Hi, everyone, and welcome to our yearly sales review meeting.」，可得知此為業務審查會議，並可從後段的「Overall sales levels have remained almost the same as last year's」知道業績成效與去年持平。由此可知，此段談話與業績有關，故正確答案為 (C)。

78

According to the speaker, what positive results were there?

(A) Overseas sales increased.
(B) Domestic sales have hit a target.
(C) Expenses were reduced.
(D) The sales force was increased.

根據說話者表示，有什麼好成果？

(A) 海外銷售量增加。
(B) 國內業績達標。
(C) 支出減少了。
(D) 銷售人員增加。

中間提及「We have significantly expanded our overseas sales . . .」，表示海外的銷售量有所增加，故正確答案為 (A)。

79

What course of action does the speaker announce?

(A) Restrictions on corporate travel
(B) Taking over another company
(C) Hiring additional employees
(D) A series of planning meetings

說話者宣布了什麼行動方針？

(A) 限制商務旅行
(B) 接管另一家公司
(C) 僱用更多員工
(D) 一連串的策畫會議

談話最後提到「Over the next month, we are going to have a series of meetings to hammer out a plan to improve our position over the next year.」，由此可知，下個月內公司將舉行會議，故正確答案為 (D)。

80-82 telephone message

80–82 電話留言

Hello, Mr. Wilson. This is Dave calling from Ace Couriers. We've received a package with your name and phone number on it, but there appears to be a problem with the address. Our driver stopped at the address we have this afternoon, but the woman there said that she did not know you. Could you please give me a call as soon as possible at 555-7142 and confirm your address for us? I'm sure you're anxious to have your package. Thanks.

威爾森先生，您好。我是王牌快遞的戴夫。我們收到了一份上面有您大名與電話號碼的包裹，但地址好像有點問題。本公司的司機今天下午到包裹上的地址，但那裡的女士說她並不認識您。可以麻煩您盡快來電555-7142給我，並幫我們確認您的地址嗎？我相信您也很焦急想拿到包裹。感恩。

• confirm 確認　be anxious to . . . 焦急地想……　shipping 運輸

80

What is the speaker calling about?

(A) Car rental
(B) Emergency arrangements
(C) Airline tickets
(D) A package delivery

說話者打電話告知何事？

(A) 租車
(B) 緊急情況的處理
(C) 航空公司的機票
(D) 包裹的運送

開頭部分提到「We've received a package with your name and phone number on it, but there appears to be a problem with the address.」，表示收到地址有誤的包裹，故正確答案為 (D)。

81

What information does the speaker require?
(A) A shipping address
(B) A telephone number
(C) A family member's name
(D) A list of contents

說話者要求什麼資料？
(A) 運送地址
(B) 電話號碼
(C) 家庭成員姓名
(D) 目錄

留言最後提到「Could you please give me a call as soon as possible at 555-7142 and confirm your address for us?」是要求對方確認地址，故正確答案為 (A)。

82

How does the speaker request that Mr. Wilson contact him?
(A) By online chat
(B) By mail
(C) By telephone
(D) By e-mail

說話者要求威爾森先生如何跟他聯絡？
(A) 線上聊天
(B) 郵件
(C) 電話
(D) 電子郵件

留言最後部分提到「Could you please give me a call as soon as possible . . .」，表示請對方以電話確認地址。題目使用的「give me a call」即選項 (C) 中的「by telephone」，故正確答案為 (C)。

83-85 talk　　　　　　　　　　　　　**83–85 談話**

Good afternoon, and thanks for tuning in. We have a fascinating lineup for you today. My first guest will be Dr. Sandra Beard. Dr. Beard has just returned from Mozambique, where she was coordinating a program that gives young doctors experience in hospitals in developing nations in Africa. This program both benefits the hospitals and provides the doctors with a different perspective. Dr. Beard will tell us about her program, and then we're going to open up the phone lines and invite any questions from our listeners.	午安，感謝您的收聽。我們今天將為您提供非常棒的陣容。第一位來賓是珊卓·比爾德博士。比爾德博士剛自莫三比克返國。她在那裡統籌了一項計畫，提供年輕醫師在非洲開發中國家醫院服務的經驗。這項計畫既有益於醫院，也提供了醫生們不同的眼界。比爾德博士將為我們說明她的計畫，然後我們會開放電話專線，歡迎聽眾提問。

• tune in 收聽節目　fascinating 很棒的　lineup 陣容　coordinate 統籌　developing nation 開發中國家
perspective 看法　construction site 工地　geology 地質學　environmental science 環境科學

83

Where would this talk most likely be heard?
(A) On the radio
(B) In a medical seminar
(C) At a construction site
(D) In a hospital

這段談話最有可能在哪裡聽到？
(A) 收音機上
(B) 醫學研討會
(C) 營造工地
(D) 醫院

開頭部份的「thanks for tuning in」，表示感謝聽眾收聽，故可推測正確答案為 (A)。

84

What field does Sandra Beard work in?
(A) Geology
(B) Chemistry
(C) Environmental science
(D) Medicine

珊卓‧比爾德在哪個領域服務？
(A) 地質學
(B) 化學
(C) 環境科學
(D) 醫學

談話中間提及「Dr. Beard has just returned from Mozambique, where she was coordinating a program that gives young doctors experience in hospitals in developing nations in Africa.」，表示珊卓‧比爾德博士剛從莫三比克回來，並且在那裡統籌醫療相關的計畫。由此可知，博士是從事醫學領域工作的人，故正確答案為 (D)。

85

What did Sandra Beard do recently?
(A) Started a company
(B) Returned from Africa
(C) Wrote a book
(D) Invented a product

珊卓‧比爾德最近做了什麼事？
(A) 設立公司
(B) 從非洲返國
(C) 寫書
(D) 發明一項產品

中間部分提到「Dr. Beard has just returned from Mozambique, where she was coordinating a program that gives young doctors experience in hospitals in developing nations in Africa.」，表示珊卓‧比爾德剛從位於非洲的莫三比克返國，故正確答案為 (B)。

86-88 telephone message

86–88 電話留言

Hello, Mr. Harrison. This is Andrea Phelps, the senior editor at the *Herald Tribune*. I've just been going over your writing samples and reviewing your résumé and cover letter. Your experience is quite impressive, and the writing work you've submitted is excellent as well. While we don't have any full-time staff writer positions available at this time, I think I can offer you some freelance assignments. If you're interested, I'd like you to come in for an interview and to discuss some of our upcoming projects. Please give me a call at 555-1244 to let me know when you can come in. If I don't pick up, dial three to talk to my secretary; she knows my schedule.

哈里森先生，您好。我是《先鋒論壇報》的資深編輯安德莉亞‧費爾普斯。我剛看過您的寫作樣稿，也審閱了您的履歷與求職函。您的經歷相當地令人矚目，您所呈交的文字作品也很出色。雖然我們目前沒有全職的寫作職缺，但我想我可以提供您一些兼職工作。如果您有興趣的話，我希望您能前來面談並討論本公司即將進行的一些計畫。請來電555-1244告知您何時能過來。若我未接電話，請撥3找我的秘書，她知道我的行程。

• **senior editor** 資深編輯 **go over** 察看 **résumé** 履歷 **cover letter** 求職函 **impressive** 令人矚目的
submit 提交 **freelance** 兼職的 **assignment** 工作 **upcoming** 即將進行的
pick up (the phone) 接聽（電話）

ACTUAL TEST 2

PART 4

中譯＋解析

08

Who is Mr. Harrison?
(A) A professional athlete
(B) A journalist
(C) A magazine editor
(D) A photographer

哈里森先生是誰？
(A) 職業運動員
(B) 記者
(C) 雜誌編輯
(D) 攝影師

從內容可知哈里森先生投寄了履歷與求職函給《先鋒論壇報》，故可推測他最可能是名記者，正確答案為 (B)。

87

What does the caller want to discuss with Mr. Harrison?
(A) Political issues
(B) Contract amendments
(C) Current affairs
(D) Writing assignments

來電者想和哈里森先生討論什麼事？
(A) 政治議題
(B) 合約修訂
(C) 時事
(D) 寫作工作

中間部分提到「If you're interested, I'd like you to come in for an interview and to discuss some of our upcoming projects.」，說話者對哈里森先生表示若有興趣可以來進行面試，並談談即將開始的計畫。前面已經提到目前沒有正職的寫作職缺，由此可知，這句話應和寫作工作有關，故正確答案為 (D)。

What should Mr. Harrison do if Ms. Phelps does not answer the phone?
(A) Press 3
(B) Leave a message
(C) Call back later
(D) Send a letter

如果費爾普斯女士沒有接電話，哈里森先生應該怎麼做？
(A) 按3
(B) 留言
(C) 稍後再回撥
(D) 寄信

留言最後說「If I don't pick up, dial three to talk to my secretary; she knows my schedule.」是費爾普斯女士告知哈里森先生，若自己沒有接到電話，可以轉撥 3 號分機。題目中使用的「dial 3」即選項 (A) 中的「press 3」，故正確答案為 (A)。

89-91 introduction

89–91 介紹

Hello, everyone. As you all know, we are here tonight to honor our colleague and friend Abdel Pratha on the occasion of his retirement after 25 years of devoted service to our company. Mr. Pratha was one of the first employees of this company when we were just starting out. He stuck with us through thick and thin and is now ready for a well-earned rest. Those of you who haven't been here that long and only know

大家好。正如各位所知，今晚我們藉著阿比多・帕爾達在公司服務屆滿25年的退休機會，齊聚在這裡表揚我們這位同事兼好友。帕爾達先生是公司剛成立時的首批員工之一。不管在任何狀況下，他始終與公司同甘共苦，而現在他已經準備好要好好休息一下了。進本公司沒那麼久，只知道帕爾

Mr. Pratha as the vice-president of Marketing might be surprised to know that he actually started out doing clerical work for the company all those years ago. **(91)Here is Mr. Pratha to say a few words.**

達先生是行銷部副總的各位可能會很驚訝發現，在許多年前，他其實一開始做的是公司的文書工作。**(91)現在就請帕爾達先生來說幾句話。**

- honor 表揚　colleague 同事　on the occasion of ... 藉著……的機會
  stick with ... through thick and thin 與……同甘共苦　well-earned 應得的　vice-president 副總
  clerical work 文書工作　executive 高階主管　reliable 可靠的

ACTUAL TEST 2　PART 4　中譯＋解析　08

89

Who is Mr. Pratha?
(A) The CEO of the company
(B) A shipping manager
(C) A clerical worker
(D) One of the executives of the company

帕爾達先生是誰？
(A) 公司執行長
(B) 物流經理
(C) 文書事務員
(D) 公司高階主管之一

段落中間部分說「Mr. Pratha as the vice-president of Marketing」，明確指出帕爾達先生為行銷部副總。題目中使用的「vice-president」屬於選項 (D) 中的「executive」，故正確答案為 (D)。

90

What does the speaker say about Mr. Pratha?
(A) He is being offered a promotion.
(B) He was with the company for 25 years.
(C) He recently joined the company.
(D) He has not been very reliable.

說話者提到什麼與帕爾達先生有關的事？
(A) 他被升職了。
(B) 他在公司已經25年了。
(C) 他最近才進公司。
(D) 他一向不太可靠。

段落開頭提到「Abdel Pratha on the occasion of his retirement after 25 years of devoted service to our company.」，表示帕爾達先生將會在工作二十五年後退休，故正確答案為 (B)。

91 [NEW]

What does the man mean when he says, "Here is Mr. Pratha to say a few words"?
(A) Mr. Pratha will install a new word processor software.
(B) Mr. Pratha will type on a keyboard.
(C) Mr. Pratha will make a speech at the ceremony.
(D) Mr. Pratha will talk to guests one-on-one.

當這位男士說：「現在就請帕爾達先生來說幾句話」，是什麼意思？
(A) 帕爾達先生將安裝新的文字處理軟體。
(B) 帕爾達先生將在鍵盤上打字。
(C) 帕爾達先生將在典禮上發表演說。
(D) 帕爾達先生將一一和賓客談話。

從開頭可知道這段內容應為公開談話，段落中間著重介紹帕爾達先生，故可推測此句應是想請帕爾達先生在典禮上致詞。題目中使用的「say a few words」即選項 (C) 中的「make a speech」，故正確答案為 (C)。

Attention, everyone. This is Dan Wilson, the building safety officer, with an important announcement. This afternoon at 3:00 we will have a fire drill. When the fire alarm goes off, please proceed out of the building in an orderly fashion and congregate out in front of the building. Please do not use the lifts. Once we are in front of the building, **(94) I will take attendance** and then we will all be able to return back to our workstations. Thanks very much.	所有人注意，我是大樓安全管理員丹·威爾森，我有重要事項宣布。今天下午3點，我們將進行消防演習。當火災警鈴響起時，請依序離開大樓，並在大樓前集合。請勿使用電梯。一旦我們到了大樓外面，**(94)我會點名**，然後大家就可以回到工作崗位上了。非常感謝大家。

• **safety officer** 安全管理員　**fire drill** 消防演習　**go off**（鈴聲）響起　**proceed out** 開始離開　**orderly** 有秩序地　**congregate** 集合　**lift** 電梯　**workstation** 工作崗位

92 --

Who most likely is the speaker?
(A) A human resources director
(B) A computer programmer
(C) A safety worker
(D) A salesperson

說話者最有可能是誰？
(A) 人力資源部主管
(B) 電腦程式設計師
(C) 保安人員
(D) 銷售人員

段落開頭的「This is Dan Wilson, the building safety officer, with an important announcement.」中，說話者直接自我介紹為大樓安全管理員。題目中使用的「safety officer」即選項中的「safety worker」，故正確答案為 (C)。

93 --

What is the announcement about?
(A) A problem with the plumbing
(B) A fire drill
(C) The elevators being serviced
(D) A staff meeting

這個宣告與什麼有關？
(A) 管線問題
(B) 消防演習
(C) 正在維修的電梯
(D) 員工會議

段落中間提及「This afternoon at 3:00 we will have a fire drill.」，表示即將舉辦消防訓練，故正確答案為 (B)。

94 (NEW) --

What does the man mean when he says, "I will take attendance"?
(A) The activity is mandatory.
(B) The activity was postponed.
(C) The activity was canceled.
(D) The activity will go smoothly.

當這位男士說：「我會點名」，是什麼意思？
(A) 這個活動是強制性的。
(B) 這個活動被延期了。
(C) 這個活動被取消了。
(D) 這個活動將順利進行。

從題幹引述的句意可以推測，所有人都需要參加訓練，故正確答案為 (A)。

Good afternoon, folks. I'd like to start off our monthly sales meeting by looking at our progress in attracting new customers here at Lucky Seven Appliances. As you can see, July was our most successful month. We can probably attribute this to the launch of the cutting-edge washing machine, Wind Wind, which came out that month. You will also see that the second-highest increase in new customers occurred during our special promotional event. This sale was a smash hit. We're now planning to hire a Web designer to make our Web site be more user-friendly for our patrons. I'm sure everything will go well.

大家午安。業務月會一開始，我想來檢視本公司「幸運七家電」招攬新顧客的進展。正如大家看到的，七月是我們營利最豐碩的月份。我們或許可以將其歸功於該月推出的尖端洗衣機——碩風的上市。各位也可以看到，新客戶增加的第二高峰就在我們特別促銷活動期間。這項銷售活動非常地成功。現在我們正計劃聘請一位網頁設計師來讓我們的網站更方便老客戶使用。我相信一切都會很順利的。

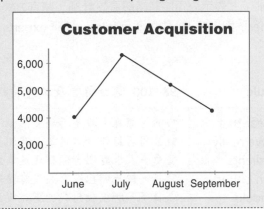

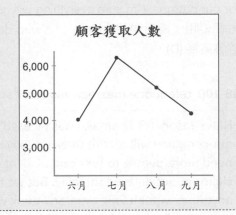

- folks 各位　start off 開始　attribute A to B 將 A 歸功於 B　cutting-edge 尖端的
  promotional event 促銷活動　smash hit 巨大的成功　user-friendly 易於使用的　patron 老客戶

95 --

Where most likely does the speaker work?

(A) At an insurance company

(B) At a home appliance company

(C) At a supermarket

(D) At a design company

說話者最有可能在哪裡工作？

(A) 保險公司

(B) 家用電器公司

(C) 超市

(D) 設計公司

談話開頭便提及「I'd like to start off our monthly sales meeting by looking at our progress in attracting new customers here at Lucky Seven Appliances.」，並從之後內容可知，說話者的公司推出了洗衣機產品，故可推測正確答案為 (B)。

96 **NEW** --

Look at the graphic. When was the promotional event held?

(A) In June

(B) In July

(C) In August

(D) In September

看一下圖表，這個促銷活動是在何時舉行？

(A) 六月

(B) 七月

(C) 八月

(D) 九月

談話中間部分説「You will also see that the second-highest increase in new customers occurred during our special promotional event.」，提到新顧客增幅第二高的地方，對照圖表可得知正確答案為 (C)。

 97

According to the speaker, what is the company going to do to improve their Web site?
(A) Hold an emergency meeting
(B) Launch a new product
(C) Conduct a promotional event
(D) Employ some experts

根據說話者表示，公司要做什麼來改善網站？
(A) 舉辦緊急會議
(B) 推出新產品
(C) 進行促銷活動
(D) 僱用一些專家

談話最後説「We're now planning to hire a Web designer to make our Web site be more user-friendly for our patrons. I'm sure everything will go well.」，表示公司將聘請網頁設計師，將官方網站改得更方便使用。題目中的「hire」與「web designer」即選項 (D) 中的「employ」與「experts」，故正確答案為 (D)。

98-100 telephone message and work schedule　　**98–100 電話留言及工作時程表**

Hello, Jason. It's Thomas. I was pleased to hear that our company will recruit three employees. We really need more people to take care of all of our clients' claims about delayed shipping. But we haven't hired anyone new for a long time. So I think we should meet to talk about the application process in detail. I'm looking at my work schedule at the moment, and I actually have some free time this Thursday. Since we'll both be at the staff meeting that morning, why don't we meet right after that meeting, which will probably take about an hour? I have time between that meeting and a lunch appointment with my client at 1:00. Please, let me know whether this is fine with you. Thanks!

哈囉，傑森。我是湯瑪士。很高興聽說公司將招聘三名員工。我們真的需要更多人來處理有關配送延誤方面的客訴。但我們已經好久沒有聘用新進人員了。所以我想我們應該碰面詳細討論一下應徵流程。我正在看我的工作時程表，事實上，這個星期四我有空。既然我們兩個都會參加當天早上的員工會議，我們何不就在會後碰面呢？員工會議大約只需要一個小時吧。我在會議與1點和客戶的午餐之約間有空檔。麻煩告訴我這樣對你來說是否可行。感謝！

Thursday Schedule

9:00	
10:00	**Staff meeting**
11:00	
12:00	
13:00	**Lunch with a client**
14:00	
15:00	**Conference call**
16:00	

週四時程表

9:00	
10:00	員工會議
11:00	
12:00	
13:00	與客戶午餐
14:00	
15:00	電話會議
16:00	

• **be pleased to V** 很高興（做某事）　　**recruit** 招聘　　**take care of** 處理　　**shipping** 運送
application process 應徵流程　　**in detail** 詳細地　　**at the moment** 此刻

98 --

Where most likely does the speaker work?
(A) At a shipping company
(B) At an accounting firm
(C) At an event planning agency
(D) At a law firm

說話者最有可能在哪裡工作？
(A) 貨運公司
(B) 會計事務所
(C) 活動策畫公司
(D) 律師事務所

留言開頭便說「We really need more people to take care of all of our clients' claims about delayed shipping.」，表示需要更多人手幫忙處理運送延遲造成的客訴。由此可知，說話者最可能在貨運公司工作，故正確答案為 (A)。

99 --

What would the speaker like to discuss with the listener?
(A) A recruiting process
(B) A staff layoff
(C) A project budget
(D) A client claim

說話者想和聽者討論什麼事？
(A) 招募程序
(B) 解僱員工
(C) 專案預算
(D) 客戶申訴

留言中間部份說「So I think we should meet to talk about the application process in detail.」，表示想見面討論應徵流程。題目中使用的「application」即選項 (A) 中的「recruiting process」，故正確答案為 (A)。

100 NEW --

Look at the graphic. What time does the speaker want to meet?
(A) At 9:00
(B) At 11:00
(C) At 12:00
(D) At 14:00

看一下圖表，說話者想於何時碰面？
(A) 9:00
(B) 11:00
(C) 12:00
(D) 14:00

留言最後說「why don't we meet right after that meeting, which will probably take about an hour? I have time between that meeting and a lunch appointment with my client at 1:00.」，表示說話者有空的時間應在 1 點之前，且在某會議後。1 點前進行的會議只有員工會議，且員工要進行一個小說多，故說話者應提議在 11 點見面，正確答案為 (B)。

ACTUAL TEST
3

1 ---

(A) The man is walking to the right.
(B) The clock is hanging on the wall.
(C) The men are working on the street.
(D) The man is looking at the bulletin board.

(A) 這位男士正往右走。
(B) 時鐘正掛在牆上。
(C) 男人們正在馬路上工作。
(D) 這位男士正看著公布欄。

• **bulletin board** 公布欄

男子正朝著照片的右方走去，且上方掛著圓形的時鐘。**(B)** 時鐘並非掛在牆上。**(C)** 此為利用與正確選項提及之「walking」發音類似的「working」誘導。**(D)** 男子並未看著告示板，所以非正確答案。正確答案為 **(A)**。

2 ---

(A) The man is walking up the stairs.
(B) The man is holding a newspaper.
(C) The windows are being opened.
(D) The man is putting on a hat.

(A) 這位男士正走上樓梯。
(B) 這位男士正拿著一份報紙。
(C) 窗戶正被打開。
(D) 這位男士正戴上帽子。

照片中的男子站在階梯上，手上拿著報紙。**(A)** 男子站在階梯上，但是並未表現出往上走的行動。**(C)** 照片中的窗戶並未打開。**(D)** 男子已是戴著帽子的狀態（wear），並未表現出正在戴帽子（putting on）的動作。正確答案為 **(B)**。

3 ---

(A) The boat is being docked.
(B) The people are walking away from each other.
(C) The women are swimming in the ocean.
(D) The man is carrying a plastic bag.

(A) 這艘船正在靠岸。
(B) 人們正走離彼此。
(C) 女士們正在海裡游泳。
(D) 這位男士正提著一個塑膠袋。

• **dock** 〔動詞〕（使）靠岸

照片中有名男子手上拿著塑膠袋，後方跟著兩名女子，三人在海邊。**(A)** 船並未處於靠岸中的狀態。**(B)** 照片中人們都往相同方向走去，所以非正確答案。**(C)** 照片中的女人們並未在海中游泳。正確答案為 **(D)**。

4

(A) The people are looking at each other.
(B) The women are clapping their hands.
(C) One of the women is smiling.
(D) The people are having a serious conversation

(A) 人們正互相對望。
(B) 女士們正在拍手。
(C) 其中一位女士正在微笑。
(D) 人們正在嚴肅地談話。

照片中有三名女子，坐在最右邊的女子臉上露出微笑。(A) 照片中的人物並沒有彼此對看。(B) 只有一名女子拍手。(D) 無法確定照片中人物談論的內容是否嚴肅。正確答案為 (C)。

5

(A) The cars are parked along the street.
(B) The building is being renovated.
(C) The windows are all open.
(D) The men are crossing the street.

(A) 車輛沿著街道停放。
(B) 大樓正在整修中。
(C) 窗戶全都開著。
(D) 男人們正在穿越馬路。

• **renovate** 整修

照片有高樓建築，且汽車排成一列停在路邊。(B) 大樓並未進行整修工程。(C) 所有的窗戶都未開啟。(D) 只有一名男子正在過馬路。正確答案為 (A)。

🎧 09

6

(A) There are no people in the restaurant.
(B) There are five tables outside.
(C) There is art being hung on the columns.
(D) There are several trees on the terrace.

(A) 餐廳裡空無一人。
(B) 外面有五張桌子。
(C) 柱子上正被掛上藝術品。
(D) 露台上有幾棵樹。

照片中有無人使用的數組桌椅。(B) 照片中並未出現五張桌子。(C) 照片中並沒有人，故藝術品不會「正被掛」上某處。(D) 照片中僅出現一棵樹。正確答案為 (A)。

7

Who is working out of the Miami office today?
(A) I am working out of Boston.
(B) He is always working.
(C) I think Ms. Gonzales is.

今天邁阿密分處裡有誰外出洽公？
(A) 我要離開波士頓去工作。
(B) 他總是在工作。
(C) 我想是岡薩雷斯女士。

• **work out of . . .** 離開……洽公

(A) 內容提及的地點與題目不同，故非正確答案。(B) 題目詢問外出洽公的人，回答「他總是在工作」並不適當。(C) 提及確切人物，為適當回覆，故正確答案為 (C)。

8

What do you say to a game of poker after dinner?
(A) Yes, I will be eating dinner.
(B) I'm afraid I'll be out of town.
(C) I enjoyed the game very much.

晚餐後來玩撲克牌怎麼樣？
(A) 是的，我將在吃晚餐。
(B) 我恐怕會去外地一趟。
(C) 我非常喜歡那場比賽。

• **be out of town** 到外地

(A) 此為利用與題目相同之單字「dinner」誤導。(B)「What do you say/think」為詢問意見的疑問句，此回覆說明具體理由拒絕提議，故為適當答案。(C) 此為利用與題目相同之單字「game」誤導。正確答案為 (B)。

9

Do you have time to help me this morning?
(A) If there's no other work to do.
(B) Yes, I helped him yesterday.
(C) It is ten o'clock.

你今天早上有空可以幫我嗎？
(A) 如果沒有其他工作要做的話。
(B) 是的，我昨天幫了他。
(C) 是十點鐘。

• **register** 註冊　**in person** 親自

(A)「Do/Does」問句通常以 Yes/No 回答，但是也有省略「Yes/No」部分的時候。選項 (A) 即以「if there is . . .」（在……情況下）的條件句回答，表示「如果沒有其他事情，就會幫忙」，此為適當回答。(B) 時態與題目不符合。(C) 回答與問題不相關。正確答案為 (A)。

10

Did you register online or in person at the school?
(A) I did it on the school's Web site.
(B) I registered last night.
(C) Because the school is far from my house.

你是線上註冊還是親自到學校註冊？
(A) 我在學校的網站上註冊。
(B) 我昨天晚上註冊了。
(C) 因為學校離我家太遠了。

(A) 此題為選擇疑問句，題目詢問註冊的方式，故回答「在學校的網站上註冊」最為合適。(B) 未回答問題。(C) 未回答問題。正確答案為 (A)。

11

When was the last time you went to Dallas?
(A) A little over 400 kilometers.
(B) About 4 months ago.
(C) Every year for the past ten years.

你上次去達拉斯是什麼時候？
(A) 略超過400公里。
(B) 大約4個月前。
(C) 過去十年裡的每一年。

(A) 回答與問題不相關。(B) 題目以「When」詢問具體的時間點，故此為適當回答。(C) 此為頻率、次數相關的回答，所以非正確答案。正確答案為 (B)。

12

Did you decide which television you want to buy?
(A) I am watching television with my friend.
(B) No, it is $750.
(C) The one with the largest screen.

你決定要買哪一台電視機了嗎？
(A) 我正和朋友一起看電視。
(B) 不是，是750元。
(C) 螢幕最大的那一台。

🎧 10

(A) 此為使用與題目相同字彙的「television」誤導。(B) 回答與問題不相關。(C) 題目為以「Which」詢問的選擇疑問句，答案常以「the one（那個）」句型出現。故正確答案為 (C)。

13

Would you please give this letter to Mr. Graham?
(A) I am writing the letter now.
(B) No problem.
(C) Yes, please hold.

可以請你將這封信轉交給葛拉翰先生嗎？
(A) 我現在正在寫信。
(B) 沒問題。
(C) 好的，請稍候。

(A) 此為利用題目出現的「letter」誘導。(B) 題目以「Would you . . .」開頭，有勸誘、拜託的作用，選項 (B) 以「no problem」接受請求，是最合適的回答。(C) 沒有回答問題。正確答案為 (B)。

14

I heard we hired a new secretary.
(A) Yes, you heard right.
(B) No, my secretary is away on leave.
(C) I am on my way.

聽說我們聘了一位新秘書。
(A) 是的，沒錯。
(B) 不，我的秘書正在休假中。
(C) 我正在路上。

• **be away on leave** 休假

(A) 題目為表示「聽說聘用了新秘書」的陳述句，選項 (A) 給予肯定答覆，故為適當回答。(B) 與題目不相關。(C) 與題目不相關。正確答案為 (A)。

15

Let's get together for lunch tomorrow.
(A) It tastes a bit strange.
(B) They will be meeting for lunch.
(C) Sounds good to me.

明天一起吃午餐吧。
(A) 吃起來有點奇怪。
(B) 他們會碰面一起吃午餐。
(C) 聽起來不錯。

(A) 題目為午餐邀約，此回答並沒有回覆邀請，故非正確答案。(B) 此為利用題目出現的「lunch」誘導。(C) 以肯定句答應邀請，故正確答案為 (C)。

16

Did you know Mary is retiring next week?
(A) Mary worked here for almost 30 years.
(B) I thought you knew.
(C) I am having lunch with Mary tomorrow.

你知道瑪莉下禮拜就要退休了嗎？
(A) 瑪莉在這裡工作快30年了。
(B) 我以為你已經知道了。
(C) 我明天會和瑪莉一起吃午餐。

(A) 題目為間接問句，詢問對方是否知道瑪莉的退休消息，此為不相關的回答，故非正確答案。
(B) 此句的語意表示已知消息，為適當回覆。(C) 與題目不相關。正確答案為 (B)。

17

I heard that you only accept cash.
(A) I have a little bit of cash.
(B) We accept credit cards as well.
(C) That is acceptable.

聽說你們只收現金。
(A) 我有一點現金。
(B) 我們也接受信用卡。
(C) 那是可以接受的。

(A) 此為利用題目出現的「cash」誘導。(B) 此回答表示除了現金還收取信用卡，為最合適答覆。對於陳述句的題目，請記得務必正確聽完三個選項再選擇答案。 (C) 此為利用與題目中的「accept」發音相似的「acceptable」誘導。正確答案為 (B)。

18

The assignment is due tomorrow, isn't it?
(A) That's what I heard.
(B) Sure, I am available tomorrow.
(C) I was assigned to write the report.

作業繳交期限是明天，對嗎？
(A) 我聽說是這樣的。
(B) 當然，我明天有空。
(C) 我被分配要寫報告。

• assignment 作業　available 有空的　assign 分配

(A) 題目為附加問句，而選項 (A) 表示同意，故最為適當回答。(B) 此為利用題目出現的「tomorrow」誘導。(C) 此為利用與題目中的「assignment」發音相似的「assign」誘導。正確答案為 (A)。

19

Where did you go for dinner yesterday?
(A) I am having dinner at home today.
(B) I wasn't very hungry.
(C) I tried a new restaurant.

你昨天去哪裡吃晚餐？
(A) 我今天在家吃晚飯。
(B) 我不太餓。
(C) 我試了一家新餐廳。

(A) 時態與題目不符。(B) 回答與問題無關。(C) 題目為「Where」疑問句，選項 (C) 告知場所，故正確答案為 (C)。

20

Are you available for a meeting this afternoon?
(A) Yes, I have lunch plans.
(B) No, the copy machine is broken.
(C) Unfortunately, I will not be in the office.

你今天下午有空開會嗎？
(A) 是的，我午餐已有安排。
(B) 不，影印機故障了。
(C) 很不巧地，我不會在辦公室。

(A) 回答與問題無關。(B) 回答與問題無關。(C) 題目為以「be 動詞」開始的疑問句，可以用 Yes/No 回答。選項 (C) 雖不以 Yes/No 開頭，但「unfortunately ＋具體理由」有拒絕之意，故正確答案為 (C)。

21

Do you have Ms. Jensen's home address?
(A) I'm afraid I don't have it.
(B) I think she leaves around 5.
(C) I will be going to a party there tomorrow.

你有詹森女士家裡的地址嗎？
(A) 我恐怕沒有。
(B) 我想她五點左右會離開。
(C) 我明天會去參加那裡的派對。

(A) 題目為「Do/Does」疑問句，回答多以「Yes/No」開始，但也可以將其省略。選項 (A) 省略「No」，但也表現出了否定之意，故為適當回覆。(B) 回答與問題無關。(C) 回答與問題無關。正確答案為 (A)。

22

Would you hand out these free samples?
(A) Okay, I will do it now.
(B) Down in the lobby.
(C) I have sampled the food before.

你可以分發這些免費的樣品嗎？
(A) 好，我現在來做。
(B) 在大廳那裡。
(C) 我以前就嚐過那樣食物了。

• **hand out** 分發　**sample** 樣品

(A) 題目以「Would you . . .」開頭，有勸誘、拜託的作用，選項 (A) 接受請求，是最合適的回答。
(B) 沒有回答問題。(C) 此為利用題目出現的「sample」誘導。故正確答案為 (A)。

23

Didn't you borrow books from the library this morning?

(A) Yes, I just got back.

(B) No, I quit my job at the library.

(C) No, we don't.

你今天早上不是去圖書館借書嗎？

(A) 是的，我才剛回來。

(B) 不，我辭掉圖書館的工作了。

(C) 不，我們沒有。

(A) 題目為否定疑問句，可先以肯定句意解釋。如果回答是肯定的，使用「Yes ＋肯定內容」，否定則以「No ＋否定內容」回覆。句意上，選項 (A) 最為合適。(B) 此為利用題目出現的「library」誘導。(C) 時態與題目不符。正確答案為 (A)。

How do I turn off this television?

(A) No, there is nothing interesting on.

(B) It's a right turn.

(C) There should be a button on the left side.

我要如何關掉電視機？

(A) 不，沒有什麼有趣的節目。

(B) 要右轉。

(C) 左邊應該有個按鈕。

(A) 疑問詞「How」的疑問句無法以 Yes/No 回答，故非正確答案。(B) 此句應是駕駛相關的情境，與題目不符。(C) 代表可以使用按鈕關掉電視，故正確答案為 (C)。

When was the carpet in the lobby replaced?

(A) Yesterday, when you were out.

(B) I was planning on washing it this afternoon.

(C) You can try next door.

大廳的地毯何時換掉的？

(A) 昨天，你出去的時候。

(B) 我打算今天下午來清洗它。

(C) 你可以試試隔壁的。

(A) 本題為「When」疑問句，詢問的是時間點，故回答確切時間最為合適。(B) 回答與問題無關，且時態不一致。(C) 回答與問題無關。正確答案為 (A)。

Are you comfortable using chopsticks?

(A) I am a fan of pork chops.

(B) Yes, I've used them before.

(C) Our reservation is for seven o'clock.

你可以用筷子嗎？

(A) 我喜歡豬排。

(B) 可以，我以前用過。

(C) 我們是訂七點的位子。

(A) 此為利用與題目中的「chopsticks」發音類似的「pork chop」誘導。(B) 本題為「be 動詞」疑問句，故回答常以「Yes/No」開頭。 (C) 回答與問題無關。正確答案為 (B)。

27 ---

Why are they rearranging the furniture?
(A) They're making room for a new workstation.
(B) No, the movers are on their way now.
(C) We're going to throw them away.

他們為什麼重新擺設家具？
(A) 他們要為新的工作站挪出位置。
(B) 不，搬家工人正在途中。
(C) 我們要把它們扔掉。

• **rearrange** 重新擺設　**make room** 挪出位置　**workstation** 工作站

(A) 本題為「Why」疑問句，回答中應敘述理由，故此為適當回覆。(B) 疑問詞問句無法用「Yes/No」回答。(C) 主詞與題目不一致。正確答案為 (A)。

28 ---

Should we buy additional equipment for the office this month?
(A) No, we already hired someone this month.
(B) We don't have the budget.
(C) We can meet this afternoon at three o'clock.

我們這個月該不該為辦公室添購設備？
(A) 不，這個月我們已經聘用了新人。
(B) 我們沒有預算。
(C) 我們今天下午三點可以碰面。

• **additional** 額外的；附加的　**equipment** 設備

(A) 此為利用題目中出的「office」的相關字彙「hire」誘導。(B) 此回答省略「No」，但告知拒絕提議的具體理由，故此為適當回覆。(C) 回答與題目無關。正確答案為 (B)。

 10

29 ---

Did Mr. Maynor assign you to the Cohen project?
(A) He likes giving assignments.
(B) Yes, just this morning.
(C) No, in the desk drawer.

梅諾先生指定你參加科恩計畫嗎？
(A) 他喜歡指派工作。
(B) 是的，就在今天早上。
(C) 不，在桌子的抽屜裡。

• **assign** 指定　**assignment** 指派的工作　**drawer** 抽屜

(A) 此為利用題目中的「assign」發音相似的「assignment」誘導。(B) 對於「Do/Did」開頭的疑問句，回答中常出現「Yes/No」，此句以「Yes」回答且句意通順。 (C) 此句雖以「No」回答，但後半部分內容與題目無關，故非正確答案。正確答案為 (B)。

30 -

Should we have chocolate cake or apple pie for dessert?

(A) Whichever you want.

(B) Help yourself.

(C) I made a reservation at the Dessert Café.

甜點要點巧克力蛋糕還是蘋果派？

(A) 你決定就好。

(B) 請自便。

(C) 我在甜點咖啡廳訂位了。

(A)「Whichever/Whatever . . .」為選擇疑問句中常見的正確答案，請務必熟記。(B) 答案與題目無關。(C) 此為利用題目中出現過的「dessert」誤導，非正確答案。正確答案為 (A)。

31 -

This is the malfunctioning copy machine, isn't it?

(A) There are a number of functions.

(B) Yes, the repairman is on his way.

(C) I need thirty copies for the meeting.

這台影印機故障了，不是嗎？

(A) 有許多功能。

(B) 是的，維修人員正在路上。

(C) 我需要30份會議用的資料。

• **malfunctioning** 故障的　**copy machine** 影印機　**repairman** 維修人員　**on one's way** 在路上

(A) 此為利用與題目中的「copy machine」相關字義「function」誘導。(B) 題目詢問影印機是否故障，回答「維修人員正在路上」，代表將有人來修理影印機，故為適當回覆。(C) 此為利用題目出現過的「copy」誘導。正確答案為 (B)。

32-34 conversation

M	Hi. I'm here to see Dr. Paulson. I don't have an appointment, but I've had a sharp pain in my knee since yesterday. Will I have to wait long?
W	I'm sorry to say Dr. Paulson is out of town at a conference and will not be in today. I can make an appointment so you can see her at 10 A.M. tomorrow morning.
M	I don't think I can wait until tomorrow. Is there another doctor available to see me?
W	Dr. Chung is in and seeing patients. There is an opening at 3 P.M. today. How does that sound?

32-34 對話

男	嗨，我來找包爾森醫師。我沒有預約，但是從昨天開始我的膝蓋就有一股刺痛。我得要等很久嗎？
女	很抱歉，包爾森醫生出城去參加研討會，今天不會進診所了。我可以幫您預約，這樣您明天早上十點就可以讓她檢查了。
男	我覺得我等不到明天了。有其他醫師有空可以幫我看診嗎？
女	鍾醫師在，而且正在看診。今天下午三點有空檔。這時間可以嗎？

• **appointment** 預約　**sharp pain** 刺痛　**patient** 病患

32

Why is the man talking to the woman?
(A) To deliver a package
(B) To see a doctor
(C) To reserve a spot at a conference
(D) To make an appointment for tomorrow

這位男士為何要和這位女士說話？
(A) 要運送包裹
(B) 要來看醫生
(C) 要預約研討會的座位
(D) 要預約明天看診

男子開頭便說「Hi. I'm here to see Dr. Paulson.」，故正確解答為 (B)。

33

Why does the man decide not to see Dr. Paulson the next morning?
(A) He will be at the conference with Dr. Chung.
(B) He needs prompt assistance.
(C) He has a meeting.
(D) He will be out of town.

這位男士為什麼決定不在明天早上給包爾森醫師看診？
(A) 他會和鍾醫師一起出席研討會。
(B) 他需要立即的協助。
(C) 他要開會。
(D) 他要出城。

男子在第二句話中提到「I don't think I can wait until tomorrow.」告知對方自己不能等這麼久，表達需要即時幫助，正確答案為 (B)。

34

What will the man most likely do?
(A) Come back tomorrow morning
(B) Visit a nearby pharmacy
(C) Meet with a different physician
(D) Call Dr. Paulson on the phone

這位男士接下來最有可能做什麼？
(A) 明天早上再來
(B) 去附近的藥局
(C) 看另一位醫生
(D) 打電話給包爾森醫師

從男子最後說的「Is there another doctor available to see me?」可知道，由於包爾森醫師無法看診，男子想和預約另一位醫生。題目中使用的「doctor」即選項 (C) 中的「physician」，正確答案為 (C)。

35-37 conversation

W	Hello. My name is Jessica Smith. Is Ms. Maeda in? I'm one of her clients.	女	你好，我是潔西卡・史密斯。前田女士在嗎？我是她的客戶。
M	Unfortunately, she is out of the country until next week. If it is regarding something urgent, I can try to reach her on her mobile phone.	男	很不巧，她出國了，要下禮拜才會回來。若是緊急的事，我可以試著用手機和她聯繫。
W	No, it's not urgent. I was just dropping off these signed legal documents. Can I leave them with you?	女	沒關係，不急。我只是來送這些簽了名的法律文件。可以放在你這裡嗎？
M	Of course. I will see that Ms. Maeda gets these as soon as she's back. It would help me if you would leave a note for Ms. Maeda saying what this is in regard to.	男	當然可以。我保證前田女士一回來就會拿到這些文件。若是妳能留個便條說明這是什麼文件，對我會有很大的幫助。

35-37 對話

• out of country 出國　urgent 緊急的　reach 聯繫　drop 送來　be in regard to . . . 與……相關

35 --

Why does the woman want to see Ms. Maeda?
(A) To ask about a court date
(B) To sign a contract
(C) To give her some documents
(D) To tell her she is leaving the country

這位女士為什麼要找前田女士？
(A) 要詢問開庭日期
(B) 要簽署合約
(C) 要給她一些文件
(D) 要告訴她她要出國

通常詢問目的的問題，答案會在一開始出現，但是本題因為想見的人不在，所以目的出現在中間部分。女子第二句台詞說「I was just dropping off these signed legal documents」，表示她送來法律相關文件，故正確答案為 (C)。

36 --

Where is Ms. Maeda?
(A) Overseas
(B) At home
(C) At a legal conference
(D) In her office

前田女士在哪裡？
(A) 國外
(B) 在家
(C) 在法律研討會
(D) 在辦公室

從男子第一句回答中的「Unfortunately, she is out of the country until next week.」可看出，前田女士現在人在海外。題目中使用的「out of the country」，表示人在國外，即選項 (A) 中的「overseas」，故正確解答為 (A)。

37 -

What will the man do next?
(A) Write a note
(B) Call Ms. Maeda
(C) Ask for assistance
(D) Deliver a message

這位男士接下來將會做什麼？
(A) 寫便條
(B) 打電話給前田女士
(C) 請求協助
(D) 轉告留言

通常在對話最後才會出現未來將發生的事件。男子最後提到「It would help me if you would leave a note for Ms. Maeda saying what this is in regard to.」，由此可知，他請女子留下便條，等前田女子回來再由他轉交，故正確答案為 (D)。

38-40 conversation

38–40 對話

M	Hi, Judy. You're preparing the agenda for the board meeting tomorrow morning, right? Let me take a look at it before you send it around to the board members.	男 嗨，茱蒂。妳正在準備明天早上董事會議的議程表，是嗎？在妳寄給董事會成員之前先給我看一下。
W	Sure, I'm still working on it. I'm waiting to hear from Cathy regarding her presentation on next year's budget. Once I insert that item, it will be ready. I'll let you know. It shouldn't be later than 2 P.M.	女 好的，我還在整理。我在等凱西要簡報明年預算報告的資料。等插入該項資料後，議程表就完成了。我會再通知你的。應該不會超過下午兩點。
M	That sounds fine. Please make sure to note on the agenda who will be speaking about each item at the meeting as well. Thanks.	男 好。麻煩務必在議程表上註明會議中每一項的報告者是誰。謝謝。

• agenda 會議議程表　board meeting 董事會議　take a look 看一看　regarding . . . 關於……

38 -

What is the woman working on?
(A) Next year's budget
(B) A set of presentation slides
(C) A meeting agenda
(D) A speech

這位女士正在準備什麼？
(A) 明年的預算
(B) 簡報投影片
(C) 會議議程表
(D) 演講

男子開頭提到「You're preparing the agenda for the board meeting tomorrow morning, right?」，由此可知，女子正在準備會議的議程，故正確答案為 (C)。

39 -

What does the woman promise to do?
(A) Reassign some work to Cathy
(B) Make a copy of the agenda
(C) Update the man on her work progress
(D) Meet the man at the board meeting

這位女士承諾要做什麼？
(A) 重新分配一些工作給凱西
(B) 影印一份議程表
(C) 向這位男士報告她的工作進度
(D) 在董事會議上與這位男士見面

女子提到「I'll let you know.」，表示她工作結束後會通知對方，故正確答案為 (C)。

What does the man ask the woman to do?

(A) Include names on the agenda
(B) Rehearse for a speech
(C) Send the agenda out before speaking to Cathy
(D) Let him revise the agenda

這位男士要求女士做什麼？

(A) 在議程表上加上姓名
(B) 為演講排練
(C) 在和凱西談話之前寄出議程表
(D) 讓他修訂議程表

題目若詢問請託的事項，可尋找段落中的「Please . . .」，通常即為答案所在。男子最後說「Please make sure to note on the agenda who will be speaking about each item at the meeting as well.」，便是在要求女子註明會議中的報告者，故正確答案為 (A)。

41-43 conversation

41–43 對話

M	Hey, Jane! Are you on your way to French class? I just heard that Professor Van Saint's class has been canceled today.	男	嗨，珍！妳正要去上法文課嗎？我剛聽說汎森教授今天的課已經取消了。
W	Really? Do you know why? She did look like she might be coming down with something when I saw her yesterday at the library.	女	真的嗎？你知道原因嗎？我昨天在圖書館看到她的時候，她看起來好像生了什麼病。
M	Apparently, her brother is getting married, and she's at the ceremony. I heard from someone else in the class.	男	似乎是她哥哥要結婚了，她去參加典禮。我從班上同學那聽來的。
W	I'm glad to hear it's not something bad. Do you want to go grab an early lunch?	女	還好不是什麼壞事。你要不要提早吃午餐？
M	That sounds great. Now we have a free hour!	男	好啊，我們有一個小時的空檔！

• **come down with** 染上（疾病）　**grab** 借機趕緊（吃）……

What does Professor Van Saint teach?

(A) Spanish
(B) Business marketing
(C) French
(D) Accounting

汎森教授教授什麼課程？

(A) 西班牙文
(B) 商業行銷
(C) 法文
(D) 會計

從一開始的「Hey, Jane! Are you on your way to French class? I just heard that Professor Van Saint's class has been canceled today.」可知道，汎森女士應為法文教授，故正確答案為 (C)。

Why is the class canceled?

(A) Bad weather
(B) Marriage of the professor's relative
(C) Sickness of the professor
(D) Public holiday

這堂課為什麼取消？

(A) 天氣不好
(B) 教授的親戚要結婚
(C) 教授生病
(D) 國定假日

從「Apparently, her brother is getting married, and she's at the ceremony.」這句話可以知道，課程取消的原因是家人的婚禮，故正確答案為 (B)。

43 --

How long was the class supposed to be?	這堂課應該是多長的時間？
(A) 60 minutes	(A) 60分鐘
(B) 90 minutes	(B) 90分鐘
(C) 30 minutes	(C) 30分鐘
(D) 2 hours	(D) 2個小時

男子最後說的「Now we have a free hour!」代表因為停課多了一小時的空檔，故可推測原本的上課時間大概為一個小時，故正確解答為 (A)。

44-46 conversation | 44–46 對話

W Hi there. I was hoping you could help me find a book that was recommended to me by a friend. It's going to be a present for my husband for his birthday. He loves a good mystery, and my friend told me about one of the current bestsellers.	女 嗨，不知道你是否可以幫我找一本朋友推薦的書。我想用它當作我先生的生日禮物。他喜歡好看的推理小說，而我朋友告訴我一本目前最暢銷的小說。
M Can you let me know the title or author of the book?	男 您可以告訴我書名或作者嗎？
W Unfortunately, I can't. I can't remember anything about the book, except that it takes place in London in the 19th century.	女 很可惜，我沒辦法。除了故事是發生在19世紀的倫敦之外，其他的我都忘記了。
M (45)**Oh, I think I know that one.** It must be the new novel by John Garvin. I haven't read it yet, but I've heard it's very good. The reviews have all been very positive. Garvin is a great writer. Well, it just so happens that we have a copy still in stock. If you wait here just a minute, I'll go get it for you.	男 (45)喔，我想我知道那本。應該是約翰·加爾文的新小說。我還沒看過，但我聽說很好看。評論都非常好。加爾文是位很棒的作家。嗯，剛好庫存還有一本。請您稍等一下，我去拿給您。

• **recommend** 推薦　**current** 目的　**unfortunately** 可惜地　**take place** 發生　**review** 評論　**in stock** 有庫存

44 --

Where does the conversation take place?	這段對話出現在哪裡？
(A) At a museum	(A) 博物館
(B) At a department store	(B) 百貨公司
(C) At a library	(C) 圖書館
(D) At a bookstore	(D) 書店

對話中，女子說自己是來購買他人推薦的書，以當作丈夫的禮物，故對話最有可能發生在書店，正確答案為 (D)。

45 NEW --

What does the man imply when he says, "Oh, I think I know that one"?

(A) He knows what she is talking about.
(B) The store has only one copy remaining.
(C) The man knows the woman well.
(D) The man will show the woman a review.

當這位男士說：「喔，我想我知道那本」，是什麼意思？

(A) 他知道她在講什麼。
(B) 店裡只剩下一本。
(C) 這位男士很了解這位女士。
(D) 這位男士要給這位女士看一篇評論。

此類掌握意圖的題目，其前後文通常是最大的線索。由於前面的對話中女子提供某書的資訊，故可推測男子此句話的意思，最有可能是在表示自己也知道那本書，故正確答案為 (A)。

 46 --

What will the woman most likely do?

(A) Go to another store
(B) Buy two copies
(C) Ask the man to call her husband
(D) Purchase a gift

這位女士接下來最有可能做什麼？

(A) 去另一家店
(B) 買兩本書
(C) 請這位男士打電話給她先生
(D) 購買禮物

對話一開始女子便提到，自己是來買書當作丈夫的禮物，故正確答案為 (D)。

47-49 conversation with three speakers NEW

47–49 三人對話

M1 Hi, Sam! Hello, Laura! Did you hear they're going to be giving us Korean classes starting next week?	**男1** 嗨，山姆！哈囉，蘿拉！你們有聽說從下週開始我們要上韓文課嗎？
M2 I hadn't heard that.	**男2** 我沒聽說。
W Oh, I thought it wasn't until next month. I'm really excited to get started.	**女** 喔，我以為下個月才會開始。我真的好興奮要開始上課了。
M1 I just heard it from the manager. The first class is next Monday, the 10th.	**男1** 我剛剛聽經理說的。第一堂課是下禮拜一，10號。
M2 Yeah, there have been a lot of tourists from Korea staying at our hotel in recent months. I've had trouble communicating with some of them.	**男2** 是啊，最近幾個月有許多來自韓國的旅客住在我們飯店裡。我和他們有些溝通上的困難。
W I agree. Picking up a few key phrases in Korean should help ease communications and improve our service.	**女** 我同意。能學會幾句關鍵的韓語詞彙應該可以讓溝通容易些，也能改善我們的服務。
M1 You know, the manager also told me that the classes are going to be mandatory. They're even going to grade us on class participation!	**男1** 你們知道嗎？經理還跟我說這些課程是強制性的，甚至會以上課出席率來評分！
M2 That doesn't sound like much fun.	**男2** 這聽起來就不太好玩了。

• **communicate** 溝通　**phrase** 詞彙　**ease** 緩解　**mandatory** 強制性的　**participation** 出席

47

What are the speakers discussing?
(A) A trip to Korea
(B) A language course
(C) Lecture schedules
(D) A management meeting

說話者在討論什麼？
(A) 去韓國旅遊
(B) 語言課程
(C) 演講時間表
(D) 管理會議

要知道對話的目的，通常可從段落開頭尋找。此題男子先問了「Did you hear they're going to be giving us Korean classes starting next week?」，三人便開始討論下周開始進行的韓語課程，故正確答案為 (B)。

48

When will the classes start?
(A) The middle of next month
(B) Tomorrow
(C) Next week
(D) On Tuesday

課程將於何時開始？
(A) 下個月月中
(B) 明天
(C) 下個禮拜
(D) 星期二

對於詢問確切時間點的問題，要仔細聆聽日期出現的部分。由「The first class is next Monday, the 10th.」可知，課程從下週開始，故正確答案為 (C)。

49

What is mentioned about the hotel?
(A) It is located in Korea.
(B) Its marketing has focused on Korea recently.
(C) It has only three employees.
(D) It has been accommodating many foreign guests.

對話中提到什麼有關飯店的事？
(A) 位於韓國。
(B) 最近的行銷策略鎖定韓國。
(C) 只有三名員工。
(D) 最近有許多外國客人來住宿。

由「Yeah, there have been a lot of tourists from Korea staying at our hotel in recent months.」可知，該處有很多觀光客投宿，故正確答案為 (D)。

50-52 conversation

W Greg, do you have a second? I've got Micron Technologies on the phone. They want to make a reservation for three single rooms from next Wednesday to Friday.

M Sure, hold on. Yes, we can accommodate that. I'll put that in the system right now. They're lucky to be calling now because we're expecting to have a large wedding here next week, and we may be all booked up.

W Greg, they also want to reserve a car and driver for Thursday.

M I'm going to have to call our usual limo service. Just tell them you'll call them back in about 15 minutes.

50-52 對話

女 貴格，你有空嗎？我正在和美光科技的人講電話。他們想要預約下星期三到五的三間單人房。

男 沒問題，等一下。可以，我們可以提供住宿。我現在就登記在系統裡。還好他們現在打來，因為下禮拜預計會有一場大型婚禮，我們可能會被訂滿。

女 貴格，他們還要預約星期四的車與司機。

男 我需要打給平常合作的轎車接送服務公司。跟他們說妳大約15分鐘後會再回電給他們。

• **make a reservation** 預約   **accommodate** 為……提供住宿   **book** 預訂   **reserve** 預約

50

Where most likely do the speakers work?

(A) At a restaurant
(B) At a limo service
(C) At a hotel
(D) At a wedding hall

說話者最有可能在哪裡工作？

(A) 餐廳
(B) 轎車接送服務公司
(C) 飯店
(D) 結婚禮堂

地點資訊通常會在對話開頭出現。此題由「They want to make a reservation for three single rooms from next Wednesday to Friday.」可知，說話者最可能位於飯店，故正確答案為 (C)。

51

Why is Micron Technologies calling?

(A) To book a wedding
(B) To reserve rooms for next week
(C) To ask about a car service
(D) To complain about poor service

美光科技為什麼來電？

(A) 預約婚禮
(B) 預約下週的房間
(C) 詢問汽車服務
(D) 抱怨服務不佳

從開頭的「I've got Micron Technologies on the phone. They want to make a reservation for three single rooms from next Wednesday to Friday」可知，正確答案為 (B)。

52

What will the man probably do next?

(A) Contact a car company
(B) Call Micron Technologies back
(C) Reschedule a wedding
(D) Clean a hotel room

這位男士接下來可能會做什麼？

(A) 聯絡汽車公司
(B) 回電給美光科技
(C) 重新安排婚禮
(D) 打掃飯店房間

通常在對話最後才會出現未來將發生的事件。男子最後說道：「I'm going to have to call our usual limo service.」，表示他將先致電汽車公司，再與美光科技聯繫，故正確答案為 (A)。

53-55 conversation with three speakers (NEW)

W	Hi, guys. Did you guys check out the review in the paper yesterday?
M1	No, I missed it. What did it say?
W	The article was extremely positive, and our restaurant got a perfect four stars!
M2	That's fabulous!
W	The critic who wrote the article described our appetizers as "delicacies from heaven" and went on and on about how creative our menu choices were—food combinations he had never seen before.
M1	I want to get my hands on a copy of that review for our kitchen wall.
M2	Definitely. I can't wait to read the article myself.

53–55 三人對話

女	嗨，大夥們。你們看了昨天報紙上的評論了嗎？
男1	沒有，我錯過了。上面寫了什麼？
女	那篇文章非常肯定我們，而且我們餐廳得到完美的四顆星！
男2	真是太好了！
女	寫這篇文章的評論家描述我們的開胃菜是「來自天堂的佳餚」，還一直談論我們的菜單選項多有創意——從沒見過的美食組合。
男1	我想要弄一份評論貼在廚房牆壁上。
男2	當然。我迫不及待想親眼看看那篇文章了。

- review 評論　paper 報紙　extremely 非常　positive 正面的；肯定的　critic 評論家　describe 描述　appetizer 開胃菜　delicacy 佳餚　go on and on 持續不斷地

53 --

What type of business do the speakers probably work in?
(A) A restaurant
(B) A hotel
(C) A newspaper
(D) A travel agency

說話者最有可能在哪種行業工作？
(A) 餐廳
(B) 飯店
(C) 報社
(D) 旅行社

地點資訊通常會在對話開頭出現。女子在對話中提及「our restaurant got a perfect four stars!」，故可知道正確答案為 (A)。

54 --

According to the woman, what did the critic say?
(A) He is friends with the chef.
(B) The menu was innovative.
(C) The service was fantastic.
(D) The food was ordinary.

根據這位女士所言，評論家說了什麼？
(A) 他是主廚的朋友。
(B) 菜單相當創新。
(C) 服務很棒。
(D) 餐點很普通。

從女子的第三句台詞「The critic who wrote the article . . . went on and on about how creative our menu choices were」可知，評論家認為餐廳的菜單相當有創意，故正確答案為 (B)。

55

What does one of the men say he will do?

(A) Close down the business
(B) Write something on the wall
(C) Think of new menu items
(D) Post the article

其中一位男士說他要做什麼？

(A) 結束營業
(B) 在牆上寫東西
(C) 想新菜單的品項
(D) 張貼文章

通常詢問「對話結束後將做什麼」的題型，大概可在對話最後的部分找到提示。

這段對話中，因為有兩名男子出現，需將兩名男子皆列入考慮。其中一名男子說：「I want to get my hands on a copy of that review for our kitchen wall.」，表示自己想要把那份評論報導張貼在廚房。另一名男子說：「Definitely. I can't wait to read the article myself.」，表示自己也想看那篇報導。故正確答案為 (D)。

56-58 conversation

56–58 對話

W I was hoping we would be able to do all of the tests right here. **M** Unfortunately, we're only equipped here to perform some of the specialized tests that you'll need. You should go to one of the larger facilities, like the municipal hospital on Gray Street. You will be able to save time and money if you have all the tests done in one place. **W** I've had a bad experience at the municipal hospital. I prefer the general hospital across the bridge. Please write me a referral that I can take there. **M** Of course. You can pick it up from the receptionist on your way out.	**女** 真希望我們可以在這裡做完所有的檢測。 **男** 很可惜，這裡的設備只能進行妳所需要的一些專科檢測。妳應該去較大的院所，像是格雷街上的市立醫院。如果能在一個地方完成所有的檢測，妳就可以省下時間和金錢了。 **女** 我在市立醫院有過不好的經驗。我比較喜歡過橋後的綜合醫院。請幫我開可以帶去那裡的轉診單。 **男** 沒問題。在妳離開時可以到接待人員那領取。

• equip 配備　perform 進行　specialized 專科的　facility 院所　municipal hospital 市立醫院
general hospital 綜合醫院　referral 轉診　receptionist 接待人員

56

Where does the conversation probably take place?

(A) At a university
(B) At a large hospital
(C) At a clinic
(D) At an exam center

這段對話可能在哪裡發生？

(A) 大學
(B) 大型醫院
(C) 診所
(D) 檢測中心

從男子第一句台詞「You should go to one of the larger facilities, like the municipal hospital on Gray Street.」中的比較級推測，對話中的地點應為較小型的醫院診所，故正確答案為 (C)。

What does the man propose that the woman do?

(A) Come back tomorrow
(B) Go to a different institution
(C) Decide which tests she wants
(D) Take medicine regularly

這位男士建議女士做什麼？

(A) 明天再來
(B) 去不同的機構
(C) 決定她要做什麼檢測
(D) 定期服藥

男子第一句台詞中說「You should go to one of the larger facilities」，代表建議女子前往不同的機構就診，故正確答案為 (B)。

What will the man probably do next?

(A) Prepare a document
(B) See another patient
(C) Call the general hospital
(D) Conduct a specialized test

這位男士接下來可能會做什麼？

(A) 準備文件
(B) 看另一位病人
(C) 打電話給綜合醫院
(D) 進行專科檢測

從女子最後說的「Please write me a referral that I can take there.」與男子回覆「Of course.」可知，男子接下來應會幫女子開立轉診單，故正確答案為 (A)。

59-61 conversation

59–61 對話

M Jenny, did you hear the news? The price of strawberries is soaring because of the snowstorm last weekend. The price has almost doubled! We should consider raising the price of our strawberry pies. They are really our only product right now.	男 珍妮，妳有聽到新聞嗎？因為上週末的暴風雪，草莓的價格飆漲。價格幾乎翻倍！我們應該要考慮調漲草莓派的價格。那是我們現在僅有的產品。
W That's too much. I'm worried we'll lose customers, though, if we reflect that cost increase in the price of our pies. Customers buy our pies because of their reasonable pricing. Let's first think of other ways to cut back on costs.	女 也派太多了吧。但是如果在派的價格上反映增加的成本，我怕會流失顧客。客戶購買我們的派是因為價格合理。我們先想想其他降低成本的方法吧。
M Okay, let's see. . . . I'll spend some time tonight reviewing our recent expenses. Maybe we can cut back on some other ingredients.	男 好吧，來想看看……今天晚上我會花點時間查看一下最近的支出。或許我們可以在其他的原料上降低成本。

• **soar** 驟升 **snowstorm** 暴風雪 **reflect** 反映 **cost increase** 成本增加 **reasonable** 合理的 **review** 查看 **expense** 支出 **ingredient** 原料

59

What does the man mention about the snowstorm?
(A) It covered the bakery in snow.
(B) The bakery is not doing very well.
(C) The price of strawberries nearly doubled.
(D) The price of strawberry pies has gone up.

這位男士提到什麼與暴風雪有關的事？
(A) 將麵包店掩埋在雪裡。
(B) 麵包店生意不太好。
(C) 草莓的價格近乎翻倍。
(D) 草莓派的價格已經調漲。

男子開頭提及「The price of strawberries is soaring because of the massive snow-storm last weekend. Prices have almost doubled!」，表示因為暴風雪導致草莓漲價，故正確答案為 (C)。

60

What does the woman imply?
(A) They may need to close down the bakery.
(B) They should apply cost-cutting measures.
(C) The price of strawberries is going to continue to rise.
(D) They have already started losing customers.

這位女士說的話意味著什麼？
(A) 他們可能要關閉麵包店。
(B) 他們應該採取降低成本的方式。
(C) 草莓的價格會持續上漲。
(D) 他們已經開始流失顧客了。

女子的台詞中提到「Let's first think of other ways to cut back on costs.」，故正確答案為 (B)。

61

What does the man say he will do tonight?
(A) Call a few customers
(B) Cut down on the number of ingredients
(C) Buy more strawberries
(D) Review financial records

這位男士說他今晚要做什麼？
(A) 打電話給一些顧客
(B) 降低原料的數量
(C) 買更多草莓
(D) 檢視財務紀錄

通常在對話最後才會出現未來將發生的事件。由男子最後說的「I'll spend some time tonight reviewing our recent expenses.」可知，他將對目前的花費明細進行檢討，故正確答案為 (D)。

62-64 conversation 　　　　62-64 對話

M Mandy, I need 30 copies of the presentation for the meeting this afternoon.	男 曼蒂，我需要30份今天下午的會議簡報資料。
W (63)**I'm way ahead of you.** Rachael will have the 30 copies ready and placed in the meeting room before the meeting starts.	女 (63)我比你先想到了。瑞秋會在會議開始前準備好30份的資料，放在會議室裡。
M That's great. It would also be a good idea to have some snacks and drinks set out in the meeting room, enough for 30 people. Most of them will be flying in for this meeting, and there will probably be some hungry people in the room.	男 太好了。如果能在會議室內放置夠30人享用的點心和飲料的話也不錯。大部分的人都是今天早上搭飛機來開會，會議中可能會有些人肚子餓。

W	No problem. I'll get right on it. How about light sandwiches and sodas?	女	沒問題。我馬上去準備。簡單的三明治和汽水，好嗎？
M	That should work. You should also get some waters and juices for those who don't drink soda.	男	好啊。也要準備水和果汁給不喝汽水的人。
W	Got it. Do you have someone helping you with the projector?	女	好。有人幫你處理投影機嗎？
M	I already told Rachael to do that.	男	我已經叫瑞秋去處理了。

• copy（印刷品的）一份　place 放置

 62

What are the speakers trying to do?
(A) Organize a group lunch
(B) Choose between soda and juice
(C) Prepare for a presentation
(D) Reserve a meeting room

說話者試著要做什麼？
(A) 規劃團體午餐
(B) 在汽水和果汁之間擇一
(C) 準備簡報
(D) 預約會議室

男子一開始先說「I need 30 copies of the presentation for the meeting this afternoon.」，要求準備會議資料，接著又要求準備零食與飲料，故正確答案為 (C)。

63 NEW

What does the woman imply when she says, "I'm way ahead of you"?
(A) She already took care of it.
(B) She is in front of the man.
(C) She is almost done.
(D) She will win the race.

當這位女士說：「我比你先想到了」，是什麼意思？
(A) 她已經處理好了。
(B) 她在這個男士前面。
(C) 她快完成了。
(D) 她會贏得競賽。

此類掌握意圖的題目，其前後文通常是最大的線索。此處引述的句子是對前一句要求準備 30 份資料的回覆。再根據後句可以得知，準備資料的工作已分配給瑞秋，故正確答案為 (A)。

64

What will the woman do next?
(A) Distribute copies of the presentation
(B) Order snacks and drinks
(C) Give a presentation
(D) Help the man with the projector

這位女士接下來會做什麼？
(A) 分發簡報資料
(B) 訂購點心和飲料
(C) 發表簡報
(D) 幫這位男士處理投影機

根據「It would also be a good idea to have some snacks and drinks set out in the meeting room, enough for 30 people」與「No problem. I'll get right on it.」可知，女子會去訂購點心與飲料。正確答案為 (B)。

65-67 conversation and schedule

W Michael, you're going to be up last today, right?
M No, I just noticed there's a mistake in the program. Martha should be performing after me.
W Why the change?
M She told me she's worried she won't be able to finish playing both of her pieces within the given 30 minutes.
W Oh, okay then. I guess you're going on after me then.
M That's right. I still need practice on the Mozart sonata. I'm just not fast enough yet.

Program	
Performer	Time
Henry	1:00–1:30
Melissa	1:40–2:10
Martha	2:20–2:50
Michael	3:00–3:30

65–67 對話及時程表

女 麥可，今天你是最後一位上場表演的，對嗎？
男 不是，我剛才注意到節目表有誤。瑪莎應該在我之後表演。
女 為什麼有異動？
男 她說她擔心沒辦法在規定的30分鐘內演奏完兩首曲子。
女 喔，好吧。我猜那你會在我之後上場表演。
男 沒錯，我還需要多練習莫札特奏鳴曲。我的速度還不夠快。

節目表	
表演者	時間
亨利	1:00 – 1:30
梅莉莎	1:40 – 2:10
瑪莎	2:20 – 2:50
麥可	3:00 – 3:30

65 (NEW)

Look at the graphic. Who will be performing right before Michael?
(A) Henry
(B) Melissa
(C) Martha
(D) Nobody

看一下圖表，麥可的前一位表演者是誰？
(A) 亨利
(B) 梅莉莎
(C) 瑪莎
(D) 沒人

男子開頭說了「Martha should be performing after me.」，表示節目順序改變後，瑪莎成為最後上場的人，而根據節目表可知道，原本在瑪莎後面的是麥可，故順序改變後，麥可變成第三位上場，而第二位上場的是梅莉莎，故正確答案為 (B)。

66

What kind of performance will Martha do?
(A) Dancing
(B) Singing
(C) Musical instrument
(D) Monologue

瑪莎要表演什麼項目？
(A) 跳舞
(B) 唱歌
(C) 樂器
(D) 獨角戲

從男子說的「she's worried she won't be able to finish playing both of her pieces within the given 30 minutes」可知，瑪莎應該會表演某項樂器，故正確答案為 (C)。

Why did the program change?	**節目表為什麼更動?**
(A) The show has been postponed.	(A) 表演被延期。
(B) Martha still needs to practice her piece.	(B) 瑪莎還需要練習曲目。
(C) Melissa is sick.	(C) 梅莉莎生病了。
(D) Martha will go over the allotted time.	(D) 瑪莎會超過指定的時間。

從男子説的「she's worried she won't be able to finish playing both of her pieces within the given 30 minutes」可知,由於瑪莎可能無法在 30 分鐘內演奏完兩首曲子,故表演順序需要調換。正確答案為 (D)。

68-70 conversation and list | 68–70 對話及表單

W Can you help me order a new desk for the head of the Accounting Department?	**女** 你可以幫我訂購一張新桌子給會計部主管嗎?
M Sure, what kind of desk is he looking for?	**男** 當然,他想要哪種桌子?
W It would need to be a large one with drawers. He likes to stack a lot of documents on his desk. But it's going to need to be less than $800.	**女** 得是有抽屜的大桌子。他喜歡在桌上堆放大量的文件。但是價錢要低於800元。
M There are plenty of good office desks for that price. We should be able to find one that he likes. Here is the catalog we usually use to order office equipment. I just used it yesterday to order some staplers.	**男** 那個價格有許多不錯的辦公桌可以挑選。我們應該可以找到一張他喜歡的。這是我們平常用來訂購辦公設備的目錄。我昨天才用它訂了一些釘書機。
W Great! Let me take a look.	**女** 太棒了!我來看看。
M What do you think about this one?	**男** 妳覺得這一張如何?

Type	Office Furniture Type	Price
A	Standard office chair	$100
B	Standard office desk with drawers	$575
C	Large, executive desk with drawers	$720
D	Large, president-style office chair	$350

種類	辦公室家具類型	價錢
A	標準型辦公椅	$100
B	標準型辦公桌（附抽屜）	$575
C	大型主管辦公桌（附抽屜）	$720
D	大型總裁款辦公椅	$350

• **head**（公司部門的）主管 **accounting department** 會計部門 **drawer** 抽屜 **document** 文件 **equipment** 設備

What does the department head want?	部門主管想要什麼？
(A) A stapler	(A) 釘書機
(B) A desk	(B) 辦公桌
(C) A new job	(C) 新工作
(D) A comfortable chair	(D) 舒服的椅子

女子在開頭提及「Can you help me order a new desk for the head of the accounting department?」
故可得知主管想要訂購辦公桌。正確答案為 (B)。

What did the man last order from the catalog?	這位男士上一次從型錄上訂購了什麼？
(A) Staples	(A) 釘書針
(B) Printer paper	(B) 列印紙
(C) An office desk	(C) 辦公桌
(D) Staplers	(D) 釘書機

男子在最後的部分說：「I just used it yesterday to order some staplers.」，由此可知正確答案為
(D)。

70 (NEW) --

Look at the graphic. What item will the woman probably order?	看一下圖表，這位女士有可能訂購什麼商品？
	(A) A
(A) A	(B) B
(B) B	(C) C
(C) C	(D) D
(D) D	

女子說：「He likes to stack a lot of documents on his desk. But it's going to need to be less than
$800.」，根據表格，不超過 800 美元的大書桌為「大型主管辦公桌」，故正確答案為 (C)。

PART 4 🎧 12

71-73 announcement

Okay, everyone. Gather around. Before we go through the main entrance, I want to remind you about a few things. The museum does not allow any touching of the artwork. Please do not make contact with any of the sculptures, artifacts, paintings, or other items on display. By that, I mean not just your hands, but your clothes and anything that you're carrying. You are allowed to take pictures, but no flash photography. Also, no eating, drinking, or smoking, unless in specially designated areas in the lobby. Those areas will close at 3:00 P.M. today. Lastly, please remember that we will be meeting back here, where we are standing now, at exactly 4:00 P.M. That gives you about four hours to enjoy the museum before we leave. Now, please follow me through the main entrance. I know you will all have a great time.

71-73 宣告

好的,請大家靠過來。在穿過大門前,我要提醒大家幾件事。博物館內的藝術品是禁止碰觸的。請不要碰觸任何的雕刻品、工藝品、畫作或其他展示的物品。我指的不只是各位的手,還有衣服與任何攜帶的物品。您可以拍照,但不要使用閃光燈。還有,除非在大廳特別指定的區域內,全館禁止飲食或抽菸。那些區域將於今天下午三點關閉。最後,請記得我們要在下午四點整回到現在所站的位置會合。在離開前,大家有四個小時左右的時間可以欣賞博物館。現在,請跟著我一起進入大門。我相信大家將度過一段美好的時光。

• **sculpture** 雕刻品 **flash** 閃光燈 **designated** 指定的

71 --

Where is the announcement being made?
(A) At a stadium
(B) At a restaurant
(C) At a university library
(D) At a museum

這段宣告出現的地點是在哪裡?
(A) 體育館
(B) 餐廳
(C) 大學圖書館
(D) 博物館

地點資訊通常會在開頭出現。從「The museum does not allow any touching of the artwork.」可知,此為在博物館正門對觀光客進行的解說,故答案為 (D)。

72 --

What does the speaker ask the listeners to do?
(A) Be careful when touching the sculptures
(B) Not eat but feel free to drink anywhere
(C) Be at the appointed place on time
(D) Go directly home after viewing the exhibits

說話者要求聽眾做什麼?
(A) 碰觸雕刻品時要小心
(B) 不可以吃東西,但可以隨處喝飲料。
(C) 準時到指定地點
(D) 看完展覽後直接回家

根據「Lastly, please remember that we will be meeting back here, where we are standing now, at exactly 4:00 P.M.」,正確答案為 (C)。

ACTUAL TEST 3

PART 4

中譯＋解析

🎧 11

🎧 12

73 -

When must the listeners leave the building?
(A) 12:00 P.M.
(B) 3:00 P.M.
(C) 4:00 P.M.
(D) 8:00 P.M.

聽眾必須在何時離開大樓？
(A) 中午12點
(B) 下午3點
(C) 下午4點
(D) 晚上8點

根據「Lastly, please remember that we will be meeting back here, where we are standing now, at exactly 4:00 P.M.」得知，必須四點回到正門以離開大樓，故正確答案為 (C)。

74-76 announcement

74–76 宣告

Attention, all monorail passengers heading to Hotel Candle Lake. This is your conductor speaking. I've just received an alert saying that the section of the track just before the hotel has been shut down due to ice from the recent snowstorm. Workers have already begun trying to defrost the track, but I understand it will take at least another two hours to have the track up and running again. Because of this, we are planning on reversing course and heading back to the last monorail station. You are all welcome to wait at the station until the track is up again. Alternatively, you are free to take the local bus or a taxi to get to the hotel if you are in a hurry. Apologies for the inconvenience, and thank you all for your patience.	所有搭乘單軌列車前往燭湖飯店的旅客請注意。這裡是列車長報告。我剛剛收到警示，由於最近暴風雪結冰的關係，飯店前的軌道區已經關閉。工人已開始試著為軌道除霜，但我知道至少還要兩個小時才能讓鐵軌恢復正常營運。因此，我們打算掉頭，返回上一個單軌列車車站。歡迎大家在車站候至鐵軌可再度通行。或者，若您趕時間的話，也可以自行搭乘本地巴士或計程車前往飯店。很抱歉造成您的不便，並感謝各位的耐心等候。

• **attention** 注意　**conductor** 列車長　**alert** 警示　**snowstorm** 暴風雪　**defrost** 除霜
reverse 倒車；(使)反向　**alternatively** 或者　**in a hurry** 趕時間　**apology**〔名詞〕道歉
inconvenience 不便　**patience** 耐心

 -

Where is the announcement being made?
(A) On a local bus
(B) At a monorail station
(C) At a hotel
(D) On a monorail train

這段通知出現的地點是在哪裡？
(A) 本地巴士上
(B) 單軌列車車站
(C) 飯店
(D) 單軌列車上

地點資訊通常會在開頭出現。從第一句「Attention, all monorail passengers heading to Hotel Candle Lake.」可知，這是單軌列車上的車長廣播，故正確答案為 (D)。

75 --

Why was the announcement made?
(A) The train will stop and wait.
(B) The train will head back.
(C) The train will continue on to the hotel.
(D) The train needs to be repaired.

為什麼會有這段通知？
(A) 列車將停駛並等候。
(B) 列車將調頭。
(C) 列車將繼續開往飯店。
(D) 列車需要修理。

廣播的中間部分說明「we are planning on reversing course and heading back to the last monorail station.」，表示因為鐵道結冰無法通行，所以要返回上一個車站，故正確答案為 (B)。

76 --

According to the speaker, what can listeners do?
(A) Wait two hours on the train
(B) Walk back to the monorail station
(C) Help the workers repair the track
(D) Take a bus or taxi to the hotel

根據說話者表示，聽眾可以做什麼？
(A) 在列車上等兩個小時
(B) 走回單軌列車車站
(C) 協助工人修復鐵軌
(D) 搭乘巴士或計程車到飯店

從廣播最後的「you are free to take the local bus or a taxi to get to the hotel if you are in a hurry.」可知，乘客可以在火車站等待，也可以搭乘巴士或計程車前往飯店，故正確答案為 (D)。

77-79 advertisement

77–79 廣告

Do you have trouble getting out of bed in the morning? Is it a struggle just to get through your day? If so, the experts at Cottonwood Clinic may be able to help you. James Cotton, our owner and chief therapist, is the author of the book *Energize Your Life*, which discusses his methods for helping you cope with stress and breathing new energy into your daily routine. Dr. Cotton has been featured in numerous health magazines and has won a number of awards for his unique treatment methods, including one last month at the Annual Conference of National Psychologists. The clinic has witnessed hundreds of patients find new meaning and vigor in their lives. Our hours are from 10 A.M. until 8 P.M., Monday through Friday, including holidays. Please give us a call at 555-1821 to meet with one of our therapists. If you set up an appointment this week, we'll take 20% off the cost of your initial consultation.

早上起床有困難嗎？只想撐完一天是件難事嗎？是的話，那卡頓伍德診所的專家們也許可以幫助您。本診所的老闆兼主任治療師詹姆士·卡頓是《振奮你的生活》一書的作者，書中討論了幫助您處理壓力和在日常生活中注入新活力的方法。卡頓醫生已經被許多健康雜誌特別報導過，其獨特的治療方式獲得許多獎項，包括上個月在全國心理治療師年度研討會上所獲得的獎項。本診所已有數百名見證的患者因此找到生命的新意義與活力。本診所營業時間是週一至週五上午十點至晚上八點，包含國定假日。請來電555-1821預約治療師。若於本週預約，將享有初診八折優惠。

• **struggle** 難事　**expert** 專家　**therapist** 治療師　**cope with** 處理　**breathe . . . into . . .** 為……注入……
daily routine 日常生活　**numerous** 許多的　**unique** 獨特的　**treatment** 治療　**annual** 年度的
witness 見證　**patient** 患者　**vigor** 活力　**set up** 安排　**initial** 最初的　**consultation** 諮詢

Who is James Cotton?

(A) A pastor

(B) A cotton farmer

(C) A therapist

(D) A magazine editor

誰是詹姆士・卡頓？

(A) 牧師

(B) 棉花農

(C) 治療師

(D) 雜誌編輯

從「James Cotton, our owner and chief therapist, is the author of the book . . .」可知詹姆士・卡頓身兼診所老闆、治療師與作家，故正確答案為 (C)。

78

What happened to James Cotton last month?

(A) He won an award.

(B) He was featured in a magazine.

(C) He opened the Cottonwood Clinic.

(D) He was out of town.

詹姆士・卡頓上個月發生了什麼事？

(A) 他獲得獎項。

(B) 他接受雜誌專訪。

(C) 他開設卡頓伍德診所。

(D) 他出遠門。

問題中的關鍵字為「last month」，請記下關鍵字，並集中於該字出現的部分。根據「Dr. Cotton . . . has won a number of awards for his unique treatment methods, including one last month at the Annual Conference of National Psychologists.」可知，他上個月剛得獎，故正確答案為 (A)。

79

How can patients get a discount?

(A) By calling next Monday

(B) By presenting a coupon

(C) By bringing a copy of a book

(D) By making an appointment this week

病患要如何獲得折扣？

(A) 下禮拜一打電話來

(B) 出示折價券

(C) 帶一本書來

(D) 本週預約

題目中的「discount」為關鍵字，段落中與折扣相關的句子為「If you set up an appointment this week, we'll take 20% off the cost of your initial consultation.」，故可以得知正確答案為 (D)。

80-82 radio broadcast

80–82 電台廣播

Welcome back, everyone. You are listening to Radio Classics this beautiful morning. We've invited into our studio today renowned performer Dimitry Olanov, a cellist who hails from Moscow. He first grabbed a cello when he was four years old, and he spent his youth winning numerous competitions. He first performed on the stage at Carnegie Hall at the young age of 16. He has traveled the world, delighting audiences everywhere, from as far west as Canada to as far east as Japan. He will perform for us here in a

歡迎大家回來。在這美麗的早晨，您現在正在收聽的是古典廣播電台。今天我們邀請到了來自莫斯科的知名大提琴演奏家迪米崔・歐藍諾來到播音室。他在四歲時就開始接觸大提琴，並在青少年時期贏得無數的比賽，年僅16歲就在卡內基音樂廳首次登場。他周遊列國，西至加拿大、東至日本，帶給世界各地的聽眾喜樂。一會後，他將為我們演奏韋瓦第。現在，

few minutes—Vivaldi. Now, with that introduction, I give you Mr. Olanov.

隨著介紹結束，讓我們歡迎歐藍諾先生。

• renowned 知名的　hail from . . . 來自……　numerous 無數的　delight 使高興　recital 演奏

80

Where can this morning's recital be heard?
(A) In the auditorium
(B) On the radio
(C) In Japan
(D) At Carnegie Hall

今天早上的演奏可以在哪裡聽到？
(A) 禮堂
(B) 收音機上
(C) 日本
(D) 卡內基音樂廳

地點資訊通常會在開頭出現。根據「You are listening to Radio Classics this beautiful morning」可以得知，這段話是對廣播收聽者說的，故正確答案為 (B)。

81

What does the speaker say about Dimitry Olanov?
(A) He lives in Russia.
(B) He does not perform outside Canada.
(C) He does not play a musical instrument.
(D) He won only one competition.

說話者說了什麼有關迪米崔・歐藍諾的事？
(A) 他住在俄羅斯。
(B) 他不在加拿大以外的地方表演。
(C) 他不會演奏樂器。
(D) 他只贏過一場比賽。

根據「We've invited into our studio today renowned performer Dimitry Olanov, a cellist who hails from Moscow.」可以得知，迪米崔・歐藍諾是來自莫斯科的大提琴家，而莫斯科又為俄羅斯首都，故正確答案為 (A)。

82

What will Dimitry Olanov most likely do this morning?
(A) Talk about his childhood
(B) Travel to Canada
(C) Discuss his love for Vivaldi
(D) Play a musical instrument

迪米崔・歐藍諾今天早上最有可能做什麼？
(A) 談論他的童年
(B) 去加拿大旅行
(C) 討論他對韋瓦地的喜愛
(D) 演奏樂器

從開頭的「You are listening to Radio Classics this beautiful morning.」可以知道這是個早晨廣播節目，再從後文得知迪米崔・歐藍諾為來賓，且「He will perform for us here in a few minutes」，表示接下來他將進行演奏，故正確答案為 (D)。

I truly appreciate all of your hard work on the project. Thanks to you, it was a huge success. The client just called to tell me that we have the best team of consultants he's ever worked with. We were able to lower their costs by over 40%, and we increased their sales by over 20% in less than one year! I know many of you are exhausted from the long hours you put into this project. I am confident that **(84)we could not have achieved this level of success without each and every one of you.** Each of you will be receiving an extra bonus for your superb efforts. I know none of you were able to take any time off this summer, but you can now enjoy some time off. The next project we have lined up is not until next month, November. Nothing for any of you to do until then.

真心感謝大家對這個專案付出的辛勞。因為有你們，這個專案相當地成功。客戶剛剛打來說我們是他合作過最棒的顧問團。一年內，我們為他們降低40%以上的成本，並將業績提升20%以上！我知道你們當中有許多人因為長時間投入這個專案而感到筋疲力盡。我相當確信，**(84)沒有在座的各位，我們就無法達成這樣的成就。** 每一位都將因傑出的努力獲得額外的獎金。我知道大家今年夏天都無法休假，但是現在你們可以享受休幾天假。我們安排的下個專案要到下個月——11月才會開始進行。在那之前，大家都不會有什麼工作要做。

- **appreciate** 感謝　**consultant** 顧問　**sales** 銷售量　**exhausted** 筋疲力盡的　**confident** 確信的
  superb 傑出的　**effort** 努力

 83

Who most likely are the listeners?
(A) Clients
(B) Consultants
(C) Salespeople
(D) Children

聽者最有可能是誰？
(A) 客戶
(B) 顧問
(C) 業務員
(D) 孩童

地點或職業資訊通常會在對話開頭出現。而根據「The client just called to tell me that we have the best team of consultants he's ever worked with.」可以知道，聽者應是顧問團的成員。正確答案為 (B)。

 84 NEW

Why does the speaker say, "we could not have achieved this level of success without each and every one of you"?
(A) She wants to achieve success.
(B) She has a new project for the team.
(C) She wants to praise the team members.
(D) She is ready for a vacation.

說話者為什麼說：「沒有在座的各位，我們就無法達成這樣的成就」？
(A) 她想要成功。
(B) 她要給團隊新專案。
(C) 她要稱讚團隊成員。
(D) 她準備好要休假了。

此類掌握意圖的題目，其前後文通常是最大的線索。題目引述的句子稱讚聽者工作表現優秀，而下句告知獎金與休假的資訊，故正確答案為 (C)。

85 -

What will the listeners do in October?

(A) Go on vacation
(B) Finish up the project
(C) Lower costs
(D) Start on a new project

聽者在十月時將做什麼？

(A) 休假
(B) 完成專案
(C) 降低成本
(D) 開始新的專案

從「you can now enjoy some time off. The next project we have lined up is not until next month, November. Nothing for any of you to do until then.」可知，到 11 月前都不會進行新的計畫，故 10 月時聽者可以休假。正確答案為 (A)。

86-88 talk

86-88 談話

Hello, guys. Thank you all for coming. As I told you yesterday, we're going to be moving our office down the street to the Conway Center in a couple of weeks. The new space will be a lot bigger than what we're using now. Also, you all know how famous and prestigious the Conway Center is. We're a boutique law firm, and the new address should help to better publicize us. Our monthly rent will be going up, but I think we're getting back solid value. Another bonus is that both the subway and the commuter train stations are connected through the basement of the Conway Center. That'll make commuting much easier for all of you who don't drive. I'll get back to you later this week with details about packing and hiring a moving company.

嗨，大家好。感謝大家的出席。如同我昨天所說的，幾週後我們公司就要搬到這條街上的康威中心。新辦公室的空間會比現有的大上許多。而且，各位也知道康威中心多有名氣。我們是一間精緻型律師事務所，新址應該更有助於宣傳。每個月的租金將會增加，但是我想我們可以獲得穩固的收益。另一個好處是，地鐵和通勤列車站都與康威中心的地下室相通。對於不開車的人來說通勤將更便利。這週稍後我會再告訴大家打包與聘僱搬家公司的相關細節。

• **prestigious** 有聲望的　**law firm** 律師事務所　**publicize** 宣傳　**rent** 租金　**solid** 穩固的　**commuter** 通勤者　**basement** 地下室　**pack** 打包　**moving company** 搬家公司

86 -

What is the speaker mainly talking about?

(A) A subway station
(B) A boutique law firm
(C) An office relocation
(D) A prestigious building

說話者主要在說明什麼？

(A) 地鐵站
(B) 精緻型律師事務所
(C) 辦公室搬遷
(D) 有名氣的大樓

談話目的通常會在對話開頭出現。根據「As I told you yesterday, we're going to be moving our office down the street to the Conway Center in a couple of weeks.」可以得知，本段文稿的主題是辦公室搬遷。正確答案為 (C)。

87

What is the merit of the change?
(A) Smaller space
(B) More publicity
(C) Decreased rent
(D) Parking

變動的優點是什麼？
(A) 空間更小
(B) 更多的宣傳
(C) 租金減少
(D) 停車

題目中的關鍵字為「merit」，故要在談話中尋找優點。根據「We're a boutique law firm, and the new address should help to better publicize us. Our monthly rent will be going up, but I think we're getting back solid value.」可以知道，「publicize」為最大的價值，故正確答案為 (B)。

88

What does the speaker say about the Conway Center?
(A) It is on top of a train station.
(B) It is next to a shopping mall.
(C) It is the tallest building in the city.
(D) It is on the other side of town.

說話者說了什麼有關康威中心的事？
(A) 它在火車站的上面。
(B) 它在購物中心的旁邊。
(C) 它是本市最高的大樓。
(D) 它位於本市的另一邊。

題目中的關鍵字為「Conway Center」，從後段內容可知「the subway and the commuter train stations are connected through the basement of the Conway Center.」，故正確答案為 (A)。

89-91 report

Good morning, everyone. You are watching *Today in Business*. I'm your host, Spencer Hawes. Our first story is about a blockbuster merger that was announced yesterday—GenuSoft and Softech. These are currently the two largest software companies in the United States, and after the merger, they will be the largest software company in the world. Yesterday's announcement stated that the reason for the merger is so that they can compete against Veriline, which is the world's largest software company today. The two merging companies have already laid out plans to come up with new global marketing strategies using social media platforms. The merger will become official this July. The new company will be called GenuTech, and it will be led by Valerie Wood, the current CEO of GenuSoft.

89–91 報導

大家早安。您現在收看的是《今日商業》。我是主持人史賓塞・霍伊斯。第一則報導是關於昨天一宣布就造成轟動的合併案——基努軟體與軟體科技合併案。這兩家是美國目前最大的兩間軟體公司，合併之後，他們將成為全世界規模最大的軟體公司。昨天的宣告中陳述了合併的原因，是為了與現今世界最大的軟體公司凡瑞萊恩相抗衡。兩間合併的公司已經訂定好計畫，要以社群媒體平台來進行新的全球行銷策略。今年七月將正式合併。新的公司名稱為基努科技，並將由基努軟體的現任執行長瓦樂利・伍德來領導公司。

• **host** 主持人　**merger** 合併案　**state** 陳述　**compete against** ... 與……抗衡　**lay out** 訂定
come up with 想出；提供（辦法）　**strategy** 策略　**official** 正式的

89 --

What is the report mainly about?
(A) A new construction project
(B) A business merger
(C) An innovative software product
(D) Social media platforms

這篇報導主要和什麼有關?
(A) 新的營建計畫
(B) 企業合併
(C) 創新的軟體產品
(D) 社群媒體平台

主題或目的通常會在開頭出現。根據「Our first story is about a blockbuster merger that was announced yesterday」可知,正確答案為 (B)。

 90 --

What can be inferred about GenuTech's future plans?
(A) It will focus more on online marketing.
(B) It will seek to merge with Veriline.
(C) It will market only in the United States.
(D) It will hire someone new as its first CEO.

關於基努科技的未來計畫,我們可推論出什麼?
(A) 將更專注於網路行銷。
(B) 將尋求與凡瑞萊恩合併。
(C) 只在美國行銷。
(D) 將聘請新人擔任首任執行長。

報導後段提到「The two merging companies have already laid out plans to come up with new global marketing strategies using social media platforms.」,表示將利用社群媒體平台來行銷,故正確答案應為 (A)。

91 -- 🎧 12

What does the speaker suggest about the reason behind GenuTech's formation?
(A) To increase sales revenues
(B) To deal with a market competitor
(C) To streamline costs
(D) To come up with global marketing strategies

說話者提到什麼與基努科技組成的背後原因有關的事?
(A) 為了增加銷售收入
(B) 為了應付市場競爭者
(C) 為了精簡成本
(D) 為了想出全球行銷策略

根據「Yesterday's announcement stated that the reason for the merger is so that they can compete against Veriline, which is the world's largest software company today.」可以知道,公司合併是為了與業界龍頭抗衡,故正確答案為 (B)。

I need your help with editing this video that I am hoping to upload onto the Internet. There is this new Web site that allows anyone to post clean, original works. I shot this video myself, but I'm having trouble getting rid of some of the noises in the background. I could really use your help with deleting those and also with adding in background music. Here is a list of the points in the video where I'd like you to insert music. Do you think you can do this? **(92)I need to make one change, though**. I've decided I want BGM 2 to be the opening music, rather than BGM 1. If you can get this done by Thursday, I'll give you $100!

Time	Music
0:00	BGM 1
2:12	BGM 2
5:25	BGM 3
5:50	BGM 4
6:41	BGM 3
7:01	BGM 1

我需要你協助我編輯這支我想要上傳到網路的影片。這是個新的網站,讓大家可以上傳完全原創的作品。我自己拍攝了這支影片,但是在去除背景雜音時碰到了困難。我真的需要你幫忙去除那些雜音,並加入背景音樂。這裡有一張清單是我希望你在影片中加入音樂的時間點。你覺得你可以接案嗎?**(92)不過我還要改一個地方。我決定要以背景音樂2作為開場音樂,而不是背景音樂1**。如果你可以在星期四前完成的話,我會支付你100元!

時間	音樂
0:00	背景音樂1
2:12	背景音樂2
5:25	背景音樂3
5:50	背景音樂4
6:41	背景音樂3
7:01	背景音樂1

• **edit** 編輯　**post** 張貼;發布(資訊)　**get rid of** 去除;擺脫

 92 NEW --

Why does the speaker say, "I need to make one change, though"?
(A) He wants to revise the chart.
(B) He has to change his background.
(C) He needs change for the vending machine.
(D) He wants to make a new song.

說話者為什麼說:「不過我還要改一個地方」?
(A) 他要修改圖表。
(B) 他要更換背景。
(C) 他需要零錢來投自動販賣機。
(D) 他想要做一首新的歌。

此類掌握意圖的題目,其前後文通常是最大的線索。段落中前一句提到請對方根據圖表加入背景音樂,後句提到想修改音樂,故說話者應該會修改圖表,好讓對方按照他的意思插入音樂。正確解答為 (A)。

93 --

What does the speaker expect the listener to do?
(A) Pay him $100
(B) Compose background music
(C) Complete the task by Thursday
(D) Help him shoot a video

說話者希望聽者做什麼事?
(A) 支付他100元
(B) 創作背景音樂
(C) 在星期四以前完成工作
(D) 幫他拍攝影片

根據最後部分的「If you can get this done by Thursday, I'll give you $100!」正確答案為 (C)。

Look at the graphic. What can you tell about the speaker's request?
(A) BGM 4 should be the opening music.
(B) BGM 2 comes after BGM 4.
(C) BGM 2 should be played in two spots.
(D) Background music should be inserted 5 times.

看一下圖表，說話者的要求為何？
(A) 背景音樂4應該是開場音樂。
(B) 背景音樂2排在背景音樂4之後。
(C) 背景音樂2應該在兩個時間點播放。
(D) 背景音樂應該安插五次。

根據「I've decided I want BGM 2 to be the opening music, rather than BGM 1.」，說話者要求將開場音樂從背景音樂1，改成背景音樂2。又因之後的檔案同樣為背景音樂2，故背景音樂2將出現兩次。正確解答為 (C)。

95-97 notice and schedule

95–97 通知及時程表

Thanks for coming, everyone. Let's get right to it. I'm going to explain to you what you need to do when picking classes this semester at Mi Amore Italian. As you know, our school is only open on Mondays and Tuesdays, and all of our classes are 120 minutes long. Students who are joining us for the first time are allowed only to take up to two classes per semester. This restriction is based on experience so you don't burn out too early. Returning students are free to take as many classes as they'd like. But some of the classes will require you to have taken another class first. For example, if you want to take Italian 201, you must already have completed Italian 101. The same thing applies to Italian 301; you must have completed Italian 201. Any questions?

感謝大家的出席。讓我們直接開始吧。我要向大家說明這學期在吾愛義大利學校選課時需要做的事。如同大家知道的，本校只開放星期一與星期二，而且所有的課程都是120分鐘。第一次來上課的學生每學期最多只可以修兩門課。這個限制是依照以往的經驗所訂定的，這樣各位才不會太早累壞。舊生可依個人意願選擇課程數量，但是部分課程規定必須先修過其他課程。舉例來說：如果你想修義大利文201的話，就必須先修完義大利文101；同樣規定也適用於義大利文301，你必須先修完義大利文201。有任何問題嗎？

	Monday	Tuesday
8:00 A.M.–10:00 A.M.	Italian Cuisine	Singing in Italian
12:00 P.M.–2:00 P.M.	Italian 101	Italian Opera
2:00 P.M.–4:00 P.M.	Italian Opera	Italian 301
3:30 P.M.–5:30 P.M.	Italian 201	Italian 101
7:00 P.M.–9:00 P.M.	Singing in Italian	Italian Cuisine

	星期一	星期二
上午8:00–上午10:00	義大利佳餚	義大利歌謠
中午12:00–下午2:00	義大利文101	義大利歌劇
下午2:00–下午4:00	義大利歌劇	義大利文301
下午3:30–下午5:30	義大利文201	義大利文101
晚上7:00–晚上9:00	義大利歌謠	義大利佳餚

• **restriction** 限制　**be based on . . .** 以……為基礎　**burn out** 累壞

Who are the listeners?

(A) Italian teachers
(B) Foreigners
(C) Students
(D) Employees

聽眾是誰？

(A) 義大利文老師
(B) 外國人
(C) 學生
(D) 員工

分辨聽眾身分的問題，通常在開頭會出現答案。從「I'm going to explain to you what you need to do when picking classes this semester at Mi Amore Italian.」可知，此段內容是向學生說明學校選課的方式，故正確答案為 (C)。

What is mentioned about the classes?

(A) New students can take up to two classes.
(B) Students may take Italian 201 and Italian 301 simultaneously.
(C) The first day of classes is on Saturday.
(D) No more than ten students are allowed in one class.

關於課程，提到了什麼事？

(A) 新生最多可以修兩門課。
(B) 學生可以同時選修義大利文201和義大利301。
(C) 上課第一天是星期六。
(D) 一堂課最多不能超過十位學生。

根據「But some of the classes will require you to have taken another class first.」，不能同時修義大利文 201 與 301，故 (B) 不正確。且「our school is only open on Mondays and Tuesdays」，故 (C) 也不正確。內容未提及上課人數，故 (D) 不正確。

從「Students who are joining us for the first time are allowed only to take up to two classes per semester.」可以知道，正確答案為 (A)。

 NEW

Look at the graphic. Which of the following combinations is possible for a new student?

(A) Italian 101 (Mon), Singing in Italian (Mon), and Italian Cuisine (Tues)
(B) Italian 101 (Mon) and Italian 301 (Tues)
(C) Italian 101 (Mon) and Italian 201 (Tues)
(D) Italian Cuisine (Mon) and Italian 101 (Tues)

看一下圖表，下列哪個組合對新生來說是可行的？

(A) 義大利文101（星期一）、義大利歌謠（星期一）和義大利佳餚（星期二）
(B) 義大利文101（星期一）和義大利文301（星期二）
(C) 義大利文101（星期一）和義大利文201（星期二）
(D) 義大利佳餚（星期一）和義大利文101（星期二）

新學生只能參加兩種科目，且參加 201 課程之前，需要先上完 101 課程，同樣上 301 課程前也需先上過 201 課程。故正確答案為 (D)。

98-100 telephone message and schedule

Hey, this is Megan calling. You know I was supposed to be flying back tomorrow, but I just got a call saying that my flight from Hawaii to Seattle has been canceled because of some unexpected bad weather. I called the airline, and they told me the soonest I can leave here is not going to be until tomorrow afternoon. But if I leave that late, by the time I land in Seattle and take public transportation to Tacoma, it's going to be after midnight. I think it makes more sense if I just enjoy this great place one extra night and fly back early the day after tomorrow. That should bring me into Tacoma that same evening. Anyway, Hawaii is just amazing. We should come together next time. I'll see you soon!

98-100 電話留言及時程表

嗨,我是梅根。你知道我本來打算明天要搭飛機回來,但是我剛接到電話,說因為天候不佳,導致我從夏威夷飛往西雅圖的班機被取消了。我打電話給航空公司,他們說最快要到明天下午才可離開這裡。但如果我那麼晚才離開,等我抵達西雅圖,再搭大眾交通運輸工具去塔科馬港市,應該已經過了午夜了。我想如果我在這麼棒的地方多待一晚,後天一早再搭飛機回去,這樣會比較合理些。我一樣會在當晚抵達塔科馬港市。不管怎樣,夏威夷真是太棒了。我們下次應該一起來的。一會兒見!

	Saturday, April 1	Sunday, April 2	Monday, April 3
Hawaii to Seattle	10:00 P.M.	4:00 P.M.	9:00 A.M.
Hawaii to Los Angeles	10:00 A.M.	11:00 A.M.	5:00 P.M.
Hawaii to Atlanta	3:30 P.M.	3:30 P.M.	3:30 P.M.

	4月1日 星期六	4月2日 星期日	4月3日 星期一
夏威夷至西雅圖	晚上 10:00	下午 4:00	上午 9:00
夏威夷至洛杉磯	上午 10:00	上午 11:00	下午 5:00
夏威夷至亞特蘭大	下午 3:30	下午 3:30	下午 3:30

- **unexpected** 出乎意料的 **land** 降落

98

Why did Megan make a phone call?
(A) To say she is going to be leaving early
(B) To say she has lost some luggage
(C) To report that her flight schedule got delayed
(D) To say she will be traveling next to Boston

梅根為什麼打這通電話?
(A) 說她要提早離開
(B) 說她有部分行李遺失
(C) 報告她的班機延誤了
(D) 說她接下來要去波士頓

目的通常會在開頭出現。根據「I just got a call that my flight from Hawaii to Seattle has been canceled because of some unexpected bad weather.」可以知道,航班因為天候不佳而取消。正確答案為 (C)。

What does Megan say about her schedule?
(A) She was originally scheduled to leave today.
(B) She is transferring in Hawaii.
(C) Her final destination is Seattle.
(D) She can depart from Hawaii tomorrow if she wants to.

梅根提到什麼和她行程有關的事？
(A) 她原本預定今天離開。
(B) 她會在夏威夷轉機。
(C) 她的最終目的地是西雅圖。
(D) 如果她要的話，明天可以離開夏威夷。

根據「I called the airline, and they told me the soonest I can leave here is not going to be until tomorrow afternoon.」，梅根最快可於明日下午搭機，離開夏威夷並前往西雅圖，故正確答案為 (D)。

(A) 她原本是預定明天離開。(B) 題目內容並沒有提到轉機一事。她只說了要在西雅圖轉乘大眾運輸工具到塔科馬港市，故西雅圖才是旅程的中繼地。(C) 最終目的地是塔科馬港市。

100 NEW

Look at the graphic. Which day will Megan go home?
(A) Saturday
(B) Sunday
(C) Monday
(D) Tuesday

看一下圖表，梅根將會在哪一天回家？
(A) 星期六
(B) 星期日
(C) 星期一
(D) 星期二

根據段落內容，梅根選擇不搭乘從夏威夷往西雅圖、下午起飛的班機，而是搭乘隔天最早的飛機，故根據時程表可得知，她應搭乘禮拜一早上的飛機回家，正確答案為 (C)。

ACTUAL TEST
4

1

(A) He is wearing a backpack.
(B) He is leaving the building.
(C) He is lifting the bag off the floor.
(D) He is getting into the vehicle.

(A) 他背著背包。
(B) 他正離開大樓。
(C) 他正從地上拿起包包。
(D) 他正要進車內。

• **lift** 拿起　**vehicle** 車輛

此為男子背著背包走在路上的照片。(B) 無法判斷男子是否從建築物裡走出。(C) 男子並未從地面提起包包。(D) 雖然出現車輛，但是男子並未表現出要進入車內的樣子。正確答案為 (A)。

2

(A) They are boarding the aircraft.
(B) They are loading luggage on the conveyor belt.
(C) They are rolling the suitcase.
(D) They are transporting the cartons.

(A) 他們正要上飛機。
(B) 他們正把行李放上輸送帶。
(C) 他們正在推行李。
(D) 他們正在搬運紙箱。

• **board** 登上（飛機）　**load** 裝載　**conveyor belt** 輸送帶　**transport** 搬運　**carton** 紙箱

此為在機場跑道上裝載行李的照片，照片背景中可以看到幾架飛機，男子們正把行李搬上輸送帶。(A) 雖然可以看到飛機，但是照片中未能看出正在登機。(C) 並非正在推行李，而是正在裝載行李。(D) 照片中並未看到紙箱。正確答案為 (B)。

3

(A) Trees are being planted in front of a building.
(B) Lines are being painted on the road.
(C) Shadows are being cast on the pavement.
(D) Lampposts are being installed by the sign.

(A) 大樓前正在種樹。
(B) 路上正在畫交通指示線。
(C) 影子投射在人行道上。
(D) 街燈柱正被裝設在標誌旁。

• **cast** 投射　**pavement** 人行道

此為街道上空無一人的風景照。道路上有影子，還可以看到幾盞路燈。大部分描寫景物的照片，選項中如果使用「being p.p.」，且搭配的動詞為人為動作，則多非正確答案。

(A) 樹木已經種植在建築物前，而不是正在被種植的狀態（being planted）。此選項若要成為正確解答，應刪去「being」。(B) 雖然道路上有線條，但是已經被漆上，並非正在上漆的狀態。此選項若要成為正確答案，應刪去「being」。(C) 由於影子的出現並非人的動作造成，所以在風景照片的題型中，可以成為正確答案。(D) 照片中僅出現一盞路燈。從主詞為複數這點開始，就可以判定非正確答案，且「being installed」必須由人表現進行（by＋人）。故正確答案為 (C)。

4

(A) One of the women is sitting on the grass.
(B) They're standing in line for a bus.
(C) They're gathered together outdoors.
(D) A man is taking a picture in the park.

(A) 其中一位女士正坐在草地上。
(B) 他們正在排隊等公車。
(C) 他們聚集在戶外。
(D) 一位男士正在公園裡拍照。

照片中人們聚集在戶外，且周圍有兩輛巴士。當照片裡出現兩個以上的人物，應先仔細觀察照片中人物的差異。 (A) 女子不是坐在草地上，而是坐在戶外椅上。(B) 並未出現排隊等候搭乘巴士的景象。(D) 並未看到男子在拍照。正確答案為 (C)。

5

(A) A flag has been hung on the exterior of the building.
(B) A car is being parked on the road.
(C) Some windows have been left opened.
(D) The stairway leads to the balcony.

(A) 一面旗子被掛在大樓外面。
(B) 一輛車正被停在馬路上。
(C) 一些窗戶打開著。
(D) 樓梯通往陽台。

• **exterior** 外部　**stairway** 樓梯

這是洋服店外觀的照片，建築物外面懸掛了一面旗幟，有車輛停放在路邊，且沒有任何人物出現。(B) 車子已經是停放的狀態，並非正在停車。此選項若要成為正確解答，應刪去「being」。(C) 窗戶都是關上的狀態。如果照片中出現門窗，請先確認是全部打開或只有部分打開。(D) 階梯延伸至店面入口，而非陽台。正確答案為 (A)。

🎧 13

6

(A) A server is taking off an apron.
(B) Patio umbrellas have been folded.
(C) They are having a conversation with a cashier.
(D) Some seats are taken at an outdoor restaurant.

(A) 一位服務生正脫下圍裙。
(B) 露臺的洋傘收起來了。
(C) 他們正在和收銀員說話。
(D) 露天餐廳有些位子已經有人坐了。

• **take off** 脫下（衣物）　**apron** 圍裙　**patio** 露臺

此為人們在戶外餐廳用餐的照片，且可看出座位並未被坐滿。

(A) 餐廳前的服務生已經穿上（wear）圍裙。(B) 戶外用陽傘為撐開狀態。如果改為「be opened」有可能成為正確答案。(C) 照片中並未出現收銀員。(D) 雖然使用「be taken」，表示被佔據使用，但是也請熟記「be occupied」的用法。正確答案為 (D)。

PART 2

7

Do you have a concert ticket?
(A) I left it in my office.
(B) Please take your seat.
(C) I booked the table.

你有演唱會的票嗎？
(A) 我放在辦公室了。
(B) 請坐。
(C) 我訂位了。

此為詢問是否持有票券的 Yes/No 問句。選項 (A) 省略「No」並告知放在家裡，故為適當答案。(B) 此為提及演唱會相關之延伸字彙的誤導答案。(C) 告知對方自己預約了餐廳，與題目毫不相關。正確答案為 (A)。

8

Could we discuss this after lunch?
(A) No, every 30 minutes.
(B) I'm meeting some clients.
(C) About launching the product.

我們可以在午餐後討論這件事嗎？
(A) 不，每30分鐘。
(B) 我要見一些客戶。
(C) 有關產品的上市。

• launch（產品）上市

此題為邀請疑問句，詢問午餐後能否進行討論。選項 (A) 雖然明確說「No」，但是後續的說明與題目情境不符。(B) 省略「No」並告知要與客戶見面，以此表示拒絕，故為適當答案。(C) 此為利用與題目「lunch」發音相似的「launch」製造陷阱。正確答案為 (B)。

9

Who can open the office supply room?
(A) I have the key.
(B) I report to Joanne.
(C) Some new supplies.

誰能打開辦公用品供應室？
(A) 我有鑰匙。
(B) 我向瓊安報告。
(C) 一些新用品。

• office supply 辦公用品

此題為以疑問詞「Who」詢問誰可以打開房間的問句。選項 (A) 告知對方自己有鑰匙，代表自己可以打開，故為正確答案。(B) 因為題目並非在詢問向誰報告，雖然選項 (B) 以人名回答，但內容和題目不相關。看見「Who」問句時，應該要判斷題目問的專有名詞為何。(C) 此為利用與題目中「supply」發音相似的「supplies」製造陷阱，其句意也和題目情境不符。正確答案為 (A)。

10

What kind of products does your company make?
(A) Sportswear mostly.
(B) The Production Department.
(C) I'll accompany you.

貴公司生產何種產品？
(A) 主要是運動服飾。
(B) 生產部。
(C) 我會陪你。

• accompany 陪伴

題目為疑問詞「What」問句，詢問公司製造何種產品。(A) 回答「主要是運動服飾」，明確說出品項，故為合適答案。(B) 如果是要求回答部門名稱的問句，應該要以「Which department/division . . .」進行詢問。(C) 此為利用與題目中的「company」發音相似的「accompany」製造陷阱。正確答案為 (A)。

11 --

When did Henry tidy the office?
(A) After we left.
(B) Soon, I hope.
(C) She cleaned the floor.

亨利是什麼時候整理辦公室的？
(A) 我們離開後。
(B) 我希望不久後。
(C) 她清理了地板。

• **tidy** 整理

題目以疑問詞「When」與過去式，詢問他人何時整理了辦公室。選項 (A) 表達「我們離開後」，故為適當答案。(B)「When」是詢問時間點的疑問詞，故應先判斷時態。選項 (B) 與題目時態不符。(C) 此為利用與題目中的「tidy」意義相近的「clean」造成混淆。題目並未詢問要清掃何處，且題目中的「Henry」為男性的名字，代名詞應使用「he」。正確答案為 (A)。

12 --

Where is your new restaurant located?
(A) In a couple of hours.
(B) It's right around the corner.
(C) I had the chicken.

你們新餐廳位於何處？
(A) 在幾個小時後。
(B) 就在轉角處。
(C) 我吃雞肉。

• **a couple of** 數個　**around the corner** 在轉角處；在附近

本題以疑問詞「Where」詢問新餐廳位置。(A) 選項若要成為正確解答，則問句應使用「When」或「What time」詢問，且詢問內容要與時間相關。(B) 表示過轉角就到，為適當答案。(C) 此為利用與題目中的「restaurant」相關的「chicken」製造陷阱。正確答案為 (B)。

13 --

How often do you visit your parents in Brisbane?
(A) For a decade.
(B) It's in Sydney, I think.
(C) They don't live there anymore.

你多久去探望一次住在布里斯本的父母？
(A) 十年了。
(B) 我想是在雪梨。
(C) 他們不住在那裡了。

• **decade** 十年

(A) 題目不是與「How long」詢問，故回答與問題無關。(B) 題目不是與「Where」詢問，故回答與問題無關。本題是用疑問詞「How often」詢問頻率的句型。常見回答應為告知「有多常」做某事，但選項 (C) 則是說明「（父母）不住在那裡」，意即不會去布里斯本，故也是合適回答，正確答案為 (C)。

14

14 --

Why is the library closing early?
(A) I checked out the books.
(B) There's a foundation day event.
(C) At ten o'clock on weekends.

圖書館為什麼提早閉館？
(A) 我借了書。
(B) 有設館紀念日活動。
(C) 在週末10點。

• **check out** 借（書）　**foundation day** 設立紀念日

(A) 此為利用題目中「library」與選項裡「books」的關聯性，試圖設下陷阱。(B) 本題用疑問詞「Why」詢問圖書館提早閉館的原因，故表示「有設館紀念日活動」為合適回應。(C) 因為題目詢問的不是時間，故非正確答案。正確答案為 (B)。

15 --

Which plant produces these umbrellas?
(A) The one in Westville.
(B) It's going to rain.
(C) Yes, water the plants.

哪間廠房生產這些雨傘？
(A) 在韋斯特維爾那間。
(B) 要下雨了。
(C) 是的，為植物澆水。

• **plant** 廠房

(A) 疑問詞「Which」後面出現的名詞即為問題的核心。本題詢問的是哪間廠房，選項 (A) 以「the one」代表「那間」工廠，且表達出地點位置，故為適當答案。

(B) 此為利用與題目中「umbrella」相關的「rain」誘導，但內容與題目無關。(C) 以「Yes」開頭即可判定錯誤。疑問詞問句不可使用「Yes/No」回答。正確答案為 (A)。

16 --

You can pick up your car after one o'clock.
(A) You are a mechanic.
(B) I can deliver it for you.
(C) Okay, I'll drop by then.

你可以在一點後取車。
(A) 你是技師。
(B) 我可以幫你遞送。
(C) 好的，我到時候會過去。

• **pick up** 取（某物品）　**mechanic** 技師　**deliver** 遞送　**drop by** 拜訪

(A) 此為利用與題目中的「car」相關的「mechanic」製造陷阱。(B) 此為利用與題目中的「pick up」相關的「deliver」製造陷阱。陳述句題型最重要的是分析。本題題目提到車子的修理工作下午就會完成，選項 (C) 回答會去把車子開回來，故正確答案為 (C)。

17 --

The prototype will be ready by next Monday, won't it?
(A) We're still working on it.
(B) Yes, I can type.
(C) I already read the novel.

這原型在下週一前會準備好，不是嗎？
(A) 我們還在進行中。
(B) 是的，我會打字。
(C) 我已經看過那本小說了。

此為附加問句題型，基本上可以用「Yes/No」回答，但是為了確定更細部的內容，需要先分析陳述句的部分。

(A) 為省略「No」的附加說明，告知對方因為仍在作業中，所以有可能無法及時準備齊全，故為合適答案。(B) 因為「Yes」後面的附加內容與題目無關，故此為利用與題目中「prototype」發音相似的「type」製造陷阱。(C) 為利用與題目中「ready」發音相似的「already read」製造陷阱，且內容與題目無關。正確答案為 (A)。

18

Do you think the new handbook contains enough information?
(A) I would have liked more pictures.
(B) No, thanks. I've had enough.
(C) I think it can be handled properly.

你認為新手冊裡有足夠的資訊嗎？
(A) 我希望有更多的圖片。
(B) 不，謝了。我夠了。
(C) 我想那可以被妥當地處理。

要掌握間接問句「Do you think . . . ?」欲詢問的訊息，必須仔細聆聽「think」後面的內容。本題欲詢問的是手冊中是否有足夠的資訊，(A) 省略了「No」，並表示需要更多照片，故為正確解答。

(B) 中的「No thanks」是慎重拒絕提議時的慣用句。然而本題並無任何提議，以此選項回答與題目無關。(C) 雖然使用與題目相同的字彙「think」，但是與題目的脈絡不符。正確答案為 (A)。

19

Are you starting your new job immediately or taking some time off?
(A) Yes, I applied for that online.
(B) Yes, I'm interested in the position.
(C) I'm going on vacation first.

你會立即開始新工作，還是先休息一陣子？
(A) 是的，我在網路上申請的。
(B) 是的，我對那職位有興趣。
(C) 我要先去度假。

• **immediately** 立即　**take time off** 休假　**position** 職位

此題利用選擇疑問句，詢問要開始新的工作還是先休假。(A) 選擇疑問句無法用「Yes/No」回答，且回答內容與題目不相關。(B) 此為利用與題目中「job」相同意思的「position」誤導。(C) 明確選擇休假，故正確答案為 (C)。

20

What did the supervisor say about the annual report?
(A) Once a year.
(B) At the staff meeting.
(C) She's satisfied with it.

主管對於年度報告說了什麼？
(A) 一年一次。
(B) 在員工會議上。
(C) 她很滿意。

此題用疑問詞「What」，詢問主管說的內容。(A) 選項中的「once a year」似乎在呼應題目中的「annual」，但是此答覆內容更適合「How often」問句。(B) 因為主管對報告的感想與場所無關，故不是正確答案。(C) 轉達「她很滿意」，故正確答案為 (C)。

21 --

Do you mind reviewing this budget proposal for me?
(A) You proposed to me.
(B) Sure, I'd be happy to.
(C) She has a different view.

你介意幫我看一下這份預算報告嗎？
(A) 你向我求婚。
(B) 當然，我很樂意。
(C) 她有不同的觀點。

 review 審查　budget 預算　propose 求婚

「Do you mind . . . ?」的實際意思為「你可以……嗎？」，表示鄭重的請託，此處解釋為「你介意……嗎？」一般而言，此狀態下的「Yes」為拒絕，而「No」為接受。

(A) 此為利用與題目「proposal」發音類似的「proposed」設下陷阱，且與題目的內容不符。
(B) 選項的「Sure」代表「不介意幫忙」，表示回答者接受請託，故為正確解答。(C) 也是利用與題目「reviewing」發音類似的「view」設下陷阱，而且題目中並未出現可以使用代名詞「she」的對象。正確答案為 (B)。

22 --

Our advertising budget was increased this month more than we expected.
(A) Yes, by 15 percent.
(B) Every Monday afternoon.
(C) By decreasing advertisements.

我們這個月的廣告預算增加超出預期。
(A) 是的，增加了15%。
(B) 每週一下午。
(C) 藉由減少廣告。

 advertising budget 廣告預算

題目為表示廣告預算增加的陳述句。(A) 表示同意並說明預算增加了 15%，此為合適解答。
(B) 描述的狀況和題目不符。(C) 則使用了與題目「advertising」發音類似的「advertisement」，和「increase」的相關字彙「decreasing」形成陷阱。題目表示廣告預算增加，此選項卻說廣告減少，故不是正確答案。正確答案為 (A)。

23 --

Let's move to a quieter place for our efficiency.
(A) Of course, the movie was great.
(B) A new apartment building.
(C) Room 81 is available.

為了效率，讓我們移到比較安靜的地方吧。
(A) 當然，這部電影很棒。
(B) 一棟新的公寓大樓。
(C) 可以用81室。

• quieter 比較安靜的　efficiency 效率　available 可用的

「Let's . . .」的意思是「一起做……」，表示提議。(A) 為使用與「move」相似發音的「movie」作陷阱，雖然表示同意，但是後面的附加說明內容與題目不符。(B) 為使用與「place」相關的「apartment」誤導。題目提議換個安靜點的場所，選項 (C) 表示附和並提議房間，故正確答案為 (C)。

24

Don't we need to set another table?
(A) Employees from the sales team won't be coming.
(B) I've never been to that place.
(C) Yes, it's a famous restaurant.

我們不需要多擺設一張桌子嗎？
(A) 銷售團隊的員工不會來。
(B) 我從沒去過那個地方。
(C) 是的，是間著名的餐廳。

• **set the table** 擺設桌子

詢問是否要佈置更多桌子的否定問句。如果需要，則回答「Yes」；如不需要，則應回答「No」，此與肯定疑問句相同。

(A) 為省略「No」的回答。表示「員工不會出席，所以沒有必要」，故此選項為正確解答。(B) 為使用帶有否定意味的「never」（從未……；絕不……）的陷阱。(C) 因為回答了「Yes」，後續的附加說明應為「需要擺設」，但此句後段內容與題目無關。故正確答案為 (A)。

25

Should we leave now, or can we wait a bit?
(A) I was a little bit late.
(B) You can leave it here, thanks.
(C) It really depends on the traffic conditions.

我們應該要現在離開，還是可以再等一下？
(A) 我有點遲到了。
(B) 你可以把它放在這，謝謝。
(C) 要看現在的交通狀況而定。

題目為詢問要現在離開還是等候的選擇疑問句。請注意，表示反問的選項也有可能是正確答案，故不可先入為主，一概視為錯誤答案。

(A) 雖然使用與題目相同的字彙「a bit」，時態卻與題目有出入。(B) 雖然也出現與題目相同的字彙「leave」，但是在本選項的意思不是「離開」，而是「留下」。請注意，雖然本題不在此例，但是大部分的選擇疑問句題型中，出現與題目相同字彙的選項成為正確答案的機率相當高。

(C) 在做出選擇之前反問路況，故正確答案為 (C)。

26

Who can show me how to install the new program?
(A) I just saw this month's figures.
(B) I will, in a few minutes.
(C) I'm not sure how to get there.

誰可以教我如何安裝新程式？
(A) 我剛看到這個月的數據。
(B) 我可以，再等一下。
(C) 我不確定要如何到那裡。

• **install** 安裝 **figure** 數據

題目用疑問詞「Who」詢問可以示範安裝方法的人。(A) 表示「我看到了」，雖然也是第一人稱，但是時態不符合，且回答的內容也與題目不符。(B) 表示稍後可以示範，故為正解。(C)「I'm not sure」等迂迴的答覆也可能是正確答案，但是後面接續的「前往方法」（how to get there）並非題目詢問的訊息。故正確答案為 (B)。

27 --

Will our proposal get to the Paris branch on time? | 我們的企畫案會準時抵達巴黎分公司嗎？
(A) In the city council. | (A) 在市議會。
(B) I sent it by overnight mail. | (B) 我用特急郵件寄的。
(C) A 20 percent increase. | (C) 20%的增額。

• **proposal** 企畫案　**branch** 分公司　**on time** 準時

題目使用未來助動詞「Will」，詢問企畫書能否及時送達。(A) 提及的「市議會」與題目無關。(B) 表達已用隔日送達的特急郵件寄送，表示可以及時送達，故為合適答案。(C) 回答與題目無關。正確答案為 (B)。

28 --

When can I receive the shipment of dress shoes? | 我什麼時候可以收到禮服鞋那批貨？
(A) From the shoe store. | (A) 從鞋店。
(B) A couple of months ago. | (B) 幾個月前。
(C) It's delayed at the airport. | (C) 它在機場被延誤了。

• **shipment** 運輸的貨物

題目以疑問詞「When」詢問可以收到物品的時間。(A) 為詢問場所時可能出現的答案，是使用了與題目中「dress」相關的「shoes」造成陷阱。(B) 與題目時態不符。(C) 表示「在機場被耽誤」，代表還需要等候一段時間，故正確答案為 (C)。

29 --

Our train will be an hour late, right? | 我們的火車會晚一個小時到，是嗎？
(A) We should push back the client meeting. | (A) 我們應該延後客戶會議。
(B) We really enjoyed the training. | (B) 我們真的很喜歡那個訓練課程。
(C) Platform 6 or 8. | (C) 6號或8號月台。

• **push back** 延後；推遲

題目為詢問火車時刻是否延遲的附加疑問句。(A) 省略「Yes」，但說明會議因為延遲應該延後，故此選項為正確答案。(B) 為使用與題目「train」相似發音的「training」誘導。(C) 此為使用「train」相關字彙的陷阱。如果回答中要提及「platform」，題目應該詢問搭乘火車的地點。正確答案為 (A)。

30 --

Where should we place the new file cabinets? | 我們應該把新的檔案櫃放哪裡？
(A) It depends on Ms. Park. | (A) 由帕克女士決定。
(B) Just across the street. | (B) 就在對街。
(C) I ordered more a few days ago. | (C) 我好幾天前有多訂。

題目用疑問詞「Where」詢問檔案櫃的放置處，(A) 表示放置地點由帕克女士決定，迂迴地告知對方應該詢問帕克女士，故此選項為合適回覆。(B) 只說明「在對街」並不夠明確。(C) 此內容與題目無關。如果要成為正確答案，題目應使用「When」並以過去式詢問。正確答案為 (A)。

31 --

Wasn't the budget report supposed to be completed this morning?
(A) I'm supposed to work.
(B) There was a mistake on page 10.
(C) By decreasing the budget.

這個預算報告不是應該在今天早上完成嗎？
(A) 我應該要工作。
(B) 第10頁有誤。
(C) 藉由減少預算。

• be supposed to V . . . 應該

題目為否定疑問句。(A) 雖然使用與題目相同的片語「supposed to」，但是內容與題目的情境不符合。(B) 省略「Yes, but . . .」並提到因為報告書第十頁有錯誤，所以還沒有完成，為合適答案。(C) 也是利用與題目相同的字彙「budget」所形成的陷阱。本題正確為 (B)。

PART 3 15

32-34 conversation

W	Good morning, Steve. This is Stella. I just came in and turned my computer on, but my screen is not working. I'm sure it's turned on because I can hear the fan blowing.
M	Are you sure the monitor is turned on? The computer and the monitor should be plugged into two separate outlets.
W	I'm not sure. I just pushed the power button and didn't touch anything else. I have to submit the weekly report first thing in the morning, so I am in real trouble now.
M	Calm down. Can you see the power light on? I mean, the one on the monitor.
W	Yes, both the computer and monitor are on. One is red and the other is blue.
M	Ah! That must be the problem. The indicator is blue if the monitor is connected to the computer properly.
W	So, you mean it's already turned on, right? What should I do to check now?
M	Do you see a blue cable coming out from the monitor? That must be plugged into the back of the computer. No, wait a minute. I'm coming to the 2nd floor. Just don't touch anything. I'll do it.

32–34 對話

女	史提夫，早安。我是史黛拉。我剛進來打開電腦，但我的螢幕壞了。我很確定電腦開機了，因為我有聽到風扇在吹的聲音。
男	妳確定螢幕有打開嗎？電腦跟螢幕應該是插在兩個不同的插座上。
女	我不確定。我剛按了電源鈕，就沒碰其他東西了。我早上得先把週報表交出去，所以我現在真的麻煩大了。
男	冷靜下來。妳有看到電源指示燈亮起嗎？我是指，螢幕上的那個。
女	有，電腦和螢幕的兩個燈都亮著。一個是紅的，另一個是藍的。
男	啊！那就是問題所在了。如果螢幕有正確地連接到電腦上的話，指示燈會是藍色的。
女	所以，你是說電腦已經開機了，是嗎？那我現在應該檢查什麼？
男	妳有看到螢幕那有條藍色的傳輸線嗎？那應該要插進電腦後面的插槽。不，等一下。我去二樓。什麼都不要碰。我來處理。

• **plug into** （插頭）插入　**separate** 個別的　**outlet** 電源插座　**submit** 呈交　**calm down** 冷靜下來　**indicator** 指示器　**cable** 電線

32

Why did the woman call the man?
(A) To get help fixing a problem
(B) To replace a device with a new one
(C) To send him an urgent document
(D) To purchase a monitor

這位女士為什麼打電話給這位男士？
(A) 要請求協助修復問題
(B) 要更換新設備
(C) 要寄給他一份緊急文件
(D) 要購買螢幕

女子撥打電話的目的請在女子的台詞中尋找。一開始，女子說：「I just came in and turned my computer on, but my screen is not working.」女子說明自己打開電腦，但是螢幕沒有出現畫面。接著，她為了解決這個問題，而繼續和另一方對話，故正確答案為 (A)。

(D) 為透過對話找到的解決方法，並非一開始女子撥打電話的目的。

33

According to the woman, what did she do in the morning?
(A) Turned on her computer
(B) Came in earlier than usual
(B) Tried connecting her monitor again
(C) Printed the weekly report from her computer

根據這位女士所言，她早上做了什麼？
(A) 打開電腦
(B) 比平常更早進公司
(C) 試著再次連接螢幕
(D) 從她的電腦列印出週報表

女子說：「I just pushed the power button and didn't touch anything else.」，由此可知，她早上打開了電腦，正確答案為 (A)。

注意題目中並未提及女子平時多早來上班，也沒有提到今日的狀況而無法進行比較，故 (B) 非正確答案。注意不要混淆「just came in」與「first thing」等慣用法。

34

What will the man probably do next?
(A) Submit the report for Stella
(B) Meet Stella in her office
(C) Bring his computer to the 2nd floor
(D) Try plugging the computer into another outlet

這位男士接下來可能會做什麼？
(A) 為史黛拉提交報告
(B) 和史黛拉在她的辦公室碰面
(C) 把他的電腦搬到二樓
(D) 嘗試將電腦插頭插進另一個插座

對話的後半部中，男子對女子說，螢幕的藍色電線應該要和主機連結。接著，又告訴女子，自己將會去幫她（I'm coming to the 2nd floor. Just don't touch anything. I'll do it.），故可推測男子將前往女子位於二樓的辦公室，親自檢查螢幕與主機。正確答案為 (B)。

35-37 conversation

W	Hi, James. One of our drivers who usually delivers our merchandise to the Arcade Bakery is off sick today. So could you fill in for him this afternoon?
M	Sure, but this would be my first time delivering to that store. I need to know how to get there. Do you have the directions?
W	Okay, here you are. Just follow the map! One more thing, when you're there, remember to have the store manager sign the delivery confirmation form.

35-37 對話

女	嗨，詹姆斯。平常送貨到拱廊麵包店的那位司機今天請病假，所以你今天下午可以代他的班嗎？
男	當然可以，不過這是我第一次送貨到那家店。我需要知道怎麼到那裡。妳有路線資訊嗎？
女	好的，在這裡。只要跟著地圖上的指示走就行了！還有一件事，到了之後，記得讓店經理在送貨單上簽名。

* deliver 運送　merchandise 商品；貨物　off sick 請病假　fill in for ... 代（某人）班
  directions 路線資訊

35 ---

Why does the woman ask the man for help?
(A) A coworker is not feeling well.
(B) She is very sick.
(C) She is out of town this afternoon.
(D) She will take some time off.

這位女士為什麼向男士求助？
(A) 一位同事身體不適。
(B) 她生了重病。
(C) 她今天下午要出城。
(D) 她要休一段時間的假。

女子的第一句台詞說：「One of our drivers who usually delivers our merchandise to the Arcade Bakery is off sick today.」，表示送貨人員因為身體不適無法來上班，隨後她又說「So could you fill in for him this afternoon?」，拜託男子代替同事執行工作。由此可知，正確答案為 (A)。

36 ---

What does the man need?
(A) A key to a truck
(B) A telephone number
(C) A director's contact information
(D) Directions to a store

這位男士需要什麼？
(A) 卡車鑰匙
(B) 電話號碼
(C) 主管的聯絡方式
(D) 去商家的路線資料

男子的台詞中提及「I need to know how to get there. Do you have the direction?」，因為男子不知道如何前往，所以向女子詢問前往店家的路線資訊。由此可知，正確答案為 (D)。

37 ---

What does the woman remind the man to do?
(A) Get a signature
(B) Notify his manager
(C) Become a member
(D) Sign the contract

這位女士提醒男士要做什麼事？
(A) 拿到簽名
(B) 通知經理
(C) 成為會員
(D) 簽合約

本題詢問女子提醒男子記得的事，應該要注意聆聽女子的台詞。對話的後半部提到：「remember to have the store manager sign the delivery confirmation form」，要男子別忘記讓客戶簽名，所以正確答案為 (A)。

特別注意當題目出現「remind」時，對話中「don't forget」或「remember」後面的內容很有可能是正確答案。

38-40 conversation

| 38–40 對話 |

M Hello, this is Robert from SM Telecom. I'm supposed to visit you around two to upgrade the router.	男 哈囉，我是SM電信的羅伯特。我大約兩點會到貴府升級路由器。
W Oops, I didn't expect you today. I thought you would come over tomorrow.	女 哎呀，我沒想到你今天會來。我以為你明天才會過來。
M Oh, I'm sorry. There seems to be a mix-up in the information. Can I have your name, please?	男 喔，很抱歉。資料好像搞錯了。可以麻煩您告訴我您的大名嗎？
W I'm Ella Spencer in unit 503, Mainwell Apartments. And if possible, I'd rather have the service today because my Internet connection has been lagging all day.	女 我是明緯大樓503室的艾拉‧史賓賽。如果可以的話，我希望今天可以維修，因為我的網路連線一整天都跑得很慢。
M Sure, Ms. Spencer. Your appointment was at 2:30 P.M. on Wednesday, but I can reschedule it right away. Is it okay to visit you at two?	男 沒問題，史賓賽女士。您預約的時間是週三的下午兩點半，但我可以立刻重新安排。下午兩點過去可以嗎？
W Two sounds fine. I'll be staying home around that time, but I need to go out at three o'clock.	女 兩點可以。那個時間我會在家，但我三點需要出門。
M No problem. The work will take no longer than twenty minutes. I'll see you then.	男 沒問題。工程時間不會超過20分鐘。到時候見。

• **upgrade** 升級　**router** 路由器　**mix-up** （混亂引起的）錯誤　**lag** 緩慢移動；滯後
reschedule 重新安排時間

38 -

Why will the man visit the woman's house? | 這位男士為什麼要造訪女士的家？
(A) To verify her name and address | (A) 要核對她的姓名與地址
(B) To reschedule an appointment | (B) 要重新安排預約
(C) To improve the network speed | (C) 要改善網路速度
(D) To sell a telecommunication device | (D) 要賣電信設備

男子一開始提到「to upgrade the router」，即告知了拜訪目的。儘管不知道路由器（router）為一種網路設備，從對話中間部分的女子台詞：「I'd rather have the service today because my Internet connection has been lagging all day.」可以得知，女子覺得網路速度慢，希望相關人員能在今天維修。意即，如果男子前往升級路由器，將可以提高女子的網路速度，故正確答案為 (C)。

(D) 的「telecommunication device」雖然也可以是「router」，但是對話中無法看出是在「sell」，故不是正確答案。

39

Why does the man ask the woman's name?
(A) He is trying to be polite.
(B) Some information is not accurate.
(C) He'll write her a letter afterwards.
(D) He wants to record the woman's voice.

這位男士為什麼詢問女士的姓名？
(A) 他試著表現禮貌。
(B) 有些資料不正確。
(C) 他之後將寫信給她。
(D) 他想錄下女士的聲音。

從內容可知道，男子原本計畫在週三拜訪用戶，但他致電告知自己將在週二前往，並在電話中提到「There seems to be a mix-up in the information. Can I have your name, please?」男子混淆了客戶資料，所以必須詢問對方的姓名，以確認目前通話對象的資訊。由此可知，正確答案為 (B)。

比起「What's your name?」，「Can I have your name, please?」更加慎重，但是「表現禮貌」本身無法成為詢問姓名的原因，故 (A) 非正確答案。

40

What time does the woman want the upgrade to be finished by?
(A) By 2:00 P.M.
(B) By 2:20 P.M.
(C) By 2:30 P.M.
(D) By 3:00 P.M.

這位女士希望升級工作幾點前可以完成？
(A) 下午2:00前
(B) 下午2:20前
(C) 下午2:30前
(D) 下午3:00前

女子說：「Two sounds fine. I'll be staying home around that time, but I need to go out at three o'clock.」，表示自己三點前要出門，暗示她希望升級工作可以在那之前完成。由此可知，正確答案為 (D)。

(A) 的兩點為男子預計來訪的時間。(C) 的兩點三十分則為原本週三的預約時間。另外，原本約定的時間是週三，而女子在對話中提到，她以為男子明天才會來訪，故可以得知今天為週二。

41-43 conversation

M	Hi, Jessica. I was just looking over the building you designed for Mr. Bradley's law firm, and you did a great job!
W	Thanks, I did my best! It was a wonderful design to work on!
M	Why don't you join my team for our new account with Commonwealth Bank? You know, maybe they could be one of the biggest banks. They're expanding the business to open new branches nationwide.
W	It sounds really interesting. But, at this time, ⁽⁴²⁾**I really can't say.** I'm having a meeting with my manager to discuss another big project tomorrow, though.

41–43 對話

男	嗨，潔西卡。我剛看過妳為布萊德利先生的律師事務所設計的大樓。妳表現得很好！
女	謝謝，我盡力了！這是一個很棒的設計案！
男	妳何不加入我們新客戶聯邦銀行的專案呢？妳知道的，他們可是數一數二的大銀行。他們正在拓展業務，在全國各地開設新分行。
女	聽起來很有趣。不過現在，⁽⁴²⁾我真的不敢肯定。我明天要和主管討論另一個大案子。

ACTUAL TEST **4**

PART **3**

中譯＋解析

15

| M | Okay. Is it possible to stop by your meeting and go over the details with both of you? This way, your manager will know how important this bank's project is as well. | 男 | 好吧。那有沒有可能讓我一起參加會議，和你們兩位說明一下細節？這樣，妳的主管也會知道這個銀行的專案有多重要。 |
| W | That sounds good! | 女 | 聽起來不錯！ |

• look over 閱覽　law firm 律師事務所　account 客戶　expand 拓展　nationwide 全國

 41 --

Where are the speakers working?
(A) At an advertising agency
(B) At a law firm
(C) At an architectural company
(D) At a design school

說話者在哪裡工作？
(A) 廣告公司
(B) 律師事務所
(C) 建築公司
(D) 設計學校

針對詢問對話者工作場所的題型，請專心聽對話的前半部。男子的第一句台詞說：「I was just looking over the building you designed for Mr. Bradley's law firm」，表示自己相當喜歡律師事務所大樓的設計。由此可知，對話雙方是在建築公司上班，因此正確答案為 (C)。

42 (NEW) --

What does the woman mean when she says, "I really can't say"?
(A) She is not allowed to reveal certain information.
(B) She should cancel the appointment.
(C) She cannot make a commitment yet.
(D) She has to revise some mistakes.

當這位女士說：「我真的不敢肯定」，是什麼意思？
(A) 她不能透漏特定資訊。
(B) 她應該取消約會。
(C) 她還無法做出承諾。
(D) 她必須修正一些錯誤。

詢問說話者意圖的題目，應先了解引號中內容的意義，再仔細聆聽對話。男子邀請女子一同參與新的專案，女子則說：「But, at this time I really can't say. I'm having a meeting with my manager to discuss another big project tomorrow, though.」，表示自己明天將和經理討論另一個大型專案，所以沒辦法立刻答應男子的提議，故正確答案為 (C)。

 43 --

What does the man propose?
(A) Making an itinerary
(B) Preparing a negotiation
(C) Delaying a meeting
(D) Reviewing the project together

這位男士提出什麼建議？
(A) 制定行程
(B) 準備協商
(C) 延後會議
(D) 一起檢視專案

對話後半部男子說：「Is it possible to stop by your meeting and go over the details with both of you?」，表示他想參與女子與經理的會議，討論專案的細節，故正確解答為 (D)。

W I got a call from Mark Dice this morning. He eventually confirmed he cannot deliver the keynote address due to an important meeting. However, he still wants to present his opinion about recent changes in the market, he said.	**女** 我今天早上接到馬克‧戴斯的電話。他最後還是確定，他因為一場重要會議，無法發表主題演講。不過，他說他還是希望能報告自己對最近市場變化的看法。
M We were expecting this from the beginning, weren't we?	**男** 我們從一開始就預期到會這樣了，不是嗎？
W Yes, we were. He hesitated to take it, saying he has another commitment that can't be missed. I should've found someone else.	**女** 是啊。他接受的很不情願，說他有另一件不能不履行的工作。我那時應該另找他人的。
M That's fine, and **(45)it was worth a try.** Then, we can list him on the last day of the conference and ask the president to take the keynote speech.	**男** 沒關係，**(45)還是值得一試。**那我們可以把他列在研討會最後一天，然後請主席發表主題演講。
W It's a relief that we have an alternative. I'll tell the president about this change. What else should we prepare?	**女** 有替代方案真是讓人鬆了一口氣。我會告訴主席這個變動。我們還需要準備什麼其他的嗎？
M The timetable on the Web site should be revised, too. And we'll have to send text messages to those registered in advance and notify them of this change. I'll take care of it.	**男** 網站上的時程表也要修訂。我們也必須傳簡訊給那些預先報名的人，告知這項異動。我會處理這件事。

• **keynote address** 專題演講　**opinion** 看法；見解　**hesitate** 猶豫　**commitment** 必須做的事情　**conference** 研討會　**president** 主席　**relief** 寬心；解脫　**alternative** 替代方案　**revise** 修訂　**register** 報名　**in advance** 事先　**notify sb of sth** 告知某人關於某事

44

What problem are the speakers mainly discussing?

(A) They must launch a Web site in a hurry.

(B) There are not as many participants as they expected.

(C) They have made a change in a plan.

(D) The president won't be able to deliver a speech.

說話者主要在討論什麼問題？

(A) 他們必須趕快發布一個網站。

(B) 與會者人數不如他們預期的多。

(C) 他們對計畫做了更動。

(D) 主席無法發表演說。

女子在開頭便告知男子講者無法出席，兩人並接著討論替代方案，最後決定讓講者的演說改期，並由他人頂替原先的時段，故正確答案為 (C)。

45 (NEW) ---

Why does the man say, "it was worth a try"?	**這位男士為什麼說：「還是值得一試」？**
(A) He is comforting the woman.	(A) 他在安撫那位女士。
(B) He doesn't want to take the risk.	(B) 他不想冒險。
(C) He knew that Mr. Dice would turn them down.	(C) 他知道戴斯先生會拒絕他們。
(D) He regrets he had to meet the speaker in person.	(D) 他懊悔自己必須親自見演講者。

「it was worth a try」在這裡可以包含多種意義。首先，馬克‧戴斯應是一位傑出人物，故雖然無法請他演講，仍然值得嘗試邀請他。前一句台詞中，女子說：「I should've found someone else.」代表女子認為當初自己應該另邀他人，而感到自責。因此男子此時的這句話是在安慰女子，即使講者無法如期出席，他們也試過邀請對方，故正確答案為 (A)。

46 ---

What does the woman say she will do?	**這位女士說她會做什麼？**
(A) Send text messages	(A) 傳簡訊
(B) Update a Web page	(B) 更新網頁
(C) Contact the president	(C) 聯絡主席
(D) Convince Mr. Dice to attend the event	(D) 說服戴斯先生參加活動

關於女子將要做的事，請在女子的台詞中尋找線索。在「I'll tell the president about this change.」中，女子表示將會告知主席此次的變更。(C) 將題目中的「tell」改成「contact」，正確答案為 (C)。

47-49 conversation (NEW)

47–49 對話

M Good afternoon. This is Pablo Ortega. I called you to ask for a prescription for glasses.	**男：** 午安，我是帕布羅‧奧爾特加。我打這通電話是想要索取配眼鏡的驗光單。
W Hello, Mr. Ortega. I've checked your voice message. By the way, you should visit us again. We have a record saying that you saw Dr. Jenkins for a checkup in April, but it is no longer valid for a new prescription. You should get your eyes checked again, which will take about 30 minutes.	**女：** 奧爾特加先生，您好。我有收到了您的語音留言。順帶一提，您應該再過來我們這裡一趟。我們的紀錄顯示，您在四月讓詹金斯醫生檢查過，但這不適用於開立新的驗光單。您應該再檢查一次眼睛，這大概要30分鐘左右。
M Oh, I see. Can I see the doctor tomorrow morning?	**男：** 喔，我懂了。我可以明天早上去看醫生嗎？
W I'm afraid all the doctors have a full schedule on Thursday morning. How about Friday instead? We are open from 10 A.M. to 8 P.M.	**女：** 週四早上所有的醫生恐怕都滿約了。改到星期五如何？我們的門診時間是早上十點到晚上八點。
M You close at 8? Then I can come in after work. Can I stop by this evening?	**男：** 你們八點休息？那我可以下班後過去。我可以今天晚上過去嗎？

W	Sure. I can schedule an appointment with the same doctor as last time. She's available from 6 to 7:30.	女：沒問題。我可以幫您預約上次同一位醫師的診。她6:00至7:30可以預約。
M	Thank you. I'll be there by 7.	男：謝謝妳。我七點前會到。

• prescription for glasses 配鏡驗光單　voice message 語音留言　no longer 不再　valid 有效的
full schedule 行程滿檔　stop by 順路造訪

47 -

Who most likely is the woman?　　　這位女士最有可能是誰？
(A) A pharmacist　　　　　　　　(A) 藥劑師
(B) An optician　　　　　　　　 (B) 配鏡師
(C) A receptionist　　　　　　　 (C) 櫃檯人員
(D) An appraiser　　　　　　　　(D) 鑑定員

女子能夠確認男子的診療紀錄，並為他預約看診，可見女子是在眼科工作的櫃台人員，正確答案為 (C)。

本題就算只聽懂「glasses」、「eye」、「doctor」等簡單的字彙，也能選出答案，但是考生可能對醫院用語不熟悉，最好事先準備，也請記住另外三個選項中的人物名詞。

48 -

When is the man supposed to come?　這位男士應該何時來看診？
(A) Wednesday morning　　　　　 (A) 星期三早上
(B) Wednesday evening　　　　　 (B) 星期三晚上
(C) Thursday morning　　　　　　(C) 星期四早上
(D) Thursday evening　　　　　　 (D) 星期四晚上

本題必須同時掌握日期與時間才能選出答案。男子在第二句台詞問道「Can I see the doctor tomorrow morning?」，而女子說「all the doctors have a full schedule on Thursday morning」，故可得知明日是週四，而今日是週三。

此外，男子說：「I can come in after work. Can I stop by this evening?」，女子答應後，他又接著說「I'll be there by 7.」，由此可知，男子將在週三晚間七點前往眼科看診，故正確答案為 (B)。

49 -

What is suggested about the clinic?　有關該診所，對話中暗示了什麼？
(A) Dr. Jenkins is the only doctor working there.　(A) 詹金斯醫生是唯一在那裡服務的醫師。
(B) This is the first time Mr. Ortega has contacted it.　(B) 這是奧爾特加先生第一次跟他們聯絡。
(C) It is open from 10 A.M. to 8 P.M. on weekends.　(C) 週末看診時間是早上十點到晚上八點。
(D) It keeps some patients' medical records.　(D) 該診所保留病患的醫療紀錄。

本題需要一一確認選項內容。遇到「What is (NOT) suggested about . . . ?」的題型時，在聽對話之前，請先瀏覽選項的內容。

(A) 因為女子說：「all the doctors have a full schedule on Thursday morning.」，可以知道該醫院有多名醫師，故此非正確答案。(B) 因男子在四月時曾經來看過診，且女子說：「Hello, Mr. Ortega. I've checked your voice message.」，由此可知，在這次通話前，男子已經打過電話並留下語音訊息，這並非他們第一次聯絡。(C) 對話中，女子說：「How about Friday instead? We are open from 10 A.M. to 8 P.M.」無法單從這句話確認週末的營業時間，故 (C) 並不確定。

(D) 女子說：「We have a record saying that you saw Dr. Jenkins for a checkup in April」，由此可知，男子在四月曾讓醫師看診，且診所保有男子的看診紀錄，故本題的答案為 (D)。

50-52 conversation with three speakers (NEW)   **50–52 三人對話**

M1 Thanks for coming, Chris and Nancy. I'm pleased you decided to come to take a look at this shop. As I told you yesterday, this property has a reasonable price because the seller wants to put the store up for sale so quickly. **W** Yes, we really like the property, but we have some concerns. **M2** We're worried about the cost of refurbishment. We think everything needs to be changed. **M1** Don't worry about that. I can recommend an interior design company that provides low prices with high quality. **M2** That's good news. I'm just wondering why the owner decided to sell at short notice. **M1** Well, she'll start a new business out of the city. **W** All right, could we sign the contract now?	**男1** 克里斯、南西，感謝你們的光臨。我很高興你們決定來看看這家店。正如我昨天告訴你們的，這個物件價格合理，因為賣家想要盡快將店面賣掉。 **女** 是啊，我們真的很喜歡這個物件，但我們還有些疑慮。 **男2** 我們擔心翻修的費用。我們覺得所有的東西都需要更換。 **男1** 別擔心這個。我可以推薦質優價廉的室內設計公司。 **男2** 那真是好消息。我只是在想屋主為什麼決定倉促出售。 **男1** 嗯，她要在城外開設新店面。 **女** 好，那我們現在可以簽約嗎？

• take a look at . . . 看一看……　property 房地產　concern 疑慮　refurbishment 翻修　interior 室內的
at short notice 在短時間內

50 -

Who most likely are Chris and Nancy?　克里斯和南西最有可能是誰？
(A) Apartment managers　(A) 公寓大樓管理員
(B) Interior designers　(B) 室內設計師
(C) Realtors　(C) 房地產經紀人
(D) Potential buyers　(D) 可能的買家

第一句台詞中，男子叫喚這兩人的名字，並說道：「I'm pleased you decided to come to take a look at this shop.」可見兩人想要購買店鋪，故正確答案為 (D)。

51 --

What are Chris and Nancy concerned about?

(A) The placement of smoke detectors
(B) The size of a property
(C) The expense of renovation
(D) The range of interior design companies

克里斯和南西擔心的是什麼？

(A) 煙霧偵測器的設置
(B) 地產的大小
(C) 整修的費用
(D) 室內設計公司的類型

女子先提出自己有所顧慮後，男子緊接著說：「We're worried about the cost of refurbishment.」
表示兩人對翻修費用感到擔心，故正確答案為 (C)。

52 --

What is mentioned about the owner?

(A) She owns several stores.
(B) She'll start a new business.
(C) She can recommend qualified workers.
(D) She wants to change the interior.

對話中提到什麼有關屋主的事？

(A) 她有好幾家店。
(B) 她將開設新店面。
(C) 她能推薦合格的工人。
(D) 她想改變室內裝潢。

男子在對話後半段提到：「she'll start a new business out of the city.」，表示屋主因為要在外地開
設新店，希望盡快將此物件賣出，故正確答案為 (B)。

53-55 conversation　　　　　　　　　　　**53–55 對話**

W Hi, Lucius. I've been trying to register for the workshop, but it said I'm using an incorrect password on my computer. I don't know what the problem is. What about your computer? **M** Really? I already signed up for it. I think the tech support team upgraded some servers last night, so it was affected by this change. **W** Oh. I guess I need to contact a technician from tech support. Who should I speak to about this? **M** I don't know, but I think the best way is to submit a request form for service first. Let me do that for you here on my computer.	女　嗨，盧修斯。我一直試著要報名研討會，但我的電腦卻顯示我輸入了錯誤的密碼。我不知道出了什麼問題。你的電腦呢？ 男　真的嗎？我已經報名了。我想是技術支援小組昨晚更新了部分伺服器，電腦因此受到影響了吧。 女　喔，我想我需要聯絡技術支援小組的技術員了。我應該和誰說這個問題？ 男　我不知道。不過我覺得最好的辦法是先提出一份申請表。讓我用我的電腦幫妳處理。

• **register for** 報名參加　**sign up for** 報名參加　**technician** 技術員　**submit** 提交

53 --

What is the woman unable to do?

(A) Log on to her computer
(B) Organize a workshop
(C) Print a document
(D) Create a password

這位女士無法做什麼？

(A) 登入她的電腦
(B) 籌辦一個研討會
(C) 列印一份文件
(D) 創建一個密碼

本題詢問女子無法做的事情，也就是詢問女子發生的問題。第一句台詞中，女子說：「I've been trying to register for the workshop, but it said I'm using an incorrect password on my computer」，也就是說，她無法登入系統，所以正確答案為 (A)。

54 --

According to the man, what happened yesterday?	根據這位男士所言，昨天發生了什麼事？
(A) The power went out.	(A) 停電。
(B) Some servers were changed.	(B) 部分伺服器被更改了。
(C) Some equipment was broken.	(C) 一些設備故障了。
(D) Computers were installed.	(D) 電腦被安裝。

男子第一句台詞說：「I think the tech support team upgraded some servers last night.」，可知昨晚更新了部分伺服器，故正確答案為 (B)。

55 --

What does the man say he will do?	這位男士說他要做什麼？
(A) Restart a computer	(A) 重新開啟電腦
(B) Install new software	(B) 安裝新軟體
(C) Call a coworker	(C) 打電話給同事
(D) Put in a help request	(D) 提出請求支援的申請

對話後半段中，男子說：「but I think the best way is to submit a request form for service first. Let me do that for you here on my computer.」，提議自己用電腦替女子提交申請表，故正確答案為 (D)。

請熟記字義為「提交」的單字有：submit、put in、hand in 和 turn in。

56-58 conversation 　　　　　　56–58 對話

M	Natalie, I just got your e-mail. The proposal looks pretty good, but we need to modify something.	男	娜塔莉，我剛收到妳的電子郵件。這個企畫案看起來很棒，但我們需要修改某些地方。
W	What do you think we should revise? Do we need to increase the estimates for the overhead?	女	你認為我們應該修改什麼？我們需要增加經常性費用的預估金額嗎？
M	I think that is fine. The quotes for expenditure in Rome seemed a little low, though. There have been some cost-of-living increases over the past few months.	男	我覺得那還好。但羅馬的經費報價有點低。過去幾個月以來生活費用略有增加。
W	Oh. Actually, I used the estimates from last year. I'll check that online and have that revised before I leave today.	女	喔。事實上，我用的是去年的預估金額。我會上網查對，在今天下班前修訂好。

* **proposal** 企劃案　**modify** 修改　**estimate** 估價　**quote** 報價　**overhead** 經常性費用
expenditure 支出　**cost-of-living** 生活費用

56

What are the speakers mainly talking about?

(A) The cost of living
(B) Overseas branches
(C) An online business
(D) A proposed budget

說話者主要在討論什麼?

(A) 生活費用
(B) 海外分公司
(C) 電子商務
(D) 擬定的預算

對話的主題通常可從開頭尋找。男子第一句台詞提到:「The proposal looks pretty good, but we need to modify something.」,故正確答案為 (D)。

 57

What does the man say about the Rome expenses?

(A) They have been underestimated.
(B) They are the same as last year's.
(C) The quotes look good.
(D) The living costs were not in the budget.

這位男士提到什麼有關羅馬經費的事?

(A) 被低估了。
(B) 跟去年一樣。
(C) 報價看起來很不錯。
(D) 生活費不在預算中。

在對話中間的部分,男子說:「The quotes for expenditure in Rome seemed a little low, though.」, 故正確答案為 (A)。

58

What does the woman say she will do?

(A) Spend less money
(B) Estimate a price
(C) Use last year's records
(D) Update some information

這位女士說她要做什麼?

(A) 花更少的錢
(B) 估算價格
(C) 使用去年的紀錄
(D) 更新部分資料

對話後半部中,女子說:「I'll check that online and have that revised before I leave today」, 表示下班前會修改預估金額,故正確答案為 (D)。

59-61 conversation

W	Hi, Edward! This is Jody from the Personnel Department. I just wanted to let you know that the projector in meeting room 5B is out of order.
M	Yes, I can come down immediately and take a look at it.
W	Right now? Umm, **(60)I'm interviewing someone here in 10 minutes.** I don't use the equipment at all for that, so can you wait until I finish?
M	No problem. In that case, I'll visit when you're done. Is there anything else you need to set up in the room?

59–61 對話

女	嗨,愛德華!我是人事部的喬蒂。我只是要通知你會議室5B的投影機壞了。
男	好。我可以馬上下去看看。
女	現在嗎?喔,**(60)**我十分鐘後就要在這裡面試人員。我不會用到這個設備,所以你可以等到我結束嗎?
男	沒問題。這樣的話,等妳結束後我再過去。那間會議室裡還有什麼東西需要裝設的嗎?

W	No, thanks. Nowadays, I try to talk to candidates in person without using equipment like video conferencing. It is important to know them well for a change.	女 沒有，謝了。我現在盡量親自跟應徵者面談，而不是使用視訊會議那類的設備。換個方式去好好地了解他們是很重要的。

- out of order 故障　immediately 立即　take a look at ... 看一看……　equipment 設備　set up 裝設
  candidate 應試者　in person 親自　interrupt 打擾

59 --

Why is the woman calling the man?
(A) To report an equipment malfunction
(B) To check a device
(C) To request personal information
(D) To set up a meeting

這位女士為什麼打電話給男士？
(A) 要回報器材故障
(B) 要檢查設備
(C) 要詢問個人資料
(D) 要安排會議

注意女子的第一句台詞：「I just wanted to let you know that the projector in meeting room 5B is out of order.」，可以知道女子是為了報告設備故障而撥打電話，所以正確答案為 (A)。

60 NEW --

What does the woman imply when she says, "I'm interviewing someone here in 10 minutes"?
(A) She needs help urgently.
(B) She does not want to be interrupted.
(C) She is not satisfied with an assignment.
(D) She will not attend another meeting.

當這位女士說：「我十分鐘後就要在這裡面試人員」，是什麼意思？
(A) 她迫切地需要協助。
(B) 她不想被打擾。
(C) 她對一項工作不滿意。
(D) 她不會參加另一場會議。

此為詢問說話者意圖的題型，應先掌握題目引用之句子的意思，再仔細聆聽對話。在對話中間部分，男子表示將馬上前往修理，而女子則說：「Umm, I'm meeting with someone in here in 10 minutes for an interview. I don't use the equipment at all for that, so can you wait until I finish?」。女子詢問男子能否面試結束後再修理，是在暗示不想要讓人打擾面試，故正確答案為 (B)。

61 --

What does the woman say is unique about the interview?
(A) It will be recorded.
(B) It will be filmed.
(C) It will be conducted face-to-face.
(D) It will last for more than an hour.

這位女士提到面試有何特點？
(A) 將被錄音。
(B) 將被錄影。
(C) 將面對面進行。
(D) 將歷時超過一個小時。

對話後半部女子提到：「I try to talk to candidates in person without using equipment like video conferencing.」，告知對方自己最近正在嘗試不使用任何設備，直接與應試者見面進行面試，所以正確答案為 (C)。

W	Thomas, have you already checked in your baggage? You'll stay three days for the conference, won't you?
M	I'm afraid I can't stay for the whole conference. I have to return for an important client meeting. It was difficult to reschedule it. So I'll be returning right after my presentation the day after tomorrow.
W	That's too bad. Anyway, don't we have to hurry if we want to catch the flight? My boarding pass says it's gate B14.
M	Let's check the departure gate. Gate B14, there it is! It says our flight's on time. We do have time to have some drinks and snacks while we're walking over there.

女	湯瑪士，你的行李已經託運了嗎？這個研討會你要待三天，不是嗎？
男	我恐怕無法待滿整個會議期間。我必須回來開一個重要的客戶會議。那個會議很難重新安排時間，所以我後天發表完就要趕回來了。
女	那真是太糟糕了。不過，如果我們想要趕上班機的話，不是應該快一點嗎？我的登機證上寫說是B14登機門。
男	我們確認一下登機門吧。B14，就在那裡！上頭顯示我們的班機是準時的。在我們走過去時，還有時間喝點東西、吃個點心。

Departure	Gate	Time	Status
Melbourne	A8	15:30	Delayed
Sydney	B14	15:45	On time
Perth	A9	16:00	Canceled
Brisbane	C10	17:00	On time

目的地	登機門	時間	狀態
墨爾本	A8	15:30	延誤
雪梨	B14	15:45	準時
伯斯	A9	16:00	取消
布里斯本	C10	17:00	準時

• **check in** 託運　**boarding pass** 登機證　**departure** 啟程　**on time** 準時

62

Where is the conversation taking place?

(A) At a bus terminal
(B) At an airport
(C) At a business conference
(D) At a train station

這段對話是在哪裡發生的？

(A) 公車總站
(B) 機場
(C) 商務會議
(D) 火車站

詢問對話場所的問題，請專心聆聽第一句台詞。「Have you already checked in your baggage?」詢問是否已經將行李託運。由此可知，對話的地點在機場，故正確答案為 (B)。

(C) 提及的會議是說話者將前往的地方。

Why isn't the man staying for the entire conference?
(A) He has a scheduling conflict.
(B) He is about to go on holiday.
(C) He has a presentation.
(D) He could not find a later flight.

這位男士為什麼不待滿整個會議期間？
(A) 他的行程有衝突。
(B) 他即將去度假。
(C) 他要發表簡報。
(D) 他找不到晚一點的班機。

男子的第一句台詞說：「I have to return for an important client meeting. It was difficult to reschedule it. So I'll be returning right after my presentation the day after tomorrow.」，告知為了和客戶開會而必須離開，故正確答案為 (A)。

64 NEW

Look at the graphic. What city are the speakers going to?
(A) Melbourne
(B) Sydney
(C) Perth
(D) Brisbane

看一下圖表，說話者要前往哪個城市？
(A) 墨爾本
(B) 雪梨
(C) 伯斯
(D) 布里斯本

解題時，請先閱讀與圖表，並記住圖表中的登機門與時間。後半段的對話中，女子提到「My boarding pass says it's gate B14.」，由此可知，對話者應該前往 B14 登機門，故正確答案為 (B)。

65-67 conversation and floor plan	65–67 對話及樓層平面圖
M Tracy, do you know when the floor plan will be posted? I'd like to check it before I leave. I'm taking the afternoon off.	男 崔西，妳知道樓層平面圖何時會公布嗎？我想在離開前確認一下。我下午要請假。
W Actually, it came out last night. Here it is.	女 事實上，昨天晚上就公布了。在這裡。
M Thank you. I should've asked sooner. Let's see. Hmm . . . The biggest room on the floor has been assigned to the Sales Department. Where are we going to move into?	男 謝謝你。我應該要早點問的。來看一下。嗯……這層樓最大的辦公室已經分配給業務部了。那我們要搬去哪？
W We're going to take the one between the copy room and the staff lounge. It's near the elevator.	女 我們會用影印室與員工休息室中間的那間，靠近電梯。
M The members would be glad to hear about this, wouldn't they?	男 大家會很高興聽到這消息的，不是嗎？
W Not exactly. As you know, the staff lounge is quite noisy in the afternoon.	女 並不盡然。你知道的，員工休息室到了下午都會很吵。
M Since they have said they are adding some soundproof insulation this time, we'll see how it turns out. I'm leaving now. I have to see a doctor at 2.	男 既然他們說這次會加裝隔音設備，我們就看看結果如何吧。我要走了。我兩點要看醫生。

W Alright, see you on Monday. We should come earlier because there is a lot of stuff to move.

女 好，週一見了。我們應該早點來，因為有很多東西要搬。

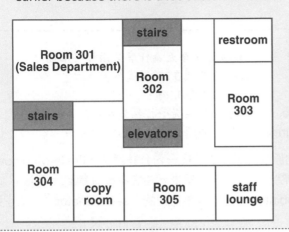

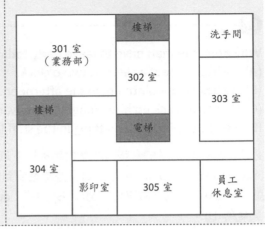

- **floor plan** 樓層平面圖 **assign** 分配 **copy room** 影印室 **staff lounge** 員工休息室
  soundproof insulation 隔音設備 **turn out** 最終成為

65 (NEW) --

Look at the graphic. Which room are the speakers moving into on Monday?

(A) Room 302
(B) Room 303
(C) Room 304
(D) Room 305

看一下圖表，說話者星期一要搬進哪間辦公室？

(A) 302室
(B) 303室
(C) 304室
(D) 305室

男子第二句台詞中提到「Where are we going to move into?」，而女子回答「We're going to take the one between the copy room and the staff lounge. It's near the elevators.」，對照圖表可知，正確答案為 (D)。

66 --

According to the woman, what would her colleagues say about their new room?

(A) They're glad to take the biggest room.
(B) They are pleased to be situated near the stairs.
(C) They're not happy to be located near the staff lounge.
(D) They enjoy the advantages of soundproof insulation.

根據這位女士所言，她的同事會說新辦公室如何？

(A) 他們會很高興能用最大的辦公室。
(B) 他們會很高興被安排在樓梯附近。
(C) 他們會不喜歡被安排在員工休息室附近。
(D) 他們會喜歡隔音設備的優點。

男子問：「The members would be glad to hear about this, wouldn't they?」，表示其他人聽了應該會很高興，而女子回應道：「Not exactly. As you know, the staff lounge is quite noisy in the afternoon.」，表示「並不會」，隨後又告知每到下午員工休息室會很吵，表示同事並不喜歡這個位置安排，因此正確答案為 (C)。

(A) 與 (B) 因為描述的事實與題目不符，所以不是正確答案。(D) 防噪音措施是男子提及的內容，且無法得知員工們對於防噪音效果的想法。

67 -

Why does the man have to leave early today? 這位男士今天為什麼必須提早離開？

(A) He has to meet a client at two o'clock. 　(A) 他必須在2點時見客戶。

(B) He has an appointment in the afternoon. 　(B) 他下午有約。

(C) He has to pack up his belongings in advance. 　(C) 他必須提早打包私人物品。

(D) He has to pick up something in the staff lounge. 　(D) 他必須去員工休息室拿東西。

必須仔細聆聽男子的台詞，才能找到提早下班的原因。男子的最後一句台詞說：「I'm leaving now. I have to see a doctor at 2.」提及他兩點要到醫院，所以今天要早退。注意不能只聽到「兩點」就選擇 (A)，此為陷阱選項。選項 (B) 中的「appointment」即為題目裡的「see a doctor」，故正確答案為 (B)。

68-70 conversation and list　　　　　68–70 對話及表單

M	Hey, Ms. Jennings, is the Internet working on your computer? I really need to check my e-mail.
W	Yeah, I'm not having any problems at all.
M	Well, whenever I log on to the Internet it freezes, so I can't see my e-mail. Have you received the data about the quarterly sales figures yet?
W	Hmm, let me see. . . . yes! Do you want me to send you the information?
M	Thanks a lot, but could you print it out for me? I just need a copy of the quarterly sales figures for the meeting this afternoon.

男	嘿，詹寧斯女士，妳電腦的網路可以用嗎？我真的需要查收我的電子郵件。
女	可以，我的一點問題也沒有。
男	嗯，每當我登入網路，它就當機了，所以我無法查看電子郵件。妳收到季銷售數據的資料了嗎？
女	嗯，讓我看看……有！你要我把資料傳給你嗎？
男	非常感謝，但是妳可以幫我列印出來嗎？我只是需要一份季銷售數據，今天下午開會要用。

From	Subject
Brian Swann	Budget Report
Yianni Ellenikiotis	Conference Agenda
Helen Yang	ATTACHED: Quarterly Sales figures
Brittany Seymour	DELAYED: Management workshop

寄件人	主旨
布萊恩・史旺	預算報告
依婭妮・艾倫尼奇歐提斯	會議議程
海倫・楊	附件：季銷售數據
布塔妮・西摩	延期：管理研討會

- **freeze** 凍結（此延伸指電腦當機）　**quarterly** 一季一次的　**sales figures** 銷售數據　**print out** 印出

68 -

Why is the man unable to access his e-mail?
(A) He's using an incorrect password.
(B) His Internet connection isn't available.
(C) He forgot to update some software.
(D) His computer is malfunctioning.

這位男士為什麼無法收電子郵件？
(A) 他用了錯誤的密碼。
(B) 他的網路無法連結。
(C) 他忘了更新部分軟體。
(D) 他的電腦故障了。

男子的第一句台詞說：「Ms. Jennings, is the Internet working on your computer? I really need to check my e-mail.」，表示他為了查收電子郵件，必須使用網路，但自己的網路卻無法連接，才會問女子確認她是否能夠開啟網路，故正確答案為 (B)。

69 (NEW) -

Look at the graphic. Who sent the e-mail the speakers are referring to?
(A) Brian Swann
(B) Yianni Ellenikiotis
(C) Helen Yang
(D) Brittany Seymour

看一下圖表，說話者所提到的電子郵件是誰寄的？
(A) 布萊恩・史旺
(B) 依婭妮・艾倫尼奇歐提斯
(C) 海倫・楊
(D) 布塔妮・西摩

本題在閱讀圖表時，不應將重點放在人名，而該仔細聆聽郵件標題，藉此查出寄件者。男子問道：「Have you received the data about the quarterly sales figures yet?」，由此可知，對話者需要查看各季銷售數值的資料，所以正確答案為 (C)。

70 -

What does the man ask the woman to do?
(A) Call the technician
(B) Present the quarterly sales figures
(C) Print out a document
(D) Arrange a meeting this afternoon

這位男士要求女士做什麼？
(A) 打電話給技術員
(B) 提交季銷售數據
(C) 印出文件
(D) 安排今天下午的會議

要知道男子提出的要求，應注意男子的台詞。後半段中，男子說：「could you print it out for me?」，請女子幫他列印各季的資料，故正確答案為 (C)。

(D) 的內容為男子該做的工作，而非要求女子做的事。

ACTUAL TEST **4**

PART **3**

中譯＋解析

 15

71-73 talk

Thank you for visiting the opening of the new American Art exhibition at the Whitney Museum. This exhibit has some modern American art. Before we see the exhibition, I'd like to hand out some audio devices to you. This player can help you to hear background information about the art. Also, we'll have a great lecture from one of the famous artists at 2 P.M. I hope you'll enjoy the talk.

71-73 談話

感謝各位參觀惠特尼博物館的新美國藝術展開幕式。這項展覽展示了一些美國現代藝術作品。在我們觀賞展覽前,我要發給各位音訊設備。這個播放器可以讓您聆聽這些藝術作品的背景知識。此外,我們在下午2點也有知名藝術家的精彩演講,希望各位會喜歡。

• exhibition 展覽　hand out 發放

71

What is the purpose of the talk?
(A) To ask for donations
(B) To publicize the museum
(C) To discuss modern art
(D) To introduce an exhibit

這段談話的目的是什麼?
(A) 請求捐款
(B) 宣傳博物館
(C) 討論現代藝術
(D) 介紹展覽

一段話的目的通常在一開始出現。開頭的部分提到:「Thank you for visiting the opening of the new American Art exhibition at the Whitney Museum.」,感謝聽者參加博物館的展覽開幕活動。由此可知,本段內容為介紹展覽活動,故正確答案為 (D)。

72

What will the speaker distribute?
(A) Entrance tickets
(B) A brochure
(C) A map of the museum
(D) An audio player

說話者將分發什麼?
(A) 入場券
(B) 小手冊
(C) 博物館地圖
(D) 音訊播放器

從「I'd like to hand out some audio devices for you」中可以看出,說話者將分發音訊設備,故正確答案為 (D)。

73

According to the speaker, what will begin at two o'clock?
(A) An auction
(B) A concert
(C) A talk
(D) A reception

根據說話者所言,什麼會在兩點開始?
(A) 拍賣
(B) 音樂會
(C) 演講
(D) 接待會

從後半段出現的 「we'll have a great lecture from one of the famous artists at 2 P.M.」 中，可以知道兩點將有一段演講，故正確解答為 (C)。

74-76 telephone message

Good morning, Sarah. This is Paul Grant from Furniture Depot. I regret to inform you that the chairs you wanted for your conference room are sold out. I ordered them for you, but they will take four weeks to get here. We do have similar style chairs in stock. If you want, I can have those delivered to you tomorrow. Give me a call and let me know what you decide. I'm going to be out all day today making deliveries, so either leave me a message or send me a text message. After returning to the store, I'll get back to you.

74–76 電話留言

莎拉，早。我是家飾店的保羅·格蘭特。很遺憾要通知您，您會議室所需要的椅子已經全部賣完了。我已經為您訂購，但需要四週的時間才能到貨。我們的庫存有類似款式的椅子。如果您要的話，我可以在明天配送給您。請來電告知您的決定。我今天全天都會在外送貨，所以請留訊息給我或傳簡訊亦可。我會在回到店裡後回電給您。

• furniture 家具　regret 遺憾　sold out 售完　order 訂購

Why did the speaker leave a message?
(A) To talk about a problem with an order
(B) To find out when to make a delivery
(C) To get more information about furniture
(D) To ask for help choosing a new chair

說話者為什麼要留言？
(A) 要談論訂單的問題
(B) 要查清楚何時可送貨
(C) 要取得更多家具的相關資訊
(D) 要求幫忙挑選新椅子

段落的目的通常會在開頭出現。「I regret to inform you that the chairs you wanted for your conference room are sold out.」，表示聽話者想要的椅子已經賣完。由此可知，說話者是為了訂單相關問題而撥打電話聯繫，故正確答案為 (A)。

When does the speaker say he can deliver similar chairs?
(A) In four weeks
(B) Tomorrow
(C) This evening
(D) In two days

說話者說他何時可以配送類似的椅子？
(A) 四週後
(B) 明天
(C) 今晚
(D) 兩天後

本題詢問說話者表示何時可以配送，聆聽時請將重點放在時間相關訊息。說話者提到：「If you want, I can have those delivered to you tomorrow.」，故正確答案為 (B)。

76 ---

What does the speaker say he will do today?   說話者說他今天要做什麼？
(A) Work at the store all day long   (A) 整天在店裡工作
(B) Record some messages   (B) 記錄一些訊息
(C) Send the package   (C) 寄包裹
(D) Deliver items   (D) 送貨

本題後半段提到「I'm going to be out all day today making deliveries」，表示今天因為負責送貨，一整天都會在外面。由此可知正確答案為 (D)。

77-79 advertisement   ## 77–79 廣告

If you're looking for a reliable travel agency with a good reputation and professional, knowledgeable staff, then look no further than Modu Travel Agency, located in the heart of Chicago. Modu has been in business for twenty years, helping customers book reasonably priced trips worldwide. We specialize in European package tours, particularly to Italy. We are currently offering discount airfares on ten-day guided trips to Venice, Florence, and Rome. All trips include accommodation and sightseeing tours. Or, if you are planning a trip to Asia or other countries in Europe, our capable staff can assist you with all of your travel arrangements. Just give us a call at 978-6418 or visit our office.	你在找信譽良好並擁有專業、博學員工的可靠旅行社嗎？那麼不用再找了，就是位於芝加哥市中心的摩度旅行社了。摩度已經營了20年，幫客戶預訂全球價格合理的旅遊行程。本公司專精歐洲套裝行程，特別是義大利地區。我們目前提供威尼斯、佛羅倫斯和羅馬十天導遊服務的優惠機票。所有的行程皆含住宿和觀光行程。或是如果您正計劃到亞洲或歐洲其他國家旅行，我們能幹的員工都能協助您做好所有旅行上的安排。只要來電978-6418或親至本公司即可。

- **reliable** 可靠的   **reputation** 名聲   **knowledgeable** 博學的   **worldwide** 遍及全球的
  specialize in . . . 專精於……   **airfare** 飛機票價   **accommodation** 住宿   **sightseeing** 觀光
  arrangement 安排

77 ---

How long has the business been operating?   這家公司經營多久了？
(A) For twelve years   (A) 12年
(B) For two decades   (B) 20年
(C) For a decade   (C) 10年
(D) For fifteen years   (D) 15年

廣告前半部分提到「Modu has been in business for twenty years」，表示該公司二十年間都在致力服務客戶，故正確答案為 (B)。

78 --

What type of business is being advertised?

(A) An airline
(B) A bus company
(C) A travel agency
(D) A bookstore

這裡宣傳的是哪一種行業？

(A) 航空公司
(B) 巴士公司
(C) 旅行社
(D) 書店

本題為詢問段落主題的題型，故應專心聆聽開頭部分的內容。一開始提到：「If you're looking for a reliable travel agency with a good reputation」，點出「旅行社」這個重點，故正確答案為 (C)。

79 --

What special offer is the business making now?

(A) Free calling cards
(B) Reduced rates on certain flights
(C) Package tours to Asia and other countries in Europe
(D) Free accommodation in Venice and Florence

這家公司現正提供什麼特別優惠？

(A) 免費電話卡
(B) 特定航班的優惠價
(C) 到亞洲與歐洲其他國家的套裝行程
(D) 威尼斯和佛羅倫斯的免費住宿

從段落中間「We are currently offering discount airfares on ten-day guided trips」可知，旅行社將會提供十天的優惠機票，故正確答案為 (B)。

80-82 news report

80–82 新聞報導

This is Channel Five News. I'm Marco DeGrassi. At this morning's press conference, Milton City Council announced a plan to build more bus lanes to solve the traffic problems all over the city. Construction on the project is scheduled to begin at the end of this month. It'll take about 3 months. According to the city mayor, Tom Kenny, new bus lanes on the main roads will reduce the traffic congestion. Many citizens have already voiced their strong support for new lanes, although they will experience inconvenience during the construction. Stay tuned for news on the governor's race after the commercial break.	這裡是第五頻道的新聞報導。我是馬可·狄格西。在今天早上的記者會中，米爾頓市議會宣布了一項計畫，內容是要設立更多公車專用道以解決全市的交通問題。這項計畫的工程預定在本月底展開，耗時約三個月。根據市長湯姆·肯尼表示，主要道路上的新公車專用道將緩解交通壅塞。雖然工程期間可能會帶來一些不便，但許多市民還是表達了對新車道的強烈支持。不要轉台，廣告後請繼續收看州長競選的新聞。

• **press conference** 記者會　**mayor** 市長　**congestion** 壅塞　**citizen** 市民　**voice** 發聲表達　**construction** 建造

ACTUAL TEST **4**

PART **4**

中譯＋解析

🎧 16

What does the speaker say will happen at the end of the month?
(A) A new City Hall will be built.
(B) Traffic congestion will take place.
(C) Construction on new bus lanes will commence.
(D) A hotel association will select a new president.

說話者說月底將發生什麼事？
(A) 要蓋新的市政廳。
(B) 將發生交通堵塞。
(C) 新公車專用道的工程將展開。
(D) 飯店協會將選出新會長。

從報導前半部的「Construction on the project is scheduled to begin at the end of this month.」可知，本月底將施工建造公車專用道，故正確答案為 (C)。

81 --

Who is Tom Kenny?
(A) A local politician
(B) A news reporter
(C) A bus driver
(D) A city spokesperson

湯姆・肯尼是誰？
(A) 當地政治人物
(B) 新聞記者
(C) 公車司機
(D) 市府發言人

詢問特定人物的題型，線索通常會出現在該人名的前後句中。從「According to the city mayor, Tom Kenny」可以知道，市長為湯姆 ・ 肯尼，所以正確答案為 (A)。

另外，也可用「city official」，表示市政府官員，請一併記住此說法。

82 --

What will listeners probably hear next?
(A) A sports game
(B) A local news report
(C) A sponsor's message
(D) A weather forecast

聽眾接下來可能會聽到什麼？
(A) 運動比賽
(B) 地方新聞報導
(C) 贊助商的訊息
(D) 天氣預報

本題詢問下一個節目為何，所以應仔細聆聽後半段的內容。「Stay tuned for the governor's race after the commercial break.」中，表示廣告後將進行州長選舉的相關報導，所以這段節目結束後會先聽到廣告，再聽地方新聞。正確答案為 (C)。

83-85 announcement

83–85 宣告

Good morning, everyone. Welcome to the Jeremy OA Training Center. We specialize in helping office employees make good use of various software and work more efficiently and conveniently. It's your first day today. You'll team up with three or four people from the same department. For each group, we'll assign a teaching assistant who is an expert in all kinds of office software and also understands the general workflow of each department. As you can see, we

大家早。歡迎來到傑若米辦公自動化訓練中心。我們專門協助上班族善用各種軟體，且更有效率與便利地工作。這是各位在此的第一天。各位將與同部門的三到四位同仁組隊。我們為每一個小組分配了一位精通所有辦公軟體，也了解各部門一般工作流程的教學助理。正如大家所見，教室前面有一本簽到簿。請確認您所屬的訓練小

have an attendance book in front. Please check which training group you are in and sign next to your name on the list. This will take some time because we have many participants today. And for those who didn't turn in the copy of your photo ID card with the application, would you please submit it now? **(84)The copier is in room 305.**

組，並於名單上您的大名旁簽名。由於今天與會者眾多，這可能會花上一點時間。那些未連同報名表一齊繳交附照片的身分證影本的人，是否可請您現在繳交？**(84)影印機就在305室。**

- specialize 專門從事　various 各種的　efficiently 有效率地　conveniently 便利地　team up 組隊　teaching assistant 教學助理　expert 專家　workflow 工作流程　attendance book 簽到簿　participant 與會者　application 報名表　copier 影印機

83 --

What type of business does the speaker work for?
(A) A recruiting agency
(B) A computer retailer
(C) An office equipment manufacturer
(D) An education center

說話者在何種行業服務？
(A) 人才招募公司
(B) 電腦零售店
(C) 辦公設備製造商
(D) 教育中心

開頭的部分提到：「Good morning, everyone. Welcome to the Jeremy OA Training Center.」對來到「傑若米辦公自動化訓練中心」的訪客表示歡迎，選項 (D) 雖將題目中的「training center」改為「education center」，但仍符合段落文意，故正確答案為 (D)。

84 [NEW] --

Why does the speaker say, "The copier is in room 305"?
(A) He was asked if a copier is available.
(B) The attendees will learn how to make copies today.
(C) The teaching assistants need to copy the roll book.
(D) Some people should go to another room to prepare some document.

說話者為什麼會說：「影印機就在305室」？
(A) 他被問到有沒有影印機。
(B) 與會者今天要學習如何影印。
(C) 助教要影印點名冊。
(D) 有些人必須去另一個房間準備文件。

最後的部分提到：「And for those who didn't turn in the copy of your photo ID card with the application, would you please submit it now? The copier is in room 305.」，表示因為 305 室有放置影印機，希望未提交身分證影本的人，前往此室將證件印出，故本題的正確答案為 (D)。

特別需要注意的是，(A) 乍看之下有道理，但是整段話中並未出現相關情節，只是依據猜測而做出的判斷，所以不是正確答案。

85

What does the speaker ask the listeners to do?
(A) Sign the contract
(B) Introduce themselves
(C) Team up with their colleagues
(D) Submit their applications in advance

說話者要求聽眾做什麼？
(A) 簽署合約
(B) 自我介紹
(C) 和同事組隊
(D) 提早繳交報名表

說話者提到：「You'll team up with three or four people from the same department.」，表示會將參加者與相同部門的同事組隊，而選項 (C) 將「people from the same department」改為同義字「colleagues」，故正確答案為 (C)。

86-88 excerpt from a meeting　　　　　　**86–88 會議摘錄**

Thanks for coming today on such a short notice. As I told you in the e-mail, we've been trying to help young students who are struggling to get through their lives without their parents' support. Thanks to the enthusiastic help and the donations from local businesses and the city council, we finally opened the Child Welfare Center last month, where we are providing meals and basic education services free of charge. Most of the beneficiaries are in their late teens; therefore, we need more education programs that are suitable for them. But unfortunately, we have insufficiency of funds and are unable to pay for this quality education. So, above all, I think we need to receive help from the current and former teachers in the area. I'll hand out a list of local schools. Please make sure to contact them, asking for help. I hope this project will be a great help for disadvantaged children, and more people join this meaningful cause.	感謝各位在臨時通知的狀況下出席會議。正如我在電子郵件中告訴各位的，我們一直在努力幫助那些在沒有雙親資助下，艱難度日的年輕學子。由於本地企業與市議會的熱情協助與捐助，我們終於在上個月開辦了兒童福利中心，在此我們免費提供餐點與基本教育服務。大多數的受惠者都在青少年晚期，因此我們需要更多適合他們的教育課程。但遺憾的是，我們資金短缺，無法支付這樣優質的教育。所以最重要的是，我想我們需要得到本地現任與前任教師的協助。我將發下一份本地學校的名單。請務必與他們聯絡，尋求協助。我希望這個計畫對弱勢孩童會有很大的幫助，讓更多人來參與這件有意義的事。

- **struggle** 掙扎　**get through** 度過　**enthusiastic** 熱情的　**donations** 捐助
  local business 本地企業　**city council** 市議會　**free of charge** 免費　**beneficiary** 受惠者
  unfortunately 遺憾地　**insufficiency** 不足　**disadvantaged** 弱勢的

86

What does the speaker mainly talk about?
(A) Building a welfare center
(B) Drawing more volunteers
(C) Organizing a fundraising event
(D) Becoming a teacher

說話者主要在談論什麼？
(A) 建立福利中心
(B) 招攬更多志工
(C) 籌備募款活動
(D) 成為教師

段落後段部分提到「I think we need to receive help from the current and former teachers in the area.」，表示需要得到當地現任與前任教師的幫助，也就是兒童福利中心需要教導孩童的教師，再考量前文提到中心的資金短缺，故可推測最可能的答案為 (B)。

 87

What problem does the welfare center have?
(A) There are not many schools in the area.
(B) It cannot afford free meals for the beneficiaries.
(C) The center hasn't launched any education programs yet.
(D) They don't have enough money for a plan.

福利中心有什麼問題？
(A) 該地區沒有很多學校。
(B) 無法為受益者提供免費餐點。
(C) 中心還沒有開辦任何教育課程。
(D) 他們沒有足夠的經費支持這項計畫。

段落中後段提到「But unfortunately, we have insufficiency of funds and are unable to pay for this quality education.」明確表示目前資金不足，而選項 (D) 將題目中的「funds」改為「money」，仍符合文意，故正確答案為 (D)。

 88

What are the listeners asked to do?
(A) Contact the schools in the area
(B) Look for a suitable contractor
(C) Attract more young teens
(D) Ask for their parents' support

聽眾被要求做什麼事？
(A) 聯絡該地區的學校
(B) 尋找適合的承包商
(C) 吸引更多青少年
(D) 尋求他們父母的支持

說話者在最後提到「I'll hand out the list of local schools. Please make sure of contacting them, and ask for help.」，表示會將當地的學校名單分配給聽眾，並請他們幫忙募集願意支援的教師。由此可知，本題的正確答案為 (A)。

89-91 telephone message　　　　　　**89–91 電話留言**

Hello, Ms. Shirley. This is Vanessa Adams from Rich Real Estate. I got the message you left while I was out of the office. It said that you need to change the moving date to earlier than you had indicated before. That means I have less time to look for an apartment that meets your requirements. **(90)But it's not a problem.** We do have many rental apartments in our listings. By the way, can you tell me when you will visit our office? I think it would be better, if you like one of the properties, to sign a rental contract on that day. Please call back as soon as possible. Thank you.

雪莉女士，您好。我是瑞麒地產的凡妮莎‧亞當斯。我收到了外出時您留下的留言。您在留言說您需要將之前指定的搬家日期再提早一點。這表示我能幫您找到符合需求公寓的時間更少了。**(90)**不過，這倒不是問題。本公司的名冊上有許多出租公寓。順道一提，您可否告訴我何時可到本公司來？我想如果您中意其中某個物件，當天就簽訂租賃合約，那是最好的。麻煩盡快回電。感謝您。

• **indicate** 指定　**meet** 符合　**rental** 租賃的　**by the way** 順道一提　**property** 房地產　**contract** 合約

16

89 --

What is the speaker doing for Ms. Shirley? | 說話者為雪莉女士做什麼事？
(A) Finding a place to live | (A) 找住的地方
(B) Reserving a hotel room | (B) 預訂飯店房間
(C) Buying an office building | (C) 購買辦公大樓
(D) Renovating an interior design | (D) 翻新室內設計

本題是詢問說話者行動的題型。從留言中間的「That means I have less time to look for an apartment that meets your requirements.」中，表示要找到符合條件的公寓，時間不太夠，故正確答案應為 (A)。

 90 (NEW) ---

What does the speaker imply when she says, "But it's not a problem"? | 當說話者說：「不過，這倒不是問題」，是什麼意思？
(A) She wants to recommend a moving company. | (A) 她要推薦搬家公司。
(B) She asks for a specific reason. | (B) 她要一個明確的理由。
(C) She feels disappointed. | (C) 她覺得很失望。
(D) She thinks that she can resolve the issue. | (D) 她認為自己可以解決這個問題。

本題為掌握意圖的題型，應注意聆聽整體內容的走向。從「I have less time to look for an apartment that meets your requirements. But it's not a problem. We do have many rental apartments in our listings.」可得知，表示雖時間不足，但是說話者認為自己手上有許多出租公寓的名單，應當足以解決問題，故正確答案為 (D)。

 91 --

What does the speaker ask Ms. Shirley to do? | 說話者要求雪莉女士做什麼？
(A) Arrange an appointment | (A) 安排會面
(B) Leave a message | (B) 留言
(C) Choose the color of the wallpaper | (C) 挑選壁紙顏色
(D) Update contact information | (D) 更新聯絡資料

留言後半段提到：「can you tell me when you will visit our office?」詢問對方何時可以來辦公室，可知說話者想和聽話者約定見面時間，故正確答案為 (A)。

Mr. Reece, this is Darius Stanton from the Colorado office. I'm calling to confirm your attendance at the board meeting here in March. The meeting is scheduled for the 10th. Your secretary mentioned last week that you might not be able to attend. So, I was wondering if this is still the case. If you are not able to come, please let me know whether you can participate in a conference call. I'll send you an e-mail with possible times for a call. With the time difference, however, please understand if they seem a little inconvenient. I'll also be attaching the proposed agenda for the meeting. I am looking forward to hearing from you.	瑞斯先生，我是科羅拉多分處的達里斯·史坦頓。我打這通電話是為了確認您是否出席三月在此舉行的董事會。會議預定於10號舉行。您的秘書上週提到您可能無法出席。因此，我想知道情況是否還是如此。如果您無法前來，請告知您是否能參加電話會議。我會寄給您一封附上可能通話時間的電子郵件。但由於時差的關係，如果時間看起來有點不便，敬請見諒。我也會附上擬定的會議議程表。期待您的回覆。

• **attendance** 出席　**mention** 提及　**participate in** 參與　**time difference** 時差　**attach** 附加
agenda 議程　**look forward to (+Ving)** 期待（做某事）

92 --

Why is the speaker calling?　　　　説話者為什麼要打這通電話？
(A) To schedule a meeting　　　　　　(A) 安排會議時間
(B) To confirm the listener's presence at a　(B) 確認聽者是否出席會議
　　conference　　　　　　　　　　　(C) 安排合適的旅遊日期
(C) To arrange suitable travel date　　(D) 重新安排電話會議
(D) To reschedule a conference call

此為詢問撥打電話目的的題型，答案通常在開頭出現。從第二句「I'm calling to confirm your attendance at the board meeting here in March.」可知，説話者想確認聽話者是否會出席三月的董事會，故正確答案為 (B)。

93 --

What did Mr. Reece's secretary tell Mr. Stanton?　瑞斯先生的秘書告訴史坦頓先生什麼事？
(A) His availability is uncertain.　　　(A) 他不確定有沒有空。
(B) His interest is negligible.　　　　(B) 他的喜好並不重要。
(C) His attendance is mandatory.　　(C) 他必須出席。
(D) His schedule is canceled.　　　　(D) 他的行程被取消了。

留言前半段提到「Your secretary mentioned last week that you might not be able to attend」，表示秘書曾告知史坦頓先生，瑞斯先生可能無法參加會議，所以史坦頓先生才會再打電話來確認，故正確答案為 (A)。

What does the speaker say he will do?	**說話者說他會做什麼？**
(A) Mail the proposed agenda	(A) 郵寄擬定的議程表
(B) Arrange a flight	(B) 安排航班
(C) Send information electronically	(C) 透過電子方式寄送資料
(D) Check the time difference	(D) 確認時差

本題為詢問說話者未來行動的推測式題型，應當注意段落的後半部分。留言中後段提及「I'll send you an e-mail with possible times for a call.」，表示會將可以通話的時間以電子郵件告知。(C) 將 e-mail 改成「以電子方式（electronically）發送資訊」，故正確答案為 (C)。

95-97 instructions and seating chart   95–97 指示及座位表

Hello, everyone. I'm so glad that all you musicians are here to perform at the City Pop Festival. I want to give everyone some instructions briefly before you perform on the stage today. We don't have designated seats, so before and after each groups performance, please feel free to take any seats in the crowd if you want to watch the rest of the show. But I recommend you get a seat close to exit 2 to avoid disturbing the rest of the audience when you make your way from the stage. One more thing, could you stay a bit longer to take pictures after the performance? These pictures will be in the next issue of *City News Magazine*.	大家好。很高興所有的樂師齊聚在此為市立流行音樂節演出。在各位今天上台表演前，我想簡短地做一些說明。我們並未指定座位，因此在每一場團體表演前後，如果各位想觀賞其他的表演，可隨意於群眾中就座。但我建議各位挑選靠近二號出口的位子，以免從舞台離開時干擾其他觀眾。還有一件事，各位在表演結束後可否留下來拍照？這些照片將刊在下一期的《市聞雜誌》中。

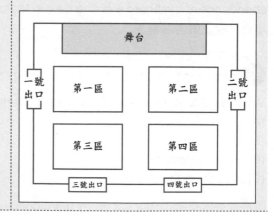

• **perform** 演出   **instructions** 指示說明   **briefly** 簡短地   **designate** 指定的   **crowd** 人群

95 ---

Who most likely are the listeners?
(A) Photographers
(B) Performers
(C) Ushers
(D) Audience members

聽者最有可能是誰？
(A) 攝影師
(B) 表演者
(C) 引座員
(D) 觀眾

本題為詢問聽者身份的問題，通常說者或聽者的職業會在一開始出現。段落開頭提到「I'm so glad that all you musicians are here」，表示很高興看到眾多音樂家聚集在此，所以可知正確答案為 (B)。

 96 NEW --

Look at the graphic. What section does the speaker want the listeners to sit in?
(A) Area 1
(B) Area 2
(C) Area 3
(D) Area 4

看一下圖表，說話者要聽者坐哪一區？
(A) 第一區
(B) 第二區
(C) 第三區
(D) 第四區

段落中間提到「But I recommend you get a seat close to exit 2」，建議與會者坐在二號出口附近的位子，對照座位表可知正確答案為 (B)。

97 ---

What are listeners asked to do when the show ends?
(A) Have some refreshments
(B) Sign autographs
(C) Revise a magazine
(D) Attend a photo shoot

聽者被要求在表演結束後做什麼？
(A) 吃些茶點
(B) 簽名
(C) 修訂雜誌
(D) 合照

段落最後提到「One more thing, could you stay a bit longer to take pictures after the performance?」，邀請聽眾在表演結束後多留片刻，以便拍照留念，故本題答案為 (D)。

I'd like to begin today's staff meeting by sharing some results of the customer survey of our running shoes recently conducted to satisfy customers. These results are very important. As you can see, what they like the most is the shoes' design. So we don't need to improve this. Here are the top four answers to the question, "What features of the product did you like most?" As you can see, the durability is the biggest problem we should upgrade. I'll let the product development team know about this. In the meantime, we can discuss the second-most-common answer. If you have any ideas, please let me know.

今天員工會議一開始，我想分享一些最近為了讓客戶滿意而進行的慢跑鞋顧客調查結果。這些結果非常重要。正如大家看到的，他們最喜歡的是鞋款的設計，所以這部份我們不需要再改進。以下是對於「你最喜歡這款產品的哪些特色？」這個問題的前四個答案。如大家所見，耐用度是我們應該提升的最大問題。我會讓產品開發小組知道這件事。在此同時，我們可以討論第二常見的答案。如果各位有任何想法，請告訴我。

Survey Results	
Design	40%
Color Scheme	25%
Durability	15%
Material	20%

調查結果	
設計	40%
配色	25%
耐用度	15%
材質	20%

 • **durability** 耐用度

98

According to the speaker, why did the company conduct the survey?

(A) To satisfy consumers
(B) To release the running shoes
(C) To cut operating expenses
(D) To correct a questionnaire

根據說話者表示，公司為什麼要進行這項調查？

(A) 為了讓客戶滿意
(B) 為了推出慢跑鞋
(C) 為了刪減營運費用
(D) 為了改正問卷

段落一開始便提到「. . . by sharing some results of the customer survey of our running shoes recently conducted to satisfy customers」，說明公司對客戶進行了產品滿意度調查。此句雖然略長，但只要能抓出最後解題關鍵的「to satisfy customers」，便可知道正確答案為 (A)。

99 [NEW] --

Look at the graphic. Which survey result does the speaker want to address now?

(A) Design
(B) Color Scheme
(C) Durability
(D) Material

看一下圖表,說話者現在想要討論的是哪一個調查結果?

(A) 設計
(B) 配色
(C) 耐用度
(D) 材質

本題需同時參照表格內的百分比數值。在段落最後,說話者提到「we can discuss the second-most-common answer」,代表說話者想探討數值第二高的項目,所以正確答案為 (B)。

100--

What does the speaker ask the listeners to do?

(A) Conduct safety inspections
(B) Give some feedback
(C) Mention some potential employees
(D) Contact the product development team

說話者要求聽者做什麼?

(A) 進行安全檢測
(B) 提供意見回饋
(C) 提名幾位有潛力的員工
(D) 聯絡產品開發小組

段落最後提到「If you have any ideas, please let me know.」,表示如果聽話者有任何想法都可以隨時提出,因此正確答案為 (B)。

ACTUAL TEST
5

1

(A) A woman is changing into a swimsuit.
(B) A woman is walking along the beach.
(C) A woman is surfing in the ocean.
(D) A woman is picking up some seashells.

(A) 一位女士正換上泳衣。
(B) 一位女士正沿著沙灘散步。
(C) 一位女士正在海裡衝浪。
(D) 一位女士正在撿貝殼。

照片中的女子正沿著海邊行走。**(A)** 女子並非正在換穿泳裝。**(C)** 女子並非正在衝浪。 **(D)** 雖然地上有貝殼，但是未能看到有人正在撿拾。正確答案為 **(B)**。

2

(A) A man is taking notes on the paper.
(B) A man is walking in the forest.
(C) A man is lying on the floor.
(D) A man is sitting on the bench.

(A) 一位男士正在紙上做筆記。
(B) 一位男士正在森林裡散步。
(C) 一位男士正躺在地板上。
(D) 一位男士正坐在長椅上。

• **take notes** 做筆記

照片中的男子趴在草地上，正在紙上書寫。**(B)** 照片的背景比起樹林，更接近草地。而且並未看出有人正在行走。**(C)** 男子不是躺在草地，而是趴在草地上。**(D)** 照片上並未出現長椅。正確解答為 **(A)**。

3

(A) Food is being prepared in the kitchen.
(B) A man is washing dishes.
(C) A man is wearing gloves.
(D) A bowl is being filled with water.

(A) 食物正在廚房準備中。
(B) 一位男士正在洗碗。
(C) 一位男士正戴著手套。
(D) 一個碗正被水盛滿。

照片中的男子正在烹調料理。**(A)** 雖然句子以被動進行式表現，但是照片中可看出廚師親自製作的樣子，故本句的敘述最符合照片。**(B)** 照片中未出現洗碗的動作。**(C)** 未出現戴著手套的人。**(D)** 雖然照片中出現碗，但是並非正被裝填。正確答案為 **(A)**。

(A) Some people are watching a movie.
(B) Some people are sitting in a line.
(C) A woman is speaking to a group of people.
(D) A woman is arranging a document.

(A) 一些人正在看電影。
(B) 一些人正坐成一排。
(C) 一位女士正對著一群人說話。
(D) 一位女士正在編排文件。

• **sit in a line** 坐成一排

此照片中間有一名女子坐在椅子上，其他人則圍繞著該女子討論事情。(A) 照片中並未出現觀賞電影的場面。(B) 照片中的人物並非並排而坐。(C) 從中間女子的立場看來，她正在向周圍的人說話，此為合適答案。(D) 桌上雖然放置著一些資料，但是並未看到有人正在整理。所以正確答案為 (C)。

⑤

(A) A customer is ringing a bell.
(B) A woman is trying on a ring.
(C) Some jewelry is on display.
(D) A telephone is ringing.

(A) 一位顧客正在按鈴。
(B) 一位女士正在試戴戒指。
(C) 一些首飾正在展示中。
(D) 電話正在響。

• **ring a bell** 按鈴　**try on** 試穿；試戴　**be on display** 展示中

照片上只出現「戒指」，故可能使用「ring」做出各種描述。因為照片中只有物體，若選項中提及人物做出的行動，皆為錯誤答案。(A) 和 (D) 中的「ring」是鈴鐺「響起」的意思，所以並不正確。(B) 照片中沒有人物。由此可見正確答案為 (C)。

⑥

(A) The armchairs are facing the artwork.
(B) The rug is being rolled up.
(C) The sitting area is brightened by lamps.
(D) Books are being stacked on the table.

(A) 扶手椅面對著藝術品。
(B) 地毯正被捲起。
(C) 燈照亮了座位區。
(D) 書本正被疊放在桌上。

• **armchair** 扶手椅　**rug** 地毯　**roll up** 捲起　**sitting area** 座位區　**brighten** 照亮　**be stacked** 被堆疊

此為房內家具擺設的圖片。(A) 兩張有扶手椅是面對面放置，而不是面向牆上的畫作。(B) 與 (D) 使用的被動進行式句型，在照片中未出現人物時，不可能成為正確解答。只要可以聽懂 (C) 中描述椅子放置空間的「sitting area」，就可以順利解題。本題的正確答案為 (C)。

PART 2 18

7

How do you come to the office every day?
(A) By the post office.
(B) No, I didn't go there.
(C) I just walk.

你每天如何來上班？
(A) 在郵局旁邊。
(B) 不，我沒去那裡。
(C) 我走路來的。

(A) 在只聽到「office」這個單字時，此選項可能會誤導考生。描述方法時，大多像「by bus」一樣使用介系詞「by」，但是如同選項 (A) 的「by」後面出現地點，此時「by」解釋為「在……旁邊」，故不是本題適合的答案。(B) 疑問詞的問句無法用「Yes/No」。正確答案為 (C)。

8

I think you really liked the volunteer we met yesterday, didn't you?
(A) Yes, we should give him a better position.
(B) He'll do it tomorrow.
(C) I received a copy of his application.

我覺得你真的很喜歡我們昨天碰到的志工，對不對？
(A) 對啊，我們應該給他更好的職位。
(B) 他明天會做。
(C) 我收到一份他的申請書。

• volunteer 志工　position 職位　application 申請書

句子以附加疑問句結束。因為是尋求對方認同的句子，回答開頭應出現「Yes/No」，所以正確答案應為 (A)。

9

Is the shareholders' meeting scheduled to be held on April 5?
(A) We should have shared them last year.
(B) To discuss our new products.
(C) No, it has been delayed.

股東會議是安排在4月5日嗎？
(A) 我們去年應該一起分享。
(B) 要討論新產品。
(C) 不，已經延後了。

• shareholders 股東　be scheduled to V... 被安排在……　hold 舉行　delay 延後

本題是確認某消息的問題，可以用「Yes/No」回答。就算不知道「shareholder」的意思，只需要注意詢問的重點（是否舉行會議），就能輕鬆解題。(A) 和 (B) 的內容與題目無關，而 (C) 表示會議已經延期，故正確答案為 (C)。

10

Who do I have to inform of my change of address?
(A) No, it doesn't change at all.
(B) Anderson, at the Reception Desk.
(C) Tom will give an address.

應該要告知誰我的地址更動了？
(A) 不，一點都沒有變。
(B) 接待處的安德森。
(C) 湯姆會發表演說。

• inform sb of sth 告知某人某事　reception desk 接待處　give an address 發表演說

此題以疑問詞「Who」詢問，不能用「Yes/No」回答，故 (A) 不正確。另外，(C) 中的「give an address」指的是演說，不同於與題目中的「address」，所以只是陷阱。題目詢問應該將地址變更一事告知誰，(B) 提及人物及其所屬單位，故正確答案為 (B)。

11

Why are your office supplies moved to another room?　你為什麼要把辦公室用品搬去其他處室？

(A) We will move to Chicago.　　　　　　　(A) 我們將搬到芝加哥去。

(B) An old piece of furniture, thanks.　　　(B) 一件舊家具，謝謝。

(C) Water is leaking through the ceiling.　(C) 天花板在漏水。

- **office supplies** 辦公室用品　　**leak** 漏水

(A) 是為了誤導只聽懂「move」的考生而設定的答案。(B) 為完全無關的句子。(C) 的回覆最為適當，故正確答案為 (C)。

12

The new products will be ready by next Friday, right?　新產品下禮拜五會準備就緒，是嗎？

(A) No, we need more time to finish them.　(A) 不，我們需要更多時間來完工。

(B) Yes, it makes a lot of products.　　　　(B) 是的，它可以做出很多產品。

(C) I will read newly-published books.　　(C) 我會閱讀最新出版的書。

- **newly-published** 新出版的

此題向對方確認產品是否已經準備好，句尾使用「right」徵求對方同意，所以使用「Yes/No」回答的機率很高。選項 (A) 即以「Yes/No」回答，表示還需要一些時間，為正確選項。(B) 雖以「Yes/No」回答，但後續內容與題目無關，並重複使用「product」造成誤導。(C) 則利用題目中的「ready」與「read」的發音相似性設陷阱。正確答案為 (A)。

13

The door to the supply room has been locked.　通往用品供應室的門鎖住了。

(A) We supply tickets.　　　　　　　　　　(A) 我們提供門票。

(B) I'll call the manager.　　　　　　　　　(B) 我會打電話給管理員。

(C) I can lock the window for you.　　　　(C) 我可以幫你鎖上窗戶。

- **supply room** 用品供應室　　**lock the window** 鎖上窗戶

(A) 出現與題目相同的字彙「supply」誘導。題目說門被鎖上了，(B) 表示會找人來開門，故為最適當的回應。(C) 出現與題目相同的「lock」誘導，內容與題目完全無關。正確答案為 (B)。

14

When will the headquarters on Main Street be remodeled?

(A) A quarter of a mile.

(B) Work begins next Monday.

(C) Yes, I enjoy walking down the street.

緬因街上的總部將於何時進行整修？

(A) 0.25英里。

(B) 工程從下禮拜一開始。

(C) 是的，我喜歡沿著街道走路。

• **headquarters** 總部　**remodel** 整修　**walk down the street** 沿著街道走

題目詢問「什麼時候」，故常見的答覆應提及「時期」或「時間點」。(A) 藉由與題目中的「headquarters」發音相似的「quarter」誤導。(B) 提到明確時間點，為合適答案。(C) 利用題目中出現的「street」試圖誤導。正確答案為 (B)。

15

Do you know who is carrying out the survey today?

(A) In Ashton's division.

(B) Winston Bale is.

(C) Please fill in the survey form.

你知道今天是誰進行問卷調查嗎？

(A) 在亞斯頓分處。

(B) 是溫斯頓‧貝爾。

(C) 請填寫問卷調查表。

• **carry out** 進行　**survey** 問卷調查　**division** 分處　**fill in** 填寫

題目詢問「誰」進行工作，故應以「對象」相關的句子回答。(A) 回答場所，故不正確。(B) 以人名回答，為正確答案。(C) 僅在利用與題目中出現過的「survey」誤導。正確答案為 (B)。

16

Could you give me a ride when you leave the office?

(A) I just placed an order for office supplies.

(B) I dropped off and missed the show.

(C) Today, I took a taxi to work.

你離開辦公室的時候，可以載我一程嗎？

(A) 我剛剛下了辦公室用品的訂單。

(B) 我打瞌睡，錯過了演出。

(C) 我今天搭計程車來上班的。

• **give sb a ride** 載某人一程　**place an order** 下訂單　**office supplies** 辦公室用品
　drop off 打瞌睡

(A) 重複題目中出現的「office」製造混淆。(B) 此處的「drop off」為打瞌睡，但若在中間加入對象（drop . . . off），就變成讓某人下車。平時熟知此種表現的考生可能會因此而受誤導。(C) 從題目中要求對方載自己一程的內容看來，告知對方自己來時搭乘計程車，是在暗示自己沒有開車過來，故為最適當的回應，正確答案為 (C)。

Which store sells these lunch boxes?
(A) Probably last year.
(B) Yes, it's going to snow heavily.
(C) The one between 5th and 6th Avenue.

這些午餐便當是哪家店賣的？
(A) 可能是去年。
(B) 是的，要下大雪了。
(C) 在第五和第六大道之間的那家。

題目詢問「Which store」，故回答中應該出現「場所」相關的訊息。(A) 只出現時期，而 (B) 只出現天氣，故皆非正確答案。告知位置的 (C) 最為適當，正確答案為 (C)。

Doesn't Mindy generally leave at six o'clock?
(A) Actually, I believe she has little.
(B) She won't take long.
(C) Yes, but she will work late into the night.

明蒂不是通常六點下班嗎？
(A) 事實上，我相信她沒有多少。
(B) 她不會花太多時間。
(C) 是的，但她要加班到深夜。

• take long 花很多時間　work late into the night 加班到深夜

此題為否定疑問句，但解讀句意時可先當作肯定疑問句，較容易選出適當回答。如果會在六點離開，須回答「Yes」，反之如果不會在該時間離開，則回答「No」即可。(A) 與 (B) 沒有回答問題。(C) 回答「Yes」，接著再進一步說明明蒂今天為了加班會晚點離開，故正確答案為 (C)。

Should we walk or drive to the shop?
(A) My car is in the parking lot right here.
(B) A few blocks from your home.
(C) The grocery store, please.

我們應該走路還是開車去商店？
(A) 我的車就停在這裡的停車場。
(B) 離你家幾條街的距離。
(C) 請到雜貨店。

題目讓對方在「徒步前往」或「開車前往」之間選擇，(A) 暗示問話者兩人可以一同搭自己的車離開，故為恰當回應。(B) 提及某地的位置，並不適當。(C) 給予指示而沒有做出選擇，故不是適合的回應。因此正確答案為 (A)。

What did Mr. Clyne say about the plan?
(A) At the press conference.
(B) He finally approved it.
(C) He plans to decline an interview.

關於計畫，克萊因先生怎麼說？
(A) 在記者會上。
(B) 他終於核准了。
(C) 他打算婉拒訪談。

• press conference 記者會　approve 核准　decline 婉拒

題目詢問他人對於計畫的想法。(A) 提及場所，與問題的內容不符合。(B) 表示他人核准計畫為適當回應。(C) 利用與題目中的「Clyne」發音相似的「decline」，以及題目出現過的「plan」誤導考生。正確答案 (B)。

18

21 ---

How often do you check your e-mail? 你多久查看一次電子郵件？
(A) Yes, I'll do that. (A) 是的，我會做。
(B) Twice a day. (B) 一天兩次。
(C) By express mail. (C) 以快遞寄送。

- express mail 快遞郵寄

由於題目用「How often」詢問，所以提及次數頻率為適當回達。(A) 以疑問詞詢問，無法使用
「Yes/No」回答，故錯誤。(C) 利用「mail」與題目中的「e-mail」發音類似而企圖誤導，內容本身
與題目完全無關。正確答案為 (B)。

22 ---

Are you getting back to work or going on a vacation? 你要回去上班還是去度假？
(A) I'm taking some time off. (A) 我要休息一段時間。
(B) I need to get it back quickly. (B) 我需要盡快取回。
(C) I applied for the job. (C) 我應徵了那份工作。

- get back to work 回到工作崗位　go on a vacation 去度假　take some time off 休息　get back 取回
  apply for . . . 應徵……

題目詢問對方工作與度假的計畫，選項中雖然找不到與此兩者用詞完全相同的內容，不過選項 (A) 中
以「take some time off」代替「go on a vacation」，故為適合的答案。(B) 中的「get . . . back」意
為「取回」，與題目「get back」的意思有所不同。(C) 根據題目可以知道，回答的人已有工作。
故正確答案為 (A)。

23 ---

When does your order arrive? 你訂購的東西何時會送達？
(A) It is being held up at customs. (A) 正被扣在海關。
(B) He arrived at the airport. (B) 他抵達機場了。
(C) A new product. (C) 一項新產品。

- be held up 被耽擱　customs 海關

題目用「When」詢問時點，雖然沒有確切提及時間點的選項，選項 (A) 表示了物品還被扣在海關，
指出物品暫時還不會送達，故為適當答案。(B) 使用人稱代名詞「He」回答，與題目不符。(C) 與題
目無關。故正確答案為 (A)。

24 ---

You could use a larger font for the presentation. 你的簡報可以用大一點的字體。
(A) The projector is ready. (A) 投影機已經準備好了。
(B) We need a wider space to accommodate them. (B) 我們需要更大的空間來容納他們。
(C) I think that would help. (C) 我想這會有幫助。

- font 字體　projector 投影機　accommodate 容納

題目給予了製作簡報的建議，(A) 與 (B) 與此建議無關，(C) 則附和此項建議，故正確答案為 (C)。

25

Where should we take our clients for the meeting?
(A) I decided yesterday.
(B) The airplane will arrive soon.
(C) He sent the file.

我們應該把客戶帶去哪裡開會？
(A) 我昨天已經決定好了。
(B) 飛機很快就要抵達了。
(C) 他把檔案送出了。

題目以疑問詞「Where」詢問「場所」，雖然選項中並沒有明確提及場所的回答，但 (A) 表示昨天已決定好地點，暗示會將客戶帶往此場所，(B) 與 (C) 則與題目內容無關，故正確答案為 (A)。

近來許多不直接提及預期回答的題型，考生答題時需要多加思考。

26

Do you mind reviewing the budget report for me?
(A) A weather report.
(B) Oh, I was about to get off work.
(C) He has a different viewpoint.

你介意幫我看一下預算報告嗎？
(A) 氣象報告。
(B) 噢，我快要下班了。
(C) 他有不同的觀點。

• **review** 審查　**budget report** 預算報告　**weather report** 天氣預報　**be about to V.** 將要（做某事）
　get off work 下班　**viewpoint** 觀點

一般而言，此類問句時常用「Yes/No」回答，但是近來常有其他形式的回覆成為正確答案。

(A) 利用題目中出現的「report」誤導。(B) 以「快要下班」暗示拒絕，故為最適當的答案。(C) 也是利用與題目中的「view」相似的「viewpoint」誤導作答，句子的意思與題目無關。正確答案為 (B)。

27

Are the clients satisfied with the proposal we revised?
(A) They'll let us know later today.
(B) In the December issue.
(C) A few suggested scenarios.

客戶滿意我們修改後的企畫案嗎？
(A) 他們今天稍晚會告訴我們。
(B) 在12月刊號。
(C) 一些建議的方案。

• **proposal** 企劃案　**revise** 修改　**issue**（報刊）期號　**suggested** 建議的

題目詢問對方是否滿意，(A) 表示對方稍晚才會告知，代表尚未收到回覆，現在也不確定對方是否滿意，此為合適答案，(B) 與 (C) 則和問題無關。此題正確答案為 (A)。

28

Who has the survey results?
(A) Jamison will meet there soon.
(B) Let me check the file.
(C) The survey form, I think.

誰有問卷調查結果？
(A) 傑米森不久後會在那裡碰面。
(B) 讓我查一下檔案。
(C) 我想是問卷調查表。

• **survey result** 調查結果　**survey form** 調查表

對於以「Who」詢問的問題，有時不直接提及人物，而是表示「不清楚」的選項也有可能成為答案。(A) 雖然提及對象，但是該人物所做的行動不適合作為本題的回答。(B) 表示將親自進行確認，為合適答案。(C) 只使用了題目中出現過的單字「survey」，並未回答題目問題。此題正確答案為 (B)。

18

Did you go to the festival last weekend?
(A) I don't like crowded areas.
(B) When is the last day?
(C) They're in good condition.

上個週末你有去慶典嗎？
(A) 我不喜歡擁擠的地方。
(B) 最後一天是什麼時候？
(C) 它們狀態良好。

此類詢問上週是否參加活動的題目，可以用三種情境回答：參加與否、參加感想，或是未參加的原因。(A) 說明自己不喜歡擁擠的場合，暗示自己並未參加活動。(B) 沒有回答到問題，且此題 (A) 更適合作為答案。(C) 因為題目中並未提及可以使用代名詞「They」的對象，故非適當的回答。正確答案為 (A)。

Can you show me how to fix the copy machine?
(A) Lucy learned about that last month.
(B) A copy of the contract will be ready.
(C) A copy machine was installed in the conference room.

你可以告訴我如何修理影印機嗎？
(A) 露西上個月有學過。
(B) 會準備好一份合約書。
(C) 會議室裡安裝了一台影印機。

• copy machine 影印機　a copy of the contract 一份合約書　install 安裝

題目詢問機器的修理方法，(A) 指出其他人知道如何修理，表示自己不會修理，此為適當的回覆。(B) 只是重複題目中出現過的單字「copy」，其內容與問題無關。(C) 沒有回答到問題。正確答案為 (A)。

What should we do to celebrate Mr. Dickson's promotion?
(A) In 2 years, probably.
(B) Let's go to the Oliver's restaurant.
(C) He is starting his new business.

我們該怎麼慶祝狄克森先生升職？
(A) 可能在兩年內。
(B) 我們去奧立佛餐廳吧。
(C) 他正開始他的新事業。

• start a business 創業

題目詢問慶祝晉升的方式，(A) 沒有回答到問題，(B) 提議前往餐廳慶祝，故為適當答案，(C) 題目並非詢問慶祝對象接下來要做的事情，故 (C) 此不適合作為本題的解答。正確答案為 (B)。

32-34 conversation **32–34 對話**

M Hi, I saw your store advertised on the Internet, so I dropped by. Your shop is having a clearance sale at the moment. Is that right? Is the sale applicable to home appliances, too?	男 嗨，我在網路上看到貴店的廣告，所以過來看看。店裡現在有清倉特賣會，沒錯吧？家用電器也都有特價嗎？
W Sure, the products on display are all 50 percent off the retail price. Did you download the coupon that came with the ad?	女 沒錯，展示的商品都享有零售價的五折折扣。您有下載廣告上面附的折價券嗎？
M Actually, I downloaded it on my mobile phone, but I left it at home. It might be better to go back there and come again to get a discount.	男 事實上，我下載在手機裡，但是我把它忘在家裡了。我最好回家一趟再來才能有折扣。

- advertise 廣告 drop by 拜訪 clearance sale 清倉特賣會 be applicable to . . . 適用於……
 home appliances 家用電器 on display 展示中 retail price 零售價 come with . . . 附帶（某物）
 get a discount 獲得折扣

32

Why does the man choose to shop at the store?
(A) It is conveniently located.
(B) The staff is very kind.
(C) He saw an online advertisement.
(D) One of his colleagues recommended the store.

這位男士為什麼選擇到這家店購物？
(A) 交通便利。
(B) 員工十分和善。
(C) 他看到網路廣告。
(D) 他的同事推薦這家店。

男子第一句便說「I saw your store advertised on the Internet」，表示他是在網路上看到廣告而來的，所以本題的答案為 (C)。

其他選項中提及的交通位置、員工、同事推薦等訊息並未出現在對話中。

33

What does the woman ask about?
(A) An identification card
(B) A receipt
(C) A discount coupon
(D) An advertisement flyer

這位女士要求出示什麼？
(A) 識別證
(B) 收據
(C) 折價券
(D) 廣告單

女子告知將提供 50％的折扣，並詢問男子是否持有廣告附帶的優惠券，故可判斷正確答案為 (C)。

34

Why does the man say he will go home?
(A) He wants to come with his parents.
(B) He has to answer the phone.
(C) He left something behind.
(D) He doesn't want to buy this product.

這位男士為什麼說他要回家？
(A) 他想和父母一起來。
(B) 他必須接電話。
(C) 他把東西忘在家裡。
(D) 他不想購買這個商品。

透過男子最後一句「I downloaded it on my mobile phone, but I left it at home. It might be better to go back there and come again to get a discount.」可知道，男子應把手機放在家裡而必須回去拿，故正確答案為 (C)。

35-37 conversation

W	Hi, Mr. Bacon. I have a blouse that should be dry-cleaned. I would like you to remove a coffee stain from it.
M	We can definitely get rid of the stain on your shirt. It will be ready by Saturday. I'll also have the skirt you requested earlier ready by then, too.
W	It would be great if I could wear the blouse and skirt for my important job interview on Friday. So . . . um . . . I was wondering if this could be done sooner.
M	I could do that. I'll start working on it immediately so both will be ready by Thursday evening.

35-37 對話

女	嗨，貝肯先生。我有一件要乾洗的上衣，希望你可以清除掉上面的咖啡漬。
男	我們絕對可以清除掉您襯衫上的污漬。星期六前就可以處理好。您先前送來的裙子那時也會處理好。
女	如果星期五我可以穿著那件上衣和裙子去參加一個重要的工作面試的話，那就太棒了。所以……嗯……我在想是不是可以早點處理好。
男	可以。我會立刻開始處理，那麼這兩件星期四晚上就會好了。

• dry-clean 乾洗　remove a stain 除漬　get rid of . . . 清除……　request 要求　by then 在那之前　job interview 工作面試　immediately 立刻

Where is the conversation most likely taking place?
(A) At a coffee shop
(B) At an office
(C) At a clothing factory
(D) At a dry cleaner's

這段對話最有可能出現在哪裡？
(A) 咖啡店
(B) 辦公室
(C) 成衣工廠
(D) 乾洗店

女子的第一句台詞中提到：「I have a blouse that should be dry-cleaned. I would like you to remove a coffee stain from it.」，表示她需要對方把襯衫上的污漬去掉，由此可知，對話的地點最可能為洗衣店，正確答案為 (D)。

36

What is the woman doing on Friday?
(A) Meeting a client
(B) Interviewing for a job
(C) Going on a vacation
(D) Visiting relatives

這位女士星期五要做什麼？
(A) 和客戶見面
(B) 面試工作
(C) 去度假
(D) 拜訪親戚

透過女子最後一句「my important job interview on Friday」可以知道正確答案為 (B)。

What does the man offer to do?
(A) Exchange a defective product
(B) Cancel a reservation
(C) Offer an express service
(D) Place a special order

這位男士提議做什麼？
(A) 更換有瑕疵的產品
(B) 取消預約
(C) 提供快速服務
(D) 下特殊訂單

因為有重要的面試，女子詢問是否可以盡快完成乾洗，男子則表示沒有問題（I could do that），並告知會立刻開始處理，故正確答案為 (C)。

38-40 conversation

38–40 對話

M	Hello, this is Harvey Harris from United Electric Service. I was scheduled to visit your office to install some refrigerators this afternoon, but what I'm doing now is taking longer than planned. Unfortunately, I won't be able to make it until 7 P.M.	男	嗨，我是聯合電器服務的哈維·哈里斯。我本來預定今天下午要到貴公司安裝冰箱，但是我現在所進行的工作比預定要花更多的時間。很遺憾地，我要到七點才能趕到了。
W	Thank you for the information. Our office closes at 6 P.M., but our security guard in the building is on duty for 24 hours. I'll ask the one on duty to let you in.	女	感謝您的告知。我們公司下午六點下班，但是大樓的保全人員會24小時值勤。我會要求值勤人員讓您進來。
M	Thank you. And when I finish the installation, how can I send the invoice?	男	謝謝您。當我安裝完成後，要如何寄送帳單？
W	I would appreciate it if you could just leave it with him.	女	若您可以將帳單留給保全人員，那我會十分感謝。

• **be scheduled to V** 預定（做某事）　**take long** 花很多時間　**make it** 準時到達　**security guard** 保全人員
be on duty 值勤中　**ask for** 要求　**installation** 安裝　**invoice** 帳單　**appreciate** 感謝
leave sth with sb 將某事留給某人　**set up** 安裝　**appliances** 電器　**deliver a speech** 發表演說
refund 退款　**estimate** 估價單

Why will the man visit the woman's office?
(A) To set up appliances
(B) To make a repair
(C) To deliver a speech
(D) To get a refund

這位男士為什麼要去女士的公司？
(A) 安裝電器
(B) 進行維修
(C) 發表演說
(D) 取得退款

男子一開始便提及要在辦公室裝設冰箱（install some refrigerators），且「refrigerators」算是「appliances」的一種，故正確答案 (A)。

39

What does the woman say she will do?
(A) Buy some refrigerators
(B) Stay in the company
(C) Talk to a security officer
(D) Provide a receipt

這位女士說她會做什麼？
(A) 買一些冰箱
(B) 待在公司
(C) 和保全人員談話
(D) 提供收據

男子告知要七點才能到達公司，而女子說公司六點便會下班，但會聯絡保全人員（Our office closes at 6 P.M., but our security guard in the building is on duty for 24 hours. I'll ask the one on duty to let you in），好讓男子進公司。由此可知，正確答案為 (C)。

40

What does the woman ask the man to leave with the security guard?
(A) An estimate
(B) A manual
(C) An invoice
(D) An agreement

這位女士要求男士把什麼交給保全人員？
(A) 估價單
(B) 使用手冊
(C) 帳單
(D) 協議書

男子最後問道「And when I finish the installation, how can I send the invoice?」，詢問裝設完成後要如何提供帳單，而女子則表示「could just leave it with him」，此處的「him」即前文提過的保全人員，故正確答案為 (C)。

41-43 conversation with three speakers [NEW]　41–43 三人對話

M1 Hi. Welcome to Burton Store. How can I be of assistance?	**男1** 嗨，歡迎光臨伯頓商店。有什麼可以為您服務的嗎？
W Well, I wonder if you could help me. I am looking for colored pencils for my daughter.	**女** 嗯，我在想你是不是可以幫我一下。我在幫我女兒找彩色鉛筆。
M1 Hmm . . . I'm not sure if we have them for children. As far as I know, we have them only for professionals, but let me check on this. Hey, Christopher, do we have children's colored pencils?	**男1** 嗯……我不確定我們是否有兒童用的彩色鉛筆。據我所知，我們只有給專業人士使用的彩色鉛筆，但讓我確認一下。嗨，克里斯多福，我們有兒童用的彩色鉛筆嗎？
M2 Yes, we do, but just not on this floor. They're upstairs. Let me show you. Please follow me.	**男2** 有的，我們有，只是不在這一樓，在樓上。讓我帶妳去。請跟我來。
W That's good news. And do you know where I can get them gift-wrapped? They are for my daughter's birthday present.	**女** 真是好消息。你知道哪裡可以做禮物包裝嗎？這是我女兒的生日禮物。
M2 Actually, we offer a gift-wrapping service for free.	**男2** 事實上，我們免費提供禮物包裝服務。
W That's perfect. Thanks!	**女** 太好了。謝謝！

• **colored pencil** 彩色鉛筆　**as far as I know** 據我所知　**professional** 專業人士　**upstairs** 樓上　**gift-wrapping service** 禮物包裝服務　**stationery** 文具　**be sold out** 銷售一空　**at a discounted price** 有特價　**express delivery** 快遞運送　**packaging** 包裝　**estimate** 估價　**on-site** 在現場的

41 ---

What is the woman shopping for?

(A) Stationery
(B) Wrapping paper
(C) Children's book
(D) Paint

這位女士要購買什麼？

(A) 文具
(B) 包裝紙
(C) 童書
(D) 顏料

女子的第一句台詞說「I am looking for colored pencils for my daughter.」，表示她正在幫女兒尋找彩色鉛筆，故女子應是想購買文具用品，正確解答為 (A)。

42 ---

What does Christopher say about the items?

(A) They're sold out.
(B) They're offered at a discounted price.
(C) They've already been delivered.
(D) They're on a different floor.

克里斯多福說了什麼關於商品的事？

(A) 已經賣完了。
(B) 有特價。
(C) 已經寄出了。
(D) 在別的樓層。

首先男 1 的第二句結尾說了「Hey, Christopher, do we have children's colored pencils?」，而男 2 接著回答，故可男 2 就是克里斯多福，且男 2 說到彩色鉛筆不在對話者所在的樓層（just not on this floor），而是在樓上。故正確答案為 (D)。

43 ---

What additional service does Christopher mention?

(A) Express delivery
(B) Free packaging
(C) A free estimate
(D) On-site repair

克里斯多福提到什麼額外的服務？

(A) 快遞運送
(B) 免費包裝
(C) 免費估價
(D) 現場維修

對話的最後部分中，女子詢問能包裝禮物的地點時，克里斯多福回覆「we offer a gift-wrapping service for free.」，表示商店提供免費包裝服務，所以本題答案為 (B)。

19

W I talked to Hugo Robbins on the phone yesterday. We were going to have him as our keynote speaker for the April conference, but he confirmed that he is unable to participate. **M** Really? That's bad news. We have to find a replacement for him as soon as possible. We don't have much time because the schedule for the conference program will be out next week. **W** Do you have any alternatives to recommend? **M** As a matter of fact, I know a qualified candidate, Tim Lee. He's a very attractive speaker and will pull in huge crowds. I'll call him and let you know if he is available.	**女** 我昨天和雨果・羅賓斯通過電話。我們要邀請他擔任四月研討會的主講人,但是他確定無法出席。 **男** 真的嗎?真是壞消息。我們必須盡快找到替代人選。我們時間不多,因為下禮拜就要公布研討會的議程表了。 **女** 你有推薦的替代人選嗎? **男** 其實,我知道一個合格的人選—提姆・李。他是很有魅力的演講者,將會吸引許多聽眾。我來打電話給他,再告訴妳他有沒有空。

• on the phone 在電話中　keynote speaker 主講人　replacement 替代　as soon as possible 盡快
　be out 公布　alternative 替代選項　qualified candidate 合格的人選　pull in 吸引　crowd 人群

What are the speakers organizing?   說話者正在籌辦什麼?

(A) A job interview   (A) 工作面試
(B) A speech contest   (B) 演講比賽
(C) A conference   (C) 研討會
(D) A career fair   (D) 就業博覽會

女子的第一句台詞「I talked to Hugo Robbins on the phone yesterday. We were going to have him as our keynote speaker for the April conference . . .」,提及她打電話邀請能參加研討會的講者,可推測她應為研討會的負責人之一,故正確解答為 (C)。

 NEW

What problem does the woman mention?   這位女士提到什麼問題?

(A) An event has been delayed.   (A) 活動延遲。
(B) A flight was canceled.   (B) 班機取消。
(C) Hotels are all booked up.   (C) 飯店被預訂一空。
(D) A speaker has canceled.   (D) 演講者取消出席。

女子第一段發言的最後部分提到,演說者已經確定無法參加(he confirmed that he is unable to participate),故正確答案為 (D)。

What most likely will the man do next?   這位男士接下來可能會做什麼?

(A) Send an invitation card   (A) 寄送邀請卡
(B) Make a phone call   (B) 撥打電話
(C) Make a reservation   (C) 預約
(D) Prepare a meeting   (D) 準備會議

由於女子邀請的講者不克出席，男子則表示他知道有個適合的替代人選，並在最後表示將致電給替代人選（I'll call him），故正確答案為 (B)。

47-49 conversation

W	Hi, Dennis. Did you check on the schedule for next month's sports program? I rearranged the schedule for you to teach two classes.	女	嗨，丹尼斯。你看過下個月運動課程的時間表了嗎？我為你重新安排了課表，這樣你可以教兩個班。

47-49 對話

W Hi, Dennis. Did you check on the schedule for next month's sports program? I rearranged the schedule for you to teach two classes.

M Great! Thanks. Hmm . . . The two classes are back-to-back.

W Right. Isn't that what you want?

M Well, we have to put the equipment away and prepare the next class in just ten minutes because the basketball class is scheduled to begin right after my table tennis class is over. Who can help me? (48)**I can't do it alone.**

W I understand. How about changing the start time of the basketball class? If it starts 10 minutes later, there'll be no problem.

女 嗨，丹尼斯。你看過下個月運動課程的時間表了嗎？我為你重新安排了課表，這樣你可以教兩個班。

男 太棒了！謝謝。嗯……這兩堂課的時間是連著的。

女 沒錯。這不是你想要的嗎？

男 嗯，我們必須在十分鐘內將器材歸位，準備好上下一堂課，因為我的桌球課一結束，就立刻要上籃球課。有誰可以幫我嗎？(48)**我無法獨自完成。**

女 我了解。那調整籃球課的上課時間如何？如果晚十分鐘上課，就沒問題了。

• check on . . . 查看…… rearrange 重新安排 back-to-back 連續的 put sth away 將某物歸位 equipment 器材 fitness center 健身中心 facility（有特定用途的）場所 pay increase 加薪 be satisfied with . . . 對……感到滿意 recruit 招募

47 --

Where do the speakers most likely work?
(A) At a fitness center
(B) At a sporting goods store
(C) At a department store
(D) At a heavy equipment facility

說話者最有可能在什麼地方上班？
(A) 健身房
(B) 運動用品店
(C) 百貨公司
(D) 重型器材廠

本題只要能抓出重點單字就可以輕鬆解題。透過對話中的「sports program」、「basketball class」與「table tennis」等字彙，可以知道對話雙方的工作地點應為運動場所，故正確解答為 (A)。

48 (NEW) --

What does the man imply when he says, "I can't do it alone"?
(A) He is asking for a pay increase.
(B) He wants to know the exact number of members.
(C) He thinks that the task is impossible.
(D) He is satisfied with his current position.

當這位男士說：「我無法獨自完成」，是什麼意思？
(A) 他要求加薪。
(B) 他想要知道確切的會員人數。
(C) 他認為這個工作不可能辦到。
(D) 他對於現職感到滿意。

這種題型必須從上下文推斷句意。前一句台詞中，男子問「Who can help me?」，表示需要幫助，也暗示此項工作無法獨自完成，因此最適當的答案為 (C)。

49

What does the woman offer to do?
(A) Change the schedule
(B) Move the equipment
(C) Clean up the facility
(D) Recruit more members

這位女士提議做什麼？
(A) 調整時間表
(B) 移動器材
(C) 打掃場地
(D) 招募更多會員

女子的最後一句台詞提到「How about changing the start time of the basketball class?」，認為調整籃球課的上課時間，男子的問題就可以解決。由此可知，女子將幫助更改時間表，正確答案為 (A)。

50-52 conversation　　　　　　　　　　50–52 對話

W	Jason, I should wrap up the quarterly sales report for the presentation on Friday. Please check to see if you need to revise it.	女	傑森，我需要總結禮拜五簡報要用的季銷售報表。請看看是否需要修改。
M	Actually, I'm still correcting some of the figures. The computer system was down for maintenance yesterday, so I'm terribly behind on my work. When do you need it by?	男	事實上，我還在修改一些數字。昨天電腦系統關閉進行維護，所以我的進度嚴重落後。妳最晚什麼時候需要檔案？
W	By tomorrow morning, if possible. I have to get the presentation ready by then because the shareholders' meeting is scheduled to be held on Friday.	女	如果可能的話，明天早上之前。我必須在那之前準備好簡報，因為股東大會預定在星期五舉行。

- **wrap up** 總結　**quarterly sales report** 季銷售報表　**presentation** 簡報　**be down**（機器等）關閉
maintenance 維護　**be behind** 落後　**shareholder** 股東　**out of town** 出遠門

50

What are the speakers discussing?
(A) Selecting a new computer system
(B) Checking maintenance information
(C) Starting a business
(D) Finishing a report

說話者在討論什麼？
(A) 挑選新的電腦系統
(B) 檢查維修訊息
(C) 開始新業務
(D) 完成報表

女子說的第一句話中，提及「wrap up the quarterly sales report」，表示需要總結季銷售報表。
(D) 將「wrap up」改成「finish」，但整體意思仍與對話內容相符，故正確答案為 (D)。

51

Why was the man unable to complete a task?
(A) Sales revenue has decreased.
(B) A system was not working properly.
(C) A colleague was out of town.
(D) A meeting was canceled.

這位男士為什麼無法完成工作？
(A) 銷售營收減少了。
(B) 系統無法正常運作。
(C) 同事出遠門了。
(D) 會議被取消了。

男子表示「I'm still correcting some of the figures.」，表示他還在修改報表的數字，並且說明原因是電腦系統昨天無法使用（The computer system was down for maintenance yesterday），故正確答案為 (B)。

52 --

What does the woman say she will do?

(A) Prepare for a meeting
(B) Change a reservation
(C) Contact the Maintenance Department
(D) E-mail a report

這位女士說她要做什麼事？

(A) 準備會議
(B) 變更預約
(C) 聯絡維修部門
(D) 將報表以電子郵件寄出

從女子的最後一句「I have to get the presentation ready by then」即可知道，她需要準備會議需要的簡報，故正確答案為 (A)。

53-55 conversation with three speakers NEW

53–55 三人對話

M Hi, I'm Richard Rose. I made a phone call yesterday to get my medical records as I need a copy of them when I go on a business trip to Singapore next month.	男 嗨，我是理查‧羅斯。我昨天打過電話要索取我的病歷，因為下個月我到新加坡出差時需要一份影本。
W1 All right, I'll check on this. Who's your doctor?	女1 好的，讓我查一下。您的醫生是哪一位？
M Doctor Mitchell.	男 米歇爾醫師。
W1 Okay, I think my colleague printed them in the morning. One second, sir. Jennifer?	女1 好的，我想我的同事早上已經將病歷印出來了。請您等一下。珍妮佛？
W2 Yes?	女2 什麼事？
W1 You printed Mr. Rose's records in the morning, right?	女1 妳今天早上列印了羅斯先生的病歷，是嗎？
W2 Yes. Please just sign this form before I give them to you.	女2 是的。在我將病歷給您之前，請在這張表上簽名。
M Sure. Could I borrow a pen?	男 沒問題。可以借我一枝筆嗎？

• **make a phone call** 打電話　**medical records** 病歷　**go on a business trip** 出差
　check on . . . 查看……　**prescribe medicine** 開藥物處方箋　**reschedule** 重新安排（時間）

53 --

What does the man say he will do next month?

(A) Participate in a medical forum
(B) Go away on business
(C) Move to a different city
(D) Finish a medical course

這位男士說他下個月要做什麼事？

(A) 出席醫學論壇
(B) 出差
(C) 搬到其他城市
(D) 完成醫學課程

男子一開始的台詞說到「I go on a business trip to Singapore next month.」，故正確答案為 (B)。

54 --

According to the conversation, what did Jennifer do in the morning?

(A) She rescheduled an appointment.
(B) She prescribed some medicine.
(C) She printed some documents.
(D) She treated a patient.

根據對話內容，珍妮佛早上做了什麼事？

(A) 她重新安排預約。
(B) 她開了藥物處方箋。
(C) 她列印了一些文件。
(D) 她醫治了一名病患。

ACTUAL TEST 5

PART **3**

中譯＋解析

 19

女1的第二句台詞「Okay, I think my colleague printed them in the morning. One second, sir. Jennifer?」她在最後呼喚了珍妮佛，而女2接著回覆，可知女2即為珍妮佛，再從此句以及兩人之後的問答中知道，珍妮佛早上印出了羅斯先生的病歷，故正確答案為 (C)。

55 --

What does Jennifer ask the man to do?
(A) Make a payment
(B) Wait for a while
(C) Sign a form
(D) Call a doctor's office

珍妮佛要求這位男士做什麼？
(A) 付款
(B) 稍候一會
(C) 在表單上簽名
(D) 打電話到醫師辦公室

珍妮佛最後向男子說「Please just sign this form before I give them to you.」，表示在交付病歷前，需要男子在資料上簽名，故正確解答為 (C)。

56-58 conversation

56–58 對話

M Hello, I placed an order for a wireless speaker on your Web site on May 5th. My credit card statement said that I was charged two times for the purchase. **W** I'm really sorry to hear that, sir. Actually, we had a problem with our electronic payment system on that date. So, online transactions were repeated automatically. **M** Oh, is that so? **W** Yes, the refund procedure is currently underway, but I can deal with yours immediately if you wish. **M** Okay, that's a relief. Thank you. **W** After I put this through . . . um . . . if you don't mind, could you take part in our survey? **M** Sure, no problem.	**男** 妳好，5月5日的時候，我在妳們的網站上訂購了無線喇叭。我的信用卡明細顯示那筆交易我被扣了兩次款。 **女** 先生，我感到非常抱歉。事實上，那天我們的電子支付系統出現問題。所以線上交易自動重複扣款了。 **男** 喔，是這樣嗎？ **女** 是的，現在正在進行退款作業，但是如果您希望我立刻處理的話，我可以現在處理。 **男** 好的，這讓我鬆了一口氣。謝謝妳。 **女** 在我處理好之後⋯⋯嗯⋯⋯若您不介意的話，可以參加問卷調查嗎？ **男** 當然可以，沒問題。

• **place an order** 訂購　**statement** 結算單　**be charged** 被扣款　**electronic payment** 電子支付
online transaction 線上交易　**automatically** 自動地　**deal with . . .** 處理⋯⋯　**relief** 放輕鬆
put through 處理好　**take part in . . .** 參加⋯⋯　**renovation** 整修　**inventory** 存貨　**shortage** 短缺
expiration date 有效期限　**receipt** 收據

56 --

Why is the man calling?
(A) He wants to buy another product.
(B) His order has not yet been delivered.
(C) He needs to know the store's Web site address.
(D) He was charged twice for a purchase.

這位男士為什麼打這通電話？
(A) 他想購買另一項產品。
(B) 他所訂購的東西還沒寄送。
(C) 他需要知道商店的網址。
(D) 他的交易被收了兩次費用。

男子第一句台詞「I was charged two times for the purchase.」，表示自己的訂單被重複扣款，所以正確答案為 (D)。

What does the woman explain about?

(A) A technical issue
(B) A renovation project
(C) An inventory shortage
(D) A credit card expiration date

這位女士解釋的原因是什麼？

(A) 技術問題
(B) 整修計畫
(C) 缺貨
(D) 信用卡有效期限

女子說明「Actually, we had a problem with our electronic payment system on that date」，故重複扣款是因為電子支付系統發生問題，所以最符合的答案為 (A)。

What does the woman ask the man to do?

(A) Return a product
(B) Respond to a survey
(C) Visit a Web site
(D) Keep a receipt

這位女士要求男士做什麼？

(A) 退還商品
(B) 回答問卷
(C) 瀏覽網站
(D) 保留收據

根據女子的最後一句「if you don't mind, could you take part in our survey?」，女子說會為男子辦理退費，並且詢問男子事後願不願意參加問卷調查，故正確答案為 (B)。

59-61 conversation　　59–61 對話

W Hey David, it's Green. I'm trying to enter the building, but the gate won't open when I swipe my ID badge. M That occurred to a few employees today. If you let me know your employee number, I'll reenter your information into the server right now. Then, the gate scanner should recognize you. W Okay, but can you let me in now? I have a meeting with a client. M (61)It's against the company policy. It'll only take a few minutes. W I understand. Then I hope it can be done as quickly as possible.	女 嗨，大衛。我是格林。我試著要進入大樓，但是當我刷識別證時，大門並未打開。 男 今天有幾位員工也碰到同樣的事。如果妳告訴我妳的員工編號，我現在就可以將妳的資料重新輸入伺服器，然後大門的掃描器應該就可以辨識妳了。 女 好的，但是你可以現在讓我進去嗎？我要和客戶開會。 男 (61)這會違反公司規定。只要花幾分鐘就好了。 女 了解。希望可以盡快完成。

 19

• **swipe** 刷（卡）　　**ID badge** 身分識別證　　**recognize** 辨識　　**be against . . .** 違反……　　**policy** 政策
make up for . . . 彌補……

Where most likely is the woman?

(A) At a building entrance
(B) In a meeting room
(C) At an airport
(D) In an elevator

這位女士最有可能在哪裡？

(A) 在大樓入口
(B) 在會議室
(C) 在機場
(D) 在電梯裡

仔細聆聽女子所說的第一句話「I'm trying to enter the building, but the gate won't open when I swipe my ID badge.」，表示她想進入大樓，但是門打不開。由此判斷，女子目前最可能身在公司大樓入口，正確答案為 (A)。

60 --

What does the man ask for?
(A) A department name
(B) An employee number
(C) A password
(D) A telephone number

這位男士要求什麼？
(A) 部門名稱
(B) 員工編號
(C) 密碼
(D) 電話號碼

男子對女子說「If you let me know your employee number, I'll reenter your information into the server right now.」，只要女子提供員工號碼，他能替她在伺服器重新輸入資料，因此正確答案為 (B)。

61 (NEW) --

Why does the man say, "It's against the company policy"?
(A) To postpone a meeting
(B) To refuse a request
(C) To ask for a help
(D) To make up for a mistake

這位男士為什麼說：「這會違反公司規定」？
(A) 要延後會議
(B) 在拒絕要求
(C) 要尋求協助
(D) 要彌補錯誤

從此句上下文可推測，女子希望男子可以直接讓她進公司（can you let me in now?），而男子回覆這樣會違反規定（against the company policy），故此句是在拒絕女子的請求，正確答案為 (B)。

W Excuse me, sir. You might be sitting in the wrong seat. According to my ticket, I'm supposed to sit in A.

M No, I'm quite certain that I'm in 8A. Let's take a look at your ticket. Hmm . . . I understand what happened. You should be seated right ahead of me.

W Oh. Thank you, and sorry about that. By the way, if you don't mind, could you change your place with me? My boyfriend is going to be sitting in 8B. It would be great if we could watch the film together.

M Sure, that's no problem. I like a seat closer to the screen anyway.

女 先生，不好意思。您可能坐錯位子了。根據我的票券，我的座位應該在A。

男 不是，我相當確定我的位子是8A。我們來看看妳的票券。嗯……我知道發生什麼事了。妳應該坐在我的正前方。

女 喔，謝謝你，真是抱歉。對了，如果你不介意，可以和我換位子嗎？我的男朋友會坐在8B。如果我們可以一起看電影的話，那就太好了。

男 當然，沒問題。反正我喜歡離螢幕近一點的位子。

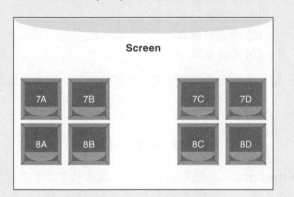

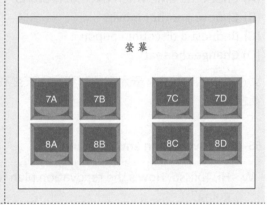

- take a look at . . . 看一看……   ahead of . . . 在……之前

62 ---

What is the purpose of the conversation?
(A) To explain refund regulations
(B) To introduce a new film
(C) To offer a special discount
(D) To resolve a problem

這段對話的目的是什麼？
(A) 說明退費規定
(B) 介紹新電影
(C) 提供特別優惠
(D) 解決問題

從「It would be great if we could watch the film together.」可知對話在電影院發生，且女子搞錯了座位，因此兩人一同確認電影票並釐清誤會，故此對話應是在解決座位問題，正確答案為 (D)。

ACTUAL TEST 5

PART 3

中譯＋解析

19

NEW --

Look at the graphic. What seat was the woman originally assigned to?
(A) 7A
(B) 7B
(C) 8A
(D) 8B

看一下圖表，這位女士原本被分配在哪個座位？
(A) 7A
(B) 7B
(C) 8A
(D) 8B

利用對話中的兩項資訊可以導出正確解答。第一，女子搞錯的座位是「8A」。第二，男子隨後表示自己的位置才是「8A」，而女子應該坐在前面的位置。由此可知，「7A」是女子本來應該要坐的位置，故正確答案為 (A)。

64 --

What does the woman ask the man to do?
(A) Check the time when the movie starts
(B) Choose another movie
(C) Request a discount coupon
(D) Change the seat

這位女士要求男士做什麼？
(A) 查看電影開始的時間
(B) 選擇另一部電影
(C) 要求折價券
(D) 更換座位

女子最後的台詞中，表示自己想和男朋友坐在一起，所以詢問男子能否與她互換座位，所以正確答案為 (D)。

65-67 conversation and schedule

65–67 對話及時程表

W Hi, Tolisso. How's the renovation plan for the hotel going?	女 嗨，托利梭。飯店的整修計畫進行得如何？
M Great. Even though the hotel is somewhat old, it was structurally sound. The plan is well under way.	男 很順利。雖然飯店有點老舊，但是結構上很穩固。計畫順利進行中。
W Good. I would like to put it up for sale on the first day of December. I think that it is the best time to sell. Will everything be finished by then?	女 很好。我想要在12月的第一天就展示出售。我認為那是最好的銷售時機。在那之前會完工嗎？
M Let me see. We've just finished the furniture, flooring, and lighting installation. And we're scheduled to start remodeling the fitness center next week. Yes, we could be done by the end of November.	男 讓我看看。我們剛安裝好家具、地板與燈具。預計下週開始整修健身中心。是的，我們可以在11月底完工。
W Could you send me the details about the total expected cost? This will help me set a price for the hotel.	女 你可以將全部預計費用的明細寄給我嗎？這可以幫助我設定飯店的售價。

Schedule	
Stage 1	Redesign lobby
Stage 2	Install furniture, flooring, lighting
Stage 3	Revamp fitness center
Stage 4	Paint outside

時程表	
第一階段	重新規劃大廳
第二階段	安裝家具、地板、燈具
第三階段	改建健身中心
第四階段	外部油漆

- renovation plan 整修計畫　structurally sound 結構穩固　be well under way 順利進行中
  put . . . up for sale 將……展示出售　flooring 地板　lighting 照明設備
  be scheduled to V 預計……　total expected cost 預估總成本　set a price 定價

65

What most likely is the man's profession?

(A) Engineer
(B) Construction manager
(C) Real estate agent
(D) Salesperson

這位男士的職業最有可能是什麼？

(A) 工程師
(B) 營建主管
(C) 不動產仲介
(D) 銷售人員

女子在對話一開始詢問飯店修理的進度，而男子表示一切都按照計畫順利進行中，接著開啟整段對話。另外，根據男子接下來告知修繕日程計畫的表現看來，男子的職業應是建物修理、修復負責人。所以正確答案最可能為 (B)。

---

66 (NEW)

Look at the graphic. What stage of the renovation will begin next week?

(A) Stage 1
(B) Stage 2
(C) Stage 3
(D) Stage 4

看一下圖表，下週將開始哪一階段的整修？

(A) 第一階段
(B) 第二階段
(C) 第三階段
(D) 第四階段

從男子最後的台詞「And we're scheduled to start remodeling the fitness center next week.」可得知，下週會開始裝潢健身房，再對照時程表可選出正確答案為 (C)。

67

What does the woman ask the man to send?

(A) An estimated price
(B) Some photos
(C) A schedule
(D) A hotel address

這位女士要求男士寄送什麼？

(A) 估價單
(B) 一些照片
(C) 時程表
(D) 飯店地址

女子最後說「Could you send me the details about the total expected cost?」是在要求對方提供總預算相關的詳細資料，故正確答案為 (A)。

M Lauren, I have read the M&A report. Have you seen the file? We considered taking over Goldman Holdings last year.	男 蘿倫，我看了合併收購報告。妳有看到那份文件嗎？我們去年考慮要接收高曼控股公司。
W Really? What else does it say?	女 真的嗎？報告上還說了什麼？
M The main topic is our company's market share. Even though we still wouldn't have the biggest market share in the industry, we're trying to improve our competitive edge.	男 主題是公司的市場占有率。雖然我們在業界還未擁有最大的市場占有率，但是我們很努力增進競爭優勢。
W So, it looks like we're already the third biggest and acquiring Goldman Holdings will definitely help our company overtake Ingram to rank second in the industry. I think taking over the company would be a good decision.	女 那麼，看起來我們已經是第三大的公司，取得高曼控股公司絕對有助於我們超越英格拉姆成為業界第二大的公司。我認為取得這間公司是個好決定。
M Well . . . I'm not sure. It isn't such a good idea. Now I'm reading the latest report. Goldman Holdings' profits has decreased for the past few months.	男 嗯……我不確定。這不是那麼好的想法。我現在正在看最新的報告。高曼控股公司的獲利在過去幾個月已經減少了。

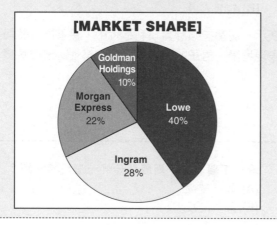 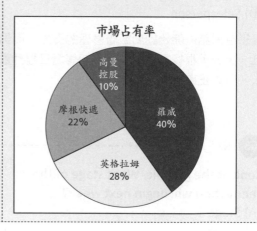

• **M&A (mergers and acquisitions)** 合併與收購　**take over** 接收　**market share** 市場占有率
competitive edge 競爭優勢　**acquire** 獲得　**overtake** 超越　**rank** 位居（某名次）　**profit** 獲利

68 --

What are the speakers mainly discussing?　　說話者主要在談論什麼？

(A) An annual plan　　　　　　　　　　　　(A) 年度計畫
(B) Unemployment rates　　　　　　　　　　(B) 失業率
(C) A business acquisition　　　　　　　　　(C) 接管公司
(D) A budget report　　　　　　　　　　　　(D) 預算報告

從男子的第一句台詞中的「M&A」以及「We considered taking over Goldman Holdings」可知，此對話整體與公司收購相關，故正確答案為 (C)。

69 NEW ---

Look at the graphic. Where do the speakers work?　看一下圖表，說話者是在哪裡工作？

(A) Lowe　　　　　　　　　　　　　　(A) 羅威
(B) Ingram　　　　　　　　　　　　　(B) 英格拉姆
(C) Morgan Express　　　　　　　　　(C) 摩根快遞
(D) Goldman Holdings　　　　　　　　(D) 高曼控股

女子在最後提到「it looks like we're already the third biggest」，表示公司現為業界排名第三，後文也提到只要收購高曼控股，市場占有率就能追上英格拉姆，由此可知對話者在摩根快遞工作，故正確解答為 (C)。

 70 ---

Why does the man say he is not convinced?　這位男士為什麼說他不認同？

(A) He didn't read the report.　　　　　(A) 他沒有看到這份報告。
(B) Some information is inaccurate.　　　(B) 有些資訊不正確。
(C) The man is not good at analyzing data.　(C) 這位男士不擅長分析資料。
(D) The company's profits have reduced recently.　(D) 那家公司最近的獲利減少了。

女子在對話最後表示收購高曼控股是個好決定，而男子回覆「Goldman Holdings' profits has decreased for the past few months」，表示因為高曼控股近期獲利減少，公司對收購失去信心，因此正確解答為 (D)。

71-73 advertisement

71–73 廣告

Do you have old electronic products that you never use, such as old computers and TVs? Why don't you bring them to Avnet Electronics? We'll make a visit to pick up your devices and recycle them. If you donate your old devices to us, you'll get a 10 percent discount coupon for any products sold in our stores. To get information on our locations or the donation process, please feel free to visit our Web site at www.avnetelectronics.com.	您有從未使用過的老舊電器產品,像是舊電腦與舊電視嗎?何不把它們帶來安富利電器行呢?我們將到府收取電器並加以回收再利用。如果您將舊電器捐至本店,將可獲得本店所有商品九折的折價券。更多關於本店門市位置或捐贈流程的資訊,歡迎至本店網站www.avnetelectronics.com 查詢。

• **make a visit** 拜訪　**pick up** 收取　**donate** 捐贈　**discount coupon** 折價券　**process** 流程
repair 維修　**take a class** 上課　**promotional video** 宣傳影片

71 --

What service is being advertised?
(A) Home delivery
(B) A recycling program
(C) Product repair
(D) An education course

廣告中提到的是什麼服務?
(A) 宅配
(B) 回收計畫
(C) 產品維修
(D) 教育課程

段落開頭便提及多次的「old」,後文又說到「recycle」與「donate」等,故廣告的主要內容應是回收老舊家電,正確答案為 (B)。

72 --

How can listeners get a discount?
(A) By making a donation
(B) By taking a class
(C) By purchasing a certain item
(D) By recommending a company

聽者要如何獲得折扣?
(A) 藉由捐贈
(B) 藉由上課
(C) 藉由購買特定商品
(D) 藉由推薦公司

答題時應專心尋找題目中的關鍵字「discount」。從「If you donate your old devices to us, you'll get a 10 percent discount coupon for any products sold in our stores.」可知,捐贈老舊電器便可獲得九折折價券,故正確答案為 (A)。

73 --

What does the speaker say is available on a Web site?
(A) A product line
(B) A discount coupon
(C) A promotional video
(D) A list of locations

說話者提到網站上有什麼?
(A) 產品線
(B) 折價券
(C) 宣傳影片
(D) 門市位置清單

從最後的「To get information on our locations or the donation process, please feel free to visit our Web site at www.avnetelectronics.com.」可知,從官方網站上可以知道店址資訊與捐贈流程,故正確答案為 (D)。

74-76 announcement

> Attention, ladies and gentlemen, the Frontier Airlines' non-stop flight from London to San Francisco has been delayed. We apologize for the inconvenience that this may have caused you. If you visit the information desk next to Gate 11 and speak to a Frontier Airlines representative, we will do our best to book you on a different flight to your final destination. While waiting, please enjoy complimentary beverages and snacks, courtesy of Frontier Airlines. Your understanding and patience are greatly appreciated. Thank you for flying Frontier Airlines.

> 各位先生女士,請注意。前鋒航空自倫敦直飛舊金山的班機已延誤。非常抱歉造成您的不便。若您前往11號登機門旁的服務台詢問本公司代表人員,我們將竭盡全力為您預訂其他班次至您欲抵達的目的地。等候期間,請享用由本公司免費招待的飲料與點心。十分感謝您的體諒與耐心。感謝您搭乘前鋒航空。

• **non-stop** 直達的 **apologize for . . .** 為……道歉 **inconvenience** 不便 **information desk** 服務台 **representative** 代表人員 **book a flight** 預訂飛機班次 **complimentary** 贈送的 **beverage** 飲料 **appreciate** 感謝 **refreshments** 茶點 **itinerary** 旅行指南

74 --

Where is the announcement probably being made? 這段宣告可能是在哪裡發布的?

(A) At an airport
(B) At a bus station
(C) At a taxi stand
(D) At a ticket office

(A) 機場
(B) 公車總站
(C) 計程車站
(D) 售票處

根據航空公司名稱、航班、航班預約內容,可以知道這段廣播應在機場出現,正確答案為 (A)。

75 --

What does the speaker ask listeners to do? 說話者要求聽者做什麼事?

(A) Meet with a representative
(B) Cancel a ticket
(C) Visit the company's Web site
(D) Book a hotel

(A) 去見公司代表人員
(B) 取消機票
(C) 瀏覽公司的網站
(D) 預訂飯店

因為航班取消,廣播說「If you visit the information desk next to Gate 11 and speak to a Frontier Airlines representative, we will do our best to book you on a different flight to your final destination.」告知旅客至服務台找公司負責人另外訂票。題目裡使用「speak to」,也就是要去前往服務處,面對面詢問公司代表的意思,故正確解答為 (A)。

76 --

According to the speaker, what will be offered? 根據說話者表示,會提供什麼東西?

(A) A free dinner
(B) Free refreshments
(C) An itinerary
(D) Maps

(A) 免費晚餐
(B) 免費茶點
(C) 旅行指南
(D) 地圖

題目裡說「please enjoy complimentary beverages and snacks」,其中「complimentary」就是「free」,而「beverages and snacks」也能解釋成「refreshments」,兩組詞語間字義相近,故正確答案為 (B)。

ACTUAL TEST 5

PART 4

中譯＋解析

20

197

77-79 telephone message

Hi, it's Mia. Can we meet at noon? We have to interview the candidates for our new branch manager position. As you already know, **(78)we have only three months left before the opening of the new branch.** I'll send you an e-mail shortly with a list of the most promising. Before we meet, please narrow the list down to three candidates. Thanks.

77-79 電話留言

嗨，我是蜜雅。我們中午可以見個面嗎？我們必須為分店經理一職面試應徵者。正如你知道的，**(78)離新分店開幕，只剩三個月的時間了。**我馬上將最被看好的人選名單以電子郵件寄給你。在我們見面前，請將名單縮減至三名。謝謝。

- **candidate** 應徵者　**branch manager** 分店經理　**as you already know** 如你所知
  promising 前景看好的　**narrow A down to B** 將 A 縮減至 B

 77 --

What is the purpose of the message?

(A) To set up a meeting
(B) To receive an order
(C) To get an approval
(D) To make a contract

這則訊息的目的是什麼？

(A) 安排會面
(B) 接受訂單
(C) 取得核准
(D) 製作合約

根據開頭和結尾的內容，便可以知道留言目的。留言者一開始問「Can we meet at noon?」，提議在午餐時見面，最後提及見面前的相關事宜，故正確解答為 (A)。

 78 (NEW) ---

What does the speaker imply when she says, "we have only three months left before the opening of the new branch"?

(A) She should find a place to conduct an interview.
(B) She wants the listener to visit a branch.
(C) A branch office should be opened soon.
(D) A decision should be made as soon as possible.

當說話者說：「離新分店開幕，只剩三個月的時間了」，是什麼意思？

(A) 她應該要找個地方進行面試。
(B) 她想要聽者去一家分店。
(C) 分處應該要盡快開設。
(D) 應該要盡快做出決定。

本句隱含的意思可由前後文推敲。前文說到必須面試新分店經理，後文要求對方將人選名單縮至三名，以利面試進行。故可知道，由於新分店即將開幕，必須盡快選出經理，因此正確答案為 (D)。

 79 --

What most likely will the speaker do next?

(A) Make a list of candidates
(B) E-mail some documents
(C) Call a branch office
(D) Fill out an application

說話者接下來可能會做什麼？

(A) 列出應徵者名單
(B) 以電子郵件寄送文件
(C) 打電話給分處
(D) 填寫申請表

(A) 為聽者要做的事。本題的重點在於說話者接下來的行動，因此根據留言最後的內容，說話者將會把有力候選人的資料以電子郵件寄給聽者，所以正確答案為 (B)。

Good morning, everyone. During your internship program, I hope you have gained a valuable experience at our museum. Today, I want you to help us promote the upcoming exhibition by Vincent Van Gogh. It will be one of the biggest exhibitions held in our museum, so I would like you all to distribute flyers not only to hotel guests and shoppers, but also to pedestrians. I'll give you a map where you can check the marked locations to visit. Please return to the museum at 6 P.M. See you then.	大家早。在實習計畫期間,希望各位可以在本博物館獲得寶貴的經驗。今天,我想要大家幫忙宣傳接下來的梵谷展。這將會是本博物館所舉辦過最大型的展覽之一,所以我希望傳單不只發送給飯店住房的賓客和購物的人,也要分發給行人。我會給你們一份地圖,各位可以查看上面標示的地點以進行作業。請在傍晚六點回到博物館。到時候見。

• internship program 實習計畫 promote 推廣 upcoming 即將到來的 exhibition 展覽
 distribute 分發 flyer 傳單 pedestrian 行人 leaflet 傳單

80 --

Where does the speaker work?   說話者是在哪裡工作?
(A) At a museum   (A) 博物館
(B) At a hotel   (B) 飯店
(C) At a store   (C) 商店
(D) At a factory   (D) 工廠

從開頭的「During your internship program, I hope you have gained a valuable experience at our museum.」可知,說話者的所在位置為博物館,所以正確答案為 (A)。

81 --

What will the listeners be doing today? 聽者今天要做什麼事?
(A) Making a flyer   (A) 製作傳單
(B) Going on a tour   (B) 參加導覽
(C) Distributing leaflets   (C) 分發傳單
(D) Taking pictures   (D) 拍照

從談話內容得知,聽者接下來將分送梵谷特展的傳單。選項 (C) 的「leaflet」與題目中的「flyer」同義,所以正確答案為 (C)。

請注意,不可因為聽到「flyer」就草率選擇 (A)。他們要負責的是分送傳單,而不是製作傳單。

82 --

What has the speaker done for the listeners? 說話者已經為聽者做了什麼事?
(A) Made a reservation for a restaurant (A) 預約餐廳
(B) Ordered gifts   (B) 訂購禮物
(C) Provided complimentary tickets (C) 提供免費票券
(D) Circled places on a map   (D) 在地圖上圈出地點

談話最後說到「I'll give you a map where you can check the marked locations to visit.」,表示將提供目的場所的地圖給聽話者,且地圖上已有標示。選項 (D) 把題目中的「marked locations」替換成「circled places」,句意仍相符,故正確答案為 (D)。

20

83-85 excerpt from a meeting   83–85 會議摘錄

As the head of the agency, I'm very delighted to announce that our agency has been named the 2017 ISAA Advertisement of the Year. It is attributable to your hard work and dedication. I personally think highly of the work that Emmy Kunis and her team did on the AVIS campaign. The company has actually increased its revenue by 15 percent due to this campaign. Please give Ms. Kunis and her team a big round of applause for what they have achieved.	身為公司主管，我很高興地宣布本公司被提名為2017年的ISAA年度最佳廣告公司。這都要歸功於各位辛勤的工作與付出。我個人對於艾米·庫妮絲和她的小組所負責的艾維斯宣傳活動給予很高的評價。由於這個活動，該公司收益實際成長了15%。請大家為庫妮絲和她的小組的成就給予熱烈的掌聲。

• **be named . . .** 被提名為……　**be attributable to . . .** 歸功於……　**dedication** 付出
  think highly of . . . 給……很高的評價　**revenue** 收益　**a big round of applause** 熱烈掌聲
  financial institution 金融機構　**resignation** 辭職　**promotion** 升遷　**retirement** 退休
  regulation 規定　**take advantage of . . .** 善加利用……　**boost profits** 提升收益

 83

What kind of business does the speaker work for?   說話者在哪種行業工作？

(A) An advertising agency	(A) 廣告公司
(B) A furniture store	(B) 家具店
(C) A library	(C) 圖書館
(D) A financial institution	(D) 金融機構

本題第一句的後半段「I'm very delighted to announce that our agency has been named the 2017 ISAA Advertisement of the Year」得知。說話者宣布公司被提名為年度最佳廣告公司，由此可知正確答案為 (A)。

84

What is the speaker announcing?   說話者宣布了什麼？

(A) An award winner	(A) 得獎者
(B) A resignation	(B) 辭職
(C) A promotion	(C) 升職
(D) A retirement	(D) 退休

說話者開頭便宣布公司成為得獎者的事實，且在後文繼續表揚特別對象，由此可知，正確答案為 (A)。

85

What does the speaker say about Emmy Kunis's work?   說話者說了什麼有關艾米·庫妮絲工作的事？

(A) It optimized the production lines.	(A) 它優化了生產線。
(B) It led to changes in a company's regulations.	(B) 它造成公司規定變更。
(C) It took advantage of the latest technology.	(C) 它利用了最新科技。
(D) It helped its client boost profits.	(D) 它幫助客戶提升利潤。

說話者中間提到「I personally think highly of the work that Emmy Kunis and her team did on the AVIS campaign.」，特別表揚艾米·庫妮絲為客戶（艾維斯）帶來巨大的宣傳成效，又說「The company has actually increased its revenue by 15 percent due to this campaign.」，表示宣傳活動讓該公司的收益實際成長了 15%，故正確答案為 (D)。

86-88 talk	86–88 談話
Thank you for participating in the meeting. We'll review results from the customer survey for our new model, ASM-1700. As you already know, this microwave has various new features that our customers will really love. The survey showed that the most popular feature of the microwave is that it has an auto sleep mode, making it easier to save energy than our previous models. Due to all the features it has, the user manual increased to 30 pages, which is too many. **(88)So the related department is now editing this.**	感謝大家出席會議。我們將檢視新型號ASM-1700的顧客問卷調查結果。正如大家所知，這個微波爐有許多顧客真的會喜歡的新特點。問卷調查結果顯示，這個微波爐最受歡迎的特點是自動休眠模式，這讓它比之前的型號更省電。由於該型號所擁有的全部特點，使用者操作手冊已經增加到30頁，這樣太多了。**(88)所以相關部門目前正在編輯中。**

• **customer survey** 客戶滿意度調查　**microwave** 微波爐　**feature** 特點　**auto sleep mode** 自動休眠模式　**user manual** 使用者操作手冊　**edit** 編輯

86 --

What is the main topic of the meeting?
(A) A new department
(B) A user manual
(C) Survey results
(D) Product defects

這個會議的主題是什麼？
(A) 新部門
(B) 使用者操作手冊
(C) 問卷調查結果
(D) 產品瑕疵

談話主題通常在開頭便會出現。首先可知道這是一場會議，且說話者表示「We'll review results from the customer survey for our new model, ASM-1700.」，表示要在會議上檢視針對新產品進行的顧客調查，由此可知，正確答案為 (C)。

87 --

What feature of the product does the speaker mention?
(A) An energy-saving function
(B) A digital display
(C) Its durability
(D) A removable rack

說話者提到產品的什麼特點？
(A) 省電功能
(B) 數位顯示
(C) 耐用度
(D) 可移動的掛架

根據說話者所說的「The survey showed that the most popular feature of the microwave is that it has an auto sleep mode, making it easier to save energy than our previous models.」可知，用戶最喜歡自動休眠功能，因為可以節省電源。考生就算不知道自動休眠模式的功能為自動關閉電源，也應可根據後文推測出正確答案。本題的正確答案為 (A)。

What does the speaker imply when she says, "So the related department is now editing this"?	當說話者說：「所以相關部門目前正在編輯中」，是什麼意思？
(A) The manual can only be viewed online.	(A) 手冊只能在線上查閱。
(B) The manual is available in multiple languages.	(B) 手冊有多種語言。
(C) The manual should be shortened.	(C) 手冊應該簡短些。
(D) Customers should read it thoroughly.	(D) 顧客應該仔細地閱讀。

根據段落中的前文可知，由於產品功能變多，操作手冊已增至 30 頁，已經太多。雖然並未直接提及「縮減內容」，但針對過長的內容進行「編輯」，此過程可視為將手冊修改得更加簡短，所以本題的正確答案為 (C)。

89-91 excerpt from a meeting	**89–91 會議摘錄**

Welcome to the Morris Park project. As many of you know, we've made an effort to build a park in the center of the city. Sadly, even though we've received donations from a large number of community groups in this area to help purchase trees, we're still lacking in funds. That means we need more funds to build amenities and buy benches. Therefore, we should make contact with some local business owners to find out their willingness to make a donation. What I am asking you to do is simple. Just make a list of local business owners interested in taking part in this project.	歡迎參加莫里斯公園計畫。正如許多人所知道的，我們努力要在市中心建造一座公園。可惜的是，雖然我們已經收到本地許多社區團體的捐款來購買樹木，但是我們仍然資金不足。這表示我們需要更多資金來打造便利設施及購買長椅。因此，我們應該與一些在地企業主聯絡，了解他們捐款的意願。我想要求各位的事很簡單。只要列出有興趣參與專案的在地企業主名單即可。

- **make an effort** 努力　**donation** 捐款　**community groups** 社區團體　**lack in . . .** 缺乏……
  amenity 便利設施　**make contact with . . .** 聯絡……　**willingness to V** （做某事的）意願
  art gallery 藝廊　**traffic congestion** 交通堵塞　**transportation** 交通運輸　**manpower** 人力
  carry out 進行　**come up with . . .** 提供……

89

What is the talk mainly about?	這段談話主要是與什麼有關？
(A) Attracting foreign companies	(A) 吸引外國公司
(B) Opening an art gallery	(B) 開設藝廊
(C) Building a park	(C) 建造公園
(D) Solving traffic congestion	(D) 解決交通壅塞

從開頭的「Welcome to the Morris Park project.」以及「we've made an effort to build a park in the center of the city.」，可知談話與建造公園有關，正確答案應為 (C)。

90

What problem does the speaker mention?

(A) A delayed schedule
(B) A transportation system
(C) Lack of funds
(D) A manpower shortage

說話者提到什麼問題？

(A) 時程延誤
(B) 交通運輸系統
(C) 資金短缺
(D) 人力不足

說話者提到「we need more funds to build amenities and buy benches.」，表示雖然有收到社區團體的捐款，但是資金不構興建便利設施及購買長椅，故正確答案為 (C)。

91

What are the listeners asked to do?

(A) Hold a meeting
(B) Carry out a survey
(C) Come up with a list of local businesses
(D) Purchase items

聽者被要求做什麼？

(A) 舉辦會議
(B) 進行問卷調查
(C) 列出當地企業名單
(D) 購買物品

說話者最後提到「What I am asking you to do is simple.」此句即為關鍵，因為答案就在後文之中，也就是接下來的「Just make a list of local business owners interested in taking part in this project.」，表示要求聽者幫忙列出有意捐款的在地企業名單，所以正確答案為 (C)。

92-94 announcement

92–94 宣告

Hello, everyone. I'm so glad you've taken time to visit the Union Staffing Agency. We specialize in finding the right position in various companies from law firms to hospitals. Today, you'll have an interview with our recruiters, who will find out which company would be best suited for you and match your professional expertise with its needs. As you may know, **(93)this process could take some time.** While waiting, please help us make a copy of your ID card. The copy machine is on the second floor.	大家好。很高興大家撥空到訪聯合人力仲介公司。本公司專精為各位在不同的公司，舉凡律師事務所到醫院，找到合適的職位。今天，各位將與我們的招募人員進行面試，他們將會媒合大家的專長與公司需求，為您找出最適合的公司。如大家所知的，**(93)這個過程可能會花點時間。** 在等候期間，請協助我們影印一份您的身分證件。影印機位於二樓。

• take time . . . 撥空（做某事）　specialize in . . . 專精於……　recruiter 招募人員
be suited for . . . 適合……　match A with B 媒合 A 與 B　expertise 專長　copy machine 影印機

92

What type of business does the speaker work for?

(A) A law firm
(B) A hospital
(C) An employment agency
(D) A manufacturer

說話者在哪種行業工作？

(A) 律師事務所
(B) 醫院
(C) 職業介紹所
(D) 製造廠

從開頭的「Hello, everyone. I'm so glad you've taken time to visit the Union Staffing Agency.」可知道說話者代表「Union Staffing Agency」發言，所以只要找出意思等同於「staffing agency」的選項即可，所以答案為 (C)。

93 NEW --

What does the speaker imply when he says, "this process could take some time"?

(A) He wants the listeners to be patient.

(B) He points out that the office is very busy.

(C) He says that the scheduled date could be canceled.

(D) He suggests that the listeners be ready anytime.

當說話者說：「這個過程可能會花點時間」，是什麼意思？

(A) 他要聽者耐心等候。

(B) 他指出辦公室很忙碌。

(C) 他說預定好的日期可能會被取消。

(D) 他建議聽者隨時準備好。

說話者告知面試過程可能會花一點時間，最有可能是希望面試者耐心配合。(B)、(C) 與 (D) 三個選項中難以找出與段落內容的關聯性，因此正確答案為 (A)。

94 --

What does the speaker ask the listeners to do?

(A) Submit their application

(B) Receive a letter of recommendation

(C) Make a copy of their identification

(D) Fill out some documents

說話者要求聽者做什麼事？

(A) 繳交申請書

(B) 取得推薦信

(C) 影印證件

(D) 填寫一些文件

在最後的部分，說話者表示「While waiting, please help us make a copy of your ID card. The copy machine is on the second floor.」，代表請聽者在等待時間去影印身分證，正確答案為 (C)。

95-97 recorded message and order form

95-97 留言錄音及訂購表

Hi, this message is for Elisha Stewart. I just received the order from your company. I was, however, surprised by the number of cups in the order form. You normally don't place an order like this. So, I will revise the number to be equal to your usual order. Please call me if you have any problems with this. By the way, I'll be away from work next week. John will cover my duties while I'm on leave. So please call John if you need anything.

嗨，這是給伊莉莎・史都華的留言。我剛接到貴公司的訂單。但是，我對於訂購單上的杯子數量感到驚訝。您通常不會下這樣的訂單。所以，我會將數量修改為您平常訂購的量。若有任何問題的話，請打電話給我。順帶一提，我下星期會休假。在我休假期間，約翰會代理我的工作。如果您有任何需要，請致電約翰。

- Order form -	
Item	**Quantity**
Chocolate bar	100
Milk in bottles	200
Cups	300
Cereal flakes	250

- 訂購單 -	
品項	數量
巧克力棒	100
瓶裝牛奶	200
杯子	300
麥片	250

• **order** 訂單　**place an order** 下訂單　**by the way** 順帶一提　**be away from work** 休假　**cover** 代理
duty 職務　**be on leave** 休假中

95 (NEW) --

Look at the graphic. Which quantity of the order form will be changed?

(A) 100
(B) 200
(C) 300
(D) 250

看一下圖表，訂購單上哪個數量會被修改？

(A) 100
(B) 200
(C) 300
(D) 250

說話者先表示「I was, however, surprised by the number of cups in the order form.」後又說「I will revise the number to be equal to your usual order」，代表他會修正杯子的訂購數量，正確答案為 (C)。

96 --

What is the speaker doing next week?

(A) She is going on a vacation.
(B) She is moving to a different country.
(C) She is remodeling her house.
(D) She is changing her job.

說話者下個星期要做什麼事？

(A) 她要休假。
(B) 她要搬到別的國家去。
(C) 她要重新裝修房子。
(D) 她要換工作。

本題可從「be away from work」、「while I'm on leave」中得到線索。由於表達要休假，所以正確答案為 (A)。

97 --

What does the speaker say about John?

(A) He will be dealing with some accounts.
(B) He will cancel an order.
(C) He will print some documents.
(D) He will introduce a new product.

說話者說了什麼關於約翰的事？

(A) 他會處理一些客戶的事。
(B) 他會取消訂單。
(C) 他會列印一些文件。
(D) 他會介紹新產品。

本題的重點在於準確掌握「account」這個單字的意思。雖然多益考題中，此字常以「帳戶」的意思出現，但是最近也會以「顧客、常客」的意思出現在題目中。本題說話者告知聽者「I'll be away from work next week. John will cover my duties while I'm on leave.」，表示約翰會在他休假期間，代為面對「顧客」。所以正確答案為 (A)。

ACTUAL TEST 5

PART 4

中譯＋解析

🎧 20

205

I'd like to start by expressing my sincere gratitude to all of you for participating in our survey. Here at Morgan Bookstore, we're dedicated to customer satisfaction. We have received many suggestions for improving our services. So, let's look into those results. As you can see, customers want lower prices, but we should comply with the government policy of fixed book prices. We can, however, accept the second-most-popular suggestion. So, we'll start working on that service right now. As an expression of our appreciation, those who participate in the survey will receive one of our best-selling novels for free.

首先，我要誠摯地感謝大家參與我們的問卷調查。在摩根書店，我們致力於讓顧客感到滿意。我們收到許多改善服務的建議。所以，讓我們來看看問卷調查的結果。如同各位所看到的，顧客想要更低的價格，但我們需要遵守政府圖書統一定價的政策。不過，我們可以接受第二多的建議。所以我們現在要開始努力推行該項服務。為了表達我們的感謝之意，參與此問卷調查的人都可以免費獲得暢銷小說一本。

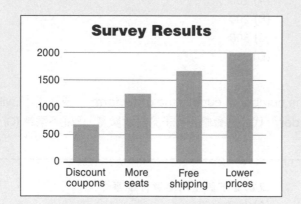

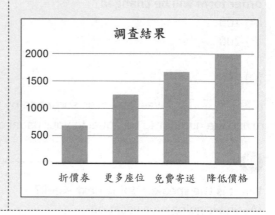

• sincere 誠摯的　participate in . . . 參與……　be dedicated to . . . 致力於……
customer satisfaction 顧客滿意度　look into 深入研究　comply with . . . 遵守……
fixed（價格）固定的　as an expression of our appreciation 以表達我們的感謝之意

98

Where does the talk take place?　這段談話在哪裡出現？

(A) At a bookstore　　(A) 書店
(B) At a factory　　　(B) 工廠
(C) At a hotel　　　　(C) 飯店
(D) At the airport　　(D) 機場

從開頭的「Here at Morgan Bookstore」可以知道地點為書店，故正確答案為 (A)。

99 NEW --

Look at the graphic. Which suggestions will the company begin to work on?

(A) Discount coupons

(B) More seats

(C) Free shipping

(D) Lower prices

看一下圖表，公司會開始推行哪一項建議？

(A) 折價券

(B) 更多座位

(C) 免費寄送

(D) 降低價格

從「We can, however, accept the second-most-popular suggestion. So, we'll start working on that service right now.」可知，說話者採納第二受歡迎的服務，並且現在要推出這項服務。根據圖表，此項目為「免費寄送」，故正確答案為 (C)。

100 --

What will the people receive for completing the survey?

(A) A complimentary book

(B) A discount coupon

(C) Refreshments

(D) A store gift card

完成問卷的人會收到什麼？

(A) 免費書籍

(B) 折價券

(C) 茶點

(D) 商店禮金卡

本題的答案可以在結尾處的「those who participate in the survey will receive one of our best-selling novels for free.」找到。說話者表示，將免費贈送一本暢銷書給參與問券調查的人，所以正確答案為 (A)。

ACTUAL TEST 5

PART 4

中譯＋解析

208

ACTUAL TEST
6

1

(A) A man is reading the magazine.
(B) A man is putting on a shirt.
(C) A man is holding some reading material.
(D) A man is boarding the plane.

(A) 一位男士正在看雜誌。
(B) 一位男士正穿上襯衫。
(C) 一位男士正拿著讀物。
(D) 一位男士正要上飛機。

• put on 穿上　reading material 讀物　board 上（船、火車或飛機）

此為一名男子在飛機內閱讀報紙的照片。(A) 男子正在閱讀的是報紙而非雜誌。(B) 不應使用表示「穿上襯衫」的動作（put on），而應使用描述狀態（wear）的動詞。除此之外，應特別注意與「穿」相關的動詞（try on）與表示「脫下」的動詞（take off、remove）也時常出現在錯誤答案，請熟知其差異。(D) 男子已經搭上了飛機，而不是正在登機。正確答案為 (C)。

2

(A) They are pushing the carts.
(B) They are using the escalator.
(C) They are riding the elevator.
(D) They are going up the stairs.

(A) 他們正在推手推車。
(B) 他們正在搭手扶梯。
(C) 他們正在搭電梯。
(D) 他們正爬上樓梯。

• escalator 手扶梯　go up 爬上　stairs 樓梯

照片中的人們正搭著手扶梯上樓。(A) 推車放置在手扶梯旁，並沒有人推著推車。(C) 人們並不是搭乘電梯，要小心不要混淆「escalator」和「elevator」的發音。(D) 照片中並無階梯。正確答案為 (B)。

3

(A) There are vehicles on the bridge.
(B) The bridge is being built over the river.
(C) The water is flowing under the structure.
(D) The boats are passing the stadium.

(A) 橋上有車輛。
(B) 橋梁正建於河上。
(C) 水從建築物下流過。
(D) 船隻正經過體育場。

• vehicle 車輛　stadium 體育場

此為水面上有一座橋梁的照片。遇到風景照時，應先觀察照片中出現了什麼。 另外，如果題目出現沒有人物的照片，通常出現「being p.p.」的選項不會是正確答案。

(A) 橋梁上並沒有車輛。(B) 橋梁已經建造完成，並非正在建造。「being built」，表示「現在正在建造」，亦即照片中應該出現正在進行工程的場面。(C) 以建築物代表橋梁，並描述橋下有水流過，為正確答案。(D) 照片中並未出現船與體育場。故正確答案為 (C)。

(A) Some balloons are hanging from the ceiling.
(B) All of the seats are occupied.
(C) The restaurant is filled with the diners.
(D) A waiter is holding the tray.

(A) 一些氣球從天花板垂掛下來。
(B) 所有的座位都坐滿了。
(C) 餐廳充滿了用餐者。
(D) 服務生正拿著托盤。

• ceiling 天花板　occupied （座位）被占據的　be filled with... 充滿……　diner 用餐者　tray 托盤

本題為餐廳內擠滿用餐人潮的照片。觀察照片時，不只是人物的樣貌，也應留意周遭的背景。照片中，牆上有一扇時鐘造型的大窗戶，而天花板上掛著華麗的照明燈飾。本題需正確掌握主詞進行消去法。

(A) 天花板上掛著的不是氣球，而是照明燈飾（light fixtures）。(B) 出現「All」時，只要描述對象在照片中少了任何一個，皆為錯誤的答案。照片中的座位大部分都有人坐，但是並非全部。實際上，「All」出現於錯誤答案的機率相當高，聆聽時請特別留意發音。(D) 照片中並未明確看到服務生端著托盤的樣子。正確答案為 (C)。

(A) Some instruments are being played on a stage.
(B) The men are trying on their uniforms.
(C) All of the people are facing each other.
(D) There are mountains in the distance.

(A) 舞台上正在演奏一些樂器。
(B) 男士們正在試穿制服。
(C) 所有人都面向彼此。
(D) 遠方有山。

• instrument 樂器　try on 試穿　in the distance 遠方

照片中，身穿制服的男子聚集在水邊，遠方還可看到高低起伏的山巒。遇到這種照片，不要把重點集中在人物上，請仔細觀察四周的背景與狀況。

(A) 照片中並未出現樂器。本句從主詞開始便為錯誤答案。(B) 已經是穿著制服的狀態，所以不該使用「try on」（表示試穿的動作）而應該使用「wear」（表示穿著的狀態）。(C) 只有一部分的人相互對視，並非所有人皆如此。正確答案為 (D)。

(A) An assortment of items is being displayed on the shop's shelves.
(B) The clerk is assisting a customer.
(C) A mask is being hung on the wall.
(D) The lights are being turned on.

(A) 各種物品被陳列在店內的架上。
(B) 店員正在協助顧客。
(C) 一張面具正被掛上牆壁。
(D) 燈正被打開。

• an assortment of 各式各樣的　display 陳列　clerk 店員　assist 協助

照片中，店鋪的陳列架上擺放了各種商品。照片中並未出現人物，這種狀況下，請以物品的位置為中心，掌握照片傳達的訊息。另外，通常在物品照片的題型，如果聽見選項出現「being p.p.」，大部分為錯誤答案，但是選項 (A) 使用「being displayed」描寫「物品陳列中」，所以可以是正確答案。(B) 店鋪中並未出現店員與客人。(C) 照片中並未出現面具。(D) 電燈已經是開著的狀態，且也未出現正要開燈的人。本題正確答案為 (A)。

211

7

Is there a pharmacy nearby?
(A) There is a prescription.
(B) It's one block away.
(C) I don't know when it opens.

這附近有藥局嗎？
(A) 有處方箋。
(B) 在一個街區外。
(C) 我不知道它何時營業。

聽到「Is there」時要多注意後面的內容。題目問附近是否有藥局，(B) 提到在下一個街區有一家，是省略「Yes」直接回答的正確答案。

(A) 為使用「prescription」與「pharmacy」的關聯性，以及和題目相同發音的「There is」設下陷阱。(C) 是迂迴的回答。只出現「I don't know」時可以是正確答案，但是如果後面有其他內容，請務必聽完完整句子，因為極有可能出現陷阱。如果 (C) 要成為正確答案，整句應該改成「I don't know where it is」。本題正確答案為 (B)。

8

Can you pass me the scissors, please?
(A) Sure, I'll have some.
(B) They are sold out.
(C) Here you are.

可以請你把剪刀遞給我嗎？
(A) 當然，我要來一些。
(B) 全售完了。
(C) 給你。

「Can you」，表示請託，須注意聆聽後面出現的動詞。(A) 內容與題目無關。(B) 題目請對方傳遞剪刀，並非詢問是否有剪刀，所以 (B) 不正確。(C) 表示將剪刀交給他人，故正確答案為 (C)。

9

Who revised these documents?
(A) A total of 24 revisions.
(B) My secretary did.
(C) Yes, I'd be happy to.

誰校定了這些文件？
(A) 共有24處修正。
(B) 我的秘書。
(C) 是的，我很樂意。

首先注意疑問詞「Who」詢問的對象為人物，並留心出現在後面的動詞，才知道題目詢問的是什麼樣的人。(A) 選項並無回答題目問題，是以與題目中「revised」相關的「revision」造成混淆。(B) 點出確切人物，為正確答覆。(C) 疑問詞疑問句的答案不能以「Yes/No」開頭。 正確答案為 (B)。

10

What date would you like to reserve the table?
(A) I prefer a non-smoking area.
(B) On the 5th of this month, please.
(C) It's upstairs.

您想預約哪一天的位子？
(A) 我偏好禁菸區。
(B) 麻煩，這個月的5號。
(C) 在樓上。

疑問詞「What」想要詢問的訊息通常緊接在後方出現，故要注意聆聽。(A) 為利用題目的最後一個單字「table」進行聯想，藉此形成陷阱。(B) 本題詢問日期，故表達月份與日期的回覆最為適當。(C) 題目詢問的並非位置。正確答案為 (B)。

11 --

When is the best time to contact Mr. Smith?

(A) In the office.

(B) Two days ago.

(C) Any time before seven o'clock.

何時與史密斯先生聯絡最方便？

(A) 在辦公室。

(B) 兩天前。

(C) 七點之前都可以。

出現疑問詞「When」時，同時上需注意時態。本題詢問什麼時間適合聯絡。因為題目的情境為「尚未聯繫」，而 (B) 表示的「兩天前」為過去時間點，故非正確答案。如果以要以 (A) 的形式回答，則題目應使用「Where」詢問。

提及「場所」的選項常常出現作為「When」問句的錯誤答案，所以需多加注意區分「When/Where」的發音。本題的正確答案為 (C)。

12 --

Where should I leave these office supplies?

(A) At 3:30.

(B) Take them to the storeroom.

(C) To San Francisco.

我應該把這些辦公用品放在哪裡？

(A) 3:30。

(B) 拿到儲藏室。

(C) 到舊金山。

遇到疑問詞「Where」時，要先熟悉美式／英式發音。英式發音 [weə] 很容易聽錯為「When」。另外，題目詢問的是何種場所，需要仔細聽「Where」後面出現的動詞。選項 (A) 與 (C) 皆非合適回答，本題正確答案為 (B)。

13 --

How much time do you need to complete the report?

(A) The reporter will be here soon.

(B) I'm almost finished.

(C) Three times a week.

你需要多少時間來完成這份報告？

(A) 記者很快就會到這裡。

(B) 我快做好了。

(C) 一週三次。

疑問詞「How much」後面連用不可數名詞，而題目中的「How much time」是在問「需要多少時間」，選項 (B) 雖然沒有指出明確時間點，但也代表「馬上就要結束」，不需要太多時間，所以為合適回覆。

(A) 為利用與題目中的「report」發音類似的「reporter」誤導。(C) 應該用於回答「How often . . . ?」的疑問句較為適當。故此題正確答案為 (B)。

14 --

Why did you recommend taking the subway instead of the bus?

(A) Across a small bridge.

(B) It will be much faster.

(C) Because they lowered bus fares.

你為什麼建議搭地鐵而不是公車？

(A) 過一座小橋。

(B) 會快很多。

(C) 因為他們調降公車票價了。

題目使用疑問詞「Why」詢問理由，(A) 只回答了位置，(C) 雖然能作為「Why」的回答，但是此選項提及的「調降票價」並非適合題目情境的理由。本題正確答案為 (B)。

此題須留意的是，聽到「Why」時，不可以只靠「because」選擇答案。練習時必須熟悉省略「because」，只依據附加說明尋找答案，以免掉入陷阱。

15 --

Which of you read this novel?
(A) David and I did.
(B) This book is really interesting.
(C) Red is better.

你們哪位讀過這本小說？
(A) 大衛和我。
(B) 這本書真的很有趣。
(C) 紅色比較好。

「Which」也可以用來詢問人物，如本題的「Which of you」，其實意思相似於「Who」。(A) 明確回答出人物，為正確答案。(B) 為利用題目的「novel」與「book」的關聯性形成的陷阱。若此選項要為正解，本題應該用「Which novel . . . ?」詢問。(C) 為使用與題目中的「read（過去分詞）」發音相似的「red」製造陷阱。本題正確答案為 (A)。

16 --

I'm eagerly looking forward to this performance.
(A) No, not here. Over there, please.
(B) Yes, we were lucky to get these tickets.
(C) I need to fill out this form.

我熱切地期待這場表演。
(A) 不，不是這裡；是那裡。
(B) 是的，我們很幸運能拿到票。
(C) 我需要填寫這張表格。

題目為表達期待公演的陳述句，並沒有詢問公演地點，所以 (A) 不正確。(B) 表示認同，且認為能拿到表演的票很幸運，為合適回覆。(C) 為利用與題目中的「performance」發音相似的「form」製造陷阱。本題正確答案為 (B)。

17 --

This meal comes with a free drink, doesn't it?
(A) I'd like to come with you.
(B) Let me check on that.
(C) I'm very thirsty.

這份餐點有附贈免費飲料，不是嗎？
(A) 我想和你一起去。
(B) 我確認一下。
(C) 我很渴。

• **check on** 確認

本題為附加問句。選項 (B) 雖迂迴答覆，但表示需要先進行確認，整體句意與題目相符，故為正確答案。(A) 為使用與題目相同的字彙「come」製造陷阱。(C) 則為利用題目中的「drink」的聯想字彙「thirsty」（口渴的）誤導。本題正確答案為 (B)。

18 --

Do you know which customer ordered this sandwich?
(A) The man at table 4.
(B) I'd prefer fried chicken.
(C) Yes, I know how to make the sandwich.

你知道哪位客人點這份三明治嗎？
(A) 4號桌的先生。
(B) 我比較喜歡炸雞。
(C) 是的，我知道怎麼做三明治。

本題為使用「Do you know . . . ?」的間接問句，通常詢問的重點會緊接在後文出現，如本題的「which customer」即為重點，故要在答覆中尋找人物相關的訊息。(A) 明確指出人物，(B) 與 (C) 皆和題目無關聯，故正確答案為 (A)。

19 --

Are you ready to leave now, or do you need more time to pack?
(A) It is packed with papers.
(B) Our plane isn't until 7.
(C) Is Kay leaving some for me?

你準備好要出發了嗎?還是需要更多時間打包?
(A) 它塞滿了文件。
(B) 我們的飛機七點才飛。
(C) 凱有幫我留一些嗎?

• **pack** 打包　**be packed with . . .** 被……塞滿　**papers** 文件

本題為給予兩個選擇的疑問句，近來選擇疑問句的題型，正確解答常是意料之外的回答，所以建議善用刪去法找出最適當的答案。

(A) 為利用與題目中「pack」發音類似的「packed」製造陷阱。(B) 表示「飛機七點才飛」，是暗示對方還有一些時間，所以不需要著急，為合適回覆。(C) 使用了與題目相同的字彙「leave」，但是題目詢問的是「you」的意願，選項中卻突然提及「Kay」，所以此選項並非適當的回答。此題正確答案為 (B)。

20 --

Which part of the plant am I working in tomorrow?
(A) The times are listed in the manual.
(B) I watered the plant this morning.
(C) Didn't your manager tell you?

我明天要在工廠的哪一區工作?
(A) 時段列在手冊上。
(B) 我今天早上幫植物澆水了。
(C) 你的主管沒有告訴你嗎?

• **plant** 工廠　**list** 列出　**manual** 手冊　**water** 給……澆水

「Which」出現時應留意後面接續的名詞。本題詢問的是「在工廠的哪裡」，但回應時並不一定要提及特定場所，像選項 (C) 提出反問，也能符合題意。

另外，(A) 沒有回答到題目詢問的地點，(B) 則是使用題目出現字彙「plant」的陷阱，此字可解釋為工廠或植物，兩者詞意相差甚大，切勿搞混。本題正確答案為 (C)。

21 --

Are you ready to get off work today?
(A) Yes, I have to work late.
(B) I just found out I have a conference call.
(C) I read it.

你今天要下班了嗎?
(A) 是的，我必須工作到很晚。
(B) 我剛發現我有電話會議要開。
(C) 我讀過了。

本題為 Yes/No 問句，但考題的答案時常出現省略「Yes/No」，而以附加說明回應的形式。
(A) 應回答「No」才符合附加說明的內容。(B) 為省略「No」並以附加說明解釋「因為要開會，所以還不能下班」，故為正確答案。(C) 為利用與題目中的「ready」發音相似的「read（過去式）it」故意誘導。正確答案為 (B)。

22 --

I left my wallet at the hotel.　　　　　　　　我把錢包留在飯店了。
(A) It's actually a right turn.　　　　　　　　(A) 事實上是右轉。
(B) I prefer to stay at the Park View Hotel.　(B) 我比較想待在園景飯店。
(C) Don't worry. I can lend you some money.　(C) 別擔心，我可以借你點錢。

陳述句題型中，出現類似發音陷阱的機率相當高。(A) 中的「right」為利用題目的「left」設下的陷
阱。left 可為動詞 leave 的過去式，表示留下，也可當作形容詞，表示左邊，但此題的字義為前者。
(B) 雖然提及題目出現過的字彙「hotel」，但是情境與題目不符。最適合的回覆為 (C)，故正確答案
為 (C)。

23 --

Let's walk to the public library.　　　　　　我們走路到公立圖書館吧。
(A) Not too fast.　　　　　　　　　　　　　(A) 別太快。
(B) It is too far to walk.　　　　　　　　　　(B) 太遠了無法用走的。
(C) I didn't know the way.　　　　　　　　　(C) 我不知道路。

「Let's . . . 」帶有勸誘對方一起做某事的意思，所以要注意後面接續的動詞。(A) 與本題的情境不
符。(B) 使用「too . . . to . . . 」句型，表達「太遠了，無法用走的（到達）」，有拒絕對方的意思。
(C) 因為時態為過去式，所以不是正確答案。此選項如果改用現在式「I don't know the way」，
則可能成為正確答案。本題正確答案為 (B)。

24 --

Couldn't we put off the conference until March?　我們不能把會議延到三月嗎？
(A) Maybe, but the hotel charges cancellation fees.　(A) 也許可以，但飯店會收取取消費用。
(B) To the nearest post office.　　　　　　　　　(B) 到最近的郵局。
(C) Yes, that was a great conference call.　　　　(C) 是的，那是場很棒的電話會議。

本題為否定疑問句，題意透露出將會議延期的請求，雖然為否定形式，但是與一般疑問句一樣，
如果答案為可以延後，則以「Yes」回答，反之則回答「No」。

(A) 省略「No」的部分，並表達將會有取消費用，暗示無法延後，為最適當的回應。(B) 提及的「郵
局」與本題狀況不符。 (C) 使用題目出現的「conference」設下陷阱，但句子內容和題目狀況不
符。本題正解為 (A)。

25 --

Would you like to make a presentation first,　你想先報告，還是我先？
or should I?　　　　　　　　　　　　　(A) 我沒有太多東西可講。
(A) I don't have much to say.　　　　　　　　(B) 這是第一次。
(B) This is the first time.　　　　　　　　　　(C) 是的，我是。
(C) Yes, I am.

本題為選擇疑問句。(A) 雖然沒有直接回答問題，但句意表示「沒有太多東西要報告」，陳述自己報
告的狀況，也是合適的回覆。(B) 利用題目出現字彙「first」設下陷阱，但句意和本題情境不符。
(C) 因為選擇疑問句基本上不可用「Yes/No」回答，故為錯誤選項。本題正確答案為 (A)。

26

Who will volunteer to organize the banquet next week?
(A) Mr. Rossi has been helping me.
(B) I'd be delighted to.
(C) She is working next week.

誰自願籌辦下週的宴會？
(A) 羅西先生一直在幫我。
(B) 我很樂意。
(C) 她下週要上班。

本題為疑問詞「Who」開頭的問句，詢問自願者，故以第一人稱回答的 (B) 為合適答案。除此之外，也請熟悉「I'll do it」的用法。

「Who」疑問句的題型中，最容易出現的陷阱就是像 (A) 一樣提及人名的肯定句。不過，題目詢問的是「下週有誰自願協助」，此選項的內容並不符合。(C) 無法確認選項中出現的「She」是誰，且沒有回答問題。本題正確答案為 (B)。

 22

27

Would you like to come in on Saturday the 15th?
(A) No, our office is located on the 10th floor.
(B) It would have to be toward the end of the working day.
(C) What was her name again?

你15號週六會進來嗎？
(A) 不，我們辦公室在10樓。
(B) 要到接近上班日的下班時間才行。
(C) 再說一次，她的名字叫什麼？

本題為提議疑問句。 (A) 的回答提及「No」，後面應出現針對「不能去」的附加說明，但是此選項卻針對地點進行說明，所以不是正確答案。(B) 省略「Yes」，並表示會在當天接近下班時間才抵達，此為合適答覆。(C) 內容與問題不符。本題正確答案為 (B)。

28

When will I receive the details about this product?
(A) From the electronics store.
(B) You will be hearing from the supplier soon.
(C) The certification was issued last week.

我何時可以收到這個產品的相關細節？
(A) 從電器店。
(B) 你很快就會收到供應商的訊息。
(C) 證書上週就核發了。

疑問詞「When」的題型中最常出現的時態為「When will」。 請特別注意不要與「Where」發音混淆。(A) 題目詢問的是時間，此處卻回答地點，所以不是正確答案。如果把「When」聽成「Where」，很容易掉入這種陷阱，請多加留意。(B) 本題詢問「何時可以收到」，回答「很快會收到訊息」最為合適。(C) 以過去式回答與題目不符合。本題正確答案為 (B)。

29

Our advertising budget was increased this month, wasn't it?
(A) Yes, by 30 percent.
(B) Every Monday morning.
(C) The advertisement was successful.

我們這個月的廣告預算增加了，不是嗎？
(A) 是的，30%。
(B) 每週一上午。
(C) 廣告很成功。

本題為附加問句。(A) 回答「Yes」並說出確切數字，為正確答案。(B) 為利用與題目中的「this month」意義相關的「morning」設下陷阱。(C) 則為利用與題目中的「advertising」發音相似的「advertisement」誘導。本題正確答案為 (A)。

Where is the report from the Accounting Department?

(A) Bring it to my office.

(B) We are still compiling it.

(C) I counted them yesterday.

會計部的報告在哪裡？

(A) 拿到我辦公室。

(B) 我們還在彙編中。

(C) 我昨天數過了。

請多留意疑問詞「Where」的英國式發音 [weə]。(A) 的句意偏向命令句，要求對方將報告拿至自己的辦公室。如果將重點放在「office」則很有可能掉入陷阱，所以請務必確實掌握題目詢問的問題以及回應。(B) 表示「還在彙編」，暗示還未完成，故為合適答案。(C) 利用與題目中的「account」發音相似的「count」設下陷阱，且句子內容也與題目不符。故此題正確答案為 (B)。

31 --

Isn't there any more space at the Springfield warehouse?

(A) Just a few kilometers down the main expressway.

(B) Yes, we'll make a delivery on Friday.

(C) I actually asked about the one in Watertown.

春田倉庫沒有多的空間了嗎？

(A) 離主要高速公路只有幾公里。

(B) 是的，我們週五會配送。

(C) 事實上，我問的是在水城的那一間。

本題為否定疑問句，詢問倉庫是否有多的空間。雖然題目為否定形式，但是與一般疑問句一樣，如果答案為「有空間」則回答「Yes」，反之則回答「No」。

(A) 題目詢問的並非倉庫的位置。(B) 回答了「Yes」，後面應該出現表示「有空間」的附加說明，但提及內容卻與題目不符。(C) 省略了「No」，並表示自己問的是另一間倉庫，暗示提問者可能錯聽資訊，故正確答案為 (C)。

PART 3 🎧 23

32-34 conversation

W	Hello, I have a problem with the tablet PC that I bought here last week. Every morning I find it turned off, although the indicator says the battery is full.
M	Hmm . . . Let me take a look. This is the Astro 7. Did you leave it plugged into an outlet overnight?
W	Yes, I did. I never forgot to recharge it every night. I think there is a problem with the battery.
M	That sometimes happens when it's overcharged. Luckily, the company has noted this issue and released an update.
W	Oh, that's nice. Can I download the update from the Internet?
M	That's right. Let me do it for you. Just five minutes will do.

32-34 對話

女	你好，我上週在這裡買的平板電腦有點問題。雖然指示器顯示電池是充飽的，但我每天早上都發現它是關機狀態。
男	嗯……我來看一下。這台是星體7。您讓它整晚都插在插頭上嗎？
女	是的。我每晚都不忘幫它充電。我想電池可能有問題。
男	有時候過度充電會發生這樣的事。幸運的是，公司已經注意到這個問題，並發布了更新軟體。
女	那太好了。我可以從網路上下載更新軟體嗎？
男	沒錯。讓我來為您服務。只要五分鐘就好。

🎧 22 🎧 23

32

Why is the woman at the shop?
(A) To buy a mobile phone
(B) To ask about a device
(C) To sell a computer
(D) To charge a battery

這位女士為什麼在店裡？
(A) 要買行動電話
(B) 要詢問裝置問題
(C) 要販售電腦
(D) 要為電池充電

第一句台詞中，女子說：「I have a problem with the tablet PC that I bought here last week.」，由此可知她是因為平板電腦的問題而來店裡。選項 (B) 把「tablet PC」換成「device」並把「inquire」換成「ask」，但句意仍相符，故正確答案為 (B)。

33

What is the problem with the computer?
(A) It turns off by itself.
(B) It ran out of battery.
(C) It is not connected to the Internet.
(D) It was not fully charged.

電腦有什麼問題？
(A) 自動關機。
(B) 沒電了。
(C) 沒有連上網路。
(D) 沒有完全充飽電。

女子說：「Every morning I find it turned off, although the indicator says the battery is full.」，表示儘管電池充飽電，早上起來發現還是關機，故可得知正確答案為 (A)。

(B) 和 (D) 因為對話中已經表示整夜都在充電，且電池標誌也顯示充滿電，所以不是正確答案。另外，雖然對話中也提到「Internet」，但並非問題所在，所以 (C) 也不是正確答案。

What will the man probably do next?
(A) Give a full refund
(B) Replace the battery
(C) Update the device
(D) Report the problem to the manufacturer

這位男士接下來可能會做什麼？
(A) 全額退費
(B) 更換電池
(C) 更新裝置
(D) 向製造商呈報問題

男子提到更新程式可以解決問題，女子則問道：「Can I download the update from the Internet?」對此，男子說：「Let me do it for you.」，由此可知，男子將幫女子下載更新程式。因此，正確答案為 (C)。請注意不要因為對話常常出現「battery」而選擇 (B)。(A) 與 (D) 的內容在對話中從未提及過，不是正確答案。

35-37 conversation

35-37 對話

M Hello, I'm calling to ask about shipping items from New York to Tokyo. We have 80 framed pictures and 10 clay statues to ship to the Edo Museum here in Tokyo.	**男** 妳好，我打來是想要詢問從紐約運送物品到東京的事宜。我們有80幅裱框的畫和10座陶土雕像要送到東京的江戶博物館。
W Sure. We specialize in shipping valuable items. They'll be handled carefully and will arrive on time. How early do you need them?	**女** 沒問題。我們專門運送貴重物品。它們會被妥善處理並準時送達。您需要多快送到？
M Well, these items are going to be displayed at the museum next month, so we'll need them by the 15th. But I was wondering how much it would cost.	**男** 嗯，這些物品下個月將於博物館展出，所以我們需要在15號前送到。但我想知道這樣需要多少錢？
W I can't actually give you a final cost estimate without the exact dimensions of each item. Could you please email me this information at smith@kccshipping.com?	**女** 沒有每樣物品的確切尺寸，我無法給您最終的報價。您可以將這份資料以電子郵件寄到 smith@kccshipping.com 嗎？

• **ship** 運送　**clay statues** 陶土雕像　**specialize in . . .** 專門從事……　**valuable** 貴重的　**handle** 處理　**on time** 準時　**display** 展出　**dimension** 尺寸

Why is the man calling?
(A) To ask about a membership card
(B) To sign up for an exhibition
(C) To check a ticket reservation
(D) To inquire about a delivery service

這位男士為什麼打這通電話？
(A) 要詢問會員卡事宜
(B) 要報名展覽
(C) 要確認票券預約
(D) 要詢問貨運服務

本題詢問男子撥打電話的目的，請將注意力集中在對話前半部的男子台詞。男子說：「I'm calling to ask about shipping items from New York to Tokyo」，由此可知，男子想詢問有關運輸的事宜，故 (D) 為正確答案。

36

What will happen next month?	下個月將發生什麼事？
(A) A museum exhibition	(A) 博物館展覽
(B) A book signing	(B) 簽書會
(C) An international music festival	(C) 國際音樂節
(D) A pottery-making demonstration	(D) 陶器製作示範

男子說：「these items are going to be displayed at the museum next month」，表示物品下個月將在博物館展示，故正確答案為 (A)。

37

What additional information does the woman ask for?	這位女士要求補充什麼資料？
(A) A price estimate	(A) 估價單
(B) An e-mail address	(B) 電子郵件信箱
(C) The sizes of some items	(C) 一些物品的尺寸
(D) The man's seating number	(D) 這位男士的座位號碼

本題詢問女子額外要求的事項，請專注對話後半部分的女子台詞。女子的最後一句台詞說：「I can't actually give you a final cost estimate without the exact dimensions of each item. Could you please e-mail me this . . . ?」，表示如果沒有物品的尺寸將無法估算費用，要求男子告知尺寸，故正確答案為 (C)。

另外，(A) 提及的估價單為男子想知道的事物，請小心不要掉入此陷阱。

38-40 conversation   **38-40 對話**

M	Hi, Sharon. This is Tim Blanks. I interviewed you last week for the reporter position at NSL Newspaper Company. I'm calling to see when you are available to finalize the next step.	男	嗨，雪倫。我是提姆‧布蘭克斯。我上週為NSL報社的記者一職為妳進行面試。我打來是想看看妳何時有空，來完成最後一關面試步驟。
W	Hi, Mr. Blanks. Thanks for calling me. I have to work all day tomorrow, but I'm free on Tuesday and Wednesday.	女	嗨，布蘭克斯先生。感謝您的來電。我明天整天都必須工作，不過週二和週三有空。
M	Right. I want you to come in to write a short article as a sample so we can get a better sense of your writing skills. Could you come in at ten o'clock on Wednesday morning? It'll take about two hours to complete.	男	好的。我希望妳過來撰寫一篇短文作為樣稿，好讓我們更了解妳的寫作技巧。妳能於週三早上10點過來嗎？完成大約需要兩個小時。

• **finalize** 完成　**sample** 樣本

38

Why is the man calling the woman?
(A) To return her résumé
(B) To reject her application
(C) To ask her to visit him again
(D) To give details about the job opening

這位男士為什麼打電話給女士？
(A) 退還她的履歷表
(B) 拒絕她的應徵
(C) 要求她再度到訪
(D) 提供職缺細節

男子説了「I'm calling to see when you are available to finalize the next step」與「I want you to come in to write a short article as a sample」，表示之前已經面試過，這次想要請女子再過去撰寫文章，以完成最後階段的面試，故正確答案為 (C)。

39

Why is the woman unavailable tomorrow?
(A) She will be traveling.
(B) She will be working.
(C) She will be giving a presentation.
(D) She will be finishing an assignment.

這位女士明天為什麼沒空？
(A) 她要旅行。
(B) 她要工作。
(C) 她要發表簡報。
(D) 她要完成任務。

本題詢問女子明天無法前往的原因，答案極有可能出現在女子的台詞中。女子説：「I have to work tomorrow all day」，表示自己明天要工作，所以正確答案為 (B)。

What does the man ask the woman to do?
(A) Submit a résumé
(B) Write an article
(C) Read an employee handbook
(D) Write a novel

這位男士要求女士做什麼？
(A) 提交履歷表
(B) 寫一篇文章
(C) 閱讀員工手冊
(D) 寫一本小說

本題詢問男子要求女子的內容，請專心聆聽男子的台詞。對話的後半段中，男子説：「I want you to come in to write a short article as a sample」，請女子前來書寫一段短文，故正確答案為 (B)。

41-43 conversation

41–43 對話

W Carlos, now I'm leaving for the airport to pick up the vice-president. Are you done with the marketing report?	女 卡洛斯，我現在要去機場接副總裁。你完成行銷報告了嗎？
M Several graphs need to be replaced. It's going to be tight for the four o'clock meeting.	男 有幾個圖表需要更換。要用在四點的會議會有點趕。
W I already revised all the figures in the tables and graphs. Is there any problem?	女 我已經修訂過表格與圖表中的數字了。有問題嗎？
M Some of the figures don't match the last quarterly report. So I'm verifying them over again and putting in the correct ones.	男 有些數字與上一季的報告不符。所以我在重新確認，並把正確的數字填上去。
W Oh, I see. I don't have time to go over it now, so I'll let you be the judge.	女 喔，我懂了。我現在沒有時間再看一次，所以交給你判斷。

| M | Don't worry, and be careful driving in the rain. Shall I make some copies when I'm finished? | 男 | 別擔心，下雨小心開車。完成後，我需要影印幾份出來嗎？ |
| W | You don't have to do that. Just send the file to the secretary's office. They'll bind it with other documents to make booklets. | 女 | 不必那樣做。只要把檔案寄到秘書室。他們會把它和其他的文件裝訂成冊。 |

• vice-president 副總裁　be done with ... 完成……　tight（時間）緊湊的　revise 修訂　verify 確認
　go over 查看　let you be the judge 給你判斷　bind 裝訂　booklet 小冊子

---

41 ---

What are the speakers mainly discussing?	說話者主要在討論什麼？
(A) The cover of a booklet	(A) 手冊的封面
(B) Bad weather	(B) 惡劣的天氣
(C) Driving to the airport	(C) 開車去機場
(D) Revising a document	(D) 修訂文件

詢問對話主題的問題，可以在對話的前半部找到線索。一開始，女子問道：「Are you done with the marketing report?」，接著對話中主要談到檢討、修改該報告書的相關內容，故正確答案為 (D)。

對話中雖然也提及 (B) 的天氣相關訊息，以及 (C) 所表示之「女子要去機場」的內容，但都不是對話的重點，故不是正確答案。

---

42 ---

What is suggested by the speakers?	說話者提到了什麼？
(A) The woman revised the marketing report.	(A) 這位女士修訂過行銷報告。
(B) The rain has finally stopped.	(B) 這場雨終於停了。
(C) The man has finished the report.	(C) 這位男士已經完成報告了。
(D) There will be a meeting at three o'clock.	(D) 三點有一場會議。

女子的台詞提到：「I already revised all the figures in the tables and graphs. Is there any problem?」，由此可知，女子已經修訂過報告書，故正確答案為 (A)。

從男子的台詞「be careful driving in the rain」中，可以看出現在正在下雨，故 (B) 不正確。另外，女子詢問報告書是否完成，男子回答說：「Several graphs need to be replaced.」，由此可知，報告書尚未完成，故可得知 (C) 不是正確答案。最後，從「It's going to be tight for the four o'clock meeting.」可以知道會議時間是四點而不是三點，故 (D) 也非正確。

---

43 ---

What will the woman probably do next?	這位女士接下來可能會做什麼？
(A) See an executive at the airport	(A) 在機場和高級主管會面
(B) Correct errors in a paper	(B) 修正報告中的錯誤
(C) Tell the man an e-mail address	(C) 告訴男士電子郵件地址
(D) Book a flight	(D) 預訂航班

女子在一開始說道：「I'm leaving for the airport to pick up the vice-president.」，故可以知道女子將開車去機場接副總裁。選項 (A) 將「vice-president」改為「executive」，並將「pick up」改為「see」，仍與文意相符，故正確答案為 (A)。

(B) 為男子將要做的事。女子因為自己沒有時間，所以將事情委託男子。(C) 因為對話中只提及男子在完成報告書之後，需將檔案寄給秘書室，並未提及電子信箱地址，所以不是正確答案。(D) 因為女子是去機場接副總裁，而不是自己要搭飛機，所以不是正確答案。

44-46 conversation　　　　　　　　　　　　　44–46 對話

W I'm really looking forward to hearing Steve Torre's speech today. I've already read many books about the financial crisis in the world. So I think this is one of the best finance conferences.	女 我真的很期待聽到史提夫‧托雷今天的演講。我已經讀過很多有關全球財務危機的書，所以我想這是最棒的金融研討會之一了。
M I think so. And there are so many attendees here! It looks like the only available seats are here in the back. **(45)Let's just sit in this row.**	男 我也這麼認為。這裡有好多與會者！看起來好像只有後面這裡有位子了。**(45)我們就坐這一排吧。**
W The last row? I think we can do better. I'd like to sit close to the presentation.	女 最後一排？我覺得我們可以坐到更好的位置。我想坐靠近演說的地方。
M Oh, don't worry about that. Look over there! There are two seats left close to the front entrance. Let's go and sit quickly.	男 喔，別擔心。看那裡！前面入口旁還空著兩個座位。我們趕快過去坐吧。

• look forward to . . . 期待……　financial 財務的　crisis 危機　attendee 與會者　row 排　entrance 入口

44 --

What type of event are the speakers attending?　說話者參加的是哪一類的活動？
(A) A professional conference　(A) 專業研討會
(B) An employee orientation　(B) 新進員工訓練
(C) A book signing　(C) 簽書會
(D) A staff meeting　(D) 員工會議

本題詢問對話者將出席的活動，通常線索會在對話開始的部分出現。女子說：「So I think this is one of the best finance conferences」，表示該活動為最棒的金融研討會之一，故正確答案為 (A)。

45 (NEW) ---

Why does the man say, "Let's just sit in this row"?　這位男士為什麼說：「我們就坐這一排吧」？
(A) He thinks they have no choice.　(A) 他認為他們別無選擇。
(B) He wants to encourage the woman to work harder.　(B) 他想鼓勵女士更認真工作。
(C) He is disappointed in the presentation.　(C) 他對演講感到失望。
(D) He thinks his team is more competent than other teams.　(D) 他認為他的團隊比其他小組更有能力。

當題目詢問對話者的意圖時，應先了解題目引用的句子，再聆聽對話。掌握意圖的題型不能只靠技巧解題，還須了解整段對話的走向。

對話中，男子說：「And there are so many attendees here! It looks like the only available seats are here in the back.」，表示參加者太多了，提議坐在後面剩下的空位。這代表男子認為已經沒有其他位子了，所以才會這麼說，故答案為 (A)。

46

What does the man say about the seats?
(A) They are all occupied.
(B) They are available near the entrance.
(C) They are not enough for everyone.
(D) They are broken.

這位男士提到什麼有關座位的事？
(A) 全都有人坐了。
(B) 入口附近有空位。
(C) 不夠給所有人坐。
(D) 都壞了。

因為題目在問男子對座位的想法，所以應該注意對話後半段的男子台詞。男子說：「don't worry about that. Look over there! There are two seats left close to the front entrance」，表示入口附近還有座位。「close to」意同「near」，故正確答案為 (B)。

47–49 conversation

47–49 對話

M	Jessica, this is Brian. I've just heard about the traffic congestion on Main Street. Will you be able to make it in time?	男	潔西卡，我是布萊恩。我剛聽說緬因街上的交通阻塞。妳能及時趕到嗎？
W	I was going to call you, Brian. I'm stuck here. I'm sorry for being late for the retirement ceremony for our president. And I have the present and flowers with me here in the taxi.	女	布萊恩，我正要打電話給你。我被卡在這裡了。很抱歉，總裁的退休典禮我要遲到了，而且我還帶著禮物跟花在計程車上。
M	**(49)They are for the last part of the event.** You still have an hour probably.	男	(49)那在活動尾聲才會用到。妳大概還有一個小時的時間。
W	Perfect. The taxi driver says it'll take about 30 minutes. By the way, what about the congratulatory message? I was supposed to hand it to Elizabeth. It's on my computer.	女	太好了。計程車司機說大概要30分鐘。對了，賀詞怎麼辦？我應該要交給伊莉莎白的。它在我的電腦裡。
M	Don't worry. She's with me, and we're almost there. I can stop by the 2nd floor and print it out from your computer.	男	別擔心。她跟我在一起，我們快到了。我可以到二樓從妳的電腦印出來。
W	Thank you so much. Just call me again when you turn on the desktop. You'll need the password.	女	太感謝你了。當你打開電腦時，再打電話給我吧。你會需要密碼的。

• traffic congestion 交通堵塞　in time 及時　be stuck 被困住的　retirement ceremony 退休典禮
president 總裁　congratulatory message 賀詞　stop by 順路造訪

47

Why will the woman probably be late?
(A) She is buying a present on the way.
(B) She is held up by a traffic jam.
(C) She had a computer malfunction.
(D) She needs to give a message to Elizabeth.

這位女士為什麼可能會遲到？
(A) 她正在途中買禮物。
(B) 她被塞車耽擱了。
(C) 她的電腦故障了。
(D) 她要轉交一則訊息給伊莉莎白。

女子遲到的理由雖然極可能出現在女子的台詞中，但是在本題中，可以在男子的台詞找到關鍵性的提示。男子問：「I've just heard about the traffic congestion on Main Street. Will you be able to make it in time?」，由此可知，現在緬因街的交通壅塞嚴重，且女子隨即說道：「I'm stuck here.」可以知道女子現在位於停滯不前的車潮裡，因此正確答案為 (B)。

(A) 禮物已經準備好，且無法確定女子是不是為了買禮物才遲到。(C) 電腦雖然曾出現在對話中，但是並非女子遲到的理由。另外，雖然對話中提及要交賀詞給伊莉莎白，但是這也不是女子遲到的理由，故 (D) 不是正確答案。

What does the woman recommend?
(A) Taking a taxi instead
(B) Going to her office
(C) Calling her again later
(D) Getting a message from Elizabeth

這位女士提出什麼建議？
(A) 改搭計程車
(B) 去她的辦公室
(C) 晚點再打電話給她
(D) 從伊莉莎白那裡取得訊息

本題詢問女子建議的做法，所以應該要集中於女子的台詞。女子説：「Just call me again when you turn on the desktop. You'll need the password.」告知因為需要密碼，所以請對方在打開電腦後，再與她連絡一次。因此，正確答案為 (C)。

(B) 雖然也有可能是正確答案，但「進入女子二樓的辦公室」這句話是男子提出的。

49 (NEW) --

What does the man imply when he says, "They are for the last part of the event"?
(A) Jessica doesn't need to prepare the congratulatory message.
(B) Jessica doesn't need to be at the event from the beginning.
(C) Jessica doesn't need to tell him the password to her computer.
(D) Jessica doesn't need to meet Elizabeth at the ceremony.

當這位男士說：「那在活動尾聲才會用到」，是什麼意思？
(A) 潔西卡不用準備賀詞。
(B) 潔西卡不需要一開始就參加活動。
(C) 潔西卡不需要告訴他她電腦的密碼。
(D) 潔西卡不需要在典禮上見到伊莉莎白。

在推測意圖的題型中，題目引用的句子如果包含代名詞，則解題重點在於掌握該代名詞指稱的對象。本題所引用的句子中，「They」指稱的對象即為前一句女子台詞「And I have the present and flowers with me here in the taxi」裡的禮物與鮮花。意即女子正帶著活動需要的禮物與鮮花前往會場，卻遇到塞車，而因為活動尾聲才需要禮物和花，所以男子認為女子不用如此著急前來，故正確答案為 (B)。

50-52 conversation

M Excuse me, I bought this book about gardening here last week, and it's missing several pages in the middle. Could I exchange it for anther copy?

W Sure, as long as it was purchased less than a month ago and you have the original receipt, it's not a problem.

M I'm afraid I don't have the receipt. I threw it out when I got home. I just opened it today, though. It hasn't been used.

W I'm sorry, sir. But store policy won't let me exchange it without a receipt.

50–52 對話

男 不好意思，我上禮拜在這裡買了這本有關園藝的書，中間有缺頁。我可以換一本嗎？

女 當然，只要是一個月內購買，並有原始收據，就不成問題。

男 我恐怕沒有收據了。我一到家就把它丟了。但是我今天才開封的。還沒用過。

女 先生，很抱歉。店內規定沒有收據就無法更換。

• **purchase** 購買　**receipt** 收據　**throw out** 丟掉

50

What is suggested about the book?
(A) It is a used book.
(B) It is expensive.
(C) It has a defect.
(D) It was on sale.

關於書籍，提到了什麼事？
(A) 是二手書
(B) 很昂貴
(C) 有瑕疵
(D) 特價中

男子的第一句台詞説：「I bought this book about gardening here last week, and it's missing several pages in the middle.」，表示他上週買了書，但是內容少了幾頁，所以正確答案為 (C)。

51

What does the man ask the woman to do?
(A) Switch the item
(B) Make a copy
(C) Buy a book
(D) Give a discount

這位男士要求女士做什麼？
(A) 更換商品
(B) 影印副本
(C) 買書
(D) 提供折扣

本題詢問男子對女子的要求，請專注聆聽男子的台詞。男子的第一句台詞「Could I exchange it for another copy?」告知書本有瑕疵，並要求換貨，所以正確答案為 (A)。

請注意 exchange、trade、switch 皆表示「交換」。

52

What does the woman ask for?
(A) A credit card number
(B) Proof of purchase
(C) A billing address
(D) An exchange

這位女士要求什麼東西？
(A) 信用卡號碼
(B) 購買證明
(C) 帳單地址
(D) 換貨

本題詢問女子提出的要求，請集中聆聽女子的台詞。女子告知男子「as long as it was purchased less than a month ago and you have the original receipt」，表示得有收據才能換貨，所以正確答案為 (B)。

M Hello, this is Sato Ahiko. I was a patient at your medical clinic, but I recently moved to Osaka. A few days ago, I asked that my medical records be sent to my new doctor here, but they haven't received them yet.

W Mr. Sato. Yes, let me check . . . I can see your request, but you didn't sign the form to transfer your records. We can't send them to your new doctor's office until that's done.

M Oh, I must have forgotten to sign it. Do I need to come in to do that?

W No, I can send you a form by e-mail. Just sign it and mail it back by express mail.

男 妳好，我是佐藤雅彥。我之前是貴診所的病患，但我最近搬到大阪了。幾天前，我要求將我的病歷寄給我在這裡的新醫師，但他們還沒有收到。

女 佐藤先生。好的，讓我查一下……我看到您的申請了，但您並沒有在轉移紀錄的表單上簽名。要等這部分完成了，我們才能把病歷寄到您新醫師的辦公室。

男 喔，我一定是忘記簽名了。我需要親自過去補簽嗎？

女 不用，我可以用電子郵件將表單寄給您，只要簽好用快遞寄回即可。

• **patient** 病患　**form** 表單　**transfer** 轉移

What has the man recently done?

(A) Relocated to a new place
(B) Sent a package
(C) Had a medical check-up
(D) Seen a doctor

這位男士最近做了什麼事？

(A) 搬到新地方
(B) 寄包裹
(C) 做健康檢查
(D) 看醫生

男子說「I was a patient at your medical clinic, but I recently moved to Osaka.」，由此可知男子以前是這家醫院的患者，最近搬到大阪。選項 (A) 將「move」換成「relocate」，「Osaka」換成「new place」，但仍與題目相符，故正確答案為 (A)。

What problem does the woman mention?

(A) An appointment was delayed.
(B) A payment was not received.
(C) An address is incorrect.
(D) A document has not been signed.

這位女士提到什麼問題？

(A) 預約被延後了。
(B) 款項沒有收到。
(C) 地址錯誤。
(D) 文件沒有簽名。

本題詢問女子提出的問題，請專心聆聽女子的台詞。女子說：「I can see your request, but you didn't sign the form to transfer your records.」故正確答案為 (D)。form 與 document 時常互相替換使用，請多加熟悉。

55 --

What does the woman say she will do?
(A) Introduce a new doctor
(B) Update the medical records
(C) Email a document
(D) Send something by express mail

這位女士說她會做什麼？
(A) 介紹新醫生
(B) 更新病歷
(C) 用電子郵件寄送文件
(D) 用快遞寄東西

本題是詢問女子在對話結束後的動作，請集中於女子後半部的台詞。她說：「I can send you a form by e-mail.」，故可知她將以電子郵件將表單寄給男子，正確答案為 (C)。

56-58 conversation with three speakers. (NEW)　　**56–58 三人對話**

 23

W1 Thanks for coming to this interview, Mr. McCarthy. I'm Olivia Barash, head of the Personnel Department at KBC film production company. **W2** And I'm Jennie Finch. I'm a film producer. Nice to meet you. **M** Nice to meet you both. And thanks for the interview opportunity. **W2** We've reviewed your résumé, and you seem to be highly qualified for the camera operator position. But we're just wondering about your requirements, since our film crews often get assigned tasks on short notice. **M** I see. Don't worry. I can be available anytime. **W1** Okay, so can we take a look at a sample of your work? You said you brought a video. Is it possible to see it now? **M** Sure, my file's right here on my laptop.	**女1** 麥卡錫先生，感謝您來參加面試。我是KBC製片公司人事部的主管奧莉維亞・巴拉什。 **女2** 我是珍妮・芬奇。我是電影製作人。很高興見到你。 **男** 很高興認識兩位。感謝您們提供這個面試機會。 **女2** 我們檢視過你的履歷，你看起來很適合攝影師這個職位。但由於我們的拍片組員常臨時接到任務，我們想知道你的要求條件。 **男** 我懂。這不是問題。我隨時可以配合。 **女1** 好。那我們可以看一下你的作品試片嗎？你說帶了一段影片。現在可以看嗎？ **男** 沒問題，我的檔案就在筆電裡。

• **head** 主管　**personnel department** 人事部門　**review** 檢視　**résumé** 履歷　**qualify** 有資格
　wonder 想知道　**crew** 全體工作人員　**on short notice** 臨時

56 --

Where do the women most likely work?
(A) At an electronics store
(B) At a movie production company
(C) At a TV station
(D) At a movie theater

這兩位女士最可能在哪裡工作？
(A) 在電器行
(B) 在電影製片公司
(C) 在電視台
(D) 在電影院

女子們工作的地方在對話的一開始出現。第一句台詞中，女子自我介紹道：「I'm Olivia Barash, head of the personnel department at KBC film production company.」，故正確答案為 (B)。

57 --

What job requirement do the speakers discuss?
(A) Being professionally certified
(B) Using the proper equipment
(C) Having camera operation skills
(D) Handling some urgent tasks

說話者討論的是什麼工作條件？
(A) 受到專業認證
(B) 使用適當設備
(C) 具攝影機操作技術
(D) 處理緊急任務

第二位女子說：「we're just wondering about your requirements, since our film crews often get assigned tasks on short notice」，題目表示公司員工偶爾會「臨時」接到任務，選項 (D) 將其改寫為「緊急」任務，與題目相符，故正確答案為 (D)。

58 --

What will the man do next?
(A) Show his work sample
(B) Make a video
(C) Meet a director
(D) Buy a laptop

這位男士接下來要做什麼？
(A) 展示他的作品試片
(B) 拍影片
(C) 和導演見面
(D) 買一台筆電

本題詢問男子在對話後將進行的活動。後半段對話的台詞中，女子問：「You said you brought a video. Is it possible to see it now?」，而男子回答說：「Sure, my file's right here on my laptop」表示立刻可以將作品給女子看，正確答案為 (A)。

59-61 conversation

59–61 對話

W Roy, I confirmed the cost to use Hyde Park for our company retreat next month. I think it's reasonable. So we'll probably choose this place. By the way, have you contacted the catering company yet?	**女** 洛伊，我確認過下個月到海德公園員工旅遊的費用了。我覺得滿合理的。所以我們可能會選擇這個地點。對了，你聯絡外燴公司了嗎？
M No, I haven't decided yet, and I'm just thinking about whether we should order food for our event. Since it's going to be at a park this year, perhaps everyone can bring their favorite food instead.	**男** 還沒有，我還沒決定要哪一家，我在想這個活動是否要訂購食物。既然今年是在公園舉行，也許大家可以改帶自己喜歡的食物。
W (61)**That's a good point.** However, we should make sure people are willing to bring their dishes to share before we make a final decision about not using a caterer.	**女** (61)有道理喔。不過在我們決定不找外燴業者前，應該先確定大家是否願意帶餐點來共享。
M I agree. I'll forward an e-mail to the staff today and find out their opinions.	**男** 我同意。我今天會轉寄電子郵件給全體職員，看看他們的意見如何。

• **confirm** 確認　**company retreat** 員工旅遊　**reasonable** 合理的　**catering company** 外燴業者

What will happen next month?
(A) A dedication
(B) A holiday party
(C) A company outing
(D) A retirement celebration

下個月將發生什麼事？
(A) 揭幕儀式
(B) 假日派對
(C) 公司郊遊
(D) 退休慶祝會

題組的第一題詢問下個月將發生的事，其答案很有可能是對話的主題。女子的第一句台詞說：
「I confirmed the cost to use Hyde Park for our company retreat next month」，由此可見，正確答案為 (C)。

What is the man considering?
(A) Whether to use a catering company
(B) Where to hold an event
(C) When to order food
(D) Who should be invited

這位男士正在考慮什麼？
(A) 是否僱用外燴公司
(B) 要在哪裡舉辦活動
(C) 要於何時訂購食物
(D) 該邀請誰

本題詢問男子正在考慮何事，請注意聆聽男子的台詞。男子說：「I'm just thinking about whether we should order food for our event」，表示正在考慮是否要訂購餐飲，故正確答案為 (A)。

61 NEW

What does the woman imply when she says, "That's a good point"?
(A) She agrees with the man's opinion.
(B) She wants to bring some food.
(C) She'll send an e-mail.
(D) She suggests ordering some food.

當這位女士說：「有道理喔」，是什麼意思？
(A) 她同意男士的看法
(B) 她想帶些食物
(C) 她將寄發電子郵件
(D) 她建議訂購食物

詢問對話者意圖的題目，應先了解引用句的意思，再聆聽對話掌握意圖。男子說：「perhaps everyone can bring their favorite food instead.」，表示所有人都可以帶他們喜歡的食物，緊接著女子說「That's a good point.」，對男子的意見表示同意，故正確答案為 (A)。

62-64 conversation and chart

62–64 對話及圖表

W Max, I'm planning to see a new play at the City Theater this weekend. Don't you want to go with me? **M** Absolutely! I've read good reviews from a recent article. It said it's a wonderful performance! How much is the ticket? **W** It depends . . . Let's look at the information. I'm a member, and one more person can get an additional discount, so both of us can buy tickets at the member's price.

女 麥克斯，我打算這週末到市立戲院看場新戲。你要不要跟我一起去？ **男** 當然要！我在最近的文章上看到了不錯的評論。上面寫說那是場很棒的表演！票價是多少？ **女** 不一定……我們來看一下資料吧。我是會員，多一個人可以得到額外的折扣，所以我們兩個都可以以會員價購票。

M	Wow, that's good news. Would that be for Saturday or Sunday?	男	哇，真是好消息。那要約週六，還是週日呢？
W	Saturday at 7 P.M. Is it possible?	女	週六晚上七點，可以嗎？
M	Sure. Could you order the tickets for me?	男	當然可以。妳可以幫我訂票嗎？
W	No problem. I'll visit the Web site and order them now.	女	沒問題。我現在就上網訂。

Admission Price per Person		個人入場費	
Children under 12	$8	12 歲以下孩童	8 元
Group of 10 or more	$12	10 人以上團體	12 元
Member	$15	會員	15 元
Non-member	$20	非會員	20 元

• **play** 戲劇 **absolutely** 當然 **review** 評論 **performance** 表演 **additional** 額外的 **admission price** 入場費

 62 ---

What type of event are the speakers discussing?
(A) A theater performance
(B) A museum exhibition
(C) A new movie
(D) A live music concert

說話者討論的是什麼活動？
(A) 劇場表演
(B) 博物館展覽
(C) 新電影
(D) 現場音樂會

第一句台詞說：「I'm planning to see a new play at the City Theater this weekend.」，說話者表示正計畫去觀賞新的戲劇演出，所以答案是 (A)。

63 NEW ---

Look at the graphic. What ticket price will the speakers probably pay?
(A) $16
(B) $24
(C) $30
(D) $40

看一下圖表，說話者可能要支付多少票價？
(A) 16元
(B) 24元
(C) 30元
(D) 40元

遇到視覺資料題型時，應先掌握題目，再研究視覺資料。先閱讀題目和選項時，偶爾會出現與圖表不同的價格，此時便需要進行計算，故須事先做好心理準備。

在對話的中間部分，女子說：「I'm a member, and one more person can get an additional discount, so both of us can buy tickets at the member's price.」，表示自己是會員，而同行的另一位朋友也是會員，所以可以享有折扣。會員的門票價格為每人 $15，所以兩人應支付 $30，正確答案為 (C)。

64

What does the woman say she will do?

(A) Leave work early
(B) Purchase the tickets
(C) Pay with a credit card
(D) Visit the theater

這位女士說她要做什麼？

(A) 提早下班
(B) 買票
(C) 用信用卡付款
(D) 去劇院

女子最後說「I'll visit the website and order them now.」，表示將會上網訂購門票，故正確答案為 (B)。

65-67 conversation and list

65–67 對話及表單

W Hi, this is Linda from SummerMax Advertising. We reserved the picnic area in Parramatta Park on April 19th for a company picnic. But I'm calling to see if we could change to another Saturday.

M Let me check the schedule. I'm sorry, but all Saturdays are booked in April. What about in May?

W No, it has to be in April because we're going to expand the production line in May. Is there another venue in the park that we could use in April?

M I'm sorry, but wait. My coworker just told me that someone called this morning to cancel their reservation. Let me check it again.

W Oh, that's perfect!

M Yes, I can see the memo here that says Amax Accounting changed their event to June. So you can use their spot.

女 嗨，我是夏馬可仕廣告公司的琳達。我們為公司的野餐活動預約了帕拉馬塔公園4月19號的野餐區。但我打來是想看看我們是否能改到其他週六？

男 讓我看一下時間表。很抱歉，四月份所有週六時間都已被預訂了。五月可以嗎？

女 不行，得在四月，因為五月我們公司要擴大生產線。公園內有沒有其他地點可以讓我們在四月使用的呢？

男 很抱歉，不過等一下。我的同事剛告訴我，有人今天早上打電話來取消預約了。讓我再確認一次。

女 喔，那太好了！

男 是的，我看到備忘錄上寫說，安邁信會計事務所把他們的活動改到六月了。所以貴公司可以使用他們原訂的場地。

Parramatta Park	
April 5	Ashifield Consulting
April 12	Burwood Church
April 19	SummerMax Advertising
April 26	Amax Accounting

帕拉馬塔公園	
4 月 5 日	艾士菲顧問公司
4 月 12 日	伯伍德教會
4 月 19 日	夏馬可仕廣告公司
4 月 26 日	安邁信會計事務所

• **reserve** 預約 **book** 預訂 **venue** 場地 **coworker** 同事 **consulting** 諮詢 **advertising** 廣告業
accounting 會計

65 -

Why is the woman calling?
(A) To cancel the event
(B) To change the location
(C) To change the date
(D) To give an invitation

這位女士為什麼打這通電話？
(A) 為了取消活動
(B) 為了更改地點
(C) 為了更改日期
(D) 為了提出邀請

題目詢問女子為何撥打電話，故應注意聆聽女子的台詞。女子說：「I'm calling to see if we could change to another Saturday.」，表示是為了將活動日期改到其他週六，故此題正確答案為 (C)。請注意，此類題型中，「I'm calling to . . .」之後的內容就會是撥打電話的目的。

66 -

According to the woman, what will her company do in May?
(A) Relocate to a different city
(B) Expand a budget
(C) Enlarge a work area
(D) Hire additional workers

根據這位女士所言，她的公司五月要做什麼？
(A) 搬到另一座城市
(B) 擴大預算
(C) 擴大工作區
(D) 僱用更多員工

女子在對話中半段說「because we're going to expand the production line in May」，說明了更改日期是因為五月將擴張生產線，選項 (C) 將「expand the production line」改寫為「enlarge a work area」，仍與題目相符，故正確答案為 (C)。

67 -

Look at the graphic. When will the woman use the park?
(A) April 5
(B) April 12
(C) April 19
(D) April 26

看一下圖表，這位女士將於何時使用公園？
(A) 4 月 5 日
(B) 4 月 12 日
(C) 4 月 19 日
(D) 4 月 26 日

對話後半提到：「I can see the memo here that says Amax Accounting changed their event to June. So you can use their spot」，對照表單上原先保留給安邁信會計事務所的日期，可知女子的公司可在 4 月 26 日使用場地，正確答案為 (D)。

68-70 conversation and map

W	What should we do for our director's retirement party next week? I think we should do something to thank him for his dedication to our company.
M	Well, let's do more than just write thank-you cards. How about buying a special gift for him?
W	That's actually a good idea. In that way, he could always remember us every time he looks at the present. So, what kind of gift is the best for him?
M	I have an idea. I know a premium gift shop on George Street that handles personalized gifts such as cups and trophies. They're only a block away from us. I'll drop by their store this afternoon.
W	Actually, they just moved to a new location at the corner of Central Avenue and Broadway, across from AnZ Bank.
M	Alright! I think I know it.

女	我們應該為主管下週的退休派對做點什麼呢？我想我們應該做點事感謝他為公司的付出。
男	嗯，我們不要只寫感謝卡。買個特別的禮物送他如何？
女	那的確是個好主意。這樣一來，每次他看到那個禮物時，就會想起我們。那麼，什麼禮物最適合他呢？
男	我有個主意。我知道喬治街上有一家優質的禮品店，可以做客製化禮物，像是杯子或獎盃。這家店離我們只有一個街區的距離。我今天下午會順道過去他們店裡。
女	事實上，他們剛搬到新址，就在中央大道與百老匯的轉角，AnZ銀行對面。
男	好的！我想我應該知道在哪裡。

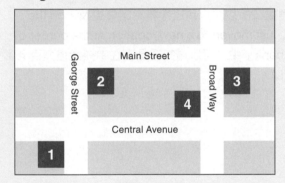

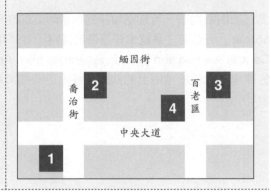

• **retirement** 退休　**dedication** 付出　**premium** 優質的　**personalized** 客製化的

What do the speakers want to do?
(A) Plan a party for customers
(B) Celebrate a company's anniversary
(C) Express their gratitude
(D) Send out invitations

說話者想做什麼？
(A) 為客戶規劃派對
(B) 慶祝公司週年紀念
(C) 表達感謝之意
(D) 寄發邀請函

詢問對話者想要做什麼的題型，有時答案就是對話的主題。對話第一句台詞說：「What should we do for our director's retirement party next week? I think we should do something to thank him for his dedication to our company.」，由此可知，對話者為了在下週主管的退休典禮上表達感謝，所以在討論進行的方式。本題答案為 (C)。

What does the man suggest doing?

(A) Making a presentation

(B) Purchasing a present

(C) Setting up a gift shop

(D) Giving an award

這位男士建議做什麼？

(A) 做簡報

(B) 買禮物

(C) 開禮品店

(D) 頒獎

本題詢問男子的提議，所以應從注意男子的台詞。男子說過：「How about buying a special gift for him?」，所以正確答案為 (B)。

請注意「How/What about . . . ? / Why don't you . . . ? / Why don't we . . . ?」皆為表達提議的典型句型。

70 (NEW)

Look at the graphic. Where is the gift shop located?

(A) 1

(B) 2

(C) 3

(D) 4

看一下圖表，禮品店位於何處？

(A) 1

(B) 2

(C) 3

(D) 4

先仔細觀察地圖，可知選項中的四個地方都在轉角處，所以可以預設等等對話會提及「on the corner」，並要注意找出是正確的道路。從「they just moved to a new location at the corner of Central Avenue and Broadway, across from AnZ bank」中，可以得知禮品店在中央大道與百老匯的轉角，故位於地圖上的四號位置，正確答案為 (D)。

PART 4

🎧 24

71-73 telephone message

71–73 電話留言

Hi, Ms. Jade. This is David Foster calling from David's Garage. When I inspected your vehicle, I noticed a problem with a light bulb that cannot be turned on. So it needs to be replaced. I ordered the part this morning, but it won't arrive at the shop until next week. So if you'd like, we can lend you a car to use until your car is fixed. Please get back to me at 333-3033.	嗨，杰蒂女士。我是大衛車廠的大衛‧佛斯特。我在檢查您車輛時，注意到有個燈泡不會亮的問題，所以需要更換。我今天早上訂購了零件，但是要到下週才會送達車廠。所以如果您願意的話，我可以先借您一台車使用，直到車子修好為止。請回電333-3033給我。

• **garage** 汽車修理廠　**inspect** 檢查　**vehicle** 車輛　**light bulb** 燈泡

🎧 23

🎧 24

71 --

Where does the speaker work?

(A) At an electronics store
(B) At a hardware store
(C) At a car repair shop
(D) At a car rental company

說話者在哪裡工作？

(A) 電器行
(B) 五金行
(C) 汽車修理廠
(D) 汽車租賃公司

說話者工作的地方常常會在開頭出現。此外，在電話留言的題型中，說話者常會以「This is ＋姓名」和「from ＋部門」的句型自我介紹，通常聽到部門就可以知道工作地點。本題提到：「This is David Foster calling from David's Garage」，所以正確答案為 (C)。

72 --

What does the speaker say he has done?

(A) Scheduled an appointment
(B) Completed a repair
(C) Replaced a light
(D) Ordered a part

說話者說他做了什麼？

(A) 安排預約
(B) 完成維修
(C) 更換電燈
(D) 訂購零件

說話者提到，維修汽車時發現燈泡有問題，並說「it needs to be replaced. I ordered the part this morning」，所以正確答案為 (D)。

73 --

What does the speaker offer?

(A) A rental car service
(B) An extended warranty
(C) A free inspection
(D) An express delivery

說話者提供了什麼？

(A) 汽車租用服務
(B) 延長保固
(C) 免費檢測
(D) 快遞

本題詢問說話者提供了什麼，應仔細聆聽文章中提到「我將（為聽者）做……」的部分。後半部的內容提到「if you'd like, we can lend you a car」，表示如果聽者有需要，說話者考慮出借車輛，所以正確答案為 (A)。

237

74-76 excerpt from a meeting　　　　　　　**74-76 會議摘錄**

Last on the agenda today, I'd like to talk about using telephone conferencing more often this year. Computers with video cameras have been set up in all meeting rooms for use during teleconferences. Staff will be trained on how to use the equipment. Our group training is scheduled for next Wednesday after lunch in meeting room C, so please mark your calendars. One more important thing, before the training, you should read the manual I passed out. It'll help you to be much more familiar with the equipment. If you are not available next week, please let me know by the end of the week. I'll arrange other sessions at a later date.	今天議程的最後，我想討論今年會更常使用電話會議一事。所有會議室都已裝設了附有錄影機的電腦，可於電話會議時使用。同仁將接受使用設備的訓練。我們的團體訓練安排在下週三的午餐後，於會議室C舉行，所以請標示在各位的行事曆上。還有一件重要的事，在訓練前，大家應該先閱讀我所發下去的使用手冊。它能幫助各位更熟悉設備。如果你下個禮拜無法出席，請於週末前告訴我。我會在之後安排其他講習。

• **agenda** 議程　**conferencing** 會議　**mark** 標示　**manual** 使用手冊　**pass out** 發放　**arrange** 安排
　session 講習　**procedure** 程序

What is the speaker mainly discussing?　　說話者主要在討論什麼？
(A) A change to project timelines　　　　　(A) 專案時間表的變更
(B) Plans to use teleconferencing　　　　　(B) 使用電話會議的計畫
(C) Some expected job opportunities　　　　(C) 可能的工作機會
(D) Camera installation　　　　　　　　　(D) 安裝相機

本題詢問文章的主題，答案通常在開頭出現。一開始提到「I'd like to talk about using telephone conferencing」，由此可知，這段內容與電話會議有關，故答案為 (B)。

According to the speaker, what will happen next week?　根據說話者表示，下週會發生什麼事？
(A) Employees will learn new procedures.　　　(A) 員工要學新操作程序。
(B) Salespeople will meet with clients.　　　　(B) 業務員要與客戶會面。
(C) Designers will create video materials.　　　(C) 設計師將創造影像素材。
(D) Technicians will replace old computers.　　(D) 技術員將更換舊電腦。

本題詢問下週將發生的事。內容提到「Staff will be trained on how to use the equipment. Our group training is scheduled for next Wednesday」，所以員工下週將學習使用設備，正確答案為 (A)。

What does the speaker ask the listeners to do?　　說話者要求聽眾做什麼？
(A) Distribute handouts　　　　　　　　　(A) 分發講義
(B) Compile sales data　　　　　　　　　　(B) 編輯銷售資料
(C) Set up the equipment　　　　　　　　　(C) 裝設配備
(D) Refer to the instructions　　　　　　　(D) 參考指示說明

從「One more important thing, before the training, you should read the manual I passed out」中，可以知道說話者要求聽眾參閱已發放的說明書，因此答案為 (D)。

77-79 tour information

Welcome to St. Cyres National Park. My name is Sean, and I'll be your guide on our hike to the top of Chester Point today. As we go, I'll show you many of the unique plants and flowers the park is famous for. I will also explain a little bit about its history. It will take about 2 hours to reach the top, but this will include several short breaks along the way. We should arrive at the top around noon and will stop for a picnic lunch there. I would ask you to please protect the environment by not throwing out your trash on the path. There aren't any trash bins on the top of the mountain, so you'll need to carry your garbage with you and discard it in the garbage cans in the parking area when we come back.

77-79 導覽資訊

歡迎來到聖賽瑞斯國家公園。我是尚恩，是各位今天到切斯特山頂健行之旅的導遊。我們一邊走，我會邊向各位介紹這座公園著名的獨特植物與花朵。我也會稍微說明它的歷史。到達山頂耗時約兩個小時，但這當中包含了沿途幾段短暫的休息時間。我們應該會在中午左右抵達山頂，並在那裡享用野餐式午餐。懇請大家不要將垃圾丟在步道中，以保護環境整潔。山頂沒有垃圾筒，因此各位必須帶著自己的垃圾，等我們回來時，再丟在停車場的垃圾桶。

• **guide** 導遊 **reach** 到達 **break** 休息時間 **along . . .** 沿著…… **throw out** 丟掉 **path** 步道
trash bin 垃圾桶 **discard** 丟棄 **garbage can** 垃圾桶 **parking area** 停車場

77 --

Where is the tour most likely taking place?

(A) At a nature center
(B) In a parking area
(C) At a flower shop
(D) At an outdoor market

這段行程最有可能在哪裡進行？

(A) 自然中心
(B) 停車場
(C) 花店
(D) 露天市場

詢問地點的題型，可以在開頭尋找線索。題目一開始便說「Welcome to St. Cyres National Park」，可知這是在國家公園裡。選項 (A) 將「national park」改寫為「nature center」，意思相近，故正確答案為 (A)。

另外，通常遇到詢問場所的題型，聽到「Welcome to . . .」時，後面出現的場所就會是答案。

78 --

Where will the group have lunch?

(A) At a mountain cabin
(B) At a waterfall
(C) At the summit
(D) In a parking lot

旅行團會在哪裡用餐？

(A) 山中小屋
(B) 瀑布旁
(C) 山頂
(D) 停車場

提供導覽資訊的文章通常會在中間部分進行行程介紹。題目介紹上午的行程後，隨即提到午餐的行程。由「We should arrive at the top around noon and will stop for a picnic lunch there.」可知，旅行團將在山頂用午餐，故正確答案為 (C)。

79

What are the listeners asked to do?

(A) Throw away trash when they return
(B) Refrain from picking flowers on the trail
(C) Not interrupt while the speaker is talking
(D) Take a group photo after the hike

聽眾被要求做什麼事？

(A) 回來後再丟垃圾
(B) 不可在小徑上摘花
(C) 不可打斷說話者說話
(D) 在健行後拍合照

題目後半段的內容提到「so you'll need to carry your garbage with you and discard it in the garbage cans in the parking area when we come back.」，表示聽眾必須將自己的垃圾帶回停車場的垃圾桶丟棄，故正確答案為 (A)。

請記得，throw out、throw away、discard 皆有「丟棄」的意思。

80-82 advertisement

80–82 廣告

Do you want to get a driver's license at a reasonable price? Then look no further. The SimPit Driving School is the answer! We're currently offering a special for new drivers. If you sign up for our three-week introductory course anytime during March, you will receive a 20 percent discount. SimPit hires only certified instructors who are friendly, patient, and experienced, and our cars are fully insured and totally dependable. The three-week course includes one week of classroom instruction in traffic laws, one week of automobile safety and basic car maintenance, and one week of hands-on driving practice. For more information, or to register for a course, please visit our Web site at www.simpitdriving.com.	你想以合理的價格取得駕照嗎？不用再找了，莫圖伊卡駕訓班就是正解！我們目前為新手駕駛提供了特別優惠。如果您在三月任何時間報名三週的入門課程，將可獲得八折優惠。莫圖伊卡只聘僱合格的指導員，友善、有耐心且經驗豐富，而且我們的汽車保有全險，完全可靠。三週的課程將包括一個禮拜的交通法規課堂教學、一個禮拜的汽車安全與汽車基本保養以及一個禮拜的實駕練習。欲知更多資訊或報名課程，請上我們的網站 www.simpitdriving.com。

- **license** 執照 **introductory course** 入門課程 **certified** 合格的 **instructor** 指導員
  experienced 經驗豐富的 **insure** 投保 **dependable** 可靠的 **instruction** 教學 **traffic law** 交通法規
  maintenance 保養 **hands-on** 實際操作的 **register** 報名

80

Who is this advertisement for?

(A) Traffic police
(B) Driving instructors
(C) Auto mechanics
(D) New drivers

這則廣告是要給誰的？

(A) 交通警察
(B) 駕訓教練
(C) 汽車技師
(D) 新手駕駛

本題詢問廣告對象，也可以視為詢問「產品主要購買者」。廣告開頭便說「Do you want to get a driver's license at a reasonable price? Then look no further. The SimPit Driving School is the answer!」詢問聽者是否想要考取駕照，可知這則廣告的對象為想要考取駕照的新手駕駛，正確答案為 (D)

81

What is being advertised?
(A) A discount on driving instruction
(B) A sale on used cars
(C) Automobile insurance
(D) A job opening for driving instructors

這是要廣告什麼？
(A) 駕訓課程的優惠折扣
(B) 二手車拍賣
(C) 汽車保險
(D) 駕訓教練的職缺

本題詢問廣告內容，此類題型通常與詢問廣告對象及廣告目的等相關題目同時出現，可以練習兩道題目一起閱讀，一次找出所有線索。廣告提到「If you sign up for our three-week introductory course anytime during March, you will receive a 20 percent discount.」，一面宣傳駕駛訓練課程，一面強調聽眾若報名三週入門課程，即可獲得八折優惠，所以正確答案為 (A)。

82

How can the listeners sign up for a service?
(A) By visiting an office
(B) By sending for a brochure
(C) By visiting a Web site
(D) By making a phone call

聽眾要如何報名？
(A) 到公司
(B) 訂購手冊
(C) 上網站
(D) 打電話

廣告通常會在後半段提及聯繫方法。如題目最後「For more information, or to register for a course, please visit our Web site」，如果需要更多詳情或報名課程，聽眾需要上官方網站，因此正確答案為 (C)。

83-85 excerpt from a meeting

83-85 會議摘錄

Thanks for attending today's meeting. I'd like to start by looking over some results of the customer survey we conducted last week. Last year, we introduced our new blender, the Brown 100. As you know well, it has many great features such as ice-grinding, low noise, and low power consumption. According to the survey, the biggest advantage of this model is that it can be disassembled into several parts so that users can wash it entirely. However, it has a higher failure rate at the same time. The most frequent problem is that customers cannot put the parts back together. Also, they may not be aware of the parts that shouldn't be washed with water, and often damage the motor. We'll be releasing the new model, the Brown 150, this year, and we ought to make it a better one. That is to say, we must **(85)strengthen the strengths and make up for the weaknesses.**

感謝大家出席今天的會議。一開始，我想來檢視上週進行的顧客問卷調查結果。去年我們推出了新的攪拌機，布朗100。正如大家都很清楚的，它具有很多優質特點，像是製作碎冰、低噪音及省電。根據調查結果顯示，這個型號最大的優點，就是可以拆解成數個部位，所以使用者可以整台清洗。但這同時也出現了較高的故障率。最常見的問題就是顧客無法將零件重組回去，而且他們也不清楚哪些零件是不可以水洗的，常讓馬達受損。今年我們將推出新型號，布朗150，我們應該讓它成為更棒的產品。也就是說，我們要**(85)強化優點，彌補缺點。**

• **customer survey** 顧客問卷調查　**blender** 攪拌機　**ice-grinding** 碎冰　**low noise** 低噪音
low power consumption 省電　**disassemble** 拆解　**failure rate** 故障率
put . . . back together 將……重組　**be aware of . . .** 注意……　**damage** 損壞　**ought to . . .** 應該……
That is to say 也就是說　**strengthen** 強化　**make up for . . .** 彌補……

83 --

What kind of business does the speaker work for?
(A) A repair center
(B) A home appliance company
(C) A market research firm
(D) A cleaning company

說話者在何種產業工作？
(A) 維修中心
(B) 家電公司
(C) 市場研究公司
(D) 清潔公司

從前半部的「Last year, we introduced our new blender, the Brown 100.」中，可以知道說話者的公司去年推出「布朗 100」攪拌機，而從後半部的「We'll be releasing the new model, the Brown 150, this year」中，可以知道今年又將推出新型號。選項中，和製造生產攪拌機相關的選項，只有「家電公司」，故正確答案為 (B)。

--- 84 ---

What is the most popular feature of the current model?
(A) Waterproof motor
(B) Self-cleaning
(C) Detachable parts
(D) High power consumption

目前型號最受歡迎的優點是什麼？
(A) 防水馬達
(B) 自動清潔
(C) 可拆解的零件
(D) 高耗電

目前的型號即布朗 100，故要尋找布朗 100 的最大優點。說話者曾提到「as ice-grinding, low noise, and low power consumption」針對功能進行說明，但是這些非本題答案，因為說話者隨後又提到「the biggest advantage of this model is that it can be disassembled into several parts so that users can wash it entirely」，表示布朗 100 最大的優點為「可拆解清洗」，所以正確答案為 (C)。請熟記「disassemble」、「detachable」、「removable」等「拆解、分解」有關的字彙。

(A) 文中提及消費者常「不清楚哪些零件是不可以水洗的」而導致「馬達受損」，故可知此型號不具防水馬達。(B) 內文提到的是「容易清潔」，而非「自動清潔」。(D) 題目中提到的是「low power consumption」，而非「high power consumption」，且對電子產品而言，耗電量高是缺點。

 85 (NEW) --

What does the speaker imply when she says, "strengthen the strengths and make up for the weaknesses"?
(A) She believes the new model has to be more expensive.
(B) She doesn't want to give up the advantages of the previous model.
(C) She regrets the Brown 150 model was designed too poorly.
(D) She doesn't agree with the customers about their complaints.

當說話者說：「強化優點，彌補缺點」，是什麼意思？
(A) 她認為新型號應該要更貴。
(B) 她不想放棄之前型號的優點。
(C) 她懊悔布朗150的設計不良。
(D) 她不認同客戶的投訴。

題目引用的句子出現在本文最後的「That is to say, we must strengthen the strengths and make up for the weaknesses.」。其中，「That is to say」（也就是說）代表此句將以相同意義轉述前文。前一句話說：「we ought to make it a better one」，表示今年上市的布朗 150 應該比去年的布朗 100 更好，所以不會刪去舊型號的優點，正確答案為 (B)。

(A)「更好」的東西並不等於是「更貴」的，所以非正確答案。(C) 使用過去式描述未上市的型號，此與文中內容不符。(D) 女子並未對客戶意見表達相反看法。

86-88 telephone message
86–88 電話留言

Hello, Ms. Cynthia. I just received your message about the problem you encountered with some of the office supplies we sent your company 3 days ago. I'm so sorry that your order arrived damaged. We'll of course stop by your office to pick up the supplies with new materials tomorrow. You don't need to do anything. **(88)We can just handle everything.** Also, I'll give you a special offer on the next purchase. Again, we apologize for the inconvenience caused. We appreciate your understanding. Thank you for your continual business with us.

辛希亞女士，您好。我剛收到您的訊息，提到三天前我們送到貴公司的某些辦公用品出了問題。很抱歉，您訂購的物品在運送時受損了。我們明天一定會帶著新品到貴公司收取物件。您無須採取任何動作。**(88)我們會處理一切問題。**此外，我也將提供您下次消費時的特別優惠折扣。我們再次為所造成的不便致歉。感謝您的諒解。也謝謝您一直以來的惠顧。

• **encounter** 遭遇 **office supplies** 辦公用品 **ship** 運送 **damage** 損害 **stop by** 造訪 **apologize** 道歉 **inconvenience** 不便 **appreciate** 感謝 **continual** 持續的

86 --

Why is the speaker calling?
(A) To receive a message
(B) To apologize to a customer
(C) To order some items
(D) To inquire about a product

說話者為什麼打這通電話？
(A) 為了接收訊息
(B) 為了向客戶道歉
(C) 為了訂購商品
(D) 為了詢問產品

詢問撥打電話目的的題型，答案通常出現在文章的前半部。從開頭可知，說話者收到辛西亞女士的訊息，表示公司運送的物品有問題，而說話者現在正針對問題提供答覆。透過「I'm so sorry that your order arrived damaged」，可以得知說話者是為了致歉而撥打電話，故正確答案為 (B)。

87 --

What problem does the speaker mention?
(A) Some items are faulty.
(B) A machine is broken.
(C) A shipment is late.
(D) Some items are out of stock.

說話者提到了什麼問題？
(A) 部分商品有瑕疵。
(B) 機器故障。
(C) 貨運延遲。
(D) 部分商品缺貨。

說話者提到「I'm so sorry that your order arrived damaged.」，表示問題點是產品出現損壞，正確答案為 (A)。

88 NEW

- -

Why does the speaker say, "We can just handle everything"?

(A) To make up for a mistake
(B) To purchase the item
(C) To provide a sample
(D) To give a special gift

說話者為什麼說:「我們會處理一切問題。」?

(A) 為了彌補錯誤
(B) 為了購買商品
(C) 為了提供樣品
(D) 為了贈送特別禮物

掌握說話者的意圖,需要掌握文章整體的動向。一開始說話者提及產品的問題點,並提到「You don't need to do anything. We can just handle everything. Also, I'll give you a special offer on the next purchase」,表示將提供特別優惠作為彌補,所以正確答案為 (A)。

89-91 news report

89-91 新聞報導

Good morning, this is Duncan Piper reporting for Channel 7 local news. I'm here in the Strathfield Plaza, just standing in front of Ruda's Delicious Ice Cream, which is celebrating its grand opening. This is the first franchise location of Ruda's Delicious Ice Cream in our city, but the Sydney-based company is already famous nationwide. To celebrate the opening this morning, the company is giving away a complimentary ice cream cone to the first 100 people. But it's only available before noon. Just come by the store and enjoy a free taste. Even if you miss the free ice cream, you can try it anytime. It's very tasty!	早安,這裡是第七頻道地方新聞,鄧肯・派柏報導。我現在就在史卓菲廣場上魯達醇冰淇淋的前面,他們正在慶祝盛大開幕。這是魯達醇冰淇淋在本市的第一家加盟店,而這家源自雪梨的公司早已聞名全國。今天早上為了慶祝開幕,公司提供前100名顧客免費的冰淇淋甜筒,但僅限中午前。只要來店,即可免費品嚐。就算錯過了免費冰淇淋,仍歡迎隨時來店品味。非常可口美味!

- **grand opening** 盛大開幕 **franchise** 加盟 **nationwide** 全國地 **give away** 免費發送
  complimentary 免費贈送的 **available** 可獲得的

89

- -

What type of business is being discussed?

(A) A fabric manufacturer
(B) An ice cream factory
(C) A local business
(D) A cooking school

談話中所談論的是何種行業?

(A) 紡織製造廠
(B) 冰淇淋工廠
(C) 地方商家
(D) 烹飪學校

本題一開始,說話者說「I'm here in the Strathfield Plaza, just standing in front of Ruda's Delicious Ice Cream.」,由此可知,這是一篇宣傳地方冰淇淋店的新聞。「store」(店家)時常在選項中改為「business」(商家),請多注意。本題正確答案為 (C)。

90

What can be inferred about the company?
(A) It has never operated in this city before.
(B) Its headquarters moved to another city.
(C) It is celebrating its 10th anniversary.
(D) It is expanding a building.

有關該公司，從談話中可推論出什麼？
(A) 從未在這個城市開業過。
(B) 總部搬遷到其他城市。
(C) 正在慶祝創店十週年紀念。
(D) 正在擴建大樓。

本題為推論該公司資訊的題型。文章中出現許多資訊，所以應集中在選項上，只要一出現相符的內容，即可將該選項選為答案。

由「This is the first franchise location of Ruda's Delicious Ice Cream in our city」可知該店鋪為此城市的第一家加盟店，所以店鋪先前並未在這個城市開業，故正確答案為 (A)。

91

What will some customers receive before noon?
(A) A free sample
(B) Some coupons
(C) A promotional brochure
(D) Complimentary recipes

部分顧客在中午前可獲得什麼？
(A) 免費試吃
(B) 折價券
(C) 宣傳手冊
(D) 免費食譜

從中間部分的「To celebrate the opening this morning, the company is giving away a complimentary ice cream cone to the first 100 people.」中可知，店家將贈送免費冰淇淋給前一百名顧客，故有些顧客可免費試吃冰淇淋，正確答案為 (A)。

92-94 announcement

92–94 宣告

Many of you have probably seen the electricians in and around the office here this week. Apparently, there was a power failure on the fourth floor last week. This means that the electricity on that floor will have to be turned off for a few hours tomorrow while technicians try to solve this problem. So, please use your laptop computer to work on and we'll use the conference room on the fifth floor as a temporary office space. Before leaving the office today, remember that you should save any important documents.

很多人可能已經看到這個禮拜電工在辦公室裡四處走動。事實上，上禮拜四樓發生了斷電。這表示在明天技術人員努力解決問題之際，該樓層的電力將關閉數小時，因此請各位使用自己的筆記型電腦辦公，我們將使用五樓的辦公室作為臨時辦公處所。今天下班前，請記得儲存所有重要檔案。

• **electrician** 電工　**apparently** 事實上　**power failure** 斷電　**electricity** 電力　**work on** 辦公
temporary 臨時的

92

What kind of work needs to be done?
(A) Electrical maintenance
(B) Computer system upgrades
(C) Software installation
(D) Floor cleaning

哪種工作需要被完成？
(A) 電力維修
(B) 電腦系統升級
(C) 軟體安裝
(D) 地板清潔

本題詢問需要完成的事情。透過「This means that the electricity on that floor will have to be turned off for a few hours tomorrow while technicians try to solve this problem」可以知道，因為公司上週發生斷電狀況，明天將會暫時斷電以進行修復電源的工程。所以正確答案為 (A)。

When will the work begin?
(A) Tonight
(B) Tomorrow
(C) This weekend
(D) Next week

工程何時開始？
(A) 今晚
(B) 明天
(C) 本週末
(D) 下週

由「This means that the electricity on that floor will have to be turned off for a few hours tomorrow」可見，明天將進行電力維修。正確答案為 (B)。

What are some listeners asked to do?
(A) Hire the technicians
(B) Use personal electronics
(C) Attend the meeting in the conference room
(D) Remove important documents from the computer

部分聽眾被要求做什麼事？
(A) 僱用技術人員
(B) 使用個人的電子設備
(C) 參加會議室的會議
(D) 移除電腦重要文件

本題詢問聽話者被要求做什麼事，請務必仔細聆聽說話者在中後半段提出要求的內容。在「Please use your laptop computer to work on」中，聽者被要求使用個人筆記型電腦辦公，故可知答案為 (B)。請特別注意此處出現的「please」。 在說話者下達指示時，「please」是慎重提出請託的用法，所以後面接續的部分很有可能是正確答案。

95-97 recorded message and order form

95–97 留言錄音及訂購表

Hello, this message is for Tim Falcon. I'm calling about the weekly order you just asked for, because I found you ordered a different one from what you usually do. I think you're still using the FX-Q1700, right? The one you've ordered doesn't work with the grayscale printer in your office. That's for the FX-Q2200C, which can print colored copies of various sizes. So I wonder whether I should change the item code to match your usual order. If you have a new printer now and this is what you want, please call me by the

哈囉，這是給提姆・孚爾肯的留言。我打來是有關您剛提出的週訂單，因為我發現您訂購了不同於以往的商品。我想您應該仍在使用FX-Q1700，是嗎？您剛訂購的商品並不適用貴公司的灰階印表機。那是給FX-Q2200C使用的，它可列印各種尺寸的彩色影印文件。因此，我在想是否該將商品編號更改成您平常訂購的產品。如果您們已經買了新的印表機，而這型號就是您們想要的產品，請

end of the day. We close at 9:30. Thank you for your business with us.

在下班前來電。我們於9:30打烊。感謝您的惠顧。

·················· **Order Form** ··················

Item	Item code	Quantity
Ink cartridge	FC505	1
Colored pencils, Set (12 colors)	PW74	3
Stapler	HK250	2
Paper cups	DC303	150

·················· **訂購單** ··················

品項	商品編號	數量
墨水匣	FC505	1
彩色鉛筆/組 (12色)	PW74	3
釘書機	HK250	2
紙杯	DC303	150

• **grayscale** 灰階　**match** 符合；相配

 95 [NEW] --

Look at the graphic. Which item does the speaker want to be checked?
(A) FC505
(B) PW74
(C) HK250
(D) DC303

看一下圖表，說話者想確認哪一項商品？
(A) FC505
(B) PW74
(C) HK250
(D) DC303

在「The one you've ordered doesn't work with the grayscale printer in your office. That's for the FX-Q2200C, which can print colored copies of various sizes.」中，表示聽者（提姆·孚爾肯）訂購的商品不適合灰階印表機，故說話者建議使用在彩色印表機。對話中不停提到印表機，而對照訂購單，最相關的品項應為墨水匣，所以正確答案為 (A)。

 96 --

What is suggested about Tim Falcon?
(A) He has ordered from this store before.
(B) He has a new printer in his office.
(C) He works for a printing company.
(D) He works until 9:30.

關於提姆·孚爾肯，提到了什麼事？
(A) 他之前跟這家商店訂過東西。
(B) 他的辦公室有了新印表機。
(C) 他在印刷公司工作。
(D) 他上班到9:30。

提姆·孚爾肯為這則語音訊息的收件人。說話者說：「I found you ordered a different one from what you usually do.」，由此可知，此人曾在商店訂購相似物品。所以正確答案為 (A)。

(B) 題目中，說話者想要確認聽者是否購入新的印表機，因此訂購不同的墨水匣，代表說話者還無法確定聽者是否有了新印表機。(C) 雖然文章提到辦公室有印表機，但不代表公司是一間印刷公司。(D) 九點半為此商店的打烊時間。

Why would Tim Falcon call back?	提姆・孚爾肯為什麼要回電？
(A) To check the working hours	(A) 要確認上班時間
(B) To order more stationery	(B) 要訂更多文具
(C) To receive a new printer	(C) 要收到一台新的印表機
(D) To confirm an item code	(D) 要確認商品編號

説話者説：「If you have a new printer now and this is what you want, please call me by the end of the day.」要求聽者若已購入新印表機，務必來電告知，代表需要聽者來電確認訂單上編號 FX-Q2200C 的彩色印表機用墨水匣是否正確。正確答案為 (D)。

請留意，(C) 選項中雖然也出現「new printer」，但是前面出現「to receive」，所以整句話的意思是「收到新印表機」，故並不正確。(B) 將各種訂購物品改寫為「stationery」，但從題目內容中，無法得知聽者是否要額外訂購其他物品，所以 (B) 非正確答案。當選項中提及無法確定的推測，請將其視為錯誤答案。

98-100 talk and graph
98–100 談話及圖表

Good morning. I'd like to commence our quarterly sales meeting by reviewing our progress in expanding new customers here at Elena beauty hair salon. As you know, March was the most successful month. We can probably attribute this to promoting big discounts for the 15th anniversary celebration. You can also see that the second highest increase in new customers occurred during our free dyeing event. So, generally, this quarter was successful. Now, we have to prepare for next quarter to continue this trend. We're planning to make our Web site more user-friendly. Therefore, many customers can get more useful information like looking at the variety of hair styles. I think it is critical for sustaining and increasing our business success.	早安，季業務會議一開始，我想來檢視本公司伊蓮娜美髮沙龍擴展新顧客的進度。正如大家所知，三月是最成功的一個月。我們或許可將其歸功於15週年慶的促銷優惠折扣。大家也可以看到，新顧客增加的第二高峰出現在我們免費染髮活動期間。因此，整體來說，這一季非常地成功。為了延續這股趨勢，我們現在必須為下一季做好準備。我們正規劃讓公司網頁更容易使用。這樣許多顧客就可以獲得更多有用的資訊，像是瀏覽各種髮型。我認為這對維持並提升本公司事業成就非常重要。

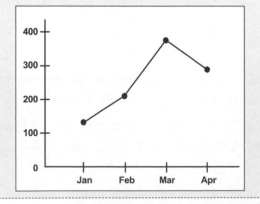
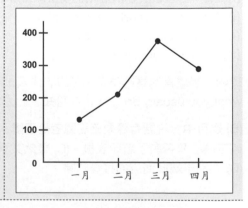

• **commence** 開始　**progress** 進度　**expand** 擴展　**attribute . . . to . . .** 將……歸功於……
promote 促銷　**occur** 出現　**user-friendly** 容易使用的

98 ---

Where most likely does the speaker work?

(A) At an advertising agency
(B) At a beauty parlor
(C) At a cosmetics store
(D) At a supermarket

說話者最可能在哪裡工作？

(A) 廣告公司
(B) 美容院
(C) 化妝品店
(D) 超市

說話者的工作場所通常出現在文章的前半部。由「here at Elena beauty hair salon」可見，正確答案為 (B)。

99 (NEW) ---

Look at the graphic. When was the discount event held?

(A) In January
(B) In February
(C) In March
(D) In April

看一下圖表，折扣活動於何時舉行？

(A) 一月
(B) 二月
(C) 三月
(D) 四月

請閱讀視覺資料解題。可先依序找出顧客最多及最少的月份，即為三月與一月，然後仔細聆聽當月發生了什麼事件以進行判斷。藉由「March was the most successful month. We can probably attribute this to promoting big discounts for the 15th anniversary celebration.」可以得知，三月顧客最多的原因是 15 週年的促銷折扣活動，故正確答案為 (C)。

100 ---

What does the business plan to do next quarter?

(A) Offer a free dyeing event
(B) Open a new branch
(C) Use eco-friendly items
(D) Upgrade a Web site

這家商家下一季打算做什麼？

(A) 提供免費染髮活動
(B) 開設新分店
(C) 使用環保產品
(D) 升級網站

藉由「we have to prepare for next quarter to continue this trend. We're planning to make our website more user-friendly.」可以得知，店家為持續吸引客戶來店，將更新官網使其更容易使用，故正確答案為 (D)。

ACTUAL TEST
7

1

(A) The woman is wearing a scarf.
(B) The woman is pushing a button on a keypad.
(C) The woman is handing over a credit card.
(D) The woman is arranging items on the shelf.

(A) 這位女士繫著圍巾。
(B) 這位女士正在按鍵盤上的按鍵。
(C) 這位女士正遞出信用卡。
(D) 這位女士正在整理架上的東西。

• **arrange** 安排；整理

照片中的地點看起來是服飾店，櫃檯上放著一個可能是男子要購買的物品，且女店員正要把信用卡交給男客人。請注意，如果敘述中出現意思為「購物、買東西」的「make a purchase」，則照片中一定要能看得出具體的購物行為，如客人交出現金或信用卡等動作。(A) 因為女子並未配戴圍巾，所以不是正確答案。(B) 女子並未按任何按鍵。(D) 女子沒有在整理架上物品。正確答案為 (C)。

2

(A) The people are dining at an outdoor patio.
(B) A dish is being passed at a table.
(C) Water is being poured into a glass.
(D) Some plates are stacked in a pile.

(A) 人們正在戶外露臺上用餐。
(B) 一道菜正在桌上傳遞。
(C) 水正被倒進玻璃杯裡。
(D) 盤子堆成一疊。

• **dine** 用餐 **outdoor** 戶外 **pass** 傳遞 **pour** 傾倒（液體） **stack** 堆疊 **pile** 疊

照片中的地點看起來是餐廳，人們圍著桌子而坐正在用餐。桌上放滿食物，且照片最前方的一名女子正將一排食物傳遞給孩子，故 (B) 為正確答案。

(A) 的場所描述錯誤。(C) 因為動詞描述有誤而不是正確答案。(D) 則是細節描寫錯誤。

3

(A) A staircase leads to the kitchen.
(B) There are some flowerpots hanging from the ceiling.
(C) A carpet has been rolled up on the floor.
(D) The sofas are unoccupied.

(A) 階梯通往廚房。
(B) 天花板上垂掛著一些花盆。
(C) 地毯被捲起放在地板上。
(D) 沙發沒有人坐。

• **staircase** 階梯 **lead to** … 通往…… **flowerpot** 花盆 **ceiling** 天花板 **roll up** 捲起
unoccupied 沒有人坐的

照片中的地點看起來是客廳，空間中擺放著沙發和桌子，左邊出現一只花瓶，右邊則可看見通往樓上的階梯，照片中並未出現人物，所以「沙發沒有人坐」為合適描述，正確答案為 (D)。此選項中的「unoccupied」還可以改寫為「not taken」或「not in use (at the moment)」等。

4 --

(A) The man is reading the label on an item.
(B) A cart is being wheeled along the aisle.
(C) Some merchandise is being loaded onto a cart.
(D) The man is carrying a can of food to the cashier.

(A) 這位男士正在閱讀物品上的標籤。
(B) 一台推車正被沿著走道推動。
(C) 一些商品正被放到推車上。
(D) 這位男士正拿著一罐食物到收銀台。

• label 標籤　cart 推車　wheel 推動（輪椅、推車等）　merchandise 商品

照片中貨架上放滿商品，看起來是在超市。有名男子一手握著推車把手，另一隻手拿著罐頭食品並讀著上面的標籤內容。(B) 照片中的推車是靜止狀態。(C) 男子並未將食物放上推車。 (D) 男子並未走向收銀台。正確答案為 (A)。

5 --

(A) The man is looking out of the window.
(B) The man is turning on the answering machine.
(C) The man is cleaning the monitor of a laptop.
(D) The man is doing some work at a desk.

(A) 這位男士正看著窗外。
(B) 這位男士正打開答錄機。
(C) 這位男士正在清潔筆記型電腦的螢幕。
(D) 這位男士正在書桌前工作。

🎧 25

• look out of . . . 朝……的外面看　answering machine 答錄機

照片中的有名男子在辦公桌前，面對電腦辦公。(A) 男子並未看著窗外。請注意，不要因為出現「window」就聯想到電腦。(B) 請注意不要聽到「machine」就聯想到電腦，此選項指的機器是答錄機。(C) 照片中的物品並不是筆記型電腦，且表示男子正在清理的動詞描述也不正確。本題正確答案為 (D)。

6 --

(A) None of the tables are vacant.
(B) The tables are covered with tablecloths.
(C) A boat is unloading passengers at the dock.
(D) The restaurant is crowded with dining guests.

(A) 沒有空桌。
(B) 桌子都鋪上了桌巾。
(C) 一艘船正在碼頭邊讓乘客下船。
(D) 餐廳擠滿了用餐的客人。

• vacant 空著的　be covered with . . . 被鋪上……　table cloth 桌巾　unload 卸下　dock 碼頭　be crowded with . . . 擠滿了……　dining guest 用餐的客人

照片中出現幾張餐桌與椅子，桌上都鋪上了桌巾，但是沒有出現人物。背景是大海，遠處可以看見一艘船。(A) 位子並未被人坐滿。(C) 描述的是照片中未出現的場景。船航行在大海中央，並未看見乘客正在下船的狀況。(D) 則因為提及照片中未出現的人物，所以非正確答案。本題正確答案為 (B)。

7 --

Do we have any extra copies of this document?　　我們有這份文件的額外影本嗎？
(A) You can place it on my desk.　　(A) 你可以把它放在我桌上。
(B) Sure, we do.　　(B) 當然，我們有。
(C) Please submit it in duplicate.　　(C) 請繳交副本。

• **extra** 額外的　**place** 放置　**submit** 繳交　**duplicate** 副本；複製品

本題詢問是否有資料的影本。(A) 不符合題目的情境。(B) 直接回答有，為合適答案。(C) 為利用題目「copies」的同義詞「duplicate」製造陷阱。本題正確答案為 (B)。請記住「submit sth in duplicate」的意思是「交出某物（文件）的副本」。

8 --

Who made the restaurant reservation?　　誰預約了餐廳？
(A) At the entrance.　　(A) 在入口。
(B) They served seafood dishes.　　(B) 他們提供海鮮餐點。
(C) Mr. Smith was supposed to.　　(C) 應該是史密斯先生。

• **reservation** 預約　**entrance** 入口　**be supposed to (V)** 應該（做某事）

本題為「Who」疑問句，所以提及「人物姓名」的為合適答案。(A) 是適合「Where」疑問句的回答。(B) 是利用與題目的「restaurant」相關之食物名稱（seafood dishes）設下陷阱。(C) 直接指出人名，故正確答案為 (C)。

9 --

What is the problem with the storage?　　庫存有什麼問題嗎？
(A) Yes, cups and plates.　　(A) 是的，杯子和盤子。
(B) We're out of stock.　　(B) 我們沒有庫存了。
(C) They haven't decided when.　　(C) 他們還沒有決定時間。

• **problem with . . .** 在……方面有問題　**storage** 庫存　**out of stock** 缺貨；沒有庫存

本題是「What」疑問句。(A) 使用與題目的「storage」相關的兩件物品製造陷阱，內容與題目無關。(B) 明確回答沒有庫存，為合適答案。(C) 回答與題目無關。故本題正確答案為 (B)。

10 --

When should we take a lunch break?　　我們什麼時候午休？
(A) At the new restaurant across the street.　　(A) 在對街的新餐廳。
(B) It's a quarter to one now.　　(B) 現在是12點45分。
(C) After we finish printing all these documents.　　(C) 在我們印好這些文件後。

• **break** 休息時間　**across the street** 對街　**a quarter** 十五分鐘

本題是詢問時間的「When」疑問句。(A) 較適合作為「Where」疑問句的回答。(B) 只回答現在時間，但內容與題目無關。(C) 雖未回答明確時間點，但明白表示午休會在文件印好後開始，故正確答案為 (C)。

11 --

You'll find an express bus terminal down the street.
(A) To use a faster delivery service.
(B) Regular mail is less expensive.
(C) How far is it to the terminal?

你會在這條街上看到快捷公車總站。
(A) 用更快的貨運服務。
(B) 一般郵件比較便宜。
(C) 到總站的距離有多遠？

• **express bus terminal** 快捷公車總站　**regular mail** 一般郵件

本題為描述路面資訊的陳述句。(A) 為利用題目中「express」意義相關的「faster delivery service」設下陷阱，並不是合適回覆。(B) 也是利用可由「express」聯想之「regular mail」誘導。(C) 反問抵達總站需要多少時間，藉此要求額外資訊，為最適回覆，故本題正確答案為 (C)。

12 --

Where are the clients from China staying?
(A) They'll be here tomorrow evening.
(B) They made a speech in Chinese.
(C) At the hotel near the company headquarters.

從中國來的客戶要住哪裡？
(A) 他們明天晚上會到這裡。
(B) 他們用中文進行演講。
(C) 在公司總部附近的飯店。

• **make a speech** 進行演講　**headquarters** 總部

本題為詢問地點的「Where」疑問句。(A) 只回答時間，作為「When」疑問句的回答較為恰當。(B) 為利用題目中「China」相關的「Chinese」誘導，實際內容完全無關。(C) 明確回答出地點，故本題正確答案為 (C)。

13 --

How many tables should we set for the banquet?
(A) I'm not sure how many will come.
(B) Forty extra chairs.
(C) There aren't any furniture stores open today.

宴會需要擺放幾張桌子？
(A) 我不確定有多少人會來。
(B) 多了40張椅子。
(C) 今天家具行都沒有營業。

• **banquet** 宴會

本題是詢問數量的「How many」疑問句。(A) 雖然沒有直接回答數量，但告知對方自己不知道參加者人數，即暗示了不知道要放幾張桌子，故為合適答案。(B) 雖然提及數字，但是題目並沒有詢問椅子的數量。(C) 是用和題目中「tables」相關的「furniture」設下陷阱。本題正確答案為 (A)。

14 --

Why did they reschedule the regular meeting?
(A) No meeting rooms are available.
(B) On the company Web site.
(C) Sometime next week.

他們為什麼要重新安排例會？
(A) 沒有會議室可以用。
(B) 在公司網站上。
(C) 下個禮拜某個時間。

• **reschedule** 重新安排　**regular meeting** 例行會議　**available** 可使用的

本題為詢問更改原因的「Why」疑問句。(A) 雖沒使用「Because」，但是告知無可用場地，此為合適回覆。(B) 內容與題目不符。(C) 則利用與題目「reschedule」意義相關的「next week」誘導。本題正確答案為 (A)。

15 --

Which smartphone would you like to buy?　　你想要買哪一隻智慧型手機？
(A) Maybe tomorrow.　　　　　　　　　　(A) 或許明天。
(B) I haven't decided yet.　　　　　　　　(B) 我還沒決定。
(C) He called me to order a blue one.　　　(C) 他打電話給我訂了藍色的。

本題使用「Which」疑問句，詢問要購買哪一支手機。(A) 僅告知時間，與題目不符。(B) 表示還沒決定，此為合適回覆。(C) 為利用與題目中「buy」意義相關的「order」設下陷阱。且此選項提及毫不相關的第三者（He），也與題目詢問的（you）不符。故本題正確答案為 (B)。

16 --

The Vegans' Delight has various vegetarian　　素食樂有各種素食餐點。
dishes.　　　　　　　　　　　　　　　(A) 我的一些同事。
(A) Some of my coworkers.　　　　　　　(B) 價格不貴嗎？
(B) Isn't it expensive?　　　　　　　　　(C) 水果旁邊可以看到蔬菜。
(C) Vegetables can be found next to the fruits.

• **vegetarian** 素食者　**coworker** 同事

本題為描述餐廳提供素食餐點的陳述句。(A) 回答與題目毫無關聯。(B) 反問餐點價格，為合適回覆。(C) 較適合「Where」疑問句，如果誤解題目是在詢問蔬菜擺放位置，可能會誤選。正確答案為 (B)。

17 --

She runs a drugstore in our building, doesn't　　她在本大樓經營藥局，不是嗎？
she?　　　　　　　　　　　　　　　　(A) 是的，她感冒了。
(A) Yes, she caught a cold.　　　　　　　(B) 是的，他們快要沒貨了。
(B) Yes, they're running out of stock.　　　(C) 是的，在二樓。
(C) Yes, on the second floor.

• **drugstore** 藥局　**catch a cold** 感冒

本題為附加問句。(A) 為利用與題目中「drugstore」相關的「cold」設下陷阱。(B) 題目中的「run」是「經營」之意，而選項中的「running out of」為「沒有……了」的意思。(C) 回答「Yes」並告知店面在大樓的二樓，故正確答案為 (C)。

18 --

Can you tell me how I can install this program?　　你可以告訴我要如何安裝這個程式嗎？
(A) The entire program ends at 4:00 P.M.　　(A) 整個節目會在下午四點結束。
(B) From the IT department.　　　　　　(B) 從資訊科技部門。
(C) I can help you after lunch.　　　　　(C) 我午餐後可以幫你。

• **install** 安裝　**entire** 整個的　**IT department** 資訊科技部門（**IT**=information technology）

本題為間接問句，詢問可否告知程式安裝方法，(C) 告知可在午餐後提供協助，故正確答案為 (C)。(A) 為使用題目出現字彙「program」的陷阱。而 (B) 利用可從「install this program」聯想的「IT department」誘導，且介系詞「from」的使用與題目不符。此選項較適合作為「Where」疑問句的回答。

19

Will you sign up for the session online or at the site?
(A) The session is currently offline.
(B) Probably in person.
(C) The same lecturer as last month.

你要在線上登記研習還是到現場登記？
(A) 研習目前是離線狀態。
(B) 可能會親自去。
(C) 和上個月同一位講師。

• **sign up** 登記　　**at the site** 現場

本題為選擇問句，詢問對方要在線上登記還是現場申請。(A) 再次出現「session」並用與題目中「online」意義相關的「offline」設下陷阱，回答與內容並不相符。(B) 把題目中的「at the site」改為「in person」，告知會親自去申請，為合適回覆。(C) 利用與題目「session」相關的「lecturer」製造混淆。本題正確答案為 (B)。

20

What is the purpose of the seminar next week?
(A) Yes, it's postponed to the following week.
(B) I didn't do it on purpose.
(C) To discuss the new service.

下週專題討論會的目的是什麼？
(A) 是的，被延到隔週了。
(B) 我不是故意的。
(C) 要討論新的服務。

• **purpose** 目的　　**on purpose** 故意地

本題為詢問下週研討會目的的「What」疑問句，所以利用不定詞（to V）表目的，告知是「為了討論新服務」的 (C) 為正確答案。

(A) 重複使用「week」，並告知行程已改變，但是本題詢問的是研討會的目的，故為與題目無關的選項。(B) 雖然反覆使用「purpose」，但是此選項中為「on purpose（故意）」之意。

21

Is there a stationery store nearby?
(A) You just missed Martin Station.
(B) There's one across the street.
(C) It's stationary and not removable.

這附近有文具行嗎？
(A) 你剛剛錯過了馬汀站。
(B) 對街有一間。
(C) 它是固定的且無法移動。

• **stationery store** 文具店　　**stationary** 固定的　　**removable** 可移動的

本題為 Be 動詞疑問句，詢問附近是否有文具店。(A) 為利用與題目「stationery」發音相似的「station」製造陷阱，且內容與題目無關。(B) 明確告知對方馬路對面有一家，故本題正確答案為 (B)。

(C) 使用與題目「stationery」發音相似的「stationary」製造混淆，其實可由後面出現的「and not removable」知道，此處的「stationary」並不是指文具店，且應為一形容詞，故非正確答案。

22

Some parts of this machine seem to be defective.
(A) Can you tell me which parts should be replaced?
(B) As soon as the parts are repaired.
(C) Yes, I'm interested in some part-time work.

這台機器有些零件好像故障了。
(A) 你可以告訴我應更換哪些零件嗎？
(B) 一旦零件修好時。
(C) 是的，我對一些兼職工作有興趣。

• **defective** 有瑕疵的　　**replace** 更換　　**repair** 修理

本題為敘述機械零件有瑕疵的陳述句。 (A) 反問需要替換的零件為哪些，故正確答案為 (A)。

(B) 雖然重複出現「parts」與相關字彙「repaired」，但是「As soon as」為表示時間點的片語，所以此選項較適合作為「When」疑問句的答案。(C) 是利用與題目中「parts」發音相似的「part-time」設下陷阱，非正確答案。

23 --

Can I help with anything?
(A) It is quite helpful.
(B) There wasn't anyone but me.
(C) No, not at the moment.

有什麼我可以幫忙的嗎？
(A) 這相當有幫助。
(B) 這裡除了我沒有別人了。
(C) 沒關係，現在不用。

• **at the moment** 現在

本題詢問是否有可以幫忙的地方， (A) 為利用與題目中「help」發音相似的「helpful」形成陷阱，內容與題目不符。(B) 同為利用與題目中「anything」發音相似的「anyone」誤導。(C) 表示目前沒有需要幫忙之處，為最適回覆，故本題正確答案為 (C)。

24 --

Don't you have to talk to your manager?
(A) You don't have any.
(B) So you managed it after all.
(C) I was just about to call her.

你不用跟你的主管說嗎？
(A) 你什麼都沒有。
(B) 所以你最後還是設法做到了。
(C) 我才剛要打電話給她。

• **manage** 設法做到　**after all** 最後　**be about to** 剛要

本題為否定疑問句。(A) 只是將題目「Don't you have . . .」重新排列為「You don't have . . .」當作回答，但內容與題目並不符合。(B) 為利用與題目中的「manager」發音相似的「managed」誤導。(C) 將題目的「talk」改成「call」，表示正要撥打電話告知主管，故正確答案為 (C)。

25 --

Would you like to try it yourself now, or do you need more practice?
(A) I was just talking to myself.
(B) I think I'm ready now.
(C) How'd you like to put it into practice?

你想要現在自己試看看，還是要多練習一下？
(A) 我剛剛只是在自言自語。
(B) 我想我現在已經準備好了。
(C) 你想要怎麼執行？

• **put sth into practice** 執行某事

本題用問句確認對方想要嘗試，或要再練習。(B) 告知自己已經準備好，暗示可以試試看，故本題正確答案為 (B)。

題目中的「yourself」雖可以聯想到 (A) 中的「myself」，但是內容與題目不符，所以 (A) 不是正確答案。 (C) 雖然重複題目中的「practice」，但是題目中的意思是「練習」，而這裡的「put sth into practice」的意思是「執行某事」。

26 --

Who should I forward the e-mail to?
(A) The assistant manager.
(B) Via express mail.
(C) Copy it on both sides.

我該把這封電子郵件轉寄給誰？
(A) 副理。
(B) 透過快捷郵件。
(C) 雙面影印。

• **forward** 轉寄　**via . . .** 透過……　**both sides** 雙面

本題是詢問要將電子郵件轉寄給誰的「Who」問句，(A) 直接以明確對象回答，故正確答案為 (A)。(B) 電子郵件（e-mail）與快捷郵件（express mail）為完全不同的東西。(C) 提到影印資料，與題目毫無相關。

27 --

Has Mr. Douglas left for his vacation?
(A) There are leftovers in the bin.
(B) It lasted three days.
(C) Yes, and he'll be back next Tuesday.

道格拉斯先生去度假了嗎？
(A) 桶子裡有剩菜。
(B) 持續三天。
(C) 是的，他下星期二會回來。

• **leftovers** 剩菜　**last** 持續

本題詢問道格拉斯先生是否去度假了，(C) 回答「Yes」，並另外告知他回來的時間，故正確答案為 (C)。(A) 是利用與題目中「left」發音相似的「leftovers」形成的陷阱。另外，聽到「vacation」可能誤會題目詢問的是假期長短，但是題目詢問的是「去度假了嗎」，且選項 (B) 使用過去式表達已經過去的三天，所以不可能是正確答案。

28 --

When can I see the final draft of the article?
(A) Wednesday evening, at the latest.
(B) It's about the U. S. government announcement.
(C) That'll be interesting.

我何時可以看到這篇文章的最終稿？
(A) 最慢星期三晚上。
(B) 是關於美國政府的公告。
(C) 那會很有趣。

• **final draft** 最終稿　**at the latest** 最慢　**government announcement** 政府公告

本題是詢問時間的「When」疑問句，(A) 用具體時間點回答，故本題正確答案為 (A)。

(B) 利用與題目中的「draft」與「article」相關的「announcement」試圖造成混淆。另外，題目的情境為檢視原稿，雖然有可能像 (C) 一樣說出「很有趣」的評價，但是本題詢問的是「何時」，所以選項 (C) 也與題目主旨不符。

29 --

We know each other, don't we?
(A) They're standing next to each other.
(B) I was going to meet you, too.
(C) No, I don't think so.

我們見過，不是嗎？
(A) 他們比鄰站著。
(B) 我也正要去找你。
(C) 不，我不這麼認為。

本題為附加問句，詢問是否見過，(C) 表示不認為見過對方，故正確答案為 (C)。

題目中的主詞「We」是結合問話者與回答者的表現方式，與選項 (A) 提及的複數第三者「They」完全無關，該選項重複「each other」也僅為誤導。(B) 選項表示「我『也』正要去找你」，但題目並未表示要相見，故此非正確答案。

---

30 --

Where is Ms. Moore's new apartment?
(A) In two weeks.
(B) Apart from her.
(C) It's in Hillsville.

摩爾女士的新公寓在哪裡？
(A) 在兩週內。
(B) 除了她以外。
(C) 在希爾斯維爾。

• **apart from . . .** 除了……以外

本題為「Where」疑問句，詢問某人的公寓地點。在聽到「new apartment」時，可能會誤以為題目問的是「何時」要搬去新家，而誤選 (A) 做為解答。不過，此選項較適合做為「When」疑問句的回答。(B) 則是利用與題目中「apartment」發音相似的「apart」設下陷阱。(C) 表示明確地點，故本題正確答案為 (C)。

---

31 --

Wasn't Patricia supposed to visit the factory in Michigan?
(A) I often go to Tokyo.
(B) I heard her flight was canceled.
(C) It is one of the most populous cities in Canada.

派翠西亞不是應該去參觀密西根的工廠嗎？
(A) 我常去東京。
(B) 我聽說她的班機取消了。
(C) 是加拿大人口最稠密的城市之一。

• **be supposed to V** 應該要（做某事）　　**populous** 人口稠密的

本題為否定問句。(A) 提及的場所與題目完全不同，且題目的主詞為「Patricia」，與此處的「I」不符。(B) 告知航班取消造成女子無法前往，故為合適答案。(C) 密西根州位於美國而非加拿大，且此與題目完全無關。本題正確答案為 (B)。

PART 3 🎧 27

32-34 conversation

M	Hello, I'm calling to check if there are any tickets available for the concert.
W	There are several concerts scheduled this month. Do you know the names of the performers or the exact date?
M	I don't remember the names. It's a jazz concert on a Friday evening.
W	The "Oldies but Goodies" jazz concert is on Friday, October 17th. We have a few seats available at the stage level, which are 115 dollars each, and in the balcony in the back they are 90 dollars each.
M	Oh, that's nice. Thank you, and I will call right back after consulting with my friends about the seats.

32-34 對話

男　嗨，我打這通電話是想看看音樂會是否還有票。
女　這個月安排了幾場音樂會。你知道表演者的姓名或是確切日期嗎？
男　我不記得名字了。是星期五晚上的爵士音樂會。
女　《經典雋永》爵士音樂會是在10月17日星期五。我們還有幾張舞台區座位的票，一張115元，以及後方包廂的位子，票價是一張90元。
男　喔，那太好了。謝謝妳，我和朋友討論一下座位後再打電話過來。

● **available** 可取得的　**concert** 音樂會　**performer** 表演者　**exact** 確切的　**jazz** 爵士樂　**balcony** 包廂

🎧 26
🎧 27

32 --

Where most likely does the woman work?
(A) At a library
(B) At a stadium
(C) At a performance hall
(D) At a music shop

這位女士最有可能在哪裡工作？
(A) 圖書館
(B) 體育館
(C) 表演廳
(D) 唱片行

詢問場所的題目，通常是需要從該場所相關的字彙或片語推論出答案。男子詢問「if there are any tickets available for the concert」，而女子回覆「We have a few seats available at the stage level, which are 115 dollars each, and in the balcony in the back they are 90 dollars each.」告知舞台層與包廂的座位價格，故正確答案為 (C)。

33 --

What is the purpose of the man's call?
(A) To ask for a refund
(B) To cancel a reservation
(C) To sign up for a class
(D) To inquire about tickets

這位男士打電話來的目的是什麼？
(A) 要求退費
(B) 取消預約
(C) 登記課程
(D) 詢問票券

對話一開始，男子告知自己是為了確認是否還有門票而撥打這通電話（I'm calling to check if there are any tickets available for the concert.）直接說出了致電目的，由此可知正確答案為 (D)。

What will the man probably do next?
(A) Verify a seating chart
(B) Check his calendar
(C) Talk with his friends
(D) Buy tickets online

這位男士接下來要做什麼？
(A) 核對座位表
(B) 查看他的行事曆
(C) 和他的朋友討論
(D) 線上購票

男子最後表示「I will call right back after consulting with my friends」，告知女子會和朋友商議過後再決定。選項 (C) 改用意義相近的「talk with his friends」，故正確答案為 (C)。

35-37 conversation

35–37 對話

W It is a pleasure to meet you, Mr. Anderson. As I let you know last time, our radio channel is running an advertising campaign for local businesses. We would like to feature your company on Monday.	女 很開心見到您，安德森先生。如同上次告訴您的，我們的廣播頻道正在為在地企業進行廣告活動。我們想在星期一特別介紹貴公司。
M Thank you for the opportunity, Ms. Taylor. What should we start with?	男 感謝您提供這個機會，泰勒女士。我們要從哪裡開始呢？
W Hmm . . . Would you please summarize the concept behind your business, Good Hands?	女 嗯……可以請您大略說明一下貴公司——好幫手的概念嗎？
M Good Hands started as a home appliance repair shop 7 years ago. Now we mainly service on-site repairs and also cover office supplies and equipment.	男 好幫手七年前是以家電用品維修店起家。現在主要服務項目是到府維修，也提供辦公用品及設備的維修服務。
W What makes your company different from other similar ones?	女 貴公司與其他相似店家有何不同之處？
M As you know, our competitors hesitate to employ experienced engineers due to the high cost. Instead of a better staff, they tend to rely on newer equipment. But at Good Hands, we believe that skilled manpower is most important in this field.	男 如您所知，由於成本高的關係，競爭同業不願聘用經驗豐富的工程師。他們傾向依賴新型設備，而非優良的員工。但是在好幫手，我們相信在這個領域，技巧熟練的人力才是最重要的。
W Sounds interesting. How do you strengthen the staff expertise?	女 聽起來很有趣。您如何強化員工的專業技能？
M We have a great staff training program similar to those at major companies. Many would argue that it is ineffective in small businesses, but we've been running our training system continually since we started the business.	男 我們擁有類似大公司的優良員工教育訓練計畫。許多人認為這對小型企業來說沒什麼效果，但是從公司創業開始，我們就持續地實施教育訓練制度。

• **pleasure** 榮幸 **feature** 以……為特色 **summarize** 大略說明 **home appliance** 家電用品 **on-site repair** 到府維修 **competitor** 競爭同業 **hesitate** 不願 **manpower** 人力 **expertise** 專業技能 **ineffective** 無效的 **continually** 持續地

35 --

Who most likely is the woman?
(A) A staff trainer in a local company
(B) A radio producer
(C) A maintenance engineer
(D) A TV reporter

這位女士最可能是誰？
(A) 在地企業的員工訓練人員
(B) 廣播製作人
(C) 維修工程師
(D) 電視記者

（右側標籤）ACTUAL TEST 7　PART 3　中譯＋解析

女子雖然未直接提及自己的職業，但是從「our radio channel is running an advertising campaign for local businesses.」這句話中，可以知道她從事的是廣播相關工作。所以，選項中最合適的是 (B)。

36 --

What items would probably be serviced by Good Hands?
(A) Toys
(B) Bicycles
(C) Photocopiers
(D) Vehicles

下列哪樣產品可能是好幫手的服務項目？
(A) 玩具
(B) 腳踏車
(C) 影印機
(D) 汽車

男子第二句話提到「Good Hands started as a home appliance repair shop 7 years ago. Now we mainly service on-site repairs and also cover office supplies and equipment.」，表示公司創業時是家電產品維修店，現在也提供辦公設備維修，故正確答案為 (C)。

37 --

According to the man, how does Good Hands differ from its competitors?
(A) It provides extended guarantees.
(B) It has a lot of state-of-the-art equipment.
(C) It provides faster on-site service than its competitors.
(D) It has very skilled employees.

根據這位男士所言，好幫手和競爭對手有什麼不同之處？
(A) 它提供延長保固。
(B) 它有許多最先進的設備。
(C) 它提供比其他競爭對手更快速的到府服務。
(D) 它擁有技巧非常熟練的員工。

男子說：「But at Good Hands, we believe that skilled manpower is most important in this field.」，由此可知，這家公司重視員工專業度，故正確答案為 (D)。

38-40 conversation

38-40 對話

W Hi, Eric. Can you do me a favor? Will you be in the office on Monday morning? I'm expecting a call from a supplier but I won't be in until after 2 P.M. due to my client meeting.	女 嗨，艾瑞克。你可以幫我一個忙嗎？星期一上午你會在辦公室嗎？我在等供應商的電話，但是因為客戶會議的關係，我要到下午兩點後才會回到辦公室。
M Yes, I will be in early on Monday. I have some data to enter onto the computer and was planning to start early. When are you expecting the call?	男 好的，星期一一早我就會進來了。我有些資料需要輸入到電腦裡，正打算早點開始做。對方大概何時會打來？

263

W They said between 9 and 10 A.M. I will reroute my calls to your phone and let them know that you will be answering. Many thanks, Eric.

女 他們說在上午九點到十點之間。我會將我的來電轉到你的電話去,也會讓他們知道你會接電話。十分感謝,艾瑞克。

• **do sb a favor** 幫某人一個忙　**expect a call** 等電話打來　**supplier** 供應商　**client** 客戶
reroute 轉接(電話)　**redirect** 轉接(電話)

38 --

What does the woman ask the man to do?　這位女士要求男士做什麼事?
(A) Accept a package　　　　　　　　　(A) 接收包裹
(B) Attend a morning meeting　　　　　(B) 出席晨會
(C) Take a phone call　　　　　　　　　(C) 接聽電話
(D) Enter some data　　　　　　　　　　(D) 輸入一些資料

一開始,女子向男子詢問「Will you be in the office on Monday morning? I'm expecting a call from a supplier but I won't be in until after 2P.M.」,表示自己週一下午兩點前不在辦公室,但上午有客戶將來電聯繫。由此可知,女子想要委託男子幫忙接聽電話,故正確答案為 (C)。

39 --

What information does the man request?　這位男士要求什麼資訊?
(A) A time　　　　　　　　　　　　　　　(A) 時間
(B) A contact number　　　　　　　　　(B) 聯絡電話號碼
(C) An address　　　　　　　　　　　　(C) 地址
(D) A price　　　　　　　　　　　　　　(D) 價格

男子說自己週一從早上開始都會待在辦公室,並詢問「When are you expecting the call?」,想知道客戶來電的時間,故正確答案為 (A)。

40 --

What does the woman say she will do?　這位女士說她會做什麼事?
(A) Postpone a meeting　　　　　　　　(A) 延後會議
(B) Redirect her phone　　　　　　　　(B) 將來電轉至其他電話
(C) Check her schedule　　　　　　　　(C) 確認她的行程表
(D) Cancel an appointment　　　　　　(D) 取消約會

本題詢問女子接下來將採取的行動。從女子最後說的「I will reroute my calls to your phone and let them know that you will be answering.」可知,她將告知其他同事,如果有人來電,可以轉接給男子代為接聽。選項 (B) 將題目中的將「reroute」改為意義相近的「redirect」,故正確答案為 (B)。

41-43 conversation

M Hello, this is Christopher Brown. I am renting a car while in Oregon for business purposes. But I just found a few scratches on the passenger's door. I hadn't noticed them when I first borrowed it yesterday. So I am worried about whether I might have to pay for the repairs.

W Well, don't worry, Mr. Brown. Our database shows you have insurance coverage, so it will reimburse the expense if needed.

M That's a relief. By the way, do I need to do anything special when I return the car tomorrow?

W There will be some papers for you to fill out at our office. So please give yourself extra time.

41–43 對話

男 嗨，我是克里斯多福・布朗。我在奧勒岡出差時租了一輛車，但是我剛剛發現後座的門上有幾道刮痕。我昨天剛租用時沒有注意到這些刮痕。我擔心自己是否得支付維修費用。

女 嗯，布朗先生，請不用擔心。我們的資料顯示這涵蓋在您的保險內，所以如果有需要的話，保險將賠償費用。

男 那我可以鬆一口氣了。對了，當我明天歸還車子的時候，需要特別做什麼嗎？

女 有一些文件需要您在辦公室填寫。所以，請預留一些額外的時間。

ACTUAL TEST 7 · PART **3** · 中譯＋解析

* rent 租用　business purpose 商業用途　scratch 刮痕　passenger's door 後座的門　insurance 保險　reimburse 賠償　That's a relief 鬆了一口氣　papers 文件　fill out 填寫　paperwork 文書工作

 27

41

What type of business does the woman most likely work for?
(A) A used car dealer
(B) A repair shop
(C) A car rental agency
(D) A paid parking lot

這位女士最有可能是在哪種行業工作？
(A) 二手車仲介商
(B) 維修站
(C) 汽車租賃公司
(D) 付費停車場

男子一開始表示自己租了一輛車（I am renting a car.），但因在車上發現了刮痕，他擔心自己需要賠償。女子則回答「Our database shows you have insurance coverage, so it will reimburse the expense if needed.」，表示男子有保險可以辦理理賠，由此可知，女子最可能在租車公司工作，故正確答案為 (C)。

42

What is the man concerned about?
(A) Being charged for a repair
(B) Doing some paperwork
(C) Attending an important meeting
(D) Driving to Oregon from his company

這位男士擔心什麼？
(A) 要被收取維修費用
(B) 做一些文書工作
(C) 出席一場重要會議
(D) 從公司開車到奧勒岡

一開始，男子說「I am worried about whether I might have to pay for the repairs.」，表示自己擔心要賠償修理費用，所以正確答案為 (A)。

43

For how long is the man renting the car? | 這位男士租車的天數為幾天？
(A) One day | (A) 一天
(B) Two days | (B) 兩天
(C) Three days | (C) 三天
(D) Four days | (D) 四天

從「I had't noticed them when I first borrowed it yesterday.」可知男子的租車日是昨天，再從「do I need to do anything special when I return the car tomorrow?」可知還車日是明天，故男子總共借了三天，正確答案為 (C)。

44-46 conversation | 44–46 對話

W	Hello, this is Donna Garcia at 16 Wilson Street. I'm calling to inform you that we will be moving out of the house on May 16. My husband has accepted a new job in Atlanta.	女 嗨，我是住在威爾森街16號的多娜‧賈西亞。我打這通電話是為了通知你我們將在5月16日搬家。我先生得到了在亞特蘭大的新工作。
M	That's great news, Ms. Garcia. However, it is stated in the rental agreement that we need to be informed at least 4 weeks before you vacate the house.	男 這是個好消息，賈西亞女士。但是，租賃協議上有註明，您需要在遷出房子至少四週前告知我們。
W	Yes, I'm aware of that. That means we are liable for the rent until the end of next month.	女 是的，我知道。這表示我們必須支付租金到下個月月底。
M	Exactly. And I'm hoping to get a new tenant very soon.	男 沒錯。我希望很快就可以找到新房客。
W	One of my friends is urgently looking for a house. Shall I call her and check if she can move in?	女 我有位朋友正急著找房子。我可以打電話給她，問問她是否可以搬進來嗎？
M	Yes, please. If she can move in without delay, I guess I can let you be exempted from the excess rent for the 15 days.	男 好的，麻煩您了。如果她可以立刻搬進來，我想我可以讓您免付那15天額外的租金。

• inform 通知 move out of . . . 搬出…… rental agreement 租賃協議 vacate 遷出
  be aware of . . . 知道…… be liable for . . . 對……有責任的 tenant 房客 urgently 急迫地
  be exempted from . . . 被免除…… excess 額外的

44

Why is the woman moving out? | 這位女士為什麼要搬走？
(A) Her rental agreement has expired. | (A) 她的租賃合約已經到期。
(B) She has found a less expensive house. | (B) 她找到一間較便宜的房子。
(C) Her husband decided to relocate. | (C) 她先生決定要轉換工作地點。
(D) She wants a bigger house. | (D) 她想要一間更大的房子。

女子說：「I'm calling to inform you that we will be moving out of the house on May 16. My husband has accepted a new job in Atlanta.」，表示因為丈夫在亞特蘭大找到新工作，他們將在五月十六日搬家，故本題正確答案為 (C)。

45

What does the woman offer to do?
(A) Move out as soon as possible
(B) Help look for a new tenant
(C) Contact a moving company
(D) Pay the rent fee for two months

這位女士提議做什麼？
(A) 盡快搬出
(B) 幫忙找新房客
(C) 聯絡搬家公司
(D) 支付兩個月的租金

男子說要找新房客，而女子說：「One of my friends is urgently looking for a house. Shall I call her and check if she can move in?」，表示自己可以問問朋友要不要搬進來，也就是幫房東找到新房客，故正確答案為 (B)。

46

According to the man, why would the woman be willing to help him?
(A) To find a new house in Atlanta
(B) To get a new job
(C) To save the excessive rental fee
(D) To renovate her house within 4 weeks

根據這位男士所言，這位女士為什麼願意幫他？
(A) 為了找到亞特蘭大的新房子
(B) 為了得到一份新工作
(C) 為了節省額外的租金
(D) 為了在四週內整修房屋

女子表示將在五月十六日搬走，但根據契約，女子必須負擔到五月三十一日的租金。男子後說：「I'm hoping to get a new tenant very soon.」，表示想找到新的房客，而女子提到自己有個朋友正在找房子。對此，男子回覆：「If she can move in without delay, I guess I can let you be exempted from the excess rent for the 15 days.」所以若那位朋友可以立刻搬進來，女子可以免付剩下十五天的租金，故正確答案為 (C)。

47-49 conversation with three speakers NEW

47–49 三人對話

W1 Many thanks for attending the interview, Edward. I'm Jennifer Davis, and this is Ruth Miller, the floor director.	**女1** 十分感謝你出席這次的面試，愛德華。我是珍妮佛・戴維斯，這位是樓層主管露絲・米勒。
M Nice to meet you, Ms. Davis, Ms. Miller. Thank you for the opportunity.	**男** 您們好，戴維斯女士、米勒女士。謝謝您們給我這次機會。
W1 As an assistant art director, you have worked for a number of companies. And some of them are very well known. However, I am a bit confused as to why you want to apply to our theater.	**女1** 你在數家公司擔任過助理藝術指導。其中一些還是非常著名的公司。但是，我有些不解你為何想要應徵本劇院。
W2 I feel the same as Ms. Davis. Do you understand this is not going to be the same as your previous work?	**女2** 我和戴維斯女士有相同的感受。你知道這和你之前的工作大不相同嗎？
M Yes, I do. I have been working as an assistant for many years. And now I feel it is time to move on. I'm eager to manage my own team and expand my area. I'm also very interested in your upcoming performances.	**男** 是的，我知道。我擔任助理多年。我覺得是該往前邁進的時候了。我急切地想要管理自己的團隊，擴展我的領域。我也對於貴團即將到來的演出十分感興趣。

W1 Very well then. This could be a good opportunity for you. But you'll be asked to do a lot of overtime work, since we are seriously understaffed.	女1 那很好。這對你來說是個好機會。但是因為我們人手嚴重不足,你將會經常被要求加班。
W2 In particular, you will be required to work on overnight shoots. Is that okay with you?	女2 特別是您會需要通宵拍攝。那樣可以嗎?
M I don't have an issue with that. I am ready to accept any out-of-hours assignments.	男 這一點我沒問題。我已經準備好接受任何需要用到下班時間完成的工作了。

• interview 面試　floor director 樓層主管　assistant art director 助理藝術指導　well known 著名的　confused 感到不解的　apply to . . . 應徵……　move on 往前邁進　be eager to V 急切想要　expand 擴展　overtime work 加班　understaffed 人手不足的　in particular 特別是　overnight shoots 通宵拍攝　out-of-hours 利用下班時間的　assignment 工作

What impressed the women about the man?　女士們對男士的什麼感到印象深刻?

(A) His appearance　　　　(A) 他的外表
(B) His managing skills　　(B) 他的管理技巧
(C) His previous career　　(C) 他之前的工作
(D) His upcoming performances　(D) 他即將到來的演出

戴維斯女士(女1)的第二句話說:「you have worked for a number of companies. And some of them are very well known. However, I am a bit confused as to why you want to work with us.」提及男子的經歷,並對男子想要應徵的動機感到不解。米勒女士(女2)也詢問男子:「Do you understand this is not going to be the same as your previous work?」可見面試官對男子先前的工作經歷印象深刻,並針對此事提出疑問,所以正確答案為 (C)。

According to the man, why did he apply to this company?　根據這位男士所言,他為什麼要應徵這家公司?

(A) He wants to earn more money.　(A) 他想要賺更多的錢。
(B) He is eager to try overnight shoots.　(B) 他渴望嘗試通宵拍攝。
(C) He wants to lead his own team.　(C) 他想帶領自己的團隊。
(D) He wants to work for a bigger company.　(D) 他想在更大的公司上班。

男子說:「I have been working as an assistant for many years. And now I feel it is time to move on. I'm eager to manage my own team and expand my area. I'm also very interested in your upcoming performances.」,由此可知,男子一直從事助理的工作,現在想要獨當一面,帶領自己的團隊,故正確答案為 (C)。

49 -

What does the new job require of the man?

(A) Excellent presentation skills

(B) Experience in health matters

(C) The willingness to work overtime

(D) Frequent overseas performances

新工作對於這位男士會有什麼要求？

(A) 絕佳的簡報技巧

(B) 健康事務方面的經驗

(C) 加班的意願

(D) 經常性的海外表演

能夠掌握對話中的關鍵字如：「overnight shoots」、「overtime work」、「out-of-hours assignments」等，應該就能選出本題答案。女子們說，因為員工人數不足，常常需要加班，想要確認男子是否可以接受，故本題正確答案為 (C)。

50-52 conversation

50–52 對話

W	Have you checked the new company Web site? The IT department has done a great job!	女	你看過公司的新網站了嗎？資訊科技部門做得真好！
M	Yes. It looks fantastic. They finally made the navigation even easier than ever. But when I clicked on the floor guide menu, it took me to a blank page. Did you face the same problem?	男	是的，看起來很棒。他們終於讓瀏覽網頁比以前更簡便了。但是當我點擊樓層導覽選單時，卻導向空白網頁。妳有碰到同樣的問題嗎？
W	No. I haven't had such problems. Did you try reloading the page? Press the F5 key and it'll be refreshed.	女	沒有，我沒碰到這類問題。你有試著重新整理網頁嗎？按F5鍵，它就會更新了。
M	(51)**It didn't work for me.** Maybe I'll send an e-mail to Jim.	男	(51)這對我來說沒用。或許我該寄一封電子郵件給吉姆。
W	Don't forget to attach a screenshot. They usually need that to fix the problem. I am sure they will reply with some positive solutions.	女	別忘了附上螢幕截圖。他們通常需要截圖來修復問題。我相信他們會提供有效的解決方法。

• navigation 瀏覽　blank page 空白網頁　reload 重新整理　attach 附上　positive 有效的
solution 解決方法

50 -

What does the man like about the updated Web site?

(A) The clear images

(B) The faster response time

(C) The easier usability

(D) The detailed floor guide

這位男士喜歡更新後的網站哪一點？

(A) 清晰的圖像

(B) 更快的反應時間

(C) 更簡便的操作

(D) 詳細的樓層導覽

女子詢問是否看過公司的新網站，而男子回答道：「They finally made the navigation even easier than ever.」，表示網頁變得更加方便瀏覽。由此可知，正確答案為 (C)。

What does the man imply when he says, "It didn't work for me"?

(A) He did not work yesterday.
(B) He already tried pressing the F5 key.
(C) He wants to consult with Jim.
(D) He had the same issue before the update.

當這位男士說:「這對我來說沒用」,是什麼意思?

(A) 他昨天沒有上班。
(B) 他已經試過按F5鍵了。
(C) 他想要請教吉姆。
(D) 他在更新前碰過一樣的狀況。

請掌握男子提及的「it」指稱的是何物。前一句台詞中,女子說:「Press the F5 key and it'll be refreshed.」,表示按下「F5」鍵即可解決問題。男子則表示這解決方法他試過了,但沒有效用,所以正確答案為 (B)。

52

What does the woman recommend?

(A) Installing some new software
(B) Checking for computer viruses
(C) Restarting his desktop computer
(D) Including an image with his report

這位女士建議什麼?

(A) 安裝一些新軟體
(B) 檢查電腦病毒
(C) 重新啟動電腦
(D) 在報告上附上圖像。

男子說會寄電子郵件給吉姆,女子則說:「Don't forget to attach a screenshot.」提醒男子要附上畫面截圖。選項 (D) 將「screenshot」改為「image」,意義仍與題目相符,故正確答案為 (D)。

53-55 conversation / 53–55 對話

M	Hello, this is Charles Harris from the Margaret Chicken Farm. We have recently hatched a large number of chickens, and I need them to be checked for any diseases, considering the latest outbreak of bird flu.	男	嗨,我是瑪格麗特養雞場的查理斯·哈里斯。我們最近孵出許多雞隻,考量到最近禽流感大爆發,所以需要檢查牠們是否有任何疾病。
W	Thank you for calling, Mr. Harris. Would you please tell me your management number?	女	感謝您的來電,哈里斯先生。可以請您告訴我您的管理編號嗎?
M	Um . . . We don't have a management number, as far as I can remember. I think this is the first time I've called you.	男	嗯……就我印象中,我們沒有管理編號。我想這是我第一次打電話給你們。
W	Oh, that's fine, Mr. Harris. Your wife called us several times last year, and we have your farm on our list. Let me check the schedule. Um . . . We're able to send our examiners to your farm either on Wednesday or Thursday this week to take blood samples from your chickens. Your farm is near the lake, right?	女	喔,沒關係,哈里斯先生。去年您太太打過幾次電話來,我們的名單上有您的農場名稱。讓我看看時程表。嗯……這個禮拜三或禮拜四,我們可以派檢驗人員到您的農場去抽取雞隻血液樣本。您的農場在湖邊,對嗎?
M	Yes, by Loufine Lake. Thursday sounds good. Can I inquire as to the cost, and also, is there any subsidy I can apply for?	男	是的,在羅凡湖旁邊。星期四沒問題。我可以詢問費用,還有是否有補助可以申請嗎?

| W | We cannot offer any subsidies directly, but the relevant government department may be able to help you. | 女 我們無法直接提供補助，但是相關政府部門或許可以協助您。 |

• chicken farm 養雞場　hatch 孵化　outbreak（疾病、危險等的）大爆發　bird flu 禽流感
subsidy 補助金　relevant 相關的　breed 繁殖　poultry 家禽

53 --

Where most likely does the man work?　這位男士最有可能在哪裡工作？

(A) At a laboratory　(A) 在實驗室
(B) At a farm　(B) 在農場
(C) At a fried chicken restaurant　(C) 在炸雞餐廳
(D) At a government agency　(D) 在政府機關

男子的第一句台詞「this is Charles Harris from the Margaret Chicken Farm.」，介紹自己是在瑪格麗特養雞場工作的查理斯‧哈里斯，由此可知男子在農場工作，故正確答案為 (B)。

54 --

What has the man recently done?　這位男士最近做了什麼事？

(A) Called to confirm the management number　(A) 打電話確認管理編號
(B) Moved to a new location　(B) 搬到新的地點
(C) Sold a number of eggs　(C) 賣掉許多的蛋
(D) Bred a lot of poultry　(D) 繁殖許多家禽

從男子說的「We have recently hatched a large number of chickens」可知，養雞場最近孵化了許多隻雞。選項 (D) 將「hatched a large number of chickens」改寫為意義相關的「bred a lot of poultry」，故正確答案為 (D)。

55 --

What does the woman say she is unable to do?　這位女士說她不能做什麼事？

(A) Vaccinate the animals　(A) 給動物注射疫苗
(B) Offer a discount　(B) 提供折扣
(C) Provide financial support　(C) 提供財務資助
(D) Verify the information of the farm　(D) 核對農場資料

男子最後一句的「Can I inquire as to the cost, and also, is there any subsidy I can apply for?」可知男子想詢問疾病檢疫所需的費用，並想確認如果需要支付費用，能否申請補助金，女子則告知「We cannot offer any subsidies directly」。選項 (C) 將「subsidy」改寫為意義相關的「financial support」，故正確答案為 (C)。

(A) 和 (B) 雖然是合理的內容，但是並未在此對話中提及。(D) 則無法成為正確答案。雖然男子表示不記得管理編號，但是女子可以從名單中找到該農場。

PART 3 中譯＋解析

27

M	Thank you for visiting our Bringham supermarket. How can I help you?	男	感謝您光臨伯林漢姆超市。您需要什麼協助嗎？
W	I ordered some groceries this morning. My name is Karen Williams.	女	我今天早上訂購了一些食材。我叫凱倫‧威廉絲。
M	**(57)I was expecting you**, Ms. Williams. Your goods are ready for you. Would you prefer to get them from the warehouse yourself, or would you like us to deliver them to you?	男	(57)我正在等您，威廉絲女士。您訂購的物品已經準備好了。您要自行到倉庫領取，還是要我們幫您配送呢？
W	I would like you to deliver them to my house. The frozen items are very heavy. Could someone help me carry them to the third floor?	女	我想要請您們幫我送到家裡。冷凍品很重。有人可以幫我搬到三樓嗎？
M	Yes, the delivery man will help you carry the items. Which time is the most convenient for you?	男	好的，送貨人員可以幫您搬運物品。您什麼時候最方便呢？
W	The sooner the better. Here is my address. It's just a ten-minute drive from here. I'll be waiting for the items at my house.	女	越快越好。這是我的地址。離這裡只有十分鐘的車程。我會在家裡等候。
M	Alright. I'll tell the delivery man to leave right now.	男	好的，我請送貨人員現在出發。

• **goods** 物品   **warehouse** 倉庫   **deliver** 配送   **frozen** 冷凍的

56 --

Where does the man most likely work?   這位男士最可能在哪裡工作？

(A) At a food store   (A) 在食品店
(B) At a car repair shop   (B) 在汽車維修廠
(C) At a cold storage facility   (C) 在冷藏處所
(D) At a delivery service   (D) 在貨運公司

男子的第一句台詞中，出現名為「Bringham supermarket」的商店名稱。且根據女子說的「ordered some groceries」，可知男子的公司是接受訂購食材的地方，故男子最可能為食品店店員，正確答案為 (A)。

57 --

What does the man imply when he says, "I was expecting you"?   當這位男士說：「我正在等您」，是什麼意思？

(A) He is ready to take the order.   (A) 他已經準備好要接訂單了。
(B) They already know each other.   (B) 他們已經認識彼此。
(C) He knew Ms. Williams would come.   (C) 他知道威廉絲女士會來。
(D) He will deliver the items to Ms. Williams' house himself.   (D) 他會親自把商品送到威廉絲女士家。

從前文的「I ordered some groceries this morning.」可知女子先訂購了冷凍食品，故可推測現在來到店裡是想領取商品。又從後文男子告知「Ms. Williams. Your goods are ready for you.」，告知他已將女子要的貨品準備好了，表示男子早就知道女子會來，故正確答案為 (C)。

58 --

What is the woman most likely to do next?

(A) Go home
(B) Provide her telephone number
(C) Pick up the items at the warehouse
(D) Ask for a door-to-door delivery

這位女士接下來最可能做什麼？

(A) 回家
(B) 提供電話號碼
(C) 去倉庫領貨
(D) 要求送貨到府

推測說話者接下來動作的題型，關鍵句通常會在題目後半部出現。女子的最後一句話說：「I'll be waiting for the items at my house.」，由此可知，她將先回家等待貨品送達，故正確答案為 (A)。(B) 與 (D) 為已經在對話過程中完成的動作。(C) 則因為女子已在對話中開口要求送貨到家，所以不可能成為解答。

59-61 conversation

59–61 對話

M Did you see the memo about the company contest? The owner wants suggestions for a theme for the new advertising campaign. **W** Yes, I have seen it. I presume the advertising agency hasn't thought of anything suitable. It needs to be attractive to the customers. To be honest, I have to finish these sales figures before the audit, so I don't think I will have time to enter. **M** You have a very creative mind and the prize is a trip to France on Eurostar, so perhaps you should find time to come up with something.	男 妳有看到公司比賽的備忘錄嗎？老闆想要新廣告活動主題的建議。 女 有，我有看到。我猜廣告商可能想不到任何合適的主題。這要能吸引顧客才行。老實說，我必須在決算前完成這些銷售數據，所以我想我不會有時間參加。 男 妳很有創意，而且獎品是搭乘歐洲之星的法國之旅，或許妳該花點時間想想看。

• theme 主題　presume 猜想　suitable 合適的　to be honest 老實說　sales figures 銷售數據
audit 決算　come up with . . . 想出……　expenditure 支出　customer base 顧客群　unsure 不確定
deadline 截止期限　plaque 徽章　voucher 票券　abroad 國外

59 --

What is the purpose of the contest?

(A) To create a themed campaign
(B) To reduce expenditure
(C) To increase the customer base
(D) To recruit additional employees

比賽的目的是什麼？

(A) 創作主題活動
(B) 減少支出
(C) 增加顧客群
(D) 增聘員工

本題詢問比賽的目的，所以請從提及「contest」的部分尋找線索。男子的第一句台詞詢問對方是否看到與公司比賽相關的公告，並說：「The owner wants suggestions for a theme for the new advertising campaign.」，表示老闆為了選出新廣告活動的主題而舉辦比賽，因此正確答案為 (A)。

60

Why is the woman unsure about participating?
(A) She is going on vacation.
(B) She will be changing jobs.
(C) She does not have any related experience.
(D) She has a deadline for work.

為什麼這位女士不確定是否參加？
(A) 她要去度假了。
(B) 她要換工作了。
(C) 她沒有任何相關經驗。
(D) 她的工作快接近截止期限。

本題詢問女子無法下定決心參加的原因，應從女子的台詞中尋找線索。

從女子台詞的後半部分：「To be honest, I have to finish these sales figures before the audit, so I don't think I will have time to enter.」可知，女子因為要在決算前完成工作，所以無法參加比賽。選項 (D) 將「have to finish these sales figures before the audit」改寫為意義相關的「have a deadline for work」，所以正確答案為 (D)。

「To be honest」或「Actually」、「In fact」等單字片語通常用於表達說話者的真正意見，所以千萬不要忽略這些單字片語後面出現的內容。

61

What will the winner receive?
(A) A plaque
(B) A hotel voucher
(C) A trip abroad
(D) A cash bonus

優勝者將獲得什麼獎品？
(A) 徽章
(B) 飯店住宿券
(C) 國外旅遊
(D) 現金獎金

優勝者可以獲得獎品，故可以注意對話內容中是否出現「winner」或「prize」。男子的最後一句台詞「the prize is a trip to France on Eurostar」，表示比賽獎勵是搭乘歐洲之星的法國之旅，因此正確答案為 (C)。

62-64 conversation and map

62–64 對話及地圖

M Hello, Betty. I'm wondering if you are still interested in joining our badminton club. We have lost a couple of members recently, so we would like to offer you the opportunity to join.	**男** 嗨，貝蒂。我在想妳是否仍然有興趣加入我們的羽毛球社？我們最近流失掉幾位社員，所以我們想要提供妳加入的機會。
W I certainly enjoy playing badminton. But as you know, I have moved to a new location, so I would have a long way to drive to your club.	**女** ：我真的很喜歡打羽毛球。但是你也知道，我已經搬到新地方，所以開車到羽毛球社有一點遠。
M Yes, I heard you've moved to a new apartment near Stanton High School. But we do have an affiliated gym running some badminton games near your place. I think they have some available spaces, too.	**男** 是啊，我聽說妳搬到史丹頓高中旁的一座新公寓。但是我們在妳家附近有一個附屬體育館，我們會在那裡舉辦一些羽毛球賽。我想那邊有一些可以使用的空間。
W Really? Where exactly is the gym?	**女** 真的嗎？體育館的確切地點是在哪裡？

274

M	I'll send you details by e-mail about the club, which meets at the Hillsberry Building. It's just next to the Community Center. Please take a look and call me back.
W	I don't know much about the neighborhood. Is it on Alton Street?
M	No, it's the new building across from the shopping mall. It's on the same block as the high school.
W	I'm confused. I'll have to check your e-mail.

男	我會把羽毛球社的詳細情況以電子郵件寄給妳，羽毛球社在西斯貝利大樓聚會。就在社區活動中心旁邊。請妳看一下，再打給我。
女	我對這鄰近地區不太熟。那是在雅頓街上嗎？
男	不是，是在購物中心對面的新大樓。和高中同一個街區。
女	我有點混亂。我得看看你的電子郵件了。

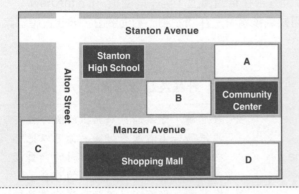

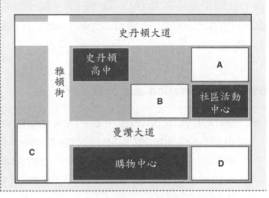

🎧 27

• **affiliated** 附屬的　**run** 舉辦　**available** 可以使用的　**exactly** 確切地　**neighborhood** 鄰近地區

---

62 ---

What are the speakers mainly talking about?	說話者最主要在討論什麼？
(A) The woman's new apartment	(A) 這位女士的新公寓
(B) Joining a sports club	(B) 參加運動社團
(C) Driving a long distance	(C) 長途開車
(D) A newly arrived student	(D) 新來的學生

一開始，男子對女子說：「I'm wondering if you are still interested in joining our badminton club.」，想知道她是否還想加入羽毛球社，接下來的內容也與這句話有關。選項 (B) 將「badminton club」改寫為意義相關的「sports club」，故正確答案為 (B)。

---

63 ---

What is the woman concerned about?	這位女士擔心的是什麼？
(A) The cost of joining a gym	(A) 加入健身房的費用
(B) The amount of spare time she has	(B) 她所擁有的空閒時間
(C) The location of the new office	(C) 新辦公室的地點
(D) The distance she would travel	(D) 她要往返的距離

本題詢問女子擔心的問題，應該從女子的台詞中尋找線索。女子說：「I have moved to a new location, so I would have a long way to drive to your club.」，表示自己已搬到其他地方，如果從家裡開車前往社團所在地，可能距離會太遠。 由此可知，女子擔心的是移動距離太遠，所以正確答案為 (D)。

Look at the graphic. Where is the Hillsberry Building?

(A) A
(B) B
(C) C
(D) D

看一下圖表，西斯貝利大樓在哪裡？

(A) A
(B) B
(C) C
(D) D

請事先瀏覽地圖上的地點名稱，再從對話中找尋線索，推導出正確的地點。男子提到「Hillsberry Building」，並説「It's just next to the Community Center」，表示該棟建築就在社區活動中心旁邊，此時可能答案為 (A)、(B) 與 (D)。女子接著反問是否在雅頓街上，男子則回應「it's the new building across from the shopping mall.」，故可知聚會場所是在購物中心對面的 B，因此正確答案為 (B)。

65-67 conversation and checklist　　65–67 對話及核對清單

W Daniel, your photos of the new branches in the newspaper advertisement were so amazing. Can you send those images to me so our web designers can put them on our homepage?	女 丹尼爾，你為新分店拍攝的照片放在報紙廣告上看起來好棒。你可以把那些照片寄給我嗎？這樣公司的網頁設計師就能把照片放到我們的首頁了。
M Sure, Jenny. Just tell me which ones you wish to use.	男 沒問題，珍妮。只要告訴我妳想要用哪幾張照片。
W I was going to use all of them. In addition, I need some related information on each, such as the names of the manager, phone numbers, and addresses.	女 我想用上全部的照片。除此之外，我需要每張照片的相關資料，像是主管的姓名、電話號碼及地址。
M But I'm worried some of them wouldn't look good on your Web site because they were taken at night. Moreover, the Glanstown branch doesn't have a phone number yet, and they haven't decided who will take charge of the McMillan branch.	男 但是我擔心有些照片放到網站上不好看，因為是在晚上拍攝的。再說，葛蘭斯城分店還沒有電話號碼，而且他們也還沒決定誰要接管麥克米蘭分店。
W I think I can handle the issues with the telephone numbers. But I agree that we should post the pictures taken during the daytime only. Are there any other issues?	女 我想我可以處理電話號碼的問題。但是我同意我們應該只放白天拍攝的照片。還有其他的問題嗎？
M I'm not sure for now. I'll just send you all the images with the information.	男 現在還不確定。我先把全部照片附上資料寄給妳。
W Thank you so much. By the way, the names of the branch managers will be finalized next Monday, right? Then we'd better post all the pictures except for those taken at nighttime.	女 非常感謝你。對了，分店主管的名單下週一就會定案了，對嗎？那除了晚上拍攝的照片以外，我們最好把所有的照片都貼到網站上去。

Attachment: Pictures Checklist			
Branch Name	Phone No.	Manager	Taken at
Alpha Center	7590-4761	Martin Clause	Nighttime
Glanstown	(N/A)	Laura Bright	Daytime
McMillan	7550-8761	(N/A)	Daytime
Unicorn Building	7575-4561	Aaron Smith	Daytime

附件：照片核對表			
分店名稱	電話號碼	主管	拍攝時間
阿爾法中心	7590-4761	馬汀・克勞斯	晚上
葛蘭斯城	無	蘿拉・布萊特	白天
麥克米蘭	7550-8761	無	白天
獨角獸大樓	7575-4561	亞倫・史密斯	白天

• advertisement 廣告　image 照片　moreover 再說　take charge of ... 接管……　issue 問題
daytime 白天　finalize 定案　except for ... 除了……以外　nighttime 晚上

 65 ---

What most likely is the man's job?

(A) Branch manager
(B) Office interior designer
(C) Photographer
(D) Web site developer

這位男士最有可能從事何種工作？

(A) 分店主管
(B) 辦公室室內設計師
(C) 攝影師
(D) 網頁開發人員

27

男子雖然未直接提及自己的職業，但是從女子的第一句台詞「Daniel, your photos of the new branches in the newspaper advertisement were so amazing.」可以得知，男子幫新分店拍攝廣告用的照片，故男子最可能為攝影師，正確答案為 (C)。

 66 ---

What does the woman ask the man to help with?

(A) Assigning a manager
(B) Photocopying some images
(C) Getting some photographs
(D) Installing a telephone

這位女士要求男士幫忙什麼事？

(A) 指派經理
(B) 複印一些圖像
(C) 取得一些照片
(D) 安裝電話

從女子第一句的「Can you send those images to me so our web designers can put them on our homepage?」可以得知，女子需要男子寄給她網頁設計師要使用的照片。所以本題正確答案為 (C)。雖然 (B) 中出現類似單字，但是本題對話中，照片已經拍攝完成，而且女子並未要求進行複印。

 67 NEW ---

Look at the graphic. Which site's photograph is not suitable to be posted on the Web site?

(A) Alpha Center branch
(B) Glanstown branch
(C) McMillan branch
(D) Unicorn Building branch

看一下圖表，哪個地點的照片不適合放在網站上？

(A) 阿爾法中心分店
(B) 葛蘭斯城分店
(C) 麥克米蘭分店
(D) 獨角獸大樓分店

男子的第二句提到「I'm worried some of them wouldn't look good on your Web site because they were taken at night.」，而女子回覆「I agree that we should post the pictures taken during the daytime only.」，所以在晚上拍攝的照片不會被放到網站上。女子最後一句「Then we'd better post all the pictures except for those taken at nighttime.」也直接表明了答案。對照核對清單可知，只有阿爾法中心為晚上拍攝，故正確答案為 (A)。

(B) 葛蘭斯城分店沒有標明連絡電話，但因為女子可以解決電話問題，所以不是正確答案。(C) 麥克米蘭分店尚未決定分店長，但女子表示人選會在下週一決定，所以也不成問題。

68–70 conversation and floor guide　　68–70 對話及樓層導覽

W This is Samantha Collins from the Silverstein Employment Agency. I'm calling to confirm that we have received your application for temporary employment, and we will expect you to come into the office to sign the paperwork on Tuesday morning.	**女** 我是希爾佛斯坦職業介紹所的莎曼珊·柯林斯。我打這通電話是要確認我們已經收到您短期就業的申請函，希望您星期二早上到辦公室來簽署文件。
M Thank you for calling, Ms. Collins. Shall I come straight up to your office?	**男** 感謝您的來電，柯林斯女士。我應該直接到您的辦公室嗎？
W No, let's meet in the administration office downstairs. You will need to bring your qualification certificates and references with you so that we can issue your work permit.	**女** 不用，在樓下的行政辦公室碰面即可。您需要攜帶您的合格證書與推薦函，這樣我們才可以核發工作許可。
M But I already submitted all the required documents when I met you at the cafeteria last time. Do I need to bring more copies?	**男** 但是上回在餐廳碰面時，我已經將全部的必要文件繳交給您了。我需要再帶幾份副本嗎？
W Oh, you are right, Mr. Thompson. Then I'll see you in my office in the Counseling Department at 1:30 in the afternoon. After a short interview, you'll take part in a 3-hour training program on the third floor.	**女** 喔，你說的對，湯姆森先生。這樣下午1:30在我諮詢部門的辦公室見面吧。在簡短面試後，你得參加位於三樓的三個小時教育訓練課程。

Floor Guide:

4F	Cafeteria
3F	Auditorium
2F	Counseling Office
1F	Administration Office
B1	Parking lot

樓層導覽：

4 樓	餐廳
3 樓	禮堂
2 樓	諮詢辦公室
1 樓	行政辦公室
地下 1 樓	停車場

- application 申請　paperwork 文件　administration office 行政辦公室　downstairs 樓下
certificate 證書　work permit 工作許可　autograph 親筆簽名

68 -

What document will be issued to the man?

(A) An application form

(B) A work permit

(C) A membership card

(D) A recommendation letter

這位男士將被核發何種文件？

(A) 申請表

(B) 工作許可

(C) 會員卡

(D) 推薦信

女子說：「You will need to bring your qualification certificates and references with you so that we can issue your work permit.」，由此可知，男子提交資料後，職業介紹所將發行工作許可，故正確答案為 (B)。

69 NEW -

Look at the graphic. Where should the man go to meet the woman on Tuesday?

(A) 1st floor

(B) 2nd floor

(C) 3rd floor

(D) 4th floor

看一下圖表，這位男士星期二應該去哪裡和女士見面？

(A) 一樓

(B) 二樓

(C) 三樓

(D) 四樓

女子一開始向男子說「let's meet in the administration office downstairs」，提議在樓下的行政辦公室見面，故可知道女子的辦公室位於行政辦公室樓上，所以正確答案為 (B)。(C) 對話最後出現的三樓不是與女子見面的地方，而是進行教育訓練的禮堂。

70 -

What does the woman ask the man to do?

(A) Submit an application as soon as possible

(B) Mail extra copies of his certificates

(C) Attend a training session

(D) Give her his autograph

這位女士要求男士做什麼？

(A) 盡快繳交申請函

(B) 郵寄額外的證書影本

(C) 參加教育訓練課程

(D) 給她他的親筆簽名

女子在最後一句說道：「After a short interview, you'll take part in a 3-hour training program on the third floor.」。選項 (C) 僅將「take part in」改寫為意義相近的「attend」、「training program」改為「session」，仍然符合題意，故本題正確答案為 (C)。

(D) 提到的「autograph」特指知名人士簽寫用來當作紀念的簽名，不是一般在「paperwork」上的簽名。

71-73 advertisement

71–73 廣告

Exo-Spices is one of the leading companies for the food service industry. We recently added quality Indian buffets and various kinds of cold noodles to our menu. With the most competitive prices in the market and the most menu choices, we have a good reputation for superb catering services. And if you are not satisfied with our food or service, we will give you your entire money back! Visit our Web site at www.exospices.ca to see our selection of set menus or create your own by using the "My Taste" option.

異香是餐飲服務界的領導公司之一。我們最近在菜單裡新增了優質的印度自助餐與多種的冷麵。有著市場上最具競爭力的價格,以及最多餐點選擇的我們,擁有一流餐飲服務的好口碑。而且若您對於我們的餐點或服務感到不滿意,我們將提供全額退費!請上我們網站www.exospices.ca查看精選套餐,或以「我的口味」選單來創造您自己的菜單。

• **competitive** 具競爭力的　**reputation** 口碑　**superb** 一流的　**be satisfied with . . .** 對⋯⋯滿意　**nutritious** 營養的

71 --

What type of business is being advertised?
(A) A cold storage facility
(B) A catering firm
(C) A web design service
(D) A cooking institute

這則廣告宣傳的是何種行業?
(A) 冷藏設備
(B) 餐飲公司
(C) 網頁設計公司
(D) 烹飪學校

廣告內容中,開頭介紹異香是「one of the leading companies for the food service industry」,因此可知公司與餐飲服務有關,因此正確答案為 (B)。

72 --

According to the advertisement, what does Exo-Spices guarantee?
(A) Unlimited beverages
(B) Discount vouchers
(C) A full refund
(D) Nutritious food

根據廣告內容,異香保證什麼?
(A) 無限的飲料
(B) 折價券
(C) 全額退費
(D) 營養的食物

藉由中間部分的「And if you are not satisfied with our food or service, we will give you your entire money back!」可以得知,如果對服務不滿意,公司將以全額退款進行補償。選項 (C) 將「give entire money back」改寫為意義相近的「full refund」,故正確答案為 (C)。

73 ---

What can listeners do online?

(A) Customize a set menu

(B) Order samples of some food

(C) Leave comments

(D) Track an order

聽者可以在網路上做什麼事？

(A) 客製化套餐

(B) 訂購一些食物樣品

(C) 留下評論

(D) 追蹤訂單

從「Visit our Web site at www.exospices.ca to see our selection of set menus or create your own by using the『My Taste』option」可以得知，官方網站上除了有套餐菜單的介紹之外，也可自由組合喜歡的料理，組成獨一無二的套餐，所以正確答案為 (A)。

74-76 news report

74–76 新聞報導

This is Eugene Wilson from the City of Eunice with the latest news. The announcement was made this morning that the public swimming pool will be reopened next summer. Local sports minister Martin Floyd announced that since several kinds of harmful substances were found in the ceiling of the pool area 2 months ago, renovation work was forced to a halt. However, thanks to a local environmental organization, they have been cleared off and the work has begun again. The swimming pool is scheduled to receive a new roof, repairs to the pool area, and a new children's pool with waterslides. Employees at local businesses are encouraged to become members of the newly-renovated facility, and a number of incentives will be offered to the residents of Eunice once the pool is reopened in July. They include a weekly prize drawing for 7 free annual memberships.

這裡是尤尼斯市的尤金‧威爾森最新報導。今天早上公共游泳池宣布將於明年夏季重新開放。當地體育部長馬汀‧佛洛伊德宣布，自從兩個月前在泳池區的天花板上發現數種有害物質後，翻修工程就被迫暫停。但是，在當地一個環保團體的努力下，有害物質已經被清除，工程又再度開始進行。游泳池預計將建造一個新屋頂、修復泳池區域，並興建一個具滑水道的全新兒童泳池。在此鼓勵當地企業員工成為新整修後場地的會員，一旦游泳池於七月重新開放後，也將提供尤尼斯市居民許多鼓勵措施，包括每週抽出七名免費年度會員的獎項。

- **latest** 最新的 **announcement** 宣布 **reopen** 重新開放 **minister** 部長 **harmful** 有害的 **substance** 物質 **halt** 暫停 **environmental organization** 環保團體 **incentive** 鼓勵措施 **prize drawing** 抽獎 **remote** 偏遠 **object to . . .** 反對…… **renovation** 整修 **detect** 偵測 **insufficient** 不足的

74 ---

What is being rebuilt in Eunice?

(A) A shopping mall

(B) A swimming pool

(C) A playground

(D) An environmental center

尤尼斯市重建了什麼？

(A) 購物中心

(B) 游泳池

(C) 遊樂場

(D) 環保中

說話者提到「The announcement was made this morning that the public swimming pool will be reopened next summer.」，表示公共泳池今天早上宣布將於隔年夏季重新開張，所以正確答案為 (B)。

75

Why was the renovation delayed?
(A) The location was too remote.
(B) Local residents objected to the renovation.
(C) Harmful substances were detected.
(D) Funding was insufficient.

整修工程為何延遲？
(A) 地點太偏僻。
(B) 當地居民反對整修。
(C) 偵測到有害物質。
(D) 經費不足。

從「since dangerous chemicals were found in the ceiling of the pool area 2 months ago, renovation work was forced to a halt」可知，兩個月前因為從天花板檢測出有害物質，游泳池不得不暫停施工，所以正確答案為 (C)。

76

According to the speaker, what will take place in July?
(A) A weekly prize drawing
(B) An opening ceremony
(C) A series of lectures
(D) A charity event

根據說話者表示，七月將發生什麼事？
(A) 每週一次的抽獎
(B) 開幕典禮
(C) 一系列的演講
(D) 慈善活動

報導最後提到「a number of incentives will be offered to the residents of Eunice once the pool is reopened in July. They include a weekly prize drawing for 7 free annual memberships.」，游泳池七月重新開張後，將每週抽獎贈送七張免費年度會員，由此可知正確答案為 (A)。

77-79 announcement

77-79 宣告

Just before we start our guitar class, I would like to bring to your attention a big event that is being held here at Jackson Community Center. As you know, we hold a number of music classes here, and we would like to encourage people to try out playing new musical instruments. So if you attend more than two different classes before the end of April, you will be eligible to join one new class free of charge. Pick up a brochure from the office on the first floor with all the details and enroll in more classes. And don't forget to swipe your student card every time you attend a class.	在吉他課開始前，我想告訴大家一個在傑克森社區活動中心舉辦的大型活動。正如大家所知，我們在這裡開設許多音樂課程，並想鼓勵大家嘗試演奏新樂器。所以如果各位在四月底前參加兩種以上不同的課程，將有資格免費參加一種新課程。請至一樓辦公室領取含有所有資訊的簡介，並加入更多課程吧。別忘了每次來上課的時候，都要刷學員證。

• **bring to one's attention** 使某人注意　**encourage** 鼓勵　**try out** 嘗試　**eligible** 有資格的　**brochure** 簡介　**enroll in . . .** 報名參加……　**swipe** 刷（卡片）　**complimentary** 免費的

What is the purpose of the upcoming event?
(A) To promote an art class
(B) To encourage class participation
(C) To introduce a new lecturer
(D) To test students' performances

即將舉辦的活動目的是什麼？
(A) 宣傳藝術課程
(B) 鼓勵參與課程
(C) 介紹新的講師
(D) 測試學生表現

說話者表示在上課之前有事情要宣布，隨後告知「we hold a number of music classes here, and we would like to encourage people to try out playing new musical instruments.」，表示中心開設各種音樂課程，並鼓勵學生多多報名參與，因此正確答案為 (B)。

What will some students receive?
(A) Tickets to a musical performance
(B) Theater discounts
(C) A complimentary class
(D) Reduced tuition fees

部分學生將獲得什麼？
(A) 音樂演出的票券
(B) 戲院折扣
(C) 免費課程
(D) 學費減價

說話者在文章的中間提到「if you attend more than two different classes before the end of April, you will be entitled to join one new class free of charge.」，表示如果在四月底前參加兩堂以上不同的課程，可以免費再參加一堂新課程。 選項 (C) 將「one new class free of charge」改寫為意義相同的「a complimentary class」，故正確答案為 (C)。

What are the listeners asked to do when entering a class?
(A) Play the guitar
(B) Accompany a friend
(C) Stop by the office
(D) Apply an ID card

聽者被要求進入課堂時要做什麼？
(A) 彈吉他
(B) 陪同朋友
(C) 去辦公室一趟
(D) 使用識別證

文章的最後提到「don't forget to swipe your student card every time you attend a class」，故每一堂課出席時，應在讀卡機上掃描學生證 ，故正確答案為 (D)。

ACTUAL TEST 7 / PART 4 / 中譯＋解析 / 28

80-82 recorded message

80–82 留言錄音

Thank you for calling the Redwood Trekking Hotline. Due to the unfavorable weather change, we are experiencing more calls than normal. Your call will be answered as soon as one of our representatives is available. To ensure that you are put through to the correct department, please consider the following options. For emergency situations, press number one. For shelter inquiries, press number two. For shuttle service inquiries, press number three. For local traffic information, press number four. For all other inquiries, press the pound sign. You can also check the real-time weather report via the Internet at weather.redwood.com.

感謝您來電紅木步旅熱線。因為惡劣的天氣變化，我們接到比往常更多的來電。當本公司代表人員有空時，將盡快接聽您的電話。為了確保您被轉接到正確的部門，請參考下列選項。緊急狀況，請按1。避難查詢，請按2。接駁車查詢，請按3。當地交通資訊，請按4。其他查詢，請按#字鍵。您也可以透過網站 weather.redwood.com 查詢即時氣象報告。

• **hotline** 熱線　**unfavorable** 惡劣的　**put through** 轉接　**emergency situation** 緊急狀況　**shelter** 避難
inquiry 查詢　**pound sign** 井字　**real-time** 即時的　**weather report** 氣象報告

Why are the callers unable to speak to a representative immediately?

(A) More people are calling than usual.
(B) A hotline system is faulty.
(C) The shuttles are out of service.
(D) The Internet connection is unavailable.

來電者為什麼無法立即與代表人員說話？

(A) 比往常有更多人來電。
(B) 熱線系統發生故障。
(C) 接駁車停止服務。
(D) 沒有網路連線。

一開始的部分提到「Due to the unfavorable weather change, we are experiencing more calls than normal.」，因為天氣惡化，公司接到比平常多的電話，所以公司無法立刻回應每個來電者，故正確答案為 (A)。

Why would callers press 4 on their phones?

(A) To check the shuttle schedules
(B) To get advice on road travel
(C) To check the weather forecast
(D) To locate a nearby shelter

來電者為什麼要按4？

(A) 要確認接駁車時刻表
(B) 要獲取道路通行的建議
(C) 要確認天氣預報
(D) 要確定附近避難所的位置。

先記住題目的關鍵字為「press 4」，並在聆聽文章內容時注意相關部分。由於出現「For local traffic information, press number four.」代表如果想瞭解當地交通狀況，可以按下 4 號鍵。從選項中，最有可能需要交通資訊的情況為 (B)，所以正確答案為 (B)。

82 --

What does the speaker mention about the Web site?
(A) It is updated every day.
(B) It is currently inaccessible.
(C) You need to log on to check the contents.
(D) It provides the current weather status.

說話者提到什麼有關網站的事？
(A) 每日更新。
(B) 目前無法連結。
(C) 需要登入才能查詢內容。
(D) 提供目前的天氣狀態。

最後一句話「You can also check the real-time weather report via the Internet at <u>weather.redwood.com</u>」提供聽話者網站的網址，並且告知可以在網站上查詢即時氣象報告，因此正確答案為 (D)。

83-85 talk

83–85 談話

Everyone worked very hard on the sales of the HeatTech Womenswear last winter. I'm so happy to announce that everyone in our branch is going to get a bonus for the best sales record. Congratulations, everyone. And now, this meeting has been arranged to inform you of the new product line that we are launching in the spring. On top of our standard collection of suits, shirts, and pants, we are also launching a new collection of knitwear this year. Your job is to present these new products to the clients successfully. However, before I explain the sales strategy, let me show you the knitwear, which is displayed in the showroom.	去年冬天，大家為了發熱科技女裝的業績都很努力。我很開心地宣布，本分店的每一位都將因最佳銷售紀錄獲得獎金。恭喜各位。現在，本次會議就是要告訴大家，我們即將發行春季的新系列產品。除了套裝、襯衫與褲子等標準系列外，我們今年也要推出針織衫新品。各位的工作就是將新展品成功地呈現給顧客。但是，在我說明銷售策略以前，讓我將目前在展示間陳列的針織衫拿給大家看看。

• **inform sb of sth** 告訴某人某事　**launch** 發行　**knitwear** 針織衫　**present** 呈現　**strategy** 策略
　showroom 展示間

83 --

Who most likely are the listeners?
(A) Fashion designers
(B) Corporate executives
(C) Factory workers
(D) Salespeople

聽者最有可能是誰？
(A) 時裝設計師
(B) 企業主管
(C) 工廠工人
(D) 銷售人員

從開頭提到的「Everyone worked very hard with the sales」可知，聽話者最可能為銷售相關人員。
另外，後半部也提到「Your job is to present these new products to the clients successfully.」，
所以本題正確答案為 (D)。

84 --

What will happen this spring?
(A) A womenswear collection will be discontinued.
(B) A new client list will be introduced.
(C) A new range will be launched.
(D) A new outlet will be opened.

今年春天將發生什麼事？
(A) 一個女裝系列將停產。
(B) 將採用新的客戶名單。
(C) 新的產品線將上市。
(D) 即將開設新銷路。

談話中間說到「the new product line that we are launching in the spring.」，由此可知，春季將推出新產品。此外，從「we are also launching a new collection of knitwear this year.」可得知，今年新推出針織類產品，所以正確答案為 (C)。

85 --

What will the listeners do next?
(A) Visit their clients
(B) View sample items
(C) Report their sales strategies
(D) Attend a regular meeting

聽者接下來將要做什麼？
(A) 拜訪顧客
(B) 觀看樣品
(C) 報告他們的銷售策略
(D) 出席定期會議

說話者的最後一句話提到：「let me show you the knit wear, which is displayed in the showroom.」，故聽者接下來將會觀看新推出的商品，所以正確答案為 (B)。

86-88 telephone message　　　　　　　**86–88 電話留言**

Hi, this is Carol Foster, head of Marketing at Murrey Outdoors. We need your help for a marketing campaign we are launching. We want you to create a montage of pictures based around a vacation theme. Please transpose as many Murrey outdoor wear items and accessories as possible in various locations—such as campsites, ski resorts, and mountains—and make them unique. At the end of the month, we will award the person with the best montage with a holiday discount voucher. Send your entry to design@murrey.com and win money-off vouchers!	嗨，我是莫瑞戶外用品店的行銷主管凱羅‧福斯特。我們需要各位協助一個即將發表的行銷活動。我們希望您依據一個度假主題來創作一份照片剪輯。請盡量在各種不同的場地變換莫瑞戶外用品的服裝與配件——如露營地、滑雪度假村及山區，並讓它們看來獨樹一格。月底時，我們將頒發節慶折價券給最佳剪輯的人。請將參賽作品寄到design@murrey.com，贏得折價券吧！

• **montage** 剪輯　**transpose** 變換　**unique** 獨樹一格的　**award** 頒發　**entry** 參賽作品　**money-off voucher** 折價券

 86 --

What type of business does the speaker work for?
(A) An advertising company
(B) A photography studio
(C) A clothing company
(D) A travel agency

說話者是在哪種行業上班？
(A) 廣告公司
(B) 攝影工作室
(C) 服裝公司
(D) 旅行社

本題詢問説話者從事的職業，如果只聽懂公司名稱中的「outdoors」，可能很難聯想到服飾業者。不過，文章中間部分提到「Please transpose as many Murrey outdoor wear items and accessories as possible in various locations」，由此可知，此公司生產的產品為「outdoor wear items and accessories」，所以説話者最可能是在服裝公司工作，正確答案為 (C)。

 87 --

What should the listener submit to join the contest?
(A) A series of photographs
(B) A sketch
(C) A video clip
(D) A travel essay

聽者要繳交什麼來參賽？
(A) 一系列的照片
(B) 素描
(C) 一段影片
(D) 旅遊短文

從「We want you to create a montage of pictures based around a vacation theme.」可知，説話者要求參賽者以度假為主題，創作照片剪輯作品，故正確答案為 (A)。

 88 --

What will the winner receive?
(A) Cash
(B) Coupons
(C) Flight tickets
(D) Camping equipment

優勝者將獲得什麼？
(A) 現金
(B) 折價券
(C) 機票
(D) 露營設備

從最後的「Send your entry to design@murrey.com and win money-off vouchers!」中可以得知，比賽優勝者可獲得折價券。選項 (B) 將「money-off vouchers」改寫成意義相近的「coupons」，故正確答案為 (B)。

89-91 radio broadcast

89–91 電台廣播

Good evening, and welcome back to Stadium Fever! I am Mike Burns, and I will be with you for the next two hours for today's match. And we have a great prize for some lucky listeners tonight. If you correctly guess the first player to score in the game, we will send twelve winners a pair of tickets to the grand final to be held at Prime Capital Stadium next month. **(91)It couldn't be simpler!** Just text us your predictions at 050-884-1291. Just make sure you're sending it only one time with one single name! You may send your message now! I will be back after this commercial.	晚安，歡迎回到狂熱球場！我是麥可·伯恩斯，將和大家一起共度今天比賽接下來的兩個小時時光。今晚我們準備了大獎要給一些幸運的聽眾。如果您正確地猜出比賽中首位得分的球員，我們將送給12位猜中的優勝者一組下個月在第一首府體育館舉行的總決賽門票。**(91)**這再簡單不過了！只要將您的預測以簡訊傳到050-884-1291即可。要確定一次只傳送一個名字喔！現在就可以傳送訊息了！廣告之後再回來現場。

• **match** 比賽　**score** 得分　**stadium** 體育館　**prediction** 預測　**commercial** 廣告

89 --

Who most likely is the speaker?
(A) A stadium vendor
(B) A sports announcer
(C) A football player
(D) A match referee

說話者最有可能是誰？
(A) 球場攤販
(B) 體育播報員
(C) 足球球員
(D) 比賽裁判

開頭說話者提到「Good evening, and welcome back to Stadium Fever! I am Mike Burns, and I will be with you for the next two hours for today's match.」，介紹節目名稱，並表示接下來兩個小時將由他進行足球賽轉播，故可推測說話者最可能是播報員，正確答案為 (B)。

90 --

What prize is being offered?
(A) Dinner with an athlete
(B) Tickets for the final
(C) A two-week trip
(D) Autographed football shirts

提供了什麼獎品？
(A) 和運動員一起用餐
(B) 決賽門票
(C) 兩週的旅行
(D) 親筆簽名的足球球衣

從中間部分的「we will send twelve winners a pair of tickets to the grand final to be held at Prime Capital Stadium next month」可知，猜對手為得分球員的聽眾可獲得決賽的門票，所以正確答案為 (B)。

91 NEW --

What does the man imply when he says, "It couldn't be simpler"?
(A) Everyone can send the message free of charge.
(B) The rules for soccer are not complicated.
(C) It is easy to join the event.
(D) All the names of the players need to be memorized.

當這個男士說：「這再簡單不過了」，是什麼意思？
(A) 每個人都可以免費傳送訊息。
(B) 足球的規則並不複雜。
(C) 參加活動很容易。
(D) 要記住所有球員的姓名。

從後文「Just text us your predictions at 050-884-1291.」可知道，只要傳送簡訊預測得分球員，就有機會獲得門票，故男子這句話最可能代表活動的參加辦法很容易，故本題的答案為 (C)。

(A) 內容沒有在文章內容中出現，所以不是正確答案。(B) 內容與文章走向無關，所以不是正解。
(D) 不須記下所有選手的姓名，只要預測第一位得分的球員即可。

92-94 announcement

I wish to inform you all about a change in policy regarding working hours. You recently completed a survey questionnaire on efficient practices in the office, and the consensus is that you would be more productive if you took a shorter lunch break and left earlier in the day. We will try out this suggestion from next week. The lunch break will be halved, but, as most of you indicated, **(94)there would be no difficulty in that.** On the other hand, you will then be able to leave the office at least 40 minutes earlier than now. This change will enable us to make more efficient use of the time spent in the office. Please note that these adjustments will come into effect following the weekend.

92-94 宣告

我想告訴大家工時規定的相關變動。各位最近完成了有關辦公室高效作業的問卷調查，其中大家一致認為，如果能縮短午餐休息時間並提早下班的話，產能會更高。我們將從下週起試行這個建議。午餐休息時間將減半，但是如大部分的人所說的，**(94)**這部分不會有問題。另一方面，大家將可以比現在提早至少40分鐘下班。這個異動將讓我們更有效率地運用在辦公室裡的時間。請注意，這些調整將於週末後開始生效。

• policy 規定　regarding . . . 關於……　questionnaire 問卷　consensus 共識
try out 試行　adjustment 調整　come into effect 生效　following . . . 在……以後　comply with 配合

92

What is being announced?
(A) A meeting schedule
(B) An increase in salaries
(C) A new working arrangement
(D) An overtime project

公告了什麼事？
(A) 會議時程表
(B) 薪水調漲
(C) 新的工作安排
(D) 加班計畫

說話者一開始表示「I wish to inform you all about a change in policy regarding working hours.」，告知此事與上班時間政策的改變有關變革，所以正確答案為 (C)。

93

Why is a change being made?
(A) To attract new employees
(B) To create a survey
(C) To improve working practices
(D) To reward hard-working employees

為什麼要變動？
(A) 為了吸引新員工
(B) 為了設計一份問卷
(C) 為了改善工作習慣
(D) 為了獎勵認真工作的員工

說話者提到「You recently completed a questionnaire on efficient practice in the office, and the consensus is that you would be more productive if you took a shorter lunch break and leave earlier in the day.」，表示根據最近的調查，員工們認為縮短午休時間並提早下班，能夠增加工作效率，可知此次變動就是以增加工作效率為目標，正確答案為 (C)。

What does the woman imply when she says, "there would be no difficulty in that"?

(A) It is impossible to comply with the change.

(B) The survey was conducted without any trouble.

(C) The change will cause some confusion.

(D) A shorter lunch break is not a big deal.

當這位女士說：「這部分不會有問題」，是什麼意思？

(A) 要配合異動是不可能的。

(B) 問卷調查進行得很順利。

(C) 異動將造成一些混亂。

(D) 縮短午餐休息時間沒有關係。

從前文可知，縮短午休時間是經過問卷調查得出的共識，故本題正確答案為 (D)。

95-97 telephone message and map

95–97 電話留言及地圖

Hello, Ms. Martinez. This is Joseph Rockwood from the Lotus real estate agency. I have located another property on Robinson Road, which looks suitable for you. It's within walking distance to White Pebbles Park, right next to a gas station. It's also close to the train station, and there's a public parking area across the road. I think it is an ideal spot for your new warehouse. But there's one problem. The area is prone to flooding, and therefore, insurance premiums may be high. I have arranged a meeting with the landlord on Friday morning to check it myself. Since the building is a bit old and in poor condition, I think you can buy it very cheaply. I advise you to sign the contract as soon as possible if it works for you.

哈囉，馬丁尼茲女士。我是蓮花房地產仲介公司的約瑟夫·洛克伍德。我已經找到位於羅賓森路上的另一件房產，看起來很適合您。就在白水晶公園的步行距離內，加油站的旁邊。距離火車站也很近，對街就有一個公共停車場。我認為這是您新倉庫的絕佳地點。不過有個問題。這個區域容易淹水，因此保險費用可能會高一點。我和房東約好星期五上午見面，我自己會過去看看。因為屋齡有點高，而且狀況不佳，我想您能以很便宜的價錢買進。如果合適的話，建議您盡快簽訂合約。

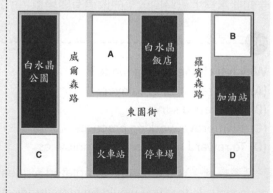

• **real estate agency** 房地產仲介公司　**property** 房產　**walking distance** 步行距離
public parking area 公共停車場　**ideal** 絕佳的　**be prone to . . .** 容易⋯⋯　**insurance premium** 保險費
landlord 房東

95 --

Why does the speaker recommend the property?
(A) It is in a flood-prone area.
(B) The landlord wants to sell it cheap.
(C) The building is in a good condition.
(D) There is a subway station nearby.

說話者為什麼建議這件房產？
(A) 它位在容易淹水的地區。
(B) 屋主想便宜出售。
(C) 房屋狀況佳。
(D) 附近有地鐵站。

從「Since the building is a bit old and in poor condition, I think you can buy it very cheaply」中可以得知，此件房產價格較低，故正確答案為 (B)。

(A) 反而為不利的條件。(C) 與 (D) 則與說話者描述的內容不同。

96 --

What disadvantage does the speaker mention?
(A) The deposit is too high.
(B) The flood risk is high.
(C) The landlord has another buyer.
(D) A parking lot is not included.

說話者提到什麼缺點？
(A) 押金太高。
(B) 淹水風險高。
(C) 屋主有其他買家。
(D) 不含停車位。

留言中間，說話者提到「But there's one problem. The area is prone to flooding, and, therefore, insurance premiums may be high.」，表示這個地區容易發生洪災，因此正確答案為 (B)。

97 (NEW) --

Look at the graphic. Where most likely is the property?
(A) A
(B) B
(C) C
(D) D

看一下圖表，這個房產最有可能在哪裡？
(A) A
(B) B
(C) C
(D) D

關於房產的位置，說話者表示「I have located another property on Robinson Road, which looks suitable for you.」，因為在羅賓森路上的只有 B 與 D，故可先刪去其他選項。再從「It's also close to the train station, and there's a public parking area across the road.」可知，這個房產最可能的位置為 D，故正確答案為 (D)。

I would like to inform everyone that the inspectors are going to assess the noise situation of the offices later today. So that employees are no longer affected by the noise coming from the factory site across the street, the office windows are to be double glazed. I ask everyone to take down the blinds and store them in the storeroom on the seventh floor until the work is finished. The replacement will begin on Thursday morning, so you have two days to remove them. And if you have curtains instead of blinds, Mr. Coleman will take them down and wash them tomorrow. Thank you in advance for your cooperation.

我要通知大家，今天稍晚時檢測員要來評估辦公室的噪音狀況。這樣一來，員工就不用再受到對街工廠傳來的噪音影響。辦公室窗戶將安裝雙層玻璃。我要請大家在完工前，將百葉窗取下，放到七樓的儲藏室去。更換作業將從星期四上午開始，所以你們有兩天的時間可以移除。若你的是窗簾而不是百葉窗的話，柯爾曼先生明天會將它們取下清洗。先感謝大家的配合。

Renovation Schedule	
Noise Inspection	May 24 (Mon.)
Painting the walls	May 25 (Tue.)
Painting the ceilings	May 26 (Wed.)
Replacing the windows	May 27 (Thu.)

整修時間表	
噪音檢測	5 月 24 日（星期一）
粉刷牆壁	5 月 25 日（星期二）
粉刷天花板	5 月 26 日（星期三）
更換窗戶	5 月 27 日（星期四）

• assess 評估　noise situation 噪音狀況　double glazed 裝雙層玻璃　take down 取下 storeroom 儲藏室　in advance 事先　cooperation 配合

What problem is the Management responding to?　管理部門回應的是什麼問題？
(A) Noise from a factory
(B) A shortage of office supplies
(C) Renovation expenses
(D) Broken windows

(A) 來自工廠的噪音
(B) 辦公用品短缺
(C) 整修費用
(D) 損壞的窗戶

説話者提到「So that employees are no longer affected by the noise coming from the factory site across the street, the office windows are to be double glazed」，故可知道，安裝雙層玻璃窗是為了阻隔噪音，所以正確答案為 (A)。

99 NEW --

Look at the graphic. When will Mr. Coleman remove the curtains?

(A) Monday
(B) Tuesday
(C) Wednesday
(D) Thursday

看一下圖表，柯爾曼先生什麼時候會拆卸窗簾？

(A) 星期一
(B) 星期二
(C) 星期三
(D) 星期四

從第一句的「the inspectors are going to assess the noise situation of the offices later today」可以得知今天是檢測噪音的日子，對照圖表可知，今天為週一。另外，再從「And if you have curtains instead of blinds, Mr. Coleman will take them down and wash them tomorrow.」可以知道，柯爾曼先生明天將前來收取窗簾並送去清洗，而明天應該為週二，所以本題的答案為 (B)。

100 --

What does the speaker encourage listeners to do?

(A) Clear the blinds
(B) Wash the curtains
(C) Change the windows
(D) Work from home

說話者鼓勵聽者做什麼？

(A) 拆卸百葉窗
(B) 清洗窗簾
(C) 更換窗戶
(D) 在家工作

說話者在最後提到「I ask everyone to take down the blinds and store them in the storeroom on the seventh floor until the work is finished.」，要求員工將百葉窗卸除，存放在儲藏室，直到替換工程結束，所以本題正確答案為 (A)。

ACTUAL TEST

8

PART 1 🎧 29

1

(A) The man has his hand on a bottle.
(B) The shelves are being dusted.
(C) The man is resting his arm on the table.
(D) Some mugs are arranged in a row.

(A) 這位男士把手放在瓶子上。
(B) 架上的灰塵正在被清掃。
(C) 這位男士把手擱在桌上。
(D) 一些馬克杯被排成一列。

• **dust** 撣掉灰塵　**rest** 擱在　**arrange** 排列　**in a row** 一列

照片中的場所看起來是某家商店，一名男子雙臂放在桌上，坐在桌前閱讀報紙。男子的桌上放著蛋糕和馬克杯，後方的架子上放著鍋具。**(A)** 男子手碰到的是馬克杯（mug）和報紙（newspaper）而不是瓶子（bottle）。**(B)** 照片中沒有正在撣灰塵的人，動詞描述錯誤。**(D)** 照片中只有一個馬克杯。本題正確答案是 **(C)**。

2

(A) One of the women is cleaning the desk.
(B) The women are wearing long-sleeved shirts.
(C) One of the women is looking out the window.
(D) The women are sitting side by side.

(A) 其中一位女士正在清理書桌。
(B) 女士們穿著長袖上衣。
(C) 其中一位女士正看著窗外。
(D) 女士們並肩坐著。

• **long-sleeved** 長袖的　**look out** 往外看

照片中的場所看起來是辦公室，有兩名女子並肩而坐，且對著電腦辦公。**(A)** 沒有人在清理書桌。**(B)** 女子穿的是短袖上衣。**(C)** 女子都看著電腦。本題正確答案為 **(D)**。

3

(A) A man is picking up a plastic bag.
(B) Different kinds of goods are displayed.
(C) Leaves are being cleared from the road.
(D) The outdoor market is crowded with people.

(A) 一位男士正撿起塑膠袋。
(B) 各種物品被陳列著。
(C) 馬路上的樹葉正在被清掃。
(D) 露天市場擠滿了人。

• **pick up** 撿起　**plastic bag** 塑膠袋　**outdoor market** 露天市場　**be crowded with . . .** 擠滿了……

照片中的場所看起來是移動式攤販，攤子上放滿各式商品，裡頭有名男子正向外看。**(A)** 男子沒有撿物品，照片中未出現塑膠袋。**(C)** 沒有人在掃樹葉。**(D)** 照片裡只看到男子一人。正確答案為 **(B)**。

4 --

(A) The women are preparing some food.
(B) One of the women is chopping some vegetables.
(C) The women are setting the dinner table.
(D) One of the women is tasting some food.

(A) 女士們正在準備食物。
(B) 其中一位女士正在切菜。
(C) 女士們正在擺設餐桌。
(D) 其中一位女士正在品嚐食物。

• **chop** 切碎　**set a table** 擺設餐桌　**taste** 品嚐

照片中有兩名女子在廚房裡製作料理。(B) 沒有女子在切菜。(C) 沒有人在擺設餐桌。(D) 沒有人在吃東西。本題正確答案為 (A)。

5 --

(A) The road passes by a wooded area.
(B) Some pots decorate the entrance to the restaurant.
(C) A wooden structure stands near a lake.
(D) The plants are being watered.

(A) 道路經過一片林區。
(B) 一些花盆裝飾著餐廳入口。
(C) 一座木造建築矗立在湖邊。
(D) 植物正被澆灌。

🎧 29

• **wooded** 長滿樹木的　**decorate** 裝飾　**wooden** 木造的　**structure** 建築　**water** 澆灌

照片裡的湖邊有木造露臺，遠處還可看到一座樹林。(A) 照片中沒有看到道路。(B) 照片中看不到入口。(C) 木造露臺就在湖邊，此為正確描述。(D) 沒有人在替植物澆水。本題正確答案為 (C)。

6 --

(A) Some people are reading documents.
(B) Some people are placing folders in a cabinet.
(C) One of the men is talking on the phone.
(D) A man is posting a notice on the wall.

(A) 一些人正在閱讀文件。
(B) 一些人正將檔案夾放進櫃子中。
(C) 其中一位男士正在講電話。
(D) 一位男士正將告示貼在牆上。

• **folder** 檔案夾　**cabinet** 櫃子　**post a notice** 張貼告示

照片中的三名男子並肩而坐，正在閱讀資料。(B) 三人皆在閱讀文件。(C) 沒有男子在講電話。(D) 照片中沒有出現告示。本題正確答案為 (A)。

7

Who left this report on my desk?

(A) In the bottom shelf.

(B) I have no idea.

(C) I'll do it later.

是誰把這份報告放在我桌上的？

(A) 在底層架上。

(B) 我不知道。

(C) 我晚點做。

• shelf 架子

本題為「Who」疑問句。(A) 為「Where」問句的回答。(B) 雖未直接提及人名，但此回答也是合理回覆。(C) 本題是發現了桌上的報告才發問的狀態，使用未來式回覆並不正確。故本題答案為 (B)。

8

When did you learn how to drive a bus?

(A) Only a month ago.

(B) I'm not sure which bus I should take.

(C) Yes, it's a big one.

你什麼時候學會開公車的？

(A) 僅一個月前。

(B) 我不確定該搭哪一班公車。

(C) 是的，很大一個。

本題是詢問時間點的「When」疑問句。(A) 明確點出時間，為合適答案。(B) 內容與題目不符。(C) 為利用題目中的「bus」能夠使用的形容詞「big」形成陷阱，且「When」疑問句不適用「Yes/No」回答。

9

Can you change a 100-dollar bill?

(A) Sure thing.

(B) That's too expensive.

(C) I'd like some small change.

你可以換一張一百元的紙鈔嗎？

(A) 沒問題。

(B) 那太貴了。

(C) 我想要一些小額零錢。

• change（將紙鈔）換零錢　bill 紙鈔　sure thing 沒問題

題目詢問可不可將 100 美元紙鈔換成零錢，(A) 雖省略「Yes」，但也表達了肯定之意，故為最適當的回答。(B) 為使用聽到「100-dollar」就會聯想到的「expensive」造成陷阱。(C) 為重複題目中的「change」誘導作答。提問者已經拿出一百美元紙鈔要求換成零錢，所以不該再要求提問者拿出零錢。故本題正確答案為 (A)。

10

My laptop needs to be fixed.

(A) Fix it to the door.

(B) What's wrong?

(C) We inspected them fully.

我的筆記型電腦需要修理了。

(A) 把它固定在門上。

(B) 怎麼了？

(C) 我們徹底地檢查過它們了。

• fix 修理；固定　inspect 檢查　fully 徹底地

本題為陳述句，筆記型電腦需要維修,(B) 反問是哪裡出了問題，為適當回覆。(A) 為利用重複題目中的「fix」誘導作答，但此處的字義為「固定」，與題目中的「修理」並不同。(C) 是利用與題目中的「fix」字義相關的「inspect」設下陷阱。本題正確答案為 (B)。

11 --

This is the serial number of your desktop, isn't it?
(A) Actually, Emma wrote it.
(B) No, it's for the copier.
(C) Yes, I need your help.

這是你桌上型電腦的序號，不是嗎？
(A) 實際上，是艾瑪寫的。
(B) 不，那是影印機的。
(C) 是的，我需要你的協助。

• **serial number** 序號　**copier** 影印機

本題為附加問句，詢問號碼是否為電腦的序號，附加問句通常會以「Yes/No」回答。(A) 沒有回答到問題。(B) 回答「No」且說明其為影印機的序號，此為最適回答。 (C) 使用「Yes」誤導，後句的內容其實與題目無關。故本題正確答案為 (B)。

12 --

Isn't it going to rain this afternoon?
(A) Yes, you'd better take your umbrella.
(B) It'll depart at three o'clock.
(C) No, I'm going to do it tomorrow morning.

今天下午不是會下雨嗎？
(A) 是的，你最好帶著傘。
(B) 它將於三點出發。
(C) 不，我明天早上會做。

• **depart** 出發

本題為否定疑問句，詢問下午是否會下雨。(A) 回答「Yes」（會下雨）並提醒對方要記得帶傘，為合適答覆。(B) 為利用題目中的「afternoon」與時間點的相關性設下陷阱，且動詞搭配也不適合。(C) 回答「No」但後文的內容與題目不符。故本題正確答案為 (A)。

🎧 30

13 --

Can you show me how to install the software?
(A) The program finishes at nine o'clock.
(B) I'd be glad to help you.
(C) He's in the training session now.

你可以告訴我如何安裝軟體嗎？
(A) 這個節目九點結束。
(B) 我很樂意幫你。
(C) 他現在在訓練講習中。

• **install** 安裝　**training session** 訓練講習

本題為請求他人幫助的問句，(B) 表示樂意協助，故正確答案為 (B)。

(A) 為使用與題目中的「software」意義相似的「program」誘導作答。(C) 雖然提及可以學習到方法的「training session」，但是此選項的主詞「He」與題目不符。如果將主詞改為「I」，表示自己正在培訓中，無法進行指導，但等培訓結束後可以幫忙，則此選項可能成為正確解答。

14 --

Should I e-mail this application now, or do you want to revise it again?
(A) I didn't e-mail it.
(B) Yes, it was issued without delay.
(C) Please send it to me.

我應該現在以電子郵件將申請表寄出，還是你想再修改一次？
(A) 我沒有用電子郵件寄出。
(B) 是的，毫無延誤地核發出去了。
(C) 請寄給我。

• application 申請表　revise 修改　issue 核發

本題為選擇疑問句。(A) 雖然再次提及「e-mail」，但是內容與題目情境不符。(B) 的「was issued」，雖然與提交申請表有關，但內容與過去式時態不符題目情境。(C) 明確做出選擇，要求提問者將申請表寄給自己，故本題正確答案為 (C)。

15 --

You've met Ms. Harvey before, haven't you?
(A) Okay, let's meet at lunch.
(B) I will pick her up at the airport.
(C) No, not yet.

你之前就見過哈維女士了，不是嗎？
(A) 好的，在午餐時碰面吧。
(B) 我會去機場接她。
(C) 不，還沒有。

• pick up 用汽車接（某人）

本題是附加疑問句，常以「Yes/No」回答。 (A) 為利用與題目中的「met」發音相似的「meet」設下陷阱。(B) 內容皆與題目無關。(C) 明確回答「No」，故此為最適合回覆。本題正確答案為 (C)。

16 --

Where can I purchase a train ticket?
(A) It comes every hour.
(B) At the automated machine over there.
(C) Sixteen dollars, please.

我可以在哪裡買到火車票？
(A) 每個小時一班。
(B) 在那裡的自動販賣機。
(C) 麻煩，16塊。

• automated 自動化的

本題為「Where」疑問句，詢問何處可以購買火車票。(A) 是利用聽到「train」可能會聯想到的火車到站頻率（every hour）所製造的陷阱。另外，此選項較適合作為「When」疑問句的回答。
(B) 回答在自動售票機可以買票，為合適回覆。 (C) 為利用聽到車票可能會聯想到的「票價」誘導作答。本題正確答案為 (B)。

17 --

Wasn't Celia at the cosmetics conference in France last week?
(A) No, I didn't see her there.
(B) Yes, she will try out the new products there.
(C) Where is the main conference room?

席莉亞沒有出席上週在法國的化妝品研討會嗎？
(A) 是的，我沒在那裡看到她。
(B) 不，她將在那裡試用新產品。
(C) 主會議室在哪裡？

• cosmetics 化妝品　conference 研討會　try out 試用

本題否定疑問句，詢問席莉亞是否出席研討會。答題時若先看作肯定疑問句，會與中文思維較接近。(A) 表示自己沒有見到席莉亞，故回答「No」，此為合適答覆。 (B) 題目詢問的是上週的事件，此選項卻以未來式回答，所以不是正確答案。(C) 重複題目中的「conference」，但內容與題目不符。本題正確答案為 (A)。

18 --

How many boxes did we order today?
(A) About five meters tall.
(B) Can I have one?
(C) More than eleven.

我們今天訂了多少箱子？
(A) 大約五公尺高。
(B) 我可以來一個嗎？
(C) 超過11個。

• . . . meters tall ⋯⋯公尺高　more than . . . 超過⋯⋯

本題為詢問數量的疑問句。 (A) 因為題目問不是尺寸，所以不是正確答案。(B) 雖然提及「one」，但此處不是指數字「一」，而是指「一個」、「一份」。(C) 具體提及數量「11 個」，故正確答案為 (C)。

19 --

Why did the workshop end so late?
(A) Some attendees will be late.
(B) We had a lot to talk about.
(C) No, the store does not close until ten.

研討會為什麼這麼晚才結束？
(A) 一些與會者會遲到。
(B) 我們有很多要討論的事情。
(C) 不，這家店十點才關門。

• attendee 與會者

本題為詢問原因的「Why」疑問。 (A) 為使用與題目「workshop」相關的「attendees」誘導作答。此外，題目詢問的是已經過去的研討會，此選項卻以未來式回答，故不適合作為本題的答案。(B) 明確解釋原因，為正確答案。(C) 疑問詞問句無法用「Yes/No」回答。本題正確答案為 (B)。

20 --

Which branch needs more staff members?
(A) About the job opening.
(B) Twenty more chairs.
(C) Most of them.

哪一間分行需要更多職員？
(A) 有關職缺。
(B) 再20張椅子。
(C) 大多數都有需要。

• branch 分行

本題為「Which」疑問句，詢問哪一間分公司需要更多員工。 (A) 為利用「need more staff members」可能聯想「求職」而誘導作答。(B) 雖然再次出現「more」，但是內容與問題毫無相關。(C) 表示大多數的分行都需要，故本題正確答案為 (C)。

21

Do you want to go out to see a movie?
(A) Oh, did you?
(B) No, I didn't move it.
(C) Sure, how about seven o'clock?

你想出去看電影嗎？
(A) 喔，你有嗎？
(B) 不，我沒動它。
(C) 好啊，七點好嗎？

題目詢問對方要不要看電影，(A) 為利用與「do」相關的「did」誘導作答；(B) 為利用發音相似的「movie」與「move」試圖造成混淆；(C) 表示答應並反問約定時間，為合適答案，故本題正確答案為 (C)。

22

Who's attending the international convention in Paris?
(A) They've been expanding overseas.
(B) In the conference center.
(C) It hasn't been announced yet.

誰要去參加巴黎的國際會議？
(A) 他們正在海外擴展。
(B) 在會議中心。
(C) 還沒宣布。

• attend　出席參加　convention 會議　expand 擴展

本題為詢問人物的「Who」疑問句。(A) 為利用聽到「international」可能會聯想到的「overseas」誘導作答。(B) 為利用與題目「convention」相關的「conference center」設下陷阱。(C) 雖然沒有直接說出人，但表示人選尚未宣布，也為合適回覆，故正確答案為 (C)。

23

What are you intending to bring to Allison's birthday party?
(A) I bought the same one.
(B) I'm afraid I can't go.
(C) She visited me last week.

你打算帶什麼去愛麗森的生日派對？
(A) 我買了同樣的。
(B) 我恐怕無法參加。
(C) 她上週來找我。

• intend to V 打算（做某事）

本題為詢問物件的「What」疑問句。(B) 雖並非直接告知攜帶的物品，但說明無法參加派對，也是合理回覆，故正確答案為 (B)。(A) 使用代名詞「one」來借指某樣物品，但前後文並未出現可以被代稱的事物，故整句句意不完整，此選項無法作為答案。(C) 內容與題目不符。

24

Should I buy the shirts online or at the clothing store?
(A) The same color.
(B) Probably at the store.
(C) It's less expensive.

我應該在網路上還是服飾店裡買襯衫？
(A) 同樣顏色。
(B) 也許在店裡。
(C) 比較不貴。

• clothing store 服飾店

本題為選擇疑問句，典型回覆方式為從題目給出的選項中挑出其一。(A) 為利用聽到「shirts」可能會聯想到的「color」製造陷阱。(B) 選了題目給的其中一個選項，此乃典型回答。(C) 則藉由與題目中的「buy」、「online」和「clothing store」相關的「less expensive」試圖誘導作答，內容與題目無關。本題正確答案為 (B)。

25 --

What was the weather like during your business trip?
(A) I lost my passport.
(B) It was hot and humid every day.
(C) Take your coat when you go out.

你出差時，天氣如何？
(A) 我弄丟護照。
(B) 每天都又熱又潮濕。
(C) 外出時要帶著你的外套。

• **business trip** 出差　**go out** 外出

本題使用「What . . . like?」句型詢問天氣狀態。(A) 利用聽到「business trip」可能聯想到的「passport」設下陷阱，但內容與題目不符。(B) 使用過去式明確告知天氣狀況，此為合適回覆。(C) 藉由題目「weather」與「coat」的相關性誘導作答。本題正確答案為 (B)。

26 --

Have you examined the marketing proposal from Benjamin?
(A) I'm looking forward to meeting them.
(B) No, it's scheduled to be submitted tomorrow.
(C) I had my van examined.

你檢查過班傑明的行銷企畫了嗎？
(A) 我正期待與他們見面。
(B) 還沒，預定明天才要呈交。
(C) 我的廂型車檢查過了。

• **examine** 檢查　**proposal** 企畫書　**look forward to Ving** 期待（做某事）　**be scheduled to V** 預定（做某事）

本題為助動詞（Have）疑問句，詢問某動作是否已完成。(A) 內容與題目無關，而且題目中並沒有可與代名詞「them」匹配的名詞。(B) 回答「No」並告知後續相關資訊，故此為合適答案。(C) 雖然重複題目中「examined」，但是內容與題目無關。本題正解為 (B)。

27 --

The flight is an hour late.
(A) Every thirty minutes.
(B) That's due to the weather problem.
(C) No, it will be rescheduled.

班機晚了一個小時。
(A) 每30分鐘。
(B) 那是因為天氣問題。
(C) 不，將會重新安排。

本題為表示飛機將延遲一個小時的陳述句，(A) 回答與題目無關，此選項應該作為詢問動作頻率時的答案；(B) 告知延遲理由，為合適答案；(C) 不應以「No」回答，本題正解為 (B)。

28 --

Would you like some orange for dessert?
(A) I don't like spicy food.
(B) Thanks, but I'm full.
(C) Yes, I can't wait for the main dish.

你要來點柳橙當甜點嗎？
(A) 我不喜歡辛辣食物。
(B) 謝謝，我飽了。
(C) 好的，我等不及要吃主餐了。

• **main dish** 主餐

本題為表示勸誘或提議的「Would you like . . . ?」問句。(A) 利用食物相關的主題聯想，內容與題目無關。(B) 雖沒有直接回答「Yes/No」，但內容委婉拒絕對方提議，故為合適答案。(C) 題目詢問的是「dessert」而不是「main dish」，且通常上菜順序中，主菜會比甜點還早出現，所以此非正解。本題正確答案為 (B)。

29 --

When are you going to review the monthly reports?
(A) No, he won't.
(B) Two days ago.
(C) As soon as I get them.

你什麼時候要檢視月報告？
(A) 不，他不會。
(B) 兩天前。
(C) 等我拿到它們時。

• **review** 檢視　**monthly report** 月報告　**. . . as soon as . . .** 一…… 就……

本題是詢問未來時間的「When」疑問句，(A) 疑問詞問句不能用「Yes/No」回答，且此選項的主詞也與題目不符；(B) 應以未來的時間點回覆，但此表示過去的時間點；(C) 使用「as soon as」，表示一拿到報告就會檢視，此為合適回覆，故本題正確答案為 (C)。

30 --

I dry-cleaned all my winter clothes last week.
(A) Yes, it suits you well.
(B) Only for regular customers.
(C) How much did that cost in total?

我上週乾洗了所有的冬衣。
(A) 是的，非常適合你。
(B) 只給常客。
(C) 那樣總共多少錢？

• **dry-clean** 乾洗（衣物）　**suit** 適合　**regular customer** 常客

本題為陳述句，告知對方自己乾洗衣物，(C) 反問乾洗花費多少錢，故正確答案為 (C)。

(A) 利用聽到「clothes」可能會聯想到的「suits」形成陷阱，但此選項中的「suits」不是「衣服」的意思，而是作為動詞表達「適合」之意。(B) 為利用「dry-clean」與「regular customers」的相關性誘導作答。

31 --

Where do you put the order forms?
(A) We don't have any.
(B) It was nearly 10 pages long.
(C) Don't write on them.

你把訂購表放在哪裡？
(A) 我們都沒有了。
(B) 將近10頁長。
(C) 別寫在上面。

• **order form** 訂購表　**nearly** 將近

本題使用「Where」疑問句，詢問某物品的放置處。(A) 雖未直接告知地點，但説明該物品已全數用完，暗示現在並不存放於任何地方，為合適答覆。(B) 內容與題目無關。 (C) 為利用題目「forms」與「write」的相關性誘導作答。故本題正確答案為 (A)。

PART 3 🎧 31

32-34 conversation

W	Justin, I found a couple of issues in the economy section in tomorrow's newspaper. We have to replace some tables with the updated ones. I need your assistance along with Kayla and Sam, who are also staying late.
M	Sure, I would be glad to do that. Tell me how I can help you.
W	Thanks. Please take some time to hear what Sam has to say about it. Meanwhile, I'll order dinner for everyone who will be staying late.

32–34 對話

女	賈斯汀，我剛在明天報紙的經濟版發現一些問題。我們必須把一些表格換成最新的。我需要你還有凱拉和山姆的協助，他們也會待到很晚。
男	沒問題，我很樂意。告訴我要怎麼幫妳。
女	謝謝。請花點時間聽一下山姆交代的事項。同時，我也會為加班的各位訂晚餐。

• issue 問題 **replace** 取代 **along with...** 還有 **meanwhile** 同時

32 --

What is the woman concerned about?
(A) A family matter
(B) A newspaper page
(C) A travel itinerary
(D) A group presentation

這位女士關心的是什麼？
(A) 家庭事務
(B) 報紙頁面
(C) 旅遊行程
(D) 團體報告

題目詢問女子關心的事，應該從女子的台詞找尋答案。從「I found a couple of issues in the economy section in tomorrow's newspaper. We have to replace some tables with the updated ones.」可知，明天發行的報紙經濟版出現問題，須更換幾個表格，故正確答案為 (B)。

33 --

What does the woman ask the man to do?
(A) Take some pictures
(B) Revise an article
(C) Buy some food
(D) Work overtime

這位女士要求男士做什麼？
(A) 拍照
(B) 校訂文章
(C) 買食物
(D) 加班

題目詢問女子要求的事項，應該要從女子的話中找出線索。女子的第一句台詞「I need your assistance along with Kayla and Sam, who are also staying late.」提到報紙版面上的問題，並請求男子以及其他同事留下來幫忙，故正確答案為 (D)。

ACTUAL TEST 8

PART 3

中譯＋解析

🎧 30
🎧 31

305

34

What does the woman say she will do?
(A) Read a proposal
(B) Mail a package
(C) Arrange for some food
(D) Create an advertisement

這位女士說她要做什麼？
(A) 看企畫書
(B) 寄包裹
(C) 準備食物
(D) 創作廣告

人物之後要做的事情通常會在對話後半段出現。女子最後一句「Meanwhile, I'll order dinner for everyone who will be staying late.」，表示會幫留下來加班的人點晚餐，選項 (C) 將「order dinner」改寫為意義相似的「arrange for some food」，故正確答案為 (C)。

35-37 conversation

35–37 對話

M I saw a television commercial with Patrick Spencer, a personal trainer. He said that we could improve a person's posture to make work more comfortable.	男 我看到私人教練派翠克·史賓塞的電視廣告。他說我們應該改善個人姿勢，使工作更舒適。
W I went to an exercise class held by Mr. Spencer last week that was useful in many ways. For instance, he explained that leaning over a computer causes lower back problems, but a simple set of exercises could help with posture. In addition, he recommended changing the height of the chair.	女 我上週去參加了史賓塞先生舉辦的健身課程，那課程在很多方面都很實用。舉例來說，他解釋身子往電腦傾斜會造成下背問題，但一組簡單的運動就可以改善姿勢。除此之外，他還建議調整椅子的高度。
M I certainly get a lot of pain from constantly working on a computer. How about arranging a lunchtime exercise class?	男 我的確因為連續在電腦上工作而感到疼痛。不如來安排個午休健身課程吧？
W That's a good idea. He gave me some DVDs of exercises with step-by-step instructions. I will hand them out to interested staff members.	女 那是個好主意。他給了我一些逐步解說的運動DVD。我會發給有興趣的同仁們。

• **posture** 姿勢 **for instance** 舉例而言 **lean over** 往……傾斜 **recommend** 建議
step-by-step 逐步的 **instructions** 解說 **hand out** 發放

35

Who is Patrick Spencer?
(A) A computer engineer
(B) A DVD seller
(C) A health trainer
(D) An ad executive

派翠克·史賓塞是誰？
(A) 電腦工程師
(B) DVD銷售員
(C) 健身教練
(D) 廣告主管

仔細聆聽開頭，可從「Patrick Spencer, a personal trainer」中，得知他是一名私人健身教練。同時，從接下來的內容可以知道，他是專門指導矯正姿勢等與等方法的人，故正確答案為 (C)。

36

What did Patrick Spencer advise the woman to do?

(A) Sit up straight in her chair
(B) Work on her computer
(C) Lean against a wall
(D) Upgrade her computer

派翠克‧史賓塞建議這位女士做什麼？

(A) 在椅子上坐直
(B) 用電腦工作
(C) 倚靠牆壁
(D) 升級電腦

女子説：「he explained that leaning over a computer causes lower back problems」，由此可知，史賓賽先生認為彎腰駝背對著電腦工作會導致下背部疼痛，所以應該端正姿勢，正確答案為 (A)。

37

What does the woman offer to do?

(A) Share some information with her colleagues
(B) Assist in preparing a demonstration
(C) Buy the man a computer
(D) Make a list of interested employees

這位女士提議做什麼事？

(A) 和同事分享一些資訊
(B) 幫忙準備操作示範
(C) 為男士買一台電腦
(D) 列出有興趣的員工名單

女子的最後一句話説：「He gave me some DVDs of exercises with step-by-step instructions. I will hand them out to interested staff members」，表示會把 DVD 分給有興趣的同事，故正確答案為 (A)。

38-40 conversation 　　　　　　　　38–40 對話

W Mr. Yates. Alexa here. Our clients from Starwood want to discuss the paperhanging work for their hotel.	女 葉慈先生，我是艾麗莎。喜達屋的客戶想討論他們飯店的壁紙裱貼工程。
M I heard everything was settled last month. Is there any problem?	男 我聽說上個月就安排好了所有事項。有什麼問題嗎？
W They've approved the color and material already, but now they think the project is too expensive.	女 他們已經核准了顏色和材質，但現在他們覺得工程太貴了。
M Well, Starwood is one of our biggest customers, so **(39)I would like to allay their worries.** Maybe if we source cheaper wallpaper for the hotel rooms, we would be able to reduce the overall cost. When is the meeting scheduled?	男 嗯，喜達屋是我們最大的客戶之一，所以**(39)我想緩和他們的憂慮。**也許我們若能為飯店房間取得便宜一點的壁紙，我們就能減少整體費用。會議安排在何時？
W Friday morning. We still have some time to come up with some alternatives.	女 星期五早上。我們還有時間想想替代方案。
M Excellent. Let's have a meeting with the supplier to see what choices are available.	男 很好。我們先和供應商開會吧，看看有哪些選擇可用。

• **paperhanging** 壁紙裱貼　**settle** 安排　**approve** 核准　**material** 材質　**wallpaper** 壁紙　**allay** 緩和　**alternative** 替代方案　**supplier** 供應商

What are the clients worried about?
(A) The color of the paint
(B) The cost of the work
(C) The deadline for the project
(D) The material of the wallpaper

客戶擔心的是什麼？
(A) 油漆的顏色
(B) 工程的費用
(C) 工程的截止日期
(D) 壁紙的材質

從女子說的「They've approved the color and material already, but now they think the project is too expensive.」可知，客戶擔心的是作業費用，故正確答案為 (B)。

 (NEW) ---

What does the man imply when he says, "I would like to allay their worries"?
(A) He wants to satisfy the clients.
(B) He needs more time to finish the project.
(C) He's going to ask for a budget increase.
(D) He doesn't want to work for Starwood.

當這位男士說：「我想緩和他們的憂慮」，是什麼意思？
(A) 他想滿足客戶要求。
(B) 他需要更多時間完成工程。
(C) 他將要求增加預算。
(D) 他不想為喜達屋工作。

此類題型可從前後文判斷。女子先說了客戶擔心費用太高，男子便在後文提到「Maybe if we source cheaper wallpaper for the hotel rooms, we would be able to reduce the overall cost.」，表示他會尋求降低成本的方法，故可推測男子想滿足客戶要求、壓低價格，故正確答案為 (A)。

40 --

What does the man suggest?
(A) Finding a different hotel
(B) Consulting with the supplier
(C) Ignoring the customer's expectations
(D) Postponing the meeting

這位男士提出什麼建議？
(A) 找其他飯店
(B) 與供應商商議
(C) 不顧客戶期望
(D) 延後會議

本題詢問男子提議的內容，應從男子的話中尋找線索。從「Let's have a meeting with the supplier to see what choices are available.」中，可以得知他將與供應商協調對策，故正確答案為 (B)。

41-43 conversation

41–43 對話

M Hello, Doctor Hopkins. I am Gary Kemp, the chief editor at Medical Tech Online. We wish to publish your article on the common cold in our online forum next month.	**男** 哈金斯醫師，您好。我是《線上醫藥科技》的主編蓋瑞・坎普。我們希望能在下個月的線上論壇刊登您有關普通感冒的文章。
W That's amazing news. I researched a lot of sources for this article, which was worthwhile and rewarding. But I feel it may be too technical for your Web site.	**女** 那是個好消息。我為這篇文章研究了很多資料，相當值得也很有回報。不過我覺得那對你們的網站可能太過專業了。
M I thought the same thing. But I can assist you in simplifying the text. If I send you some easier vocabulary, you can make a start on rewriting the article.	**男** 我有同感。但我可以幫您簡化原文。如果我給您一些淺顯的字彙，您就可以著手改寫那篇文章了。

- **publish** 刊登　**common cold** 普通感冒　**source** 資料　**worthwhile** 值得的　**rewarding** 有回報的
  technical 專業的　**simplify** 簡化　**text** 文字　**make a start** 著手

What is the conversation mainly about?
(A) Getting a general checkup
(B) Designing a book
(C) Publishing an article
(D) Giving a talk

這段對話主要是與什麼有關？
(A) 接受健康檢查
(B) 設計書籍
(C) 刊登文章
(D) 發表演說

男子開頭介紹自己是主編，並向對方說：「We wish to publish your article on the common cold in our online forum next month.」，故可知道，這段對話的主題與刊登文章相關，正確答案為 (C)。

What are the speakers worried about?
(A) The length of a text
(B) The difficulty of an article
(C) The access to an online forum
(D) The deadline for publishing

說話者擔心的是什麼？
(A) 內文的長度
(B) 文章的難度
(C) 線上論壇的使用
(D) 出版截止日期

女子的最後一句話說：「But I feel it may be too technical for your Web site.」，表示自己的文章內容可能太過艱深，故正確答案為 (B)。

如果不懂「technical」的字義，也能從後文男子說的「But I can assist you in simplifying the text. If I send you some easier vocabulary, you can make a start on rewriting the article.」推論，原文應過於困難，男子才會提議簡化文章。

What does the man offer to do?
(A) Participate in the research
(B) Carry a different article
(C) Provide a list of words
(D) Vaccinate the patients

這位男士提議要做什麼？
(A) 參與研究
(B) 刊登另一篇文章
(C) 提供字彙表
(D) 為病人注射疫苗

從「If I send you some easier vocabulary, you can make a start on rewriting the article.」可知，男子將寄送簡易單字表給女子，故正確答案為 (C)。

44-46 conversation	44-46 對話
W Have you noticed how quiet the remodeling work of our office has been?	女 你有注意到辦公室的整修工程進行得有多安靜嗎？
M Yes, I know. It was even tough to say that there was construction going on.	男 沒錯，我知道。甚至很難感覺到有工程正在進行。
W I'm very impressed with the workers because they've been so professional and they managed their working schedule so wonderfully that it never overlapped with ours. They even cleaned the workspace every day.	女 我對這些工人印象深刻，因為他們很專業，而且對工作進度的掌控也完美到從不和我們的工作時間重疊。他們甚至每天都清掃工作區域。
M I agree. I'm going to suggest using the same company in the future.	男 我同意。我會建議將來聘用同一家公司。

• **notice** 注意　**professional** 專業的　**overlap** 重疊　**professionalism** 專業度

What are the speakers discussing?
(A) A renovation project
(B) A job interview
(C) A road development
(D) A work schedule

說話者在討論什麼？
(A) 整修工程
(B) 工作面試
(C) 道路開發
(D) 工作時程表

女子開頭以「Have you noticed how quiet the remodeling work of our office has been?」詢問對方有沒有注意到改裝工程進行得很安靜，藉此開啟話題。(A) 將「remodeling work」改寫為意義相近的「renovation project」，故正確答案為 (A)。

What is the woman impressed by?
(A) The improved environment of the office
(B) How quickly the job was performed
(C) The professionalism of the workers
(D) How little the construction cost

這位女士對什麼感到印象深刻？
(A) 辦公室改善後的環境
(B) 工作執行的速度
(C) 工人的專業度
(D) 工程費用的微薄

女子的第二句台詞「I'm very impressed with the workers because they've been so professional . . .」直接提示了線索，故本題正確答案為 (C)。

雖然對話中女子也稱讚工人能準確分配工作時間，而不與女子重疊，但不代表工人工作執行快速，故 (B) 非正確答案。

46 -

What does the man say he will suggest?
(A) Rescheduling some appointments
(B) Moving to a new building
(C) Calling the maintenance office
(D) Employing the same company again

這位男士說他將提出什麼建議？
(A) 重新安排一些預約
(B) 搬到新大樓
(C) 打電話給維修部門
(D) 再次聘用同一家公司

男子最後說：「I'm going to suggest using the same company in the future.」，提出以後也要讓同一家業者承包的想法，故正確答案為 (D)。

47-49 conversation　　　　　　　　　　**47–49 對話**

W Hello, Glenn. I see you have safely returned from your visit abroad. Did you find any good suppliers for our overseas venture? **M** Yes, I think a firm in Copenhagen is ideal for our company. And there are two other manufacturers in Malmo that make high-quality products. However, Copenhagen is nearer to the harbor and is better placed for transportation. **W** Can you show me the full report when it's finished? Oh, and remember that tomorrow is your last chance to submit your travel expense report. Make sure all of the receipts are sent to the Finance Department.	**女** 哈囉，葛蘭。我得知你已經從海外探訪平安歸來了。你有為我們的海外企業找到不錯的供應商嗎？ **男** 有的。我覺得哥本哈根有家公司很適合我們。另外，在馬摩爾也有兩家生產高品質產品的廠商。但哥本哈根離港口比較近，也較方便運輸。 **女** 在你完成整份報告後，可以給我看一下嗎？噢，記得明天是你提交差旅支出報告的最後一天。務必把所有的收據都送到財務部去。

• **abroad** 海外　**overseas** 海外的　**venture** 企業　**ideal for . . .** 適合……　**transportation** 運輸
finance department 財務部　**source** 獲取

 31

47 -

What was the purpose of the man's trip?
(A) To look at the new factory sites
(B) To source new suppliers
(C) To sell goods abroad
(D) To arrange interviews

這位男士出差的目的是什麼？
(A) 查看新廠址
(B) 獲取新供應商
(C) 賣商品到海外
(D) 安排面談

對話開頭女子便以「Did you find any good suppliers for our overseas venture?」詢問男子是否找到適合的海外供應商，男子回覆了一些廠商的資料，由此可知，男子剛結束尋找供應商的出差旅程，所以正確答案為 (B)。

48

What does the man say about the company in Copenhagen?

(A) It has many manufacturing plants.

(B) It is favorably located.

(C) It welcomes business from abroad.

(D) It is close to an airport.

關於哥本哈根的公司，這位男士提到什麼事？

(A) 有很多製造廠

(B) 地點適宜

(C) 歡迎海外企業

(D) 靠近機場

男子提及位於哥本哈根與馬爾摩的兩家業者，並說「However, Copenhagen is nearer to the harbor and is better placed for transportation.」，表示哥本哈根的業者離港口比較近，方便運送物品，所以正確答案為 (B)。

49

What does the woman remind the man to do?

(A) Ask for an extended vacation

(B) Report the loss of his luggage

(C) Submit his report

(D) Update his current client details

這位女士提醒男士做什麼？

(A) 請求延長假期

(B) 呈報行李遺失

(C) 送交報告

(D) 更新現有客戶資料細節

女子最後說：「Oh, and remember that tomorrow is your last chance to submit your travel expense report. Make sure all of the receipts are sent to the Finance Department.」，告知明天是報銷出差費用的最後機會，要男子不要忘記繳交資料，所以正確答案為 (C)。

50-52 conversation

50–52 對話

M	Hi, Ms. Warren. My name is Tim Rhodes, from the Human Resources Department at Morris Shipping Service, calling regarding your application as head receptionist. Following consultation with our interviewers, I am delighted to offer you the job.
W	That is excellent news. However, as I am working now, I must hand in my notice to my current company. What is the start date for the job?
M	Ideally, we want someone to start immediately, but with your experience, we can try to sort a suitable time frame out for you. How soon do you think you could begin?
W	Luckily, I have a capable successor who is to be appointed to my position here. It will take about two weeks to train her properly, so that would be the earliest I can start.

男	華倫女士，妳好。我是莫利斯貨運公司人力資源部的提姆·羅德斯，我打這通電話是有關妳應徵首席接待員一職的事宜。在與我們的面試官討論後，我很樂意提供妳這份工作。
女	那真是太好了。不過，由於我現在還有工作，我必須預先通知目前的公司。該職的起始日是什麼時候？
男	最理想的狀況是立刻開始。不過，由於妳的經驗豐富，我們可以試著為妳安排一個合適的時間範圍。妳認為妳多快可以開始？
女	幸運的是，已經有一個能幹的接班人指派到我的職位了。訓練她上手大概需要兩週的時間，所以那會是我最快可以上班的時間。

• **human resources department** 人力資源部　**receptionist** 接待員　**following . . .** 在……之後
hand in one's notice 繳交通知（引申為遞交辭呈）　**ideally** 理想地　**sort . . . out** 挑出……
time frame 時間範圍　**capable** 能幹的　**properly** 徹底的

50

What department does the man work in?
(A) Maintenance
(B) Customer Service
(C) Reception
(D) Human Resources

這位男士在哪個部門工作？
(A) 維修部
(B) 客戶服務部
(C) 接待處
(D) 人力資源部

男子的自我介紹提到「My name is Tim Rhodes, from the human resources department」，
直接告知自己隸屬人事部，故正確答案為 (D)。

51

What does the woman ask about?
(A) The start date of a job
(B) The qualifications for a job
(C) The name of the Human Resources Manager
(D) The location of the training session

這位女士詢問何事？
(A) 開始上工的日期
(B) 工作的資格條件
(C) 人力資源部的主管姓名
(D) 訓練講習的地點

從女子說的「What is the start date for the job?」可知，她在詢問男子新工作的上班時間，
故正確答案為 (A)。

52

What does the woman say she will probably do?
(A) Hand over her present duties to her colleague
(B) Teach the man how to do his job properly
(C) Move to a new location
(D) Submit a job application

這位女士說她可能會做什麼？
(A) 將她目前的職務移交給同事
(B) 教導這位男士如何做好工作
(C) 搬到新址
(D) 遞交求職申請書

女子說：「Luckily, I have a capable successor who is to be appointed to my position here.」
表示自己目前擔任的職務已經找到優秀的繼任者，(A) 將「capable successor」根據文意改為
「her colleague」，故正確答案為 (A)。

53-55 conversation

M I'm moving to the second floor to get started on the painting work in the hallway. Do you know of any other maintenance requests that I've somehow missed?

W Yes, there is a request I just received. Ms. Stone has informed me that the lights in the meeting room, which is just next to her office, won't turn on.

M Okay, I will have a look. Do I need to check it before I start painting, or would it be okay if I checked it this afternoon?

W I think it would be better if you checked it right now because Ms. Stone will be attending a meeting with her clients in there from one o'clock today.

53–55 對話

男 我要去二樓著手進行走廊的油漆工作。妳覺得我有漏掉其他需要維修的申請嗎？

女 有，我剛收到一項申請。史東女士告訴我她辦公室旁邊那間會議室的燈不亮了。

男 好，我會去看一下。我需要在開始油漆前去檢查，還是今天下午再去就可以了？

女 我想你最好現在去看一下，因為史東女士今天一點要跟客戶在那裡開會。

• maintenance 維修　defective 壞的

Who most likely is the man?
(A) An administrative assistant
(B) A sales representative
(C) An interior designer
(D) A maintenance employee

這位男士最有可能是誰？
(A) 行政助理
(B) 業務代表
(C) 室內設計師
(D) 維修人員

男子開頭說：「I'm moving to the second floor to get started on the painting work in the hallway. Do you know of any other maintenance requests that I've somehow missed?」，表示自己將開始進行走道的油漆工程，並詢問女子有沒有其他需要維修的部分，故可推測男子從事的是維修相關的工作，所以正確答案為 (D)。

What problem does the woman mention?
(A) A project is not complete.
(B) An office is locked.
(C) Some electric equipment is defective.
(D) Some materials are not available.

這位女士提到了什麼問題？
(A) 計畫不完整
(B) 辦公室鎖住了
(C) 一些電力設備壞了。
(D) 少了一些材料。

女子說：「lights in the meeting room, which is just next to her office, won't turn on.」，表示會議室的燈不會亮，所以正確答案為 (C)。

According to the woman, what is scheduled to take place in the afternoon?
(A) A safety check
(B) A meeting
(C) A job interview
(D) A power outage

根據這位女士所言，什麼事情被安排在今天下午？
(A) 安全檢查
(B) 會議
(C) 工作面試
(D) 停電

如果題目中提及時間點，請專心聆聽對話中提到時間的部分並找出線索。女子的最後一句台詞提到「Ms. Stone will be attending a meeting with her clients in there from one o'clock today.」，表示史東女士將在今天下午一點和客戶開會，因此要求男子先去檢查會議室的電燈。由此可知，正確答案為 (B)。

56-58 conversation with three speakers (NEW)

56–58 三人對話

W	Seth, I am unable to make any telephone calls from the office.	
M1	I have the same problem. The message states that the network is unavailable.	
M2	I have contacted the telephone company, and the manager explained that the cables have been damaged, which is affecting the communication system on this floor. It won't be fixed until later today.	
W	(57)**That's no good to me.** I have to call two of our clients at lunchtime.	
M1	Oh, no. Are there some time-sensitive issues?	
W	Yes, I need to explain to them about the urgent changes to be made. But it can't be done in this situation.	
M2	Here's a solution. Why don't you try using the phone in the conference room downstairs? As I remember, that allows a three-way call.	
W	What a relief! Thank you. I'll go to the conference room to check it right now.	

女　賽斯，我無法從辦公室撥打電話出去。
男1　我也有同樣的問題。消息說網路線路不通。
男2　我已經聯絡電信公司了，經理解釋說纜線受損，影響了這層樓的通訊系統。要到今天稍晚才能修復完成。
女　(57)那我就慘了。我得在午餐時間打電話給兩個客戶。
男1　不會吧。是急迫的問題嗎？
女　是的，我得跟他們說明緊急更動的事。但看來在這種狀況下是無法了。
男2　有個解決辦法。妳何不試試樓下會議室的電話？我記得那可以三方通話。
女　那真是鬆了一口氣！感謝你。我現在就去會議室看一下。

• **communication system** 通訊系統　**time-sensitive** 急迫的　**urgent** 緊急的　**conference room** 會議室
three-way call 三方通話　**What a relief** 鬆了口氣

ACTUAL TEST 8

PART 3

中譯＋解析

31

What problem is the woman talking about?

(A) She cannot meet her manager today.
(B) She cannot find any problem with her mobile phone.
(C) She cannot contact her clients from the office.
(D) She cannot fix the defective cables.

這位女士提到什麼問題？
(A) 她今天無法與經理碰面
(B) 她不知道她的手機怎麼了
(C) 她無法從辦公室與客戶聯絡
(D) 她無法修復受損的纜線

從女子一開始説的「I am unable to make any telephone calls from the office.」即可知道，女子正在描述沒辦法撥打電話的問題，所以正確答案為 (C)。

57 NEW --

What does the woman imply when she says, "That's no good to me"?

(A) She has to leave early today.
(B) She can't wait for the cables to be repaired.
(C) She will visit the clients in person.
(D) She doesn't want to use a three-way call.

當這位女士説：「那我就慘了」，是什麼意思？
(A) 她今天必須提早下班。
(B) 她無法等到纜線修復好。
(C) 她將親自拜訪客戶。
(D) 她不想使用三方通話。

請注意女子在説這句話之前出現的台詞。男子説：「the cables have been damaged, which is affecting the communication system on this floor. It won't be fixed until later today.」，告知今天稍晚的時候線路才會修復。就算線路可以修復，女子仍説「no good」，因為她必須在中午使用電話。由此可知，正確答案為 (B)。

58 --

What will the woman probably do next?

(A) Check the telephone downstairs
(B) Contact the telephone company again
(C) Make a speech at the conference
(D) List some time-sensitive issues

這位女士接下來可能會做什麼？
(A) 確認樓下的電話
(B) 再次聯絡電信公司
(C) 在會議上發表演說
(D) 列出有時效性的問題

男子建議「Why don't you call them using the phone in the conference room downstairs?」，女子則回覆「I'll go to the conference room to check it right now.」，表示女子將去會議室確認那裡的電話能否使用，故正確答案為 (A)。

M	Erin, have you decided to redecorate your office yet?	男	艾琳，妳已經決定好要重新裝修辦公室了嗎？
W	Yes, I have contacted a company called Amberhues. I got a number of estimates from several companies, all within a similar price range. But because the company has been established for over a decade, I decided to use Amberhues.	女	是的，我已經聯絡一家名叫琥珀色的公司。我跟好幾家公司拿了一些估價單，價位都差不多。不過因為這家公司已經成立十多年了，所以我決定聘用琥珀色。
M	I wondered if you had changed your mind since you have been asked to travel to Miami for work over the next few weeks.	男	我還在想妳是不是改變主意了，因為妳接下來幾週必須去邁阿密工作。
W	Amberhues was very accommodating and has agreed not to start work on the office until I return in July.	女	琥珀色非常地隨和親切，他們已經同意等我七月回來再開始動工。

• **redecorate** 重新裝修　**estimate** 估價單　**decade** 十年　**accommodating** 隨和親切的

59 --

What type of company is Amberhues?　　　琥珀色是哪一類型的公司？
(A) A travel agency　　　　　　　　　　　(A) 旅行社
(B) A moving company　　　　　　　　　　(B) 搬家公司
(C) A decorating firm　　　　　　　　　　(C) 裝潢公司
(D) A hotel　　　　　　　　　　　　　　　(D) 飯店

男子詢問女子是否決定要裝潢辦公室，而女子說：「Yes, I have contacted a company called Amberhues.」，由此可知，琥珀色應是辦公室裝潢公司的名字，所以正確答案為 (C)。

60 --

Why did the woman choose Amberhues?　　這位女士為什麼選擇琥珀色？
(A) It has been in operation for a long time.　(A) 它已經營業很久了。
(B) It is convenient to her office.　　　　　(B) 就在她辦公室附近。
(C) It has a branch in Miami.　　　　　　　(C) 它在邁阿密有分公司。
(D) It is the most competitively priced.　　(D) 價格最實惠。

從女子說的「because the company has been established for over a decade.」可知，正確答案為 (A)。

61 --

Why will the work start in July?　　　　工程為什麼七月才開始？
(A) The company has to give approval.　　　(A) 那家公司必須授予許可。
(B) Furniture cannot be delivered earlier.　(B) 家具無法提早送達。
(C) The woman will be away until then.　　(C) 這位女士在那之前都不在。
(D) The company is busy with other work.　(D) 那家公司忙著其他工程。

從男子說的「you have been asked to travel to Miami.」可知，女子將前往邁阿密出差。且隨後女子回覆「Amberhues . . . has agreed not to start work on the office until I return in July.」，表示裝潢公司答應會等女士七月歸來後再開始工作，所以正確答案為 (C)。

W	James, next Monday is the birthday of our president. Do you think we should arrange a party for him?	女 詹姆士，下星期一就是總裁的生日了。你認為我們應該幫他辦個派對嗎？
M	Let's have a nice dinner together. How about one of his favorite restaurants? Monsoon Lounge, for example. They're offering a 10% discount on their buffet.	男 大家一起吃頓好吃的晚餐吧。到他最喜歡的餐廳如何，像是季風飯店？他們的自助餐有提供九折優惠。
W	But that's just for lunchtime. And some of us don't like Thai food. How about the newly opened Japanese restaurant?	女 但那僅限於午餐時間，而且有些人不喜歡泰式料理。那家新開的日本餐廳如何？
M	Hikaru? I doubt he'll enjoy those raw fish. We'd better have some sort of Western food.	男 光芒嗎？我不覺得他會喜歡生魚片。我們最好找西式料理。
W	This isn't easy. Maybe we should take some suggestions.	女 那可不容易。也許我們該徵詢一些意見。
M	You're right. And we need to book a place that can accommodate 15 people in a separate room.	男 妳說的沒錯。而且我們需要預訂一個可以容納15個人的包廂。

Restaurant Suggestions

Wang's Castle	Chinese	Delicious noodles, Not spicy
Beefy Porky	Barbecue	Outdoor restaurant, Fairly cheap
Indiana's	Steakhouse	Lunchtime discount, Rooms available
Chili Chili	Spicy Ribs	Best for spice lovers, Mexican style

建議餐廳

王堡	中菜	麵食很好吃 不辣
牛豬雙味	烤肉	戶外餐廳 價格實惠
印第安納	牛排館	午餐時段有折扣 有包廂
紅番椒	辣肋排	適合嗜辣者 墨西哥式

• **president** 總裁 **arrange a party** 辦派對 **newly opened** 新開幕的 **doubt** 不能肯定 **raw fish** 生魚
Western food 西式料理 **accommodate** 容納 **separate room** 包廂

62 --

According to the woman, what is the purpose of the event?

(A) To organize an awards ceremony
(B) To taste some exotic food
(C) To open a new business
(D) To celebrate a birthday

根據這位女士所言，這個活動的目的是什麼？
(A) 安排頒獎典禮
(B) 品嚐異國食物
(C) 開新店家
(D) 慶祝生日

女子開頭說：「next Monday is the birthday of our president. Do you think we should arrange a party for him?」，表示下週是總裁老闆的生日，並提議舉辦派對。由此可知，正確答案為 (D)。

63 NEW

Look at the graphic. Which place would be most suitable for the event?

(A) Wang's Castle
(B) Beefy Porky
(C) Indiana's
(D) Chili Chili

看一下圖表，哪一個地方最適合舉辦這個活動？
(A) 王堡
(B) 牛豬雙味
(C) 印第安納
(D) 紅番椒

根據男子說的「We'd better have some sort of Western food.」可知，他們想選的是西餐廳。再從男子最後說的「And we need to book a place that can accommodate 15 people in a separate room.」知道，餐廳必須有包廂，所以既是西餐廳又有包廂的只有印第安納，故本題正確答案為 (C)。

64

Why does the woman disagree with the man's idea?

(A) The restaurant is not big enough.
(B) They won't be able to get a discount.
(C) The president doesn't like Japanese food.
(D) They have no time to book a room.

這位女士為什麼不認同男士的意見？
(A) 餐廳不夠大。
(B) 他們無法得到優惠折扣。
(C) 總裁不喜歡日式料理。
(D) 他們沒有時間訂包廂。

此段對話雙方正進行討論，所以本題的解題重點在找出男子提出意見，而女子表達反對看法的部分。男子的第一句台詞說「How about one of his favorite restaurants? Monsoon Lounge, for example. They're offering a 10% discount on their buffet.」提議選擇有優惠的季風飯店，而女子回答「But that's just for lunchtime.」，表示只有午餐時段才有優惠，故正確答案為 (B)。

 31

65-67 conversation and map

W	You know what? I've just found the ideal location for your culinary school. It's in the Diana Complex, directly to the north of the city.
M	I've never heard of the Diana Complex. Where is it located?
W	Just across from Tinderbox, where we had dinner together last Wednesday.
M	Hmm . . . I thought there was a gas station across from the restaurant.
W	No, it's on the other side. It's a five-story building right next to the hotel.
M	I'm not sure which hotel you're talking about. By the way, is it large enough?
W	You would be surprised at the size inside. Can you find some time later today to visit the site with me?

65–67 對話及地圖

女	你知道嗎？我找到你烹飪學校的理想地點了。就在黛安娜大樓，在本市的正北方。
男	我沒聽過黛安娜大樓。它在哪裡？
女	就在我們上週三吃晚餐的打火匣對面。
男	嗯……我以為餐廳的對面是加油站。
女	不，那是另一邊。它是飯店旁的一棟五層樓大樓。
男	我不確定妳說的是哪一間飯店。順道一提，它夠大嗎？
女	你一定會對內部的空間感到驚訝。你今天稍晚有時間跟我去看一下那場地嗎？

| M | Tomorrow afternoon is better, as I am in cooking lessons all day today. | 男 | 明天下午比較適合，因為我今天一整天都要上烹飪課。 |

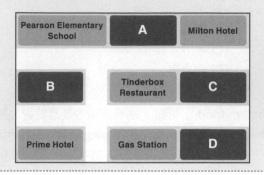
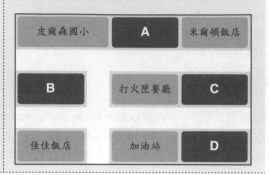

• **ideal** 理想的　**culinary school** 烹飪學校　**complex** 綜合大樓　**directly** 筆直地

65 --

What most likely is the man's occupation?
(A) Real estate agent
(B) Building constructor
(C) Cooking teacher
(D) Hotel worker

這位男士最有可能是做什麼的？
(A) 不動產經紀人
(B) 大樓營建商
(C) 烹飪老師
(D) 飯店員工

女子的第一句台詞中提及「your culinary school」，故可推測男子正在尋找料理教室開幕或移轉的地點。此外，男子的最後一句話說：「Tomorrow afternoon is better, as I am in cooking lessons all day today.」，由此可知，男子今天一整天都有料理課程，所以選項中最符合的為 (C)。

66 (NEW) --

Look at the graphic. Where most likely is the Diana Complex?
(A) A
(B) B
(C) C
(D) D

看一下圖表，黛安娜大樓最有可能在哪裡？
(A) A
(B) B
(C) C
(D) D

男子詢問黛安娜大樓的位置，女子回答道：「Just across from Tinderbox, where we had dinner together last Wednesday.」，表示該建築為打火匣餐廳的對面，並告知「It's a five-story building right next to the hotel.」，表示該建築位於飯店隔壁，故可推測，黛安娜大樓最可能位於 (A)。

67 --

When does the man say he can visit the Diana Complex?
(A) This evening
(B) Later tomorrow
(C) The day after tomorrow
(D) The week after

這位男士說他何時可以參觀黛安娜大樓？
(A) 今天傍晚
(B) 明天稍晚
(C) 後天
(D) 下週

從男子說的「Tomorrow afternoon is better」可知，男子明天下午比較方便參觀，故正確答案為 (B)。

M Ma'am, your orders are now ready. Is there anything else you need?	**男** 女士，您訂購的東西都備好了。還有其他需要的嗎？
W No, that's all I want. How much do they cost?	**女** 不，就這些了。這些多少錢？
M They're 265 dollars. The speakers are 30 dollars each, since we're offering a 25% discount. Check them on the monitor here.	**男** 這樣是265元。因為有七五折的優惠，喇叭每組是30元。您可以在螢幕上確認一下。
W It's strange. I can't find the webcam on the list.	**女** 真奇怪。我找不到清單上的網路攝影機。
M Really? You've chosen 6 speakers, 2 keyboards, and a mouse. Oh, I have missed the X-cam 64. It's added onto the list. Now that'll be 340 dollars in total.	**男** 真的嗎？您挑了六組喇叭、兩個鍵盤和一個滑鼠。喔，我漏掉X-cam 64了。已經加到清單上了。這樣總共是340元。
W It's more expensive than I thought. I'll take 2 speakers out of my order. Will you accept a company check? I appear to have forgotten the company credit card.	**女** 比我想的還貴。我要拿掉兩個喇叭。你們收公司支票嗎？我好像忘了帶公司信用卡了。
M A company check is fine. We need to arrange the shipping schedule. When would be the best time to deliver them to your office?	**男** 公司支票可以。我們需要安排配送時間。什麼時候最適合配送到貴公司呢？

Item	Quantity	Subtotal
Speaker	6	$180
Keyboard	2	$50
Mouse	1	$35
Webcam	1	$75
Delivery		$0
Total		**$340**

品項	數量	小計
喇叭	6	180 元
鍵盤	2	50 元
滑鼠	1	35 元
網路攝影機	1	75 元
運費		0 元
總計		340 元

• **webcam** 網路攝影機　**company check** 公司支票　**shipping schedule** 配送時間

68

Who most likely is the man?

(A) A storekeeper
(B) A bank teller
(C) A delivery man
(D) A computer repairman

這位男士最有可能是誰？

(A) 店員
(B) 銀行行員
(C) 送貨員
(D) 電腦維修員

女子購買喇叭、鍵盤、滑鼠等看起來是電腦週邊用品的物品，而男子依照女子購買的項目結算總金額，故可推測男子最可能為商店店員，所以正確答案為 (A)。

69 -

What does the woman ask about?　　　這位女士詢問何事？
(A) The delivery time　　　　　　　　(A) 運送時間
(B) The payment options　　　　　　(B) 付款方式
(C) The availability of items　　　　　(C) 有無現貨
(D) A card approval　　　　　　　　(D) 卡片核准

女子最後以「Will you accept a company check?」詢問結帳的方式，故正確答案為 (B)。

(A) 的內容是男子間的問題，而不是女子。(C) 的狀況雖然有可能發生，但是對話中，女子並未詢問「有沒有某個物品」，所以不是正確答案。(D) 女子並未攜帶信用卡。

70 -

Look at the graphic. Which information on the list has to be changed now?　看一下圖表，清單上哪一項資料需要更改？
(A) \$180　　　　　　　　　　　　　(A) 180元
(B) \$50　　　　　　　　　　　　　(B) 50元
(C) \$35　　　　　　　　　　　　　(C) 35元
(D) \$75　　　　　　　　　　　　　(D) 75元

女子本來要買六個喇叭，但最後說「I'll take 2 speakers out of my order.」，表示要少買兩個，故喇叭項目的金額應需要修改，正確答案為 (A)。

PART 4 🎧 32

71-73 announcement

May I have everyone's attention? The new tire-fitting machine is being delivered on Thursday. **(72)Without any doubt, this is good news!** This state-of-the-art machine can fit tires to cars in half the normal time. In order to ensure that it is installed and is fully functional, we will need to remain in the garage after hours. We are therefore asking as many employees as possible to stay late in order to catch up with any work. If you wish to volunteer, please add your name to the list. As usual, you will be paid overtime rates.	請各位注意一下。新輪胎安裝機將於週四送達。**(72)毫無疑問地,這是個好消息!** 這台最先進機器將輪胎安裝到汽車上的時間是正常時間的一半。為了確保安裝妥當並充分運作,我們需要在下班時間後留在車廠內。因此我們希望盡量有愈多人員留置,以趕上工作進度。如果你自願幫忙,請將名字填到名單上。你將和平常一樣可以領到加班費。

71-73 宣告

- **tire-fitting machine** 輪胎安裝機　**state-of-the-art** 最先進的　**ensure** 確保　**functional** 正常運作的　**garage** 車廠　**after hours** 下班時間後　**catch up with** 趕上……　**volunteer** 自願　**as usual** 和平常一樣　**overtime rates** 加班費　**closure** 倒閉　**opening ceremony** 開幕典禮

71 --

What is the announcement mainly about?
(A) A machine installation
(B) A company closure
(C) A safety inspection
(D) A vehicle check

這個公告主要和什麼有關?
(A) 機械安裝
(B) 公司倒閉
(C) 安全檢測
(D) 車輛檢查

本題詢問文字主旨,答案可從開頭的部分尋找。「The new tire-fitting machine is being delivered on Thursday.」,表示新的輪胎安裝機會在週四送達,且中間部分提到「In order to ensure that it is installed and is fully functional, we will need to remain in the garage after hours.」,代表機器架設在車廠裡,所以才需要下班後留在車廠監督安裝工程,故正確答案為 (A)。

72 [NEW] ---

What does the man imply when he says, "Without any doubt, this is good news"?
(A) He can fix his car by himself now.
(B) He will gladly do the overtime work.
(C) They have purchased the machine at a low price.
(D) The new machine will help them complete the work in less time.

當這位男士說:「毫無疑問地,這是個好消息」,是什麼意思?
(A) 他現在可以自己修理汽車了。
(B) 他很樂意加班。
(C) 他們以低價購得機器。
(D) 新機器將協助他們以較短的時間來完成工作。

從後文「This state-of-the-art machine can fit tires to cars in half the normal time.」可知,新機器能使輪胎更換的時間縮短,所以正確答案為 (D)。

ACTUAL TEST 8 / PART 4 / 中譯+解析

🎧 31
🎧 32

323

73

What does the speaker ask the listeners to do? | 說話者要求聽者做什麼事？
(A) Attend an opening ceremony | (A) 參加開幕典禮
(B) Welcome a new supervisor | (B) 歡迎新主管
(C) Work overtime hours | (C) 加班
(D) Review an operations manual | (D) 檢視操作手冊

本題為詢問說話者對聽話者所提出的要求，所以要特別注意與要求有關的表現法，如：「I ask you to」、「I ask for」、「I need to」、「I want you to . . . 」，「please、you should」等等。

從中間提到的「In order to ensure that it is installed and is fully functional, we will need to remain in the garage after hours.」可知，為了確保機器安裝妥當，需要有人在車廠加班，故正確答案為 (C)。

74-76 radio broadcast | **74–76 電台廣播**

This is *The Voice* of *London* on PrimeTime Radio. Today, we will be talking to Aiden Elder, Marketing Director of Angel Hearts U.K. This charity specializes in finding employment for homeless youths. Mr. Elder will be talking about the latest figures to be released about the number of homeless on Britain's streets and asking for the public's help for a major new initiative being launched. Angel Hearts is looking for a number of volunteers to mentor young people in the workplace. Keep listening; the interview will follow these commercials.	這裡是黃金電台的《倫敦之聲》。今天我們將訪問英國天使之心的行銷主管艾登・埃爾德。該慈善團體專為年輕遊民尋找就業機會。埃爾德先生將談論最新公布的英國街頭遊民數量的統計數據，並為一項即將發起的新大型行動尋求大眾協助。天使之心正在徵求大批志工，指導職場上的年輕人。請繼續收聽，廣告後即將開始我們的訪談。

• **charity** 慈善團體　**employment** 就業　**homeless** 無家可歸的　**release** 公布　**initiative** 新措施
volunteer 志工　**mentor** 指導　**fundraising** 募款

74

Where does the speaker most likely work? | 說話者最有可能在哪裡工作？
(A) At a radio station | (A) 廣播電台
(B) At an employment agency | (B) 職業介紹所
(C) At a charity organization | (C) 慈善機構
(D) At a publishing house | (D) 出版社

本題為詢問說話者工作場所的題型，可以透過有關職種的描述推敲出來。說話者一開始介紹自己是在「PrimeTime Radio」的「Voice of London」節目，且段落最後還預告將有廣告，故可推測說話者最可能是廣播節目主持人，故正確答案為 (A)。

According to the speaker, what will Mr. Elder discuss?

(A) A community building
(B) A fundraising event
(C) A marketing report
(D) A new plan

根據說話者表示，埃爾德先生將談論什麼事？

(A) 社區建設
(B) 募款活動
(C) 行銷報告
(D) 新計畫

注意本題的關鍵字「Mr. Elder」。說話者表示今天訪問的埃爾德先生將探討最新公布的英國遊民數據統計，並「asking for the public's help for a major new initiative being launched」，即針對最近推動的全新計畫尋求大眾的幫助，故本題正確答案為 (D)。

Why are volunteers needed?

(A) To advise young people
(B) To distribute brochures
(C) To conduct interviews
(D) To recruit office workers

為什麼需要志工？

(A) 為了提供年輕人建議
(B) 為了分發手冊
(C) 為了進行訪談
(D) 為了招募職員

從最後的「Angel Hearts is looking for a number of volunteers to mentor young people in the workplace.」可知，天使之心需要志工輔導年輕人，故正確答案為 (A)。

77–79 talk

77–79 談話

As chairperson of the local anti-crime society, I welcome you to this meeting. I especially welcome any new members. This is our fifth monthly meeting regarding the safety of our neighborhood. I am delighted to inform you that we have been granted permission to apply for a grant for street lighting in the Willis District, adjacent to the railway track. Our next challenge is to come up with a bid to the grant association to persuade them to give us funding. If you think you can help prepare a bid, please contact Megan Bishop, our treasurer at meganbishop@anticrime.org by November 10.	身為本地打擊犯罪協會的主席，本人歡迎各位參加這場會議。我要特別歡迎所有的新成員。這是本社區安全問題的第五次月會。我很高興地告訴各位，我們已經成功申請到鐵路附近的威利斯區街道照明設備的補助金許可。我們下一個挑戰就是要向補助協會出價，以說服他們提供我們資助。如果您認為自己能協助準備出價，請於11月10日前來信meganbishop@anticrime.org聯絡我們的財務主管梅根・碧夏。

• **chairperson** 主席　**anti-crime** 打擊犯罪　**society** 協會　**be granted permission** 獲准　**grant** 補助金
street lighting 街道照明設備　**district** 地區　**adjacent** 附近的　**railway track** 鐵道
come up with a bid 出價　**funding** 資助　**treasurer** 財務主管　**sponsor** 贊助　**contribute** 投稿

77 --

Who is the speaker?
(A) A government officer
(B) A head of a certain society
(C) A police officer
(D) A lighting expert

說話者是誰？
(A) 政府官員
(B) 某個協會主席
(C) 警官
(D) 照明設備專家

說話者一開始便介紹自己為「chairperson of the local anti-crime society」，並歡迎參加者前來參加會議，(B) 將「chairperson」改寫為意義相近的「head」，故正確答案為 (B)。

78 --

What permission has the group received?
(A) Hosting a fundraising event
(B) Supporting a sports team
(C) Submitting a bid for funding
(D) Sponsoring a lighting company

這個團體得到什麼許可？
(A) 舉辦募款活動
(B) 資助一個運動隊伍
(C) 提交出價以申請補助
(D) 贊助燈光公司

說話者提到「we have been granted permission to apply for a grant for street lighting in the Willis District, adjacent to the railway track.」，表示威利斯區的路燈設置補助金申請已經通過，選項 (C) 將「apply for a grant」改寫為意義相近的「submit a bid for funding」，故正確答案為 (C)。

79 --

Why should listeners contact Megan Bishop?
(A) To apply to the committee
(B) To help in preparing the bid
(C) To purchase some lighting
(D) To contribute to the newsletter

聽者為什麼要聯絡梅根·碧夏？
(A) 要向委員會申請
(B) 要幫忙準備出價
(C) 要購買照明設備
(D) 要投稿至社訊

注意本題的關鍵字「Megan Bishop」。談話最後出現「If you think you can help prepare a bid, please contact Megan Bishop, our treasurer . . .」，表示若聽者能協助準備出價，可連絡梅根·碧夏，正確答案為 (B)。

80-82 excerpt from a meeting　　　　　　　　　**80–82 會議摘錄**

Today's meeting is about our marketing campaign for the new book launch. This is the third novel in the best-selling series by Jessica Fox, one of the leading authors in the world, and we need to make sure that we market it well. What makes this book so special is that it is a prequel to the previous stories, and therefore, charts the history of the characters and the plot. We have exclusive rights to this book, and I am sure that you will be able to come up with a dynamic and hard-hitting marketing campaign to

今天的會議是有關我們新書出版的行銷活動。這是世界重量級作家，潔西卡·福斯暢銷系列的第三本小說，我們必須確保能成功地銷售出去。這本書的特別之處就是它是先前作品的前傳，因此裡面記載了人物與情節的演變。我們有這本書的獨家版權，我相信各位一定能夠想出轟動又有力的行銷活動來確保本書暢銷。我將發給每人一本小說。請各位仔細閱讀，激盪出新穎的點子來。

ensure that the book sells. I am giving each one of you a copy of the novel. Please read it carefully and come up with some original ideas.

• leading 重量級的　author 作家　prequel 前傳　chart 記載　character 人物　plot 情節
exclusive rights 獨家版權　come up with … 想出　dynamic 轟動的　hard-hitting 有力的
original 新穎的；原創的　prospective 未來的　proofreading 校對　serialize 使連載
work assignment 工作任務　work out …計算出……

80 --

Who is the intended audience for the talk?
(A) Prospective writers
(B) A proofreading team
(C) A book club
(D) A Marketing Department

這段談話所針對的聽眾是誰？
(A) 未來的作家
(B) 校對小組
(C) 讀書會
(D) 行銷部門

本題是詢問談話對象的題型。說話者一開始提到「Today's meeting is about our marketing campaign for the new book launch.」可知今天的會議與書本發行的行銷活動有關，故對象聽眾是與行銷業務有關的人。正確答案為 (D)。

81 --

According to the speaker, why is the new book unique?
(A) It is being serialized in the newspaper.
(B) It is available in e-book format.
(C) It is the prequel to a series.
(D) It is written in a different language.

根據說話者表示，這本新書為什麼特別？
(A) 它正在報上連載。
(B) 它可以電子書形式取得。
(C) 它是一系列叢書的前傳。
(D) 它是以其他語言寫成的。

本題的關鍵字為「book」、「unique」。中間部分提到，這本書之所以特別，是因為「What makes this book so special is that it is a prequel to the previous stories」。(C) 將「previous stories」改寫為符合文意的「a series」，故正確答案為 (C)。

82 --

What will the speaker most likely do next?
(A) Review work assignments
(B) Meet with the editing team
(C) Distribute copies of a book
(D) Work out a budget

說話者接下來最可能做什麼？
(A) 檢視工作任務
(B) 與編輯小組會面
(C) 分發書本
(D) 編製預算

詢問說話者接下來將採取什麼行動的題型，大部分可以在後半部找到線索。最後，說話者表示「I am giving each one of you a copy of the novel. Please read it carefully and come up with some original ideas.」，由此可知，說話者接下來會發放書籍，所以正確答案為 (C)。

83-85 announcement

Good afternoon. I have a special announcement regarding the promotions we are running, offering customers a 10-minute makeup class. Now I believe you are all proficient in applying makeup. We need to spread the word about this promotion. We have advertised on local radio, and we are offering visitors a free lipstick every day this week. I'm sure this will attract more customers into the salon. But, I am a little worried that we will run out of stock. Can I ask for volunteers to purchase some more stock from the wholesalers on Thursday? Please let me know if you can.

83-85 宣告

午安,關於我們正在進行的促銷活動——提供顧客十分鐘的化妝課程,我有特別事項要宣布。我相信各位對化妝都非常熟練了。我們需要把這個促銷活動的消息散播出去。我們已經在地方電台上宣傳了,而且在本週,我們將每天免費贈送來賓一支口紅。我相信這可以吸引更多客人到美容院來。但我有點擔心我們會缺貨。我想徵求自願者星期四到批發商那裡進貨。請告訴我大家是否有空。

- **run a promotion** 進行促銷活動　**makeup** 化妝　**proficient** 熟練　**apply makeup** 上妝
  spread 散播　**salon** 美容院　**run out of stock** 缺貨　**wholesaler** 批發商　**recall**（商品）回收
  cosmetic item 化妝品　**makeover** 美容服務　**continuous** 不間斷的

What is the announcement mainly about?

(A) A product recall
(B) A brand introduction
(C) A store promotion
(D) A sales training session

這則通知主要和什麼有關?

(A) 商品回收
(B) 品牌介紹
(C) 店家促銷
(D) 銷售訓練講習

説話者一開始提到「I have a special announcement regarding the promotions we are running, offering customers a 10-minute makeup class.」,所以可知談話內容與促銷活動有關,故正確答案為 (C)。

What were employees recently trained to do?

(A) Design a new promotion
(B) Prepare some cosmetic items
(C) Offer makeovers
(D) Inspect some equipment

員工最近被培訓做什麼事?

(A) 設計新促銷活動
(B) 準備化妝品
(C) 提供美容服務
(D) 檢測設

説話者前半部分提到:「Now I believe you are all proficient in applying makeup.」,故可推測,員工最可能接受過的是化妝方法培訓,故正確答案為 (C)。

85

What is the speaker concerned about?

(A) Finding a new supplier
(B) Having sufficient seating
(C) Lowering operating costs
(D) Providing continuous supplies

說話者擔心的是什麼?

(A) 要尋求新供應商
(B) 要有足夠的座位
(C) 要降低營運成本
(D) 要有不間斷的供應量

說話者曾提到「we are offering visitors a free lipstick every day this week. I'm sure this will attract more customers into the salon.」，接著又說「But, I am a little worried that we will run out of stock.」，表示說話者是擔心口紅庫存可能不足，所以正確答案為 (D)。

86-88 telephone message

86-88 電話留言

Hello, this is a message from Adam Barnes. Is the Santa Claus costume still available? I noticed it in the window of your clothing store in Lloyd Street. I desperately need one for a party at my children's school. Can you advise me of the measurements as soon as possible? And if it fits, then I can pick it up. My e-mail address is abarnes@tol.net. Thank you.

您好，這是亞當‧巴恩斯所留的訊息。請問還有聖誕老人的服裝嗎？我在您們位於洛伊德街上的服飾店櫥窗看到這款服裝。我極需要一套去參加孩子學校的派對。您可以盡快告訴我尺寸嗎？如果合適的話，我就可以過去購買。我的電子郵件信箱是 abarnes@tol.net。感謝您。

• costume 服裝　desperately 極度地　measurement 尺寸　fit 合適　notice board 布告欄

86 --

What item is the speaker calling about?

(A) An outfit
(B) A wardrobe
(C) A television
(D) An e-mail account

說話者打電話詢問何種商品？

(A) 服裝
(B) 衣櫃
(C) 電視
(D) 電子郵件信箱

從說話者開頭便詢問的「Is the Santa Claus costume still available?」可知，正確答案為 (A)。

87 --

Where has the item been advertised?

(A) In a magazine
(B) In a local shop
(C) On a bus window
(D) On a notice board

這件商品在哪裡宣傳？

(A) 雜誌
(B) 當地商店
(C) 公車窗戶
(D) 布告欄

說話者說，他曾經看過聖誕老人的服裝放在洛伊德街上的服裝店櫥窗裡，故可知正確答案為 (B)。

88 --

What does the speaker request?

(A) Some photographs
(B) A delivery date
(C) Pricing information
(D) The size of the item

說話者要求什麼東西？

(A) 一些照片
(B) 配送日期
(C) 價格資料
(D) 商品尺寸

說話者表示，自己非常需要一套可以在派對上穿的衣服，並要求「Can you advise me of the measurements as soon as possible?」。(D) 將「measurements」改寫為意義相似的「size」，故正確答案為 (D)。

89-91 telephone message

Hello, Dr. Lawrence. This is Mason Murray from Darwin Medical Supplies. You recently inquired about our physiotherapy equipment for your clinic. I am visiting your region next week, and I would be more than happy to bring some brochures for you to look at. All of our products come with a three-year warranty, which covers accidental damage and on-site repair. If you are interested, please call me to arrange an appointment at 6551-8918.

89–91 電話留言

羅倫斯醫生，您好。我是達爾文醫療器材的梅森・莫瑞。您最近為貴診所詢問了我們的物理治療設備。我下週會至您所在的地區拜訪，我非常樂意帶一些手冊供您參考。我們所有的產品都附有三年保固，其中涵蓋了意外損害與現場維修服務。如果您有興趣的話，請來電6551-8918給我以安排會面。

• **equipment** 設備　**region** 地區　**come with . . .** 附有⋯⋯　**warranty** 保固　**accidental damage** 意外損害　**on-site repair** 現場維修　**highly recommended** 高度推薦　**guarantee** 保固　**transportable** 可運送的

What does the speaker's company produce?
(A) Medical appliances
(B) Office equipment
(C) Drug supplies
(D) Audio systems

說話者的公司生產什麼東西？
(A) 醫療器材
(B) 辦公設備
(C) 藥物供應
(D) 音效系統

本題並不一定要聽得懂「physiotherapy」才可作答。從開頭說話者自我介紹為「This is Mason Murray from Darwin Medical Supplies」就可知道，說話者的公司是生產醫療相關器材的，(A) 將「medical supplies」改寫為意義相近的「medical appliances」，故正確答案為 (A)。

What does the speaker want to arrange?
(A) An on-site demonstration
(B) A factory tour
(C) A payment plan
(D) A meeting schedule

說話者想要安排什麼事？
(A) 現場示範
(B) 工廠導覽
(C) 付款方案
(D) 會面時程

說話者在一開始提到，自己可以前往聽話者所在的地區，藉由宣傳冊進行說明。另外，在最後的部分提到「If you are interested, please call me to arrange an appointment」，表示可以來電預約會面，故正確答案為 (D)。

What does the speaker say about the company's products?
(A) They are highly recommended.
(B) They are covered by a guarantee.
(C) They can be replaced every year.
(D) They are easily transportable.

說話者提到什麼有關公司產品的事？
(A) 受到高度推薦。
(B) 有保固。
(C) 可以每年做更換。
(D) 方便運送。

説話者表示「All of our products come with a three-year warranty, which covers accidental damage and on-site repair.」意為產品都享有三年保固。選項 (B) 將「warranty」改寫為意義相近的「guarantee」，故正確答案為 (B)。

92–94 recorded message

92–94 電話錄音

Thank you for calling Woodcock Art Center. We have been established in the region for many years, and we hold regular meetings to share our paintings and artistic works with other artists. **(93)We are always looking for new people**, so if you would like to find out more about us, you can attend our meetings, which are held on the first and third Wednesday of every month. For information on our schedule of artistic events, visit our Web site.

感謝您來電伍卡克藝術中心。我們在本地成立多年，並定期舉辦聚會，與其他藝術家交流我們的畫作與藝術品。**(93)**我們隨時徵求新成員，所以如果您想更了解本中心，可以參加我們每個月第一週與第三週星期三的聚會。欲了解本中心藝文活動時間相關資訊，請參考我們的網站。

• artistic works 藝術品　organization 單位　tutoring 輔導

What type of organization did the listener call?

(A) An artistic group
(B) A writers' community
(C) A tutoring program
(D) A sporting club

聽者致電的是何種單位？

(A) 藝術團體
(B) 寫作社群
(C) 輔導計畫
(D) 運動社團

本題詢問聽話者致電的機關，回答時可藉由機關從事的活動進行推理。說話者在開頭提到「Thank you for calling Woodcock Art Center.」且告知聽話者「we hold regular meetings to share our paintings and artistic works with other artists.」，表示為了分享畫作與藝術品，會有定期交流活動。由此可知，此處最可能為藝術相關團體，所以正確答案為 (A)。

 NEW

What does the woman imply when she says, "we are always looking for new people"?

(A) To inform the listener that they are newly opened
(B) To find a new place to hold an exhibition
(C) To reschedule the next event
(D) To invite more members to the meeting

當這位女士說：「我們隨時徵求新成員」，是什麼意思？

(A) 要告訴聽者他們新開幕。
(B) 要找一個新處所舉辦展覽。
(C) 要重新安排下一個活動。
(D) 要邀請更多成員參加聚會。

仔細聆聽該句的前後文。從「We are always looking for new people, so if you would like to find out more about us, you can attend our meetings」中可以發現，該藝術中心正在尋找新成員參加聚會，因此正確答案為 (D)。

According to the speaker, what is available on the organization's Web site?

(A) A display of artwork
(B) A calendar of events
(C) An application form
(D) A date for the next meeting

根據說話者表示，機構的網站上有什麼？

(A) 藝術品展示
(B) 活動行事曆
(C) 申請表
(D) 下一次聚會的日期

本題的關鍵字為「Web site」。錄音最後，說話者表示「For information on our schedule of artistic events, visit our Web site.」，請聽話者造訪官方網站，以獲得藝術活動的時間資訊，所以正確答案為 (B)。

95-97 excerpt from a meeting and graph

95–97 會議摘錄及圖表

I see everyone here now, so let's start the meeting. You may already know that our sales declined severely last quarter, and the conditions did not improve this month. As indicated in this graph, the sales of refrigerators, which definitely were our best seller, have been dropping over the past six months. To make matters worse, the sales of televisions seem to pass their peak in November and have started to decrease. On the other hand, the computer line, which was a nuisance to us last quarter, is up slightly, but it still didn't meet our expectations. The company is launching a new laptop in February, when the computer sales usually show an explosive increase. So today, we are here to come up with marketing plans to boost the sales of the new item, for this is a good chance to reverse the situation.

我看大家都到了，那會議就開始吧。大家可能已經知道，我們上一季的業績嚴重地下滑，而這個月狀況並沒有改善。如圖所示，過去顯然是我們最暢銷的冰箱，在過去六個月以來，銷售量一直在下滑。更糟的是，電視機的銷售量看來也過了11月的旺季，開始下降。另一方面，上一季讓我們頭痛的電腦微幅地上升了，但仍未達我們的預期。公司將於二月推出新的筆記型電腦，電腦的銷售量通常會在那時呈現暴增。所以今天我們開會，就是要想出提高新品銷售量的行銷計畫，因為這是一個反轉情勢的好機會。

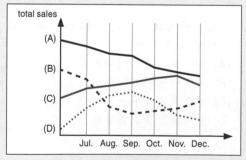

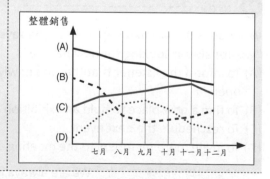

- **severely** 嚴重地 **quarter** 季 **conditions** 狀況 **indicate** 顯示 **to make matters worse** 更糟的是 **peak** 高峰 **on the other hand** 另一方面 **nuisance** 惱人的事物 **slightly** 稍微地 **meet** 符合 **expectation** 期待 **explosive increase** 暴增 **boost** 提高 **reverse** 反轉

95

What does the speaker want to discuss in this meeting?

(A) Moving up the release date of the new item
(B) Criticizing the Sales Department for the poor performance
(C) Making a successful marketing plan
(D) Deciding which products should be discontinued

說話者想在這場會議中討論什麼？
(A) 提前新品的上市日期
(B) 批評業務部門績效欠佳
(C) 制定成功的行銷計畫
(D) 決定哪些產品應該停產

通常，談話的目的會在一開始提及，但本段內容一開始先說明目前低迷的經營成果，接著才說明今天會議的目的。最後的部分中，提及：「So today, we are here to come up with marketing plans to boost the sales of the new item」。由此可知，今天召開會議是為了討論提高新產品銷售量的行銷方法，正確答案為 (C)。

96 NEW

Look at the graphic. Which line indicates the sales results of the computers?

(A) A
(B) B
(C) C
(D) D

看一下圖表，哪一條線指的是電腦的銷售成果？
(A) A
(B) B
(C) C
(D) D

本題的關鍵字為「computer」。從「the computer line, which was a nuisance to us last quarter, is up slightly, but it still didn't meet our expectations.」中可得知，電腦在上一季的銷售成績令人頭痛，但是目前已出現小幅上升。對照圖表，在近期呈現上升趨勢的只有 (B)，故正確答案為 (B)。

(A) 為持續呈現下降趨勢的洗衣機。(C) 為十一月達到高峰，但是後來開始出現降幅的電視。(D) 為到九月為止仍出現增幅，但是後來開始減少的產品。此產品並未在內容中提及，所以不知道是何種產品。

97

What does the speaker say about the new item?

(A) It will be released in February.
(B) It won't meet the customers' expectations.
(C) It is the bestseller as usual.
(D) It only took 6 months to be developed.

說話者提到什麼有關新產品的事？
(A) 將於二月上市。
(B) 無法滿足顧客的期待。
(C) 跟以往一樣暢銷。
(D) 只花六個月的時間開發。

根據中間部分的「The company is launching a new laptop in February」可知，正確解答為 (A)。

必須留意的是，其他選項提及的的關鍵字也出現在內容中。(B) 的「expectations」在文章中指的是說話者的期盼，並非客戶的期望。(C) 的「bestseller」是指「冰箱」。(D) 的「6 months」是指冰箱的銷售量持續減少的期間。

Good morning, everyone. This is Zoe Miller in Human Resources. I'd like everyone to remember that today is the first day of the lunchtime speaker series, which was designed to give us a good opportunity to learn about all the running projects in the company. We have three sessions this week, and the first speaker will be Leah Bennett, who represents the Research Department. I regret notifying you that Mr. Hunt is now at the Chicago branch to take care of an urgent matter. So, those who are interested in the recent changes in the Marketing Department, please expect his speech on Thursday. To make the session more interactive and informative, he has asked all attendees to send any questions about the new marketing projects. Please send your questions to his assistant, Julia Watson, by the end of today.

大家早。我是人力資源部的柔伊‧米勒。我要提醒大家今天是午休系列講座的第一天，這是為了讓大家了解公司所有正在推行的計畫而規劃的。我們這禮拜有三場講習，第一位講者是代表研究部門的利亞‧班內特。很遺憾告訴大家，杭特先生目前正在芝加哥分公司處理一件緊急事務。所以對行銷部門最近變動有興趣的人，請期待週四的演說。為了讓講習更具互動性、內容更充實，他要求所有與會者提出關於新行銷計畫的問題。請在今天下班前，將您的問題寄給他的助理茉莉亞‧華森。

Lunchtime Speaker Series

Room 407

12:15 P.M. – 12:45 P.M.

Mon.	Research Dept.	Leah Bennett
Wed.	Marketing Dept.	Justin Hunt
Fri.	Sales Dept.	Brody West

* Refreshments provided

午休系列講座

407 室

中午 12:15–12:45

星期一	研究部門	利亞‧班內特
星期三	行銷部門	賈斯汀‧杭特
星期五	業務部門	布洛迪‧威斯特

＊ 提供茶點

• **human resources** 人力資源   **running** 推行中的   **represent** 代表   **notify** 告訴
urgent matter 緊急事務   **interactive** 具互動性的   **informative** 內容充實的   **attendee** 與會者

98 --

What will happen later today?
(A) Mr. Hunt will leave for Chicago.
(B) The current marketing plans will be changed.
(C) A speech will be given by Ms. Bennett.
(D) A seminar will be postponed to the following week.

今天稍晚將發生什麼事？
(A) 杭特先生將前往芝加哥。
(B) 目前的行銷計畫將變更。
(C) 班內特女士將發表演說。
(D) 研討會將延至隔週。

從「I'd like everyone to remember that today is the first day of the lunchtime speaker series」可知，今天是午休講座的第一天，再從之後「the first speaker will be Leah Bennett」知道第一位報告人即為班內特女士，故正確答案 (C)。

(A) 杭特先生「已經」在芝加哥。(B) 與 (D) 的內容皆未被提及。

99 NEW ---

Look at the graphic. Which information needs to be changed?

(A) Room 407
(B) Leah Bennett
(C) Wed.
(D) Refreshments provided

看一下圖表，哪一項資料需要變更？

(A) 407室
(B) 利亞・班內特
(C) 星期三
(D) 提供茶點

從「So, those who are interested in the recent changes in the marketing department, please expect his speech on Thursday.」中可以得知，杭特先生的演說改為週四進行，所以需要修正的部分為 (C)。

100 ---

According to the speaker, why would the listeners contact Julia Watson?

(A) To report an urgent matter
(B) To notify her of their availability
(C) To reschedule a session
(D) To make inquiries to Mr. Hunt

根據說話者表示，聽者為什麼要聯絡茱莉亞・華森？

(A) 報告緊急事件
(B) 告訴她他們是否有空
(C) 重新安排講習
(D) 向杭特先生提問

最後的部分中提到「he (Mr. Hunt) has asked all attendees to send any questions. . . . Please send your questions to his assistant, Julia Watson, by the end of today.」。由此可知，杭特先生希望與會者積極發問，但是因為他目前人在芝加哥分公司出差，故聽者若要可將問題先寄給他的秘書茱莉亞・華森小姐。所以正確答案為 (D)。

32

ACTUAL TEST
9

PART 1

🎧 33

1

(A) The woman is looking at the white board.
(B) The woman is standing next to an office machine.
(C) The woman is folding a piece of paper.
(D) The woman is placing a notebook on the shelf.

(A) 這位女士正看著白板。
(B) 這位女士正站在事務機旁。
(C) 這位女士正在折紙。
(D) 這位女士正把筆記本放到架上。

照片中的地點看起來是辦公室,有一名女子站在影印機前影印東西。遇到同時出現人物與物品的照片,選項常常針對兩者的關係進行描述,所以最好先掌握相對位置或人物姓名等訊息。(A) 的動作描述錯誤。(C) 的動作也描寫錯誤。(D) 則是場所描述錯誤。故正確答案為 (B)。

2

(A) The woman is doing the dishes.
(B) The man is fastening the woman's apron.
(C) The woman is preparing some food for the man.
(D) The man is cooking something on a grill.

(A) 這位女士正在洗碗。
(B) 這位男士正在為女士繫圍裙。
(C) 這位女士正在為男士準備食物。
(D) 這位男士正在烤架上料理食物。

• **apron** 圍裙　**grill** 烤架

照片裡有一名男子正在幫女子繫圍裙,所以正確答案為 (B)。其餘選項的動作皆描述錯誤。

3

(A) Heavy machinery has been brought in to dig the ground.
(B) Some people are strolling along the road.
(C) The vehicles are parked in a line on the ground.
(D) The workers are fixing a defective machine.

(A) 重型機械被引進要開挖地面。
(B) 一些人正沿著馬路散步。
(C) 車輛在地面上停放成一排。
(D) 工人正在修理故障的機器。

• **heavy machinery** 重型機械　**dig** 挖　**stroll** 散步　**defective** 故障的

照片中有兩台重裝備,其中一台正在進行鑽地作業,所以正確答案為 (A)。

(B) 照片裡沒有人。(C) 照片裡的車並未排成一排。(D) 照片裡沒有工人,也看不出機器故障。

4

(A) The man is posing for a photo.
(B) The man is painting a fence rail.
(C) Paintings have been hung on the fence.
(D) Benches are positioned under the paintings.

(A) 這位男士正在為拍照擺姿勢。
(B) 這位男士正在粉刷籬笆的圍欄。
(C) 畫作被掛在籬笆上。
(D) 長椅被擺在畫作下。

• pose 擺姿勢　position 擺放

照片背景看起來是在戶外，有一名男子正坐著畫畫。男子面前擺放著顏料等繪畫工具，而後方的欄杆上並排掛著他的畫作，所以正確答案為 (C)。

(A) 與 (B) 男子正在畫圖。(D) 照片中沒有出現長椅。

5

(A) Glass doors lead out to a garden.
(B) A conversation is taking place near a doorway.
(C) People are gathered for a meeting.
(D) The office is separated by a wooden partition.

(A) 玻璃門通往花園。
(B) 門口旁正在進行一場對談。
(C) 人們被召集在一起開會。
(D) 辦公室被木頭隔板隔開。

• lead to 通往　take place 進行　doorway 門口　gather 召集　separate 隔開
partition 隔板

照片背景是室內，可看到玻璃門前有三名男女站在一起聊天，所以正確答案為 (B)。

(A) 無法得知玻璃門外的通道是否通往花園。(C) 無法確認人物是否正在開會。(D) 照片中沒有出現木頭隔板。

6

(A) Curtains are flapping in the wind.
(B) Cushions are being removed from the sofas.
(C) Chairs have been positioned around the table.
(D) A light fixture is being installed in the room.

(A) 窗簾在風中飄動。
(B) 坐墊正從沙發上被移開。
(C) 椅子圍著桌子擺放。
(D) 房間正在安裝燈具。

• flap 飄動　remove 移開　position 擺放　light fixture 燈具

本題看起來是張客廳的照片，裡面有窗簾和照明燈具。中央的部分可以看到擺了一張桌子，周圍還放了幾張椅子。描述事物的照片雖然會針對特定的一件物事進行描寫，但是本題呈現物品的相對位置，所以必須熟知各種物品的名稱與排列狀態。

特別要注意的是，一般而言，應該要有人對物品做出某種行為，才可以用物品當作主詞並使用「be being p.p.」句型。因此如果遇到未出現人物的照片，請先將大部分使用「be being p.p.」進行描述的選項列為錯誤答案。(A) 窗簾並未飄動。 (B) 出現 being removed，但圖片中並沒有人物，故非正確。(D) 出現 being installed，但沒有人在照片中，故也非正確描述。正確答案為 (C)。

33

339

7

I see that you have a teaching qualification.
(A) Sure, I'll look through it.
(B) Yes, from Caroline University.
(C) Are they qualified teachers?

我得知你有教師資格。
(A) 當然,我會瀏覽一下。
(B) 是的,卡洛林大學發的。
(C) 他們是合格教師嗎?

• **teaching qualification** 教師資格 **look through** 瀏覽 **qualified** 合格的

本題為陳述句,表示知道對方擁有教師資格證。對方回應「Yes」並且額外補充他得到教師資格的地點,所以正確答案為 (B)。

(A) 內容與題目無關。(C) 則是將「teaching qualification」改寫為「qualified teachers」,但內容不符題目。

8

Would you like a mug or a disposable cup to drink from?
(A) On the label.
(B) I prefer a mug.
(C) Some coffee with milk.

你要用馬克杯喝,還是免洗杯?
(A) 在標籤上。
(B) 我比較喜歡馬克杯。
(C) 咖啡加牛奶。

• **mug** 馬克杯 **disposable cup** 免洗杯 **label** 標籤

本題為選擇問句,回答者常常選出兩者之一作為回應,但也不可以只聽到重複題目字彙的選項就選為答案。(A) 與題目無關。(B) 明確做出選擇,為合適回覆。(C) 是利用與題目中的「mug」和「drink」相關的「coffee with milk」誘導作答。本題正確答案為 (B)。

9

Who closes the main entrance to the firm?
(A) The security staff.
(B) Enter the code.
(C) It is closed all day.

誰關了公司的大門?
(A) 保全人員。
(B) 輸入密碼。
(C) 整天都關閉。

• **main entrance** 大門

本題是詢問人物的「Who」疑問句,(A) 回答人物名稱,故為合適回覆;(B) 與題目無關;(C) 利用與題目「close」發音相近的「closed」誘導作答。本題正確答案為 (A)。

10

How will you get to the theater?
(A) I'll take a bus.
(B) I haven't got it yet.
(C) I'm on stage.

你要怎麼到劇院?
(A) 我會搭公車。
(B) 我還沒有拿到。
(C) 我在舞台上。

• **get to** 到達(場所)

本題為詢問交通手段的「How」疑問句。(A) 回答搭乘公車，是合適回覆。(B) 為利用與題目「get」發音相似的「got」設下陷阱。(C) 則利用題目中的「theater」與「stage」的聯想關係誘導。本題正確答案為 (A)。

11

Where did Sean go on holiday?
(A) He left yesterday.
(B) Yes, he did.
(C) To Japan.

尚恩去哪裡度假？
(A) 他昨天離開的。
(B) 是的，他有。
(C) 去日本。

本題為詢問休假地點的「Where」疑問句，(A) 應為「When」疑問句的回答；(B) 疑問詞疑問句無法用「Yes/No」回答；(C) 明確提及場所，故正確答案為 (C)。

12

Did you talk to Ms. Collins when you were transferred to our headquarters?
(A) No, not yet. I'm eager to see her.
(B) No, just through Friday.
(C) We haven't talked about it yet.

你被調到總公司時，和柯林斯女士談過了嗎？
(A) 不，還沒。我很期待見到她。
(B) 不，只到星期五。
(C) 我們還沒討論過。

• transfer 調職　headquarters 總公司　eager to V 期待做……

本題為助動詞問句，通常可用「Yes/No」回答。(A) 回答「No」，並添加說明，故為正確答案。(B) 題目中的「when」並不是疑問詞，所以此選項非合適答案。(C) 雖然重複題目中的「talk」，但是題目問的是「是否已經和某人談話」，所以此選項回答「尚未討論某事」並不恰當。故本題正確答案為 (A)。

13

I heard Blake got the Employee of the Year at the awards ceremony.
(A) A celebration for new employees.
(B) No, early this week.
(C) I'm glad to hear that.

我聽說布萊克在頒獎典禮上得到了年度最佳員工獎。
(A) 給新進人員的慶祝活動。
(B) 不，這週稍早時。
(C) 我很高興聽到這事。

• awards ceremony 頒獎典禮　celebration 慶祝活動

本題為表達自己聽聞某事的陳述句。(A) 為重覆題目中的「employee」並用從「awards ceremony」可能聯想到的「celebration」刻意誤導，但內容與題目無關。(B) 內容與題目不符。(C) 附和「很高興聽到這事」，為最自然的回應，故本題答案為 (C)。

14

Who does this jacket belong to?
(A) About 50 dollars.
(B) It's Chase's.
(C) It's too short.

這件夾克是誰的？
(A) 大約50元。
(B) 是雀斯的。
(C) 太短了。

34

本題詢問人物名的「Who」問句。(A) 應為「How much」問句的回答。(B) 直接告知人名，故為正確答案。(C) 為陷阱，利用與題目中「belong」發音相似的「long」誘使考生聯想到「short」，但內容與題目根本不符。本題正解為 (B)。

15

You've been to that seminar, haven't you?
(A) On the semiconductor.
(B) Which one?
(C) Let me introduce myself.

你參加過那場研討會，不是嗎？
(A) 有關半導體。
(B) 哪一場？
(C) 容我自我介紹一下。

• semiconductor 半導體

本題為確認對方是否參加研討會的附加疑問句。(A) 為利用與題目的「seminar」發音相似的「semiconductor」設下陷阱，且題目並不是在詢問研討會的主體。(B) 反問提問者是哪一場研討會，為合適回覆。(C) 與題目無關。正確答案為 (B)。

16

Where did Mr. Brown work before joining us?
(A) Much larger than I expected.
(B) Yes, Ms. Adams employed him.
(C) At a marketing agency in Canada.

布朗先生在到本公司前，是在哪裡服務？
(A) 比我預期的大很多。
(B) 是的，亞當斯女士僱用他的。
(C) 在加拿大的行銷公司。

本題為詢問地點的「Where」問句。(A) 與題目無關。(B) 疑問詞無法用「Yes/No」回答。(C) 以具體場所答覆，故正確答案為 (C)。

17

Didn't Maya already sign the lease contract?
(A) To rent a two-bedroom apartment.
(B) No, she'll do it tomorrow.
(C) The sign on the corner.

馬婭還沒簽租賃合約嗎？
(A) 要租一間兩房的公寓。
(B) 還沒，她明天會簽。
(C) 在轉角的標誌。

• sign a contract 簽合約　lease 租賃　sign〔名詞〕標誌

本題為否定疑問句，詢問是否完成簽約。與肯定疑問句的邏輯相同，若要表示「已完成」，則回答「Yes」，反之回答「No」。

(A) 為利用與題目中的「lease」意義相關的「rent a two-bedroom apartment」誤導作答。(B) 明確回答「No」，且說明預計簽約的時間點，故為合適答案。(C) 重複題目的「sign」，但題目中為動詞，指「簽下」，選項中的則為名詞，為「標誌」的意思。本題答案為 (B)。

18

When can I expect to receive my travel expenses?
(A) In two days.
(B) In the office.
(C) It's not that expensive.

我何時可以收到差旅費？
(A) 兩天內。
(B) 在辦公室。
(C) 沒有那麼貴。

• travel expense 差旅費

本題為詢問時間點的「When」疑問句，(A) 回答確切時間，故為合適答案。 (B) 較適合作為
「Where」疑問句的回答。(C) 使用與題目中「expenses」意義相關的「expensive」誤導作答。
本題答案為 (A)。

19 --

My review article will be issued in tomorrow's newspaper.
(A) A new editor will be employed.
(B) I'll certainly look out for it.
(C) You've run out of paper.

我的評論文章將刊登在明天的報紙上。
(A) 將聘用一位新編輯。
(B) 我一定會留意。
(C) 你的紙已經用完了。

• **issue** 刊登　**employ** 聘用　**certainly** 一定　**look out for . . .** 留意……　**run out of . . .** 用完……

本題利用陳述句告知對方，自己撰寫的社論將刊登在明日的報紙。(A) 利用聽到「review article」
便可聯想到的「editor」造成陷阱，內容與題目無關。(B) 表示自己會留意對方的文章，故為合適答
案。(C) 利用「newspaper」與「paper」的相似發音誤導作答。本題答案為 (B)。

20 --

Will you come to our company banquet on Saturday?
(A) They always provide excellent service.
(B) I have plans that day.
(C) It was really interesting.

你會參加本公司週六的宴會嗎？
(A) 他們一向提供極佳的服務。
(B) 我那天有事。
(C) 那真的很有趣。

• **banquet** 宴會

本題為助動詞疑問句，詢問對方是否參加公司宴會。遇到助動詞疑問句時，要特別注意時態、主詞
與動詞等。(A) 與題目毫無關聯。(B) 告知對方自己當天另有計畫，暗示不克出席，故為正確答案。
(C) 利用聽到「banquet」便可能聯想到的「interesting」造成陷阱。本題答案為 (B)。

21 --

When will my dress suit be ready?
(A) I already met him.
(B) In another hour.
(C) On Jeremiah Street.

我的禮服什麼時候可以好？
(A) 我已經見過他了。
(B) 再一個小時。
(C) 在耶利米街。

• **dress suit** 禮服

本題為詢問時間點的「When」疑問句。(A) 利用「ready」與「already」的類似發音形成陷阱。
(B) 以「In」加上表示一段期間的名詞（another hour）告知時間，故為合適答案。(C) 告知地點，
應作為「Where」疑問句的答案。本題正解為 (B)。

22 --

Does the utility bill include maintenance costs?
(A) He led the public utilities.
(B) No, it doesn't.
(C) It's priceless.

水電費有包含維修費嗎？
(A) 他帶領公用事業。
(B) 不，沒有。
(C) 是無價的。

• **utility bill** 水電費　**maintenance cost** 維修費　**public utilities** 公用事業　**priceless** 無價的

本題為助動詞「Does」疑問句，常以「Yes/No」。(A) 為使用與題目中的「utility」發音相似的「utilities」誤導作答。(B) 回答「No」並強調沒有，為合適回覆。(C) 是利用費用相關的主題誤導。故本題正確答案為 (B)。

23 --

Why did the seminar start so early?
(A) Mr. Rogers will be in late today.
(B) No, the shop is closed at seven.
(C) We had a lot to discuss.

研討會為什麼這麼早開始？
(A) 羅傑斯先生今天將晚到。
(B) 不，店家七點就休息了。
(C) 我們有很多要討論的。

本題為詢問研討會為何提前開始的「Why」疑問句。(A) 利用反義詞「early」與「late」造成混淆。(B) 也是利用反義詞「start」與「closed」形成的陷阱。(C) 表示有很多事項需要討論，故正確答案為 (C)。

24 --

Isn't Sam out of the office this week?
(A) Actually, his trip was rescheduled.
(B) It's close to the office building.
(C) More samples will arrive tomorrow.

山姆這禮拜不是不在辦公室嗎？
(A) 事實上，他的行程重新安排了。
(B) 靠近辦公大樓。
(C) 明天會有更多樣品送達。

• **out of the office** 不再辦公室　**reschedule** 重新安排（行程）　**be close to . . .** 靠近……

本題為否定疑問句，詢問山姆是否在辦公室。若要回答「不在」，則使用「No」，反之則使用「Yes」。(A) 雖省略「No」，但說明山姆重新安排了行程，委婉告知對方山姆並沒有不在辦公室，故為合適答案。「Actually」常常用來表達與提問者不同的意圖或事實，請多留意相關用法。本題正確答案為 (A)。

(B) 利用「out of the office」與「close to the office」的意思造成混淆。(C) 利用人名「Sam」與「sample」的發音相似性製造陷阱，且內容與題目沒有任何相關。

25 --

Which parking area is for our customers?
(A) The one that is on the corner.
(B) It's twenty-five dollars a day.
(C) Into the cabinet.

哪一個停車場是提供給我們客人的？
(A) 轉角的那一個。
(B) 一天25元。
(C) 進櫃子裡。

• **corner** 轉角　**cabinet** 櫃子

本題以「Which」詢問哪一個為客戶使用的停車場。「Which」疑問句的回覆可以是「The one under/next to/that is . . .」（在……下面的／旁邊的／……的那個）。(A) 使用「the one」代指停車場，並補述「on the corner」，明確告知對方，故為正確答案。

(B) 為利用從「parking area」可能聯想到的費用訊息（twenty-five dollars a day）設下陷阱。(C) 雖然回答了一個地點，但是題目詢問的主題為停車空間，而此選項回答的主要內容則為櫃子，故並非合適的回答。本題正解為 (A)。

26

What department do you work in?

(A) Research and Development.

(B) It stopped working.

(C) There's a part missing.

你在哪個部門工作？

(A) 研發部。

(B) 停止運轉了。

(C) 有個零件不見了。

本題為詢問在什麼部門工作的「What」疑問句，(A) 直接提及特定部門，故為正確答案。(B) 的主詞（It）與題目的主詞（you）不一致。(C) 則利用「department」與「part」的相似發音造成混淆。本題正確答案為 (A)。

27

Patrick's been working hard recently, hasn't he?

(A) I would rather work on it later.

(B) Actually, I thought it was simple.

(C) Yes, he certainly has.

派屈克最近工作很認真，不是嗎？

(A) 我寧可晚點處理。

(B) 事實上，我覺得很簡單。

(C) 是的，他的確如此。

本題為附加問句，重點在於前方類似陳述句的部分。通常其中一方知道某項訊息，但會使用附加問句向對方確認。(A) 使用「working」與「work」的相似發音試圖造成混淆。(B) 雖然使用常常出現在正解選項中的「Actually」，但是後續描述的內容與題意不符。本題的「hard」為形容工作認真的意思，和「困難的」無關。(C) 回答「Yes」，並表示「的確如此」，故正確答案為 (C)。

28

How do I know when the machine has finished washing the dishes?

(A) You will hear a beeping sound.

(B) Put them on top of the shelf.

(C) Yes, I have finished working on it.

我要怎麼知道機器已經洗好碗盤了？

(A) 你會聽到嗶一聲。

(B) 把它們放在架子最上方。

(C) 是的，我已經處理好了。

本題以「How」疑問句詢問如何得知盤子已全部洗好，(A) 告知對方會有聲響，故為合適答案。

(B) 利用聽到「dishes」可能會聯想到的內容造成混淆。(C) 重複題目中的「finished」，但疑問詞疑問句無法使用「Yes/No」回答。本題正解為 (A)。

29 --

Why don't we leave for the theater right after dinner?

(A) It leaves at noon.

(B) That might be too late.

(C) No, we can have dinner instead.

我們為什麼不在晚餐後前往戲院呢？

(A) 它在中午離開。

(B) 那可能太晚了。

(C) 不，我們可以改吃晚餐。

• leave for . . . 前往……　　right after 緊接著

本題為表示勸誘或提議的「Why don't we . . .？」問句。此題型幾乎每個月的考試中都會出現，請務必多加熟悉。(A) 為重複出現「leave」誤導作答。(B) 給予合理理由婉拒對方邀請，故為合適答案。(C) 重複使用「dinner」，但內容與題目不符。本題答案為 (B)。

30 --

Will you be stopping by the post office or the bank?

(A) Both actually.

(B) Around eleven.

(C) Yes, they're in the corner.

你會順路去郵局，還是銀行？

(A) 事實上，兩者都會。

(B) 大約11點。

(C) 是的，它們就在轉角處。

• stop by 順路去（地點）　　in the corner 在轉角

本題為詢問對方會去郵局還是銀行的選擇疑問句，(A) 回答「兩個地方都去」，為正確答案。(B) 適合作為「When」疑問句的回答。如果誤解題目詢問的是「前往的時間」，很有可能會誤選此選項。(C) 題目並沒有詢問地點。本題正確答案為 (A)。

31 --

What time does the gallery open on Monday?

(A) Actually, it's closed on Mondays.

(B) There is a lot of artwork.

(C) On Melissa Street.

藝廊星期一幾點營業？

(A) 事實上，週一休息。

(B) 有很多藝術品。

(C) 在梅莉莎街。

• gallery 藝廊　　artwork 藝術品

本題為詢問週一營業時間的「What time」問句，通常回答時會提及具體時間，但是也可能有另外的答案。(A) 雖未直接回答時間點，但回答週一休息，即表示週一並不營業，故本題答案為 (A)。

(B) 利用容易從「gallery」聯想的「artwork」設下陷阱。(C) 較適合作為「Where」疑問句的回答。

32-34 conversation

W I would like to discuss the campaign for exhibiting at the trade show in April. Have you checked the rates for exhibiting at the venue yet?	**女** 我想討論一下四月在貿易展的展覽活動。你查過那裡的展覽費用了嗎？
M I spoke with the event manager last week. The rates have increased dramatically since last year. Unfortunately, our budget does not allow us to take the same-sized display stand as last time.	**男** 上週我和活動經理談過了。從去年起，費用開始大幅調升。很遺憾地，我們的預算無法租用上次那種大小的展示台。
W We can save money by having a smaller stand. Last time, our display involved thirty products. We can reduce that number to twenty.	**女** 我們可以使用較小的架子來節省經費。上次我們展示了30項產品。我們可以降低到20樣。

• **exhibit** 展覽 **trade show** 貿易展 **rate** 費用 **venue** 會場 **dramatically** 大幅地 **unfortunately** 很遺憾地 **budget** 預算 **display stand** 展示台

32 --

What type of event are the speakers planning to attend?
(A) A trade exhibition
(B) An opening ceremony
(C) A budget committee
(D) An office opening

說話者打算要參加什麼活動？
(A) 貿易展覽
(B) 開幕儀式
(C) 預算委員會
(D) 辦公室開幕

由「exhibiting at the trade show in April」可知，他們想參加的是四月的貿易展。選項中最適當的只有 (A)。

33 --

What problem does the man mention?
(A) A venue is fully booked.
(B) The cost has increased.
(C) A company has gone bankrupt.
(D) An exhibition has been canceled.

這位男士提到什麼問題？
(A) 場地被訂滿了。
(B) 費用調升了。
(C) 一家公司已破產。
(D) 一個展覽已被取消。

男子說：「The rates have increased dramatically」，且接著談論與此相關的對策，故由此可知是費用相關的問題。本題的正確答案為 (B)。

34 --

What does the woman recommend?
(A) Reducing the size of the display
(B) Contacting other venues
(C) Promoting the event on television
(D) Asking for a discount

這位女士提供什麼建議？
(A) 縮小展示規模
(B) 聯絡其他場地
(C) 在電視上宣傳活動
(D) 要求折扣

對於男子提及的費用問題，女子表示：「Last time, our display involved thirty products. We can reduce that number to twenty.」，提出可以減少展出品項數量的意見，故正確答案為 (A)。

35-37 conversation

W This is the manager of the Sunrise Hotel here. I have received a brochure about your marble floor tiles, and I would like to see some samples, if possible.

M I can send you a selection of what we have on offer if you would like to specify the color range you are interested in.

W Yes, please, that would be great. I also need someone who would be able to fit the tiles onto our floors. Do you offer that service?

35-37 對話

女 我是日昇飯店主管。我收到了貴公司大理石地磚的介紹手冊，如果可以的話，我想看看一些樣品。

男 若是您可以具體說明有興趣的色系，我可以寄給您我們販賣的系列商品。

女 好的，麻煩你，那真是太好了。我還需要有人能夠幫忙鋪設地板瓷磚。貴公司有提供該項服務嗎？

• brochure 手冊　marble 大理石　floor tile 地磚　sample 樣品　a selection of ... 一系列的……
on offer 販賣中　specify 具體說明　color range 色系　fit 鋪設

35 --

What kind of product is the woman inquiring about?　這位女士詢問哪種產品？

(A) Computer software　(A) 電腦軟體
(B) Flooring materials　(B) 地板材料
(C) Lab equipment　(C) 實驗室器材
(D) Hotel pieces　(D) 飯店用品

本題詢問女子諮詢的產品種類，請從女子的台詞中尋找線索。一開始，女子的台詞提到「I have received a brochure about your marble floor tiles, and I would like to see some samples, if possible.」希望能看看對方生產地大理石地磚，所以正確答案為 (B)。

36 --

What does the man offer to do?　這位男士提議要做什麼？

(A) Stop by the hotel　(A) 順路造訪飯店
(B) Send the woman an order form　(B) 將訂購表寄給這位女士
(C) Provide some samples　(C) 提供一些樣品
(D) Consult a flooring expert　(D) 諮詢地板材料專家

本題詢問的是男子提議之事項，故應在男子的台詞中尋找答案。男子說：「I can send you a selection of what we have on offer」，表示如果告知想要的顏色，他將會提供目前擁有的產品樣本。此處的「what」即為選項 (C) 中的「samples」，故正確答案為 (C)。

37 --

What does the woman request?　這位女士要求什麼？

(A) An instruction manual　(A) 操作手冊
(B) A use of a product　(B) 產品的使用權
(C) An online tutorial　(C) 線上個別指導
(D) A tile specialist　(D) 地磚專門人員

本題詢問的是女子要求之事項，故應在女子的台詞中尋找答案。從女子的最後一句台詞「I also need someone who would be able to fit the tiles onto our floors.」可知，她需要的是鋪設地磚的人手，所以正確答案為 (D)。

38-40 conversation　　　　　　　　　38-40 對話

M Look at the line. The check-in area for the airline is full of people, and there is only one person at the check-in counter. It will take us ages to check our baggage.	男 看看排隊隊伍。航空公司報到區擠滿了人，而且只有一個人在報到櫃台。託運行李會花上好多時間。
W Yes, and we have less than 40 minutes before our flight. Why don't we use the express check-in service over there? It may be quicker.	女 沒錯，我們的班機時間不到40分鐘了。我們何不利用那邊的快速報到服務呢？那可能會快一些。
M Good plan. But what if we have to pay extra? I only have traveler's checks on me. I wonder if they accept other forms of payments.	男 好計畫。但是如果我們需要額外付費呢？我只有旅行支票。我不知道他們是否接受其他付款方式。
W I doubt it. But don't worry about it. I have a company credit card we can use.	女 我也懷疑這點。但是別擔心。我有公司信用卡可以用。

• **check-in counter** 報告櫃台　**traveler's check** 旅行支票　**I doubt it** 我懷疑

 38 ---

What problem is mentioned about the airport?　對話中提到機場有什麼問題？

(A) The check-in line is too long.　(A) 報到隊伍太長。
(B) The baggage area is blocked.　(B) 行李區被圍起來了。
(C) An airplane has been delayed.　(C) 飛機延誤了。
(D) An employee has not arrived.　(D) 員工尚未抵達。

一開始，男子向女子說「Look at the line. The check-in area for the airline is full of people. . . . It will take us ages to check our baggage.」，表示登機報到櫃台擠滿了人，且檢查行李所花費的時間太久。故可知道有許多人在等著報到，正確答案為 (A)。

39 ---

What does the man ask the woman about?　這位男士詢問女士什麼事？

(A) Payment options　(A) 付款選項
(B) Business hours　(B) 營業時間
(C) Round-trip airfares　(C) 來回機票費
(D) Beverage choices　(D) 飲料選項

聽男子說登機報到櫃台前擠滿了人，女子提議可以利用快速報到櫃台。接著，男子擔心「But what if we have to pay extra?」，並告知女子「I only have traveler's checks on me. I wonder if they accept other forms of payments.」，表示他身上只有旅行支票，想知道是否有其他可行的付款方式，所以正確答案為 (A)。

 40 ---

What does the woman say she will do?　這位女士說她要做什麼？

(A) Find another airline　(A) 找另一家航空公司
(B) Lend the man some money　(B) 借錢給這位男士
(C) Contact her office　(C) 與辦公室聯絡
(D) Use a credit card　(D) 使用信用卡

對於男子提出的支付方式相關疑慮，女子先請男子不用擔心，並告知「I have a company credit card we can use.」，表示她帶了可以使用的公司信用卡，所以正確答案為 (D)。

41-43 conversation

41-43 對話

W	I see you have a new vacuum cleaner. Which brand is it? I need to buy one, but I have no idea which one is best.
M	It's the Hurricane Power. Although it costs a little more than other models, I chose it because it seemed to perform better than the others.
W	The Hurricane Power has received a lot of comments on the online forum. A lot of people complained about the accessories that come with it. Apparently, they can be quite difficult to attach.
M	Yes, I heard that, but I haven't found that to be a problem. Why don't you visit the Elan Store? I got my cleaner from there, and they have a large selection.

女	我看到你有一台新的吸塵器。那是哪個牌子？我需要買一台，但是不知道哪一種最好。
男	這台是暴風動力。雖然比其他型號貴一些，但我選它是因為它看起來比其他的好用。
女	在網路論壇中，有許多關於暴風動力的評論。許多人對於它附的配件有怨言。看樣子配件很難固定。
男	沒錯，我有聽說，但是我覺得這不是問題。妳何不去埃朗商店看看？我是在那邊買吸塵器的，而且他們有許多商品可供選擇。

• **cost** 需花費 **comment** 評論 **accessory** 配件 **apparently** 看樣子 **attach** 固定 **complicated** 不容易的 **post** 張貼 **browse** 瀏覽

What does the woman want to do?
(A) Purchase a product
(B) Read a product review
(C) Complain about a device
(D) Return an item

這位女士想要做什麼？
(A) 購買產品
(B) 閱讀產品評論
(C) 抱怨設備
(D) 退貨

一開始，女子對男子說：「I see you have a new vacuum cleaner. Which brand is it? I need to buy one, but I have no idea which one is best.」，由此可知，女子想要購入吸塵器，故正確答案為 (A)。

What did the woman read about the Hurricane Power?
(A) It is inexpensive.
(B) It is complicated to use.
(C) It is unreliable.
(D) It is the most popular model.

這位女士閱讀到什麼有關暴風動力的評論？
(A) 價格不高。
(B) 不容易使用。
(C) 不可靠。
(D) 是最受歡迎的型號。

女子的第二句台詞提到，她在網路上看到許多有關暴風動力的評價，並說：「A lot of people complained about the accessories that come with it. Apparently, they can be quite difficult to attach.」，故可知許多人認為它的附件不易使用。

選項 (B) 將「difficult to attach」改寫為意義相近的「complicated to use」，故正確答案為 (B)。

350

43

What does the man suggest the woman do?
(A) Post messages on a forum
(B) Browse online
(C) Contact a sales assistant
(D) Visit a specific store

這位男士建議女士做什麼？
(A) 在討論區張貼訊息
(B) 在網路上瀏覽
(C) 聯絡業務助理
(D) 去某家商店看看

最後，男子表示自己在使用上並未發現任何問題，同時向女子提議「Why don't you visit the Elan Store?」所以正確答案為 (D)。

44-46 conversation

44–46 對話

M Good morning, Ms. Ross. I am Jeffrey from B&P Books. The diaries you ordered from our bestseller list are now ready. I can have them delivered on Friday afternoon.	男 早安，羅斯女士。我是B&P書店的傑佛瑞。您從暢銷排行榜上所訂購的日誌現在已經準備好了。禮拜五下午可以送貨。
W That would be great. I may be a little late, but please just put them through the mailbox.	女 那太棒了。我可能會有點來不及，但是請放進信箱內。
M Unfortunately, it is against policy not to get a signature when delivering our merchandise. Perhaps Saturday would be better?	男 不幸地，送貨時若是沒有簽名，是違反規定的。或許星期六會比較適合一點？
W Leave it with my son. I believe my son will be at his home on Friday, and he can sign for the items instead. Let me call him immediately, and I'll let you know if it's possible to deliver to his house then.	女 那交給我兒子。我想我兒子禮拜五會在他家，他可以代為簽收。我現在打電話給他，再告訴你是不是可以送到他家。

• **policy** 規定　**signature** 簽名

44

What type of business does the man work for?
(A) A food supply company
(B) A post office
(C) A bookstore
(D) A courier service

這位男士在何種行業工作？
(A) 食品供應公司
(B) 郵局
(C) 書店
(D) 快遞服務

一開始，男子向女子自我介紹：「I am Jeffrey from B&P Books. The diaries you ordered from our bestseller list are now ready. I can have them delivered on Friday afternoon.」，並說已準備好女子訂購的日誌。由此可推斷，男子最可能在書店工作，所以正確答案為 (C)。

What policy does the man mention?
(A) Delivered goods must be put in the mailbox.
(B) The invoice must be issued on delivery.
(C) Damaged items must be returned to the supplier.
(D) A signature must be provided.

這位男士提到什麼規定？
(A) 運送的貨品必須放在信箱中。
(B) 貨到時需附上帳單。
(C) 損壞物品必須退還給供應商。
(D) 必須簽名。

一開始，男子告知商品將在週五下午送達，女子則說自己可能會比較晚到家，所以請男子將包裹放在信箱。但是，男子表示無法接受女子的請求，因為「Unfortunately, it is against policy not to get a signature when delivering our merchandise.」故正確答案為 (D)。

「Unfortunately」、「But」與「However」後面的內容常是解題線索，故需要多加留意。

46 --

What does the woman want to check?　　這位女士要確認什麼？
(A) Her shipping receipt　　　　　　　　(A) 她的裝貨收據
(B) Her son's availability　　　　　　　(B) 她兒子是否有空
(C) Her order form　　　　　　　　　　(C) 她的訂購單
(D) Her tracking number　　　　　　　　(D) 她的追蹤編號

女子說，如果自己無法及時到家，可以請她的兒子代為簽收，並且表示「Let me call him immediately, and I'll let you know if it's possible to deliver to his house then.」，所以她將與兒子確認時間，正確答案為 (B)。

47-49 conversation　　　　　　　　　**47–49 對話**

W	Mark, according to the present need, I have to make some changes in my schedule, as the regional director wants me to visit the newly purchased production facility, where I have to stay one more day. So I won't be able to return on Thursday.
M	Okay. I guess it won't be a problem. I will change your flight and hotel reservations. A rescheduled taxi will take you to the airport.
W	Actually, I'm thinking it would be better for me to rent a car near here. The facility is over 100 miles from the airport, and it would be easier and cost less to get there if I have my own vehicle.
M	**(48)That makes sense.** I'll make all the necessary changes and get back to you.

女	馬克，根據目前情勢所需，我必須調整我的時程表，因為區經理要我去查看最新買進的生產設備，我必須在那多留一天。所以我無法在禮拜四回去。
男	好。我想沒問題。我會更改妳的航班和預約飯店。重新安排後的計程車會載妳去機場。
女	事實上，我想我自己在附近租車會比較方便。那個地點距離機場超過100哩，如果自己有車的話，會比較方便，花費也較少。
男	(48)有道理。我會完成所有必須調整的事項，再回覆妳。

• **production facility** 生產設備　　**That makes sense** 有道理　　**get back to sb** 回覆某人　　**coworker** 同事

47 --

What was the woman asked to do?　　這位女士被要求做什麼？
(A) Drive a coworker to the airport　　(A) 載同事去機場
(B) Prepare a presentation　　　　　　(B) 準備簡報
(C) Hire additional workers　　　　　　(C) 聘用更多工人
(D) Visit a production facility　　　　(D) 查看生產設備

一開始，女子說到需要變更行程，並提到「the regional director wants me to visit the newly purchased production facility」，表示受到指派，她需要去查看新買的生產設備，故正確答案為 (D)。

48 (NEW) -

What does the man imply when he says, "That makes sense"?

(A) He will pick the woman up at the airport.
(B) He thinks renting a car is a good idea.
(C) He knows taking a taxi costs less.
(D) He can send a taxi for the woman.

當這位男士說：「有道理」，是什麼意思？
(A) 他會去機場接這位女士。
(B) 他覺得租車是個好主意。
(C) 他知道搭計程車花費較少。
(D) 他可以幫這位女士叫計程車。

男子建議女子搭乘計程車，但是女子說：「I'm thinking it would be better for me to rent a car near here」，提出不同意見，男子後文更說了會為女子調整安排，故可知他認同女子的說法，所以正確答案為 (B)。

49 -

What does the woman decide to do?

(A) Leave a meeting early
(B) Get back to a branch manager
(C) Use another form of transportation
(D) Make extra copies of a report

這位女士決定要做什麼？
(A) 提早離開會議
(B) 回覆分公司主管
(C) 使用另一種交通方式
(D) 多印幾份報告

一開始，女子要求變更行程，而男子便報告將更改航班飯店，並說：「A rescheduled taxi will take you to the airport.」，但女子回覆「I'm thinking it would be better for me to rent a car near here.」，表示比起計程車，她更想自己租車，故正確答案為 (C)。

50-52 conversation

W	Hi, I am calling to check on an insurance claim for my laptop. I misplaced it on a visit to Hawaii in June, and I still haven't received a check.
M	I'm sorry about that. When did you put the claim in?
W	I will have to check the exact date in my diary. But I am sure it was about four weeks ago.
M	Okay. Usually, it takes longer for us to pay claims for items lost abroad. There is a lot of paperwork to be examined. Let me take your claim number, and I will contact you tomorrow.

50-52 對話

女	嗨，我打這通電話是為了確認我的筆電保險理賠。我在六月去夏威夷旅遊時遺失了，而我還未收到支票。
男	很抱歉。您是什麼時候提出理賠申請的？
女	我要看看日誌上寫的確切日期。但是我確定大約是四週前。
男	好的。通常在海外遺失的理賠需要花較長的時間來辦理。有許多書面文件需要審查。讓我記下您的理賠編號，明天將與您聯繫。

• **insurance claim** 保險理賠　**misplace** 遺失　**paperwork** 書面文件　**examine** 審查

ACTUAL TEST 9 | PART 3 | 中譯＋解析

What does the woman want to discuss with the man?
(A) A refund policy
(B) A travel itinerary
(C) A checklist sheet
(D) An insurance claim

這位女士想要和男士談論什麼？
(A) 退款規定
(B) 旅行計畫
(C) 核對清單表
(D) 保險理賠

女子開頭便提到「I am calling to check on an insurance claim for my laptop.」，且後面的內容也與保險理賠有關，所以正確答案為 (D)。

51

When does the woman say she submitted the paperwork?
(A) In June
(B) Yesterday
(C) Last week
(D) Last month

這位女士說她什麼時候繳交書面文件？
(A) 六月
(B) 昨天
(C) 上週
(D) 上個月

男子詢問女子「When did you put the claim in?」，而女子表示雖然確切時間需要進一步查詢，但是「I am sure it was about four weeks ago.」，故可知選項中最符合的為 (D)。

52

According to the man, what may have caused the delay?
(A) Regular procedure
(B) Computer errors
(C) Lost paperwork
(D) Staff negligence

根據這位男士所言，造成延誤的原因是什麼？
(A) 正常程序
(B) 電腦錯誤
(C) 遺失書面文件
(D) 員工疏失

女子表示，距自己提出申請已經過了四週，而男子解釋「Usually it takes longer for us to pay claims for items lost abroad. There is a lot of paperwork to be examined.」，表示在海外遺失的物品，理賠審核過程通常需要較長的時間，因為需要核對的資料比較多。故可知延誤的原因是流程本身就需花費較多時間，正確答案為 (A)。

53-55 conversation

W When can we expect our foreign clients? We could entertain them on Friday evening. What do you think of the Cebuana Lounge? I went there last week, and they served exquisite food.

M I understand that it is excellent, but we need to check what is available on the menu. It's possible for some of them to dislike Filipino dishes.

W They also serve Spanish dishes as well as a selection of seafood and pasta, but why don't we check the full menu online? It will be quicker to use my smartphone for the Internet.

53–55 對話

女 國外客戶什麼時候會到？我們禮拜五晚上可以招待他們。你覺得塞布安納酒吧如何？我上禮拜去過，那裡提供了精緻的餐點。

男 我知道那邊很棒，但是我們需要確認一下菜單。有些人可能不喜歡菲律賓料理。

女 他們也提供西班牙料理，還有各種海鮮和義大利麵，不過我們何不上網查看完整菜單呢？用我的智慧型手機上網查會比較快。

• **entertain** 招待　**serve** 提供　**exquisite** 精緻的　**dish** 料理　**a selection of** 各種

 53

Who does the woman want to take to the Cebuana Lounge?

(A) Clients
(B) The management team
(C) Family members
(D) Colleagues

這位女士想帶誰去塞布安納酒吧？

(A) 客戶
(B) 管理團隊
(C) 家庭成員
(D) 同事

從「we expect our foreign clients」與「What do you think of the Cebuana Lounge?」中可以得知，女子將帶外國的客戶前往酒吧，故正確答案為 (A)。

54

What does the man want to know about the restaurant?

(A) Its menu
(B) Its opening hours
(C) Its prices
(D) Its location

這位男士想知道什麼有關餐廳的事？

(A) 菜單
(B) 營業時間
(C) 價格
(D) 地點

如同「we need to check what is available on the menu」所示，本對話的大部分內容皆與飲食菜單有關，故正確答案為 (A)。

55

What does the woman suggest?

(A) Using her mobile phone
(B) Booking a table
(C) Making a phone call
(D) Checking room availability

這位女士提出什麼建議？

(A) 用她的手機
(B) 訂位
(C) 打電話
(D) 查詢空房

女子建議可以先上網瀏覽菜單，並說：「It will be quicker to use my smartphone for the internet.」。由此可知，女子同時也建議男子使用她的手機，故正確答案為 (A)。

 35

56-58 conversation with three speakers (NEW)

56–58 三人對話

W	Mike, Henry, the director told me to inform you to discard unwanted items in accordance with the updated recycling guidelines.
M1	Okay, that's nice. I heard that we are going to have new guidelines.
M2	Then, we need to recycle all the documents from now on, right?
W	Except for financial documents. Those are considered confidential materials. You should store them in the green bin at the corner of the hall.
M1	Where should we put the others?
W	Other documents, cardboard, and magazines can go in the regular recycling bins. Is it clear, Mike?
M2	Yes. **(58)Thanks for the information.** Now that I have a clear idea about what to do, I can throw out all the unwanted papers now without worrying about it.

女	麥克、亨利,主管要我通知你們,要依照更新後的回收指導原則來丟棄不要的物品。
男1	好的。我聽說將有新的指導原則。
男2	那從現在開始,我們需要回收所有的文件,是嗎?
女	除了財務文件外,那些被視為機密文件。你們應該把它放在大廳角落的綠色桶子內。
男1	那其他的要放在哪裡?
女	其他文件、紙板與雜誌放在一般的回收桶裡。麥克,這樣清楚嗎?
男2	是的。**(58)**感謝告知。現在我清楚知道要怎麼做了,我可以毫無疑慮地丟掉所有不要的報告了。

- **discard** 丟棄　**unwanted** 不要的　**in accordance with** 依照　**guidelines** 指導原則　**confidential** 機密的　**recycling bin** 回收桶

What is the woman mainly notifying the men of?

(A) Financial confidentiality
(B) Recycling guidelines
(C) Client information
(D) Presentation schedules

這位女士主要告知男士們什麼事?

(A) 財務機密
(B) 回收指導原則
(C) 客戶資訊
(D) 簡報時程表

女子告知兩名男子「the director told me to inform you to discard unwanted items in accordance with the updated recycling guidelines.」,要他們根據回收指導原則將不必要的物品丟棄,故正確答案為 (B)。

57

What are the men advised to do with confidential documents?

(A) Keep them in their desk
(B) Give them to the director
(C) File them in a locked cabinet
(D) Keep them in a special container

男士們被建議如何處理機密文件?

(A) 收在桌子裡
(B) 交給主管
(C) 歸檔在上鎖的櫃子裡
(D) 保存在特殊容器裡

女子說了「Except for financial documents.」,表示財務相關資料不用回收,並說「You should store them in the green bin at the corner of the hall」。題目的「the green bin」即為選項 (D) 的「a special container」,所以正確答案為 (D)。

58 (NEW)

What does Mike imply when he says, "Thanks for the information"?

(A) He's glad to be informed about the change.

(B) He's not asked to comply with the regulations.

(C) He's going to update all the financial documents.

(D) He's allowed to store all the documents in a cabinet.

當參克說：「感謝告知」，是什麼意思？

(A) 他很開心收到變更通知。

(B) 他沒被要求遵守規定。

(C) 他要更新全部的財務文件。

(D) 他被允許將所有文件收在櫃子裡。

麥克在這句話之後說：「Now that I have a clear idea about what to do with the papers, I can throw out all the unwanted papers now without worrying about it.」，表示多虧女子的告知，他知道了新的回收辦法，以後可以毫無擔憂地處理不必要的資料，所以正確答案為 (A)。

59-61 conversation

59–61 對話

M	Excuse me. Do you have this sweater in a different color? I'm looking for blue, but I can only find it in black.	男	請問一下，這件毛衣有其他顏色嗎？我要找藍色，但只有看到黑色。
W	My apologies, sir. Black is the only color we have left. It is now part of the clearance sale, and we are not ordering any more of these items.	女	先生，很抱歉。我們只剩下黑色了。它現在正在出清特價中，而且我們不會再訂購這類商品了。
M	That's a shame. I like the style of this sweater. There's nothing else like it in other shops.	男	真可惜。我喜歡這件毛衣的款式。其他商店都沒有類似的了。
W	You could try looking at our online store, then. We may have some left in the color that you want and if so, you will still only be charged the sale price.	女	那麼您可以看看我們的網路商店。可能會有您想要的顏色，如果有的話，您依舊能以特價購買。

- **clearance sale** 出清特價 **That's a shame** 真可惜 **charge** 收費 **misplace** 將……放錯位置
  check on sth 查看某物

59

What is the man interested in purchasing?

(A) A coat

(B) A hat

(C) A sweater

(D) A scarf

這位男士想購買什麼商品？

(A) 外套

(B) 帽子

(C) 毛衣

(D) 圍巾

本題詢問男子有意購買的物品為何，所以應從男子的話中尋找答案。一開始，男子詢問：「Do you have this sweater in a different color?」，由此可知，男子想要購買的物品為毛衣，故正確答案為 (C)。

60

What is the problem?

(A) A product is faulty.

(B) An item is unavailable in a certain color on site.

(C) Some merchandise has been misplaced.

(D) Some clothes are too expensive.

出現了什麼問題？

(A) 產品有瑕疵。

(B) 現場特定顏色的商品已售完。

(C) 有些商品被放錯位置。

(D) 有些衣服價格太高。

男子說：「I'm looking for blue, but I can only find it in black.」，表示自己正在尋找藍色毛衣，但是只看到黑色，女子則對此表達歉意，並告知「Black is the only color we have left.」，由此可知，藍色毛衣已經賣完了。正確答案為 (B)。

61

What does the woman suggest the man do?　這位女士建議男士做什麼？

(A) Check on the store's Web site　(A) 查看商店的網站
(B) Go to a different store　(B) 去其他商店看看
(C) Return within a week　(C) 一個禮拜之內退貨
(D) Choose another color　(D) 選另一個顏色

本題詢問女子提議之內容，所以應該從女子的台詞中尋找線索。對話最後，女子提到「You could try looking at our online store, then.」，建議男子到網路商店尋找想要的物品。選項 (A) 將「try looking at our online store」改寫為意義相近的「check on the store's Web site」，故正確答案為 (A)。

62-64 conversation and report　**62–64 對話及報告**

M　Good morning, Jasmine. It's Aiden George from the Accounts Department. I want to make an appointment to discuss your expense claim. Can you come down between 10 and 11 A.M.?

W　I heard that I only need to submit the expense report. What did I miss?

M　You've missed one of the receipts. Let's see, that's the largest amount on the report.

W　That's not good. I'm afraid I'm going out to visit a client now. I can make it in the afternoon, though.

M　I will be in a meeting all afternoon. Let me check to see if my colleague Brandon is free then. I will call him now and get back to you.

男 早安，潔絲敏。我是會計部的艾當‧喬治。我想跟妳約時間討論支出報銷。妳可以在上午10至11點間下來一下嗎？

女 我聽說我只需要繳交支出報告。有遺漏什麼嗎？

男 妳漏了一張收據。我看看，是報告上金額最大的那一張。

女 那還真不妙。我現在恐怕要出門拜訪客戶了。但是我下午可以去找你。

男 我整個下午都會在開會。讓我看看我同事布蘭登是否有空。我現在打電話給他，等一下回覆你。

Expense Report, 6–9 May

Round-trip ticket	$340
Hotel (2 nights)	$300
Car rental (with insurance)	$120
Meals (2.5 days *3)	$85

支出報告，5月6–9日

來回車票	$340
飯店（2晚）	$300
租車（含保險）	$120
餐費（2.5天*3）	$85

• accounts department 會計部　appointment 會面　expense claim 支出報銷　colleague 同事

What does the woman have to do in the morning? 這位女士早上要做什麼事？

(A) Meet with a client　　(A) 和客戶見面
(B) Fill out an expense form　　(B) 填寫支出表單
(C) Use her computer　　(C) 使用電腦
(D) Organize a training session　　(D) 安排訓練課程

男子的第一句台詞最後說了「Can you come down between 10 and 11 A.M.?」，表示自己希望與女子在上午見面，而女子卻說「I'm afraid I'm going out to visit a client now」，表示自己上午得去拜訪客戶，故正確答案為 (A)。

63 (NEW)

Look at the graphic. Which item didn't the woman attach a receipt for? 看一下圖表，這位女士未附上哪一項的收據？

(A) Round-trip ticket　　(A) 來回車票
(B) Hotel　　(B) 飯店
(C) Car rental　　(C) 租車
(D) Meals　　(D) 餐費

男子說了「You've missed one of the receipts. Let's see, that's the largest amount on the report.」，告知女子遺漏了金額最大的收據。對照表格，可知金額最大的支出項目為「Round-trip ticket」，故正確答案為 (A)。

64

What does the man say he will do? 這位男士說他要做什麼？

(A) Contact a colleague　　(A) 聯絡同事
(B) Create a database　　(B) 建立資料庫
(C) Reschedule his meeting　　(C) 重新安排會議
(D) Meet the woman in the afternoon　　(D) 下午和這位女士見面

對話者接下來要做的事通常出現在對話的最後部分。男子說：「Let me check to see if my colleague Brandon is free then. I will call him now . . .」，表示將與同事聯絡，故正確答案為 (A)。

65-67 conversation and table　　**65–67 對話及表格**

W Hi, this is the first time I've visited the art gallery. I heard that "Body Worlds" is now on display here.	女 嗨，這是我第一次參觀藝廊。聽說現在這裡正在展出〈身體世界〉。
M Indeed, the exhibition has been attracting a lot of attention. The only drawback is that currently there are too many people visiting this specific event, even though the tickets are expensive.	男 沒錯，這個展覽引起了許多人的注意。唯一的缺點是即使票價昂貴，還是有太多人來參觀這個特定活動。
W No wonder. It's not common to see such a great exhibit in this town. I've always looked forward to it.	女 難怪。要在這城裡看到這麼棒的展覽並不常見。我一直很期待。

M	In that case, can I book you in for the next available guided tour? It starts at 7 P.M.	男	如果這樣的話，我可以幫妳預約下一場導覽？晚上七點開始。
W	Is there any additional charge?	女	要額外收費嗎？
M	No, it's free but must be booked in advance.	男	不用，那是免費的，但是需要事先預約。
W	That's perfect. I can be here then. In the meantime, I will look around the other halls.	女	太棒了。到時候我會到場。在這期間，我可以到其他廳看看。

	Admission	Guided Tour
Event Hall A	$60	Not available
Event Hall B	Free	Free. 11:00 A.M., 7:00 P.M.
Event Hall C	$50	Free. 10:00 A.M., 3:00 P.M., 7:00 P.M.
Event Hall D	$20	$10, booklets provided

	入場費	導覽
活動A廳	$60	無
活動B廳	免費	免費，上午11點、晚上7點
活動C廳	$50	免費，上午10點、下午3點、晚上7點
活動D廳	$20	$10元，提供小冊子

- art gallery 藝廊　on display 展出　exhibition 展覽　drawback 缺點　specific 特定的
  in the meantime 在這期間　piece 藝術品

 65

What problem does the man mention?
(A) A piece of art is missing.
(B) A staff member is unavailable.
(C) Some displays are faulty.
(D) An exhibition is crowded.

這位男士提到什麼問題？
(A) 有件藝術品不見了。
(B) 員工沒有空。
(C) 部分展示品有瑕疵。
(D) 展覽太擠了。

男子第一句提到「The only drawback is that currently there are too many people visiting this specific display.」，可知展覽的缺點在於太多人參觀，故正確答案為 (D)。

 66 [NEW]

Look at the graphic. Where is the exhibition the woman wants to see being held?
(A) Event Hall A
(B) Event Hall B
(C) Event Hall C
(D) Event Hall D

看一下圖表，這位女士要看的展覽在哪裡？
(A) 活動A廳
(B) 活動B廳
(C) 活動C廳
(D) 活動D廳

根據對話內容，可以從「參觀人數最多」、「門票金額高」、「七點有導覽活動」、「導覽為免費參加」等線索知道展覽位置。特別注意，價格是本題最關鍵的陷阱。入場費高不一定代表是「最高的」。

雖然 (A) 的門票最貴，但是沒有提供導覽活動，所以此選項無法成為答案。(B) 雖然在七點提供導覽，但是入場免門票，所以不是正確答案。(D) 導覽要收費，所以也不是正確答案。滿足所有條件的是在活動 C 廳舉辦的活動，所以正確答案為 (C)。

What will the woman do next?
(A) Stay with the man
(B) Get a free ticket at the box office
(C) Come back tomorrow
(D) Go and see another exhibit

這位女士接下來要做什麼事？
(A) 和這位男士待在一起
(B) 在售票室索取免費門票
(C) 明天再來
(D) 去看另一個展覽

最後，女子提到「I can be here then. In the meantime, I will look around the other halls.」因為導覽從七點開始，在這之前有一些空檔，她會去其他展館看看。因此，本題的答案為 (D)。

注意「Go and see」並不代表女子會離去不再回來看展覽。

68–70 conversation

| 68–70 對話及價格表

M Good morning, my name is Austin Phillips. I'm calling about the sports classes you advertised in the local paper.

W Hello, Mr. Phillips. The gym is right next to the Graham Complex, and we currently have boxing and yoga classes available.

M I'm interested in boxing classes. What time does the earliest class start?

W We have one at 6 A.M. if that suits your schedule. It's on Tuesdays and Thursdays.

M 6 A.M. is convenient for me. The Graham Complex is not that far from my office. How much is the tuition fee?

W It's $60 per month. If you pay for three months in advance, we give you a 10 percent discount.

M Okay, I'll do that. However, I don't have a decent pair of boxing shoes. Do you sell them or rent them out?

W No, we don't, but there's a sports shop on the first floor. And if you tell them you're our member, they take $10 off the regular price.

M I'll stop by in the evening and pay for three months, and get those shoes, too.

男 早安，我是奧斯汀·菲利浦。我打來是想詢問妳們在本地報紙上廣告的運動課程。

女 哈囉，菲利浦先生。健身房就在葛拉漢綜合大樓旁，而且我們目前提供拳擊和瑜珈課。

男 我對拳擊課有興趣。最早的課程幾點開始？

女 如果時間可以的話，早上六點有一班。是在星期二和星期四。

男 我上午六點可以。葛拉漢綜合大樓離我辦公室不遠。學費是多少錢？

女 每個月60元。如果您預付三個月的學費，我們將提供九折優惠。

男 好的，那就這樣。但是，我沒有像樣的拳擊鞋。你們有販售或租用嗎？

女 沒有，但一樓有運動用品店。如果您說明是我們的會員，他們會折價10元給您。

男 我晚上會過去，支付三個月的學費，再順道買鞋子。

Boxing Equipment	Regular price
Boxing Gloves	$54
Protective Gear	$64
Sandbags	$152
Boxing Shoes	$162

拳擊器材	定價
拳擊手套	$54
護具	$64
沙袋	$152
拳擊鞋	$162

• **advertise** 廣告　**available** 有提供的　**suit one's schedule** 符合時間規畫　**convenient**（時間）方便的　**tuition fee** 學費　**in advance** 預先　**decent** 像樣的　**regular price** 定價

68 --

What is the man calling about?
(A) Taking sports lessons
(B) Moving into the Graham Complex
(C) Returning a pair of boxing gloves
(D) Leaving his office earlier than usual

這位男士打電話來詢問什麼？
(A) 上運動課程
(B) 搬進葛拉漢綜合大樓
(C) 歸還拳擊手套
(D) 比平時提早離開辦公室

在電話中，通常談話目的會在一開始出現。如開頭男子說「I'm calling about the sports classes you advertised in the local paper.」，故可知男子是為了運動課程致電，故正確答案為 (A)。

69 NEW --

Look at the graphic. How much is the man going to pay for the equipment he needs?
(A) $44
(B) $64
(C) $152
(D) $162

看一下圖表，這位男士需要支付多少錢來購買他所需要的配備？
(A) 44元
(B) 64元
(C) 152元
(D) 162元

請注意本題詢問的不是「tuition fee」，而是「equipment」。對話中提到，男子需要的物品是「boxing shoes」，且如果是健身房的會員，購買時可以享有每雙折抵 $10 的優惠，所以請找到價格表上的拳擊鞋項目，並從標示的價格減去 $10，故正確答案為 (C)。

70 --

What is suggested about the gym?
(A) It closes at 6 P.M.
(B) It's on the first floor.
(C) It's near the Graham Complex.
(D) It is far from Mr. Phillips's office.

關於健身房，提到了什麼事？
(A) 晚上六點結束營業。
(B) 位於一樓。
(C) 靠近葛拉漢綜合大樓。
(D) 離菲利浦先生的辦公室很遠。

從女子說的「The gym is right next to the Graham Complex」可知，健身房就在葛拉漢綜合大樓隔壁，所以正確答案為 (C)。

(A) 對話中雖然提及早上六點有拳擊課，但是無法確認打烊時間是不是為下午六點。(B) 位於建築物一樓的是運動用品店，但是無法確認健身房是不是也在一樓。(D) 男子曾說過自己的辦公室離綜合大樓不遠，又健身房就在大樓旁邊，故可推測男子的辦公室也離健身房不遠，所以 (D) 也非正確答案。

71-73 announcement

Welcome to all members of staff. Thank you for attending this event, which is celebrating the promotion of Charles Bailey to the general manager of IT. Charles has spent over 15 years with the company, beginning as a technician in the factory before working his way up the ladder to specialize in the computerization of this manufacturing company. Now he will be able to spend more time in the office rather than the factory floor. I would like to congratulate Charles for the dedication and loyalty that he has shown to this company and present him with a special gift that marks 15 years of service. Charles, please join me to accept this gift.

71–73 宣告

歡迎全體同仁。感謝大家參與這場盛會，慶祝查爾斯・貝里榮升IT公司的總經理。查爾斯已經在公司服務超過15年，他從工廠的技術師開始，一路平步青雲，並專心鑽研本製造商的電腦化。現在他能夠花更多時間待在辦公室，而不是廠區。我要祝賀查爾斯對本公司所展現的奉獻與忠誠，並頒給他這個象徵服務15年的特別賀禮。查爾斯，請上台接受這份賀禮。

• **celebrate** 慶祝　**promotion** 升遷　**work one's way up the ladder** 平步青雲　**specialize in . . .** 鑽研……　**computerization** 電腦化　**congratulate** 祝賀　**dedication** 奉獻　**loyalty** 忠誠　**operative** 工人

71

What special event is being held?
(A) A retirement event
(B) A training session
(C) A grand opening ceremony
(D) A promotion party

正在舉辦何種特殊活動？
(A) 退休慶祝會
(B) 教育訓練講習
(C) 盛大開幕典禮
(D) 升遷派對

在開頭便可聽到「Thank you for attending this event, which is celebrating the promotion of Charles Bailey to the general manager of IT.」，由此可知，正在進行的是慶祝升職相關的活動，故正確答案為 (D)。

72

What is Charles Bailey's profession?
(A) Computer specialist
(B) Office manager
(C) Mechanic
(D) Factory operative

查爾斯・貝里的工作是什麼？
(A) 電腦專門人員
(B) 部門經理
(C) 技工
(D) 工廠工人

本題詢問查爾斯・貝里的職業。從第三句的「specialize in the computerization of this manufacturing company」可以知道他的職業與電腦有關，故正確答案為 (A)。

73

What will most likely happen next?
(A) Some refreshments will be offered.
(B) An interview will be conducted.
(C) A seminar will take place.
(D) A gift will be presented.

接下來最可能發生什麼事？
(A) 提供一些茶點。
(B) 進行訪談。
(C) 舉行研討會。
(D) 頒發禮物。

在談話最後，說話者提到「I would like to congratulate Charles . . . and present him with a special gift that marks 15 years of service.」，表示為了表彰查爾斯‧貝里對公司的奉獻，將贈送一份紀念禮物，故正確答案為 (D)。

74-76 telephone message

74–76 電話留言

Good morning! I am calling to make an appointment with Dr. Stevenson. I was released from Kenwood Hospital last week, but I am still not well enough to return to work. Kenwood Hospital is too far from my house, so I want to consult Dr. Stevenson about what kinds of painkillers are more suitable for me. I'm out to buy something soon, so I would like to make an appointment to see the doctor this afternoon if that is possible. Please call me back at 765-4803. Thank you.

早安！我打這通電話是想跟史蒂文森醫生預約。我上週剛從肯伍德醫院出院，但我還沒恢復到可以上班。肯伍德醫院離我住的地方太遠了，所以我想請教史蒂文森醫生哪一種止痛藥比較適合我。我等等要外出購物，所以如果可以的話，我想預約今天下午看醫生。請回電765-4803給我。感謝您。

• **sb be released** 出院　**consult sb about sth** 請教某人關於某事　**painkiller** 止痛藥　**suitable** 適合的

74

What kind of business is the speaker calling?
(A) A holiday resort
(B) A medical clinic
(C) An employment agency
(D) A pharmaceutical company

說話者致電給何種行業？
(A) 度假中心
(B) 醫療診所
(C) 職業介紹所
(D) 製藥公司

從一開始的「I am calling to make an appointment with Dr. Stevenson.」以及「so I would like to make an appointment to see the doctor this afternoon」都可知道，說話者聯絡的地方是醫院或診所，故正確答案為 (B)。

75

What does the speaker ask about?
(A) Vaccination requirements
(B) Better medication
(C) A medicine price
(D) A return to work

說話者詢問何事？
(A) 疫苗接種規定
(B) 更合適的用藥
(C) 藥價
(D) 復工

本題解題關鍵為單字「painkiller」。説話者提到「I want to consult Dr. Stevenson about what kinds of painkillers are more suitable for me.」，故正確答案為 (B)。

考生若遇到不會的單字，也可從全文判斷。説話者提到上週剛出院，但還沒完全恢復，記住這點後使用刪去法，應該可以選出正確答案。

76

When does the speaker say she will be available?	説話者説她何時有空？
(A) This morning	(A) 今天早上
(B) This afternoon	(B) 今天下午
(C) Tomorrow morning	(C) 明天早上
(D) Tomorrow afternoon	(D) 明天下午

本題詢問説話者可以預約的時間。説話者的後半部內容提及「I would like to make an appointment to see the doctor this afternoon if that is possible.」，由此可知，説話者提出的會面時間是今天下午，所以正確答案為 (B)。

77-79 instructions　　77–79 指示

This week, every member of the front-of-shop sales team has to attend a demonstration on operating the new electronic cash register. The session will take place on Thursday, October 11, during the lunch break. **(78)This also applies to the temporary staff.** I am also handing out a leaflet on the new cash register, which I want you to familiarize yourselves with before Thursday. This will explain how the new equipment works and how it is directly connected to the Order Department. You will see how it works in detail at the demonstration.	這禮拜，前台銷售小組的所有成員，都必須參加一場新電子收銀機的操作示範。這個講習將於10月11日星期四中午休息時間舉行。**(78)這項任務亦適用於臨時聘雇人員。**我也會發下一張有關新收銀機的傳單，希望各位在週四前先熟悉一下。這説明這個新裝置的運作方式，以及如何直接與訂購部門連結。示範時，各位會更詳細地看到它的運作方式。

• demonstration 示範　cash register 收銀機　hand out 發送　leaflet 傳單
familiarize oneself with . . . 熟悉……　in detail 詳細地

 36

77

What will happen on October 11?	10月11日會發生什麼事？
(A) Lunchtime will be extended.	(A) 延長午餐時間。
(B) Paychecks will be distributed.	(B) 發薪水。
(C) A leaflet will be sent out.	(C) 分發傳單。
(D) A demonstration will take place.	(D) 舉行示範。

答題時若遇到時間相關資訊，最好在題本上做筆記，以便之後對照解題。一開始，説話者告知聽者必須參加「a demonstration on operating the new electronic cash register」，並提到「The session will take place on Thursday, October 11, during the lunch break.」，由此可知，在 10 月 11 日當天有操作示範，故正確答案為 (D)。

78 (NEW)

What does the woman imply when she says, "This also applies to the temporary staff"?

(A) They are not included in a lunchtime session.
(B) They are required to fill out a form.
(C) They will receive less pay.
(D) They must be in attendance.

當這位女士說：「這項任務亦適用於臨時聘雇人員」，是什麼意思？

(A) 他們不包含在午間講習中。
(B) 他們必須填寫一張表單。
(C) 他們將獲得較少的薪資。
(D) 他們必須出席。

解讀句子意圖的題目務必從前後文來解題。本題引用的句子出現前，說話者提到「The session will take place on Thursday, October 11, during the lunch break.」，由此可知，後句「This also applies to the temporary staff.」中的「This」指的應是「The session」，表示臨時職員也需要在規定時間參加培訓。選項 (D) 將「has to attend」改寫為意義相近的「must be in attendance」，故正確答案為 (D)。

79

What are listeners asked to read?

(A) A customer questionnaire
(B) A health and safety document
(C) An instruction flyer
(D) Dismissal procedures

聽者被要求閱讀什麼？

(A) 顧客問卷
(B) 健康安全文件
(C) 使用說明傳單
(D) 解僱程序

從「I am also handing out a leaflet on the new cash register, which I want you to familiarize yourselves with before Thursday.」可知，說話者要求聽者閱讀收銀機操作相關的傳單。
選項 (C) 將「leaflet」改寫為符合文意的「instruction flyer」，故正確答案為 (C)。

80-82 introduction

80-82 介紹

Welcome, everyone, to our annual awards ceremony at the Guild of Master Practitioners. This year, we have been concentrating on the theme of sustainable development without damage to the environment, and tonight, those who have effected a change in the workplace using sustainable methods will be awarded. All of the nominations and categories can be found in the booklets you will find on your seats. And *Good Energy Magazine* has kindly sponsored tonight's event.

歡迎各位來到高階執業者協會的年度頒獎典禮。今年我們持續關注永續發展，且不造成環境破壞的主題，而今晚將頒獎給那些利用永續方式在職場上產生影響力的人士。所有的提名者與項目可參考在各位座位上的手冊。而今晚的活動由《優能雜誌》友善贊助。

- **awards ceremony** 頒獎典禮 **guild** 協會 **practitioner** 執業者 **concentrate on . . .** 關注……
sustainable 永續的 **effect** 使……發生 **nomination** 提名 **category** 項目 **booklet** 手冊
sponsor 贊助

What will happen at the event?
(A) A sustainable program will be reviewed.
(B) A magazine will be introduced.
(C) Awards will be presented.
(D) New legislation will be announced.

活動中將發生什麼事？
(A) 審查一個永續發展的計畫。
(B) 介紹一本雜誌。
(C) 頒獎。
(D) 宣布新法規。

一開始，說話者說：「Welcome, everyone, to our annual awards ceremony at the Guild of Master Practitioners.」，由此可知此為頒獎典禮，故正確答案為 (C)。

What can listeners find on their seats?
(A) Information about past projects
(B) Results of a questionnaire
(C) A membership form
(D) A list of nominations

聽眾可以在座位上找到什麼？
(A) 之前計畫的資料
(B) 問卷調查的結果
(C) 會員申請表
(D) 提名者名單

本題的關鍵字為「seats」。說話者在後半段內容提到「All of the nominations and categories can be found in the booklets you will find on your seats.」，表示聽者的座位上皆有記載所有提名者與獎項的手冊，故正確答案為 (D)。

What is mentioned about _Good Energy Magazine_?
(A) It is a leading magazine in the environment.
(B) It is supporting the event.
(C) It is recruiting new practitioners.
(D) It is found on the seats.

談話中提到什麼和《優能雜誌》有關的事？
(A) 是有關環境的一本重要雜誌。
(B) 資助這場盛會。
(C) 正在招募新的執業者。
(D) 可在座位上看到。

最後一句話提到「Good Energy Magazine has kindly sponsored tonight's event.」故可知《優能雜誌》贊助了今日的頒獎活動。選項 (B) 將「sponsored tonight's event」改寫為意思相近的「supporting the event」，故正確答案為 (B)。

ACTUAL TEST 9

PART 4

中譯＋解析

36

83-85 excerpt from a talk 　　　　　　　　　83–85 談話摘錄

One more thing before you leave. Can you ensure that all items are properly stored away when you lock up? This mainly concerns the factory staff. I have posted a Health and Safety brochure on the noticeboard that explains how to safely store chemicals and preservatives. It also details correct handling techniques for these hazardous substances when using the items in the automobile painting shop. If the items are properly stored in the correct place, we can begin work much more efficiently in the mornings.	在各位離開前還有一件事情。大家都確定，所有的物品在上鎖前都已儲放妥當了嗎？這主要和工廠裡的職員有關。我已經在布告欄張貼了一份健康與安全手冊，說明如何安全地存放化學物品與防腐劑。裡面也詳細說明在汽車油漆間使用這些物品時，正確處理這些危險物質的方法。如果這些物品妥善地存放在正確的位置，那我們在早上就可以更有效率地開工了。

* **store . . . away** 儲放　**lock up** 上鎖　**concern . . .** 與⋯⋯有關　**post** 張貼　**noticeboard** 布告欄　**chemicals** 化學物品　**preservatives** 防腐劑　**handling techniques** 處理方法　**hazardous** 危險的　**substance** 物質　**painting shop** 油漆間

83 --

Who is the speaker most likely addressing?　說話者最可能在向誰說話？
(A) Safety inspectors　　　　　　　　　　(A) 安全檢測員
(B) Interior designers　　　　　　　　　　(B) 室內設計師
(C) Factory workers　　　　　　　　　　　(C) 工廠工人
(D) Laundry staff　　　　　　　　　　　　(D) 洗衣店員工

本題詢問說話者所指的對象。和場所、對象與職業有關的問題，可以從相關內容推敲出答案。本題在一開始即要求聽者在離開前確認物品是否妥善存放，並且提到「This mainly concerns the factory staff.」，已直接點出聽者的身份。由此可知，選項 (C) 將「factory staff」改寫為意義相同的「factory workers」，故正確答案為 (C)。

84 --

What is the main topic of the talk?　這段談話的主題是什麼？
(A) Car painting　　　　　　　　　　　　(A) 汽車油漆
(B) Appliance repairs　　　　　　　　　　(B) 電器維修
(C) Factory inspections　　　　　　　　　(C) 工廠檢測
(D) Safety procedures　　　　　　　　　　(D) 安全程序

說話者一開始要求聽者確認物品是否妥善存放，並說到自己張貼了與健康安全有關的手冊，說明化學物品與防腐劑的安全存放方式，故可知道本題的正確答案為 (D)。

本題的解題關鍵字彙為「a Health and Safety brochure」與「safely store chemicals and preservatives」，只要聽到這些應該就能判斷出答案。

85

Where will listeners find the guidelines?
(A) Near the chemicals
(B) In the preservatives
(C) On a bulletin board
(D) In front of the paint shop

聽者可以在哪裡找到指示說明？
(A) 化學物品附近
(B) 防腐劑裡
(C) 布告欄上
(D) 油漆店前

本題的關鍵字為「guidelines」。從「I have posted a Health and Safety brochure on the noticeboard」可知，說話者張貼指示說明在布告欄上。選項 (C) 將「noticeboard」改寫為意義相同的「bulletin board」，故正確答案為 (C)。

86-88 recorded message

86–88 留言錄音

Thank you for contacting the Doris Fitness Center. We are located in the Tintroy Building near the Danao subway station, a block away from the city hall. We offer a range of sports classes, such as aerobics, yoga, table tennis, and squash. We are currently offering a new tae-bo class, with two experienced trainers from Korea. We are open every weekday between 6 A.M. and 9 P.M. If you wish to sign up for the new class, please press one now.

感謝您來電朵瑞絲健身中心。我們就在達瑙地鐵站附近的提特伊大樓，離市政廳只有一個街區的距離。我們提供一系列運動課程，像是有氧運動、瑜伽、桌球和壁球。我們現正開設一種新的拳擊有氧課程，配有兩位經驗豐富的韓國教練。我們營業時間為平日上午六點至晚上九點。如果您有意報名新課程，請現在按一。

• **a range of** 一系列的 **experienced** 經驗豐富的 **sign up for . . .** 報名……

86

Where is the fitness center located?
(A) In the vicinity of Danao City
(B) Near a subway station
(C) Right next to the city hall
(D) In front of the community center

健身中心位於何處？
(A) 緊鄰達瑙市
(B) 地鐵站附近
(C) 市政廳隔壁
(D) 社區活動中心前

由「We are located in the Tintroy Building near the Danao subway station, a block away from the city hall.」可得知，健身中心位於達瑙地鐵站附近的提特伊大樓裡，故正確答案為 (B)。

「Danao」這個專有名詞雖然也在 (A) 中出現，但是這個名字是地鐵站名，無法確認是否也是城市名稱。而 (C) 中出現的「city hall」則在一個街區之外，無法用「right next to」描述。(D) 則為沒有提及的內容。

87

What class is newly offered?
(A) Aerobics
(B) Yoga
(C) Squash
(D) Tae-bo

最新提供的是哪一種課程？
(A) 有氧運動
(B) 瑜伽
(C) 壁球
(D) 拳擊有氧

ACTUAL TEST 9 PART 4 中譯＋解析

369

從「We offer a range of sports classes, such as aerobics, yoga, table tennis, and squash. We are currently offering a new tae-bo class. . . .」可以得知，新推出的課程為拳擊有氧，正確答案為 (D)。

若不確定「tae-bo」為何，也可使用刪去法。(A)、(B) 與 (C) 都不是加在「new」後的名詞，故應非正解。

88 -

Why would listeners press one?　　　　聽者為什麼要按一？
(A) To cancel a class　　　　　　　　　　(A) 取消課程
(B) To arrange a tutorial　　　　　　　　(B) 安排個別指導
(C) To enroll in a class　　　　　　　　　(C) 報名課程
(D) To get directions　　　　　　　　　　(D) 得到路線指引

錄音最後，說話者表示「If you wish to sign up for the new class, please press one now.」，告知聽者若想報名新課程，可以按下電話的一號鍵。選項 (C) 將「sign up for」改寫為意義相同的「enroll in」，故正確答案為 (C)。

89-91 excerpt from a meeting　　　　　**89–91 會議摘錄**

Lastly, **(91)I have good news for everyone.** We began this current quarter aiming to increase the market share of our Shiny Clean range in the eastern region by 10 percent. I am delighted to announce that this has been achieved. Due to a larger client base, we are expanding operations and opening a new branch in Wilmington. The store needs experienced staff, and we would like to hire those who are currently working here at headquarters. If you are interested in relocating to Wilmington, please let me know as soon as possible. The final date for receiving applications is in three weeks' time, on June 15, and the following week, we will be shortlisting candidates.	最後，**(91)我有好消息要告訴各位。**這一季一開始，我們的目標是在東部地區增加閃亮清潔系列產品10%的市占率。我很高興地宣布這個目標已經達成了。由於更廣大的客戶群，我們要擴大營運，並在威明頓開設新分店。這家店需要經驗豐富的員工，我們想聘用目前正在總部服務的人員。如果你對調職至威明頓有興趣的話，請盡快告訴我。接受申請的最後日期是三週後的6月15日。隔週，我們將列出入選候選人。

- aim to . . . 目標是……　**market share** 市占率　**delighted** 高興的　**client base** 客戶群　**operations** 營運
  headquarters 總部　**relocate** 調職　**shortlist** 列出　**candidate** 候選人　**recruit** 招募　**willing to** 有意願

89 -

What has Shiny Clean accomplished over the quarter?　閃亮清潔這一季完成了什麼事？
(A) It launched a new range of products.　　(A) 推出新系列產品。
(B) It relocated to Wilmington.　　　　　　(B) 搬遷至威明頓。
(C) It increased its share in a specific market.　(C) 增加特定市場的占有率。
(D) It recruited more employees.　　　　　(D) 招募更多員工。

本題可從第二與第三句的內容得知答案。說話者提到「We began this current quarter aiming to increase the market share of our Shiny Clean range in the eastern region by 10 percent. I am delighted to announce that this has been achieved.」，由此可知，公司已完成本季提高市占率的目標，故正確答案為 (C)。

90

Who is encouraged to apply for the new position in Wilmington?

(A) Employees with several years' experience
(B) Current staff willing to relocate
(C) Sales managers with an interest in cleaning products
(D) Those with experience in managing stores

誰被鼓勵申請威明頓的新職？
(A) 有數年經驗的員工
(B) 有意願調動工作地點的在職員工
(C) 對清潔產品有興趣的業務經理
(D) 具門市管理經驗者

前面的內容中，說話者提到將在威明頓建立新的分公司，並說「we would like to hire those who are currently working here at headquarters.」，希望由目前任職於總公司的員工前往任職，同時也表示「If you are interested in relocating to Wilmington, please let me know as soon as possible.」，所以只要是有意願的員工都可以提出申請，本題最合適的答案為 (B)。

 91 NEW

What does the man imply when he says, "I have good news for everyone"?

(A) He's pleased to let everyone know about their success.
(B) He's willing to move to the headquarters.
(C) He's glad to have more staff in the new branch.
(D) He's happy to have a lot of candidates.

當這位男士說：「我有好消息要告訴各位」，是什麼意思？
(A) 他很樂意讓大家知道他們的成就。
(B) 他願意搬到總部。
(C) 他很高興新分店有更多員工。
(D) 他很高興有很多應徵者。

從後文可知，說話者所謂的「好消息」，指的是達成提高市占率目標一事。選項 (A) 將達成目標改寫為符合文意的「their success」，正確答案為 (A)。

92-94 advertisement

92-94 廣告

Come and join Aerial Helicopters on a journey across the city of Cairo. This exciting tour encompasses the sites along the Nile, covering the ancient monuments and the mighty structures as dusk begins to fall on them. We are the only aerial tour in the city that operates at sunset. Our tour guides will take you on an audio journey, explaining the history of the city's rise from a Middle Eastern village to the center of trade and commerce. The helicopter tour leaves from Cairo Airport and lasts 50 minutes. In order to comply with health and safety regulations, we ask you to arrive 30 minutes prior to the stated departure times.	歡迎來參加空中直升機橫越開羅市之旅。這趟令人興奮的旅程包含了尼羅河沿岸的遺址，以及在黃昏降臨時巡禮古代紀念碑與偉大的建築。我們是全市唯一提供日落時分空中行程的旅行社。我們的導遊將帶領您進行語音導覽，說明這座城市從中東村落晉升至商業貿易中心的歷史。直升機行程將自開羅機場出發，歷時50分鐘。為符合健康安全法規，我們要求您於指定的出發時間前30分鐘報到。

• **aerial** 空中的　**encompass** 包含　**ancient** 古代的　**monument** 紀念碑　**mighty** 偉大的　**dusk** 黃昏
sunset 日落　**trade and commerce** 商業貿易　**comply with** 符合　**exclusively** 僅僅　**daytime** 日間
brand-new 全新的　**health certificate** 健康證明

What kind of service is being advertised?
(A) Online reservations
(B) Aerial tours
(C) Vehicle rental
(D) Boat rides

這裡宣傳的是何種服務？
(A) 線上預約
(B) 空中導覽
(C) 汽車租賃
(D) 船遊

本題詢問廣告內容。一開始，說話者邀請聽者「Come and join Aerial Helicopters on a journey across the city of Cairo.」，由此可知，這是一則有關搭乘直升機進行空中之旅的廣告，所以正確答案為 (B)。

According to the speaker, what is special about the service?
(A) It is exclusively a daytime trip.
(B) It is a brand-new service.
(C) It takes off once a week.
(D) It takes place at dusk.

根據說話者表示，這項服務的特別之處是什麼？
(A) 僅為日間行程。
(B) 是一項全新的服務。
(C) 一週出團一次。
(D) 在黃昏時舉行。

本題詢問此項服務有何特點。說話者在前半部分提到「We are the only aerial tour in the city that operates at sunset.」，標榜自己是該城市唯一在向晚時分進行空中導覽的旅行社，故正確答案為 (D)。

94

What are listeners asked to do?
(A) Provide a health certificate
(B) Carry identification
(C) Reserve a place
(D) Arrive early

聽眾被要求做什麼事？
(A) 提供健康證明
(B) 帶身分證
(C) 預約座位
(D) 提早到達

說話者最後提到「In order to comply with health and safety regulations, we ask you to arrive 30 minutes prior to the stated departure times.」，請參加者在出發前三十分鐘抵達集合地點，所以正確答案為 (D)。

Good afternoon. This is Harold Scott, and I am the manager of the George Fisher Restaurant. I have received a leaflet from your business and would like some details. We have recently been unhappy with our current supplier, so I would be very interested in your organic flour if you can guarantee daily deliveries to us. My telephone number is 567-0271. Can you call me back, as I would like to get some samples?	午安，我是哈洛德‧史考特，是喬治漁夫餐廳的經理。我拿到了貴公司的傳單，想了解一些細節。我們最近對目前的供應商不甚滿意，所以如果您能保證每天配貨給我們的話，我對貴公司的有機麵粉非常有興趣。我的電話號碼是 567-0271。我想索取一些樣品，您方便回電給我嗎？

Suppliers list

Miller's Joy	657-0932	Organic bakery
Herbalist's Delight	458-4273	Artificial flowers, other decorations
Mrs. Millers'	352-1853	Flour, Oil, Spices
Harmony	574-3753	Fruits & Vegetables

供應商名單

喬麥麥	657-0932	有機麵包店
草木樂	458-4273	人造花、其他裝飾品
磨坊太太	352-1853	麵粉、油、香料
怡好	574-3753	水果蔬菜

• **leaflet** 傳單　**organic** 有機的　**flour** 麵粉　**guarantee** 保證

Who is the speaker?

(A) A delivery man
(B) A restaurant manager
(C) A grocer
(D) A millworker

說話者是誰？

(A) 送貨員
(B) 餐廳經理
(C) 雜貨商
(D) 工廠工人

一開始，說話者說了「This is Harold Scott, and I am the manager of the George Fisher Restaurant.」，直接告知自己的身分為餐廳經理，所以本題正確答案為 (B)。

What does the speaker intend to do?

(A) Offer an online service
(B) Alter a menu
(C) Deliver to local bakeries
(D) Change his supplier

說話者想做什麼事？

(A) 提供線上服務
(B) 修改菜單
(C) 送貨到本地麵包店
(D) 更換供應商

說話者表示「We have recently been unhappy with our current supplier, so I would be very interested in your organic flour if you can guarantee daily deliveries to us.」，可從此段內容推測，說話者由於對目前配合的供貨商有所不滿，故考慮更換合作業者，所以正確答案為 (D)。

Look at the graphic. Which store is the man most likely calling?

(A) Miller's Joy
(B) Herbalist's Delight
(C) Mrs. Millers'
(D) Harmony

看一下圖表，這位男士可能打電話給哪個店家？

(A) 喬麥麥
(B) 草木樂
(C) 磨坊太太
(D) 怡好

本題的關鍵線索為「I would be very interested in your organic flour」。對照名單可知，提供有機麵粉的業者，只有在供貨清單中標有麵粉、油、調味料的「磨坊太太」，故正確答案為 (C)。

(A) 為麵包店，不代表能提供麵粉。(B) 為提供人造花與裝飾品的商店。請注意「flour」（麵粉）與「flower」（花卉）的發音相同。(D) 為提供水果與蔬菜的「green grocer」（蔬果商）。

98-100 telephone message and schedule

98–100 電話留言及時程表

Hello, this is Walter James calling for Professor Bonnie Holt. I am a presenter on YSBC TV and I am doing a research for a feature on adult obesity. I saw your lecture on "Eating Habits of Adults" live yesterday, and I would like to talk to you about your views on eliminating fats from the diet. I understand that as a university lecturer and a regular newspaper columnist you are very busy, but I would like to come and see you. I'm visiting your university the day after tomorrow. We would very much like to feature your opinions and research within the broadcast.

您好，我是華特·詹姆斯致電邦妮·霍爾特教授。我是YSBC電視的主持人，目前正在為一個有關成人肥胖的專題節目進行研究。我昨天看到了您有關〈成人的飲食習慣〉的現場演說，想跟您討論您對於飲食消脂的看法。我了解，身為一位大學講師兼報紙定期專欄作家，您非常忙碌，但我想過去拜訪您。我將於後天拜訪貴校。我們非常希望能在節目播出時特別介紹您的見解與研究。

Healthy Habits

11:00–11:45 P.M., Mon.–Fri.

Weekly Schedule	
Mon.	Child Obesity – A New Threat
Tue.	LIVE Lecture: Eating Habits of Adults
Wed.	Smoking, a Silent Killer
Thu.	LIVE Lecture: Vegetarianism. Is It a MUST?
Fri.	Dietholic

健康習慣

週一至週五 晚上11:00–11:45

每週時程表	
星期一	孩童肥胖——一種新的威脅
星期二	現場演講：成人的飲食習慣
星期三	抽煙——沉默的殺手
星期四	現場演講：素食主義——這是必要的嗎？
星期五	暴食

• **presenter** 主持人　**feature** 〔名詞〕專題節目；〔動詞〕特別介紹　**obesity** 肥胖　**eliminate** 消除　**broadcast** 節目播出

According to the speaker, what has Professor Holt recently done? 根據說話者表示，霍爾特教授最近做了什麼事？

(A) Delivered a lecture
(B) Organized a seminar
(C) Participated in a university debate
(D) Published an article

(A) 發表演說
(B) 籌辦研討會
(C) 參加大學辯論
(D) 發表文章

說話者提到「I saw your recent lecture on "Eating Habits of Adults"」，說明霍爾特教授最近正在發表了與成人飲食習慣有關的演說，所以正確答案為 (A)。

 99 (NEW)

Look at the graphic. When does Mr. James say he wants to meet Professor Holt? 看一下圖表，詹姆斯先生說他希望何時能與霍爾特教授見面？

(A) Tuesday
(B) Wednesday
(C) Thursday
(D) Friday

(A) 星期二
(B) 星期三
(C) 星期四
(D) 星期五

詹姆斯先生在電話中說自己昨天收看了霍爾特教授的演講，而根據圖表，該節目在週二播出，所以今天應為週三。故詹姆斯先生說「I would like to come and see you. I'm visiting your university the day after tomorrow.」，其中的「後天」可推測為「週五」，故正確答案為 (D)。

 100

What does the speaker ask Professor Holt to do? 說話者要求霍爾特教授做什麼？

(A) Contribute to a TV program
(B) Undertake a newspaper interview
(C) Review some books
(D) Take a university lecture

(A) 參加電視節目
(B) 進行報紙訪談
(C) 評論一些書
(D) 修大學課程

從最後的「We would very much like to feature your opinions and research within the broadcast.」可知，說話者想邀請教授參加自己的電視節目，所以正確答案為 (A)。

According to the speaker, what has reduced him to such a state?

(A) a boring lecture
(B) ...too a seminar
(C) participated in a university debate
(D) a class interrupted

Look at the ...
to write in each dinner class?
(A) notice
(B) ...
(C) ...
(D) ...

Who does the speaker ...
(A) ...
(B) ...
(C) ...
(D) ...

ACTUAL TEST
10

1 --

(A) He's serving food in a restaurant.
(B) He's cooking meat on a grill.
(C) He's pouring water into a container.
(D) He's holding a mixing bowl.

(A) 他正在餐廳上菜。
(B) 他正在烤架上料理肉品。
(C) 他正把水倒進容器裡。
(D) 他正拿著攪拌碗。

• grill 烤架　container 容器　mixing bowl 攪拌碗

因為照片中男子正在進行燒烤，故可預測會出現「roast」、「barbecue」、「grill」、「cook」等動詞。(A) 照片並未顯示正在運送食物的樣子。(C) 照片描述的並非正在倒水的場景。(D) 照片中並未出現碗。故本題正確答案為 (B)。

2 --

(A) Some people are looking for their bags.
(B) Some people are staring at their notebooks.
(C) Some people are standing next to the chairs.
(D) Some people are waiting on the subway platform.

(A) 一些人正在找他們的包包。
(B) 一些人正盯著他們的筆記本。
(C) 一些人正站在椅子旁。
(D) 一些人正在地鐵月台上等候。

• look for sth 尋找　stare at sth 盯著　platform 月台

照片中，一些人拿著行李，像在等候大眾交通運輸的樣子。(A) 看不出照片中的人物有尋找物品的樣子。(B) 照片中未出現筆記本。(C) 照片中未出現椅子。故本題正確答案為 (D)。

3 --

(A) Clothes are hanging on some racks.
(B) Clothes are being carried upstairs.
(C) A customer is trying on a dress.
(D) Clothes are being stacked neatly on the shelves.

(A) 衣服正掛在架子上。
(B) 衣服正被帶上樓。
(C) 顧客正在試穿洋裝。
(D) 衣服正整齊地疊放在架上。

• hang 掛　rack 架子　upstairs 上樓　try on 試穿　stack 疊放　neatly 整齊地　shelf 櫃架

當選項中出現被動式句型，如果照片沒有正在執行該動作的人物，則通常該選項非正確答案。然而本題中，由於 (A) 描寫衣服被掛著的狀態，與圖片相符，故正確答案為 (A)。

(A) A man is reaching over his chair.   (A) 一位男士正伸手越過他的椅子。
(B) A man is opening a book.   (B) 一位男士正打開書本。
(C) A man is writing something down.   (C) 一位男士正在寫東西。
(D) A man is turning on a lamp.   (D) 一位男士正打開檯燈。

• **reach over . . .** 伸手越過……   **write . . . down** 寫下……

照片中有一名男子坐在沙發上，手捧著書本專心書寫，故正確答案為 (C)。

(A) 男子周圍並未出現椅子；(B) 男子並不是正在打開書本；(D) 檯燈已開啟，不是正被男子打開，故這些皆非正確答案。

(A) A woman is admiring a painting.   (A) 一位女士正在欣賞畫作。
(B) A woman is hanging up a picture.   (B) 一位女士正在掛上畫作。
(C) A woman is leaning against a wall.   (C) 一位女士正靠著牆壁。
(D) A floor is being mopped.   (D) 地板正被拖洗。

• **admire** 欣賞   **hang up** 掛上   **lean against the wall** 靠著牆壁   **mop** 拖洗

照片中的女子正坐著欣賞畫作。(A)「admire」雖然常常以「感嘆」、「稱讚」的意思出現，但是也有「欣賞」的意思。除了「look at」、「stare at」之外，也請熟記此用法，本題正確答案為 (A)。

另外，畫面中未出現 (B)、(C) 與 (D) 的動作，所以這些選項皆非正確答案。

(A) A roof is being repaired.   (A) 屋頂正在修理中。
(B) People are sweeping the floor.   (B) 人們正在掃地。
(C) Lights are being turned on.   (C) 燈正被打開。
(D) Columns line a walkway.   (D) 柱子沿著走道排列。

• **roof** 屋頂   **repair** 修理   **sweep the floor** 掃地   **column** 柱子   **line . . .** 沿……排列   **walkway** 走道

以物品為主詞的被動式描述出現時，通常應該要有人物執行該行動。照片中可以看出，柱子整齊地沿著走道排成長長一列，所以正確答案為 (D)。

(A) 與 (C) 描述的內容無法在照片中找出正在做該行動的人，所以無法成為答案。另外，雖然照片中出現人物，但是 (B) 因為無法看出正在掃地，所以此選項也非正解。

7

When did Kelly clean out the living room?
(A) After we left.
(B) She lived there.
(C) She cleaned the supply room.

凱莉什麼時候打掃客廳的？
(A) 我們離開後。
(B) 她住在那裡。
(C) 她打掃了器材室。

• clean out 打掃　supply room 器材室

本題詢問「何時」打掃過了，所以答案中必須提及時間相關的資訊。(A) 表示「我們離開後」進行了清掃，為適當的答覆。(B) 使用與題目「living」發音相似的「live」形成陷阱。(C) 雖然重複字彙「clean」，但是清掃的地點與題目不符。此外，該選項較適合成為詢問場所時的答覆。因此本題的正確答案為 (A)。

8

Where is your new house located?
(A) Two hours from now.
(B) It's next to the post office.
(C) I don't think he's late in the morning.

你的新家在哪裡？
(A) 從現在開始兩個小時。
(B) 郵局旁邊。
(C) 我覺得他早上沒有遲到。

本題詢問場所，所以需出現告知場所的答覆。(A) 是詢問「什麼時候」時的答覆。(B) 告知位於郵局旁邊，所以是正確答案。(C) 則為與題目毫無相關的句子。故本題正解為 (B)。

9

How much did sales revenue increase this year?
(A) Yes, it is now on sale.
(B) By year's end.
(C) By 20%.

今年業績收入增加了多少？
(A) 是的，現在正在拍賣。
(B) 年底之前。
(C) 20%。

本題詢問業績上升多少，所以回答內容應同時提及「數字」與「上升程度」。(A) 重複出現「sale」；(B) 重複使用「year」，但是內容皆完全與題目無關。(C) 中的介系詞「by」當和數字一起出現，表示上升或減少的幅度，故正確答案為 (C)。

10

Would you have more dessert?
(A) No, he didn't.
(B) At the restaurant.
(C) Yes, that would be great!

你還要再來點甜點嗎？
(A) 不，他沒有。
(B) 在餐廳。
(C) 好的，那會很棒！

本題的「Would」應視為情態動詞，表示客氣的提議或邀請，當用來詢問對方意願，對方可用「Yes/No」回答。(C) 回答「Yes」並表達要繼續吃，所以本題正確答案為 (C)。

(A) 題目以「you」詢問，應以「I」回答，而非第三人稱的「he」，且由於此處的「Would」並非表示過去式，故此處應用現在式回答。(B) 更適合作為詢問「場所」時的回答。

11 --

Who informed the employees of the schedule changes?

(A) The Human Resources Department.
(B) A lot of changes.
(C) With their colleagues.

是誰通知員工時程表的異動？
(A) 人力資源部。
(B) 很多異動。
(C) 和他們的同事。

• **inform sb of sth** 通知某人關於某事　**employee** 員工　**schedule change** 時程表異動　**colleague** 同事

本題是「Who」疑問句，所以回答中必須告知對象。(B) 只是重覆題目中的「changes」，而 (C) 則利用「employees」與「colleagues」的相似性造成混淆，但兩者皆非答案。選項 (A) 指出對象為「人事部」，故本題正解為 (A)。

12 --

Which dates do you want to reserve a restaurant table for?

(A) I placed an order for a table.
(B) From the 14th to the 15th, please.
(C) It's downstairs.

你要預約哪一天的餐廳座位？
(A) 我下了一張桌子的訂單。
(B) 麻煩，從14號到15號。
(C) 在樓下。

• **reserve** 預約　**place an order for . . .** 下⋯⋯的訂單

本題使用「Which dates」的句型詢問，所以如果選項出現具體日期，則該選項為正確答案。(A) 只是重複出現「table」，實際內容與題目無關。(B) 出現「14th」、「15th」，由此可知，此處不是一般的數字，而是日期形式的數字。(C) 內容與題目無關。正確答案為 (B)。

13 --

The dinner comes with free side dishes, doesn't it?

(A) He wants to come with me.
(B) That's right.
(C) It's excellent and tasty.

晚餐有附免費的配菜，不是嗎？
(A) 他想跟我一起去。
(B) 沒錯。
(C) 很棒又美味。

• **come with . . .** 附有⋯⋯　**tasty** 美味的

本題為附加問句，確認是否會有免費的配菜，所以回答中應該出現「Yes/No」，或是其他與此呼應的答覆。 (A) 只是重複片語「come with」，其他人物與事物的描述與題目完全無關。(B) 明確表示出肯定，代表會有免費配菜。(C) 此句像是對食物的評價，與題目不符。故本題正確答案為 (B)。

14 --

Aren't we waiting for the same bus?　　我們不是在等同一輛公車嗎？
(A) No, mine departs earlier.　　　　　　(A) 不，我的較早出發。
(B) The food truck is at the corner of the street.　(B) 餐車就在街角。
(C) You can wait for some of these.　　　(C) 你可以等其中一些。

本題為否定疑問句，詢問對方是否與自己在等候同班的公車。否定疑問句通常會以「Yes/No」
回答，且在本題中，當回答「Yes」，表示為「在等同一班」，反之回答「No」。(A) 回答「No」並
表示公車的出發時間不同，其他兩選項的內容皆與題目不符，故正確答案為 (A)。

15 --

Do you know which dish the customer ordered?　你知道客人點了哪一道菜嗎？
(A) The pasta on the blue plate.　　　　(A) 藍色盤子的義大利麵。
(B) I'd prefer pizza.　　　　　　　　　(B) 我比較喜歡披薩。
(C) In the dining room.　　　　　　　　(C) 在飯廳。

• **dish** 菜餚　**order** 點（餐）　**prefer** 比較喜歡

本題詢問的是客人選擇的餐點種類，故答案中應包含餐點名稱相關的資訊。(A) 表示為特定盤子的餐
點，故為合適答案。(B) 題目詢問的是客人的選擇，用「I」回覆並不正確。 (C) 為適合詢問「地點」
時的回答。本題正確答案為 (A)。

16 --

Do you have the shirts in stock?　　你們有襯衫現貨嗎？
(A) Under 10 dollars.　　　　　　　　　(A) 不到10元。
(B) They are all sold out.　　　　　　　(B) 全都賣光了。
(C) You wear the red shirts.　　　　　　(C) 你們穿紅色襯衫。

• **have . . . in stock** ……有現貨　**be sold out** 賣光

本題詢問是否有庫存，(A) 為詢問價格時會出現的回答；(C) 只是重複「shirts」，內容與題意不符；
(B) 表示襯衫已賣光，暗示並沒有現貨，故本題正解為 (B)。

17 --

Please let us know when you finish using the copy machine.　當你使用完影印機，麻煩告訴我們一聲。
(A) Sure, I'll be done in a minute.　　　(A) 好，我再一下就好了。
(B) For the new supply room.　　　　　(B) 為了新器材室。
(C) No, it isn't working now.　　　　　(C) 不，現在沒有在運作。

• **copy machine** 影印機　**supply room** 器材室　**work** 運作

題目為陳述句，請對方使用完影印機通知自己。(A) 表示答應請求，並解釋很快會用完，故為合適回
覆。(B) 內容與題目無關。(C) 題目並非詢問機器是否啟動，故此選項也與題意不符。本題正確答案
為 (A)。

18 ---

Should we provide a free dinner at the
conference or just cold beverages?

(A) He provided me with a gift.

(B) It would be great to serve some food.

(C) At 9 in the morning.

會議時，我們應該提供免費晚餐，還是冷飲就好？

(A) 他給我一份禮物。

(B) 提供一些食物應該不錯。

(C) 早上九點。

• **provide sb with sth** 提供某人某物　　**beverage** 飲料

本題為從兩者中選擇其一的題型，所以回答中必須出現兩種選擇之一，或是提出其他替代方案。
(A) 重複「provide」但內容與題意不符。(B) 表示贊成提供食物，暗示選擇「提供免費晚餐」，故為適當的回答。(C) 本題並非詢問「時間」的題型。故正確答案為 (B)。

19 ---

What was Tim from the R&D department
asked to submit this Monday?

(A) Right, I'll ask him to do it.

(B) The report on last month's test results.

(C) Late on Monday evening.

研發部的提姆這週一要交什麼？

(A) 好，我會要他做。

(B) 上個月的測試結果報告。

(C) 週一晚上稍晚時。

• **department** 部門　　**be asked to V** 被要求……　　**submit** 繳交　　**result** 結果

本題為「What」疑問句，回答中應提及物品。(A) 重複「ask」，但內容與題目無關。(B) 回答出「報告」，所以是適當的答案。(C) 重複「Monday」，但本題並非詢問時間的題目。故正確答案為 (B)。

20 ---

Serena took a test, didn't she?

(A) I failed the test.

(B) After the result came out.

(C) I'll ask her.

瑟琳娜參加了考試，不是嗎？

(A) 我沒通過考試。

(B) 在結果出來之後。

(C) 我會問她。

• **take a test** 參加考試　　**come out** （結果）出來

本題為確認資訊的附加問句，常用「Yes/No」回答，但也可能出現其他回覆形式。(A) 的主詞與題目不符。(B) 沒有回答問題，與題目的情境不符。(C) 告知會替問話者確認，表示回答者並不知道此資訊，故本題的正確答案為 (C)。

21 ---

How did a new delivery man enter the building?

(A) The security team let him in.

(B) The building was opened last month.

(C) It was not delivered on time.

新送貨員怎麼進入大樓的？

(A) 保全讓他進來的。

(B) 大樓上個月開放。

(C) 它沒有準時送達。

• **delivery man** 送貨員　　**security** 保全　　**let sb in** 讓某人進來　　**on time** 準時

本題詢問送貨員如何進入大樓，(A) 明確提及方法，故為合適答案；(B) 與 (C) 分別重複「building」與「deliver」試圖造成混淆，但內容與題目不符，故本題正確答案為 (A)。

22

Where should I hang the accounting certificate? 我應該把會計證書掛在哪裡？

(A) This Wednesday. 　　　　　　　　　　(A) 這星期三。

(B) Maybe behind the desk on the wall? 　(B) 也許書桌後面的牆上？

(C) For a gift certificate. 　　　　　　　(C) 為了禮券。

• **hang** 掛　**accounting certificate** 會計證書　**gift certificate** 禮券

本題詢問懸掛證書的位置，所以只要選出告知位置的選項即可。(A) 僅回答時間點，與題目不符。
(B) 明確表示「書桌後面的牆上」的位置，所以是正確答案。(C) 只是重複「certificate」，內容與題
目無關。本題正解為 (B)。

We had better let Kimberley find the location. 我們最好讓金柏莉找出那個地方。

(A) At the post office. 　　　　　　　　　　　　(A) 在郵局。

(B) Please get on the bus. 　　　　　　　　　　(B) 請上公車。

(C) But Karen knows this area better than anyone. (C) 但凱倫比任何人都了解這區域。

• **had better V** 最好……　**post office** 郵局　**get on the bus** 上公車

本題為陳述句，提議讓某人去找到正確地點，(A) 與 (B) 內容與題目無關，(C) 表示有另一人更了解區
域，委婉否決了提議，故正確答案應為 (C)。

24

How do you know if the food is safe? 你怎麼知道這食物是否安全？

(A) Food and beverage, I think. 　　　　　(A) 我想是食物和飲料。

(B) Check the date marked on the container. (B) 檢查容器上標示的日期。

(C) At the store. 　　　　　　　　　　　　(C) 在商店。

• **beverage** 飲料　**marked** 被標示的　**on the container** 容器上

本題詢問如何知道食物安全可食用，(B) 提到方法為透過標示的日期確認，故為最適當的回答，
(A) 與 (C) 內容則都與題目無關。因此正確答案為 (B)。

Why was Mr. Anthony out of town? 安東尼先生為什麼出城？

(A) The town held a festival last year. (A) 這城市去年舉辦了一個慶典。

(B) They will be there within an hour. (B) 他們一個小時內會到那裡。

(C) He went on a business trip. 　　　(C) 他去出差。

• **be out of town** 出城　**go on a business trip** 出差

本題以「Why」詢問原因，注意題目中的人物為「安東尼先生」。(A) 雖然重複單字「town」，
但是整體句意與題目不符。(B) 本題詢問的是已經過去的事件，以未來將發生的事回答與題目矛盾。
(C) 以「He」代稱安東尼先生，並解釋原因，故正解為 (C)。

26

Would you like to stay here or go to a hotel?
(A) I don't want to walk anymore.
(B) The hotel is all booked up.
(C) Yes, I do.

你要住在這裡，還是去飯店？
(A) 我不想再走了。
(B) 飯店全訂滿了。
(C) 是的，我是。

本題為「二選一」的題型，所以無法用「Yes/No」回答，故 (C) 不正確。(A) 提到不想繼續走，迂迴表達不想去飯店，故為合適答案；(B) 只是重複「hotel」，內容與題目無關。故本題正確答案為 (A)。

27

I can't reach the top shelf.
(A) Maybe it's next to the restroom.
(B) No, you don't need a top score.
(C) You can use the ladder from a warehouse.

我搆不到最上面的架子。
(A) 也許就在洗手間旁邊。
(B) 不，你不需要得最高分。
(C) 你可以用倉庫的梯子。

• **reach** 搆到　**score** 分數　**ladder** 梯子　**warehouse** 倉庫

本題為陳述句，最好聽過每個選項，再選出最適合的回覆作為答案。題目表示碰不到上方的架子。(A) 本題與位置資訊無關；(B) 本題不適合用「Yes/No」回答；(C) 回答可以使用梯子，為發問者提供解決方法，故正確答案為 (C)。

28

Can we delay our dinner until next Tuesday?
(A) The restaurant will charge a cancellation fee.
(B) For a dinner reservation.
(C) Yes, it was an excellent dinner.

我們可以把晚宴延到下週二嗎？
(A) 餐廳會收取消費。
(B) 為了預約晚餐。
(C) 是的，那是很棒的晚餐。

• **delay** 延期　**charge** 收費　**cancellation fee** 取消費　**reservation** 預約

本題為提議、請求問句，雖然可以用「Yes/No」回答，但要注意之後的內容是否與題目相符。(A) 雖然沒有明確表示可否，但回覆該提議會造成的負面結果，故可推測在暗示否定提議。(B) 重複「dinner」但內容與題目無關。(C) 雖回答了「Yes」，後面接續的內容卻和題目無關，故正確答案為 (A)。

29

How soon will I receive the results of the request?
(A) Yes, I left home earlier than usual.
(B) Your proposal will be accepted.
(C) We'll call you next Thursday.

我多快可以收到申請的結果？
(A) 是的，我比平常更早離開家。
(B) 你的企畫案將被採用。
(C) 我們下週四會打電話給你。

• **request** 申請　**earlier than usual** 比平常更早　**proposal** 企畫案　**be accepted** 被採用

本題以「How soon」詢問可以得到結果的時間，通常會回答出時間點，但也可能出現別種形式的回覆。(A) 本題型無法用「Yes/No」回答，故 (A) 不正確。(B) 表示提案被採用，但一樣與時間無關。(C) 儘管沒有直接告知特定時間，但是表達會再致電通知，也是合理的回覆，故本題的正確答案為 (C)。

38

30

Are you ready to end the test, or do you still need some more time?

(A) We will arrive at the classroom.

(B) We'd like to check over our work before turning it in.

(C) Is Mr. Button moving to Australia?

你們準備好要交卷了，還是需要更多時間？

(A) 我們要到教室。

(B) 我們想在繳交之前檢查一次。

(C) 巴頓先生要搬到澳洲嗎？

• **be ready to V** 準備好要……

本題為要求「二選一」的題型，但是答案卻不是典型的從中選一，這種較為困難的類型在第二部分的後半段常常出現。(A) 與 (C) 內容與題目無關。(B) 沒有明確說出選擇，但表示想再檢查一次，故可合理推測需要更多時間，故本題的正確答案為 (B)。

31

The hotel cannot accommodate any more tourists.

(A) Just a few kilometers from the city hall.

(B) Yes, we'll book a reservation for a restaurant tomorrow.

(C) I will call other hotels to see if they are available.

那家飯店容納不下更多的觀光客了。

(A) 離市政府只要幾公里。

(B) 是的，我們要預約明天的餐廳。

(C) 我會打電話給其他飯店看看有沒有空房。

• **accommodate** 容納　**tourist** 觀光客　**book a reservation** 預約

題目表示飯店已經滿房，無法接待其他觀光客，(C) 表示將尋找其他住宿地點，故正確答案為 (C)。本題並非詢問距離或位置相關資訊，故 (A) 不適當，且本題無法使用「Yes/No」回答，所以 (B) 也非正確答案。

32-34 conversation

W Mr. Dickerson, this is Jane Roberts from Mulberry Publishing. I am calling to let you know that we'd like to publish some recipes from your blog.

M That's fantastic. I've been a big fan of your company for a long time. You have published some great cookbooks. So it would be a great opportunity for me, and I think my recipes would be a good fit.

W We do believe they would be suitable for publication. Actually, I'd like you to visit our company to discuss details about your book. So please let me know when you are available.

32–34 對話

女 狄克森先生，我是邁寶瑞出版社的珍·羅伯茲。我打這通電話是想告訴您，我們有意出版您部落格中的一些食譜。

男 那太好了。長期以來，我一直是貴公司的超級粉絲。妳們出版過一些不錯的烹飪書，所以這對我來說是一個很棒的機會，而且我覺得我的食譜應該頗為合適。

女 我們的確認為它們非常適合出版。事實上，我希望您能到本公司來討論有關書本的細節，所以請告訴我您方便的時間。

• **publishing** 出版社　**recipe** 食譜　**for a long time** 長期以來　**be suitable for . . .** 適合……
publication 出版　**make dishes** 烹煮菜餚　**favorable review** 好評　**be promoted** 被升職

32 --

What did the man write about?
(A) His favorite pets
(B) Visiting famous museums
(C) How to make various dishes
(D) Writing stories on a blog

這位男士從事哪方面的寫作？
(A) 他最喜歡的寵物
(B) 參觀著名博物館
(C) 如何烹煮各式菜餚
(D) 在部落格寫故事

從女子第一句台詞中的「some recipes from your blog」可以知道男子的部落格寫著食譜，選項 (C) 將「recipe」改寫成意義相關的「make dishes」，故正確答案為 (C)。

33 --

Why is the man delighted?
(A) He was given a prize for his writings.
(B) His work will be published.
(C) His articles earned favorable reviews.
(D) He was promoted to editor in a publishing company.

這位男士為什麼很開心？
(A) 他因為寫作得獎。
(B) 他的作品將被出版。
(C) 他的文章獲得好評。
(D) 他晉升為出版社的編輯。

透過「That's fantastic」可以知道男子感到喜悅，而其原因可從前一句女子台詞中的「publish your recipes」知道。本題的正確答案為 (B)。

34

Why does the woman want to meet with the man? 這位女士為什麼想見男士？
(A) To talk about a future project　(A) 為了討論未來的計畫。
(B) To ask for some cooking advice　(B) 為了請教烹飪建議。
(C) To receive some samples　(C) 為了拿到樣本。
(D) To organize an exhibition　(D) 為了籌備展覽。

女子最後的台詞中，邀請男子前來自己的公司，並提到「discuss details about your book」，選項 (A) 將「discuss details about your book」改寫為符合文意的「talk about a future project」，故本題正確答案為 (A)。

35-37 conversation　35–37 對話

W	I think your pharmacy received a prescription for some medicine from my doctor nearly 30 minutes ago. I'm wondering if the order is ready for me. My name is Jane Wilkins.	女	我想你們藥局應該在30分鐘前就收到我醫生開的處方箋了。我想知道我的藥準備好了嗎。我的名字是珍‧威金斯。
M	Let me check on that. Yes, we got the order. But I'm sorry, it's not ready yet. Monday is the busiest day for our pharmacy, so we're getting behind with our work. If you wait ten more minutes, it will be ready.	男	讓我查一下。是的，我們收到訂單了。但很抱歉，還沒有準備好。星期一是我們藥局最忙的一天，所以我們的工作進度有點落後。如果妳再等個10分鐘，應該就好了。
W	All right. I will spend some time shopping at a nearby store and come back in a little while to pick up my prescription.	女	好，我花點時間到附近的商店購物，一會兒再回來領我的處方藥。

• prescription 處方箋　be ready 準備好的　get behind with sth 在某事上進度落後
in a (little) while 一會兒　pick up 領　behind schedule 進度落後

35

What are the speakers discussing? 說話者在討論什麼？
(A) A shopping list　(A) 購物清單
(B) A tourist attraction　(B) 觀光景點
(C) A doctor's prescription　(C) 醫生處方箋
(D) A canceled appointment　(D) 取消的預約

對話談論主題通常在開頭便會出現。從「I think your pharmacy received a prescription for some medicine from my doctor nearly 30 minutes ago.」可知，女子推測藥局應該收到了處方箋，所以想要向男子領取處方藥。因此，本題最合適的答案為 (C)。

Why is the man behind schedule?
(A) A staff member is out sick.
(B) A doctor didn't write him a prescription.
(C) He went out for lunch.
(D) The pharmacy has been busy.

這位男士為什麼進度落後？
(A) 一名員工請病假。
(B) 醫生沒有開給他處方箋。
(C) 他外出吃午餐。
(D) 藥局很忙。

男子表示「Monday is the busiest day for our pharmacy」，所以正確答案為 (D)。

37 --

What does the woman say she will do?
(A) Visit the doctor's office
(B) Go to a nearby store
(C) Make a phone call
(D) Make an appointment

這位女士說她要做什麼？
(A) 到醫生辦公室
(B) 去附近的商店
(C) 打電話
(D) 預約

男子表示要再多等十分鐘，女子則說：「 I will spend some time shopping at a nearby store」，
表示她會去附近晃晃，以消磨等待時間，所以正確答案為 (B)。

38-40 conversation

38–40 對話

M Hello, this is Timothy Adams from AIF Electronics. Our records indicate that you've purchased a product in our store before, so we'd like to inform you of our special promotion this week. We will give you a 15 percent discount coupon for newly-released TVs through your online account. **W** Unfortunately, I just bought a TV, but I am planning to buy another air conditioner soon. **M** Umm . . . If you'd like, I can send you a text message about any future promotions.	男 您好，我是AIF電器的提摩西·亞當斯。我們的紀錄顯示，您以前曾在本店購買過商品，因此，我們想通知您我們本週的特別促銷活動。我們將透過您的網路帳戶，贈送新上市電視的八五折優惠折價券。 女 很遺憾，我才剛買了電視。不過，我打算近期內要再買一台冷氣機。 男 嗯……如果您願意的話，我可以透過簡訊方式通知您以後的促銷活動。

• **purchase** 購買　**inform sb of sth** 告訴某人某事　**promotion** 促銷　**discount coupon** 優惠折價券
newly-released 新上市的　**online account** 網路帳戶　**text message** 簡訊

38 --

Why is the man calling?
(A) To schedule a meeting
(B) To complain about a product
(C) To check a delivery schedule
(D) To advertise a special promotion

這位男士為什麼打這通電話？
(A) 為了安排會議
(B) 為了抱怨商品
(C) 為了確認貨運時程
(D) 為了宣傳特別促銷活動

男子告知女子「we'd like to inform you of our special promotion this week」，由此可知，
這通電話的目的為 (D)。

39

What types of products does the man's company sell?

(A) Home appliances
(B) Computers
(C) Office supplies
(D) Furniture

這位男士的公司販售的是哪種商品？

(A) 家用電器
(B) 電腦
(C) 辦公用品
(D) 家具

先從公司的名稱「AIF Electronics」即可知道此為一家電子公司，所以 (C) 與 (D) 不是正確答案。
接著，從後續出現的電視與冷氣，可以知道該公司是販賣家電的廠商，故正確答案為 (A)。

(B) 是電子產品，但是男子工作的公司並非專門銷售電腦的公司，所以此選項不是最適合的答案。

40

What does the man offer to do for the woman?

(A) Send a message
(B) Refund her in full
(C) Offer free delivery
(D) Call her office

這位男士提議為女士做什麼事？

(A) 傳訊息
(B) 全額退款
(C) 免費運送
(D) 打電話到她辦公室

男子在最後一句台詞表示「I will send you a text message about any future promotion.」，
所以未來將以簡訊告知優惠活動相關消息，正確答案為 (A)。

41-43 conversation

41–43 對話

M Hello, this is Jonathan Edwards in room 1213. The air conditioner in this room isn't working properly. Although the unit turns on, the air isn't cold.	**男** 妳好，我是1213號房的強納生‧艾德華茲。這間房間的空調故障了。雖然機器開著，卻不冷。
W I'm sorry, sir. Sadly, none of our repairmen is available right now. Instead, I can change your room, and I'll upgrade you to an exclusive suite free of charge. Would that be okay?	**女** 很抱歉，先生。糟糕的是，我們的維修員現在都在忙。不過，我可以為您更換房間，並免費為您升級至獨家套房。這樣可以嗎？
M Great. But would you send someone to move my luggage to the new room immediately? Because I don't have time to do it myself. I have to go to a client meeting right away.	**男** 好，但妳可以馬上派人幫我把行李搬到新客房嗎？因為我自己沒有時間處理。我馬上就要跟客戶開會。

• **not work properly** 故障　**free of charge** 免費　**broken** 壞的

41

What is the man's complaint?

(A) His room is dirty.
(B) His reservation was canceled.
(C) His air conditioner is broken.
(D) His room is too small.

這位男士投訴什麼？

(A) 他的房間很髒。
(B) 他的預約被取消了。
(C) 他的冷氣機壞了。
(D) 他的房間太小。

從男子的第一句台詞中的「The air conditioner in this room isn't working properly」可以知道正確答案為 (C)。

42 --

What does the woman offer to the man?
(A) A free meal
(B) A free shuttle bus to the airport
(C) A room upgrade
(D) A gift certificate

這位女士提供男士什麼？
(A) 免費餐點
(B) 到機場的免費接駁公車
(C) 房間升級
(D) 禮券

女子告知目前所有的維修員皆無法前往處理，但是可以「upgrade you to an exclusive suite」，故正確答案為 (C)。

43 --

What does the man request?
(A) Help with his luggage
(B) A room change
(C) Free Internet service
(D) A discount coupon

這位男士要求什麼事？
(A) 幫他搬行李
(B) 更換房間
(C) 免費網路服務
(D) 折價券

從男子最後的「But would you send someone to move my luggage to the new room immediately?」可知，男子因為要和客戶開會，沒有時間搬行李，故要求女子幫忙，本題答案為 (A)。

注意「Would/Will/Could/Can you . . .」後面常接續表示提議與請求的句子，其中「Would/Could」語氣較為客氣委婉。

44-46 conversation

44–46 對話

W	Thank you for calling Boston Clinic. This is Carey speaking. How can I help you?
M	Hi, my name is Michael Kane. I am scheduled to go on a trip to Africa next month, so I need to get vaccinated. Is it possible to make an appointment?
W	Unfortunately, we are fully booked this week, Mr. Kane, but we have several openings available next week. Does 11 A.M. work for you on Tuesday?
M	Sorry, **(46)that's not going to work.**
W	Okay. Then, what about 3 P.M. on Wednesday? Can you make it?
M	That works for me. Thank you. I'll see you then.

女	感謝您來電波士頓診所。我是凱莉。有什麼可以為您效勞的嗎？
男	妳好，我叫麥可‧凱恩。我預計下個月要到非洲旅行，所以需要注射疫苗。方便安排預約嗎？
女	很遺憾，凱恩先生。我們這個禮拜的預約已經滿了。但我們下週有幾個空檔。星期二早上11點，您方便嗎？
男	抱歉，(46)那時間不行。
女	好。那星期三下午3點呢？您可以嗎？
男	可以。感謝妳。到時候見。

• **be scheduled to V** 預計要……　　**go on a trip** 旅行　　**get vaccinated** 注射疫苗
　make an appointment 安排預約　　**be fully booked** 預約滿了　　**openings** 空檔　　**make it** 趕得上

44

Where does the woman work?
(A) At a travel agency
(B) At a department store
(C) At a national museum
(D) At a health clinic

這位女士在哪裡工作？
(A) 旅行社
(B) 百貨公司
(C) 國立博物館
(D) 健康診所

本題的答案可以從第一句台詞中的「clinic」得知。另外，從「get vaccinated」也可以看出女子工作的地方是醫院或診所，故正確答案為 (D)。

45

What does the man say he will be doing next month?
(A) Participating in a conference
(B) Making a presentation
(C) Traveling overseas
(D) Getting vaccinated

這位男士說他下個月要做什麼？
(A) 參加會議。
(B) 發表簡報
(C) 到海外旅行
(D) 注射疫苗

對話中找到提及「next month」的部分為男子說到「I am scheduled to go on a trip to Africa next month」，由此可知正確答案為 (C)。

46 (NEW)

What does the man imply when he says, "that's not going to work"?
(A) He needs a different appointment.
(B) He does not work on that day.
(C) He prefers to work on schedule.
(D) He will go abroad.

當這位男士說：「那時間不行」，是什麼意思？
(A) 他需要約不同時間。
(B) 他那天不上班。
(C) 他偏好按時程表工作。
(D) 他要出國。

對話中出現題目引用之句子的原因，可以從上下文意推敲得知。

題目中引用的句子原本是「某事將無法成功」的意思，但是在本對話中，是男子對於先前診所確認預約時間的回應，表示那一天不能預約。接著，診所再詢問隔天是否可預約時，男子又表示可行。由此可見，原本預約的時間男子無法配合，故正確答案為 (A)。

M Hi, Monica. How are you?	男 嗨，莫妮卡，妳好嗎？
W Fine. I've been waiting to talk to you. I'm saving up my money to buy a house. I've heard that you bought one recently.	女 很好，我一直想找你說話。我在存錢買房子。我聽說你最近買了一間。
M Right, and I'm thrilled. It was really tough for me to cut down on expenses and save up for it. I was able to do it thanks to an online money-saving program.	男 沒錯，而且我很開心。要縮減花費、為此存錢真的很辛苦。還好有一個線上省錢程式，讓我能夠辦到。
W And it helped?	女 有用嗎？
M Absolutely. If you want to try it, I recommend money-saving.com.	男 絕對有。如果妳想試試，我建議 money-saving.com。
W Hmm . . . How much does it cost? It might not be a good idea to spend money to save money.	女 嗯……要多少錢？為了省錢而花錢，可能不是個好主意。
M Well, they are now offering a one-month free trial. It would be a good opportunity for you to see if you like it. And it's only $50 a year.	男 他們現在提供一個月免費試用。這對妳來說是個好機會，可以看看妳喜不喜歡。而且它一年只要50塊。
W I'll take a look at it. Thank you.	女 我再看看。謝謝你。

• **save up money** 存錢 **thrilled** 極度開心的 **cut down on expenses** 縮減花費 **thanks to . . .** 還好有……
free trial 免費試用 **take a look at . . .** 看看…… **expiration date** 到期日

47 --

Why does the woman want to save money?	這位女士為什麼想存錢？
(A) To replace a computer	(A) 為了換電腦
(B) To purchase a house	(B) 為了買房子
(C) To go on vacation	(C) 為了度假
(D) To buy a car	(D) 為了買車

本題詢問女子相關的問題，故要注意女子說的內容。女子在開頭說了「I'm saving up my money to buy a house.」，表示自己為了買房正在存錢，故正確答案為 (B)。

48 --

What does the man recommend?	這位男士提出什麼建議？
(A) Applying for a loan	(A) 申請貸款
(B) Selling a house	(B) 賣房子
(C) Using an online program	(C) 使用線上程式
(D) Cutting down on expenses	(D) 縮減花費

男子說了「I was able to do it thanks to an online money-saving program.」，推薦了線上程式給女子，故正確答案為 (C)。

(A) 與 (B) 的內容並未出現在對話中。(D) 只提到男子為了買房子而減少支出，未能看出男子對此進行推薦。

ACTUAL TEST **10**

PART **3**

中譯＋解析

39

What is the woman concerned about?
(A) Web site reliability
(B) Service costs
(C) Scheduling conflicts
(D) A program's expiration date

這位女士在意的是什麼？
(A) 網站可靠性
(B) 服務費用
(C) 行程上的衝突
(D) 程式的到期日

男子推薦使用線上程式省錢，而女子表示「How much does it cost? It might not be a good idea to spend money to save money.」，覺得為了存錢而花錢不是個好方法，所以正確答案為 (B)。

50-52 conversation　　　　　　　　　　　**50-52 對話**

M Hi, Ms. Fox? It's Gabriel Silva. Have you looked at the final version of the design for your online advertisement?	男 嗨，福斯女士嗎？我是加百列·希瓦。您看過網路廣告設計稿的最終版了嗎？
W Yes, I thought the design matches what I wanted. I particularly like the way you modified the logo of my store.	女 是的，我認為這設計符合我想要的。我特別喜歡你對本店商標所做的修改。
M I'm pleased that you like it. Before we finalize this project, what about making the logo a little bigger?	男 我很高興您喜歡。在我們定案之前，把商標再放大一點如何？
W Yes! It's a good idea! I think an ad with a larger logo enables people to recognize the store's name better.	女 好啊！這是個好主意！我想有大一點商標的廣告可以讓人們更容易辨識出商店名稱。

• online advertisement 網路廣告　**modify** 修改　**finalize the project** 定案　**recognize** 辨識

Who most likely is the woman?
(A) A graphic designer
(B) An advertising agent
(C) A store owner
(D) A writer

這位女士最有可能是誰？
(A) 平面設計師
(B) 廣告商
(C) 店主
(D) 作家

從女子台詞中的「the logo of my store.」可推測她是一名商店主人，故正確答案為 (C)。

What is the woman pleased about?
(A) A final draft of an advertisement
(B) Recent online reviews
(C) A store location
(D) Contact information

這位女士喜歡什麼？
(A) 廣告的最終草案
(B) 最近的網路評論
(C) 商店位置
(D) 聯絡資訊

男子先問了「Have you looked at the final version of the design for your online advertisement?」，而從女子回覆的「Yes, I thought the design matches what I wanted. I particularly like the way you modified the logo of my store.」可知，女子喜歡廣告設計稿的最終版，本題的正確答案為 (A)。

52 -

What does the man offer to do?
(A) Install a computer program
(B) Confirm service request
(C) Print an advertisement
(D) Enlarge an image

這位男士提議做什麼事？
(A) 安裝電腦程式
(B) 確認服務申請
(C) 列印廣告
(D) 放大圖像

最後，男子提議「what about making the logo a little bigger?」，故本題正確答案為 (D)。

53-55 conversation

53–55 對話

M Amie, why are you still at your office? Aren't you participating in the company charity event today? **W** I took part in the event last year, but this time around I should take care of some delays regarding some of our translation service last month. **M** Oh, that's too bad. What happened? **W** Some customers complained about receiving their translations too late. And **(53)I'm really concerned**, as I'm not sure how to handle this issue to resolve their inconvenience. **M** I understand. I'm pretty sure you'll do all right. Actually, I've done this same thing before. I need to volunteer at the charity event now, but I'll discuss this at the next staff meeting tomorrow to find the best ways to make up for the customers' inconvenience.	**男** 艾咪，妳怎麼還在辦公室？妳不是要參加公司今天的慈善活動嗎？ **女** 我去年有參加，但這陣子我要處理上個月翻譯工作的一些延誤狀況。 **男** 喔，那真糟糕。發生什麼事了？ **女** 一些客戶抱怨太晚收到翻譯了。**(53)**我真的很擔心，因為我不太知道要怎麼處理這個問題，來解決此事帶給他們的不便。 **男** 我懂。我相信妳可以處理得當。事實上，我之前也做過同樣的事。我現在得去慈善活動義務幫忙了，不過我會在明天的員工會議上討論這件事，以找出最好的方法來補償客戶的不便。

• participate in . . . 參加……　charity event 慈善活動　take part in . . . 參加……
take care of sth 處理某事　regarding 關於　translation 翻譯　resolve 解決　inconvenience 不便
volunteer 義務幫忙　make up for . . . 補償……

53 (NEW) -

What does the woman imply when she says, "I'm really concerned"?
(A) She is able to do volunteer work.
(B) She is proud of attending the event.
(C) She is indifferent about the matter.
(D) She is worried about the complaints.

當這位女士說：「我真的很擔心」，是什麼意思？
(A) 她能夠做義工服務。
(B) 她以參加活動為榮。
(C) 她對那件事漠不關心。
(D) 她擔心那些客訴。

只要觀察題目引用句的前後文，就可以掌握引用句的意圖。前一句表示翻譯進度落後，讓客戶感到不便，而後一句則表示不知道該如何善後。由此可知，女子是在擔心客訴，故正確答案為 (D)。

What is the woman concerned about?
(A) Making a presentation
(B) Responding to client complaints
(C) Translating a different language
(D) Doing multiple tasks at the same time

這位女士擔心什麼？
(A) 發表簡報
(B) 回應客戶投訴
(C) 翻譯不同的語言
(D) 同時做多項工作

「I'm really concerned, as I'm not sure how to handle this issue to resolve their inconvenience.」，表示女子不知道該如何解決對客戶造成的不便，本題的答案是 (B)。

What does the man say he will do tomorrow?
(A) Submit some paperwork
(B) Bring a problem up at a meeting
(C) Prepare the event
(D) Conduct a customer survey

這位男士說他明天要做什麼？
(A) 繳交一些書面報告
(B) 在會議上提出問題
(C) 籌備活動
(D) 進行顧客問卷調查

從男子最後說的「I'll discuss this at the next staff meeting tomorrow to find the best ways to make up for the customers' inconvenience.」可以知道，男子將在員工會議上提出討論，以解決客戶不滿，故正確答案為 (B)。

56-58 conversation with three speakers. (NEW)

56–58 三人對話

W1 Thank you for coming to an interview on such short notice, Mr. McCain. I'm Amber Hayek, manager of the Human Resources Department here at ABF Books.	**女1** 馬侃先生，謝謝你在臨時通知的狀況下來參加面試。我是ABF書籍人力資源部經理安柏·海耶克。
W2 And I'm Kate Stone. I am in charge of the Children's Books Division.	**女2** 我是凱特·史東，負責童書部。
M Good to see you.	**男** 很高興見到您們。
W2 We've looked your résumé and career history, and you seem to be eligible for the director of the design team. However, we're concerned that you might not want the position, as it requires some overtime work. We have a new series due out in November.	**女2** 我們已經看過你的履歷及工作資歷，你看起來頗適合設計團隊的主管一職。但是，我們擔心你或許不會想要這個職務，因為它會需要加班。我們有個新系列即將在11月推出。
M I understand that. That's no problem.	**男** 我了解。這不是問題。
W1 Okay, so let's take a look at some of your work. I heard that you brought a portfolio. Can you show us?	**女1** 好，那讓我們來看一下你的作品吧。我聽說你帶了作品集來。可以讓我們看看嗎？
M Sure, just a minute.	**男** 當然，稍等一下。

• **on such short notice** 在臨時通知的狀況下 **human resources department** 人力資源部
be in charge of . . . 負責…… **résumé** 履歷 **career description** 工作資歷 **be eligible for . . .** 適合……
require 需要 **overtime work** 加班 **due** 預計的 **portfolio** 作品集

56

Where do the interviewers most likely work?

(A) At a bookstore

(B) At a kindergarten

(C) At a publisher

(D) At a broadcasting company

面試官最可能在哪裡工作？

(A) 書店

(B) 幼稚園

(C) 出版社

(D) 廣播公司

從對話內容可知，兩名女子為面試官，且而她們的所屬公司是「ABF Books」，此時可刪去 (B) 與 (D)。又因為這場面試徵求的職位是設計師，且從後面的「We have a new series due out in November.」可以得知，該公司有預計出版的書籍，所以最合適的答案為 (C)。

What job requirement do the speakers discuss?

(A) Possessing the proper license

(B) Owning some film equipment

(C) Having related experience

(D) Being able to work extra hours

說話者討論的是什麼工作條件？

(A) 具備合適的執照

(B) 擁有攝影設備

(C) 具備相關經驗

(D) 能夠加班

三人互相打招呼後，女 2 便說明「we're concerned that you might not want the position, as it requires some overtime work.」，故可以知道，該公司需要在工作時間以外加班，所以正確答案為 (D)。

58

What does the man agree to do next?

(A) Show some previous work

(B) Conduct a survey

(C) Watch a presentation

(D) Meet a president

這位男士同意接下來做什麼？

(A) 展示之前的作品

(B) 進行問卷調查

(C) 看一段簡報

(D) 與總裁見面

最後，女 1 表示「I heard that you brought a portfolio. Can you show us?」請男子展示他的作品集，而男子回覆「Sure, just a minute.」請對方稍等，故本題的正確答案為 (A)。

ACTUAL TEST **10**

PART **3**

中譯＋解析

39

W Okay, Lemar. Here's our problem. For the past three months, the number of customers visiting our restaurant has decreased by 15 percent compared to last year. So, we need to do something to attract more customers. I'd like to hear your opinions, as you're the head chef of our restaurant. **M** Well, how about offering a discount for Friday and the weekend? I'll create healthy and appealing menus that are not too expensive. **W** Okay, that's a good idea! Let's get started. I want you to prepare samples before putting them on the menu.	女 好了，利馬。這就是我們的問題。過去三個月以來，我們餐廳的顧客人數較去年減少了15%。因此，我們需要做點什麼來吸引更多顧客。既然你是本餐廳的主廚，我想聽聽你的意見。 男 嗯，在週五跟週末提供優惠如何？我會設計出不那麼貴，但卻健康又吸引人的菜單來。 女 好，那是個好主意！讓我們著手進行吧。我希望你在把新菜色加入菜單前，先準備好樣品。

• compared to . . . 相較……   opinion 意見   head chef 主廚   offer a discount 提供優惠
  appealing 吸引人的   get started 著手進行   put . . . on the menu 將……加入菜單

What problem does the woman mention?
(A) Business is unusually slow.
(B) A restaurant received several complaints.
(C) A restaurant is short-staffed.
(D) The rent has been gone up.

這位女士提到什麼問題？
(A) 生意反常地清淡。
(B) 餐廳接到了幾起客訴。
(C) 餐廳人手不足。
(D) 租金上漲了。

根據女子第一句的「For the past three months, the number of customers visiting our restaurant has decreased by 15 percent compared to last year.」可以得知客戶數量減少，故正確答案為 (A)。

What does the man suggest?
(A) Offering an outdoor event
(B) Moving into a different location
(C) Lowering prices
(D) Acquiring popular restaurants

這位男士提出什麼建議？
(A) 提供戶外活動
(B) 搬到另一個地點
(C) 降價
(D) 效法受歡迎的餐廳

從男子表示的「how about offering a discount for Friday and the weekend?」可知，本題的正確答案為 (C)。

What does the woman ask the man to do?
(A) Hire a manager
(B) Train employees
(C) Get ready for the holiday season
(D) Prepare some food samples

這位女士要求男士做什麼？
(A) 聘僱一位經理
(B) 訓練員工
(C) 為假日旺季做好準備
(D) 準備一些食物樣品

從女子最後一句的「I want you to prepare samples」可以得知，本題的正確答案為 (D)。

M	Linsey, I want to talk about my presentation for the medical science conference.	男	琳賽，我想討論一下在醫療科學會議上的發表。
W	I'm so sorry; it slipped my mind.	女	非常抱歉，我忘了這件事。
M	That's okay. I heard that you've been busy doing pioneering research into the new medicine for liver cancer.	男	沒關係。我聽說妳一直忙著進行肝癌新藥的開創性研究。
W	Yeah. The results are impressive. We'll be able to create the medication within two years.	女	是的。成效非常顯著。我們可以在兩年內開發出新藥。
M	That's fantastic! So, can I show you some slides right now? They are related to your research.	男	那太好了！所以，我可以現在讓妳看一下投影片嗎？它們和妳的研究有關。
W	Great.	女	太好了。
M	All right. Would you please check if all the researchers' names are included on the final page of the slides?	男	好。可以麻煩妳確認，是否所有的研究者姓名都列進投影片的最後一頁了嗎？
W	Okay. Let me see . . . um . . . Wait! **(64)Didn't Martial participate in this project?**	女	好。讓我看一下……嗯……等一下！**(64)馬斯亞沒有參加這個計畫嗎？**
M	Oh, you're right! Thanks for the help.	男	喔，妳說的沒錯！感謝協助。

• presentation 發表　medical science 醫療科學　sth slip one's mind 某人忘記了某事
pioneering 開創性的　liver cancer 肝癌　impressive 令人欽佩的　medication 藥物

62

What industry do the speakers most likely work in?

(A) Pharmaceutical
(B) Finance
(C) Construction
(D) Entertainment

說話者最可能從事何種行業？

(A) 製藥業
(B) 金融業
(C) 營造業
(D) 娛樂業

透過「medical science conference」、「new medicine」、「medication」可以得知，對話者應為醫學或製藥產業的從業人員，因此選項中最恰當的為 (A)。

63

What does the woman say will happen within two years?

(A) Some research will receive a prize.
(B) A new product will be introduced.
(C) A company will hire more employees.
(D) Another conference will be held.

這位女士說兩年內可能會發生什麼事？

(A) 研究將獲獎。
(B) 將推出新產品。
(C) 公司將僱用更多員工。
(D) 將舉行另一場會議。

女子提到「We'll be able to create the medication within two years」，因為新藥上市也可以視為新產品上市，故正確答案為 (B)。

ACTUAL TEST 10

PART 3

中譯＋解析

🎧 39

What does the woman imply when she says, "Didn't Martial participate in this project"?
(A) Some results are not promising.
(B) A project will be finished soon.
(C) A slide is missing some information.
(D) The man must attend the conference.

當這位女士說:「馬斯亞沒有參加這個計畫嗎」,是什麼意思?
(A) 一些結果前景不看好。
(B) 計畫即將完成。
(C) 一張投影片漏了一些資料。
(D) 這位男士必須參加會議。

此類題型請注意前後文。男子先以「Would you please check if all the researchers' names are included on the final page of the slides?」請女子幫忙確認姓名。作為此問題的答覆,女子反問此句,代表投影片應是遺漏了馬斯亞的名字,所以本題的正確答案為 (C)。

65-67 conversation and building directory | **65–67 對話及樓層說明**

W Hi, I had an appointment to see the doctor at 11 A.M. I was a bit late because parking was tricky in this building, and I couldn't find where I should pay for parking.	**女** 你好,我預約了上午11點看醫生。因為這棟大樓停車有點複雜,所以我晚到了一點,而且我找不到付停車費的地方。
M As a matter of fact, parking fees are free for visitors in this building, and we will validate the tickets you received when you entered the building.	**男** 其實,這棟大樓的訪客可以免費停車,而且我們會驗證你在進入大樓時所拿到的停車券。
W That's great. This is the first time I'm visiting Dr. Lauren. Her name is not listed on the building directory, though. Please tell me where I should go.	**女** 那太好了。這是我第一次來看羅倫醫師,但她的名字沒有列在大樓樓層說明上。請告訴我該到哪裡。
M Dr. Lauren just moved in just three days ago, so we didn't have much time to change it. We will ask the building manager to list her name as soon as possible. She's in Suite 114.	**男** 羅倫醫師三天前才剛搬進來,所以我們還沒有太多時間變更。我們會要求大樓管理員盡快列上她的大名。她在114室。

Office	Location
Prudential Finance	Suite 101
York Foods	Suite 108
UK Express	Suite 111
Morris International	Suite 114

營業單位	位置
謹明金融	101室
約克食品	108室
英國快遞	111室
莫里斯國際	114室

• **have an appointment** 預約看診　**tricky** 複雜的　**parking fee** 停車費　**validate** 驗證
be listed 被列出來的　**building directory** 樓層說明　**move in** 搬進(某處)　**package** 包裹
pharmacy 藥局　**tenant** 住戶

What is the purpose of the woman's visit?
(A) To deliver a package
(B) To have a client meeting
(C) To go to the pharmacy
(D) To have a medical appointment

這位女士來訪的目的是什麼？
(A) 遞送包裹
(B) 舉行客戶會議
(C) 去藥局
(D) 看醫生

從女子第一句的「I had an appointment to see the doctor」可以知道她的訪問目的是看診，所以正確答案為 (D)。

What does the man say about parking?
(A) It is available on the street near the building.
(B) It is free for visitors with a validated parking ticket.
(C) It is for tenants in the building.
(D) It has a time limit.

這位男士說了什麼有關停車的事？
(A) 大樓附近的街道有位置。
(B) 停車券通過驗證的訪客可免費停車。
(C) 是給大樓住戶停的。
(D) 有時間限制。

男子說了「parking fees are free for visitors in this building, and we will validate the tickets you received when you entered the building.」，表示大樓訪客可享有免費停車服務，並請女子出示停車券確認。由此可知，持有停車券的訪客可享有免費停車服務，故正確答案為 (B)。

67 (NEW) --

Look at the graphic. Which office name has to be updated on the building directory?
(A) Prudential Finance
(B) York Foods
(C) UK Express
(D) Morris International

看一下圖表，大樓樓層說明上哪一個單位的名字必須更新？
(A) 謹明金融
(B) 約克食品
(C) 英國快遞
(D) 莫里斯國際

女子表示在樓層說明上沒有看見醫師的名字，而男子則回答說「She's in Suite 114.」，對照表格可知，應該更新 114 室的「莫里斯國際」為醫師的名字，故正確答案為 (D)。

W	Will that be all, sir? Just the new computer, a computer bag, and a case?
M	I'd like to ask you one last question before I buy the laptop. Do I have to pay for this all at once? I want to buy this on an installment plan, if possible.
W	Yes, you can. I can set that up for you. For this week only, we are offering an interest-free installment plan for up to 12 months.
M	Okay, that's great! Umm . . . I've changed my mind, though. I don't think I really need the extended warranty. It already comes with a two-year warranty. Could you remove that from my invoice?
W	Yes. No problem.

女	先生，還需要其他的嗎？就一台新電腦、一個電腦包和一個保護殼？
男	在我買這台筆電前，我想請問妳最後一個問題。我必須立刻付清嗎？如果可以的話，我想以分期的方式購買。
女	是的，可以的。我可以為您設定。我們提供高達12個月的零利率分期方案，但僅限本週。
男	好，那太好了！嗯……但是我改變心意了。我想我不需要延長保固。已經附有兩年保固了。妳可以把它從帳單上取消嗎？
女	好的，沒問題。

ITEM	PRICE
Computer hard case	$50
Computer bag	$80
Extended warranty	$200
Computer	$1500
Total	**$1830**

品項	價格
電腦保護殼	50元
電腦包	80元
延長保固	200元
電腦	1,500元
總計	1,830元

- all at once 立刻　on an installment plan 分期　interest-free 零利率的　up to . . . 高達……
change one's mind 改變心意　extended warranty 延長保固　come with . . . 附有……　invoice 帳單

 68

Who most likely is the woman?
(A) A salesperson
(B) An engineer
(C) A bank clerk
(D) A computer programmer

這位女士最有可能是誰？
(A) 銷售員
(B) 工程師
(C) 銀行職員
(D) 電腦程式設計師

從對話內容可知，男子想要購買電腦，而女子則是幫助男子結帳的人，由此可知女子最可能為銷售店員，故本題的正確答案為 (A)。

69

What does the man ask about?
(A) A contract renewal
(B) A payment method
(C) Computer accessories
(D) The price of a computer

這位男士詢問何事？
(A) 合約續約
(B) 付款方式
(C) 電腦配件
(D) 電腦價格

男子說道：「I'd like to ask you one last question before I buy the laptop. Do I have to pay for this all at once?」，詢問可否分期付款，可知男子正在詢問付款方式，所以正確答案為 (B)。

70

Look at the graphic. Which amount will be removed from the invoice?
(A) $50
(B) $80
(C) $200
(D) $1500

看一下圖表，哪一個金額會從帳單上移除？
(A) 50元
(B) 80元
(C) 200元
(D) 1,500元

男子的最後一句台詞說：「I don't think I really need the extended warranty. . . . Could you remove that from my invoice?」，因此可知男子想取消延長保固的費用，故答案為 (C)。

PART 4 🎧40

71-73 information

Welcome back to *The Interviews* on AKSP Radio Station. Today's guest is Dr. Kasper Dooling, professor of business administration at the University of Copenhagen and author of the recently-released best seller *How to Use Your Time Wisely*. Today, Dr. Dooling will share his insights into the best ways to manage your valuable time. From now on, he will be asked questions from listeners over the phone. Please call us here at 555-0198 if you have any questions for Dr. Dooling.

71-73 資訊

歡迎回到AKSP廣播電台的《訪談錄》。今天的來賓是哥本哈根大學企業管理系教授，也是最近出版暢銷書《如何聰明運用時間》的作者卡斯柏．杜林博士。今天杜林博士將提出他的深度見解，分享一些管理寶貴時間的最佳方法。從現在開始，他將接受聽眾透過電話提問。如果您有任何問題想請教杜林博士，請來電555-0198。

• **guest** 來賓　**business administration** 企業管理　**author** 作者　**recently-released** 最近出版的
wisely 聰明地　**share one's insights into sth** 提出對某事的深度見解　**manage time** 管理時間
valuable 寶貴的　**from now on** 從現在開始　**over the phone** 透過電話　**call in** 來電

71

Where does the speaker work?
(A) At a radio station
(B) At a bookstore
(C) At a university
(D) At a consulting firm

說話者在哪裡工作？
(A) 廣播電台
(B) 書店
(C) 大學
(D) 顧問公司

🎧39
🎧40

本題詢問的是說話者工作的地方，而非來賓，故可從「Welcome back to *The Interviews* on AKSP Radio Station.」知道說話者最可能為廣播主持人，所以正確答案為 (A)。

72 --

What will Dr. Dooling be discussing?	杜林博士將討論什麼？
(A) Career management	(A) 職涯管理
(B) Publishing books	(B) 出版書籍
(C) Communication skills	(C) 溝通技巧
(D) Time management	(D) 時間管理

從「Today, Dr. Dooling will share his insights into the best ways to manage your valuable time.」可知，杜林博士將談論管理時間的方法，所以正確答案為 (D)。

73 --

What does the speaker encourage listeners to do?	說話者鼓勵聽眾做什麼？
(A) Call in with questions	(A) 來電提問
(B) Register in advance	(B) 提早報名
(D) Save money	(C) 存錢
(D) Buy more books	(D) 買更多書

說話者的最後一句話說「Please call us here at 555-0198 if you have any questions for Dr. Dooling.」，表示博士將開始接受提問，聽眾若有問題可以打電話進來。由此可知，正確答案為 (A)。

74-76 telephone message	**74–76 電話留言**
Hi, Ms. Ederson, it's Wagner. I'm still waiting for the airline to find my suitcase, which has our new microwave oven in it. Given the circumstances, I think that they bring me nothing before my presentation on Monday. And if so, without a prototype, the presentation won't make a deep impression on the audience. At this point, therefore, I think the best option is for you to bring another prototype here in person.**(76) I know it's a difficult job**, but I think there's no other way.	嗨，埃德森女士，我是瓦格納。我還在等航空公司找我的行李箱，那裡頭放了我們的新款微波爐。在此情況下，我想在我星期一的簡報前，他們應該沒辦法給我。如果這樣的話，沒有樣機，就無法讓觀眾留下深刻印象了。此刻，我認為最好的選擇就是您親自帶另一台樣機到這裡。**(76)我知道這是件棘手的事**，但我覺得也別無他法了。

- **suitcase** 行李箱　**microwave oven** 微波爐　**given the circumstances** 在此情況下　**presentation** 簡報　**prototype** 樣機　**at this point** 此刻　**issue a passport** 核發護照　**press conference** 記者會　**apologize for . . .** 為……致歉　**remind sb of sth** 對某人提醒某事

 74 --

What is the man waiting for?	這位男士在等什麼？
(A) His passport to be issued	(A) 他的護照被核發
(B) His airline ticket to be purchased	(B) 買好他的機票。
(C) His colleagues to arrive	(C) 他的同事抵達。
(D) His luggage to be returned	(D) 他的行李被歸還。

男子一開始表示自己「still waiting for the airline to find my suitcase」，故可以知道正確答案為 (D)。

75 --

What is scheduled for Monday?
(A) A meeting
(B) A product presentation
(C) A doctor's appointment
(D) A press conference

星期一安排了什麼事？
(A) 一場會議
(B) 產品簡報
(C) 醫生預約
(D) 記者會

從「before my presentation on Monday」可以知道說話者將在週一進行簡報發表。接著，下一句話出現「without a prototype」，由此可知原將在發表時展示樣品，故本題的答案為 (B)。

76 (NEW) --

Why does the man say, "I know it's a difficult job"?
(A) To advise the listener to finish the job quickly
(B) To warn that the job is unnecessary
(C) To apologize for an inconvenience
(D) To remind the listener of its risks

這位男士為什麼說：「我知道這是件棘手的事」？
(A) 建議聽者快點完成工作
(B) 提醒這工作是不必要的
(C) 為不便致歉
(D) 對聽者提醒風險

從題目引用句的前一句「I think the best option is for you to bring another prototype here in person.」可知道，男子麻煩聽者再準備一份樣品親自送來，並認為這會給對方造成不便，而略表無奈與歉意，故本題答案為 (C)。

77-79 excerpt from a meeting

77–79 會議摘錄

As you know, we are now installing fingerprint reader devices at the entrance to enhance the security of the building. Employees will have to scan their enrolled finger on the fingerprint reader whenever they enter the building, starting next Tuesday. So, please make sure that all employees register their fingerprints by the end of this week. It won't take long to register, but this registration process will have to be finished before the new system is introduced on Tuesday.

正如各位所知，目前我們正在入口處安裝指紋辨識器，以加強大樓安全。自下週二開始，所有員工在進入大樓時，都必須在指紋辨識器上掃描所登錄的指紋。因此，全體員工務必於本週末前登錄自己的指紋。登錄不需要太多的時間，但登錄手續必須在星期二新系統啟用前完成。

• **install** 安裝 **fingerprint reader device** 指紋辨識器 **scan** 掃描 **enrolled** 已登錄的 **registration process** 登錄手續 **introduce** 啟用 **head office** 總部 **relocation** 搬遷

 77 --

What is the talk mainly about?
(A) A wage system
(B) Security enhancements
(C) Head office relocation
(D) A training schedule

這段談話主要和什麼有關？
(A) 工資制度
(B) 加強安全防衛
(C) 總部搬遷
(D) 教育訓練時程表

從女子第一句的「we are now installing fingerprint reader devices at the entrance to enhance the security of the building」可知，指紋識別器是為了加強安全，所以正確答案為 (B)。

78

According to the speaker, what will happen on Tuesday?
(A) Additional staff will be employed.
(B) An inspection will be carried out.
(C) Office supplies will be purchased.
(D) New procedures will take effect.

根據說話者表示，星期二將發生什麼事？
(A) 將聘用更多員工。
(B) 將進行檢測。
(C) 將購買辦公用品。
(D) 新程序將生效。

從中間的「Employees will have to scan their enrolled finger on the fingerprint reader whenever they enter the building, starting next Tuesday.」和最後的「the new system is introduced on Tuesday」都可知道，公司週二開始實施新的進出程序，所以正確答案為 (D)。

79

What must employees do this week?
(A) Use a different entrance
(B) Update a company's accounts
(C) Register their fingerprints
(D) Apply for the program

員工這禮拜必須做什麼？
(A) 使用另一個入口
(B) 更新公司帳目
(C) 登錄他們的指紋
(D) 申請計畫

文章中間提及「please make sure that all employees register their fingerprints by the end of this week」意即員工必須在本週內登錄指紋，正確答案為 (C)。

80-82 excerpt from a meeting　　　　**80–82 會議摘錄**

As you already know, employees are using our coffee makers in the staff lounge all day long. As they are old models, we're thinking about changing these coffee machines. So tomorrow, three providers will be offering different coffee machines in the lobby. You can taste free cups of coffee from these devices. What we want to do is just gathering some feedback. It will help us know which one you prefer. Plus, the feedback form only takes around 5 minutes to complete, and you can leave the forms with Belotti in the Maintenance Department.	如大家已經知道的，同仁們整天都會使用員工休息室裡的咖啡機。因為它們都已經是舊機種了，我們正在考慮更換這些咖啡機。所以明天將有三家供應商在大廳提供不同的咖啡機。各位可以品嚐這些機器煮出的免費咖啡。我們要做的就是收集一些意見回饋。這將有助於我們了解各位偏好哪一款。另外，意見回饋表只需要大約五分鐘的時間即可完成，各位可將表單交給維修部的貝羅蒂。

• **staff lounge** 員工休息室　**lobby** 大廳　**feedback** 意見回饋　**prefer** 偏好
  maintenance department 維修部

80

What does the speaker say the company is considering?
(A) Buying a new product
(B) Changing the lunch time
(C) Starting a new business
(D) Extending business hours

說話者表示公司正在考慮什麼？
(A) 買新產品
(B) 更動午餐時間
(C) 開始新業務
(D) 延長營業時間

從第二句「As they are old models, we're thinking about changing these coffee machines.」可知，因為咖啡機太老舊，所以公司正在考慮更換，正確答案為 (A)。

 81 ---

What can listeners receive for free tomorrow?
(A) A laptop
(B) A T-shirt with a company logo
(C) Stationery
(D) Beverages

聽者明天可以免費獲得什麼？
(A) 筆記型電腦
(B) 有公司商標的T恤
(C) 文具
(D) 飲料

從「So tomorrow, three providers will be offering different coffee machines in the lobby. You can taste free cups of coffee from these devices.」可知，聽者明日將試喝咖啡，所以正確答案為 (D)。

 82 ---

Why should listeners visit Belotti's office?
(A) To pick up an employee ID card
(B) To sign up for an employee program
(C) To donate money
(D) To submit a form

聽者為什麼要到貝羅蒂的辦公室？
(A) 領取員工識別證
(B) 報名員工專案計畫
(C) 捐錢
(D) 繳交表單

文章的最後提及「the feedback form only takes around 5 minutes to complete, and you can leave the forms with Belotti in the Maintenance Department.」要求聽者試喝填寫回饋表，並交給貝蘿蒂，故正確答案為 (D)。

83-85 announcement

83–85 宣告

Attention, employees in the production line. As you know, the operation of the conveyor belt is temporarily suspended. The staff from the Maintenance Department said that belt repairs will take approximately six hours. The production line will resume after the completion of its repairs. Meanwhile, all production line employees will be assigned to special duties. Assembly managers will call you to offer more details about schedule changes for tomorrow's work.	生產線人員，請注意。如各位所知，輸送帶的運作已暫時中斷。維修部的人員說，修復傳送帶將花上約六小時的時間。生產線將於修復完成後恢復運作。在此同時，生產線的所有人員將被分配執行特殊職務。裝配主管將召集各位，說明明天工作時間異動的相關細節。

• **production line** 生產線　**operation** 運作　**conveyor belt** 輸送帶　**temporarily** 暫時　**suspend** 中斷　**maintenance department** 維修部　**repair** 修復　**approximately** 大約　**resume** 恢復運作　**completion** 完成　**meanwhile** 在此同時　**be assigned to V** 被分配去……　**duty** 職務　**assembly** 裝配

Where most likely is this announcement being made?

(A) At a customer service center
(B) At a factory
(C) At a department store
(D) At an auto repair shop

這段公告最有可能在哪裡發布？
(A) 顧客服務中心
(B) 工廠
(C) 百貨公司
(D) 汽車修理廠

儘管只聽懂第一句中的「employees in the production line」也可以知道，這段廣播最可能出現的地方是工廠，正確答案為 (B)。

另外，雖然 (C) 與 (D) 分別重複了文中的「department」與「repair」，但意義不盡相同，皆不是正確答案。

What problem does the speaker mention?

(A) Some supplies are sold out.
(B) A manager is sick.
(C) Inclement weather is expected.
(D) Some equipment is not working.

說話者提到什麼問題？
(A) 部分庫存已售完。
(B) 一位經理生病了。
(C) 將出現惡劣天氣。
(D) 部分設備無法運作。

第二句的「the operation of the conveyor belt is temporarily suspended」即點出輸送帶已中斷運作，輸送帶為工廠設備之一，故正確答案為 (D)。

What will employees be informed about by assembly managers?

(A) Test results
(B) Safety regulations
(C) Work schedule changes
(D) Hygiene inspection

裝配主管將告訴員工什麼事？
(A) 測試結果
(B) 安全守則
(C) 工作時程異動
(D) 衛生檢查

仔細聆聽最後的「Assembly managers will call you to offer more details about schedule changes for tomorrow's work.」可以知道，主管將透過電話告知工作時間的變動，故答案為 (C)。

86-88 news report | **86–88 新聞報導**

> Good morning. This is Prime News on Channel 11. According to a recent study released by *UPG Food Magazine*, the best healthy food is homemade meals. Those who participated in the survey were asked about their eating habits and the results revealed that people eating food cooked at home tended to consume more fruits and vegetables compared to people eating food at restaurants. Dr. Jessie Watson, who led the study, said that individuals have to make their own meals to control what they eat better. You can check a full list of questions participants answered on the *UPG Food Magazine* Web site.

> 早安。這裡是第11頻道的《首要新聞》。根據《UPG食品雜誌》最近公布的研究指出，最健康的食物就是自製餐點。參與研究的人被問及他們的飲食習慣，結果顯示，相較於那些在餐廳用餐的人，食用自家烹調食物的人攝取較多的蔬果。主導這項研究的潔希·華森博士表示，個人必須自己製作餐點，才更能控制自己吃什麼。大家可以在《UPG食品雜誌》的網站上查看參與者所回答的完整問卷內容。

- recent 最近的　release 公布　participate in . . . 參與……　eating habits 飲食習慣
  tend to . . . 傾向……　consume 攝取　compared to . . . 相較於……　lead 主導　individual 個人
  recipe book 食譜

86 --

What is the news report about?
(A) A celebrity's recipe book
(B) A new seafood restaurant
(C) Tips for selecting vegetables
(D) Healthy eating habits

這則新聞報導和什麼有關？
(A) 名人的食譜
(B) 新的海鮮餐廳
(C) 挑選蔬菜的秘訣
(D) 健康的飲食習慣

從報導第二句的「According to a recent study released by *UPG Food Magazine*, the best healthy food is homemade meals.」開始，通篇講述飲食習慣相關的資訊，故正確答案為 (D)。

87 --

What does Dr. Watson recommend that people do?
(A) Prepare meals at home
(B) Buy special equipment
(C) Enroll in a cooking class
(D) Download recipes online

華森博士建議人們做什麼事？
(A) 在家準備餐點
(B) 添購特殊設備
(C) 報名烹飪課程
(D) 線上下載食譜

華森博士表示「individuals have to make their own meals to control what they eat better」，建議自己烹調料理，以控制攝取的食物，故正確答案為 (A)。

88 --

According to the speaker, what can listeners do on a Web site?
(A) Make a reservation
(B) Place an order
(C) Read some survey questions
(D) Sign up for a subscription

根據說話者表示，聽眾可以在網站上做什麼？
(A) 預約
(B) 下訂單
(C) 查看問卷問題
(D) 申請訂閱

根據最後提到的「You can check a full list of questions participants answered on the *UPG Food Magazine* Web site.」，聽眾可以在該雜誌的官網看到完整的問卷內容，所以正確答案為 (C)。

89-91 excerpt from a meeting　　　　89-91 會議摘錄

Before we start the staff meeting, I have an announcement to make. I've just found out that our president, Jessica Stewart, will make a visit to our office next Monday. As you already know, the renovation project was just finished, and it was designed to enhance the working environment in branch offices as well as at the headquarters. The president is making visits to all our offices, and we're next. Now, as **(90)this is not a formal visit**, extensive preparations are not necessary. However, there will be a luncheon for her. Please come and give her a warm welcome and let me know your availability by Thursday.	在我們員工會議開始前，我有個公告要宣布。我剛得知，本公司總裁潔西卡·史戴華將於下週一到訪本辦公室。如各位所知，整修工程剛完成，這是為了提升分公司及總部的工作環境而設計的。總裁正在訪視所有分公司，而我們就是下一站。由於 **(90)**這不是一個正式訪視，所以不需要大規模的準備工作。但還是有一場為她安排的午餐會。請踴躍到場並熱烈歡迎她。請於週四前告訴我是否方便出席。

* **staff meeting** 員工會議　**find out** 得知　**make a visit** 拜訪　**renovation** 整修　**enhance** 提升　**working environment** 工作環境　**headquarters** 總部　**branch office** 分公司　**formal visit** 正式訪視　**luncheon** 午餐會　**facility** 處所　**settle a dispute** 解決紛爭　**reassure** 使(人)放寬心　**apologize for sth** 為某事道歉　**procedure** 流程　**welcome reception** 接待會

Why is the president coming for a visit?　總裁為什麼來訪視？
(A) A project has been completed.　(A) 一項工程剛完成。
(B) A facility has been moved.　(B) 一個處所搬遷了。
(C) A manager will retire.　(C) 一位經理將退休。
(D) A sales record has been accomplished.　(D) 銷售紀錄已經完成。

根據中間的「As you already know, the renovation project was just finished. . . . The president is making visits to all our offices, and we're next.」可知，因為辦公室整修結束，所以總裁將到訪巡視，故本題的答案為 (A)。

90 (NEW) --

Why does the speaker say, "this is not a formal visit"?　說話者為什麼說：「這不是一個正式訪視」？
(A) To settle a dispute　(A) 為了解決紛爭
(B) To reassure employees　(B) 為了使員工放寬心
(C) To apologize for problems　(C) 為了問題道歉
(D) To check a procedure　(D) 為了確認流程

根據接續在題目引用句後面的內容，可以知道這句話的目的。整句話為「Now, as this is not a formal visit, extensive preparations are not necessary.」，後句表示無須盛大的準備，意即雖然總裁將到訪，但是無須比照正式訪視大費周章地準備，此為安撫員工的意思，因此正確答案為 (B)。

91 --

What event have the listeners been invited to?

(A) A retirement party
(B) An opening ceremony
(C) A welcome reception
(D) A dinner party

聽眾被邀請去參加什麼活動？

(A) 退休派對
(B) 開幕典禮
(C) 歡迎接待會
(D) 晚宴

從「However, there will be a luncheon for her. Please come and give her a warm welcome and let me know your availability by Thursday.」可知，說話者邀請聽眾出席午餐會，以對總裁表示歡迎，故正確答案為 (C)。

92-94 information and floor plan

92–94 資訊及樓層平面圖

And that completes the tour of the oil painting collections. If you want to learn more about the exhibition, you can find a museum guidebook in our gift shop. I hope you stop by and purchase the book. That's because it is highly recommended by renowned artists and critics. Now that we have finished the tour, please continue exploring the artworks on your own. For your convenience, a map of the museum is ready at the entrance. And you don't want to miss the opportunity to see Chagall's work in our modern art gallery, which is located next to the museum entrance.

我們的油畫典藏導覽就到此結束。若各位想對展出更深入了解，在我們的禮品店可以找到博物館導覽手冊。希望各位可以前往購買該書，因為本書受到知名藝術家與評論家的熱烈推薦。既然我們已經結束了導覽，請各位自行繼續瀏覽藝術作品。為了您的方便起見，入口處備有博物館地圖。您絕對不想錯過觀賞夏卡爾畫作的機會，就在博物館入口旁的現代藝術陳列室。

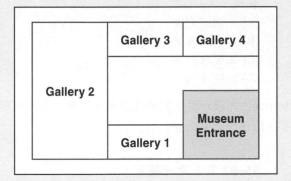

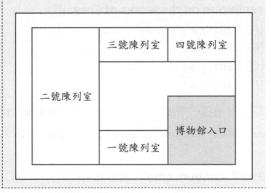

• **oil painting** 油畫　**collections** 典藏　**exhibition** 展出　**stop by** 停留　**renowned** 知名的　**critic** 評論家
for your convenience 為了您的方便起見　**art gallery** 藝術陳列室

What did the listeners see on the tour?
(A) Sculptures
(B) Paintings
(C) Photographs
(D) Pottery

聽眾在導覽中看到了什麼？
(A) 雕刻品
(B) 畫作
(C) 照片
(D) 陶器

從第一句中的「the tour of the oil painting collections」即可知道本題的正確答案為 (B)。

What does the guide recommend listeners do to learn more about the exhibition?
(A) Visit a Web site
(B) Attend a program
(C) Buy a book
(D) Watch a related movie

導覽員建議聽眾如何可以更了解展覽？
(A) 上網站
(B) 參加課程
(C) 買書
(D) 看相關電影

導覽員開頭不久便說：「If you want to learn more about the exhibition, you can find a museum guidebook in our gift shop. I hope you stop by and purchase the book.」，表示若聽眾想了解作品，可以在禮品店購買導覽手冊，故正確答案為 (C)。

 NEW

Look at the graphic. In which room is the exhibition on the works of Chagall?
(A) Gallery 1
(B) Gallery 2
(C) Gallery 3
(D) Gallery 4

看一下圖表，夏卡爾的作品在哪一個陳列室中展出？
(A) 一號陳列室
(B) 二號陳列室
(C) 三號陳列室
(D) 四號陳列室

導覽員最後一句話中的「next to the museum entrance」，表示夏卡爾的作品在入口處，再對照平面圖覽圖，便可知導覽員指的最可能是一號陳列室，故正確答案為 (A)。

95-97 announcement and map

95–97 宣告及地圖

Attention, Delta Controls employees. As announced last Friday, there will be a street parade this afternoon. And because of this, the streets in the area will be closed to traffic this afternoon, from two o'clock. It will end by five, so you don't need to worry about your commute home. However, those who have parked their cars in the basement, please keep in mind that you cannot take your cars out

達美控制的全體員工，請注意。如上週五所宣布的，今天下午將有一場街頭遊行。因此本地區的街道自今天下午兩點起將禁止通行。管制將於五點前結束，所以各位不用擔心通勤回家的問題。但將車子停在地下室的人，請記得活動期間無法取車。特別是如果您必須外出洽公，請現在就將車子移到梅費爾公園旁的付費停車場。停車費將由公司支付。

during the event. In particular, if you have an off-site duty, please move your car into the paid parking area right next to Mayfair Park now. The parking fee will be covered by the company.

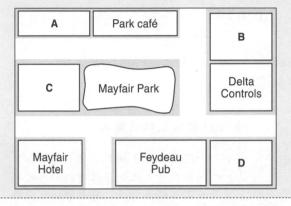
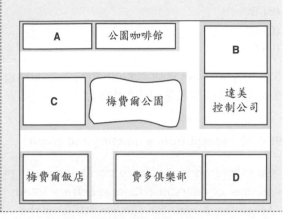

• **street parade** 街頭遊行　**commute** 通勤　**basement** 地下室　**off-site duty** 在外的公務
cover 支付（費用）

---

95 ---

Why is the announcement being made?
(A) To inform listeners about a change in working hours
(B) To encourage employees to take part in the parade
(C) To notify listeners of the unavailability of a parking space
(D) To check the off-site duties for today

為什麼會發布這項公告？
(A) 通知聽者上班時間的異動
(B) 鼓勵員工參加遊行
(C) 告訴聽者無法使用停車場
(D) 確認今天外出勤務

由「those who have parked their cars in the basement, please keep in mind that you cannot take your cars out during the event.」可知，因為遊行的關係，下午開始便無法將車子從地下停車場移出，後文中說話者又提出其他停車空間，故此項公告環繞著停車的主題，本題正確答案為 (C)。

---

96 ---

According to the speaker, what is going to happen in the area today?
(A) Delta Controls will be closed.
(B) There will be a big parade all day long.
(C) Vehicles will be regulated for about 3 hours.
(D) The streets will get jammed with cars during rush hour.

根據說話者表示，該地區今天將發生什麼事？
(A) 達美控制將關閉。
(B) 整天都有大型遊行。
(C) 車輛管制約三小時。
(D) 尖峰時間街道將塞滿車輛。

文章中提及「there will be a street parade this afternoon. And because of this, the streets in the area will be closed to auto traffic this afternoon, from two o'clock. It will end by five,」，由此可知，遊行時間為下午兩點到五點。所以，將有三個小時進行車輛管制，正確答案為 (C)。

(A) 並未提到此事。(B) 雖然有提到「遊行」，但是文中的遊行期間並非整天。(D) 活動舉辦期間並非上下班時間，而且從「It will end by five, so you don't need to worry about your commute home.」可以知道，遊行將在下午五點前結束，所以不用擔心下班時間的交通。

Look at the graphic. Which parking area was recommended by the speaker?
(A) A
(B) B
(C) C
(D) D

看一下圖表，說話者建議哪一個停車場？
(A) A
(B) B
(C) C
(D) D

從「please move your car into the paid parking area right next to Mayfair Park now.」可知，公司建議的停車場緊鄰梅費爾公園，所以正確答案為 (C)。

98-100 excerpt from a meeting and graph

98–100 會議摘錄及圖表

Good afternoon, I'd like to start by reviewing the number of new subscribers at *Leisure Trends Magazine*. As you can see, we attracted the most subscribers last month. The same thing has happened every year, and this August was not an exception. On the other hand, the special feature articles in our 5th anniversary edition didn't seem to be very successful compared to our expectations. The figures show the discount event in June worked even better, but we should not jump to conclusions. The marketing team is planning a survey next month to analyze the exact factors. I hope this can explain why the special edition showed the worst result in the past four months.

午安，一開始我想來檢視《休閒趨勢雜誌》的新訂戶量。正如各位看到的，我們上個月吸引了最多訂戶。每年都發生同樣的狀況，今年八月也不例外。另一方面，我們的五週年紀念特刊似乎不如預期的成功。數據顯示六月的優惠活動效果還更勝一籌，不過我們也不該驟下結論。行銷團隊正在規劃下個月的問卷調查，以分析確切因素。我希望這能夠解釋過去這四個月以來特刊銷售最為慘澹的原因。

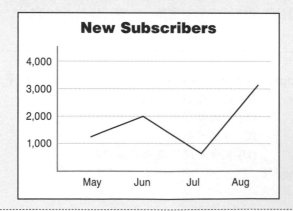

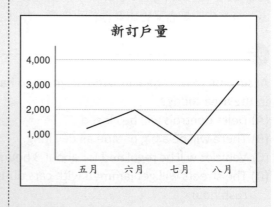

• subscriber 訂戶　sth is not an exception ……也不例外　expectation 預期
jump to conclusions 驟下結論　exact 確切的　factor 因素　worst 最慘的

98 --

Where most likely does the speaker work?
(A) At an advertising company
(B) At a magazine publisher
(C) At a leisure supplies manufacturer
(D) At a market research institute

說話者最可能在哪裡工作？
(A) 廣告公司
(B) 雜誌社
(C) 休閒用品製造商
(D) 市場研究機構

透過一開始的「new subscribers at *Leisure Trends Magazine*」可以得知，說話者上班的地方最可能為發行雜誌的公司，故正確答案為 (B)。

99 (NEW) --

Look at the graphic. When did the company have its 5th anniversary?
(A) In May
(B) In June
(C) In July
(D) In August

看一下圖表，這家公司的五週年紀念是在何時？
(A) 五月
(B) 六月
(C) 七月
(D) 八月

從「On the other hand, the special feature articles in our 5th anniversary edition didn't seem to be very successful compared to our expectations.」已能得知，五週年紀念特刊上的文章回響不如預期。但答案得從「I hope this can explain why the special edition showed the worst result in the past four months.」才能確切知道，紀念特刊的銷售成績創下過去四個月的新低。圖表上創下最低訂戶量紀錄的為七月，故正確答案為 (C)。

100 --

According to the speaker, what does the business plan to do next month?
(A) Offer a promotional event
(B) Launch a new product
(C) Get new advertisers
(D) Conduct a survey

根據說話者表示，這家公司下個月打算做什麼？
(A) 推出促銷活動
(B) 上市新產品
(C) 找新廣告商
(D) 進行問卷調查

從「The marketing team is planning a survey next month to analyze the exact factors.」可以得知，下個月將進行問卷調查分析原因，所以正確答案為 (D)。

Answer Sheet

ACTUAL TEST 01

LISTENING SECTION

1	Ⓐ Ⓑ Ⓒ
2	Ⓐ Ⓑ Ⓒ
3	Ⓐ Ⓑ Ⓒ
4	Ⓐ Ⓑ Ⓒ
5	Ⓐ Ⓑ Ⓒ
6	Ⓐ Ⓑ Ⓒ
7	Ⓐ Ⓑ Ⓒ
8	Ⓐ Ⓑ Ⓒ
9	Ⓐ Ⓑ Ⓒ
10	Ⓐ Ⓑ Ⓒ

11	Ⓐ Ⓑ Ⓒ Ⓓ
12	Ⓐ Ⓑ Ⓒ Ⓓ
13	Ⓐ Ⓑ Ⓒ Ⓓ
14	Ⓐ Ⓑ Ⓒ Ⓓ
15	Ⓐ Ⓑ Ⓒ Ⓓ
16	Ⓐ Ⓑ Ⓒ Ⓓ
17	Ⓐ Ⓑ Ⓒ Ⓓ
18	Ⓐ Ⓑ Ⓒ Ⓓ
19	Ⓐ Ⓑ Ⓒ Ⓓ
20	Ⓐ Ⓑ Ⓒ Ⓓ

21	Ⓐ Ⓑ Ⓒ Ⓓ
22	Ⓐ Ⓑ Ⓒ Ⓓ
23	Ⓐ Ⓑ Ⓒ Ⓓ
24	Ⓐ Ⓑ Ⓒ Ⓓ
25	Ⓐ Ⓑ Ⓒ Ⓓ
26	Ⓐ Ⓑ Ⓒ Ⓓ
27	Ⓐ Ⓑ Ⓒ Ⓓ
28	Ⓐ Ⓑ Ⓒ Ⓓ
29	Ⓐ Ⓑ Ⓒ Ⓓ
30	Ⓐ Ⓑ Ⓒ Ⓓ

31	Ⓐ Ⓑ Ⓒ Ⓓ
32	Ⓐ Ⓑ Ⓒ Ⓓ
33	Ⓐ Ⓑ Ⓒ Ⓓ
34	Ⓐ Ⓑ Ⓒ Ⓓ
35	Ⓐ Ⓑ Ⓒ Ⓓ
36	Ⓐ Ⓑ Ⓒ Ⓓ
37	Ⓐ Ⓑ Ⓒ Ⓓ
38	Ⓐ Ⓑ Ⓒ Ⓓ
39	Ⓐ Ⓑ Ⓒ Ⓓ
40	Ⓐ Ⓑ Ⓒ Ⓓ

41	Ⓐ Ⓑ Ⓒ Ⓓ
42	Ⓐ Ⓑ Ⓒ Ⓓ
43	Ⓐ Ⓑ Ⓒ Ⓓ
44	Ⓐ Ⓑ Ⓒ Ⓓ
45	Ⓐ Ⓑ Ⓒ Ⓓ
46	Ⓐ Ⓑ Ⓒ Ⓓ
47	Ⓐ Ⓑ Ⓒ Ⓓ
48	Ⓐ Ⓑ Ⓒ Ⓓ
49	Ⓐ Ⓑ Ⓒ Ⓓ
50	Ⓐ Ⓑ Ⓒ Ⓓ

51	Ⓐ Ⓑ Ⓒ Ⓓ
52	Ⓐ Ⓑ Ⓒ Ⓓ
53	Ⓐ Ⓑ Ⓒ Ⓓ
54	Ⓐ Ⓑ Ⓒ Ⓓ
55	Ⓐ Ⓑ Ⓒ Ⓓ
56	Ⓐ Ⓑ Ⓒ Ⓓ
57	Ⓐ Ⓑ Ⓒ Ⓓ
58	Ⓐ Ⓑ Ⓒ Ⓓ
59	Ⓐ Ⓑ Ⓒ Ⓓ
60	Ⓐ Ⓑ Ⓒ Ⓓ

61	Ⓐ Ⓑ Ⓒ Ⓓ
62	Ⓐ Ⓑ Ⓒ Ⓓ
63	Ⓐ Ⓑ Ⓒ Ⓓ
64	Ⓐ Ⓑ Ⓒ Ⓓ
65	Ⓐ Ⓑ Ⓒ Ⓓ
66	Ⓐ Ⓑ Ⓒ Ⓓ
67	Ⓐ Ⓑ Ⓒ Ⓓ
68	Ⓐ Ⓑ Ⓒ Ⓓ
69	Ⓐ Ⓑ Ⓒ Ⓓ
70	Ⓐ Ⓑ Ⓒ Ⓓ

71	Ⓐ Ⓑ Ⓒ Ⓓ
72	Ⓐ Ⓑ Ⓒ Ⓓ
73	Ⓐ Ⓑ Ⓒ Ⓓ
74	Ⓐ Ⓑ Ⓒ Ⓓ
75	Ⓐ Ⓑ Ⓒ Ⓓ
76	Ⓐ Ⓑ Ⓒ Ⓓ
77	Ⓐ Ⓑ Ⓒ Ⓓ
78	Ⓐ Ⓑ Ⓒ Ⓓ
79	Ⓐ Ⓑ Ⓒ Ⓓ
80	Ⓐ Ⓑ Ⓒ Ⓓ

81	Ⓐ Ⓑ Ⓒ Ⓓ
82	Ⓐ Ⓑ Ⓒ Ⓓ
83	Ⓐ Ⓑ Ⓒ Ⓓ
84	Ⓐ Ⓑ Ⓒ Ⓓ
85	Ⓐ Ⓑ Ⓒ Ⓓ
86	Ⓐ Ⓑ Ⓒ Ⓓ
87	Ⓐ Ⓑ Ⓒ Ⓓ
88	Ⓐ Ⓑ Ⓒ Ⓓ
89	Ⓐ Ⓑ Ⓒ Ⓓ
90	Ⓐ Ⓑ Ⓒ Ⓓ

91	Ⓐ Ⓑ Ⓒ Ⓓ
92	Ⓐ Ⓑ Ⓒ Ⓓ
93	Ⓐ Ⓑ Ⓒ Ⓓ
94	Ⓐ Ⓑ Ⓒ Ⓓ
95	Ⓐ Ⓑ Ⓒ Ⓓ
96	Ⓐ Ⓑ Ⓒ Ⓓ
97	Ⓐ Ⓑ Ⓒ Ⓓ
98	Ⓐ Ⓑ Ⓒ Ⓓ
99	Ⓐ Ⓑ Ⓒ Ⓓ
100	Ⓐ Ⓑ Ⓒ Ⓓ

ACTUAL TEST 02

LISTENING SECTION

1	Ⓐ Ⓑ Ⓒ
2	Ⓐ Ⓑ Ⓒ
3	Ⓐ Ⓑ Ⓒ
4	Ⓐ Ⓑ Ⓒ
5	Ⓐ Ⓑ Ⓒ
6	Ⓐ Ⓑ Ⓒ
7	Ⓐ Ⓑ Ⓒ
8	Ⓐ Ⓑ Ⓒ
9	Ⓐ Ⓑ Ⓒ
10	Ⓐ Ⓑ Ⓒ

11	Ⓐ Ⓑ Ⓒ Ⓓ
12	Ⓐ Ⓑ Ⓒ Ⓓ
13	Ⓐ Ⓑ Ⓒ Ⓓ
14	Ⓐ Ⓑ Ⓒ Ⓓ
15	Ⓐ Ⓑ Ⓒ Ⓓ
16	Ⓐ Ⓑ Ⓒ Ⓓ
17	Ⓐ Ⓑ Ⓒ Ⓓ
18	Ⓐ Ⓑ Ⓒ Ⓓ
19	Ⓐ Ⓑ Ⓒ Ⓓ
20	Ⓐ Ⓑ Ⓒ Ⓓ

21	Ⓐ Ⓑ Ⓒ Ⓓ
22	Ⓐ Ⓑ Ⓒ Ⓓ
23	Ⓐ Ⓑ Ⓒ Ⓓ
24	Ⓐ Ⓑ Ⓒ Ⓓ
25	Ⓐ Ⓑ Ⓒ Ⓓ
26	Ⓐ Ⓑ Ⓒ Ⓓ
27	Ⓐ Ⓑ Ⓒ Ⓓ
28	Ⓐ Ⓑ Ⓒ Ⓓ
29	Ⓐ Ⓑ Ⓒ Ⓓ
30	Ⓐ Ⓑ Ⓒ Ⓓ

31	Ⓐ Ⓑ Ⓒ Ⓓ
32	Ⓐ Ⓑ Ⓒ Ⓓ
33	Ⓐ Ⓑ Ⓒ Ⓓ
34	Ⓐ Ⓑ Ⓒ Ⓓ
35	Ⓐ Ⓑ Ⓒ Ⓓ
36	Ⓐ Ⓑ Ⓒ Ⓓ
37	Ⓐ Ⓑ Ⓒ Ⓓ
38	Ⓐ Ⓑ Ⓒ Ⓓ
39	Ⓐ Ⓑ Ⓒ Ⓓ
40	Ⓐ Ⓑ Ⓒ Ⓓ

41	Ⓐ Ⓑ Ⓒ Ⓓ
42	Ⓐ Ⓑ Ⓒ Ⓓ
43	Ⓐ Ⓑ Ⓒ Ⓓ
44	Ⓐ Ⓑ Ⓒ Ⓓ
45	Ⓐ Ⓑ Ⓒ Ⓓ
46	Ⓐ Ⓑ Ⓒ Ⓓ
47	Ⓐ Ⓑ Ⓒ Ⓓ
48	Ⓐ Ⓑ Ⓒ Ⓓ
49	Ⓐ Ⓑ Ⓒ Ⓓ
50	Ⓐ Ⓑ Ⓒ Ⓓ

51	Ⓐ Ⓑ Ⓒ Ⓓ
52	Ⓐ Ⓑ Ⓒ Ⓓ
53	Ⓐ Ⓑ Ⓒ Ⓓ
54	Ⓐ Ⓑ Ⓒ Ⓓ
55	Ⓐ Ⓑ Ⓒ Ⓓ
56	Ⓐ Ⓑ Ⓒ Ⓓ
57	Ⓐ Ⓑ Ⓒ Ⓓ
58	Ⓐ Ⓑ Ⓒ Ⓓ
59	Ⓐ Ⓑ Ⓒ Ⓓ
60	Ⓐ Ⓑ Ⓒ Ⓓ

61	Ⓐ Ⓑ Ⓒ Ⓓ
62	Ⓐ Ⓑ Ⓒ Ⓓ
63	Ⓐ Ⓑ Ⓒ Ⓓ
64	Ⓐ Ⓑ Ⓒ Ⓓ
65	Ⓐ Ⓑ Ⓒ Ⓓ
66	Ⓐ Ⓑ Ⓒ Ⓓ
67	Ⓐ Ⓑ Ⓒ Ⓓ
68	Ⓐ Ⓑ Ⓒ Ⓓ
69	Ⓐ Ⓑ Ⓒ Ⓓ
70	Ⓐ Ⓑ Ⓒ Ⓓ

71	Ⓐ Ⓑ Ⓒ Ⓓ
72	Ⓐ Ⓑ Ⓒ Ⓓ
73	Ⓐ Ⓑ Ⓒ Ⓓ
74	Ⓐ Ⓑ Ⓒ Ⓓ
75	Ⓐ Ⓑ Ⓒ Ⓓ
76	Ⓐ Ⓑ Ⓒ Ⓓ
77	Ⓐ Ⓑ Ⓒ Ⓓ
78	Ⓐ Ⓑ Ⓒ Ⓓ
79	Ⓐ Ⓑ Ⓒ Ⓓ
80	Ⓐ Ⓑ Ⓒ Ⓓ

81	Ⓐ Ⓑ Ⓒ Ⓓ
82	Ⓐ Ⓑ Ⓒ Ⓓ
83	Ⓐ Ⓑ Ⓒ Ⓓ
84	Ⓐ Ⓑ Ⓒ Ⓓ
85	Ⓐ Ⓑ Ⓒ Ⓓ
86	Ⓐ Ⓑ Ⓒ Ⓓ
87	Ⓐ Ⓑ Ⓒ Ⓓ
88	Ⓐ Ⓑ Ⓒ Ⓓ
89	Ⓐ Ⓑ Ⓒ Ⓓ
90	Ⓐ Ⓑ Ⓒ Ⓓ

91	Ⓐ Ⓑ Ⓒ Ⓓ
92	Ⓐ Ⓑ Ⓒ Ⓓ
93	Ⓐ Ⓑ Ⓒ Ⓓ
94	Ⓐ Ⓑ Ⓒ Ⓓ
95	Ⓐ Ⓑ Ⓒ Ⓓ
96	Ⓐ Ⓑ Ⓒ Ⓓ
97	Ⓐ Ⓑ Ⓒ Ⓓ
98	Ⓐ Ⓑ Ⓒ Ⓓ
99	Ⓐ Ⓑ Ⓒ Ⓓ
100	Ⓐ Ⓑ Ⓒ Ⓓ

Answer Sheet

ACTUAL TEST 03

LISTENING SECTION	1	Ⓐ Ⓑ Ⓒ Ⓓ	11	Ⓐ Ⓑ Ⓒ Ⓓ	21	Ⓐ Ⓑ Ⓒ Ⓓ	31	Ⓐ Ⓑ Ⓒ Ⓓ	41	Ⓐ Ⓑ Ⓒ Ⓓ	51	Ⓐ Ⓑ Ⓒ Ⓓ	61	Ⓐ Ⓑ Ⓒ Ⓓ	71	Ⓐ Ⓑ Ⓒ Ⓓ	81	Ⓐ Ⓑ Ⓒ Ⓓ	91	Ⓐ Ⓑ Ⓒ Ⓓ
	2	Ⓐ Ⓑ Ⓒ Ⓓ	12	Ⓐ Ⓑ Ⓒ Ⓓ	22	Ⓐ Ⓑ Ⓒ Ⓓ	32	Ⓐ Ⓑ Ⓒ Ⓓ	42	Ⓐ Ⓑ Ⓒ Ⓓ	52	Ⓐ Ⓑ Ⓒ Ⓓ	62	Ⓐ Ⓑ Ⓒ Ⓓ	72	Ⓐ Ⓑ Ⓒ Ⓓ	82	Ⓐ Ⓑ Ⓒ Ⓓ	92	Ⓐ Ⓑ Ⓒ Ⓓ
	3	Ⓐ Ⓑ Ⓒ Ⓓ	13	Ⓐ Ⓑ Ⓒ Ⓓ	23	Ⓐ Ⓑ Ⓒ Ⓓ	33	Ⓐ Ⓑ Ⓒ Ⓓ	43	Ⓐ Ⓑ Ⓒ Ⓓ	53	Ⓐ Ⓑ Ⓒ Ⓓ	63	Ⓐ Ⓑ Ⓒ Ⓓ	73	Ⓐ Ⓑ Ⓒ Ⓓ	83	Ⓐ Ⓑ Ⓒ Ⓓ	93	Ⓐ Ⓑ Ⓒ Ⓓ
	4	Ⓐ Ⓑ Ⓒ Ⓓ	14	Ⓐ Ⓑ Ⓒ Ⓓ	24	Ⓐ Ⓑ Ⓒ Ⓓ	34	Ⓐ Ⓑ Ⓒ Ⓓ	44	Ⓐ Ⓑ Ⓒ Ⓓ	54	Ⓐ Ⓑ Ⓒ Ⓓ	64	Ⓐ Ⓑ Ⓒ Ⓓ	74	Ⓐ Ⓑ Ⓒ Ⓓ	84	Ⓐ Ⓑ Ⓒ Ⓓ	94	Ⓐ Ⓑ Ⓒ Ⓓ
	5	Ⓐ Ⓑ Ⓒ Ⓓ	15	Ⓐ Ⓑ Ⓒ Ⓓ	25	Ⓐ Ⓑ Ⓒ Ⓓ	35	Ⓐ Ⓑ Ⓒ Ⓓ	45	Ⓐ Ⓑ Ⓒ Ⓓ	55	Ⓐ Ⓑ Ⓒ Ⓓ	65	Ⓐ Ⓑ Ⓒ Ⓓ	75	Ⓐ Ⓑ Ⓒ Ⓓ	85	Ⓐ Ⓑ Ⓒ Ⓓ	95	Ⓐ Ⓑ Ⓒ Ⓓ
	6	Ⓐ Ⓑ Ⓒ Ⓓ	16	Ⓐ Ⓑ Ⓒ Ⓓ	26	Ⓐ Ⓑ Ⓒ Ⓓ	36	Ⓐ Ⓑ Ⓒ Ⓓ	46	Ⓐ Ⓑ Ⓒ Ⓓ	56	Ⓐ Ⓑ Ⓒ Ⓓ	66	Ⓐ Ⓑ Ⓒ Ⓓ	76	Ⓐ Ⓑ Ⓒ Ⓓ	86	Ⓐ Ⓑ Ⓒ Ⓓ	96	Ⓐ Ⓑ Ⓒ Ⓓ
	7	Ⓐ Ⓑ Ⓒ Ⓓ	17	Ⓐ Ⓑ Ⓒ Ⓓ	27	Ⓐ Ⓑ Ⓒ Ⓓ	37	Ⓐ Ⓑ Ⓒ Ⓓ	47	Ⓐ Ⓑ Ⓒ Ⓓ	57	Ⓐ Ⓑ Ⓒ Ⓓ	67	Ⓐ Ⓑ Ⓒ Ⓓ	77	Ⓐ Ⓑ Ⓒ Ⓓ	87	Ⓐ Ⓑ Ⓒ Ⓓ	97	Ⓐ Ⓑ Ⓒ Ⓓ
	8	Ⓐ Ⓑ Ⓒ Ⓓ	18	Ⓐ Ⓑ Ⓒ Ⓓ	28	Ⓐ Ⓑ Ⓒ Ⓓ	38	Ⓐ Ⓑ Ⓒ Ⓓ	48	Ⓐ Ⓑ Ⓒ Ⓓ	58	Ⓐ Ⓑ Ⓒ Ⓓ	68	Ⓐ Ⓑ Ⓒ Ⓓ	78	Ⓐ Ⓑ Ⓒ Ⓓ	88	Ⓐ Ⓑ Ⓒ Ⓓ	98	Ⓐ Ⓑ Ⓒ Ⓓ
	9	Ⓐ Ⓑ Ⓒ Ⓓ	19	Ⓐ Ⓑ Ⓒ Ⓓ	29	Ⓐ Ⓑ Ⓒ Ⓓ	39	Ⓐ Ⓑ Ⓒ Ⓓ	49	Ⓐ Ⓑ Ⓒ Ⓓ	59	Ⓐ Ⓑ Ⓒ Ⓓ	69	Ⓐ Ⓑ Ⓒ Ⓓ	79	Ⓐ Ⓑ Ⓒ Ⓓ	89	Ⓐ Ⓑ Ⓒ Ⓓ	99	Ⓐ Ⓑ Ⓒ Ⓓ
	10	Ⓐ Ⓑ Ⓒ Ⓓ	20	Ⓐ Ⓑ Ⓒ Ⓓ	30	Ⓐ Ⓑ Ⓒ Ⓓ	40	Ⓐ Ⓑ Ⓒ Ⓓ	50	Ⓐ Ⓑ Ⓒ Ⓓ	60	Ⓐ Ⓑ Ⓒ Ⓓ	70	Ⓐ Ⓑ Ⓒ Ⓓ	80	Ⓐ Ⓑ Ⓒ Ⓓ	90	Ⓐ Ⓑ Ⓒ Ⓓ	100	Ⓐ Ⓑ Ⓒ Ⓓ

ACTUAL TEST 04

LISTENING SECTION	1	Ⓐ Ⓑ Ⓒ Ⓓ	11	Ⓐ Ⓑ Ⓒ Ⓓ	21	Ⓐ Ⓑ Ⓒ Ⓓ	31	Ⓐ Ⓑ Ⓒ Ⓓ	41	Ⓐ Ⓑ Ⓒ Ⓓ	51	Ⓐ Ⓑ Ⓒ Ⓓ	61	Ⓐ Ⓑ Ⓒ Ⓓ	71	Ⓐ Ⓑ Ⓒ Ⓓ	81	Ⓐ Ⓑ Ⓒ Ⓓ	91	Ⓐ Ⓑ Ⓒ Ⓓ
	2	Ⓐ Ⓑ Ⓒ Ⓓ	12	Ⓐ Ⓑ Ⓒ Ⓓ	22	Ⓐ Ⓑ Ⓒ Ⓓ	32	Ⓐ Ⓑ Ⓒ Ⓓ	42	Ⓐ Ⓑ Ⓒ Ⓓ	52	Ⓐ Ⓑ Ⓒ Ⓓ	62	Ⓐ Ⓑ Ⓒ Ⓓ	72	Ⓐ Ⓑ Ⓒ Ⓓ	82	Ⓐ Ⓑ Ⓒ Ⓓ	92	Ⓐ Ⓑ Ⓒ Ⓓ
	3	Ⓐ Ⓑ Ⓒ Ⓓ	13	Ⓐ Ⓑ Ⓒ Ⓓ	23	Ⓐ Ⓑ Ⓒ Ⓓ	33	Ⓐ Ⓑ Ⓒ Ⓓ	43	Ⓐ Ⓑ Ⓒ Ⓓ	53	Ⓐ Ⓑ Ⓒ Ⓓ	63	Ⓐ Ⓑ Ⓒ Ⓓ	73	Ⓐ Ⓑ Ⓒ Ⓓ	83	Ⓐ Ⓑ Ⓒ Ⓓ	93	Ⓐ Ⓑ Ⓒ Ⓓ
	4	Ⓐ Ⓑ Ⓒ Ⓓ	14	Ⓐ Ⓑ Ⓒ Ⓓ	24	Ⓐ Ⓑ Ⓒ Ⓓ	34	Ⓐ Ⓑ Ⓒ Ⓓ	44	Ⓐ Ⓑ Ⓒ Ⓓ	54	Ⓐ Ⓑ Ⓒ Ⓓ	64	Ⓐ Ⓑ Ⓒ Ⓓ	74	Ⓐ Ⓑ Ⓒ Ⓓ	84	Ⓐ Ⓑ Ⓒ Ⓓ	94	Ⓐ Ⓑ Ⓒ Ⓓ
	5	Ⓐ Ⓑ Ⓒ Ⓓ	15	Ⓐ Ⓑ Ⓒ Ⓓ	25	Ⓐ Ⓑ Ⓒ Ⓓ	35	Ⓐ Ⓑ Ⓒ Ⓓ	45	Ⓐ Ⓑ Ⓒ Ⓓ	55	Ⓐ Ⓑ Ⓒ Ⓓ	65	Ⓐ Ⓑ Ⓒ Ⓓ	75	Ⓐ Ⓑ Ⓒ Ⓓ	85	Ⓐ Ⓑ Ⓒ Ⓓ	95	Ⓐ Ⓑ Ⓒ Ⓓ
	6	Ⓐ Ⓑ Ⓒ Ⓓ	16	Ⓐ Ⓑ Ⓒ Ⓓ	26	Ⓐ Ⓑ Ⓒ Ⓓ	36	Ⓐ Ⓑ Ⓒ Ⓓ	46	Ⓐ Ⓑ Ⓒ Ⓓ	56	Ⓐ Ⓑ Ⓒ Ⓓ	66	Ⓐ Ⓑ Ⓒ Ⓓ	76	Ⓐ Ⓑ Ⓒ Ⓓ	86	Ⓐ Ⓑ Ⓒ Ⓓ	96	Ⓐ Ⓑ Ⓒ Ⓓ
	7	Ⓐ Ⓑ Ⓒ Ⓓ	17	Ⓐ Ⓑ Ⓒ Ⓓ	27	Ⓐ Ⓑ Ⓒ Ⓓ	37	Ⓐ Ⓑ Ⓒ Ⓓ	47	Ⓐ Ⓑ Ⓒ Ⓓ	57	Ⓐ Ⓑ Ⓒ Ⓓ	67	Ⓐ Ⓑ Ⓒ Ⓓ	77	Ⓐ Ⓑ Ⓒ Ⓓ	87	Ⓐ Ⓑ Ⓒ Ⓓ	97	Ⓐ Ⓑ Ⓒ Ⓓ
	8	Ⓐ Ⓑ Ⓒ Ⓓ	18	Ⓐ Ⓑ Ⓒ Ⓓ	28	Ⓐ Ⓑ Ⓒ Ⓓ	38	Ⓐ Ⓑ Ⓒ Ⓓ	48	Ⓐ Ⓑ Ⓒ Ⓓ	58	Ⓐ Ⓑ Ⓒ Ⓓ	68	Ⓐ Ⓑ Ⓒ Ⓓ	78	Ⓐ Ⓑ Ⓒ Ⓓ	88	Ⓐ Ⓑ Ⓒ Ⓓ	98	Ⓐ Ⓑ Ⓒ Ⓓ
	9	Ⓐ Ⓑ Ⓒ Ⓓ	19	Ⓐ Ⓑ Ⓒ Ⓓ	29	Ⓐ Ⓑ Ⓒ Ⓓ	39	Ⓐ Ⓑ Ⓒ Ⓓ	49	Ⓐ Ⓑ Ⓒ Ⓓ	59	Ⓐ Ⓑ Ⓒ Ⓓ	69	Ⓐ Ⓑ Ⓒ Ⓓ	79	Ⓐ Ⓑ Ⓒ Ⓓ	89	Ⓐ Ⓑ Ⓒ Ⓓ	99	Ⓐ Ⓑ Ⓒ Ⓓ
	10	Ⓐ Ⓑ Ⓒ Ⓓ	20	Ⓐ Ⓑ Ⓒ Ⓓ	30	Ⓐ Ⓑ Ⓒ Ⓓ	40	Ⓐ Ⓑ Ⓒ Ⓓ	50	Ⓐ Ⓑ Ⓒ Ⓓ	60	Ⓐ Ⓑ Ⓒ Ⓓ	70	Ⓐ Ⓑ Ⓒ Ⓓ	80	Ⓐ Ⓑ Ⓒ Ⓓ	90	Ⓐ Ⓑ Ⓒ Ⓓ	100	Ⓐ Ⓑ Ⓒ Ⓓ

Answer Sheet

ACTUAL TEST 05

LISTENING SECTION

1	Ⓐ Ⓑ Ⓒ Ⓓ	11	Ⓐ Ⓑ Ⓒ Ⓓ	21	Ⓐ Ⓑ Ⓒ Ⓓ	31	Ⓐ Ⓑ Ⓒ Ⓓ	41	Ⓐ Ⓑ Ⓒ Ⓓ	51	Ⓐ Ⓑ Ⓒ Ⓓ	61	Ⓐ Ⓑ Ⓒ Ⓓ	71	Ⓐ Ⓑ Ⓒ Ⓓ	81	Ⓐ Ⓑ Ⓒ Ⓓ	91	Ⓐ Ⓑ Ⓒ Ⓓ
2	Ⓐ Ⓑ Ⓒ Ⓓ	12	Ⓐ Ⓑ Ⓒ Ⓓ	22	Ⓐ Ⓑ Ⓒ Ⓓ	32	Ⓐ Ⓑ Ⓒ Ⓓ	42	Ⓐ Ⓑ Ⓒ Ⓓ	52	Ⓐ Ⓑ Ⓒ Ⓓ	62	Ⓐ Ⓑ Ⓒ Ⓓ	72	Ⓐ Ⓑ Ⓒ Ⓓ	82	Ⓐ Ⓑ Ⓒ Ⓓ	92	Ⓐ Ⓑ Ⓒ Ⓓ
3	Ⓐ Ⓑ Ⓒ Ⓓ	13	Ⓐ Ⓑ Ⓒ Ⓓ	23	Ⓐ Ⓑ Ⓒ Ⓓ	33	Ⓐ Ⓑ Ⓒ Ⓓ	43	Ⓐ Ⓑ Ⓒ Ⓓ	53	Ⓐ Ⓑ Ⓒ Ⓓ	63	Ⓐ Ⓑ Ⓒ Ⓓ	73	Ⓐ Ⓑ Ⓒ Ⓓ	83	Ⓐ Ⓑ Ⓒ Ⓓ	93	Ⓐ Ⓑ Ⓒ Ⓓ
4	Ⓐ Ⓑ Ⓒ Ⓓ	14	Ⓐ Ⓑ Ⓒ Ⓓ	24	Ⓐ Ⓑ Ⓒ Ⓓ	34	Ⓐ Ⓑ Ⓒ Ⓓ	44	Ⓐ Ⓑ Ⓒ Ⓓ	54	Ⓐ Ⓑ Ⓒ Ⓓ	64	Ⓐ Ⓑ Ⓒ Ⓓ	74	Ⓐ Ⓑ Ⓒ Ⓓ	84	Ⓐ Ⓑ Ⓒ Ⓓ	94	Ⓐ Ⓑ Ⓒ Ⓓ
5	Ⓐ Ⓑ Ⓒ Ⓓ	15	Ⓐ Ⓑ Ⓒ Ⓓ	25	Ⓐ Ⓑ Ⓒ Ⓓ	35	Ⓐ Ⓑ Ⓒ Ⓓ	45	Ⓐ Ⓑ Ⓒ Ⓓ	55	Ⓐ Ⓑ Ⓒ Ⓓ	65	Ⓐ Ⓑ Ⓒ Ⓓ	75	Ⓐ Ⓑ Ⓒ Ⓓ	85	Ⓐ Ⓑ Ⓒ Ⓓ	95	Ⓐ Ⓑ Ⓒ Ⓓ
6	Ⓐ Ⓑ Ⓒ Ⓓ	16	Ⓐ Ⓑ Ⓒ Ⓓ	26	Ⓐ Ⓑ Ⓒ Ⓓ	36	Ⓐ Ⓑ Ⓒ Ⓓ	46	Ⓐ Ⓑ Ⓒ Ⓓ	56	Ⓐ Ⓑ Ⓒ Ⓓ	66	Ⓐ Ⓑ Ⓒ Ⓓ	76	Ⓐ Ⓑ Ⓒ Ⓓ	86	Ⓐ Ⓑ Ⓒ Ⓓ	96	Ⓐ Ⓑ Ⓒ Ⓓ
7	Ⓐ Ⓑ Ⓒ Ⓓ	17	Ⓐ Ⓑ Ⓒ Ⓓ	27	Ⓐ Ⓑ Ⓒ Ⓓ	37	Ⓐ Ⓑ Ⓒ Ⓓ	47	Ⓐ Ⓑ Ⓒ Ⓓ	57	Ⓐ Ⓑ Ⓒ Ⓓ	67	Ⓐ Ⓑ Ⓒ Ⓓ	77	Ⓐ Ⓑ Ⓒ Ⓓ	87	Ⓐ Ⓑ Ⓒ Ⓓ	97	Ⓐ Ⓑ Ⓒ Ⓓ
8	Ⓐ Ⓑ Ⓒ Ⓓ	18	Ⓐ Ⓑ Ⓒ Ⓓ	28	Ⓐ Ⓑ Ⓒ Ⓓ	38	Ⓐ Ⓑ Ⓒ Ⓓ	48	Ⓐ Ⓑ Ⓒ Ⓓ	58	Ⓐ Ⓑ Ⓒ Ⓓ	68	Ⓐ Ⓑ Ⓒ Ⓓ	78	Ⓐ Ⓑ Ⓒ Ⓓ	88	Ⓐ Ⓑ Ⓒ Ⓓ	98	Ⓐ Ⓑ Ⓒ Ⓓ
9	Ⓐ Ⓑ Ⓒ Ⓓ	19	Ⓐ Ⓑ Ⓒ Ⓓ	29	Ⓐ Ⓑ Ⓒ Ⓓ	39	Ⓐ Ⓑ Ⓒ Ⓓ	49	Ⓐ Ⓑ Ⓒ Ⓓ	59	Ⓐ Ⓑ Ⓒ Ⓓ	69	Ⓐ Ⓑ Ⓒ Ⓓ	79	Ⓐ Ⓑ Ⓒ Ⓓ	89	Ⓐ Ⓑ Ⓒ Ⓓ	99	Ⓐ Ⓑ Ⓒ Ⓓ
10	Ⓐ Ⓑ Ⓒ Ⓓ	20	Ⓐ Ⓑ Ⓒ Ⓓ	30	Ⓐ Ⓑ Ⓒ Ⓓ	40	Ⓐ Ⓑ Ⓒ Ⓓ	50	Ⓐ Ⓑ Ⓒ Ⓓ	60	Ⓐ Ⓑ Ⓒ Ⓓ	70	Ⓐ Ⓑ Ⓒ Ⓓ	80	Ⓐ Ⓑ Ⓒ Ⓓ	90	Ⓐ Ⓑ Ⓒ Ⓓ	100	Ⓐ Ⓑ Ⓒ Ⓓ

ACTUAL TEST 06

LISTENING SECTION

1	Ⓐ Ⓑ Ⓒ Ⓓ	11	Ⓐ Ⓑ Ⓒ Ⓓ	21	Ⓐ Ⓑ Ⓒ Ⓓ	31	Ⓐ Ⓑ Ⓒ Ⓓ	41	Ⓐ Ⓑ Ⓒ Ⓓ	51	Ⓐ Ⓑ Ⓒ Ⓓ	61	Ⓐ Ⓑ Ⓒ Ⓓ	71	Ⓐ Ⓑ Ⓒ Ⓓ	81	Ⓐ Ⓑ Ⓒ Ⓓ	91	Ⓐ Ⓑ Ⓒ Ⓓ
2	Ⓐ Ⓑ Ⓒ Ⓓ	12	Ⓐ Ⓑ Ⓒ Ⓓ	22	Ⓐ Ⓑ Ⓒ Ⓓ	32	Ⓐ Ⓑ Ⓒ Ⓓ	42	Ⓐ Ⓑ Ⓒ Ⓓ	52	Ⓐ Ⓑ Ⓒ Ⓓ	62	Ⓐ Ⓑ Ⓒ Ⓓ	72	Ⓐ Ⓑ Ⓒ Ⓓ	82	Ⓐ Ⓑ Ⓒ Ⓓ	92	Ⓐ Ⓑ Ⓒ Ⓓ
3	Ⓐ Ⓑ Ⓒ Ⓓ	13	Ⓐ Ⓑ Ⓒ Ⓓ	23	Ⓐ Ⓑ Ⓒ Ⓓ	33	Ⓐ Ⓑ Ⓒ Ⓓ	43	Ⓐ Ⓑ Ⓒ Ⓓ	53	Ⓐ Ⓑ Ⓒ Ⓓ	63	Ⓐ Ⓑ Ⓒ Ⓓ	73	Ⓐ Ⓑ Ⓒ Ⓓ	83	Ⓐ Ⓑ Ⓒ Ⓓ	93	Ⓐ Ⓑ Ⓒ Ⓓ
4	Ⓐ Ⓑ Ⓒ Ⓓ	14	Ⓐ Ⓑ Ⓒ Ⓓ	24	Ⓐ Ⓑ Ⓒ Ⓓ	34	Ⓐ Ⓑ Ⓒ Ⓓ	44	Ⓐ Ⓑ Ⓒ Ⓓ	54	Ⓐ Ⓑ Ⓒ Ⓓ	64	Ⓐ Ⓑ Ⓒ Ⓓ	74	Ⓐ Ⓑ Ⓒ Ⓓ	84	Ⓐ Ⓑ Ⓒ Ⓓ	94	Ⓐ Ⓑ Ⓒ Ⓓ
5	Ⓐ Ⓑ Ⓒ Ⓓ	15	Ⓐ Ⓑ Ⓒ Ⓓ	25	Ⓐ Ⓑ Ⓒ Ⓓ	35	Ⓐ Ⓑ Ⓒ Ⓓ	45	Ⓐ Ⓑ Ⓒ Ⓓ	55	Ⓐ Ⓑ Ⓒ Ⓓ	65	Ⓐ Ⓑ Ⓒ Ⓓ	75	Ⓐ Ⓑ Ⓒ Ⓓ	85	Ⓐ Ⓑ Ⓒ Ⓓ	95	Ⓐ Ⓑ Ⓒ Ⓓ
6	Ⓐ Ⓑ Ⓒ Ⓓ	16	Ⓐ Ⓑ Ⓒ Ⓓ	26	Ⓐ Ⓑ Ⓒ Ⓓ	36	Ⓐ Ⓑ Ⓒ Ⓓ	46	Ⓐ Ⓑ Ⓒ Ⓓ	56	Ⓐ Ⓑ Ⓒ Ⓓ	66	Ⓐ Ⓑ Ⓒ Ⓓ	76	Ⓐ Ⓑ Ⓒ Ⓓ	86	Ⓐ Ⓑ Ⓒ Ⓓ	96	Ⓐ Ⓑ Ⓒ Ⓓ
7	Ⓐ Ⓑ Ⓒ Ⓓ	17	Ⓐ Ⓑ Ⓒ Ⓓ	27	Ⓐ Ⓑ Ⓒ Ⓓ	37	Ⓐ Ⓑ Ⓒ Ⓓ	47	Ⓐ Ⓑ Ⓒ Ⓓ	57	Ⓐ Ⓑ Ⓒ Ⓓ	67	Ⓐ Ⓑ Ⓒ Ⓓ	77	Ⓐ Ⓑ Ⓒ Ⓓ	87	Ⓐ Ⓑ Ⓒ Ⓓ	97	Ⓐ Ⓑ Ⓒ Ⓓ
8	Ⓐ Ⓑ Ⓒ Ⓓ	18	Ⓐ Ⓑ Ⓒ Ⓓ	28	Ⓐ Ⓑ Ⓒ Ⓓ	38	Ⓐ Ⓑ Ⓒ Ⓓ	48	Ⓐ Ⓑ Ⓒ Ⓓ	58	Ⓐ Ⓑ Ⓒ Ⓓ	68	Ⓐ Ⓑ Ⓒ Ⓓ	78	Ⓐ Ⓑ Ⓒ Ⓓ	88	Ⓐ Ⓑ Ⓒ Ⓓ	98	Ⓐ Ⓑ Ⓒ Ⓓ
9	Ⓐ Ⓑ Ⓒ Ⓓ	19	Ⓐ Ⓑ Ⓒ Ⓓ	29	Ⓐ Ⓑ Ⓒ Ⓓ	39	Ⓐ Ⓑ Ⓒ Ⓓ	49	Ⓐ Ⓑ Ⓒ Ⓓ	59	Ⓐ Ⓑ Ⓒ Ⓓ	69	Ⓐ Ⓑ Ⓒ Ⓓ	79	Ⓐ Ⓑ Ⓒ Ⓓ	89	Ⓐ Ⓑ Ⓒ Ⓓ	99	Ⓐ Ⓑ Ⓒ Ⓓ
10	Ⓐ Ⓑ Ⓒ Ⓓ	20	Ⓐ Ⓑ Ⓒ Ⓓ	30	Ⓐ Ⓑ Ⓒ Ⓓ	40	Ⓐ Ⓑ Ⓒ Ⓓ	50	Ⓐ Ⓑ Ⓒ Ⓓ	60	Ⓐ Ⓑ Ⓒ Ⓓ	70	Ⓐ Ⓑ Ⓒ Ⓓ	80	Ⓐ Ⓑ Ⓒ Ⓓ	90	Ⓐ Ⓑ Ⓒ Ⓓ	100	Ⓐ Ⓑ Ⓒ Ⓓ

421

Answer Sheet

ACTUAL TEST 07

LISTENING SECTION

1	Ⓐ Ⓑ Ⓒ Ⓓ
2	Ⓐ Ⓑ Ⓒ Ⓓ
3	Ⓐ Ⓑ Ⓒ Ⓓ
4	Ⓐ Ⓑ Ⓒ Ⓓ
5	Ⓐ Ⓑ Ⓒ Ⓓ
6	Ⓐ Ⓑ Ⓒ Ⓓ
7	Ⓐ Ⓑ Ⓒ Ⓓ
8	Ⓐ Ⓑ Ⓒ Ⓓ
9	Ⓐ Ⓑ Ⓒ Ⓓ
10	Ⓐ Ⓑ Ⓒ Ⓓ

11	Ⓐ Ⓑ Ⓒ Ⓓ
12	Ⓐ Ⓑ Ⓒ Ⓓ
13	Ⓐ Ⓑ Ⓒ Ⓓ
14	Ⓐ Ⓑ Ⓒ Ⓓ
15	Ⓐ Ⓑ Ⓒ Ⓓ
16	Ⓐ Ⓑ Ⓒ Ⓓ
17	Ⓐ Ⓑ Ⓒ Ⓓ
18	Ⓐ Ⓑ Ⓒ Ⓓ
19	Ⓐ Ⓑ Ⓒ Ⓓ
20	Ⓐ Ⓑ Ⓒ Ⓓ

21	Ⓐ Ⓑ Ⓒ Ⓓ
22	Ⓐ Ⓑ Ⓒ Ⓓ
23	Ⓐ Ⓑ Ⓒ Ⓓ
24	Ⓐ Ⓑ Ⓒ Ⓓ
25	Ⓐ Ⓑ Ⓒ Ⓓ
26	Ⓐ Ⓑ Ⓒ Ⓓ
27	Ⓐ Ⓑ Ⓒ Ⓓ
28	Ⓐ Ⓑ Ⓒ Ⓓ
29	Ⓐ Ⓑ Ⓒ Ⓓ
30	Ⓐ Ⓑ Ⓒ Ⓓ

31	Ⓐ Ⓑ Ⓒ Ⓓ
32	Ⓐ Ⓑ Ⓒ Ⓓ
33	Ⓐ Ⓑ Ⓒ Ⓓ
34	Ⓐ Ⓑ Ⓒ Ⓓ
35	Ⓐ Ⓑ Ⓒ Ⓓ
36	Ⓐ Ⓑ Ⓒ Ⓓ
37	Ⓐ Ⓑ Ⓒ Ⓓ
38	Ⓐ Ⓑ Ⓒ Ⓓ
39	Ⓐ Ⓑ Ⓒ Ⓓ
40	Ⓐ Ⓑ Ⓒ Ⓓ

41	Ⓐ Ⓑ Ⓒ Ⓓ
42	Ⓐ Ⓑ Ⓒ Ⓓ
43	Ⓐ Ⓑ Ⓒ Ⓓ
44	Ⓐ Ⓑ Ⓒ Ⓓ
45	Ⓐ Ⓑ Ⓒ Ⓓ
46	Ⓐ Ⓑ Ⓒ Ⓓ
47	Ⓐ Ⓑ Ⓒ Ⓓ
48	Ⓐ Ⓑ Ⓒ Ⓓ
49	Ⓐ Ⓑ Ⓒ Ⓓ
50	Ⓐ Ⓑ Ⓒ Ⓓ

51	Ⓐ Ⓑ Ⓒ Ⓓ
52	Ⓐ Ⓑ Ⓒ Ⓓ
53	Ⓐ Ⓑ Ⓒ Ⓓ
54	Ⓐ Ⓑ Ⓒ Ⓓ
55	Ⓐ Ⓑ Ⓒ Ⓓ
56	Ⓐ Ⓑ Ⓒ Ⓓ
57	Ⓐ Ⓑ Ⓒ Ⓓ
58	Ⓐ Ⓑ Ⓒ Ⓓ
59	Ⓐ Ⓑ Ⓒ Ⓓ
60	Ⓐ Ⓑ Ⓒ Ⓓ

61	Ⓐ Ⓑ Ⓒ Ⓓ
62	Ⓐ Ⓑ Ⓒ Ⓓ
63	Ⓐ Ⓑ Ⓒ Ⓓ
64	Ⓐ Ⓑ Ⓒ Ⓓ
65	Ⓐ Ⓑ Ⓒ Ⓓ
66	Ⓐ Ⓑ Ⓒ Ⓓ
67	Ⓐ Ⓑ Ⓒ Ⓓ
68	Ⓐ Ⓑ Ⓒ Ⓓ
69	Ⓐ Ⓑ Ⓒ Ⓓ
70	Ⓐ Ⓑ Ⓒ Ⓓ

71	Ⓐ Ⓑ Ⓒ Ⓓ
72	Ⓐ Ⓑ Ⓒ Ⓓ
73	Ⓐ Ⓑ Ⓒ Ⓓ
74	Ⓐ Ⓑ Ⓒ Ⓓ
75	Ⓐ Ⓑ Ⓒ Ⓓ
76	Ⓐ Ⓑ Ⓒ Ⓓ
77	Ⓐ Ⓑ Ⓒ Ⓓ
78	Ⓐ Ⓑ Ⓒ Ⓓ
79	Ⓐ Ⓑ Ⓒ Ⓓ
80	Ⓐ Ⓑ Ⓒ Ⓓ

81	Ⓐ Ⓑ Ⓒ Ⓓ
82	Ⓐ Ⓑ Ⓒ Ⓓ
83	Ⓐ Ⓑ Ⓒ Ⓓ
84	Ⓐ Ⓑ Ⓒ Ⓓ
85	Ⓐ Ⓑ Ⓒ Ⓓ
86	Ⓐ Ⓑ Ⓒ Ⓓ
87	Ⓐ Ⓑ Ⓒ Ⓓ
88	Ⓐ Ⓑ Ⓒ Ⓓ
89	Ⓐ Ⓑ Ⓒ Ⓓ
90	Ⓐ Ⓑ Ⓒ Ⓓ

91	Ⓐ Ⓑ Ⓒ Ⓓ
92	Ⓐ Ⓑ Ⓒ Ⓓ
93	Ⓐ Ⓑ Ⓒ Ⓓ
94	Ⓐ Ⓑ Ⓒ Ⓓ
95	Ⓐ Ⓑ Ⓒ Ⓓ
96	Ⓐ Ⓑ Ⓒ Ⓓ
97	Ⓐ Ⓑ Ⓒ Ⓓ
98	Ⓐ Ⓑ Ⓒ Ⓓ
99	Ⓐ Ⓑ Ⓒ Ⓓ
100	Ⓐ Ⓑ Ⓒ Ⓓ

ACTUAL TEST 08

LISTENING SECTION

1	Ⓐ Ⓑ Ⓒ Ⓓ
2	Ⓐ Ⓑ Ⓒ Ⓓ
3	Ⓐ Ⓑ Ⓒ Ⓓ
4	Ⓐ Ⓑ Ⓒ Ⓓ
5	Ⓐ Ⓑ Ⓒ Ⓓ
6	Ⓐ Ⓑ Ⓒ Ⓓ
7	Ⓐ Ⓑ Ⓒ Ⓓ
8	Ⓐ Ⓑ Ⓒ Ⓓ
9	Ⓐ Ⓑ Ⓒ Ⓓ
10	Ⓐ Ⓑ Ⓒ Ⓓ

11	Ⓐ Ⓑ Ⓒ Ⓓ
12	Ⓐ Ⓑ Ⓒ Ⓓ
13	Ⓐ Ⓑ Ⓒ Ⓓ
14	Ⓐ Ⓑ Ⓒ Ⓓ
15	Ⓐ Ⓑ Ⓒ Ⓓ
16	Ⓐ Ⓑ Ⓒ Ⓓ
17	Ⓐ Ⓑ Ⓒ Ⓓ
18	Ⓐ Ⓑ Ⓒ Ⓓ
19	Ⓐ Ⓑ Ⓒ Ⓓ
20	Ⓐ Ⓑ Ⓒ Ⓓ

21	Ⓐ Ⓑ Ⓒ Ⓓ
22	Ⓐ Ⓑ Ⓒ Ⓓ
23	Ⓐ Ⓑ Ⓒ Ⓓ
24	Ⓐ Ⓑ Ⓒ Ⓓ
25	Ⓐ Ⓑ Ⓒ Ⓓ
26	Ⓐ Ⓑ Ⓒ Ⓓ
27	Ⓐ Ⓑ Ⓒ Ⓓ
28	Ⓐ Ⓑ Ⓒ Ⓓ
29	Ⓐ Ⓑ Ⓒ Ⓓ
30	Ⓐ Ⓑ Ⓒ Ⓓ

31	Ⓐ Ⓑ Ⓒ Ⓓ
32	Ⓐ Ⓑ Ⓒ Ⓓ
33	Ⓐ Ⓑ Ⓒ Ⓓ
34	Ⓐ Ⓑ Ⓒ Ⓓ
35	Ⓐ Ⓑ Ⓒ Ⓓ
36	Ⓐ Ⓑ Ⓒ Ⓓ
37	Ⓐ Ⓑ Ⓒ Ⓓ
38	Ⓐ Ⓑ Ⓒ Ⓓ
39	Ⓐ Ⓑ Ⓒ Ⓓ
40	Ⓐ Ⓑ Ⓒ Ⓓ

41	Ⓐ Ⓑ Ⓒ Ⓓ
42	Ⓐ Ⓑ Ⓒ Ⓓ
43	Ⓐ Ⓑ Ⓒ Ⓓ
44	Ⓐ Ⓑ Ⓒ Ⓓ
45	Ⓐ Ⓑ Ⓒ Ⓓ
46	Ⓐ Ⓑ Ⓒ Ⓓ
47	Ⓐ Ⓑ Ⓒ Ⓓ
48	Ⓐ Ⓑ Ⓒ Ⓓ
49	Ⓐ Ⓑ Ⓒ Ⓓ
50	Ⓐ Ⓑ Ⓒ Ⓓ

51	Ⓐ Ⓑ Ⓒ Ⓓ
52	Ⓐ Ⓑ Ⓒ Ⓓ
53	Ⓐ Ⓑ Ⓒ Ⓓ
54	Ⓐ Ⓑ Ⓒ Ⓓ
55	Ⓐ Ⓑ Ⓒ Ⓓ
56	Ⓐ Ⓑ Ⓒ Ⓓ
57	Ⓐ Ⓑ Ⓒ Ⓓ
58	Ⓐ Ⓑ Ⓒ Ⓓ
59	Ⓐ Ⓑ Ⓒ Ⓓ
60	Ⓐ Ⓑ Ⓒ Ⓓ

61	Ⓐ Ⓑ Ⓒ Ⓓ
62	Ⓐ Ⓑ Ⓒ Ⓓ
63	Ⓐ Ⓑ Ⓒ Ⓓ
64	Ⓐ Ⓑ Ⓒ Ⓓ
65	Ⓐ Ⓑ Ⓒ Ⓓ
66	Ⓐ Ⓑ Ⓒ Ⓓ
67	Ⓐ Ⓑ Ⓒ Ⓓ
68	Ⓐ Ⓑ Ⓒ Ⓓ
69	Ⓐ Ⓑ Ⓒ Ⓓ
70	Ⓐ Ⓑ Ⓒ Ⓓ

71	Ⓐ Ⓑ Ⓒ Ⓓ
72	Ⓐ Ⓑ Ⓒ Ⓓ
73	Ⓐ Ⓑ Ⓒ Ⓓ
74	Ⓐ Ⓑ Ⓒ Ⓓ
75	Ⓐ Ⓑ Ⓒ Ⓓ
76	Ⓐ Ⓑ Ⓒ Ⓓ
77	Ⓐ Ⓑ Ⓒ Ⓓ
78	Ⓐ Ⓑ Ⓒ Ⓓ
79	Ⓐ Ⓑ Ⓒ Ⓓ
80	Ⓐ Ⓑ Ⓒ Ⓓ

81	Ⓐ Ⓑ Ⓒ Ⓓ
82	Ⓐ Ⓑ Ⓒ Ⓓ
83	Ⓐ Ⓑ Ⓒ Ⓓ
84	Ⓐ Ⓑ Ⓒ Ⓓ
85	Ⓐ Ⓑ Ⓒ Ⓓ
86	Ⓐ Ⓑ Ⓒ Ⓓ
87	Ⓐ Ⓑ Ⓒ Ⓓ
88	Ⓐ Ⓑ Ⓒ Ⓓ
89	Ⓐ Ⓑ Ⓒ Ⓓ
90	Ⓐ Ⓑ Ⓒ Ⓓ

91	Ⓐ Ⓑ Ⓒ Ⓓ
92	Ⓐ Ⓑ Ⓒ Ⓓ
93	Ⓐ Ⓑ Ⓒ Ⓓ
94	Ⓐ Ⓑ Ⓒ Ⓓ
95	Ⓐ Ⓑ Ⓒ Ⓓ
96	Ⓐ Ⓑ Ⓒ Ⓓ
97	Ⓐ Ⓑ Ⓒ Ⓓ
98	Ⓐ Ⓑ Ⓒ Ⓓ
99	Ⓐ Ⓑ Ⓒ Ⓓ
100	Ⓐ Ⓑ Ⓒ Ⓓ

Answer Sheet

ACTUAL TEST 09

LISTENING SECTION

1	Ⓐ Ⓑ Ⓒ Ⓓ
2	Ⓐ Ⓑ Ⓒ Ⓓ
3	Ⓐ Ⓑ Ⓒ Ⓓ
4	Ⓐ Ⓑ Ⓒ Ⓓ
5	Ⓐ Ⓑ Ⓒ Ⓓ
6	Ⓐ Ⓑ Ⓒ Ⓓ
7	Ⓐ Ⓑ Ⓒ Ⓓ
8	Ⓐ Ⓑ Ⓒ Ⓓ
9	Ⓐ Ⓑ Ⓒ Ⓓ
10	Ⓐ Ⓑ Ⓒ Ⓓ

11	Ⓐ Ⓑ Ⓒ Ⓓ
12	Ⓐ Ⓑ Ⓒ Ⓓ
13	Ⓐ Ⓑ Ⓒ Ⓓ
14	Ⓐ Ⓑ Ⓒ Ⓓ
15	Ⓐ Ⓑ Ⓒ Ⓓ
16	Ⓐ Ⓑ Ⓒ Ⓓ
17	Ⓐ Ⓑ Ⓒ Ⓓ
18	Ⓐ Ⓑ Ⓒ Ⓓ
19	Ⓐ Ⓑ Ⓒ Ⓓ
20	Ⓐ Ⓑ Ⓒ Ⓓ

21	Ⓐ Ⓑ Ⓒ Ⓓ
22	Ⓐ Ⓑ Ⓒ Ⓓ
23	Ⓐ Ⓑ Ⓒ Ⓓ
24	Ⓐ Ⓑ Ⓒ Ⓓ
25	Ⓐ Ⓑ Ⓒ Ⓓ
26	Ⓐ Ⓑ Ⓒ Ⓓ
27	Ⓐ Ⓑ Ⓒ Ⓓ
28	Ⓐ Ⓑ Ⓒ Ⓓ
29	Ⓐ Ⓑ Ⓒ Ⓓ
30	Ⓐ Ⓑ Ⓒ Ⓓ

31	Ⓐ Ⓑ Ⓒ Ⓓ
32	Ⓐ Ⓑ Ⓒ Ⓓ
33	Ⓐ Ⓑ Ⓒ Ⓓ
34	Ⓐ Ⓑ Ⓒ Ⓓ
35	Ⓐ Ⓑ Ⓒ Ⓓ
36	Ⓐ Ⓑ Ⓒ Ⓓ
37	Ⓐ Ⓑ Ⓒ Ⓓ
38	Ⓐ Ⓑ Ⓒ Ⓓ
39	Ⓐ Ⓑ Ⓒ Ⓓ
40	Ⓐ Ⓑ Ⓒ Ⓓ

41	Ⓐ Ⓑ Ⓒ Ⓓ
42	Ⓐ Ⓑ Ⓒ Ⓓ
43	Ⓐ Ⓑ Ⓒ Ⓓ
44	Ⓐ Ⓑ Ⓒ Ⓓ
45	Ⓐ Ⓑ Ⓒ Ⓓ
46	Ⓐ Ⓑ Ⓒ Ⓓ
47	Ⓐ Ⓑ Ⓒ Ⓓ
48	Ⓐ Ⓑ Ⓒ Ⓓ
49	Ⓐ Ⓑ Ⓒ Ⓓ
50	Ⓐ Ⓑ Ⓒ Ⓓ

51	Ⓐ Ⓑ Ⓒ Ⓓ
52	Ⓐ Ⓑ Ⓒ Ⓓ
53	Ⓐ Ⓑ Ⓒ Ⓓ
54	Ⓐ Ⓑ Ⓒ Ⓓ
55	Ⓐ Ⓑ Ⓒ Ⓓ
56	Ⓐ Ⓑ Ⓒ Ⓓ
57	Ⓐ Ⓑ Ⓒ Ⓓ
58	Ⓐ Ⓑ Ⓒ Ⓓ
59	Ⓐ Ⓑ Ⓒ Ⓓ
60	Ⓐ Ⓑ Ⓒ Ⓓ

61	Ⓐ Ⓑ Ⓒ Ⓓ
62	Ⓐ Ⓑ Ⓒ Ⓓ
63	Ⓐ Ⓑ Ⓒ Ⓓ
64	Ⓐ Ⓑ Ⓒ Ⓓ
65	Ⓐ Ⓑ Ⓒ Ⓓ
66	Ⓐ Ⓑ Ⓒ Ⓓ
67	Ⓐ Ⓑ Ⓒ Ⓓ
68	Ⓐ Ⓑ Ⓒ Ⓓ
69	Ⓐ Ⓑ Ⓒ Ⓓ
70	Ⓐ Ⓑ Ⓒ Ⓓ

71	Ⓐ Ⓑ Ⓒ Ⓓ
72	Ⓐ Ⓑ Ⓒ Ⓓ
73	Ⓐ Ⓑ Ⓒ Ⓓ
74	Ⓐ Ⓑ Ⓒ Ⓓ
75	Ⓐ Ⓑ Ⓒ Ⓓ
76	Ⓐ Ⓑ Ⓒ Ⓓ
77	Ⓐ Ⓑ Ⓒ Ⓓ
78	Ⓐ Ⓑ Ⓒ Ⓓ
79	Ⓐ Ⓑ Ⓒ Ⓓ
80	Ⓐ Ⓑ Ⓒ Ⓓ

81	Ⓐ Ⓑ Ⓒ Ⓓ
82	Ⓐ Ⓑ Ⓒ Ⓓ
83	Ⓐ Ⓑ Ⓒ Ⓓ
84	Ⓐ Ⓑ Ⓒ Ⓓ
85	Ⓐ Ⓑ Ⓒ Ⓓ
86	Ⓐ Ⓑ Ⓒ Ⓓ
87	Ⓐ Ⓑ Ⓒ Ⓓ
88	Ⓐ Ⓑ Ⓒ Ⓓ
89	Ⓐ Ⓑ Ⓒ Ⓓ
90	Ⓐ Ⓑ Ⓒ Ⓓ

91	Ⓐ Ⓑ Ⓒ Ⓓ
92	Ⓐ Ⓑ Ⓒ Ⓓ
93	Ⓐ Ⓑ Ⓒ Ⓓ
94	Ⓐ Ⓑ Ⓒ Ⓓ
95	Ⓐ Ⓑ Ⓒ Ⓓ
96	Ⓐ Ⓑ Ⓒ Ⓓ
97	Ⓐ Ⓑ Ⓒ Ⓓ
98	Ⓐ Ⓑ Ⓒ Ⓓ
99	Ⓐ Ⓑ Ⓒ Ⓓ
100	Ⓐ Ⓑ Ⓒ Ⓓ

ACTUAL TEST 10

LISTENING SECTION

1	Ⓐ Ⓑ Ⓒ Ⓓ
2	Ⓐ Ⓑ Ⓒ Ⓓ
3	Ⓐ Ⓑ Ⓒ Ⓓ
4	Ⓐ Ⓑ Ⓒ Ⓓ
5	Ⓐ Ⓑ Ⓒ Ⓓ
6	Ⓐ Ⓑ Ⓒ Ⓓ
7	Ⓐ Ⓑ Ⓒ Ⓓ
8	Ⓐ Ⓑ Ⓒ Ⓓ
9	Ⓐ Ⓑ Ⓒ Ⓓ
10	Ⓐ Ⓑ Ⓒ Ⓓ

11	Ⓐ Ⓑ Ⓒ Ⓓ
12	Ⓐ Ⓑ Ⓒ Ⓓ
13	Ⓐ Ⓑ Ⓒ Ⓓ
14	Ⓐ Ⓑ Ⓒ Ⓓ
15	Ⓐ Ⓑ Ⓒ Ⓓ
16	Ⓐ Ⓑ Ⓒ Ⓓ
17	Ⓐ Ⓑ Ⓒ Ⓓ
18	Ⓐ Ⓑ Ⓒ Ⓓ
19	Ⓐ Ⓑ Ⓒ Ⓓ
20	Ⓐ Ⓑ Ⓒ Ⓓ

21	Ⓐ Ⓑ Ⓒ Ⓓ
22	Ⓐ Ⓑ Ⓒ Ⓓ
23	Ⓐ Ⓑ Ⓒ Ⓓ
24	Ⓐ Ⓑ Ⓒ Ⓓ
25	Ⓐ Ⓑ Ⓒ Ⓓ
26	Ⓐ Ⓑ Ⓒ Ⓓ
27	Ⓐ Ⓑ Ⓒ Ⓓ
28	Ⓐ Ⓑ Ⓒ Ⓓ
29	Ⓐ Ⓑ Ⓒ Ⓓ
30	Ⓐ Ⓑ Ⓒ Ⓓ

31	Ⓐ Ⓑ Ⓒ Ⓓ
32	Ⓐ Ⓑ Ⓒ Ⓓ
33	Ⓐ Ⓑ Ⓒ Ⓓ
34	Ⓐ Ⓑ Ⓒ Ⓓ
35	Ⓐ Ⓑ Ⓒ Ⓓ
36	Ⓐ Ⓑ Ⓒ Ⓓ
37	Ⓐ Ⓑ Ⓒ Ⓓ
38	Ⓐ Ⓑ Ⓒ Ⓓ
39	Ⓐ Ⓑ Ⓒ Ⓓ
40	Ⓐ Ⓑ Ⓒ Ⓓ

41	Ⓐ Ⓑ Ⓒ Ⓓ
42	Ⓐ Ⓑ Ⓒ Ⓓ
43	Ⓐ Ⓑ Ⓒ Ⓓ
44	Ⓐ Ⓑ Ⓒ Ⓓ
45	Ⓐ Ⓑ Ⓒ Ⓓ
46	Ⓐ Ⓑ Ⓒ Ⓓ
47	Ⓐ Ⓑ Ⓒ Ⓓ
48	Ⓐ Ⓑ Ⓒ Ⓓ
49	Ⓐ Ⓑ Ⓒ Ⓓ
50	Ⓐ Ⓑ Ⓒ Ⓓ

51	Ⓐ Ⓑ Ⓒ Ⓓ
52	Ⓐ Ⓑ Ⓒ Ⓓ
53	Ⓐ Ⓑ Ⓒ Ⓓ
54	Ⓐ Ⓑ Ⓒ Ⓓ
55	Ⓐ Ⓑ Ⓒ Ⓓ
56	Ⓐ Ⓑ Ⓒ Ⓓ
57	Ⓐ Ⓑ Ⓒ Ⓓ
58	Ⓐ Ⓑ Ⓒ Ⓓ
59	Ⓐ Ⓑ Ⓒ Ⓓ
60	Ⓐ Ⓑ Ⓒ Ⓓ

61	Ⓐ Ⓑ Ⓒ Ⓓ
62	Ⓐ Ⓑ Ⓒ Ⓓ
63	Ⓐ Ⓑ Ⓒ Ⓓ
64	Ⓐ Ⓑ Ⓒ Ⓓ
65	Ⓐ Ⓑ Ⓒ Ⓓ
66	Ⓐ Ⓑ Ⓒ Ⓓ
67	Ⓐ Ⓑ Ⓒ Ⓓ
68	Ⓐ Ⓑ Ⓒ Ⓓ
69	Ⓐ Ⓑ Ⓒ Ⓓ
70	Ⓐ Ⓑ Ⓒ Ⓓ

71	Ⓐ Ⓑ Ⓒ Ⓓ
72	Ⓐ Ⓑ Ⓒ Ⓓ
73	Ⓐ Ⓑ Ⓒ Ⓓ
74	Ⓐ Ⓑ Ⓒ Ⓓ
75	Ⓐ Ⓑ Ⓒ Ⓓ
76	Ⓐ Ⓑ Ⓒ Ⓓ
77	Ⓐ Ⓑ Ⓒ Ⓓ
78	Ⓐ Ⓑ Ⓒ Ⓓ
79	Ⓐ Ⓑ Ⓒ Ⓓ
80	Ⓐ Ⓑ Ⓒ Ⓓ

81	Ⓐ Ⓑ Ⓒ Ⓓ
82	Ⓐ Ⓑ Ⓒ Ⓓ
83	Ⓐ Ⓑ Ⓒ Ⓓ
84	Ⓐ Ⓑ Ⓒ Ⓓ
85	Ⓐ Ⓑ Ⓒ Ⓓ
86	Ⓐ Ⓑ Ⓒ Ⓓ
87	Ⓐ Ⓑ Ⓒ Ⓓ
88	Ⓐ Ⓑ Ⓒ Ⓓ
89	Ⓐ Ⓑ Ⓒ Ⓓ
90	Ⓐ Ⓑ Ⓒ Ⓓ

91	Ⓐ Ⓑ Ⓒ Ⓓ
92	Ⓐ Ⓑ Ⓒ Ⓓ
93	Ⓐ Ⓑ Ⓒ Ⓓ
94	Ⓐ Ⓑ Ⓒ Ⓓ
95	Ⓐ Ⓑ Ⓒ Ⓓ
96	Ⓐ Ⓑ Ⓒ Ⓓ
97	Ⓐ Ⓑ Ⓒ Ⓓ
98	Ⓐ Ⓑ Ⓒ Ⓓ
99	Ⓐ Ⓑ Ⓒ Ⓓ
100	Ⓐ Ⓑ Ⓒ Ⓓ

ANSWER KEY

ACTUAL TEST 01

1	(D)	21	(A)	41	(D)	61	(D)	81	(C)
2	(B)	22	(C)	42	(B)	62	(A)	82	(C)
3	(B)	23	(B)	43	(C)	63	(C)	83	(A)
4	(A)	24	(B)	44	(C)	64	(C)	84	(A)
5	(D)	25	(C)	45	(D)	65	(C)	85	(B)
6	(B)	26	(A)	46	(B)	66	(C)	86	(A)
7	(A)	27	(B)	47	(A)	67	(D)	87	(B)
8	(C)	28	(C)	48	(B)	68	(D)	88	(C)
9	(A)	29	(C)	49	(C)	69	(D)	89	(C)
10	(C)	30	(B)	50	(D)	70	(B)	90	(A)
11	(C)	31	(A)	51	(A)	71	(A)	91	(D)
12	(A)	32	(A)	52	(C)	72	(D)	92	(C)
13	(C)	33	(B)	53	(B)	73	(B)	93	(C)
14	(B)	34	(D)	54	(D)	74	(D)	94	(D)
15	(B)	35	(C)	55	(B)	75	(B)	95	(D)
16	(C)	36	(C)	56	(A)	76	(B)	96	(A)
17	(B)	37	(A)	57	(C)	77	(C)	97	(B)
18	(C)	38	(D)	58	(A)	78	(B)	98	(C)
19	(B)	39	(D)	59	(B)	79	(B)	99	(D)
20	(A)	40	(B)	60	(A)	80	(B)	100	(D)

ACTUAL TEST 02

1	(D)	21	(A)	41	(C)	61	(C)	81	(A)
2	(A)	22	(C)	42	(C)	62	(B)	82	(C)
3	(D)	23	(C)	43	(B)	63	(D)	83	(A)
4	(B)	24	(A)	44	(B)	64	(A)	84	(D)
5	(B)	25	(B)	45	(C)	65	(B)	85	(B)
6	(C)	26	(A)	46	(D)	66	(C)	86	(B)
7	(C)	27	(C)	47	(B)	67	(B)	87	(D)
8	(A)	28	(C)	48	(C)	68	(A)	88	(A)
9	(A)	29	(B)	49	(D)	69	(D)	89	(D)
10	(C)	30	(C)	50	(A)	70	(D)	90	(B)
11	(B)	31	(A)	51	(A)	71	(C)	91	(C)
12	(B)	32	(B)	52	(C)	72	(D)	92	(C)
13	(B)	33	(A)	53	(B)	73	(B)	93	(B)
14	(A)	34	(B)	54	(D)	74	(A)	94	(A)
15	(C)	35	(B)	55	(A)	75	(C)	95	(B)
16	(B)	36	(B)	56	(C)	76	(B)	96	(C)
17	(A)	37	(A)	57	(D)	77	(B)	97	(D)
18	(A)	38	(B)	58	(B)	78	(A)	98	(A)
19	(B)	39	(C)	59	(A)	79	(D)	99	(A)
20	(A)	40	(A)	60	(C)	80	(D)	100	(B)

ACTUAL TEST 03

1	(A)	21	(A)	41	(C)	61	(D)	81	(A)
2	(B)	22	(A)	42	(B)	62	(C)	82	(D)
3	(D)	23	(A)	43	(A)	63	(A)	83	(B)
4	(C)	24	(C)	44	(D)	64	(B)	84	(C)
5	(A)	25	(A)	45	(A)	65	(B)	85	(A)
6	(A)	26	(B)	46	(D)	66	(C)	86	(C)
7	(C)	27	(A)	47	(B)	67	(D)	87	(B)
8	(B)	28	(B)	48	(C)	68	(B)	88	(A)
9	(A)	29	(B)	49	(D)	69	(D)	89	(B)
10	(A)	30	(A)	50	(C)	70	(C)	90	(A)
11	(B)	31	(B)	51	(B)	71	(D)	91	(B)
12	(C)	32	(B)	52	(A)	72	(C)	92	(A)
13	(B)	33	(B)	53	(A)	73	(D)	93	(C)
14	(A)	34	(C)	54	(B)	74	(D)	94	(C)
15	(C)	35	(C)	55	(D)	75	(B)	95	(C)
16	(B)	36	(A)	56	(C)	76	(D)	96	(A)
17	(B)	37	(D)	57	(B)	77	(C)	97	(D)
18	(A)	38	(C)	58	(A)	78	(A)	98	(C)
19	(C)	39	(C)	59	(C)	79	(D)	99	(D)
20	(C)	40	(A)	60	(B)	80	(B)	100	(C)

ACTUAL TEST 04

1	(A)	21	(B)	41	(C)	61	(C)	81	(A)
2	(B)	22	(A)	42	(C)	62	(B)	82	(C)
3	(C)	23	(C)	43	(D)	63	(A)	83	(D)
4	(C)	24	(A)	44	(C)	64	(B)	84	(D)
5	(A)	25	(C)	45	(A)	65	(D)	85	(C)
6	(D)	26	(B)	46	(C)	66	(C)	86	(B)
7	(A)	27	(B)	47	(C)	67	(B)	87	(D)
8	(B)	28	(C)	48	(B)	68	(B)	88	(A)
9	(A)	29	(A)	49	(D)	69	(C)	89	(A)
10	(A)	30	(A)	50	(D)	70	(C)	90	(D)
11	(A)	31	(B)	51	(C)	71	(D)	91	(A)
12	(B)	32	(A)	52	(B)	72	(D)	92	(B)
13	(C)	33	(A)	53	(A)	73	(C)	93	(A)
14	(B)	34	(B)	54	(B)	74	(A)	94	(C)
15	(A)	35	(A)	55	(D)	75	(B)	95	(B)
16	(C)	36	(D)	56	(D)	76	(D)	96	(B)
17	(A)	37	(A)	57	(A)	77	(B)	97	(D)
18	(A)	38	(C)	58	(D)	78	(C)	98	(A)
19	(C)	39	(B)	59	(A)	79	(B)	99	(B)
20	(C)	40	(D)	60	(B)	80	(C)	100	(B)

ACTUAL TEST 05

1 (B)	21 (B)	41 (A)	61 (B)	81 (C)
2 (A)	22 (A)	42 (D)	62 (D)	82 (D)
3 (A)	23 (A)	43 (B)	63 (A)	83 (A)
4 (C)	24 (C)	44 (C)	64 (D)	84 (A)
5 (C)	25 (A)	45 (D)	65 (B)	85 (D)
6 (C)	26 (B)	46 (B)	66 (C)	86 (C)
7 (C)	27 (A)	47 (A)	67 (A)	87 (A)
8 (A)	28 (B)	48 (C)	68 (C)	88 (C)
9 (C)	29 (A)	49 (A)	69 (C)	89 (C)
10 (B)	30 (A)	50 (D)	70 (D)	90 (C)
11 (C)	31 (B)	51 (B)	71 (B)	91 (C)
12 (A)	32 (C)	52 (A)	72 (A)	92 (C)
13 (B)	33 (C)	53 (B)	73 (D)	93 (A)
14 (B)	34 (C)	54 (C)	74 (A)	94 (C)
15 (B)	35 (D)	55 (C)	75 (A)	95 (C)
16 (C)	36 (B)	56 (D)	76 (B)	96 (A)
17 (C)	37 (C)	57 (A)	77 (A)	97 (A)
18 (C)	38 (A)	58 (B)	78 (D)	98 (A)
19 (A)	39 (C)	59 (A)	79 (B)	99 (C)
20 (B)	40 (C)	60 (B)	80 (A)	100 (A)

ACTUAL TEST 06

1 (C)	21 (B)	41 (D)	61 (A)	81 (A)
2 (B)	22 (C)	42 (A)	62 (A)	82 (C)
3 (C)	23 (B)	43 (A)	63 (C)	83 (B)
4 (C)	24 (A)	44 (A)	64 (B)	84 (C)
5 (D)	25 (A)	45 (A)	65 (C)	85 (B)
6 (A)	26 (B)	46 (B)	66 (C)	86 (B)
7 (B)	27 (B)	47 (B)	67 (D)	87 (A)
8 (C)	28 (B)	48 (C)	68 (C)	88 (A)
9 (B)	29 (A)	49 (B)	69 (B)	89 (C)
10 (B)	30 (B)	50 (C)	70 (D)	90 (A)
11 (C)	31 (C)	51 (A)	71 (C)	91 (A)
12 (B)	32 (B)	52 (B)	72 (D)	92 (A)
13 (B)	33 (A)	53 (A)	73 (A)	93 (B)
14 (B)	34 (C)	54 (D)	74 (B)	94 (B)
15 (A)	35 (D)	55 (C)	75 (A)	95 (A)
16 (B)	36 (A)	56 (B)	76 (D)	96 (A)
17 (B)	37 (C)	57 (D)	77 (A)	97 (D)
18 (A)	38 (C)	58 (A)	78 (C)	98 (B)
19 (B)	39 (B)	59 (C)	79 (A)	99 (C)
20 (C)	40 (B)	60 (A)	80 (D)	100 (D)

ACTUAL TEST 07

1 (C)	21 (B)	41 (C)	61 (C)	81 (B)
2 (B)	22 (A)	42 (A)	62 (B)	82 (D)
3 (D)	23 (C)	43 (C)	63 (D)	83 (D)
4 (A)	24 (C)	44 (C)	64 (B)	84 (C)
5 (D)	25 (B)	45 (B)	65 (C)	85 (B)
6 (B)	26 (A)	46 (C)	66 (C)	86 (C)
7 (B)	27 (C)	47 (C)	67 (A)	87 (A)
8 (C)	28 (A)	48 (C)	68 (B)	88 (B)
9 (B)	29 (C)	49 (C)	69 (B)	89 (B)
10 (C)	30 (C)	50 (C)	70 (C)	90 (B)
11 (C)	31 (B)	51 (B)	71 (B)	91 (C)
12 (C)	32 (C)	52 (D)	72 (C)	92 (C)
13 (A)	33 (D)	53 (B)	73 (A)	93 (C)
14 (A)	34 (C)	54 (D)	74 (B)	94 (D)
15 (B)	35 (B)	55 (C)	75 (C)	95 (B)
16 (B)	36 (C)	56 (A)	76 (A)	96 (B)
17 (C)	37 (D)	57 (C)	77 (B)	97 (D)
18 (C)	38 (C)	58 (A)	78 (C)	98 (A)
19 (B)	39 (A)	59 (A)	79 (D)	99 (B)
20 (C)	40 (B)	60 (D)	80 (A)	100 (A)

ACTUAL TEST 08

1 (C)	21 (C)	41 (C)	61 (C)	81 (C)
2 (D)	22 (C)	42 (B)	62 (D)	82 (C)
3 (B)	23 (B)	43 (C)	63 (C)	83 (C)
4 (A)	24 (B)	44 (A)	64 (B)	84 (C)
5 (C)	25 (B)	45 (C)	65 (C)	85 (D)
6 (A)	26 (B)	46 (D)	66 (A)	86 (A)
7 (B)	27 (B)	47 (B)	67 (B)	87 (B)
8 (A)	28 (B)	48 (B)	68 (A)	88 (D)
9 (A)	29 (C)	49 (C)	69 (B)	89 (A)
10 (B)	30 (C)	50 (D)	70 (A)	90 (D)
11 (B)	31 (A)	51 (A)	71 (A)	91 (B)
12 (A)	32 (B)	52 (A)	72 (D)	92 (A)
13 (B)	33 (D)	53 (D)	73 (C)	93 (D)
14 (C)	34 (C)	54 (C)	74 (A)	94 (B)
15 (C)	35 (C)	55 (B)	75 (D)	95 (C)
16 (B)	36 (A)	56 (C)	76 (A)	96 (B)
17 (A)	37 (A)	57 (B)	77 (B)	97 (A)
18 (C)	38 (B)	58 (A)	78 (C)	98 (C)
19 (B)	39 (A)	59 (C)	79 (B)	99 (C)
20 (C)	40 (B)	60 (A)	80 (D)	100 (D)

ACTUAL TEST 09

1	(B)	21	(B)	41	(A)	61	(A)	81	(D)
2	(B)	22	(B)	42	(B)	62	(A)	82	(B)
3	(A)	23	(C)	43	(D)	63	(A)	83	(C)
4	(C)	24	(A)	44	(C)	64	(A)	84	(D)
5	(B)	25	(A)	45	(D)	65	(D)	85	(C)
6	(C)	26	(A)	46	(B)	66	(C)	86	(B)
7	(B)	27	(C)	47	(D)	67	(D)	87	(D)
8	(B)	28	(A)	48	(B)	68	(A)	88	(C)
9	(A)	29	(B)	49	(C)	69	(C)	89	(C)
10	(A)	30	(A)	50	(D)	70	(C)	90	(B)
11	(C)	31	(A)	51	(D)	71	(D)	91	(A)
12	(A)	32	(A)	52	(A)	72	(A)	92	(B)
13	(C)	33	(B)	53	(A)	73	(D)	93	(D)
14	(B)	34	(A)	54	(A)	74	(B)	94	(D)
15	(B)	35	(B)	55	(A)	75	(B)	95	(B)
16	(C)	36	(C)	56	(B)	76	(B)	96	(D)
17	(B)	37	(D)	57	(D)	77	(D)	97	(C)
18	(A)	38	(A)	58	(A)	78	(D)	98	(A)
19	(B)	39	(A)	59	(C)	79	(C)	99	(D)
20	(B)	40	(D)	60	(B)	80	(C)	100	(A)

ACTUAL TEST 10

1	(B)	21	(A)	41	(C)	61	(D)	81	(D)
2	(D)	22	(B)	42	(C)	62	(A)	82	(D)
3	(A)	23	(C)	43	(A)	63	(B)	83	(B)
4	(C)	24	(B)	44	(D)	64	(C)	84	(D)
5	(A)	25	(C)	45	(C)	65	(D)	85	(C)
6	(D)	26	(A)	46	(A)	66	(B)	86	(D)
7	(A)	27	(C)	47	(B)	67	(D)	87	(A)
8	(B)	28	(A)	48	(C)	68	(A)	88	(C)
9	(C)	29	(C)	49	(B)	69	(B)	89	(A)
10	(C)	30	(B)	50	(C)	70	(C)	90	(B)
11	(A)	31	(C)	51	(A)	71	(A)	91	(C)
12	(B)	32	(C)	52	(D)	72	(D)	92	(B)
13	(B)	33	(B)	53	(D)	73	(A)	93	(C)
14	(A)	34	(A)	54	(B)	74	(D)	94	(A)
15	(A)	35	(C)	55	(B)	75	(B)	95	(C)
16	(B)	36	(D)	56	(C)	76	(C)	96	(C)
17	(A)	37	(B)	57	(D)	77	(B)	97	(C)
18	(B)	38	(D)	58	(A)	78	(D)	98	(B)
19	(B)	39	(A)	59	(A)	79	(C)	99	(C)
20	(C)	40	(A)	60	(C)	80	(A)	100	(D)

TOEIC 成績換算對照表

LISTENING 答對題數	LISTENING 分數	READING 答對題數	READING 分數
96-100	480~495	96-100	460~495
91-95	435~490	91-95	410~475
86-90	395~450	86-90	380~430
81-85	355~415	81-85	355~400
76-80	325~375	76-80	325~375
71-75	295~340	71-75	295~345
66-70	265~315	66-70	265~315
61-65	240~285	61-65	235~285
56-60	215~260	56-60	205~255
51-55	190~235	51-55	175~225
46-50	160~210	46-50	150~195
41-45	135~180	41-45	120~170
36-40	110~155	36-40	100~140
31-35	85~130	31-35	75~120
26-30	70~105	26-30	55~100
21-25	50~90	21-25	40~80
16-20	35~70	16-20	30~65
11-15	20~55	11-15	20~50
6-10	15~40	6-10	15~35
1-5	5~20	1-5	5~20
0	5	0	5

註：上述表格僅供參考，實際計分以官方分數為準 。

挑戰 NEW TOEIC
新制多益
聽力滿分
10回模擬試題1000題 解析版

作　者	Kim su hyeon
譯　者	林育珊／關亭薇（前言）
編　輯	王采翎／賴祖兒
校　對	吳思薇／黃詩韻／申文怡
主　編	丁宥暄
內文排版	洪伊珊／謝青秀／林書玉
封面設計	林書玉
製程管理	洪巧玲
發 行 人	黃朝萍
出 版 者	寂天文化事業股份有限公司
電　話	+886-(0)2-2365-9739
傳　真	+886-(0)2-2365-9835
網　址	www.icosmos.com.tw
讀者服務	onlineservice@icosmos.com.tw
出版日期	2024年6月 二版一刷 (寂天雲隨身聽APP版)

挑戰新制多益聽力滿分：10回1000題模擬試題(寂天雲隨身聽APP版) / Kim su hyeon作；林育珊, 關亭薇譯. -- 初版.
-- [臺北市] : 寂天文化, 2024.06
　面；　公分
ISBN 978-626-300-259-3 (16K平裝)

1.多益測驗

805.1895　　　　　　　　113007282